I'm really not ⟨...⟩ ⟨...⟩ ⟨...⟩ ⟨...⟩ ⟨...⟩ ⟨...⟩ now. This boy is getting in.

"Jason, will you please read my book? It would mean a lot to me."

He grins. "Sure, baby. I got you."

Whoa. Wasn't ready for the term of endearment. "So . . . my experience has been with liars. What's yours been?"

"I'm not the type to be all bitter. But generally, I'd say the thing that hurts the most for me, and for most men, is when your woman isn't down for you when things get rough."

"But to be fair to the sistas, y'all have a lot more rough periods than we do. We tend to have our shit together, waiting for y'all to catch up."

"Is that what love's about? Keeping score? Love is unconditional . . . or at least, it should be." He returns his gaze to me. His green eyes are shining, and he bites his full bottom lip. Oh God. I can't take it.

I place one hand on the back of his neck, the other on his chest. Damn, this man's muscles are a thing of beauty. He reaches back and rubs my hand on his neck, and this time I can't hide the tiny shiver that runs down my spine. Suddenly, his free arm is around my waist, pulling me closer.

Des, don't do it. Don't do it. We are eye to eye, nose to nose. One small lean in from being lip to lip. He flashes both rows of teeth and winks at me. It's over. I pull him closer and kiss him . . . .

No More Lies

To: Danielle

RACHEL SKERRITT

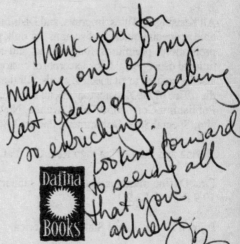

Thank you for
making one of my
last years of teaching
so enriching.
looking forward
to seeing all
that you
achieve

Kensington Publishing Corp.
http://www.kensingtonbooks.com

ACKNOWLEDGMENTS

To my family for all the gifts you've given me. Thank you for the numerous meals, from Mom and Donald especially, that you've made over the past few years when I have been too busy to cook my own food. (I know, I know. I never knew how to cook at all, but do we have to tell all of my secrets?) Special thanks to Grandma for keeping me in her prayers, to Nadine for being my not-no-real twin, and to Leah for working part time as my biggest cheerleader.

To my school family in Boston for championing my causes. Colleagues, you have supported me as a teacher, a writer, and a general free spirit. (No, I will never be excited by pension plan discussions in the lunchroom, but you know that and love me anyway.) Students, you've enriched my life in ways I'd never imagined. I look forward to seeing what you accomplish.

To my Penn family, for being there despite our physical distance from each other: Brandi, Cheeks, Dayle, Jamal, Jen, Jon, Kendall, Kenyatta, Malik, Kim, Mike, Nikki, Patrice, Rhonda, Stan. See you at the next wedding.

To my high school and college classmates who have inspired many through their creative risk taking: Angela Nissel, DeVon Harris, John Legend, Luam Keflezgy, Nkechi Okoro, Omekongo Dibinga, Rob Murat. You keep me thinking big.

To the folks who, through trips, dinners, (long) phone conversations, e-mails, and text messages, have challenged my thinking and pushed me along: Alvin, Andre, Anita, Asha, Ayanna, Ben, Dawud, Eugenia, Gena, Hassan, Heidi, Jenee, Joanne Skerrett, Joanne Soulouque, Kate, Keira, Keith, Kelly, Lynn, Marc Johnson, Matt, Maya, MJ, Nabulungi, Nyvette, Ron Gwiazda, Sabrina, Shahid, Sharifa, Sonia, and my Women On Wine. If you're not listed, either I forgot and I'm genuinely sorry, or you're some wack dude who didn't call when you said you would and therefore deserves no mention.

To my editor, John Scognamiglio, the world's fastest returner of emails (as well as an excellent discerner of reality television), and to my agent, Claudia Menza, who believed in my work since *Truth Be Told*.

I am so lucky to have all of these people whom I respect and admire in my life. My sincerest apologies for distorting you in my novels for sheer entertainment's sake.

PART 1

Chapter 1

Desiree

Imani tends to be heavy on the vodka and light on the cranberry when she mixes cosmopolitans, and my mouth puckers when I take an oversized sip from the glass she hands me. By the second swallow, my taste buds have adjusted, and I settle into her plush plum-colored couch with my martini glass.

Once Imani assumes her position, seated against the opposite arm of the couch, we start our usual dishing. "So I'm walking here from the subway on 125th," I say, "and this dude practically breaks his neck to catch up with me."

Looking past me with a bored expression, she sets her drink on the coffee table, twists her long dreadlocks into a bun at the back of her head, and scans the room for something to fasten them in place. "What else is new, Desiree?"

"Just listen, smart ass," I tease, tossing her a discarded pencil from the floor. She catches it with one hand, still holding her dreads with the other, and sticks the pencil through the twisted mass, the slender yellow stick miraculously securing the makeshift ponytail. "The guy cuts me off and stands in my path, talkin' 'bout, 'Excuse me, miss. I just have to ask. Your hair is so pretty. Is you mixed?'"

Imani chokes a little bit on her cosmo and pounds her chest to guide the alcohol in the right direction. "He did not say, '*Is* you mixed.'"

"Oh, but he did, girl."

"A bad pick-up line combined with bad grammar? I know you told him about himself."

"I let him off easy. I just told him that I *am* a mix—between totally turned off and amused by his ignorance."

"Classic Desiree," Imani chuckles. "Was the brotha at least good-looking?"

"Does it even matter? Like I would talk to some dude who's interested in me for my hair, and who thinks that black women are incapable of growing it!"

"Oh, please. Like you would talk to *any* dude, period."

I roll my eyes, because I know where this is going. "How long has it been, Des?" she asks right on cue.

I tilt the martini glass so that the stem points toward Imani's bright red ceiling, feeling the last few drops of warmth drizzle down my throat. Then I decide to let out a really loud sigh, to let her know how frustrated I get with this topic. Finally, I speak, making my voice as firm as possible without causing a fight. "I really don't want to talk about this today."

I don't know what I was thinking, trying to intimidate the only woman who can give more attitude than I can. "Well, too bad. It is not normal for a twenty-three-year-old woman to go five years without any male contact whatsoever."

I decide to try another angle. "You have a nerve to talk, seeing how you've gone twice that long without touching a man." I force a grin, hoping to receive one in return.

No such luck. "*I* have an excuse. I love women, and

have a wonderful partner in Sheila. You, on the other hand, are actually attracted to men. Yet no boyfriend, no sex buddy, not even an occasional date with a kiss good night. All because you refuse to let go of the past and—"

I put both hands up to stop her right there. "Change the subject. I'm serious."

At the sound of the tension rising in my voice, her eyes soften. That's why we're such good friends. We're both testy, often bitchy, always aggressive people, but we know one another's limits. "Fine," she says soothingly. "I just worry about you, that's all."

Of course, she has to go making me feel guilty for snapping at her. Launching a second attempt at lightening the mood, I motion my head to a standing sculpture near the fireplace, of two women in an affectionate embrace. Unable to hide the smirk, I ask, "Think I should adopt your lifestyle?"

Imani howls in laughter. "Hell no! We don't want anyone as cold-blooded as you on our team. It gives our people a bad name."

I'm about to argue back that she's not the warmest of folks herself, but I hold my tongue. She rises from the couch and stretches her arms behind her, arching her back and moaning in pleasure. I try not to connect her body movement and consequent sound effects to what she probably does with Sheila behind closed doors, but it's difficult. I'm progressive and all, but the thought of my homegirl getting it on with another woman—it still kind of weirds me out. Her African printed shawl that she has wrapped around her ample hips has started to come loose, so she unties it completely, tossing the fabric on the couch. The fact that she has jeans on underneath doesn't take away from the image that has now popped in my mind of Imani disrobing in front of her lover. Desperately wanting to redirect my own course of thought,

I pull my hair over my shoulder and examine the tips, searching for split ends.

Imani disappears into the kitchen with our empty glasses, and I hear ice cubes falling into the stainless-steel martini shaker. I finger comb my hair away from my face, satisfied that I can go another couple of weeks without a trim. I gaze around the room, searching for a new knick-knack or piece of art that Imani has picked up since I've last visited. Instead, I notice a colorful set of sheets and a fluffy pillow neatly piled on an ottoman in the corner.

"Thanks for letting me stay at your place tonight." I project my voice into the next room. "I'd much rather get to Midtown in the morning from here than to drive in from Jersey."

Imani returns with the glasses, walking like it's a charm school contest, taking baby steps so as not to spill the pinkish liquid. "No problem. You nervous about the meeting?"

I'm tempted to tell her that she has brought up yet another subject that I don't want to discuss, but I don't think that's allowed twice in one night. "That's the understatement of the century."

"You just have to go in there tomorrow and say what you gotta say. Don't beat around the bush."

"Yeah, piece of cake," I answer sarcastically. Assuming the professional tone I reserve for work-related matters, I say, "Hi, Paula. Good to see you. Look, I know you worked your ass off to get me a two-book contract, but I've had writer's block for the past year and have decided to give up writing the second novel. Hope this isn't an inconvenience for you."

"Okay, okay, it's most likely that Paula is gonna flip. But, you never know. Maybe she'll be supportive. I know there have been times where I've had problems with my writing, and Paula really coached me through them.

That's not even in an agent's job description, but she did it anyway."

I look around at the pencils and pads of yellow lined paper resting on flat surfaces all over the apartment. Each memo pad has at least a few lines scribbled on it. Imani's place is immaculate, except for these yellow squares. She says that she doesn't like to have to walk far when she gets a good idea for a character or a new story. I have never even heard her utter the words "writer's block," "stuck," or "uninspired." Unless, of course, we were talking about me. "Girl, don't act like you struggle with finishing your projects. You're the female E. Lynn Harris, remember?"

Imani sucks her teeth and swigs her drink. "I am so sick of that nickname. Paula wants to put it on the cover of my next book. I had to tell her that I'm interested in forging my own identity as an author."

"And what did she say to that?"

In a high-pitched, very girly voice, Imani recites, "Honey, it's about selling books. Put your ego in check." Not a bad impression of Paula, I must say.

"See, Paula's all about the bottom line. And I'm screwing us both outta some serious cash. She's gonna kill me." I know I'm whining, but I can't help it. Imani's being six years older than I am often results in her having to play the big sister role. Tonight is no exception.

"Maybe she'll get you an extension with your publisher." She peers into my face to see if her words have a cheering effect, but I can't even muster a hopeful look. We sit there in silence until a soulful saxophone slowly seeps into the apartment. A haunting ballad is being played live next door, and I can feel the vibrations in the tips of my fingers and toes.

"I love Harlem," I say wistfully. "Next-door neighbors sure don't sound this good in Weehawken."

Imani listens contentedly for a few more moments before responding. "That's Nicole. White chick. Real sweetheart. Her parents said they'd give her one year after high school to pursue a career in music. It's only been two months, and the girl's got gigs left and right."

I try to picture her, some pale-faced teenager with long hair and flushed cheeks, doing Charlie Parker proud at some darkened lounge. "Wow! Good for her."

After a thoughtful pause, Imani says, "She kinda reminds me of you, the way you just busted onto the literary scene right outta college."

I dismiss the notion. "I was twenty-two. This girl is what, eighteen? I just hope she doesn't get a case of artist's block, like I did."

Imani looks as if she's seriously considering that idea, and I begin tracing the patterns on the cushion that I'd been propped against. She taps me, and I meet a mischievous expression on her face. "Hey Des, ever think that you might just need a fine-ass man to 'unblock' your behind?"

I don't know whether to giggle or to tell her off, so I settle for throwing my cushion at her. She storms to her bedroom for effect, but promptly returns to help me convert the couch. I toss and turn for quite a while once she says good night, trying to script my speech for Paula tomorrow. Finally, I let Nicole soothe me to sleep with a killer rendition of "My Funny Valentine," leaving the next day in fate's hands.

CHAPTER 2

JASON

Nothin' beats the twelve to eight. Sleep in, roll to work, put in a couple hours before a lunch break, close out the shift, and reward yourself with a late dinner. A big one.

Actually, I might switch it up this morning. I'm feeling the hunger pangs already, and an English muffin on the run ain't gonna do it. Lemme get my ass up early and catch some real breakfast. Or, even better . . .

Nailah. A beautiful name for a beautiful girl. It's like as soon as I sat up in bed just now, she was calling to me. Seeing her this morning would definitely start my day right. After holding her close to me for just a few minutes, I could work a twelve-hour shift, and it would feel like a walk through Central Park on a sunny afternoon.

I throw off the covers and walk to the bathroom. The sunlight pouring in my bedroom window made me hot, so the coolness of the hardwood floor and bathroom tiles feels good on my feet. On my way out of the bathroom, I glance at my exercise bike and wonder if I should have gotten on it before I took my shower. Never mind, I'll just get that done at work. Maybe I should call

Nailah and let her know I'm coming by. But she should be home, and she'll love the surprise.

I walk out of the apartment and jog down the two flights of stairs, pausing on each landing and taking in the sounds of the other folks who live in my brownstone. On the second floor, cartoon noises emerge from the living room. I smile, knowing that little Ty is enjoying his morning routine. His parents are laughing in another room. The first floor makes me stop even longer, because there's a saxophone solo going on, and it sounds good as hell. I need to knock on Nicole's door later and find out where her next show will be.

As I turn around to face the street after locking the outer door, the first thing I notice is the green. That shiny dark emerald green with a hint of olive, mixed with a dash of army. Army green. That is a color, right? Anyhow, we'll name the blend after me since it's my favorite. So I see this Jason green Jaguar 2000 S-Type in front of my stoop. Then I see the girl.

Watching her standing there, with her hands on her hips, slightly crouched down to examine what looks to be her back tire, I'm not initially impressed. Too typical. Too Jay-Z video. That's not my steelo. But my line of work does inspire an appreciation for muscle tone, and this woman's body is practically reciting her entire workout out loud.

Clearly, a fan of the curl. No surprise there. She gives her triceps equal love, though, with some dumbbell kickbacks. Calves lookin' like she done raised 'em a thousand times. She's obviously in the gym on the reg, but it's that perfect balance—still slim, still feminine.

Shit. She felt my eyes on her. Now that she's facing me, she actually looks kind of familiar. *Is she here to see me?*

"I'm sorry. Do I know you?" Man, I meant for that to

come out upbeat and curious. Instead, I sound like I'm
about to start a turf war.

She takes her time assessing what my deal is. Scans the
running pants and the wife-beater. Doesn't seem like
she's as appreciative of my body as I am of hers. Turns
away and walks to her trunk. "Nope." At last, she speaks.
One word, cool as a cucumber. I'm about to just say
"Fuck it," cuz she seems rude, and I was supposed to be
all about Nailah this morning. But then I notice the
source of her distraction.

Her beautiful J-green automobile is slightly tilted
toward the sidewalk due to a flat-as-a-pancake rear tire
on the driver's side. I try to give her a sympathetic look,
but her head is buried in the trunk as she leans way in to
. . . get a jack? Who knows? But I know that thanks to the
position she's in, her dress is that much shorter. Defined
quads and hamstrings. Damn, does this chick do squats,
too? Impressive. It's enough to try again.

"Need a hand?" *Keep it short and casual.*

She removes her head from the trunk and regards me
once more. Am I looking all right this morning? The
cornrows are only two days old. And I just got out of the
shower, but it's not like she's close enough to smell me
anyhow. Her mouth opens at last to deliver a snippy
"Nope."

Now it's a warm July morning, but after that second
one-word answer, I swear the temperature just got ten
degrees hotter. It's like there's steam rising up off me. I
don't care if she sees the pissed-off look on my face,
either. But she ain't looking, anyhow. And that gets me
even hotter.

I was about to get on the subway to see my baby, but
now my attitude's not correct. Lemme go grab some
food and cool off. I think I feel her eyes on me as I walk
down 122nd, but it'll be a cold day in . . . damn, what

country sits right on the equator? Ecuador. It'll be a cold day there when I look back.

Starbucks and Mickey D's wave to greet me as I turn on to Lenox. I had been sleeping on Starbucks for a minute after it got large. I wasn't into all that expresso plus hazelnut divided by skim milk times three sugars. But Monique dragged me in there over a year ago, bought me some scones and one of those Frappuccinos with whipped cream, and I got hooked. Monique. It is too early in the morning to be going there. I need to replace those thoughts with a mental picture of that gorgeous girl of mine. Cool. I'm cool.

Today, I go with McDonald's, though. Gotta reaffirm my manhood with grease and biscuits after Flat Tire Trick tried to strip it from me. This place is packed at 10:45. Don't folks in Harlem have jobs? I love my people, but I know this dude behind me does not work the twelve-to-eight shift. He's probably worked twelve to eight days in his whole life. Lemme just order my Egg McMuffin and get out of here.

Damn, completely forgot that breakfast stops at ten. Krispy Kreme is two whole avenues over. I can definitely mess with a couple of their glazed donuts. Not too healthy, but I'll mix a protein shake back at the crib.

Tire Trick had actually been erased from my thoughts until I get back to my street, and she's sitting on the steps next door to my brownstone, reading a book. I don't break my stride as I stroll past, but as I pull my keys out of my pocket, there's that even-toned, emotionless voice again. "Do you have a wrench I can borrow?"

I'm a big fan of payback. So there's no way I'm not going to stare at her for a few seconds, look as bored as I possibly can, and say, "Nope." *Ha.*

Unfortunately, I don't get the injured look I was going for. She looks back down at her book and calmly turns a page. Revenge isn't sweet when it has no effect on your victim. So I decide to drop the cold front.

"To change a tire, you need a jack, not a wrench." My voice has a bit of mockery in it, although I didn't mean it to.

"Since my jack is bolted to the trunk of my car, I think I do need that wrench," she says, not looking up from her book until she finishes her sentence. Yo, she really does look familiar.

"Oh. Yeah, I'll get one from inside." I can tell that this morning is totally done for. It's always when you have big plans for a span of time that the hours get killed most violently. I jog up the stairs, open my front door, then the inner one. I peer under the kitchen sink for my toolbox, pull it out, and remove the adjustable wrench. When I come back outside, Tire Trick is on her cell phone.

"I called y'all two freakin' hours ago. Yeah, well I'm busy too, and I need to be somewhere soon. You know what? No wonder AAA has the monopoly on this market. Your PR sucks." A pause in the conversation. "You're kidding, right? PR means public relations. Lemme give you some letters you'll understand. F. U. Cancel my membership."

Have you ever watched a person try to hang up on someone when on a cell phone? This girl clearly wants to slam down the phone, but all she can do is press END. I can't help but smile. "So you can tell the service not to come now that you found a sucker like me to change it for you?"

She stands up and removes the tool from my hand. "No one asked you for anything but a wrench." It may be my imagination, but she might be half smiling.

"I'm Jason," I say as she walks down to the sidewalk and opens her trunk. Why I'm still trying with this girl, I have no idea.

Silence floats upwards from the inside of her trunk. Finally, "Desiree."

It hits me like my momma's palm used to when I back-talked. I do know this girl. I'm so excited that I practically jump the stairs to be by her side. "Desiree Thomas?"

She bolts up so fast that she hits her head on the trunk. I wanna laugh, but I'm already on thin ice. "How the hell do you know me?" Damn. She actually looks scared.

"Calm down. You act like your face hasn't been plastered all over Barnes & Noble, and there wasn't an article about you in *Ebony*."

"*Essence*." She corrects me with a look of relief, and perhaps even flattery. "Have you read the book?"

"No." I don't know why I lie. It comes out of my mouth before I can think about it.

"Oh." The mildly pleased look is gone, but she tries to hide her disappointment. "My picture hasn't been posted in the bookstore for over a year. You have a good memory."

She's not acting nearly as bitchy as she was a few minutes ago, and I did like the woman's book. Maybe I should try to be nice. "Look, you seem to be headed somewhere important, all dressed up. How about you let me put on your spare so that you don't get all sweaty?"

"Thanks, but I don't sweat." She laughs at the shocked look on my face, and that's when I realize she's joking. She shows her agreement to my plan by handing me the wrench and returning to sit on the steps.

"Just so you know, though, I'm fully capable of changing my own tire. To get my license in high school, I had to pass two tests: the DMV's and my dad's. Before I could use his car, I had to be able to put on a spare, cool down the car if it overheated, and change the oil."

"Change the oil?" I repeat with surprise as I remove

the jack from its storage area in her trunk. "Damn. Is your dad a mechanic?"

"No," she clips back at me. This girl is weird. One minute she's all normal, and the next it's like she's mad that she was even talking in the first place. I can't be too upset, though, cuz I get the same way. Actually, I should keep the conversation going so she doesn't start asking *me* questions.

"Do you live around here?" I ask as I secure the jack under the car.

"No. I was visiting a friend last night."

"One of my neighbors?"

"Uh-huh. Imani Grace. Know her?"

I swear, God is a dude with a killer sense of humor. Here I am actually checking this girl out, trying to see where her head's at, knowing that my ass needs to be at Nailah's. And God decides to teach me a lesson by making this girl Imani Grace's "friend." Imani. The most out-there gay woman in Harlem.

"Yeah, I know her. She's a . . . writer, isn't she?" I don't look at her; I just concentrate on hoisting up the Jag.

"Yup. We have the same agent, which is how we know each other."

"I see." Hell yeah, my view sure ain't cloudy anymore. No wonder she was acting all frosty before. The chick hates men! Even her book has all the brothers acting shady. Although I gotta say, her girlfriend is nothing like her. Imani's real cool, and we've had some chill conversations from our stoops on warm days. She's even told me about her fly-ass woman and how in love they are. Although I would've pictured her with someone a little more easygoing than Tire Trick. Maybe Desiree's nicer to people she knows well. Or to people she's sleeping with.

Well, the good thing is that this revelation takes the

pressure off. I can just get these bolts off and throw on this spare in silence. No sense wasting G on her. I'll be finished with enough time to at least give my girl a phone call.

A few minutes pass before I hear that creamy smooth voice again. "So what do you do, Jason?"

"I work at a gym."

"Personal trainer?"

"Something like that." Damn, these bolts are crazy tight. I can barely concentrate on her questions. Let me position myself to get some leverage. Take it back to eleventh-grade physics. Umph! Well, clearly I shouldn't have cut so many classes in high school, because my theory on force ain't workin'.

"So you work with weights all day but can't loosen that bolt, I see."

The comment is enough to put some juice in my muscles, and I get the last bolt off the tire. "Desiree, how did your tire get this flat, anyway? Did you piss someone off with that mouth of yours?" No need to try to be nice anymore.

She doesn't answer and instead rises from the steps to pass me the spare, enhancing the definition in her biceps. I wonder what her abs look like. Refocusing on the task at hand, I complete the job without saying anything else.

It feels good to stand up and stretch. Desiree stands up also, and for the first time, I feel like we're looking right at each other.

"Listen, Jason. Thank you. I have a tough day ahead of me, and this flat tire was an added stress. I appreciate the help." I take it back. Looking into her eyes, I see she's not a hip-hop video girl at all. There's a seriousness to her. A depth. Maybe even sadness.

"Not a problem. Good meeting you, and tell Imani what's up for me." I head up my steps.

"You probably see her more than I do," she calls as I open the door.

"I doubt it," I reply, without turning around.

When I get inside, I need to crash on the couch for a second. It's 11:10, I didn't see Nailah, and I'm gonna be late for work since I need to take a second shower. But on the bright side, I cracked the tough exterior of a lipstick lesbian. I can hear God chuckling.

CHAPTER 3

HUNTER

Dr. Hunter Gregory. Hunter Gregory, MD. "Dr. Gregory, the patient in Trauma One is crashing. Get in here, stat!"

Some days, when I get off a thirtysome-hour shift and my eyes are as dry as elbows in the wintertime and my feet can barely support my body, I start with the name calling. One more year. Go through a few more rotations, pass my boards, and the names I've dreamed about for so long will actually be real. Today I recite the fancy titles in my head as I wait in line at Kenny's Soul Food Restaurant for some baked chicken.

Yeah, just think about the delicious food you'll be eating in a few minutes and the bomb-ass job you'll have in a few years. The pain of the horrible shift you just came off will go away.

It's not working. I can still see Miranda, the girl I left behind in pediatrics today. She was admitted late last night by some of her friends in boarding school. Sixteen years old. Anorexic. Skin cold, heart rate low. Her screams are still resonating in my head. "No! No!" she pleaded when the doctors force-fed her.

Well, no one's gonna have to ask me twice to eat this meal I'm about to get. I gotta cheer the hell up. Go to

Plan B. First, scrap the baked chicken, and go with the fried. You only live once, after all. Then, abandon the "where Hunter will be in the near future" fantasy, and move to the "look at all Hunter has sacrificed to get here" routine.

There was the senior class trip to the Bahamas in high school, which I had to miss because of a scholarship that required me to spend that same week at a conference. There was that frat disappointment sophomore year, when I had to drop the Kappa line cuz I couldn't keep getting my ass beat and showing up to Orgo on time the next morning. Can't forget the track meet on the same day as the MCATS, which might have cost my school the championship. All in the name of med school.

And it didn't stop there, although I thought it would have. I'd made it to Columbia Med, choosing it over the Big H because I missed New York. I thought I could finally get my life back, although I wasn't quite so sure that I remembered what life was like before the doctor dream. Oh, wait. There it is. Standing in the middle of my street with some kids from the block, throwing around a football that we'd found abandoned in Central Park. Nothing to worry about till Mom shouts out the window to come eat. That's living.

Now my entire life is a punched clock. I even enter my sessions on the toilet into my Palm Pilot. Can I really blame Alicia for getting fed up? She works nine to five; her nights and weekends belong to her. It was just a matter of time before she had to be out.

I swear, the only chance I have to find a female who understands my situation is to date a med student. And I don't know about the idea of two future doctors linking up. Between schedules and egos, that could get ugly . . . .

"Fried chicken, yams, greens, mac and cheese, and

corn bread." I'd throw a "please" on it, but that's not
how it works at Kenny's. They have long lines and aren't
into extra pleasantries. But you come here for the food,
not the hospitality. You gotta go to a real Southern
restaurant for that. That's the one thing I miss about
going to Duke. Folks were friendly. Sometimes you can
find that same homely vibe in Harlem, but it's completely missing from everywhere else in the city.

I carry my tray to a table in the corner and take a huge
bite of fried chicken before I discover that I forgot to
order a drink. Maybe I can order one without having to
get back in line. If Kenny were here, he'd give me a
break, but I don't see him today. I'll just walk up to the
register and give it a . . .

Damn. About ten feet in front of me, a goddess is ordering meat loaf and mashed. I take in her red toenail
polish, move up her buttery beige legs to her gray pin-
striped fitted dress, with a deep V-neck revealing enough
to have fantasies about the rest, and finally reach a face
that would make Stevie Wonder do a double take.

I command my legs to keep moving, and as I get
closer, it becomes clear that this girl is upset. What someone who looks that good could be upset about, I have no
idea, but I'm about to find out.

"I can't believe there's no money in my wallet." Her
voice is smooth and silky, like the hair that she brushes
off her face exasperatedly. "I meant to go to the ATM
this morning, but I had a lot on my mind." She looks at
the woman behind the register, with an expression that
reads, "You understand, right?" But she gets nothing in
return.

"Can I use a credit card?"

"Machine's broken."

"Is there an ATM nearby?" Her voice doesn't sound so

smooth anymore. The people behind her are visibly losing patience.

Now it's been a long time since I've had to pull out my A game. I reserve it for those rare occasions when I can't get by on profile alone. Every guy has a profile. It's the report that a woman gives her friends when they ask what the guy she's dating is like. The Hunter Gregory profile sounds something like this: "Girl, he's tall, dark, handsome, and his body is on point. He has no kids and no baggage. *And* he's going to be a doctor." Most of the time girls only need that much info before they start picking out names for their beautiful, brilliant babies-to-be.

But I'm not taking the risk of riding on the profile with this one. On three, executing A game. One, two . . .

"Excuse me, miss." I first direct my attention to the cashier lady so that my damsel in distress has a chance to check me out without having to worry about carrying on a conversation. Ladies appreciate a chance to assess the package without distraction. "I'll take care of this woman's meal." I hand her a crisp twenty. The only twenty in my wallet, but it's all good. Cashier lady raises her eyebrows as a response and gives me my change. It's not until I put my $13.26 back into my wallet that I look at her.

"You didn't have to do that," she says as she takes her tray and walks toward an empty table. Her tone of voice doesn't sound grateful at all. It could be she's just embarrassed by the situation. Either way, she doesn't appear impressed. I guess this girl's affection can't be bought. Or maybe it costs more than seven dollars.

She sets her meal on the table and begins fishing through her purse. I watch her and feel awkward, clumsy. My A game has dropped to about a C-. Gotta boost the grade. "I wanted to. I don't like to see beautiful ladies in distress."

At this comment she moves her gaze from the inside of her black Kenneth Cole bag and settles it on my face. "Really. So if I were unattractive, you would've let me suffer?" She returns her attention to Kenneth.

I'm thrown but refuse to show it. "Good point. The suffering of any human being pains me, and I would have helped you no matter what you . . ."

"Crap." Okay, my game has quickly reached the point of failure. "Sorry to cut you off, but I realized that I don't have my checkbook, either. Can I mail you what I owe?"

This chick has officially lost goddess status. She interrupts my admissions spiel for med school to inform me that she plans to pay me back? "Look, you don't owe me anything. You said you had a rough morning, right? Consider this the good deed that changed the course of your day."

She smiles. Goddess once more. Aphrodite has nothing on her ass. "Believe it or not, I've already had one of those." At the sight of my intrigue, the pearly whites disappear. "Long story. Not important. Anyhow, I insist on paying you back, so can you write down your address?"

Now it's my turn to show what three-thousand-dollar braces and Ultra Brite toothpaste gave me. "Wouldn't you rather have my phone number?"

I get a smirk and a shake of the head, not as a response to my question, but as a sign of disbelief that I asked it. She pulls out a miniature spiral-bound red notebook from her bag, flips to the first empty page, and hands it to me. I'm about to ask for a pen when I realize there's a tiny one stuck inside the spiral.

"Interesting phone book you got here," I say as I debate what to include in addition to my address.

"Flip through the pages and you're a dead man." I get the feeling that she's only half kidding.

Once I include my first name, last name, and middle

initial, addresses (residence and e-mail), and home and cell numbers, I write, "Because of you, my chicken is cold. How about repaying me with a hot meal?"

I hand her the notebook with a wink. Either she's an expert at masking her curiosity, or she has no interest at all in what I wrote, because she returns the little red book to its rightful place and sits down to her meal.

Lord knows, I want to sit across from her. Watch her pouty, painted lips wrap themselves around the fork. Observe her tongue retrieving a crumb of corn bread from the corner of her mouth. Ef that. I'm just gonna go get my tray, come back to this table, and sit my ass down. I don't have to ask for her permission. After all, she wouldn't even have a meal to eat if it weren't for me.

But as I turn away to execute my plan, there's that voice, once again silky smooth. "Thanks . . . I'm sorry. I didn't catch your name."

I'm heated, so I get flip with her. "It's in your little notebook." Then I try to fix my answer, cuz I know I sound like a little bitch. "And your name?"

"It'll be on the check I send you, won't it?"

"I guess it will." And I walk back to my table. It occurs to me that I never even got my drink. So I eat my food, still thirsty. Still hungry, too, but not for chicken and corn bread. Hungry for more conversation. Maybe I should go back and tell her I'm in med school. Or maybe I should just forget about the meat loaf goddess. She already cost me seven dollars. I'll be damned if she costs me my pride.

CHAPTER 4

DESIREE

Sometimes I feel bad about how harsh I can be with men. Like right now I feel a slight twinge in my stomach, which is most likely due to guilt. Either that, or I'm eating this meat loaf too fast.

I glance over at my latest victim, sitting at the corner table by himself, picking at a plate of cold food. I suppose I could've been kinder to him since he saved my ass, albeit for superficial reasons. But he caught me at a bad moment. This meeting with Paula has me all stressed, and I was totally starving because I haven't eaten yet today. But who am I kidding? Ninety percent of the reason I was so cold is because that boy looks a little too much like Trevor for me. Trevor. A name I try not to allow into the paths of my memory, but that occasionally slips past the gatekeepers.

Just the thought of Trevor brings me back to a time in my life when I knew nothing, thought everything was possible, and would do anything for love. I can still recall the stars in my eyes when he approached me in the dim light of a basement party off campus. And the tears in my eyes when it all ended six months later are just as fresh.

But I know I'm not right for being mad at a man because he's Henessey brown, bald-headed, and six feet two. I'm supposed to be working on my issues. Maybe I'll put this guy's check inside of a thank-you card or something.

Or maybe not. Perhaps I *am* too extreme with men, but I still come first. And in about an hour, my career as a young writer diva will be officially over. That's what I need to be thinking about right now, not this man's little hurt feelings.

It's been quite a while since I've considered any career besides novelist. I used to be really good at the violin. If I practice super hard, are there openings around for violinists? For an orchestra or something? Because after being creative for a living, it's hard to go to a punch in, punch out situation.

I wonder what my knight in shining chicken grease does for a living. He's in a shirt and tie, which doesn't really say too much. He could be anything from financial tycoon to manager at KFC. Although if he works there, I should hope he wouldn't order fried chicken from somewhere else on his lunch break. But judging from his cocky swagger and corny lines, I'd guess his occupation is on the higher end of the class spectrum. He doesn't seem used to rejection, either, because he just walked past me and out the door without even a nod in my direction. Well, good for him. I like a man who refuses to play himself. He's climbed a notch in my esteem. Maybe I'll write a note of thanks after all.

In this fleeting spirit of goodwill, I really should send a card to tire guy, too. What's his name? James? No, Jason. Now he's an interesting one. First of all, I didn't even think people with bodies like that existed outside of Torso Track infomercials. I go to the gym damn often, but never have I seen a body that displayed each and every muscle that clearly. If he ever decides to change careers, he could be the anatomical model for first-year medical students. Just stand there naked as the professor uses a pointer and asks the class to note the lateral muscles. I know my girl Robyn would never complain about how dry her lectures are anymore.

And homeboy actually has a face that can compete with the beauty of his neck-down. Green eyes don't usually do it for me (I'm more of a dark chocolate lover myself), but on a deep caramel complexion, and with some cornrows to make it all seem a little less pretty . . . that's hot. And who would think that a guy like that would know who the hell I am? Impressive.

It's definitely a good thing that I'm not looking for a guy to be with, because Jason's the type that would have you wide open. Open. I love that word because it really exemplifies the perils of getting romantically attached to someone. You're just leaving yourself open to pain. It's like when you leave a wound uncovered. It's exposed to elements that can leave you infected and scarred. If that doesn't capture what being in love is like, I don't know what does. Hey, I should jot that down. But then again, why pull out the red notebook? In an hour, Desiree the writer will cease to be.

No sense in prolonging the inevitable. Let me dump this tray and get on out of here. I hope my car will be okay where it's parked. There was no meter, but I think it's legal. I swear, if Wall Street folks had any sense, they'd all park in Harlem and take the subway downtown. But, on the other hand, as I scan the streets and watch the brown river of bodies ebb and flow, I can imagine that they have their reasons for keeping their distance. Not every Joe Schmo has what it takes to be a Bill Clinton of the world. I heard he's chilled at soul food restaurants around the way many times.

I walk to the subway station at a snail's pace. I tell myself that it's because I'm taking in the sights and smells that only up-uptown Manhattan can provide. But I know the real reason is because I'm nervous about the meeting.

As I near the station at 135th Street, I manage to take my mind off of things momentarily just by people-watching. A couple walking down the street provides me with the most amusement. The woman is in a tighter-than-tight miniskirt and fur jacket, rocking a long, silky ponytail (bought the day before). She could be anywhere from thirty-five to sixty, depending on how rough the years have treated her. Proud as a peacock as she sucks on a cigarette like it's the tastiest thing since Now and Laters. The man is a cross between a kind grandpa and a blaxploitation film pimp. He has his arm around his lady's waist like someone might steal her if he lets go. I'm actually smiling by the time I'm on the train.

When I step out of the subway downtown, I rationalize that I shouldn't be nervous to meet with Paula. This is my girl. She's always been supportive, and everything's going to be fine. I repeat this over and over in my head until I reach her office.

Paula Moy is a fabulous woman. In all ways that a woman can be the bomb, Paula is. First, she's gorgeous. Slender with subtle curves, she turns heads with her five-foot-nine stature (a very unusual height for a Chinese female). Her sleek, long layers of jet-black hair are always perfect, and we won't even go into her Fifth Avenue wardrobe.

Next, she's crazy successful. She started out as a journalist—not the boring kind, though. Pieces for *Cosmo* and *Glamour*, just breaking down all of men's secrets.

Another thing that makes her fantastic is that she understands men more than most men do! Although when people read my book, they think I understand men, too. But I think Paula's the real deal. After she got tired of that gig, she began reviewing books for a bunch of magazines. That's how she made all these connections that she's been taking advantage of since she opened her own agency four years ago.

One of the reasons Paula has been such a good businesswoman is she has a knack for making you feel like you're the most important person on earth. She gives compliments with sincerity, does favors without a second thought, and laughs harder at jokes than anyone I know. But there's not a thing about her that seems fake. She's just a true people person.

"Desi! Kisses," she says dutifully as she holds my arms and smooches the air on either side of my face. "You look to die for, as usual."

"Just trying to keep up with you, Paula." I force a smile and check out her black capris with huge cuffs at the calf, stiletto Jimmy Choos, and a red button-down blouse with three-quarter sleeves that cuff at the elbows.

"Well, sit! Actually, don't sit. I got some new pieces since you were last here." Another thing that makes Paula an exceptional female is that she possesses the whole decorating talent that women are supposed to have. Now me, I've definitely tried to step it up since college, putting my posters in frames and replacing my halogen lamps with track lighting and candles. But Paula's on another level; she makes a twenty-five-square-foot office space look like a museum curator's wet dream. No artwork, just photographs. Framed black-and-whites, mostly. Her husband's a photographer. And you know Paula couldn't marry some starving artist. She had to get with one of the most notable photographers in New York. I saw one of his shots of a chain-link fence, with some guys on a basket-ball court behind it, in a gallery once. It was going for two grand.

There's only one photo in color on the wall, and it's new. Paula is sitting on the beach at what looks like sun-rise. It's taken from behind, though there's a touch of a side profile. But the focus of the shot is obviously the colors exploding over the ocean. "Wow," is all I can say.

"Peter's newest. He calls it P.M. Dawn. Get it? Me at sunrise? Goodness, my sweetie is corny," she giggles.

I giggle back as a response, but it comes out funny. I practically choke on it. She notices.

She takes a seat and motions for me to do the same. "Desi, I'm pretty sure why you called this meeting. You haven't started the next book, have you?"

I'm speechless. I never thought Paula was on to me. Over the past several months, I have always had upbeat reports on my writing progress. Maybe the lack of detail clued her in. I don't know whether to feel guilty, re-lieved, or offended that she had guessed my failure.

"Listen, Desi. If you came here to tell me you want out of your contract, I'm here to say hell no. You're too tal-ented a writer to receive such a blemish on your career. Not to mention that I have some news for you myself. Ya ready?" She smiles, relaxing my nerves a little bit. I manage a nod.

"*No More Lies* . . . the *movie*, hon! New Line wants the rights. . . ."

Paula's still talking, but it sounds like it's coming through a tunnel. My book made into a movie. Well, it's what I've dreamed about since I first started writing it in college. My girl Kahli and I would sit up late at night after reading over my latest chapter, trying to cast the movie, and daydreaming about attending the Academy Awards with some sexy Hollywood star.

I command myself to listen to Paula's words. If I had to choose a handwriting to match the tone of her voice, it would be that bubbly, swirly cursive that I trained myself to use in ninth grade. Hearts dotting the i's. But as perky as she sounds, there's no question, she's the most sensible person I know next to Imani, and I can trust her with anything related to my career.

"You can *not* flake out on this deadline for book number two. With the movie on the way, the next book is guaranteed to be a hit! Are you sure you can't write a sequel?" she asks hopefully.

"Paula, we've been through this. I refuse to revisit that part of my . . . I just want to do something different." I'm flustered, the way I always get when I think about the real-life events that inspired the book. You'd think that after hundreds of interviews and readings I'd be used to it, but no one ever seems to have a problem with my standard white lie of "all characters and events are purely fictional." Paula had tried to convince me that it would be great for publicity to admit that the novel had been based on my own life, but I just had too much pride. A sequel will always be out of the question. Writing about my college drama the first time was therapy. The second time would just be an exercise in torture.

"Well," Paula says, interrupting my internal monologue, "there's another option. Publishers are taking notice of all these male authors writing from the female perspective. But they feel that female writers aren't crossing the gender line as often, or as effectively."

"Hey! I take offense to that. I told parts of *No More Lies* from the guys' points of view."

"You're exactly right, but the key word is 'parts'. Most of your book was told through the eyes of a young woman. Gerry, a marketing exec at Random House, says that they're looking for a young black female to write a novel about relationships, using the voice of a man, or of several men. He called me because you're one of the writers they thought of."

"Why me?" I think I know the answer, but I could use the flattery.

"Because reader response to *No More Lies* indicates that you seem to really understand the twenty-something demographic, male and female. Do you think you could do a little stretching and push yourself to write a man's novel?"

This is hysterical. Random House is asking me—someone who has not gone on a date in five years, someone who doesn't even have a male platonic friend, even a gay one—they're asking me to think like a guy for at least 250 pages.

"Paula, I've had writer's block for a year. What the hell makes you think that I can do this? I couldn't even come up with something when I had no restrictions!"

Paula puts her finger to her lips thoughtfully. Her nails are painted red—red enough to stand out, but not red enough to look tacky. I look at my toenails in hopes that the shade matches hers. Close enough.

"Desi, maybe the reason you haven't been able to write is because there haven't been *enough* restrictions. With the first book, you were bound by your real life story. That was your guide through the process. You could be the type of author who needs an assignment, kind of like a journalist. I know I'm like that. And as far as using your own experience, I'd have to disagree. Think of all the stuff you and your friends complain about when it comes to guys and relationships. Then try to imagine why they do those things."

At this, I have to smile. "If I knew why men do the things they do, none of my girls would be single, and I'd probably be the richest woman on earth."

She laughs. "Let's talk in a week. Over the next few days, talk to friends. Ask them about their boyfriends, their brothers, their dads. Try to come up with a story line." Upon seeing my look of doubt, she hurriedly adds, "Just the skeleton."

Sighing, I consider my options. Break my contract and ruin my hopes of seeing my book made into a movie? Hell no. Come up with an original story line that is both interesting and writeable? I've been trying that forever, and it hasn't happened. I guess I could give Paula's idea a try and see how it goes.

"All right. I'll e-mail you next week." I stand up and so does she. I must look like I need encouragement, because she gives me a hug, which she doesn't ordinarily do. I know she has a lot riding on me, too, both in terms of money and reputation, but I feel like the hug is genuine. My self-confidence is momentarily boosted as I leave her office. But as I step into the glaring sun, the reality of the situation hits me. I want to get right to work, but I don't even know exactly what that consists of. I'm anxious to get home and jump on my computer, but I have to get a new tire first. Hopping on the New Jersey Turnpike with a spare sounds like a recipe for disaster.

Wow, has it really only been a few hours since Jason changed my flat? Or since Trevor's twin bought my lunch? I wonder why they stuck their necks out for me. Probably because I'm an attractive woman in a fitted dress. It can't be because I'm sweet and nice, because I'm not. Did they regret helping me once they realized that my bitchiness was here to stay? But men like challenges, so maybe they were intrigued. Hey! I should be writing all this down.

My pace quickens.

CHAPTER 5

To: *kahlila@alumni.franklin.edu, lloyd@philosophy.*
franklin.edu, robyn@med.columbia.edu,
jt_steinway@alumni.franklin.edu
From: *desiree@alumni.franklin.edu*
Time: Sunday, July 8, 2001 10:18 a.m.
Subject: research—IMPORTANT!

Message:
hi all-
hope everyone is doing well. here's the deal. i'm
trying to start this new book. i know i say this every
week, but this time it's serious. it's a real challenge
because i have to write it from a male point of
view.

what i was hoping was that you guys could e-mail
me any thoughts you have on men. kahli and
robyn, what would you want to see addressed in
a book about guys and relationships? lloyd and
j.t., i'm hoping you can maybe give me the inside
scoop on anything your species does that mysti-
fies us. or you can tell us about the things women

do that drive y'all crazy. and sorry for hitting you up for info, even though we're technically not friends. being that the two of you are best friends with my girlfriends, you're the closest things to guy friends i have. pathetic, i know.

anyhow, i know i haven't been really clear about what i'm looking for, but that's because i'm not even sure.

looking forward to hearing from you
des

To: *desiree@alumni.franklin.edu*
From: *jt_steinway@alumni.franklin.edu*
Time: Sunday, July 8, 2001 4:04 p.m.
Subject: almost deleted your mail

Message:
Hey Des,
   Your e-mail almost went in the trash because I was going through my messages so quickly, hitting delete. Somehow the friggin' groupies got a hold of this address (I just changed it last month).
   Anyhow, what I'm about to write probably won't help you, since you're probably not writing a book about NBA players, but it's what's on my mind, so too damn bad. It's about these girls clogging up my e-mail accounts, waiting outside my hotel rooms, calling my dad! A few years ago, I would've thought that a dude was crazy complaining about girls ready to hook up at a moment's notice, but it really does get old. I want to know why girls think they're going to be my future wife by making

themselves pieces of meat. I also wanna know why they like me so much, being that none of them seem to know anything about basketball. You'd think that if you were trying to snag somebody, you'd do a little research on what you know the person's interests are.

I guess my beef is that girls seem to go about seeking us out the wrong way. We don't want the girl at the bar who's the first one to walk over. We want the one across the room, laughing with her friends, not paying us any mind. I want the girl in the stands at my games, with her little brother, eating a hot dog, cheering her hardest for us to beat the other team.

But in all fairness, maybe I'm to blame, because I never find that girl after the game. I always end up with someone who is a lot more aggressive, but half as impressive. Hey, that rhymes!

Sorry for the ranting. Good luck with your book. Let's get together when Kahlila comes to town.

J.T.

To: *desiree@alumni.franklin.edu*
From: *kahlila@alumni.franklin.edu*
Time: Sunday, July 8, 2001 9:46 p.m.
Subject: wasn't it all so simple then?

Message:
desiree,

my time in arizona is coming to a close. the school year is over, the teach for america program has concluded for me, and i have to figure out where i'm going in september. the good news is that i am definitely making a trip to new york in the next few weeks.

watching my middle schoolers fall in "love" over and over again, i've decided that i want to go back to the way relationships used to work back then. if someone likes someone else, a note is passed or a middle man is implemented. suddenly, the boy and girl are a couple, which consists of meeting between classes and talking for hours on the phone. when one person is ready to break up, the note or the middle man is again utilized, and all parties have moved on by lunchtime.

now that we're adults, everything has such dire consequences. women are so anxious to make that final love connection. we meet a guy with a decent resume, and we're already placing our last name with his, evaluating his potential to be a capable father, a strong provider, a lifelong lover. you use information about his past ("so why did you break up with your ex-girlfriend?") to provide clues about his future potential. and though all of this takes place through searching looks and subtle "i see's," the guy feels it. and he resents it. then the relationship ends, with the woman still thinking that she was the one for him. and a lot of times, the guy knows that she was indeed the one. but he just wasn't ready.

but here's the most hilarious part: when a guy decides that the timing is right for him to settle down, he'll turn to the closest woman available and make her his wife. soul mate be damned.

and i know what you're thinking, girl. this is not bitterness about dave marrying joy. well, maybe it is a little bit. even though it's been five years since my brief college romance with dave, i still stay up nights, trying to figure out why he would get back with his ex. and here's what i've decided: guys are scared of loving a woman too much. they'd rather have a woman adore them. oh, sure, they'll reciprocate the feelings enough to be content. but getting swept off your feet implies that you're not in control. dave was scared by how deep it was between us, so he returned to what was safe and comfortable.

or maybe what we had was just all in my head.
kahli

To: *desiree@alumni.franklin.edu*
From: *robyn@med.columbia.edu*
Time: Monday, July 9, 2001 9:58 a.m.
Subject: Re: research—IMPORTANT!

Message:
You know I'm the practical one in our little Three Musketeers crew. So while Kahli will probably send some dreamy, head in the clouds ruminations, here's what I want you to address in your book:

Why do guys say they'll call and then never do?

Why do educated men say that they want successful women but run with their tails between their legs when they hear Columbia med school?

Why are their egos ten times more fragile than ours?

How come sex doesn't necessarily come with an emotional price tag for them?

Why do men seem to have so much less drama with their friends than we do?

I'll try to think of more, but right now I need to get back to this lab experiment.

Robyn

To: *desiree@alumni.franklin.edu*
From: *lloyd@philosophy.franklin.edu*
Time: Monday, July 9, 2001 1:11 p.m.
Subject: Pressure!

Message:
Hi Desiree,

I'm really glad to hear that you're seriously work-ing on this next novel. I ask Robyn all the time when your sophomore work is coming out, since I loved the first one so much.

Anyway, I feel a bit of pressure responding to your request, partly because I'm one of only two men from whom you're seeking input, and I'm the only black one. Also, people tend to think that I have deep things to say just because of what I'm study-ing in school. In any case, I'll try my best to be useful.

My basic feeling is that women are hypocrites. That's right. Sweet little Lloyd is actually insulting the fairer sex. Here's why: everything that you say you want is a lie. You lament the behavior of the majority of men, but when you meet an atypical guy, you don't want him.

Minor example: women say that men are too concerned with the superficial. But without fail, women I'm dating will ask me why I insist on wearing Miles Davis T-shirts instead of Nike athletic wear, or if I can trade in my Converse sneakers for a pair of Tims. What difference does it make?

Major example: women say that men don't express their feelings. Yet they continually choose to pursue those men who are the least communicative. They apparently like to have to guess what the man they love is thinking. Look at Kahlila. In college, she fell in love with Dave—a man who never told her how he felt and broke up with her by writing her a letter. I know what you're thinking, Desiree: that's a personal beef as opposed to a general observation. Okay, maybe a little bit. But what I'm saying is still the truth.

How about this as a plot for your book: a woman meets her ideal partner, but because she doesn't even know what she wants or needs, she lets him go. Only to realize too late that she'd held forever in her hand and tossed it on the ground.

Lloyd

CHAPTER 6

DESIREE

It's one of those summer nights where you're rewarded for the sweltering daytime heat with a beautiful evening, and the cardigan you brought just in case it gets chilly uselessly rests in the crook of your arm. My skinny-heeled, strappy sandals click down Adam Clayton Powell Boulevard, while Imani's shoes, which look an awful lot like ballet slippers, are an almost inaudible shuffle.

I suddenly notice that I forgot to put my rings on my fingers, which makes me automatically touch my earlobes to check for earrings. "Damn it. I forgot to put on my jewelry. Think I should take my hair down?"

Imani doesn't even look at me. "You look great with your hair pulled back. Don't fall victim to the notion that you have to wear long tresses in your face to be pretty."

"I don't think I said all that, but whatever. You're wearing *your* hair down," I say, fondling the braid at the nape of my neck. She wears a colorful band around her hairline, her wavy dreadlocks flowing past her shoulders, resting on her not-so-modest bustline.

"I don't count. My hair is natural, which automatically discounts me from being classically beautiful by society's standards."

"That's bullshit."

"Is it? When was the last time you saw Tyra or Naomi rocking an Afro?"

I inhale and exhale loudly. She thinks the sigh means that I've seen the light and have surrendered the argument. It really means that I'm too annoyed to continue talking. This way we both win.

She begins fishing in her bag, a hand-beaded sack with a long shoulder strap. "Thanks for coming with me tonight. Sheila's in Chicago for work. What was I thinking, falling in love with a corporate stiff?" Pulling out two tickets, she reads them closely, checking the numbers on the buildings as we pass.

I decide not to answer her question about Sheila, partly because it was rhetorical, and also because I don't know the answer. I had been just as surprised as she was when she first told me that she had a crush on the lawyer working with Paula on her book contract. One year later, they still seem pretty mismatched. "It was really nice of Nicole to give you tickets. B Sharp has been the hottest jazz spot in Harlem since it opened last month."

"Wasn't it sweet of her? She said she felt like it was the least she could do for her neighbors, since we have to endure her incessant practicing. She actually used the word endure, like it's torture or something. Sheila loves hearing Nicole through my walls so much that she started buying jazz albums to play at her apartment. *Endure* my ass."

At the sound of the word "neighbors," I become a little distracted. Isn't Jason her neighbor also? Maybe Nicole gave him tickets, too. I can't picture him at B Sharp. Would he wear his undershirt and running pants? And what would his date look like? Probably some around-the-

way girl who buys all her clothes from the hip-hop stores
on 125th, scoring Gucci bags and shoes from the shady
guy on the corner, selling his wares out of trash bags. I
want to gossip with Imani about Jason, but I know she'll
blow the whole thing out of proportion.

There's a smattering of well-dressed folks on the
corner, and my ears perk up at the soft strains of music
floating down the street to greet us. The clicking of my
heels on the sidewalk increases its tempo as we near B
Sharp. I'm suddenly excited to spend an evening in the
company of good people and good music.

It doesn't take long for the hostess to seat us at a
round table for two in front of the stage, where instruments have been set up, but the musicians are missing.
Once I position my bag and sweater on the back of my
chair and order a glass of pinot grigio from our waiter, I
take a slow swivel around the room.

There's something spectacular about the sight. Maybe
it's the lighting—the candles casting a glow on the face
of each patron, yet creating a dim enough atmosphere
for couples to feel a sense of privacy. It could be the
people themselves. Of the forty or so bodies in this
place, none of them shares the exact same skin color.
Brown comes in so many gorgeous variations, and as a
writer, I'm constantly trying to find new ways to describe
complexion. The food words are overused: honey,
caramel, buttermilk. So are the wood/nut words: oak,
mahogany, acorn, almond. I close my eyes and listen to
the voice of Jill Scott sneaking out of the speakers, the
clinking of glasses as toasts are made, the soft bass tones
of men trying to spit their smoothest game, the shrieks
of laughter that only come from a girls' night out. And
at that moment, though my career is hanging on a ledge,
and I can barely recall the feeling of a man's arms
around me, I am so happy. The phrase "young, gifted,

and black" pops into my head and makes me smile. It's like every person in this place embodies that idea.

Then I see him. Seated in the far corner of the room, almost behind the stage, staring off into space, holding what looks like a glass of vodka on the rocks. Alone. I can feel the pulse in my wrists, and one in my neck that I'd forgotten I had. I force a casual tone as I lean toward Imani. "Jason's here."

She slowly turns in the direction of my eyes and rotates to her original position just as smoothly. "Oh, right. He changed your tire the other day, didn't he? Go say hi."

"No need." She gives me a smug look, which I ignore. "So I got some interesting responses from my college friends when I asked for ideas about my new book."

"What did they say?" she asks, smiling at the waiter, who has just arrived with our drinks.

"They said all types of things. It basically boiled down to the women wanting to understand men, and vice versa. They think my book should give some insight as to why men and women just can't ever get it right. Of course, they all have personal experiences that impact their opinions."

"Exactly, Desiree. Which is why you haven't written anything in so long. You have no experiences to pull from yourself. If you want this book to ring true, you can't just rely on interviewing people you know. You have to get out there and live life. That's what makes the writing fresh."

"So you're saying that all stories have to be auto-biographical?"

She takes a sip of her shiraz and considers the question. "In a literal sense, no. But when you're writing about relationships, especially romantic ones, you have to remember what it feels like: the excitement, the pain. . . ." She leans in closer and whispers, "The sex."

We both collapse into giggles, earning the attention of a few nearby tables.

"Excuse me, ladies. If you can't get yourselves under control, I'm going to have to ask you to leave," says a voice standing over us.

Embarrassed and alarmed, I look up and meet Jason's eyes. They remind me of the glass eyes of the only white doll I ever had, a gift from a patient of my mom's. They caught the light like a crystal prism, as his are doing right now. His cornrows are just as tight as the first time I saw him, though his outfit is drastically different. A simple black silk short-sleeved shirt falls nicely on his broad shoulders, and the open top button reveals a thick silver link chain, which shines brightly against his skin. I spend a few more seconds taking in his linen pants and dress shoes. I didn't think it was possible, but he looks sexier today than he did on his doorstep last week.

I can tell that Imani is trying to peer inside my skull and read my mind, so I force myself to look away. "How ya doin', Jason? You scared us for a second there," she says brightly.

"I'm doing well, Imani. And how are you, Desiree? Good to see you again." His voice alone quickens my heart, a rich baritone with a scratchy edge to it—the handwriting of a note scrawled with both haste and care before a lover's departure. I gotta get away from this guy.

"Fine, thank you. Excuse me for a moment." I rise from the table and walk toward the bathroom as fast as I possibly can without busting my ass. Once I'm in there, I fix a stray hair in the mirror, wondering if he'll be gone by the time I get back. Hoping that he won't be.

CHAPTER 7

JASON

I wasn't even gonna roll tonight, but Nailah's out of town visiting her grandparents, so I figured I'd come check out Nicole at B Sharp. It was supposed to be a night out with my muddled thoughts, a glass of water, and maybe a Muddy Waters tune from the band to bring it all together. But everything got thrown off when I saw her.

The candle on the table lit up her face, her hair braided down her back. I couldn't see what she had on, but whatever it was revealed what must have been hours of work on her delts. She was leaned in close, chatting with Imani, who had her back to me. I don't know why I got up and walked over there. But I felt myself being yanked across the room to their table, and it crossed my mind for the second time in one week that God was truly messing with me.

Now here I am, watching Desiree's back as she practically runs away from me to the bathroom. It was a mistake to come say hello, no doubt, but if I go back to my table all quick, I'll look like a damn fool. Imani offers me Desiree's chair while she's gone, so I take it. Just for a minute, though. I don't want to be here when she gets back.

"Lookin' good tonight, Imani." And it's true. Her cocoa skin always looks tasty, but she put on some kind of nighttime make-up that chicks wear to hypnotize you with their suddenly sparkly eyes. She's also displaying mad cleavage in a low-cut top that's begging for my attention, but I make sure not to allow myself more than a quick glance.

"You too, Jason. As always." I hate compliments, and I look around at the crowd so I don't have to say anything. Then she adds, "Like my opinion counts," and we both share a chuckle.

"Yo, I can't even believe that Nicole got a guest spot with the Quarter Notes. Do you think she'll just do a set, or is she sitting in with the band all night?"

Imani gives me a look that says, "Do I look like I would fall for some small-talk bullshit?" and moves in closer, but not before hurriedly looking over her shoulder. "You did not come over here to talk about Nicole. I saw the way you looked at my girl. You're trying to get at her."

My heart's racing a little bit now. Not many things make me nervous, but the idea of having to convince a woman that I'm not trying to steal *her* woman, well, that kind of shit doesn't happen every day. "Honest, Imani, I wouldn't play you like that. You're cool peoples. And I'd just be playing myself, anyway—"

"Hold up, hold up, hold up," she interrupts, her forehead all scrunched up. "Why would you be playing me by trying to kick it to Des?"

She's really gonna make me spell it out. This mess couldn't get any more awkward. "Cuz you two are together." Her jaw drops. "Aren't you?"

"Did she tell you that?"

I try to think back to the morning that I changed

Desiree's tire. Did she ever come out and say that she and Imani were a couple? "I guess not. But she never said that you weren't, either."

Now Imani's looking amused, but there's sympathy in her face as well. Her pity makes me embarrassed, but I'm kinda grateful for it, too. "Listen, Jason." I can hardly wait for her to continue, but she studies the area near the restrooms first. "I am in a relationship, but it's not with Desiree. Do not let that girl try to convince you that she likes women. She's not gay in the least."

The sensation of my top teeth touching my bottom lip lets me know that I'm smiling. I force my mouth shut. "So why would she want to come off that way?"

"Come off what way?" Desiree is standing at our table, with her hands on her hips. My mind races, trying to come up with some clever lie to tell, but it ain't coming fast enough.

Imani to the rescue. "We were just talking about Nicole and what she wants her image to be in the industry. She looks like Britney Spears but plays like Wynton Marsalis." Desiree seems to buy the story, and I breathe a sigh of relief. "Des, what the hell did you do to your hair?"

I look up and notice that while Desiree was in the bathroom, she took her braid out. Her hair is kinda wavy, I guess from having the braid in it before, and it's falling all down her back and around her face. Desiree looks flustered by her friend's question. Imani shifts her stare to my direction. "Jason, tell this girl that she looks just as good with her hair pulled back."

"She looks better, cuz you can see her face more." Imani is looking all victorious as Desiree gathers her hair and places it behind her shoulders. I didn't mean to make her feel self-conscious.

Time for my exit. "Looks like we're one chair short, so I'm gonna head back to where I was sitting."

"Actually," Imani says slyly, "would you mind keeping Desiree company until I get back? That wine went right through me." She doesn't even wait for me to answer before she leaves the table, motioning for Desiree to take her seat.

Homegirl looks downright salty as she plops down in the chair and fiddles with one of the coasters on the table. My usual reaction would be to give attitude right back, but for some reason, I want nothing more than to lift her mood.

"Come here often?" I say in my best Billy D. voice. Bingo. A slow smile from the beauty across the table.

"This is my first time, actually. So be gentle, okay?"

Oh, really. "No doubt. I got you." I try to meet her eyes, but she's looking everywhere but at me. She crosses and uncrosses her legs a few times. I can't believe I'm actually making this ice queen nervous. "So how's the writing coming along?"

She sighs and shakes her head. "I need some inspiration badly."

The wheels in my brain are turning as I try to come up with something cool to say back. But before I can put it together, her eyes light up like she just got this bright idea. "Hey. You really saved me last week, you know that?"

The unexpected kindness has me cheesing again. "It was no big thing."

"Maybe not, but I'm grateful anyway. How about you let me take you out for a drink . . . as a thank you?" She stops playing with the coaster and looks me dead in my eyes.

What the hell is going on? First, she's a total biatch, then she's borderline flirting, now she's almost pressed. Somethin' ain't right. "I don't drink."

She doesn't bat an eyelash. "Dinner, then."

"And how would Imani feel about that?"

"Why would she feel any way?"

"Isn't that your girlfriend, or partner, or whatever?" It's kinda fun watching her squirm.

After a long pause, "Oh. Right. Um, she's not a jealous person."

Perfectly on cue, Imani approaches, dragging an extra chair from a nearby table. She places it to Desiree's left, forcing her to move closer to me. "Who's not jealous?"

Desiree looks at her sweetly. "You, honey. I was just telling Jason that he should let me buy him a meal as payment for helping me the other day." I pretend to look away, and out of the corner of my eye, I catch her shooting Imani a raised eyebrow and a pleading look.

"Uh-huh. As long as Jason doesn't get any ideas." Imani winks at me, and I bite my lip. It's all I can do to keep from cracking up.

"Don't worry, Imani. I'm clearly not your girl's type, and she's not mine, either." I steal a glance at Desiree, who's trying to act casual but can't mask how offended she is by my comment.

The place gets dark at that moment, and all attention shifts to the stage.

The Quarter Notes' first set is all up-tempo tunes, from classics like "Take the A Train" to their own original pieces. For a quartet, they sure produce a nice, full sound. Heads are boppin' in this place like it's a hip-hop concert. The drummer is just sick with it, soloing for about five minutes, making beats from the floor to his music stand, never losing the rhythm. It's getting hot in this tight space, but ain't a soul complaining.

After five or six songs, the lead horn player gets on the mike. "We're gonna slow it down for y'all right now." A few women hoot and holler. "But before we do, I think we could use the help of a sexy alto sax. What do y'all think?" Everybody claps and cheers. "Let me introduce a young woman who's gonna be a household name before you know it. Making her first appearance at B Sharp, the Quarter Notes are honored to welcome Nicole McKie!"

The applause is thick as she takes the stage. Folks who didn't know whisper to their table mates, shocked by what they see. I can't lie. It does look pretty strange. This girl is *white*. Now there are white people, and there are *white* people. Like to me, Jewish people aren't always *white*. They've been through some rough shit in their history, lots of 'em marched with us on Washington, and quite a few have some serious kink and curl to their hair. But Nicole—she's a midwestern, blond-haired, blue-eyed white girl. Looks like she should be doing a commercial for suntan lotion or something.

But the whispers and snickers stop on a dime when she starts blowing into that instrument. Her first number is a slow-as-molasses version of "Summertime" that just makes you wanna cry. I manage to glimpse Desiree's profile next to me, her eyes closed as she sways to the sound. Meanwhile, Nicole is so into her solo that her back is arched and her sax is moving every which way. It's crazy. This girl was born in Ohio to some white-bread parents and discovers that she has more soul in her pinky finger than most of us do in our whole CD collection. Guess I'm not the only one God likes to mess with.

The crowd is actually on its feet when the song is through. Nicole's cheeks are flushed—probably for a variety of reasons. But she takes the mike in her hand and breathlessly utters a thank you. "This next song came out when I was in elementary school. Hope you guys like it."

It only takes about three notes on the keyboard before I recognize it to be "Weak" by SWV. Everyone in the place starts saying stuff like, "Awwwww, shit!" and "This was my *song!*" Elementary school? Nicole is really a baby. I close my eyes and take myself back to where I was when this song was hot. Senior prom. Holding Monique in my arms, our bodies pressed against each other, barely moving to the music. *Your love is so sweet, it knocks me right off of my feet.* That was the jam. And those were the days.

I feel someone staring at me and open my eyes in time to see Desiree turn away. What this girl's agenda is, I have no idea. But it don't matter. Cuz I sure don't let myself get weak for anybody anymore. With one exception. And I'm not going to let some pretty face try to break me while Nailah's out of town. In the middle of the song, I get up and walk back to my table in the corner.

CHAPTER 8

HUNTER

Every once in a while, I step out from the stifling smell of urine, disinfectant, hot meal trays, and recycled air into the warm breeze of early evening, and I actually feel like the ten hours just spent inside the hospital were truly special. Today is one of those days.

It's a natural high watching a resident save his first patient on his own, or observing the attending diagnose something that has gone untreated for years. But the patients and the rest of the hospital workers are the ones who make me feel like my being a medical student really means something.

I remember back in high school, when I'd meet with the other kids in Prep for Prep, a program that gets poor kids from the city into prestigious private schools, and we'd bitch about being the only black student in our classes. We used to hate having to be the "spokesperson for the race." It was a burden that we felt was unfairly placed on us at such a young age, an age where many of us hadn't even fully figured out what we wanted our identity to be.

Now, as the only black male going through my rotation

at Presbyterian, I feel no bitterness at having to rep the race. Only pride. The thankful look from the black woman whose son suffers from juvenile diabetes, the sigh of relief from the Cuban girl with an ovarian cyst who learns that I'll be shadowing her doctor—those small tokens of appreciation make the experience worthwhile.

And then there's the staff, who are all too happy to see a soon-to-be black doctor in their midst. I mean, 80 percent are people of color themselves. And they look out for me any time they can. Rita, the middle-aged unit clerk on the floor, helped me out at the beginning, when I was overwhelmed by all the charts and notation that I had to do. Now that I have that together, she rewards me with leftovers from the dinners she makes for her husband and teenaged daughters, calling me the son she never had. Valerie, the twenty-something nurse who I think may have a crush on me, always lets me nap longer than I should when things are slow.

Even the male workers are cool. Like today, I was put on the spot when the head of pediatrics, Dr. Silver, asked me to present a case. I took a deep breath and launched into the patient's history, not getting all thrown off when dude interrupted to ask questions. It went pretty well, I thought, but you can never tell from the doctor's reaction. I swear, physicians should all take a trip to Atlantic City and clean up on the tables, cuz their poker faces are no joke. Anyhow, this lab tech named Carlos found me later to tell me that he overheard a conversation between two doctors in the call room about how Dr. Silver was sweatin' me. I'm sure they didn't use those words, but I was pretty gassed regardless.

On the walk home, I reach in the pocket of my lab coat, pull out my cell phone, and turn it on. I have a new message. After entering my password and deleting a message from my niece that I'd archived, an unfamiliar voice begins to talk to me. It's a woman. Young. Speaking in low-pitched tones that can only be described as unintentionally sultry:

"Hello, Hunter. This is the person whom you saved from starving at Kenny's. If you remember, that person isn't very nice, but her stomach insisted that she call to thank you properly." And then she laughs. A soft, natural laugh that comes out as easily as breathing. "Anyway, I was going to mail you that check, but I thought that maybe I could buy you a meal instead. Call me if you're interested. 908-555-3809. Oh, my name is Desiree, by the way. Take care."

I can't be completely sure if I'm walking or skipping down 170th Street. It's official. This is a great day. I know that I should wait until I'm in the comfort of my own apartment to return her call, but that's not happening. I replay the message, this time entering and saving her number into my cell. Then I highlight her name in my phone book and hit SEND, trying to ignore the knot that I feel right below my chest. With every ring, it's like someone is pulling the rope tighter and tighter. Damn. Voice mail. I barely hear what she's saying because I'm trying to plan out what I'm going to say before the beep.

Here we go. "How you doin'? This is Hunter, calling for Desiree's stomach. I was very surprised to hear from you, partly because I'm not familiar with many highly intelligent internal organs, and also because the body which you inhabit is not particularly friendly. Still, I am more than willing to risk a meal with both of you. Have your host give me a shout." Flipping the phone shut, I smile at my own humor. The next moment the smile has disappeared as I second-guess my message. One misstep when trying to achieve cleverness can throw you headfirst into the corny zone.

I should've listened more closely to her voice mail

greeting, just to make sure that she didn't end her message with the increasingly popular "God bless." Call me a heathen, but when I hear that on a girl's voice mail, I usually don't call back. I've never been a very religious person, and I think it's been made worse by the field I chose. As a doctor, you're altering nature on a daily basis. Not to mention that you're committing all kinds of sins by counseling women on things like birth control and abortion. And after a few days in a burn unit, or on the oncology floor, you witness way too much tragedy to fully believe that there's a loving, benevolent God watching over us.

I take the death-trap elevator in my building up to my fifth-floor apartment and immediately head for the shower. The hot water blasts my tired muscles, and the tiny bathroom is steamy in no time. It's like a massage and a sauna in one.

Damn it. Is that my cell phone ringing? I almost slip in the porcelain tub as I hop out as quickly as possible, wrapping a towel around my waist on the walk to the bedroom. On the phone's fluorescent screen, Desiree's name is flashing, and I scramble to answer it before it's too late. "Hello?"

"Hi, Hunter? This is Desiree." That voice again. It's what a sexy blues singer should sound like when she talks between songs.

"Hey. Good to hear from you." I plop down on my bed, disregarding the water that I'm dripping on the sheets.

"Did you want me to call you back? You sound kind of out of breath." A slight mocking tone, as if she knows I just broke my neck to catch her call.

"Nah. I'm good. I just got home a little while ago from the hospital." Trying to regain control of the conversation.

"Oh. Is everything okay?" A hint of concern, more out of politeness than anything.

"I'm fine. I'm actually a medical student." How do you like me now?

"Really. What year?"

"Just beginning my third."

"So you're starting rotations. What floor are you on?"

"Pediatrics. Are you in the medical field as well?"

"Oh God, no." She says it like it's the furthest possible thing from what she does, which makes me very happy for some reason.

"So what is it that you do?"

A pause. "I take overworked medical students to dinner, that's what I do. What's your schedule like this week?"

As we iron out a time that works for both of us, I get more and more excited about the prospect of seeing the meat loaf goddess again. I can't wait to ask what made her call me, because I sure wasn't expecting to ever hear from her. She hangs up, leaving me wanting more. More of that voice. And more information. But I'm consoled by the fact that I'll get those things on Saturday.

I throw on some clothes, suddenly wanting to make it outside to catch the last few rays of sunshine. Grabbing my wallet and keys off the dresser, I leave my place, practically jogging down a flight of stairs to the fourth floor. I knock cheerfully on the door marked 4D, and it swings open within a few seconds.

"What's up with the Kool-Aid smile?" says Robyn skeptically.

"My day was the bomb. So we're going to get ice cream."

"Are you paying?"

"For sure." I hold up the wallet still in my hand as evidence.

"Cool. Let me put on some shoes." That's why I like Robyn. She's down-to-earth and always ready to roll. We met at a minority medical student meeting at Columbia last fall and realized that we lived in the same building off campus. We've been studying together ever since. She just finished her first year, which means that she's sympathetic, but not competitive.

"Okay. I'm ready." Robyn looks cute, standing just a little over five feet tall in her jean shorts and fitted Columbia T-shirt. We wait about five minutes for the cage-like elevator before we decide to take the stairs. I'm tempted to tell her about my phone call from the meat loaf goddess, but there really isn't much to report yet. Then she asks me about my day, and suddenly we're talking about IV tubes and BP readings. Which makes me think about how hearing Desiree's voice on the phone made my pulse start racing. Which makes me think that I need to chill.

CHAPTER 9

DESIREE

"So let me get this straight. You met two guys who are interested in you, and you've decided to date them both after a five-year stint of abstinence to like the tenth power. But the only reason you're giving them the time of day is so you can get ideas for your book." Kahlila is clearly about to give me a speech condemning my entire plan, but that's okay. I'm still excited to see her. Last time we hung out was when I visited her in Phoenix this past winter. She had a boyfriend who was also in Teach for America, a pleasant enough do-gooder named Eugene, but I have a feeling from the tone of her recent e-mails that things have fallen apart.

"Incorrect. Only one of them is interested in me. The other one is just . . . *interesting*, shall we say. The plan is not to date that one. It's to befriend him. Wouldn't it be a fascinating experiment to see how a man handles a platonic relationship with an attractive woman?" The sun has just emerged from behind a hefty cloud, and I reach in my purse for my shades. Sunglasses are also useful for people watching, and we have a prime seat for just that at an outdoor café on Columbus Avenue.

"And why do you think this poor guy will be satisfied with just being buddies?" She sucks down her coffee milk shake, trying as always to put on weight, oblivious to the stares that she's receiving from male passersby on the street. Since I've seen her last, she's cut her hair down to a jet-black curly crop, perfectly suited for her delicate features. Her time out West has bronzed her skin to the color of a copper bracelet I have in my jewelry box at home. She looks amazing. Robyn told me once that the difference between Kahlila and me is that men admire me and I know it, while Kahli is completely unaware of how much attention she gets.

"He has no choice but to be satisfied with it. He thinks I'm a lesbian." I smirk, knowing exactly what Kahli's reaction is going to be.

And there it is: the wide-eyed, shocked expression for which Kahli is legendary. She opens her mouth to ask a follow-up question but then shuts it, apparently at a loss for words. Talking to her like this totally takes me back to our college days, when I felt like I was constantly waking her up to life's harsh realities. It's so different from my friendship with Imani, where I'm the one getting schooled all the time.

Kahli finally gets her voice. "If you want to know about male/female friendships, why not just examine Robyn's relationship with Lloyd? Or mine with J. T.?"

"Been there. Done that. I think I've exploited our college antics as much as I possibly could in my first book. It's time for some fresh material."

She smiles in spite of herself, revealing her only physical flaw that I've ever detected: a grin that twists slightly left. "I see. So tell me, what do you plan to learn from the other victim in this charade?"

"Oh, Hunter. Well, at first, I wasn't sure what I wanted to get out of him. But then, during our first phone conversation, he made such a point to let me know that he's a med student. Like I was supposed to be so blown away by that fact. And I thought back to something Robyn had e-mailed me, about how 'ballers in training' claim to want a girlfriend on their level, but they seem turned off when women are *too* together."

"Yeah, I've heard her talk about that before. So you're going to see if he gets intimidated by the fact that you're a successful author?"

"Not exactly." I signal the waitress for the check. "Think about this, Kahli. What if he didn't know I was a writer? What if he didn't even know I've been to college? How would he feel about me then?"

Kahli's crooked smile morphs into a frown as she pulls the wallet from her bag. I motion for her to put her money away, and she does so without a fight. That was way too easy, which means she'll insist on paying for something twice as expensive later. "So you're not only lying about your intentions with this guy. You're lying about your identity."

When she puts it that way, I get a little nervous. Not because I feel guilty about this plot in any way, but because these days, it just takes one quick surf on the Internet to expose the truth about who somebody is. I'm too busy trying to figure out how to get around this problem to respond. After paying for our midday snack, I lead us toward Broadway for a leisurely stroll.

It's been a year since Kahlila's been to New York, so for a couple of blocks, she is successfully distracted by the clothes in store windows, dogs on leashes, and babies in strollers, classic characteristics of the Upper West Side. But she eventually returns to the topic of my deception. "What med school does Hunter go to?"

On the corner of Eighty-sixth and Broadway, I nod my head toward the Gap, and we proceed inside. We both detest the Gap. She's more Urban Outfitters, and I'm a Bloomingdale's kinda girl. But it's pushing ninety degrees outside, and air-conditioning is a must. "Columbia, I hope. Then I can get the scoop on him from Robyn," I reply as I absentmindedly sift through a rack of khakis.

"Are you crazy? You'd better hope that boy doesn't go to Columbia. Robyn will bust your scheme right open. She will not think your little game is cute in the least."

Kahli's right. I can't let Robyn know what I'm doing, which further complicates things. For a brief moment, I consider scrapping the plan—canceling the date with Hunter, leaving Jason alone. Then I feel a tap on my arm. It's the security guard, a black woman about my age, with long nails and even longer hair extensions. My stomach flips, even though I know I've done nothing wrong.

She smacks her gum a few times before deciding to speak. "Ain't you the girl who wrote *No More Lies*?" She spits her words with the same intonation she would use to say something like, "What'd you say about my momma?" But I feel a wave of relief in spite of her attitude.

"Yup, I am. Have you read the book?" I ask in my sweet-as-pie voice, reserved for my readers and my little brother Desmond, who's now twenty years old and hates that I still talk to him like he's twelve.

She touches my arm again, this time in that sister girl way that black women do when they're sharing a secret. "Oh shoot, that is my favorite book, for real. That dude was a straight-up asshole, the way he did ol' girl like that. You base that on some stuff in yo' life or somethin'?"

The air-conditioning isn't helping the heat I feel in my cheeks when she asks that question. "Nope. Just my imagination," I respond a little too quickly.

She purses her lips to one side and looks at me skeptically. "Mm-hmm. When you comin' out with another book?"

I smile warmly, back in the driver's seat. "Soon. Keep an eye out. It was nice meeting you." She smiles back, and I rush out of the store, with Kahli right behind me. Outside a hot gust of wind smacks me in the face.

"Listen, I know you don't approve of what I'm doing, and that Robyn will approve even less. But this is my career on the line, Kahlila." I hate that I sound like I'm begging for her approval, but honestly, it would make me feel a lot better.

Sighing and folding her arms, she shows signs of softening. "What does Imani say about all this? I thought she was supposed to be your voice of reason now that Robyn's busy with school."

"She's totally supportive of anything that will aid my creative process," I say with assertion. Okay, this is not completely true. I haven't even told her about the Hunter half of the plan. I just casually mentioned that I might try to get to know Jason better, for research purposes. Imani got unusually happy and hyper, saying what a fabulous idea it was. But I'm on to her. She thinks I'm going to fall for him. All I know is that she'd better not blow my lesbian cover.

A couple passes us on our left, the guy carrying all of the shopping bags, with his free hand on his girlfriend's back to guide her along the congested sidewalk. Kahlila shoots them a look of longing and annoyance all at once. Perfect opportunity to change the subject.

"Enough about me. What's going on with you and Eugene? When I saw you guys together in Phoenix, y'all seemed really well matched."

She nods, acknowledging the truth in my statement. "He was a great guy. But I had to end it. It just wasn't . . . right." I debate for about thirty seconds whether to say what I'm thinking, and I finally decide that I have to. "It wasn't right . . . or he wasn't Dave? Which one was it?"

There's fire in her eyes as she turns to face me, but when she sees my comment wasn't intended to be malicious, her eyelids lower in surrender. "Why can't we put these men out of our minds, Des? I mean, here I am sabotaging relationships five years after Dave dumped me. And you . . . Look at the effect Trevor had. You transformed into an entirely different person after . . . the situation."

How the hell did this conversation come right back to me and my issues? It's not like I'm prepared to argue this point with my girl at this exact moment, but I'd have to say that designing the Desiree Self-Improvement Plan (D.S.I.P.) after the disaster with Trevor was probably my best decision to date.

During the post-Trevor summer, I thought about how much time I'd wasted waiting for guys to call, going out on meaningless dates, spending hours dishing dirt on some loser with my girls. All of this could've been time spent on me. So I cut 'em off. And damn it if my schedule didn't open right up like a flower in the sun.

The things we sacrifice to be social butterflies! When I was little, before boys infiltrated my life like enemy missiles, I was addicted to books. I devoured Judy Blume, Beverly Cleary, the Sweet Valley twins, even *Little Women*—all of that wonderful preteen literature that makes girls realize that their problems are natural and normal. By high school, I was reading Cliffs Notes in exchange for more free time to learn the fine art of doing hair and applying make-up. College ignited a passion for reading again, but it wasn't until I swore off the male species that I really devoted myself to the great African-American authors: Hurston, Morrison, Wright, Baldwin. After turning thousands of pages by the lamplight by my bed, I began to think that maybe I should take a next step in my love of literature.

The book had actually been Kahlila's suggestion. We were up late one night, gossiping about boys (the one habit I wasn't able to shake), and Kahli said that our collective drama freshman year (mine, hers, and Robyn's) could be a soap opera. She suggested that I be the one to write the script. So the soap opera brainchild evolved into a book idea. I'd been writing poetry for a few years, and I decided to take a fiction writing class my sophomore year. I told my professor about my idea for a coming-of-age novel set at Franklin University, and she was totally supportive.

Once I began writing, I really started reaping the benefits of D.S.I.P. I declared my English major, worked on the novel, worked out at the gym, worked summers at Kahli's program for high-school kids, worked on loving Desiree Thomas. And don't you know, all my working, it worked.

So I'll nod my head sympathetically for Kahli's sake, but Trevor served his purpose. Like Sade sings, "It's a lover's revenge, but out of the pain come the best things." The same thing that had me sobbing under my covers for months turned out to be quite the page-turner. People loved the story: popular girl meets smooth-talking guy who turns out to be too good to be true, makes her feel worthless, and leaves her to pick up the pieces. With *No More Lies*, I successfully turned my heartbreak into profit. And if I have to break a couple of hearts to cash in a second time, so be it.

CHAPTER 10

JASON

I stand near the entrance and watch the men and women lined up to pay their cover. The guys are all co-ordinated in their Sean John outfits, and the girls are showing mad skin in sports bras and short shorts. A Dr. Dre video on *106th and Park* is playing pretty loud on the hanging televisions, but I manage to overhear a snippet of conversation between two dudes taking in the sights. "You know Jay's is always jumpin' right after work." I smile on the inside, realizing that at a quick glance, you can barely tell the difference between my gym and a nightclub.

When I opened Jay's Gym last year, mad heads doubted the pay-as-you-go concept. They kept telling me to charge an annual membership fee like everybody else. But I knew my idea was a can't miss. Four dollars a day. Stay as long as you want. Use the equipment; utilize the personal trainers on-site; take a class if you want. No wasted money if you slack off on coming to work out. And more incentive to work long and hard when you get here.

At first, by nature of the people I know, the place was

attracting nothing but dudes. Hard-ass niggas at that, throwin' up prison weight like it was nothing. But Monique started spreading the word around the professional set, and soon guys rolling up in Armani suits were at the bench right alongside my Newark peeps, spotting each other and trading jokes. It was a beautiful thing to see. And the sights got even better when we bought some additional machines and hired a couple of aerobics teachers to attract the ladies. The cheap classes pulled them in, and the number of muscular men kept them here.

I take a walk around, surveying the space at what is always my busiest hour. All my trainers are working with female clients. Dudes hate to admit that they could use some help with their workouts. Through the glass windows of the mirrored room in the far corner, I can see Aisha doing her thing, teaching her African aerobics class. The fifteen women in there are sweating to the rhythms of some drumbeats playing on a boom box.

"Everybody else in this place is working hard, while you stand here staring at the half-naked ladies shaking their stuff." I know the voice before I turn around, but I must have it wrong. There's no way that Desiree is in Secaucus, at my job. I turn slowly, ready to laugh at myself when I learn the speaker's true identity.

Nope. It's really her. Not looking too glamorous wearing a New Jersey Nets T-shirt and some loose-fitting cotton pants, with her hair in a messy ponytail. "What are you doing here?" I know that sounds rude, but I can't help it.

If she senses my attitude, she sure doesn't show it. "I live in Weehawken. My neighbor told me about this gym where you didn't have to be a member. I have a gym in my condo complex, but I decided to check this place out for a change of pace. You work here?" She does sound kind of surprised to see me, so maybe it's not like she's stalking me after all. I actually didn't know she lived in North Jersey.

"Oh. Well, I can give you the tour without moving from this spot. Over there, where you came in, you passed the cardio stuff. Nothing too fancy, just treadmill, StairMaster, bikes. Right here are the machines. We got 'em for just about everything you can think of—arms, legs, abs, whatever. Over there are free weights, bench press, that kinda thing. And toward the back, as you can see, we got two rooms for classes. There's a step aerobics class starting in about twenty minutes in the empty one."

She laughs. "I'll pass. I tried it one time and almost tripped over the step."

"So you mean to tell me that you're a klutz on the low?"

"Not quite a klutz. Just a little awkward sometimes." I don't buy it. The only thing awkward about this chick is the way she makes other people feel.

"Well, I'm gonna go get my money's worth," she says, walking back in the direction of the cardio equipment. I make myself turn away.

"Yo, Jay." Hakim, my boy from way back and right-hand man at the gym, jogs up to me. "Don't forget Charles has to leave early today. You want me to take over for him at the register?"

"Yeah. Thanks." There's some hollering going on at the bench press, the kind of noise that means someone is about to try to beat their max. Hakim and I walk up just as one of my regular customers successfully does 315 for two reps.

"Real nice, Nigel. That went up so smooth, I thought you had another rep in you," I say, giving him a pound when he gets off the benches.

"Just tryin' to be like you, big man," he says all out of breath.

I wave my hand to brush off his comment and continue my stroll through the gym. Hakim catches up with me, putting his hand on my shoulder. "So check it, Jay. Who's the dime you was rappin' to before?"

"My neighbor's friend." *Keep it short. Don't encourage further questions.*

Hakim gets this sly grin on his face and pushes up his sleeves like he's about to begin something strenuous. "Introduce me, dawg." Shit. I was afraid of this.

"For what?"

"Nigga, what do you think for what?"

"Nah." I try to make it as casual as possible. "Forget about it, man."

"Why?" Hakim sounds shocked, which is understandable. Growing up, he pulled all the girls with his fast talking and fast cars. He still believes that any female is just an Escalade ride away from being had.

"Honestly, player, she's kind of crazy." It's the best explanation I can give. I really do think the girl is nuts. Split personalities, all that.

We've now walked within viewing distance of Desiree as she warms up on the treadmill, and Hakim is scoping her out something serious. "Bullshit. If you want to holla at her yourself, just say so."

I debate giving him a clearer picture, complete with attitude problems and lesbian fraud. Just when I'm about to fill him in, Desiree increases the speed on her treadmill to a brisk jog. While her legs are pumping, she pulls her T-shirt over her head, showing off a tight Everlast tank top. The way she pulled that shirt off while she was running—it was like a scene outta Black *Baywatch*. Awkward my ass. The chick looks like she's training for a fuckin' marathon.

Hakim slaps me on the back. "If it doesn't work out with you two, just let me know. I ain't above leftovers in special situations. And that"—he pauses, motioning his head in her direction and licking his lips—"is a special situation." I have to chuckle as he goes to relieve Charles at the front. Sometimes I swear Hakim thinks he's auditioning for a part in somebody's movie.

I watch her a little longer after he leaves. She once joked around that she doesn't sweat, but that's clearly not true. Her skin is shining by the time she cools down. I must admit, she looks even better stepping off that treadmill than she did at B Sharp that night. When she walks past me to the free weights, I begin inspecting the abductor machine with my full concentration. Once I can't do that anymore, I go make small talk with some of my regular patrons.

As I listen to Ms. Hardaway complain about her bad-ass grandkids while she does a set of pulldowns, I watch Desiree go through her upper-body routine. She's one of the only females in the area with the free weights, and men look like they might drop a dumbbell on their toes from staring. When she's forced to make eye contact with them, she gives a polite enough nod. But as soon as they turn their heads, her eyes get real cold. Something about the way she acts around these dudes who ain't even disrespecting her . . . yeah, she's definitely crazy.

I tune back to Ms. Hardaway's ranting in time to give a standard "kids will be kids" response and decide to tackle some paperwork in my office. If only I'd made that decision five minutes earlier, because suddenly, Desiree is standing in front of me. "This is a cool spot. I like the layout."

"Yeah. They do a good job."

"*They*? Aren't you the Jay in Jay's Gym? This isn't your

place?" Not only is this chick a little crazy, but she's pretty damn nosey, too.

"Uh, yeah. The staff gets most of the credit, though."

"You mean *your* staff." Why is she stressing the fact that I own this place? *I don't care how good you look. You shouldn't be allowed to be this annoying.*

"Whatever." I honestly want to just walk right around her and go to my office, but this is still my place of business. I can't be acting all rude like that on the job.

"Wow," she says in this kind of amazed voice, looking at me all strange. "Here I was, thinking you were just a blue-collar guy tryin' to make ends meet. Meanwhile, you're probably sittin' back with some business degree, building up your fortune." I can't believe she's saying this stuff out loud. "Actually, it does make sense. That brownstone you live in is not cheap."

All right. I'm being set up here. For some unexplainable reason, this girl wants to know my story. And she thinks I'm so dumb that it'll just take a few off-base comments to get me pouring my heart out? She obviously doesn't know who she's dealing with.

"So you're a Nets fan?" I ask, pointing to the balled-up T-shirt in her hand.

"Uh-huh. What's that got to do with anything?"

"I'm just wondering how someone as educated as you would choose to support the Nets over the Knicks. You're a Jersey girl for real, huh?" I'm starting to have a little fun now.

"I'm actually from Baltimore. But I have a friend on the team."

"Who? Steinway?" I laugh a little bit at my choice—the rookie with more endorsements than Tiger Woods, it seems like.

She smiles. "Actually, yes. We went to college together."

Damn. She got me. "For a white boy, he has a nice game."

"Well, if you like basketball, I can let you know when I get tickets." I'm speechless, so after a few silent moments, she goes on. "Imani hates sports, so I could use the company." Here she goes again with the gay charade.

"Why me?"

"Imani likes you." She can't even meet my eyes when she says that one.

"And what about you?" I tilt my head to the side, forcing her to look at me.

"You have four dollars of my hard-earned money. I must think you're okay." And she's gone, putting on the wrinkled Nets shirt as she heads toward the locker room. I wonder if she's bullshitting about getting tickets this season. I hope she is, because I might not be strong enough to refuse a night with a psycho for some courtside seats.

CHAPTER 11

DESIREE

Stepping out from Grand Central Station onto Lexington Avenue, I'm greeted by sheets of rain. When I left Jersey, the sky was perfectly clear. Now my hair is getting soaked, and I have neither jacket nor umbrella to protect me. This is a bad sign. The Lord is trying to tell me not to play with Hunter's head. Even worse sign: I used the wrong exit at Grand Central, which means tacking on an extra three blocks to my walk.

At the corner of the block, I spy a folding table with mini-umbrellas for sale. Excellent. It may not be a permission slip from God to deceive Hunter on this date, but it isn't exactly a condemnation, either.

Using my internal compass to decide the direction I should be walking, I begin the trek to East, a Japanese restaurant that Hunter suggested. I've never been there, but I love sushi, so his choice was fine with me. He'd originally wanted to do gourmet soul food at Jimmy's Uptown in Harlem. But I've been to Jimmy's too many times to fake my identity in there.

I review my plan as I walk down the dark gray sidewalks, sidestepping puddles and trying not to hit anyone with my umbrella. I've constructed an alter ego to use with Hunter—a secretary from New Jersey who's very excited to be working in the big city. Remembering what J. T. had told me about wanting a girl who shows interest in his profession, I've got to be completely awestruck by the fact that he's going to be a doctor. The goal is to gauge his reaction to my phony profile and get him to answer as many questions as possible about his relationship history. I've gotta work fast, because this song and dance can't go on for more than one date, especially since I found out during our second phone conversation that he does go to Columbia. I don't know if he knows Robyn, but she could be a huge risk factor if he does.

I'm starting to feel a bit nauseated. What did I eat today? Nothing out of the ordinary. Maybe I'm just hungry. I need to stop fooling myself; these stomach pangs are nothing but nerves. To be fair, I have every right to be nervous. It's been over five years since I've even been on a date. And I've pretended to be a different person, um, how many times in my life? Ah yes, that's right. None.

But it's not like I don't have experience in lying. Like last night at Jason's gym, when I told him I was there by coincidence. He seemed to believe me, although common sense should've told him that Imani told me where he worked. He puts flyers for Jay's Gym under her door, for goodness sake! Making friends with him is going to be harder than I thought, though. The only time he seemed even half intrigued by anything I had to say was when I brought up basketball tickets. Which reminds me, I have to call J. T. and see if he can hook me up. But the season is still a couple months away. I can't wait that long to make some progress. Maybe I can convince J. T. to swing by the gym, boost Jason's business a little bit.

Okay, I need to concentrate. Even if I get all types of valuable information tonight with Hunter, how is this going to translate into a book? I suppose I can just keep an open mind and shape my characters based on how this all plays out.

Of course, the rain slows to a drippy drizzle just as I see the sign for East between Second and Third Avenue. I fold the umbrella and shake it out right before I enter, giving myself a once-over in the glass reflection. Hair hasn't frizzed out too much. Outfit is cool—a turquoise off-the-shoulder top and a pair of jeans. The sandals are killin' 'em, but between the long walk and the rain, I'm wishing I'd put on some galoshes instead.

Hunter and hostess excitedly greet me at the exact same time. There's so much going on, I can barely squeeze in a hello. The hostess is asking us whether we want a table or seats at the bar, and Hunter is telling me how pretty I look. Pretty. That's a nice word. I wonder why men don't use it so much anymore. Sure beats scrumptious, or off the chain, or fine as hell. He looks pretty good himself—head freshly shaven, blue button-up shirt, and a crisp pair of jeans. I don't remember him being this tall. I must be five feet eleven in these heels, but I'm still looking up at him.

Once we sit down, I take a few quiet moments to check out my surroundings. Most of the tables are taken, and there's a significant Asian clientele. Always a good indicator of quality. He tells me that a classmate recommended the place, and I have no time to compliment his choice before the waiter is asking us if we want drinks. I would love a glass of plum wine or sake, but it's important that my head be completely clear tonight. I get a Sprite instead, and he orders a Sapporo.

"So, Desiree, I'm so glad we're getting to sit down to a meal together."

"Me too."

"One thing I realize I didn't get to ask you on the phone is what do you do?" This boy wasted no time with that one. No surprise there.

"I work at a law firm downtown."

"You're an attorney. Impressive," he says, nodding his head up and down like Cliff Huxtable used to when he heard a good jazz record. Can't blame him for hoping I'm his Claire.

"Oh no," I say, with a giggle.

"I guess you do look a bit young to be practicing law. So you're a paralegal, then?" He looks right into my eyes when he's talking, which makes it a lot harder than I thought it would be to tell bald-faced lies.

"No. I'm an administrative assistant." Pause. "You know, like a secretary."

Damn it. The drinks couldn't have come at a worse time. The waiter is blocking Hunter's face, and by the time my view becomes unobstructed again, I can't read a thing from his expression.

After a few sips of our beverages, he clears his throat. "I'm sure working at a firm gives you a lot of insight into the profession. Are you thinking about law school?"

I laugh a kind of cynical chuckle. "I'd have to go to college first."

Now he looks completely embarrassed. I'll give him credit. He's clearly more ashamed of his own presumptuousness than he is of me. "My bad. That was stupid of me to—"

"Don't worry about it." Why am I letting him off the hook? This is exactly the type of stuff I should be letting him elaborate on. "I did go to college for a couple semesters, but it wasn't for me. I've been working as the office manager at a mortgage company near my house in Jersey for the past few years, but the place closed down a couple months ago. My uncle's friend got me a job at his law firm. It's so great to be working in New York City. I feel like a real career woman, you know?"

He smiles. Goodness, he has some perfect teeth. Whether the smile is genuine or just polite is anybody's guess. "Where do you live in Jersey?"

"Weehawken. Just past the tunnel." Don't tell lies where you don't have to.

"Oh yeah? How's the rent out there?"

"I bought a condo." Shit shit shit. What am I doing? I can't afford to buy squat based on what I just told him. "I mean, my parents. They bought a condo. I live with them."

He really can't hide the disappointment on his face with that one. All the fantasies of us having passionate make-out sessions at my Jersey shore hideaway just got dashed from his poor little head.

I think I've broken enough bad news for now. Let me look at this menu. They have a nice selection here, and my stomach is getting happy as my eyes scan the pages of pictures. I think all restaurants should take a cue from sushi places and photograph all of their dishes.

"So don't feel like because we're at a sushi restaurant that you have to do the raw fish thing. A lot of the meat is cooked, and there are some vegetarian options also." He then elaborates on the difference between nigiri sushi and maki sushi, and advises how much I might need to order to fill me up. No, this negro is not. I tell him I didn't go to college, so he assumes I never ate sushi before? I so want to tell this brother about himself, but it might be fun to play along. There's definitely some pride in his voice as he's explaining everything, like he deserves a gold star for exposing me to something new.

"Wow. It's all so overwhelming. Maybe you can order

for me? I trust your opinion." His head is about to burst from flattery.

"Sure," he says, with a dazzling smile. "We can share." He signals the waiter over to the table and chooses a good beginner's selection: steamed dumplings and teriyaki strips for appetizers, and an assortment of maki sushi for our main dish, including California, spider, and shrimp tempura rolls. I'm disappointed that I won't be eating my usual spicy tuna and eel avocado rolls, but it was worth it to see how gassed he got when he was allowed to take control. I almost wish I could take notes on this guy so I don't forget anything.

"So Hunter is an interesting name. Is there any significance to it?"

Looks like I asked the right question, because he sits up straighter to tell the story. "My mom was eighteen when she had me. She had just graduated and was tryin' to make things work with her high-school sweetheart, who had started "steppin' out" on her, as she calls it, as soon as she got pregnant. But when he found out the baby was a boy, he was all amped about passing on the Hunter name. He and Moms got in a huge fight about it because, she said, since it was obvious they'd never be getting married, she wanted me to have her maiden name, which is Gregory. They settled the argument by giving me his last name as a first name."

There are some elements of his mom's story that ring a few disturbing bells. The guy "steppin' out" when times get rough . . . Suddenly, I'm eighteen years old again, pleading with Trevor not to make me go through hell by myself.

I force myself to press on with the conversation. "Do you have a nickname?"

"When I used to run track, all the guys just called me

Gregory, Greg, or G. Actually, almost everybody calls me Gregory, except my mom, who calls me Doc."

Time to make a bold move. "You don't mind if I call you Hunter, do you?" I give him my best seductive look, the look I learned from the photographer who took my author photo for *No More Lies*.

"Not at all. Not at all." He gives me a sexy stare right back, although I don't think his had to be taught. Seems like he's had some hands-on experience at seductive looks.

He breaks the gaze abruptly, swigs his beer, and sets it down with a loud clink. "So tell me. You work all the way downtown. What were you doing in Harlem, at Kenny's, the day we met? You weren't in the best mood, I must say."

I see the waiter in the distance with our food, and I begin to ramble, distracted by the rumble in my stomach. "It was the day from hell. I'd gotten a flat tire, then I forgot to get money from the ATM, as you know, and I was on my way to an important meeting with my agent, so I was nervous about that. . . ." Fuck. Friggin' friggity frick.

He shakes his head, with a knowing smile. *Nice going, Desiree. You blew your cover in twenty minutes.* "I just had a feeling this whole time."

"A feeling about what?" I can hear the tremble in my own voice. This is the most humiliating moment of my life. And the moment is now prolonged because the waiter is placing the appetizers in front of us. Mm, they smell good. I hope Hunter doesn't get so mad about the fact that I'm a liar that I don't get to eat this food.

Once the saucers and sauces are in place, he begins dipping and munching immediately. I actually have to repeat my question. "What is it that you had a feeling about?"

He waits to swallow the chicken teriyaki before responding. I swear, he must be chewing the prescribed thirty-two times. Wait. Is it thirty-two chews, or do we have thirty-two teeth? I can't remember. And I can't believe I have time to think about all of this before he answers the question.

In true detective fashion, he points at me with his chopstick. "You're a model. Or an actress."

I don't know whether to laugh or cry. On one hand, he's given me the perfect way to save myself. Then again, I know nothing about being a model, actress, or even a video ho. But what choice do I have? "It's nothing major. Just a few gigs here and there."

"I'll bet you blow up, for real. What's that Destiny's Child chick's name?"

"Beyoncé."

Talking through a mouthful of dumpling, he says, "Anybody ever say that you look like her?" Only once a day since "Bills, Bills, Bills" came out.

"No, never. You really think so?"

"No doubt."

Time to shift the focus. This Hunter has got to become the prey. One thing I must say, he's not like a lot of egotistical guys, who insist on talking about themselves for hours at a time. But when I begin to ask him questions about medicine, he's all too happy to answer them. He tells me that he's wanted to be a doctor since he was seven years old and his younger sister, Jasmine, was plagued with really bad asthma. As unpleasant as those frequent hospital visits were, he was always fascinated by the emergency room.

I use the mention of his sister to get him to open up more about his family. Apparently, his mother got married a few years after Hunter was born. She got divorced ten years later, and now Jasmine is twenty-two, with a three-year-old daughter. He is such the proud uncle, although I can tell he's disappointed that his sister got tied down so young. I think it's safe to label him a pretty protective person.

When the main course arrives, he spends some time helping me with the chopsticks and advising me on the appropriate wasabi–to–soy sauce ratio. Once I pretend to get the hang of everything, I launch back into the questioning. "So do you want to set up a private practice someday?"

"Definitely not. I'll be working in a hospital, most likely in an impoverished area, probably in emergency medicine. I was never in this to get paid." He lays a piece of ginger on top of his California roll and pops the whole thing in his mouth. "You seem to know a lot about the field," he says once he digests the crab, avocado, rice, and cucumber.

So not only does he think that the girl with the high-school diploma wouldn't know sushi, but he also thinks that she wouldn't know phrases like private practice. "My friend's mom is a psychiatrist." Now that lie isn't too far off, being that my own mom's the shrink.

I take a look at the sushi boat in the middle of the table. The pieces are depleting fast, and I still haven't gotten his take on anything related to dating or relationships. Time to cut to the chase. "So why isn't a handsome, successful man like yourself already taken?"

Works like a charm. The grin is ear to ear. "Honestly, Desiree, I really don't have much time for a social life these days."

Cop out. "Come on, Hunter. You're out with me tonight, which means you're able to make time if you want." I use my coaxing voice, the one I employ when I want Robyn to drive with me to the shopping outlets, even though I know she has a midterm to study for.

"Sometimes the hours you're able to squeeze in just aren't enough, though. I was in a relationship for over a year, but she eventually got tired of having to accommodate my schedule."

"That's crazy. She should respect that you're doing something worthwhile, to better yourself. And to help other people." Let's see if he likes me bad-mouthing the ex.

"True, but I can see her side, too. Lonely nights are damn lonely, no matter the reason, n'ah mean?" He chuckles, and I have to smile. Not a bad answer.

We have a little tiff about who should eat the last shrimp tempura roll. He wins, and I begrudgingly stuff the piece into my mouth. It's funny how you can be starving one moment and full enough to want to puke the next.

"Now it's your turn, Desiree. What do you eventually want to do? Where do you see yourself a bunch of years from now?" He puts his fist in front of my mouth like a microphone.

This is the easiest question of the evening because the answer my alter ego gives is the same one that the real me would. "Honestly, Hunter, I have no idea."

He takes back the microphone, speaking into his own fist. "And there you have it, folks. Model. Actress. Office wizard. The possibilities are endless."

It's while I'm laughing at this silly boy's corny joke that I know I'm going to agree to go out with him again.

CHAPTER 12

HUNTER

Juxtaposition. I once had a minor obsession with that word. I remember the first time I heard it, in eleventh-grade English class. I was never much of a literature person, always preferring science and math. But when Ms. Shillingford talked about the juxtaposition of Gatsby's crowded parties and his internal loneliness, I was impressed. I immediately started looking for interesting juxtapositions to point out. My boys thought it was hilarious, because my comments would mostly be things like, "It's odd, isn't it? The juxtaposition of her big ol' titties with that flat ass?"

I haven't thought about that word in a long time. But it's the perfect way to describe the impressions that Desiree left with me the other night. She's a bunch of intriguing juxtapositions: her childish awe of New York and the expert way that she holds her chopsticks; the bashful eyes she gives when I tell her she looks nice and the sexy stare she sends my way at dinner; her lack of college experience and the way her voice carries so much thoughtfulness and . . .

Insight. Staring at my letters—*A, I, G, H, N, S, T*—I

realize that I can make the word INSIGHT, if I can find an open *I* on the board. Checking the score, I see that Robyn is ahead by seventeen points, which means I really need a double word score or something. The first time that I spotted Robyn's Scrabble game in the corner of her living room, she seemed real surprised that I would want to play. But I've always dug Scrabble. People think you need to have this big old vocabulary, but to me, the game is more about probability than anything. What are the odds that you will pull an *E* out of the bag when four *E*'s have already been used? How many permutations can be made with seven letters, and which combination is going to earn the most points?

Ah, here we go. I can build INSIGHT off of QUICK, which is the word that put Robyn in the lead on her last turn. I put the letters down with force, like I'm playing a game of dominoes with the fellas or something. Robyn tallies the points, unimpressed, and adds eighteen to my score. She hands me the bag, and I remove six letters, only to be disappointed by the fact that I've picked all vowels except for the letter *L*.

"It's a conspiracy, man," I announce. "You've gotten the *Q*, the *Z*, and the *J*. I've had to try to make power moves with the letter *H*."

Robyn squints her eyes, concentrating on her letters, then looks at the board, then at me. "You are the sorest loser. The *X* is still out there. Maybe you can do something with that." She makes her word, VOW, and fishes in the bag for replacement letters. "Um, forget what I just said about the *X*," she says, with a giggle.

"That's it. Game over." I fold the Scrabble board in half, dislodging all the pieces and causing Robyn to scream in outrage. From the look on her face, I'd better start running. I take off into the kitchen, and she's right on my heels. We do a little bit of cat and mouse around the table before I manage to escape back to her living room. I land on the couch and shield myself with a cushion as she throws a few fake punches my way.

"Robyn, grow up. Seriously. You're so childish." I swallow a laugh in my throat, and she rolls her eyes. It's nice to unwind over here sometimes. She has so many things at her place that I don't, like food, games, and comfortable furniture. I rationalize that I don't need any of those things, since I'm hardly ever home, but the more I chill at her spot, the more I miss the finer things at my own apartment.

After surveying the damage on the floor and realizing that the game cannot be saved, she resigns herself to sitting next to me in a huff. I ignore it. "So how's the job, Rob?" I nudge her with my elbow and keep doing it until she cracks. Robyn has the best smile I've ever seen, even better than mine. Her teeth are celebrity white. You know how famous people always use that good shit to bleach their teeth. And then she has the dimples going on. It's real special.

"I love the job. It's a great resume builder, and the work is really cool. Diabetes runs in my family, so it's kind of nice to be in a lab that's working on cures."

"So I guess the G-Man really hooked you up, huh?" When Dr. Eisengrath asked me in the spring if there were any first-year students who would want the lab position that I had last summer, I immediately thought of Robyn. She seemed to have her stuff together more than the other folks in her class, maybe because she took a year off before she started med school.

"Damn it, Gregory, I thanked you for the job a million times. Stop sweatin' it." Suddenly, she's off the couch, cleaning up the Scrabble pieces, which are all over the floor.

"I should've known your anal ass couldn't look at that

mess for too long," I say as I crouch on the carpet to help her.

"Um, isn't every ass anal? Otherwise, you'd have serious problems." I pretend to be ashamed of her corny joke but eventually give in with a chuckle.

"How's Eisengrath treating ya?" I ask as I spy what I think is a Scrabble tile in the corner of the room, but it turns out to be a Cheez-It. Dr. Webster Eisengrath is this extremely disorganized man, with unkempt hair and thick, plastic-rimmed glasses, who literally rubs his hands together like Gargamel when a lab experiment goes according to plan.

"Crazy. Eisengrath's idea of fun is to pore over scientific journals until he finds a discrepancy, then compose a two-page letter to the editor, complete with footnotes. It scares me, because I'm interested in pursuing research after graduation, and I wonder which comes first: working in the lab or being a total dork? Am I destined to become just like that guy?"

Robyn is way too high maintenance about her hair to turn into Eisengrath, who looks like he lets birds sleep on his head at night. If Robyn's in the house, her dome is always wrapped mad tight with a black scarf. When she combs it out, she looks like the woman on my mom's home perm kit. But I know that's not the answer she wants, and before I can give her one, she adds, "It's really sad when the mice in the lab are getting more action than I am." I don't know if she meant it as a joke, but I crack up laughing anyway.

"Seriously, Greg! You don't know how hard it is for a black female medical student to find a decent man." She leans tiredly against the base of the couch.

"And it's just another story for the guys, huh?"

"Hell yeah! It kills me how the men in med school get such a social boost just for being here. A future doctor is attractive to all types of females—from the chicken head who wants to ride your financial coattails to the career woman who's looking for her baller counterpart."

Desiree crosses my mind as I listen to Robyn's complaints. Desiree isn't exactly a career woman, but I sure wouldn't call her a chicken head, either. "What about the person who falls in the middle? That's your best bet, I think."

"You would think so. But when I try to meet guys with "average" professions, they get all nervous and intimidated when they hear I'm gonna be a doctor. Or they don't understand my studying obligations and think I'm dissing them."

"Stop whining, little girl." She hates when I call her that, which is why I use it as often as possible. "I experience the same difficulties with getting girls to cope with my hectic schedule."

Robyn does stop whining and stares straight ahead, with plenty of thoughts obviously still swirling around in her head. I really want to go back to thinking about Desiree, but I try to focus and offer Robyn some suggestions. "You know, there are a few good brothers right here at Columbia."

"Whatever. You guys want someone to be impressed by what you do, which doesn't happen if your girlfriend does the exact same thing." I know she's right. My buddies always say that any time they date one of the girls at school, all they end up talking about is medicine, and it turns into a contest of who's more successful.

"So who is it that you think we want?"

She thinks about this for a second, staring at me, with her head tilted to the side, like she's trying to see inside my head. "You want a beauty queen with substance. Enough substance that you consider her an intellectual equal, but not enough that she'll surpass you professionally. You want her to cook for a dinner party you're hosting for coworkers, and you also want her to be able to participate in all of the debates and discussions at that party. Yeah, Gregory, and you wonder why you're single?"

I space out for a second, trying to picture Desiree with an apron on, talking politics with another doctor's wife. "I may not be single for long. I met somebody."

Robyn raises her eyebrows and gives the "hurry up" motion with her arms.

"Her name is Desiree. She's beautiful, easy to talk to—"

She grabs my arm excitedly. "Oh my goodness! Desiree what?"

I rub my forehead a little bit, realizing that I don't even know the girl's last name. "Um, I can't remember. Why? You think you might know her?"

"Yes! One of my closest friends from college is named Desiree."

"Well, it's not her then. This Desiree definitely didn't go to Franklin." I'm a little relieved. I don't need Robyn and Desiree knowing each other. I prefer to keep my worlds separate.

"Okay. Come to think of it, actually, my Desiree wouldn't be dating you, anyhow. No offense or anything. She just doesn't go out much. So what's your Desiree all about?"

I'm not sure how much I want to tell her. I'm excited about this girl, and people sometimes have a way of killing your high, even if they don't mean to. At the same time, I've been wanting to talk to someone about her since our date. I'll give her the short version. "She's a secretary at a law firm. And a model."

She gives a little snort at the word "model." Strike one for Desiree. "A model. Really. Have I seen her anywhere before?"

"She's just getting started. But she's bangin', though."

"What's she look like?"

"Um, she's sorta tall, real toned body, not skinny but not thick, either, light-skinned. She got these naturally full red lips, eyelashes that are as long as hell—"

"Don't forget the hair down to her butt crack," Robyn says, with what's obviously an attitude. Here we go. Why did I even start to tell her about Desiree? Now she's clearly thinking that I'm all into this chick because she fits into some prototype of what all black men secretly want. That's bullshit. I mean, look at Robyn. She's, like, the exact opposite of Desiree. She's super short, the same color as me, and her jet-black hair stops right at her chin. But all the dudes I roll with think she looks good as hell, including me.

"I know what you're getting at. Let's just drop it then." I really don't feel like defending myself tonight, and if I point out that I find Robyn attractive in order to back my point, that could lead to a conversation I surely don't want to have.

"Fine, but let me just say one thing. Whenever you ask a guy what he's looking for in a woman, he gives some bullshit answer about being down-to-earth, a good listener, strong-minded, all these lofty traits. But as soon as someone bright and beautiful comes along, everything he said he wanted is out the window." It's not even worth giving her a response. I'm just grateful that Robyn is the only woman I know who has such a cynical view of what men are all about.

CHAPTER 13

JASON

I've never seen this many excited white girls in one place before in my whole life. It looks like an *NSYNC concert up in here. I gotta give Desiree her props. She promised a big crowd, and the line is stretching out the door to get some face time with J. T. Steinway.

When she stopped by a few days ago to ask if I'd be interested in having Steinway make a promotional appearance at the gym, I figured she was just talking to have some shit to say. But I said sure, on the off chance that she was actually for real. She asked me for my cell number, "in case I have to catch you off-hours, cuz these things tend to fall into place pretty quickly," and that's when I got real suspicious. But Hakim was standing right next to me, getting all hyped up about a pro ballplayer coming to Jay's, so I gave her the digits.

True to her word, Desiree called the next day with all the details. She said J. T. could come for two hours on Thursday evening, sign some autographs, use some of the equipment, whatever we wanted. She warned not to advertise too much, because we wouldn't be able to handle the crowds if too many people got word. But I

kept it on the low for a different reason: I wasn't about
to play myself and tell the whole state of New Jersey that
their hero would be here, only to have him not show up.
I told my staff to promote the appearance through word
of mouth only, forgetting what a big-ass mouth Hakim
has.

So here we are, with the parking lot overflowing and
the building capacity on the verge of being tested. I must
admit, this Steinway kid is a cool cat. He rode to the spot
in a Pathfinder. Go figure. You'd think a dude with a
seven-figure salary would be driving something a little
more souped-up than a Nissan. Desiree was already here,
met him at the back entrance, and brought him right
to my office. He gave me a pound, took a quick tour of
the place, and asked me some questions about how I got
the gym off the ground. Said he might be interested in
starting a chain of health clubs someday. I must say, I was
pretty pumped, talking business with an NBA player. I
even told him about my plan to add onto the property
so we can build an indoor basketball court by next
summer, something I haven't spoken to a single person
about, except for the contractors.

While we were rapping in the back, Desiree was setting
up, designating jobs for the staff. We'd shut down the
workout equipment for the rest of the day, so all of the
trainers were free to lend a hand with crowd control.
Luckily, I had just reordered all of our logo items—
T-shirts, sweatshirts, and running pants—because folks
were buying those up like crazy so J. T. would have something to autograph. Between the four dollars we charged
to get in, plus the money from clothing sales, it's my most
successful day in terms of revenue yet. And J. T. is having
a ball, flirting with the ladies, trash talking with the Knicks
fans, and even agreeing to a bench-press contest with one

of my trainers. I put a stop to it before one of them gets hurt, but they seem about evenly matched to me.

Desiree points at her watch from across the room when the two hours are up, and I get the attention of the crowd to announce that the man of the hour has to be leaving. Folks are real cool about it, clapping and everything, and no one even presses him for any extra conversation when we walk toward the back of the gym. In my office, I have to give dude a hug. "Yo, man, I don't even know how to thank you. You really didn't have to roll through here like this."

"No sweat, dude. Really. It was a blast." He looks around to see if anyone else is listening. "You *can* do something for me, though," he says softly.

"Anything. For real."

"The girl who works here, with the long black hair. She's hot. What's her deal?" I know who he's talking about right away. She's my only female trainer, Marisol. Puerto Rican chick, real fun girl. He has good taste; if I didn't have my own shit going on, I might have kicked it myself.

"Let me put you down." I hang out of my office door and shout her name. She walks in wearing our standard uniform—a Jay's Gym T-shirt with the sleeves cut off. Her hair is in a ponytail that begins at the top of her head and ends at her waist.

"What's up, Jay?" she says cheerily, nodding in greeting to J. T., who's looking kind of shy all of a sudden.

"Hey, Marisol, I thought you might wanna meet J. T. before he breaks out. You're a basketball fan, right?"

She shakes his hand, scanning him from head to toe with her eyes. "Most definitely. Great to meet you. What the hell brings you to Jay's?"

He's a little thrown off by her question, but he gets his

cool pose back pretty quick. "Just doing a favor for a friend."

"Well, it's nice to see you in the flesh. I thought you'd be taller, though." God, I want to laugh, but my boy is tanking, and I can't clown him like that.

He's a stronger man than I am, though, since he manages a chuckle. "I still got Iverson beat."

"True. You know, I'm Jersey born and bred, so the Nets are my heart. And you've been an asset to my team, I gotta tell ya." She smiles at him, and I can tell this dude's already sprung. "I just got one beef with you. I nicknamed you 747 this season. You know why?"

Trying to imagine what Steinway and a plane have in common, I guess, "Cuz he got mad hops?"

"Nope," she answers all smug, with her hands on her hips.

"Cuz forty-seven is my number?" he asks hopefully.

"Nope. Because you love to travel! Three times during regular season, you got called for traveling. And that's three too many times, in my opinion." She's poking him in the chest as she reviews his mistakes.

The poor cat is speechless. Bad enough that she's hating on his game, never mind with me in the room to hear it. I take that as my cue to give them some alone time. "Yo, Marisol, after you finish putting him through the wringer, you mind walking him out?"

"No sweat, boss." I give J. T. another pound, with some extra heart in it for encouragement, and leave the office, closing the door behind me.

Desiree is waiting in the hallway. "You're just a regular Chuck Woolery, aren't you?"

"Huh?" Am I supposed to know who that is?

"The host of *Love Connection* . . . the game show? Forget it."

"Oh yeah, yeah, yeah. I remember that show. Nah, it's

not at all like that. I'm just making some introductions is all." She's smiling, which I realize I haven't seen her do too much in the past. It's a nice smile. Nothing spectacular, but it softens her out.

"That's very nice of you," she says, adjusting the bag on her shoulder. The shoulder of her gray tank top moves out of place, revealing a black bra strap underneath.

"And it was more than very nice of you to organize this whole event today." She shakes her head to protest, but I shake mine harder. "No, no, I'm not gonna let you downplay how big what you did for me was."

"It wasn't all for you, I'll have you know." She crosses her arms, and I can't help but notice that her chest is all pushed up because of it. "Hakim told me about the mentoring program in Newark that your gym sponsors. How'd you get involved in that?"

Hakim's a trip. Dude is running point for me when I'm not even trying to score. "I remember what it was like growing up in those streets, and I just told myself that if I was ever in a position to help out the boys in my old neighborhood, I would do it. I just wish I had more time to get out there myself and talk to the kids, you know?" She's looking really interested in this topic of conversation, and the last thing I need is for her to be pressing for information about my younger years. "So what are you about to get into?"

"I'm going to do what every red-blooded New Jersey woman does in her spare time: go to the mall."

I chuckle. The Garden State is definitely king of the shopping center. "That's too bad, cuz I was thinking that I owed you a meal as a thank you."

"Don't worry about it. I owed you dinner from when you changed my tire."

"Yeah, but you paid me back with interest today." I

look through my office window to see J. T. and Marisol exchanging a laugh. Her hand is resting on his arm. I guess playa has some moves off the court, after all.

"So I think we're even then." That smile again, and then a soft punch in the stomach. "But if you want, I could use some company."

"At the mall?"

She laughs. It's a mellow laugh—not too giggly or screechy. Just cool. "You don't have to sound so disgusted by the thought."

"It's not you. I just hate shopping." That's the truth, too. For Christmas and her birthday, I buy all of Nailah's gifts on the Internet. I hate crowds; I hate lines; I hate those damn directories with the YOU ARE HERE signs, which just make me more lost than I was before.

"Who said anything about shopping? I'm going to people-watch." Seems like she's already started that activity. With her heels on, she's exactly my height, which puts us eye to eye. I feel very person-watched right now.

"So you're just gonna sit on a bench at the mall and stare at the people walkin' by?" Every time I start thinking that this girl may not be crazy . . .

"I watch, and I write. It's an exercise. When I'm trying to design characters for a new project, I like to observe people in everyday activities and try to describe them, using as much detail as possible, in my journal."

I gotta admit, that sounds kind of interesting. I've probably read about one hundred books in the past five years, and I always wonder how the good writers do their thing. "I won't be in your way?"

"Not at all. Maybe you can give me some ideas."

I doubt that. I read a lot, but I sure ain't nobody's writer. Last time I put pen to paper, it was a long letter to Monique, telling her to find somebody new. Actually, maybe I do have some lyrical skills, after all, because she sure moved on pretty damn quick. My note must have been real convincing.

In the parking lot, we can't decide which car to drive. I'm ready for her to jump in my Acura, but on second thought, Nailah was just riding in it yesterday, and she's known for leaving some little trinket of hers behind whenever she rolls with me. So I tell Desiree that I want to see how her Jay green Jag drives, which isn't a lie. She tosses me the keys and walks to the passenger side. I keep the expression on my face neutral, but I'm definitely surprised that she would relinquish control of her car like that. I'm feeling big time as I hop in, trying not to readjust her seats and mirrors too much.

The ride to the outlets is pretty quiet. But not quiet in that uncomfortable way that it has been with Desiree in the past. It's that relaxed quiet, with the radio playing and the girl humming and the guy enjoying the feel of a beautiful car purring down the highway. I notice that her legs are crossed, and I wonder how comfortable that could be in a confined space. I read in some book once that when a girl crosses her legs toward you, it means she's interested. Her crossed leg is pointing toward the passenger window. That's probably a good thing, anyhow. It's random enough that I'm driving some girl's car to the mall so we can "people-watch." If she liked me, it would go from random to risky.

We park and go inside, making our way through the maze of people on their after-work strolls, and we wind up at the food court. Why does every food court in America look the same? There's the McDonald's or Burger King, pizza place, Chinese place, ice cream/smoothie/health drink place, the regional specialty (in Jersey, that's usually Roy Rogers), and that bizarre new place that's popped up lately: the Cajun/Asian place. They serve bourbon chicken, spicy fries, and lo mein as a meal. Hey, I'm not gonna hate on what's making money. I just wouldn't have called that one.

We grab a seat near the Orange Julius, and she pulls a plain red notebook out of her bag. I offer to get her some food, but she says that if she starts eating, she won't be writing, which is the whole point. I'd feel bad eating fried chicken in her face while she's trying to work, so I just buy two sodas from the Pizzeria Regina. Sipping and staring. Sipping and staring. I wonder what comes next.

"See that woman with the stroller near the trash can?" she asks, without looking at me.

I see her. Midthirties; long, greasy brown hair; bags under her eyes; huge hips; flat ass. "Yeah."

"How would you describe her body?"

I laugh, kind of awkwardly, cuz this must be a trick question. "Well, it ain't great."

She reaches across the table to flick my shoulder. Second time she's touched me today. "Real descriptive, Jason. You're supposed to be the body expert. Tell me about her shape."

I study her some more as she's bending over to tend to the chubby toddler in the stroller. "I'd say she's definitely bottom heavy. In a wide way, not in a juicy booty way."

"So she's pear-shaped?"

"Exactly. Pear-shaped."

"See, pear-shaped is a term people use all the time. If you wanted to use language that was more unique, what would you say?" Desiree looks like a schoolgirl, with her head tilted and her pen in her mouth.

"Shit if I know! You're the writer."

She sucks her teeth and continues staring at the woman. "What about a cello?"

I picture a cello in my mind—its roundness, especially in the lower half. "That's pretty good. How'd you think of that?"

"I used to play the violin, so instruments often come to mind when I'm trying to brainstorm images." She scribbles in her notebook as she talks.

I don't want to be deadweight in this little exercise, so I come up with a comment to contribute. "The problem with the cello, though, is it's so . . . sleek, and . . . classy. Makes the woman sound all lusciously curvy. That lady is just borderline fat."

"Good point. Wrong connotation with cello. Although all the characters in my book are gonna look good. And a woman doesn't have to be skinny to be fly. So I could have a female who's 'lusciously curvy,' as you say. I'll keep cello on reserve." She jots down a few more words before finding a new target.

For the next half hour, we take turns pointing out people's physical features, trying to come up with inventive ways to paint those people on paper. There's this kid with a head shaped like a lightbulb. We feel bad laughing, but we can't help it. There's a black girl with freckles, whose skin is even lighter than Desiree's, and we struggle to come up with a way to describe her color. I suggest a rubber band, and she writes it down. We agree that noses are the hardest things to describe; other than wide, hooked, or button, you're kind of at a loss. She asks me what my favorite physical feature is.

"On women or on myself?"

"Both."

"Obviously, a woman with a beautiful face gets my attention. Bodywise, I'm into toned arms and shoulders. It's the exercise junkie in me." An honest answer, but I wonder if she thinks I was trying to give her a compliment on the low. If I had, I would've said legs, because the two times I've seen her in a dress, she looked like a young Tina Turner from the waist down.

"And what about *your* best feature?"

I rub my hand over my head, tracing the cornrows from front to back. "I'd probably say my braids."

She leans closer and studies them carefully, to the point where I wonder if she's checking my scalp for dandruff. "They do always look freshly done. Who braids your hair for you?"

"Why do you think it's what I'm most proud of?" I ask, tossing her a wink. "I braid it myself."

She mushes me in the forehead. That's touch number three. "Shut up. No, you don't."

"I'm not playin'. I don't like depending on people." Still, I do miss the feel of Monique's fingers massaging my head, the gentle tug as she started each braid. But until Nailah learns how—and who knows when that will be—I'm on my own.

"How do you get the parts straight?" she marvels.

"Mirrors, love." I'm just trippin' out, being cocky, so I hope she doesn't think I mean anything by calling her love.

"I've never heard of a guy braiding his own hair in my life. That's impressive. I'm feelin' that."

She writes a few lines in the notebook kind of frantic, like she can't get the words down fast enough. She's probably writing that she thinks the fact that I braid my own hair is fruity or something. Who cares what she thinks, anyhow.

"Okay," she says, flipping to a clean page in the small spiral book. "Look at the way people are interacting with each other. Body language, facial expressions, that kind of thing. What do you see?"

I scan the crowd, landing on a young couple at the Cajun/Asian place. "Those teenagers over there."

She follows my gaze to the pair. "What about them?"

"They're just starting out, and he's diggin' her."

Desiree squints her eyes, trying to see whatever invisible signals she thinks I'm picking up on. "I'm listening."

"See, the girl's ordering her meal, pointing to the dishes, asking the employees questions. And he's just staring at her. Not at the food, not at the workers, just at her. With that stupid half smile on his face. If they'd been going out for a long time, he wouldn't even be paying attention to what she was doing. And if he didn't really like her, he might even think she was being annoying, acting all picky, like she's at a gourmet restaurant or something."

Desiree had stopped looking at them a while ago and is practically tearing her notebook page, pressing down so hard on the paper. I watch her write until she finishes, giving me a quick smile of gratitude.

"Do me," I say as she takes a sip of her Sprite.

"Excuse me?" She practically spits out her drink.

"Write me. Describe me in your little notebook. I wanna see what kind of skills you got." I sit back in my chair and fold my arms, posing like she's about to sketch a portrait.

She rests her chin in her hand, thinking about it for a while. Then she gives me a long look, starting at my braids and going all the way down to the pair of Jordans I have on. Her pen flies into motion.

I try to keep people-watching while she does her thing, but I can see out of the corner of my eye that her white lined paper is filling up with blue ink. It seems like forever, but it's probably more like five minutes when she pushes the notebook across the ring-stained table.

He rubs a calloused hand on a stubbled face. His piercing eyes, the color of an emerald sky on a rainy day, are cold. Staring into the distance to catch a glimpse of the past, to peer into days long gone. His gray green oval windows get misty from the memory.

Hard, soft, proper, street, honest, guarded, strong, hurt. To try to label him would be moronic, for he is a walking oxymoron. He regards her regarding him, distrustful of her intentions,

*and rightfully so. He slathers himself with an extra layer
of defensiveness and nervously feels it rubbing off. Their
words and smiles are causing him to shed his skin. "Be careful," he says to himself. "She'll expose you if you let her."*

I keep staring at the paragraphs even after I'm done
reading, not ready to talk to her just yet. It's a creepy feeling, realizing that every time someone's been looking at
you, they've really been looking through you. Reading
you. I don't know what I was expecting when I asked her
to "write me," but it sure wasn't anything this . . .
personal. No, not even personal. Invasive. It's like she's
been trying to get in my head since we met.

"Interesting," is all I can say. I don't even want to look
at her, out of fear of what she might see.

"I hope you're not offended. I was just trying to be creative, based on things I've seen you do." She slides the
notebook back to her side of the table, rereading the
passage, using her capped pen to scan the lines.

"And what kind of things are those?" I can hear the
tightness in my voice. There was a point in my life where
I used that voice for three years straight, and I'm pissed
that she has me using it again.

"Sometimes in the middle of a conversation, you kind
of space out, like you're thinking about somebody.
Somebody special." She pauses, like she's expecting me
to verify what she's saying. She better keep talking. "And
then, the way you talk—it's slang and it's sophisticated at
the same time. I like that."

I don't think I've said much sophisticated shit to her
at all, which makes me think that she's just trying to flatter a brother. For what reason, I have no idea. Which
brings me to the most disturbing part of what she wrote.
"So why'd you diss yourself in the last paragraph? You
practically called yourself shady."

For a minute, I don't think she's going to answer, because she closes her notebook and puts it back in her bag. Then she finishes what's left in her cup of soda. Finally, she says, "I have a confession to make. A couple of confessions, actually." She scoots her chair a few inches back so she can cross her legs. This time her dangling foot, with silver-painted toenails, is pointed right at me. And my foot starts tapping, cuz I'm getting nervous.

"First of all, Imani's not my girlfriend."

Over the course of the past few hours, I'd completely forgotten that girlie was trying to play gay in the first place. My mind goes back and forth over the course of about three seconds, deciding whether to pretend like I'm hearing this information for the first time. Unfortunately, even though my mouth is closed, a laugh manages to escape through my nose.

Her mouth opens wide, and she shakes her head, embarrassed by my reaction. "So you knew all along."

"Pretty much. What else you got?"

Another long pause, this time to adjust the silver bracelets on her wrist and to twirl a piece of hair around her finger. "When I planned the whole J. T. thing, it was originally to get in your good favor so I could use you."

Use me? "For what?"

"Material for my book."

"So what we're doing right now, me helping you people-watch—that's you using me?" Because if that's the case, she can use me all she wants. It wasn't so bad.

"No. My plan was a lot more complicated than that. I wanted to see how guys handled friendships with women they couldn't have, which is why I let you think I was with Imani."

She's acting like she's at a Catholic church, waiting to see how many Hail Marys she has to say for forgiveness, and all I can do is laugh. "That's the dumbest shit I ever heard. I'm sorry, I don't mean to be ill, but that really is a stupid-ass idea."

She slaps my knee kind of hard. We're at four touches and counting. "Stop laughing at me!"

"All right, all right. So what made you change your mind? Because you really had me fooled." I move my leg before she can hit it again.

"I realized that you're too sharp for me to play games with."

"This is true," I respond with a smirk. She's looking down in her lap, and I hope she's not regretting her little confession. I'm flattered that she felt like she had to be real with me. "Look, Desiree, if you want ideas for your book, you can just ask my opinion. As a friend. You don't have to go to all kinds of drama just to see what I'm thinking."

"A friend," she repeats softly. "I've never had a guy friend before." She looks and sounds about twelve years old, nothing like the way she usually carries herself. I can't say that I'm surprised that she doesn't have any dudes as friends. From the way she acts half the time, I wouldn't be surprised if she didn't have any friends at all. But I still feel kind of bad for her, until I realize that I haven't had any female friends before, either, with the exception of Monique. And that's almost too complicated to even call a friendship.

"I'll break you in slowly then," I answer before I even recognize the sexual connotation. But from the way she laughs and looks at me with this fake scolding expression, I can tell that she does. I may be new at this, but I don't think the best way to begin a friendship is by flirting. This could be trouble.

CHAPTER 14

To: *imanigrace@aol.com*
From: *desiree@alumni.franklin.edu*
Time: Friday, July 20, 2001 11:33 a.m.
Subject: checking in

Message:
whatzup, girlie. i haven't been in the city too much lately, trying to buckle down at home and make some headway with this story. i think i actually have a story line down. that's the good news. the bad news is that i have a confession to make.

i know when i told you about hunter a while back, i promised you that it was only going to be one date. but the date went so well that i agreed to go out with him again. imani, i'm going to base my main character on him. and if i'm gonna do that, i need to get to know him better. two more dates at the most, maybe three.

i figured if i e-mailed you, i wouldn't have to deal with you yelling at me.
des

* * *

To: *paula@moyagency.com*
From: *desiree@alumni.franklin.edu*
Time: Friday, July 20, 2001 12:01 p.m.
Subject: summary

Message:
Hi Paula,

Just wanted to give you an idea of what I've been
working on since we last spoke:

The handsome, brilliant, and extremely wealthy
attorney Russell Montgomery has never met a
woman who could live up to his impossible standards. But when he hires a no-nonsense secretary
at his firm to reorganize his office, she ends up
turning his whole world upside down instead.
Russell's attraction to her is undeniable, but is he
ready to let go all of his preconceptions with what
his ideal woman should be?

Let me know what you think.
Desiree

To: *desiree@alumni.franklin.edu*
From: *robyn@med.columbia.edu*
Time: Friday, July 20, 2001 12:14 p.m.
Subject: Miss ya!

Message:
How ya doin', girl? I'm sure you're busy trying to
get that book done.

This crazy doctor in charge of the lab is running me ragged. I never get off campus these days.

Feel like I haven't seen you in forever. Hope I haven't missed anything too big.

Robyn

To: *desiree@alumni.franklin.edu*
From: *paula@moyagency.com*
Time: Friday, July 20, 2001 3:40 p.m.
Subject: Re: summary

Message:
   Honey,
   It could work, but you need some twists and turns. What's the deal with the secretary? Does she return Russell's feelings? What's her home life like? Give her a child or an abusive ex-husband or something.
   Are you writing in the third person? It will give you more leeway for us to see both perspectives—male and female. You could always do alternating first-person narrative, but that style ends up being so contrived most of the time.
   Keep me posted.

   Paula

To: *desiree@alumni.franklin.edu*
From: *imanigrace@aol.com*
Time: Friday, July 20, 2001 4:19 p.m.
Subject: bad, bad girl

Message:

Desiree, I hope that boy does a Google search on your ass and exposes you for the fake that you are. You are too talented of a writer to feel like you have to create exact scenarios to then recount in a book. It's about using emotions as inspiration, not using an innocent guy as a pawn in your twisted game. Not to mention, what the hell is going to happen when this dude wants to kiss your face? Or get in your pants?

I guess the only good news is that Jason is not the sucker getting played in all this. What made you decide to exclude him from your plan?

Imani

To: *desiree@alumni.franklin.edu*
From: *jason@jaysgym.com*
Time: Saturday, July 21, 2001 2:25 p.m.
Subject: Thanks again

Message:
Yo, I wanted to say thank you one more time for organizing that event the other night. Since then, there has been a whole mess of new faces around here. Morale and profits are up. When you get a chance, hit me up with J. T.'s address. I want to send him something as a thank you. What do you send another dude as a gift? I don't think flowers are the way to go. On a different note, so how is this friends stuff gonna work with us? Do we braid each other's hair and tell secrets? Let me know.-J

* * *

To: *imanigrace@aol.com*
From: *desiree@alumni.franklin.edu*
Time: Saturday, July 21, 2001 2:45 p.m.
Subject: Re: bad, bad girl

Message:
>I guess the only good news is that Jason is not
the sucker getting played in all this.
>What made you decide to exclude him from
your plan?

i think i realized that as much as i need a subject
for my book, i need a guy in my life whom i can
trust even more. and don't get all geeked, either.
it's a friendship, and that's all.

To: *desiree@alumni.franklin.edu*
From: *kahlila@alumni.franklin.edu*
Time: Saturday, July 21, 2001 3:17 p.m.
Subject: another visit

Message:
hey des,

   that last visit was way too short. i didn't even get
to see robyn, and i barely squeezed in a dinner with
j. t. (who, by the way, told me about hanging out
with you the other day. he wanted me to tell you
that he's gone out with marisol already and likes her
a lot). so i'm going to leave boston a couple days
early to head to new york one more time before i
start my job in philly. see you in a couple weeks.

kahli

* * *

To: *robyn@med.columbia.edu*
From: *desiree@alumni.franklin.edu*
Time: Saturday, July 21, 2001 5:03 p.m.
Subject: miss u 2!

Message:
what's up doc,

i know how hectic things can get. don't worry. it's been same ol' same ol' with me. did you hear from kahli about her paying us another visit? we'll definitely get together when she comes, if not before.

des

To: *jason@jaysgym.com*
From: *desiree@alumni.franklin.edu*
Time: Saturday, July 21, 2001 5:21 p.m.
Subject: no problem

Message:
jason,

it really wasn't that big of a deal getting j. t. to come down. but i'm glad that his visit has had such positive results.

just give j. t. a sweatshirt from the gym. he lives in athletic wear. besides, he's the one who should be thanking us. he's already had one really good date with the girl he met. nice work, chuck.

braiding each other's hair sounds like fun. we might have to work up to the telling secrets part, though. i don't think either of us is too big on pouring our hearts out.

desiree

CHAPTER 15

DESIREE

For the past year and a half, I've spent at least two weekends out of every month in New York City. I've been to hundreds of restaurants and thousands of stores, but I've never bothered with the Empire State Building, the Statue of Liberty, or Madison Square Garden. And I can count the number of museums I've visited on one hand (one finger, to be exact). Which made it all the better when Hunter suggested that we engage in a "classic New York activity" for our second date. I told him that this date was going to be my treat, but he completely refused to entertain that idea, saying that he's an old-fashioned guy and believes in courting a woman properly. Hearing him say that made me feel like a hot mess, being that this is not a courtship, but an experiment. So we compromised by agreeing that whatever he chose had to be free, because he's a struggling student, and I didn't want him wasting his money. Of course, the real reason was that I felt too guilty having him pay for dates that weren't leading anywhere, but I kept that to myself, for obvious reasons.

We're supposed to meet at his place, which means I

have to take the subway. First of all, there is no way that
Hunter can see I drive a Jag. Second, when he told me
his address, I realized that he lives in the same building
as Robyn. I can't take the chance of her seeing my car.
Plus, their neighborhood isn't the greatest, and I
wouldn't want to be stressed about some shady characters messing with my baby. I can hear my dad's voice in
my head, reminding me how impractical it was to buy
such a fancy car when I'd be parking it all over New
York. But I'd just gotten my advance for *No More Lies* and
decided to treat myself to something I've fantasized
about. The Jaguar has always been, in my opinion, the
most beautiful car ever made. People have called me an
old soul for preferring it to something younger and
sportier, and maybe I am. But I haven't gotten tired of
the feeling I get when I'm behind the wheel, like I'm the
classiest woman on the planet. Tonight, I'd have to settle
for being just an average chick, since there's not a damn
thing glamorous about the A train uptown.

   Approaching his building, I try to focus on my goals
for the date, but I'm distracted by the thought that I
could run into Robyn. His apartment is just one floor
above hers, and my stomach is flip-flopping by the time
I reach the rickety elevator in their high-rise. As much as
I would be completely mortified if I got caught by my
girl, I think there's a small part of me that wants to be exposed so this charade can be over. Imani's probably
right: I don't need to do all of this to write my book. My
imagination is strong enough. But at the same time,
Paula told me that I have to develop my female character more. What better way to get inside her head than to
take on her identity in a real-life situation? So my mission
this evening is simply to see how he reacts to me—what
he finds attractive, and what he wishes he could change.
What we have in common and what sets us worlds apart.

I use the walk from the elevator to arm myself with one more layer of lip gloss.

My eyebrows rise when Hunter opens the door. He's looking quite good in a long-sleeved T-shirt, baggy jeans, and Adidas flip-flops. The casual look works really well for him, contrasting with his clean-cut head and face nicely. I tend to like when guys switch up their usual style, and this is the first time I've seen Hunter in kicking-it clothes. Jason, on the other hand, lives in tank tops and sweats, which is why I had to wipe the drool from my mouth the time I saw him dressed up at B Sharp. Okay, Jason needs to get the hell out of my head, because I have work to do.

"Hey. You look great," I say, with a smile. Now that's something I would never do as the real me—compliment a guy.

"Yeah, right," he answers modestly. "I haven't even changed yet. I just didn't want to get my clothes dirty while I was cooking."

"You cooked?" I can't believe this. The only man who's ever cooked for me in my life is my dad. And everything he makes is on the grill. It figures that as soon as I pretend to be someone else, I get showered with unexpected treats. "I just figured we'd grab something to eat when we were out."

"Nope. You told me you didn't want me spending any money while we were out. So I decided that this was a way to sidestep your rule. Anyhow, come on in." His eyes are boring holes through me as I walk past him into the apartment. Tonight I decided to sport a Paula Moy–inspired ensemble: capri pants, a fitted button-down short-sleeved blouse, and high-heeled sandals. "You look gorgeous."

I wave off his comment and walk around his living room, a tiny box of a space that barely fits the couch and

TV. Only his degree from Duke and an eight-by-ten picture, both framed, adorn the wall. In the photo, he's posing with an attractive girl, very tall and slender, and a toddler sits in front of them. My mind is jumping to all types of conclusions, but then I remember what he told me on our first date about his family history.

"Your sister and your niece, right?" He looks pleased that I remembered.

"Yup. Jasmine and Asha. We took that picture as a gift for my mom last year."

I wander into the adjoining kitchen and see that the table is already set for two. Relief floods my body that it's not a romantic affair with champagne and candles, but a cozy supper with cracked china and juice glasses.

"You hungry?" he asks. "I know it's kind of early for dinner."

"Starved." He takes a tray out of the oven and uncovers a few pots on the stove, revealing baked salmon, rice pilaf, and spinach. I insist on serving myself, and we make small talk as we dish the food onto our plates. It feels great, hanging out in a warm kitchen, chatting about our weeks at work, sitting down to eat a nice meal. I know, I know. I'm an absolute fraud. My week at "the firm" is aided by a talk I had with Imani's girlfriend Sheila the other day about her job. But I try not to think about the fact that I'm spewing lies.

I listen as he explains that he only has one more week in his pediatric rotation before he moves on to the ER, which is what he expects to pursue when he graduates. "I'm gonna miss peds, though. I liked it a lot more than I expected."

"Did you have a favorite patient?" I'm forgetting about the task at hand. My character, Russell Montgomery, isn't even a doctor, so this whole line of conversation is pointless.

"Manny, no doubt. That kid is a trip." He smirks and shakes his head, like he's remembering something Manny said or did, which puts a smile on my face as well.

"What's he like?"

"Thirteen-year-old black male with familial hyperlipidemia," he says in one breath before taking a swig of fruit punch.

"English, please." I'd meant for him to tell me about Manny's personality, not his condition.

"My bad," he apologizes, with a chuckle. "It's a cholesterol thing. Genetics screwed him over, and he has too much fat in his blood. He has to come in every few weeks to basically get his blood cleaned out." I wince, trying to imagine what that life must be like for the poor boy. "I know," he says. "Not fun at all. But that's what's so cool about Manny. He's a jokester, real easy to talk to. It's like the hospital staff is his second family. We hit it off right away."

"He's probably so glad to have a young black doctor to talk to. It doesn't happen often, I'll bet."

"I'm not a doctor yet," he reminds me. "And I don't know if it's so much that I make him feel better, or that he makes me feel better. The other day he said to me, 'Doc Greg, I've seen a lot of med students come and go, but you definitely got what it takes.' That was better than any accolade I could've gotten from staff."

He's doing it, the two things that turn me on most with men: using impressive vocabulary and gushing about kids. Sophistication and sensitivity, a lethal combination. I could fall for Hunter. He's a decent guy—funny, good-looking, charming. But it's so easy to put up a barrier, because he doesn't know me. The real me—Desiree Thomas. He knows Desiree . . . Oh goodness, I'd better think of a last name. Smith. Too plain.

Let's go with a color. Green. Black. White. White is good. Add a suffix. Whiteman.

When dinner is finished, I insist on washing the dishes, something that Desiree Thomas would do just as quickly as Desiree Whiteman. He sponges down the table and the stove as I lather and rinse the plates and glasses, letting the pots and trays soak. "That was a terrific meal, Hunter. I'm impressed."

He grabs a hand towel and begins drying the dishes as I stack them on the counter next to the sink. "Don't be too impressed. I got some help."

"Don't tell me your mom came by and cooked all the food before I came."

He laughs the kind of laugh where no sound comes out, but his shoulders jerk up and down. "Not quite. But I was on the phone with my friend Robyn for an hour before you got here, making sure I was doing everything right."

And there it is. My stomach is seizing, and I'm afraid the salmon in my tummy might end up in the garbage disposal if I don't get it together. This moment of silence is stretching way too long.

He sets down the dish towel and moves behind me, putting his hands on my waist. I jump a little. Can't help it. It's been ages since I've felt a man's touch on my skin. "Sorry," I mumble. "Your hands are cold." He removes them from my hips and rubs his palms together.

"I know what you're thinking." He pauses. "Robyn and I are just friends. I swear."

"That's not what I was thinking." I turn around to face him, a little bothered by how close to me he's standing. "I was just thinking that you shouldn't have gone through all that trouble for me."

He flashes this torturously dazzling smile and kisses me on the forehead before I even know what hit me.

"No trouble at all, sweetheart. Robyn's a year behind me at the med school, and I give her all my old textbooks for free. I've saved her crazy dollars. She could at least help me out with one dinner."

I'm calming down a bit, but I'm still not at the point where I can have a casual conversation about Robyn. Add that to his comfortable use of the word "sweetheart," and suddenly, the room is stifling. He looks at me strangely. "Are you okay? You don't look like you're feeling too well."

"I'm fine," I say too quickly. "Could just use a little fresh air, I think."

He glances at his watch and begins to move in fast-forward. "Good idea. The sun's setting in about an hour, so we gotta get out of here, anyway." I open my mouth to inquire where we're going, but he anticipates my question. "Don't even bother asking. You'll see when we get there." He looks down at his clothes and then back at me. "Do you mind if I just wear this?" I shake my head to say that I don't, and we head out the door.

My sick feeling increases once we leave the safety of his apartment. What if he decides to stop by Robyn's place to thank her for the help with the meal? What if she's coming into the building as we're walking out? What if he's already told her about the fake Desiree, and she's figured out that it's really me? Fortunately, we make it to the subway unseen, and my breathing becomes a little less ragged. I'm still fairly quiet, though, thinking about this friendship between Robyn and Hunter. What if she has feelings for him? I mean, why wouldn't she? He's great. But if she did, I would've heard about this guy. And I've definitely never heard Hunter's name before. But wait, she probably calls him Gregory. Have I heard about a Gregory? Or a Greg? I don't think so. Still, I haven't had a long conversation with Robyn in . . . goodness, over a month now. Maybe they've gotten closer recently. *Okay, Des. Calm down.* It's not a big deal. After all, this is the last time I'm going to see him. It's getting way too complicated, and he's not giving me much useful information, anyhow.

We're on the train for a long time. Seems like we're going all the way downtown. When we finally get off and reach above ground, I realize that we're at the Brooklyn Bridge.

He looks at me with a big grin, awaiting my reaction. "I hope those shoes are comfortable."

My BCBG pumps are a lot of adjectives: colorful and cute, for instance. Comfortable is not one of them. "We're walking across the bridge?"

"Yup. Just in time for sunset." And he starts toward it, leaving me to do nothing but follow. I debate complaining about having to walk in my heels, just to see how Hunter responds to such a diva move. But he's been so nice tonight, cooking dinner and all, I can't bring myself to be a bitch.

Once we're walking across, my mood immediately begins to improve. It had been a sweltering day, and the early evening breeze feels so refreshing. It's also fun watching the other people on the bridge—tourist families, lovey-dovey couples, athletic Rollerbladers. "You made a good choice, Hunter. This is definitely a New York activity I've never done, and probably would have never done if you hadn't brought me. Thanks."

"I'm glad you approve. People usually take the subway to Brooklyn so they can walk across the bridge facing Manhattan, but I feel like that's discriminating against my old neighborhood. So have you ever thought about moving to New York?"

Every day. Each time I jewelry shop in the Village, or find another amazing restaurant in SoHo, or get my hair done for twelve dollars in Harlem, I ask myself why I don't live in the city. Other than my dad and my brother, the only man in my life is Manhattan. But as is true with any relationship that's going well, you don't want to rock the boat. Manhattan and I do well living apart. I don't get sick of him, and he's always happy to see me when I do come around. This is all way too much to explain to Hunter, however. "Can't afford it."

"What if money were no object? What part of the city would you live in?"

"Probably in a renovated brownstone in Harlem, or in a high-rise on the Upper West Side."

He shakes his head, obviously disappointed by my answers. "Typical. What about Brooklyn?"

"Honestly, I haven't spent enough time there to feel any way about it." He pretends to look injured, as all New Yorkers are so protective of and defensive about their boroughs.

"Well, I'll have to do something about that, won't I?" Oh, Lord. I can't even bring myself to respond to that one, I'm feeling so guilty. Luckily, he takes this moment to guide me to the edge of the bridge to watch the sun set. It had been a fairly clear day, with just a few puffy clouds in the sky, making for a spectacular mix of fiery oranges and reds now that the big yellow ball is retiring for the evening.

"Wow. It's spectacular," is all I can say.

"So are you," he answers. And even though I'm still looking straight ahead at the last cloud the sun has to travel through before it completely disappears, I can tell that Hunter lost interest in the sunset long ago. If I turn to face him, he's going to kiss me. I just know it. But the crazy thing is, I'm actually debating whether I should. That's when I notice that he's laughing. The silent laugh with the shaky shoulders.

"What's funny?" I'm relieved to be relieved of the kissing decision, but I'm fully aware that I'm going to have to return to the issue in my mind later on. I haven't kissed anyone in five years, and I was about to kiss this man who doesn't even know who I am. What the hell? After Trevor, I decided not to let any man into my life romantically until I could fully trust him, and until I could trust myself not to let my own bitterness and anger ruin things. I would've thought that if I were going to eventually surrender my asexual streak for anybody, it would be Jason, not Hunter. Jason and I spent such an amazing day together last week. But he was the one who suggested being friends. Which is probably a much better idea than kissing him, anyway.

"I don't even know your last name, Desiree."

I congratulate myself on anticipating this question and answer with confidence. "Whiteman."

"Kind of ironic, isn't it?" I stare at him blankly. "A black woman named white man?"

I force a chuckle. "Yeah, I get that a lot." Stupid, stupid, stupid. Why the heck did I pick that name?

We begin walking again, and he begins the "favorite" conversation. Favorite book, favorite song, favorite city. Let the lies continue. I can't answer any of these questions truthfully. My favorite book is *Mama Day* by Gloria Naylor. A little too obscure for my alter ego. Favorite song: "Four Women" by Nina Simone. Again, not likely for the sheltered secretary. And my favorite city is Paris, which I've been to twice since college, once with Kahlila and once alone. There's no freakin' way the local Jersey girl made two trips to Europe on her salary. I go with *Waiting to Exhale* (one of the books that motivated me through writing *No More Lies*), "One in a Million" by Aaliyah (a song that my girls and I wore out sophomore year), and New York City (the only city in which Desiree Whiteman would have realistically spent any time).

He tells me that the only books he reads are for school, which is a plus for me. Reduces the chance of his stumbling across my book. His favorite song is anything off of Stevie Wonder's *Songs in the Key of Life*—a stellar choice, I must say. And while D.C. and Atlanta rank high for him, he has to go with New York, the hometown favorite.

When we get to the subject of movies, I don't have to bend the truth at all. My favorite of all time is *Love Jones,* and he excitedly tells me that it's his, too. We quote a few lines, laughing and being silly. I explain that I believe the film to be the catalyst for a whole wave of movies and TV shows that followed, portraying a subculture for twenty-something African Americans that was both intellectual and creative. Uh-oh. He looks impressed. Maybe I said too much. I guess I won't mention how unrealistic it was for Larenz Tate's character to have written an entire novel, secured a book deal, and published it in hard-cover in less than a year. I mean, I loved the movie, but damn.

In the contented silence that follows, he confidently takes my hand in his. Women, especially black women, pray every day for moments like this. *Dear Lord, please send me an ambitious black man who treats me with respect, and if it's not too much trouble, let him be good-looking. And tall.* Please forgive me, Lord, for monopolizing the subject of another woman's prayers.

"So, when are we going to get to do this again?" The dreaded question. There's no way we can keep doing this. He's getting caught up, and so am I. And it's not even really helping me with the book. I have to rely on my own abilities. Besides, if I need a male perspective, maybe my new buddy Jason can help me out.

"Whenever. Just call me." It kills me to sound this evasive. I never intended on hurting feelings when I made my exit from this charade. Actually, I guess I never intended on caring whether anyone got hurt or not.

"I'll be in the hospital a lot this week. What's your e-mail address? I can hit you up tomorrow."

Crapola. I certainly can't give him my real e-mail address with my real last name and my real college. "You know, I have to type all day for work. I hate e-mail. Just call me when you can."

Goodness, half of me wants him to call me on my inconsistencies. To make me come clean. But he accepts my answer with no visible suspicion and continues walking in the dark.

CHAPTER 16

JASON

I set down my ginger ale to give Nicole a standing ovation as she wraps up her set at B Sharp. Just over a month ago, she was sitting in with the Quarter Notes, and now she's headlining, with cats playing backup for her. This is also the first time she's performing any original music, and I must say that while I knew the girl was talented before, she's on genius level now that I've heard two of her own songs. I don't know much about writing music, but it's gotta be hard to write for an entire jazz band.

Desiree, Imani, and Sheila are hooting and hollering, but that just ain't my style. So I clap my hands together as loud as I can and give Nicole a thumbs-up when she looks in our direction. Finally, we settle back into our seats—Imani and Sheila pulling their chairs close together—and I try to convince myself for the millionth time tonight that I'm not on a double date. Even though it sure feels like one.

Before this evening, I hadn't seen Desiree since the day J. T. rolled through the gym. But we've been talking on the phone a little bit, just casual "how was your day" type stuff. One thing I've noticed about her from our phone conversations is that she's a real good listener. I'll mention something to her once, an errand I have to run or a problem at work, and she'll always follow up on it the next time we speak. It's kind of nice having someone who seems to care about the little details of my life. And even though she takes an interest in what I tell her, she still respects my privacy. When I don't answer my cell, or I'm vague about what I've been up to, she never asks me where I was or whom I was with. She could just be following my lead on that, being that I've never been one to try to dig up what folks want to stay buried. And it's not like she doesn't have shady moments. On Sunday she stayed the night at Imani's, and when I asked her what she was doing in the city, she said, "Research." All short and snippy, like I better not ask nothin' else. So I didn't.

Coming here tonight as a group was her idea, but I wasn't against it at all. I was actually a little curious about Imani's girl, being that I've been hearing about her for so long and never met her. This probably isn't PC, but she pretty much looks like the textbook lesbian, with a short, natural haircut, no jewelry on, and a pantsuit that hides any small curves she may possibly have. Although she did come straight here from work, so maybe this is just her in professional mode. Desiree did say that Sheila and Imani were an odd couple, and they do look like complete opposites. But none of this is even my business, and I can't believe I'm even giving it this much thought. I think this is what happens when you spend too much time gossiping with women on the phone.

I glance over at Desiree, who has just put her hand on my arm in the middle of telling what looks to be a pretty funny story to Imani and Sheila. As soon as I look over, she moves her hand as if she just realized it was there. She's looking completely lopsided tonight. Now I'm not big on fashion at all. Gucci, Guess, GAP, it doesn't make a bit of difference to me. As long as a woman's clothes fit her nice, it's all good. But there's this one style that came out recently that I just don't dig at all: the one-sleeve shirt. What the hell is that shit? It looks like the designer just fell asleep on the job and put the shirt on sale before it was even finished. Well, Desiree has on one of those shirts—one long sleeve and nothing on the other side. And to make it worse, the skirt she has on is longer on one side, like the bottom of it ripped all crooked. When I met her outside my brownstone earlier, I couldn't hide the look of displeasure on my face.

"What's wrong?" she'd asked me. "Do I have something in my teeth or something?"

"I just hate that whole 'I'm hot/I'm cold' steelo. I mean, decide whether you want to wear long sleeves or not. It's that simple." I don't know why I had been so honest, but she didn't seem bothered at all. She even laughed.

"So you're not a fan of the asymmetrical look, huh?" And she took a black elastic from her wrist, pulled all her hair to the side, and put it in a ponytail that hung over one shoulder. "How do you like that?" she said, with a devilish smile.

I don't think I'm ever going to like the "asymmetrical look," as she called it, but it was real cool of her not to give a shit what I thought. I dig that about her.

Nicole has been making her way to our table since she left the stage, but it's taking a while with everyone stopping her to give her props on a job well done. Scanning the crowd and watching the way she interacts with people, it's clear that no one in the audience is a friend of hers. Wow. I guess we're the closest things to friends that she has in this city. I feel bad for her, because even though I don't have too many friends myself, I'm twenty-seven years old. And I know how to fill that alone time. Shit, I even enjoy my alone time. But for an eighteen-year-old, it must be tough not having a social life.

She finally joins us, getting hugs and kisses from Imani and Sheila, a pound from me, and a handshake from Desiree, who is just officially meeting her for the first time. Nicole is all giddy to meet Desiree, telling her that she read her book twice and loved it. Desiree, of course, returns the compliment with real positive comments about Nicole's performance, and it seems like forever before we all sit down again for a normal conversation.

"So, Nicole, how are you handling all of this craziness?" Desiree asks in between sips of white wine.

Nicole opens her mouth wide and closes it, like she just picked up on the fact that everyone in the place came to hear her play. That's when I notice that she has braces—the clear ones, and only on her bottom teeth. I wanna ask her if they get in the way when she plays the sax, but that might be a rude question. "I'm just so excited, like all the time. It's a dream come true," she says, like she just won a Miss Teen USA pageant.

"I'll bet it is," Sheila chimes in. "How many people your age get to live on their own and make money doing what they love? That's really fabulous."

"Thank you," Nicole says in a shy voice and orders a seltzer water from the waitress.

"Still, it must be difficult. That's a lot of pressure for a young person. Do you ever feel overwhelmed?" The concern on Desiree's face looks for real, but I'm still a little annoyed. Everyone at the table was in a great mood, smiling and giving Nicole her due props. Then Desiree gets all serious, like she's Barbara Walters and just has to make the girl cry.

"Sometimes I do, yeah. But then I think of the alternative. I could be back in Ohio, doing the community college thing, when school was never my favorite place to be." I can feel her on that. Other than English class, nothing in high school ever got me too excited.

"Well, credit to your parents for allowing you to take the road less traveled," Imani says, raising her glass for a toast. Everyone except Nicole clinks in agreement. I don't know if it's because she doesn't have her drink yet, or because she doesn't agree.

"Let's not even talk about my folks," she mutters. I've never heard Nicole sound like that before. She's usually all perky, the way white girls on TV sound when they're trying to sell pimple cream.

It's almost like I can feel the nosiness rising off Desiree's body in waves as soon as Nicole says that. I swear, it's like the girl stays looking for people to be troubled about some shit. "Are you sure you don't want to talk about it?"

Nicole looks down at her lap while the others shoot these all-knowing looks at each other, like the three wise women or something. She takes a deep breath, and when she breathes out, all of her bottled-up frustration comes out with it. "I'm just really mad at my parents. I mean, I call them all super excited about stuff that's going on here in New York, and they can't even be happy for me. They're just so disappointed that their only daughter isn't satisfied staying in Ohio, going to school, and meeting some boring guy to marry so I can live a boring life just like them."

"Have they come out and said all that, Nicole?" asks Imani in a motherly tone. I feel like I'm trapped inside an episode of Oprah.

"They don't have to. It's . . . What's the word? Like hidden but not hidden—"

"Implicit," Desiree interrupts.

Nicole makes a funny face. "Um, that's not what I was

thinking of, but okay. It's implicit in the way they talk to me, ya know? Like they never ask about my shows, or if I tell them some really good news, they're not even happy for me."

"They're probably just sad that you're so far away," chimes in Sheila.

"If they miss me so much, they should come visit. When I told them to come to a performance, my mom was like, 'Well, you know your father isn't that well.' Gimme a break. Please explain to me how my dad's high blood pressure relates to them not coming to see me in New York."

She looks like she really wants an answer, so I try to give her one. "Well, it *is* kinda hectic in the city. Maybe—"

I'm silenced by a hit under the table from Desiree, who begins talking over me just to be completely sure that I'll shut up. "They can't be that much against what you're doing. They're footing the bill, right?"

Nicole is sipping her drink, but when she hears Desiree say that, her eyes open all wide, and she sets the glass on the table. "Ha! That's what you think. They're not even paying for my 'little experiment,' as they call it. My grandfather had an account set up for me when I turned eighteen."

"Must be nice," I say under my breath, resulting in another smack from my right.

"And I'm not even using that much of the money since I've been getting steady paying gigs since I got here."

Desiree has her head tilted in that sympathetic way, and I wonder if she had sensed how down Nicole had been feeling. It pisses me off the way she seems to read people when she barely knows them. Actually, more than it makes me mad, it scares me.

No one seems to have any words of wisdom for the

girl, so I risk getting hit again for the sake of trying to make the kid feel better. "Look, Nicole, your folks are going to be real uptight about this music thing. That ain't going to change for a while. But as soon as you make it big, like real big, they're gonna be so damn proud, telling everyone that they believed in you from jump street. That's what parents do."

Nicole smiles, and I figure I must've done good since Desiree keeps her hands to herself. "Thanks, Jason."

"He's right, Nicole," says Imani, throwing me a wink, which I realize just may be her trademark. "You think you're disappointing your parents by not going to college? Well, imagine coming home from college to announce that you're a lesbian. Can't say that went over too well."

"Oh my God! What did they say?" asks a wide-eyed Nicole.

Putting on the countryfied voice of her mother, Imani says, "First, you twist up your beautiful hair. Now this!" We all laugh, imagining her siddidy parents all tied up in knots.

"Please, hon. You got off easy," says Sheila, clearly trying to outdo her partner in storytelling. Then directing her tale to Nicole, she continues. "I was actually married to a very kind man for two years before I came out. So not only did I have to tell my mom and dad that I was divorcing a son-in-law whom they loved, but I had to add on that I wouldn't be marrying another man ever again."

"My parents would've freakin' died. They would've just dug graves for themselves and died," Nicole says in a dazed voice.

"They didn't die, but they sure did tell me off. My dad yelled, 'You could've at least given us a grandchild before you decided to ruin your life!'" I want to ask her if she plans on having any kids in the future, but that might be stepping over a couple lines. Desiree's nosiness is really rubbing off on me.

"But the bigger point, Nicole," Imani says, reaching across the table to pat her hand, "is that they come around. I never thought my parents would accept my lifestyle, but they read my novels that contain gay characters and gay experiences, and they're proud of me."

"Really?" Nicole looks a bit encouraged. "What about you, Sheila? Are your parents okay now?"

Sheila sighs a long tired sigh before responding. "My parents prefer to pretend like my relationship with Imani doesn't exist." Upon seeing Nicole's face fall with disappointment, she quickly adds, "But it doesn't stop them from bragging about my professional success, stuff like that."

"You're so lucky, Desiree," Nicole says wistfully. "Your parents must just think you're so awesome."

Desiree doesn't look so comfortable now that the focus is on her. Yeah, that's right, Nicole. Put her in the hot seat for once. "I've had awesome moments and not so awesome moments."

Since Nicole is so young, she hasn't yet learned to pick up on the signs that someone wants to change the subject. She just keeps poking. "What do you mean?"

Imani squirms a little in her seat, and Desiree starts playing with her hoop earrings. She gets fidgety when she's uncomfortable. "The college years weren't without drama, let's just say."

"Oh! Are you a lesbian, too?" Nicole asks, with an innocence that is so real, it makes us all double over laughing.

"No, nothing like that. Just . . . growing pains kinda stuff. But my mom's a psychiatrist, and my dad's a social worker. You can't get a reaction outta them if you tried. Between the two of them, there's so much nodding and pensive thought, you almost need a straightjacket to keep yourself from going crazy." This is definitely news to me. Desiree has never mentioned her parents before. I don't know why I'm surprised that her mom's a doctor. A head doctor at that. No wonder Desiree's so good at picking people apart. Runs in the family.

"Better to have parents who nod all quiet than to have some screaming, yelling mo-fos up in your face," I point out.

"Is that how it was at your house?" Leave it to Desiree to shift the sharing time to me.

"Nah. I lived with my aunt and uncle, growing up, and they were pretty cool." That's all they need to know.

Black people seem to know to leave issues of parenting alone. You never know who has a daddy or who got raised by Grandma or what. But I guess I can't fault Nicole for wanting more information. "Where were your mom and dad?"

"In the West Indies, where I was born. They sent my brother and me to Jersey cuz Moms was sick and couldn't really handle us."

"Where in the West Indies, Jason? My family's from Barbados," says Sheila.

"Montserrat. Real tiny island."

"I know Montserrat," she responds. "It's been all over the news the last few years cuz of the volcano."

"Yeah, my folks moved to Aruba after it erupted. Their old house is still covered in ash."

Sheila raises her eyebrows. "Aruba? Lucky them. It's supposed to be really expensive to live there, right?"

I hesitate, not wanting to get into how my brother footed the bill for my parents' pricey relocation. Luckily, I'm saved by Nicole. "I'm sorry, are you guys talking about a real volcano?" Poor girl. I don't think she expected all this when she sat down to chat with us. But she's saved from any more worldly exposure when the manager of B Sharp comes over and asks her to come meet a few "important people."

Just as Nicole is stepping away from the table, she turns back suddenly. "Jason, tell Nailah I said hi. I haven't seen her in a while." Shit. I'd managed to dodge the Nailah conversation the whole time Nicole was sitting with us, and she somehow manages to slip it in at the end. Nicole and Nailah have hung out a few times, and I had a feeling she was going to call me out.

"I will," is all I say, ignoring the curious looks of the other ladies, especially Desiree. As nosy as the girl is, I know she doesn't have the audacity to push the issue. She stays quiet for now, but I can practically see the wheels turning in her head.

Things would probably be easier if I just came clean about Nailah. Maybe then all this sexual tension could be deadened. Desiree wouldn't be touching my arm anymore. That's a definite. Which is exactly why I keep my mouth shut.

CHAPTER 17

To: *desiree@alumni.franklin.edu*
From: *jason@jaysgym.com*
Time: Friday, July 27, 2001 1:32 p.m.
Subject: The Buddy System

Message:
Hey, I ran into Imani today, and I asked her what I can do as a friend to get your creative juices flowing. She told me that it's helpful to write all the time, even if you're not working on the book. Just write about whatever. She's the big-time writer, so I trust her advice. So I figured we could have some online conversations, which might get the wheels spinning. How about doing a question of the day? We ask the other person a question, which they have to answer in an e-mail. I'll start it off. What are you proudest of?-J

To: *jason@jaysgym.com*
From: *desiree@alumni.franklin.edu*

Time: Friday, July 27, 2001 4:58 p.m.
Subject: answer of the day

Message:
jason,
it's really nice of you to try to help me out. at this point, i'll try anything. so to answer your question, i'd have to say that i'm proudest of *No More Lies*. but that's the obvious, predictable response. another accomplishment of mine that i think is pretty unusual is that i've never gotten into a serious disagreement with one of my girls.

in high school, it was pretty easy to stay drama free with my girlfriends because my friendships were pretty superficial. but in college, living with females allowed bonds to deepen. kahli and robyn were, and are, my true friends. sisters, even. i did go a couple months freshman year without speaking to them, but i was going through some stuff and shut everybody out. but they understood that it wasn't about them.

aside from that, though, no drama with females, and i'll tell you why. ninety percent of conflict between women involves men. either "she wants my man," "she's hating on my relationship with my man," "my man doesn't like her, so i don't have time for her," or some remix of one of those tunes. and i've always known never to dip into my girls' relationships. women only ask for advice in hopes of hearing what they were planning to do, anyhow. when you tell them otherwise, they either ignore your warnings, or heed them and blame you when things don't turn out right.

i also forbid myself from having any friendships with guys to whom my friends have connections. even if they're not tied romantically to them, a rivalry for their attention always starts. kahli and j. t. are like brother and sister; robyn and this guy lloyd behave like an old married couple. i can count the conversations i've had with lloyd without robyn being there, and the time j. t. came to your gym was the most quality time we've ever spent together. i mean, they seem like cool people, but they aren't worth causing a rift between my girls and me.

the other 10 percent of the time that girls fight is because someone has a personality trait that the other takes issue with. meddling, bossy, hypocritical, insecure, whatever. and then a situation arises that reveals that trait. the reason i don't engage in these tiffs is not because my friends are perfect. robyn is controlling, and kahli is absurdly naïve for someone so brilliant. and as for me, well, i think you're slowly getting to know all my defects ☺, but we recognize our own faults and the flaws of each other, and therefore, we don't get annoyed when they pop up at times.

wow. this email has gotten pretty long. i guess the question of the day really does get me writing.

thanks
des

* * *

To: *desiree@alumni.franklin.edu*
From: *jason@jaysgym.com*
Time: Saturday, July 28, 2001 8:27 a.m.
Subject: Question #2

Message:
So you and your girls live in harmony, huh? I
guess you save all your fire for the dudes. Just
playing. Next question: Aside from being somewhat cool with J. T., do you have any other friendships with white people? How do you feel about
them in general?-J

P.S. At some point, you're gonna have to tell the
rule about when to use who and whom. You seem
to have it all figured out, with your "to whoms"
and all that fancy shit in your e-mails.

To: *jason@jaysgym.com*
From: *desiree@alumni.franklin.edu*
Time: Saturday, July 28, 2001 11:40 a.m.
Subject: on the subject of the fairer people

Message:
if i were white, i wonder what kind of white
person i'd be. i hope i'd be one of the socially conscious ones who realizes the world is not a land of
equal opportunity. i wouldn't want to have such
a guilty conscience about it that i feel the need
to make up for the fact that i'm privileged by kissing black folks' asses. on the flip side, i'd hate to
be one of those oblivious folks who believe race is

a 1960s issue, and that with the exception of a few southern hicks, racists are a thing of the past. equally annoying are the white boys who've adopted hip-hop culture to the extreme, quoting rap lyrics, complete w/nigga, etc., and white girls with black girl hairstyles. they annoy me. you can spot them from miles away. hair cornrowed or gelled into some complex design. a mating call for black men. not that i'm against interracial relationships or anything. people just shouldn't have to try to hard so get into one.

what determines which type of white person one becomes? upbringing mostly, i think. that's why i try not to trip too much when they say something ridiculous. but at the same time, i don't let them get too close, either. kahli has j. t., and they're like best friends, but i've never been that cool with a white person. and the idea of having a white female friend . . . i just don't feel like we could relate. but then again, nicole seems like a great person from the little i've spoken to her. maybe if i were eighteen, we'd be girls. remember, i'm from baltimore. it's not like my city was exactly swarming with white people with whom i could bond.

and speaking of "with whom," you use who for the subject and whom for the object.
ex. who broke the china? who is the subject.
ex. whom did you tell about my breaking the china? this time "you" is the subject.
ex. on whom was the blame placed? whom is the object of the preposition "on."

was that confusing? sorry. kahli's the teacher,
not me.
anyhow, i realized that i shouldn't be the only one
answering questions here. so here's your question
of the day: what got you interested in working
out? see, i'm starting you off easy.

des

To: *desiree@alumni.franklin.edu*
From: *jason@jaysgym.com*
Time: Saturday, July 28, 2001 7:01 p.m.
Subject: Don't quit your day job.

Message:
Yeah, your grammar lesson needs work. Stick to
writing. I thought I was gonna get away with not
answering any questions, since the whole point
was to stimulate your creativity. I don't need any
of that to run my gym. But being that your question wasn't too hard, I'll humor you. I should've
started working out way before I actually did.
When I was little, I used to be real chubby. My
brother, Jamal, was always more athletic. As a
teenager, the only exercise I ever got was running
the streets. Then I got real skinny and started feeling like a runt around all the big dawgs I was
tryin' to roll with. So I guess it was just a matter of
time before I got into lifting. The ultimate motivation wasn't my size, though. Honestly, I was
pissed off. My brother and I . . . well, we had a
falling out, to say the least. I needed something to
do to release all this steam I had built up. So that's
what it was at first—an outlet for my anger. But

then I started enjoying setting new goals and meeting them. Not to mention the physical results. I hope that answer is good enough for you, cuz my fingers are tired. I have a feeling you type real fast, don't you? Well, I don't, so I don't wanna hear shit about my short messages. Anyhow, next question—talk about one thing that men don't understand about women.-J

To: *jason@jaysgym.com*
From: *desiree@alumni.franklin.edu*
Time: Sunday, July 29, 2001 11:10 a.m.
Subject: demystifying the fairer sex

Message:
jason,

for the record, i can picture you neither chubby nor skinny. and as for your clowning my grammar lesson, go to hell. you could use some instruction on when to use the colon instead of the dash, but i'm going to let you suffer.

on to the issue at hand: your question. men think women agonize too much over when and how often a guy calls them. what they don't realize is that while it may appear minor—a measly check in to say hi—a phone call is actually the last step in a series of events that are really quite meaningful.

a woman's mind-set is that for a man to call her, she would've had to have crossed his mind for whatever reason. we can fantasize for hours about what made a guy think of us. an engagement ring commercial? a girl on the street who is almost as pretty as we are, but not quite?

then there's the question of setting. where was the guy when he called? if he calls from home, that's cool, because we know at least he's there alone. a call from the car is the least impressive, because there aren't that many options when you're on the road. it's almost like a "keep me company while i drive" type of thing. not very special. the most surprising (and pleasing) calls are when he is with his boys. for him to give you a quick shout out during male bonding is a huge deal, especially if he says something sweet or mushy.

finally, we have to consider the time of day. of course, late-night calls are the least desirable. we all know that after-midnight rings are booty calls. evening is fine, especially if he's calling with the intention of scooping you up for a spontaneous dinner or movie. but we get most excited about a midday call, because he clearly just wanted to hear your voice, being that you're both caught up at work and have no chance of any face time.

and there you have it. you should have to pay me for such valuable information. remember this stuff, and you'll score huge with the ladies. which brings me to my question of the day: do you have a girlfriend? nicole mentioned a female at the jazz club the other day, so i was just curious. trust me, i'm not making a move or anything.

des

* * *

To: *desiree@alumni.franklin.edu*
From: *jason@jaysgym.com*
Time: Sunday, July 29, 2001 8:31 p.m.
Subject: Re: demystifying the fairer sex

Message:
How is someone who doesn't even use capital letters in her e-mails gonna be trippin about proper
punctuation?

Don't worry. I know better than to think you're
trying to get at me, being that you just stopped
being a lesbian two weeks ago. But no, I don't
have a girlfriend.-J

CHAPTER 18

HUNTER

The sun is strong as I stumble out of Presbyterian at 4:30 in the afternoon. That's a good thing, though, because as I walk down the street, wiping the tears from my face, it probably looks like I'm trying to get the sweat out of my eyes. I can't believe that I'm crying right now. In public. When was the last time I cried? I guess when Grandpa passed last year. But that was different. There was a time and place for mourning. My shit was under control. This time, I think I might lose it.

I want something to throw or kick, or something to punch. My eyes catch a fence that looks great for punching, but I could really jack up my hand if I do. It might mess me up for this rotation, and for surgery after that. Then again, who the hell cares? I never want to go back to that hospital again. Breaking my fingers could give me an excuse.

I talk myself out of punching the fence. Not sure if I'm actually talking out loud or to myself. People are staring at me, but it could be because I'm dressed in a lab coat, sniffling and wiping my nose. I look like such a punk, but it doesn't matter. I just wanna get in my bed, pull the sheets over my head, and block out all the fucked-up shit in the world.

When I get to the lobby of my building, I decide to take the steps. I can't imagine being stuck in the smelly, confined space of the elevator. The stairwell isn't much better, but I take each flight as fast as I can and find myself on the fourth-floor landing in no time. It's not my floor, but I tear through the hallway and locate Robyn's apartment, knocking on the door like a crazy person. She throws open the door, with a disgusted stare.

But one look at my eyes, all red and swollen, and at my chest, heaving from the run from the lobby, and her expression changes to worry. "Greg, oh my goodness. What's wrong?" She opens the door wider for me to enter, and I feel my way to the couch like a blind man, sinking into it like it's my salvation.

As soon as I feel the soft cushions support my body, I collapse into sobs. Sobs that prohibit me from talking. Sobs that almost stop me from breathing. Sobs that make my rib cage ache. I can hear Robyn's terrified voice next to me, asking a million questions, but there's no way I can answer them. "Where are you coming from? Are you hurt? Is someone else hurt? Did you see something? Did you get a phone call?" It soon becomes clear to her that she's not getting anything out of me, so she starts putting pieces together on her own.

"Greg, wasn't today your first day of ER rotation?" My head is buried in my hands, but I manage to nod yes. "It was? Okay. Was there a big trauma? Should I turn on the news?" I shake my head no, slowly regaining control of my ragged breathing. With much concentration, I whisper, "Manny," before I lose control again.

"Manny? Who's Manny? I've heard you say that name before, but I just can't . . . Emmanuel. Manny." She paces back and forth in front of the couch, muttering to herself. Suddenly, she stops in her tracks. "Oh! The kid in peds, right? The really funny one?"

I've got to get myself together if I want to explain to Robyn what happened. Not to mention that I'm being a total bitch right now, crying like a baby. The story comes out in spurts, sometimes incoherent, but Robyn patiently wades her way through, prompting me with gentle questions at first, then simply hanging on my every word. I start at the middle and reach the end, doubling back to the beginning. They told me Manny was paralyzed, and I had to get out of there. I just ran out of the emergency room in the middle of my shift. No one tried to stop me.

They wheeled him in at about 2:30, with three of his boys from school screaming and crying alongside him. They had been hanging out after school, laughing and talking while they were crossing the street. It was an ambulance that hit him. Threw him straight into the air. Fell to the concrete on his back. The ambulance wasn't even going to the scene of an injury. No siren. Just heading to the hospital. Some crazy shit.

I'd been having a perfect day. The chief resident had already singled me out to answer a couple of questions, and I nailed them no problem. There hadn't been any traumas, but we did have to tell a woman that she had cancer, and it had already spread to her bones. Her husband was a wreck, and it was real sad. It really was. But I was okay. I've wanted to work in the ER my whole life. I knew this was the kind of stuff you had to deal with. When the EMTs came in all panicked with Manny, I'd actually been excited to see them. Before I knew who it was, I was happy that I was going to get to see some action. How sick is that?

He was unconscious. I wasn't in the room when they were working on him. They realized I knew him and told me to keep my distance. I stayed with his friends. Then his mom showed up, and she was so happy to see me. Like I was going to make the situation better. Asking me over and over again if he was going to be all right. I didn't fucking know! What was I supposed to say?

Doctors came out after what seemed like forever. Said he was awake and groggy. His mom started praising Jesus. We were all hugging each other and crying, we were so happy. But I noticed the doctor wasn't smiling. He was just waiting, with his hand in the air, as if to say, "Hold up. Don't celebrate yet." When it got quiet again, he said it softly. That they couldn't be a 100 percent sure as yet, but it looks like Emmanuel has no ability to move from the neck down. His mom screamed. Straight up screamed. The waiting room went into a panic. Thought someone was being attacked or something. Staff came out of nowhere to try and calm her down. Manny's little friends were speechless. That's when I got the hell outta there.

Robyn just lets me talk, rubbing my hand with both of hers, only taking one away every once in a while to wipe her eyes. My mind flashes back to days in my childhood when my mom would take me in her wiry arms and rock me till I fell asleep and forgot how my stepfather reminded me, in everything he said and did, that I wasn't his real son. Something about the way Robyn rubs my hand gives me the same comfort I felt on my living-room couch twenty years ago. I wish I could curl up in her arms, but she's too tiny. But her presence still soothes me to the point where I can think again and talk out my feelings rationally.

"Robyn, so many times when I was chillin' with Manny in peds, I thought, wow. Life isn't fair. This really great kid has to come into the hospital every few weeks for his entire life for tedious procedures. And he doesn't even seem bitter. Then I finally made peace with it. I said to myself, 'Manny's fine. He's a well-adjusted kid. Who am I to be upset when he's handling it all in stride?' So you tell me, what kind of twisted dude is a God who would paralyze such a wonderful person? A person who's done nothing bad to anybody his whole life."

Robyn sighs and scoots closer to me on the couch. "You can't think of it that way, Greg. What about looking at it like Manny could've died today, and God blessed him with his life?"

"What kind of life is he gonna lead, Robyn? He can't move a damn thing below his neck!" I'm practically screaming, but she doesn't flinch. I lower my voice before I add, "He'd be better off dead."

"Don't say that. Don't say that," she murmurs. "He has his mind and all the people who love him. He needs those people's strength right now. And that includes you."

"Me? I can't do anything for him."

"Maybe not medically, but you can be there." She reads my face to see if I agree, but I know my expression is blank.

We just sit for a while. Somewhere in the process of our sitting and talking, she ends up in my arms. Her back in my chest, my hands on her stomach. The feel of her breathing relaxes me.

The clock on the wall above her bookcase says 5:15, and I realize that she should still be at work. "Why are you home, anyway?" I ask, with a nudge.

"Left the lab early today. No particular reason. Something just told me to go home. Eisengrath didn't even seem surprised when I told him I'd see him tomorrow." The back of her head fits perfectly in the small of my shoulder. She repositions her whole body so she can look me in the eye. "And you really don't think there's a God, Greg?"

I'm too exhausted to debate the difference between good luck and divine intervention, so I close my eyes in response. The next thing I know, Robyn's shaking my arm, and the clock says 7:30.

"You rested?" I nod, looking around the room, which is much dimmer than it had been a few hours ago. She turns on the lamp, and I wonder if she's been sleeping the whole time as well. I notice the blanket draped over me, and I'm so grateful for everything she did for me today. I open my mouth to tell her, but she walks out of the room before any sound comes out.

"I cooked dinner," she shouts from the kitchen. As soon as she says it, I smell what I guess to be fried chicken. I feel guilty for having an appetite, but I'm starving. She comes back into the room and gives me her hand to help me up from the couch. Once I'm on my feet, I'm looking down at her, like usual. But she still seems larger than life.

"Once we eat, you're going back to the hospital. You know that, right?" I can feel my heart beating in my chest as soon as she says it, but I still nod yes.

"Yeah. I know." Manny's whole life turned upside down in one afternoon. He at least deserves a familiar face.

I want to ask her for a favor, but I don't want to put her in a difficult position. She's done so much for me today already. But I guess that's what makes Robyn a true friend, because I don't have to ask. "I'd like to come with you, if that's okay."

I want to pick her up and squeeze her as tight as I can, and say thank you over and over again in her ear. But I think I've displayed enough emotion today as it is. "That's cool. Thanks."

Chapter 19

Desiree

I've figured out the theme of my novel: nice guys finish last. Hunter has been leaving me messages since our last date, and I just don't return the calls. It might be easier to call him and say that it's over, but he's so smooth and persuasive that I don't want to be convinced to give it another try. A part of me wonders how he would react if I told him the truth right now. It might not be too late for him to forgive and forget.

Meanwhile, all of the time that I'm not tossing around story ideas with Imani or stationed in front of my laptop is spent with Jason. Not that he's not a nice guy, *too*. But he's the guy with the edge. While Hunter's face is clean shaven, Jason has a five o'clock shadow. While Hunter was telling me unpleasant family history on our first date, Jason has yet to tell me anything about his past beyond a few funny childhood stories. While Hunter slathered me with compliments, Jason only comments on how I look when it's something he doesn't like.

But none of these differences has to do with why Jason wins out. I can chill with Jason, because Hunter was trying to get with me, and Jason isn't. The fact that I'm even spending time with a man is such a dramatic departure from what I've been doing the past five years that I don't need to throw myself into a romantic relationship. Experiencing a mental connection with a man is a first for me, and I'm enjoying it. Even during my good times with Trevor, the happiness was so linked to the physical. From our first passionate kiss on the dance floor of a crowded party to our late-night session in a locked library seminar room, our bond was entirely dependent on sex. I didn't realize this at the time, but after years of discussion on the living-room couch with my psychiatrist mom, a lot of things have come to light.

Anyway, trying to be with Hunter would be too much pressure. He's so damn wonderful that I wouldn't be able to be myself. My flawed, issuefied self. Something tells me that while Jason doesn't talk much about his personal life, he has just as many flaws and issues as I do. So it's like a no-judgment zone when we spend time together.

Most of our hang time is spent at his place, and tonight is no exception. He's never been to my place, and I'd prefer to keep it that way. I believe in the opposite of home-court advantage. If I'm at his apartment, I don't have to play host or make him feel comfortable. And more importantly, I can leave whenever I want.

I've noticed that I tend to feel overdressed when I'm with Jason, being that I love clothes, and he just strives to be comfortable. So I show up at his door wearing a pair of jeans with a hole in the knee and a white fitted T-shirt. I even wear sneakers, which only see the light of day when I'm going to the gym. Still, Jason manages to surpass me in chill mode, wearing a T-shirt with the sleeves cut off and a pair of sweats. He even has a doo-rag on his head, which looks surprisingly sexy on him. My sneakers make him taller than I am for a change, and

I'm a little overwhelmed at first sight by the rugged brawniness of it all.

At first, I'm skeptical of Jason's nonchalant insistence on watching "whatever," but I have to take him at his word when he agrees to check out an episode of *Sex and the City*. Usually, I won't watch the show, because I get jealous of their clever, hilarious plots and become afraid that I might unknowingly steal an idea from their writers, but today I make an exception. I figure it'll be fun watching four women discuss love and sex in the company of a guy.

And it is fun. We laugh at Samantha's sexual conquests and debate the fine points of who's right and who's wrong in the never-ending battle of the sexes.

"Why do females lie about what they want? Like they say to dudes that they're not looking for a serious relationship and then get mad when dudes don't give them one."

"Oh, and men don't lie to women? Give me a break."

"We lie because y'all don't wanna hear the truth. You'd rather hear that we were out with our boys than out with some other chick."

I had been reclining in the corner of the couch, but at this, I sit right up. "But that's the same reason *we* lie! We know guys will be scared off if we admit that we're looking for commitment."

He removes himself from the other corner of the couch, with a grunt, and scoots right next to me. I try to ignore the mixture of soap and Cool Water that floats my way when he changes position. "But is that the type of man you want, anyway?"

"True." I really enjoy my conversations with Jason. He's smart, in a commonsense kind of way. I like that. I find myself wanting to know more about him. It's probably just because of this book I'm trying to write, though. I'm so caught up in my own thoughts that I don't immediately realize that he's talking again.

" . . . And sometimes guys do try the honest approach! They'll tell a girl that they're only out for a good time, and the girl will think that she can change him."

"Hmm, I'm more familiar with the liars and cheaters myself."

"I can tell that from your book."

I try not to act too excited. I'd been hoping that Jason would read my book. I sneaked a peek in his bedroom before, and he has quite an extensive library in there. His being a reader and his down-to-earth intelligence would make for great feedback. "So you read it?"

He hesitates. "Nah. I meant that I could tell from the title, *No More Lies.*"

I try not to show my disappointment, but it must be showing through a little bit, because he puts his hand on my knee and kind of squeezes it. It feels really good, and I struggle not to have a physical reaction to his touch. "Desiree," he says in a voice that's even raspier than usual, "if you want me to read your book, just ask me."

I'm really not liking what's happening right now. This boy is getting in. He's penetrating the icy exterior, patiently chipping away. And all I can do is melt.

"Jason, will you please read my book? It would mean a lot to me." I bat my eyelashes to add some humor to the request.

He grins. I've seen him smile before. I've watched him smirk many times. But never have I seen this grin. It's hysterical. I can see both rows of teeth. "Sure, baby. I got you."

Whoa. Wasn't ready for the term of endearment. He just made one big ol' hack with that ice pick of his. Time to change the subject before I'm one big puddle on his hardwood floor. "So . . . my experience has been with liars. What's yours been?"

He hesitates again, but I know the reason this time. I've crossed that line: he has to share something personal, and he doesn't know if he wants to. I've been there. I'm about to let him off the hook when he starts talking. "I'm not the type to be all bitter. But generally, I'd say the thing that hurts the most for me, and for most men, is when your woman isn't down for you when things get rough."

"Like a fair-weather friend?"

"Yeah. Like that. Only it's worse, because that's supposed to be your friend *and* your lover." He's not looking at me anymore, but past me. I'm not sure when it happened, but his hand isn't on my leg anymore, either. It helps me to return to room temperature.

"But to be fair to the sistas, y'all have a lot more rough periods than we do. We tend to have our shit together, waiting for y'all to catch up." I say it in a bit of a lecturing tone and regret it when I see that he looks angry.

"Is that what love's about? Keeping score? Love is unconditional . . . or at least, it should be." He returns his gaze to me pleadingly, almost begging me to agree. His green eyes are shining, and he bites his full bottom lip. Oh God. I can't take it. The best way to melt the ice is to do so unintentionally.

I place one hand on the back of his neck, the other on his chest. Damn, this man's muscles are a thing of beauty. He reaches back and rubs my hand on his neck, and this time I can't hide the tiny shiver that runs down my spine. Suddenly, his free arm is around my waist, pulling me closer.

Des, don't do it. Don't do it. We are eye to eye, nose to nose. One small lean in from being lip to lip. He flashes both rows of teeth and winks at me. It's over. I pull him closer and kiss him.

CHAPTER 20

JASON

I knew the kiss was coming, but I still wasn't ready. It's as if neither of us has kissed anyone in years. Well, actually, it's practically true for me. A couple of meaningless encounters here and there, but nothing like this. Her tongue searches my mouth, and mine greets hers playfully. I take her bottom lip in my mouth, feeling its softness as I nibble and suck. She returns the favor, and then our mouths are in full contact, tongues meeting in passionate sweeps.

I use my hand on her waist to push up the bottom of her tank top. The smoothness of her back is warm on my skin for a split second before she jumps off the couch. We're both gasping for air, and I wait for her to explain.

"I gotta go," she whispers out of breath, tugging on the back of her top. She walks around the room, collecting her purse, shoes, keys.

I don't know why I don't speak. Well, maybe I do. I'm still all thrown off by that kiss, first of all. Plus, I don't want to say the wrong thing. She can be so touchy. If I make some insensitive comment, I might never see her again. And, damn, I have to see her again. I watch her walk briskly to the front door and shut it behind her.

How the hell did I get here with Desiree? One day she was a complete stranger, and a bitchy one at that. Who doesn't even like men. Then she becomes a cool person to kick it with, and even though she does like dudes, she doesn't ever act on it for some mysterious reason. But at the same time, she seems to like me. And she just acted on it. Which I'm not too upset about, because I'm feeling this girl, too.

She's smart—it's not like we sit around discussing politics or anything—but you can just tell. She gets all my jokes, which most people miss. And her writing . . . As much as I clown her for male bashing, the girl has mad talent. Monique had told me to read the book last year because she thought the author and I had the same sense of humor, and because she thought the story touched on some things about men and women that we used to rap about.

I agreed to check it out for neither of those reasons. When I read the back cover, I saw it was about black folks in college. Something I always wondered about. What are classes like? How's the social scene? I swear, Des really took me there. By the time I finished *No More Lies*, I felt like I'd been through it—gained some knowledge from professors, played ball at a D1 school, macked on some females at college parties . . . fallen in love.

Anyhow, I can't even front that my feelings for Des are all on that mental/emotional tip. The woman is flat-out sexy. When she rolls to the gym, brothers almost cause accidents, straining to look. I saw a dude almost drop 215 pounds right on his chest when she walked by. Some of them try to help her out, not knowing that she probably knows more about lifting than they do. And then I get this really stupid pride, like she's mine or something.

But she's not. Even though she pops into my head at the strangest times. Her smile when I'm brushing my teeth. A sarcastic comment she made when I'm watching TV. The way she tucks her hair behind her ears when I'm braiding Nailah's hair.

Shit. I forgot about Nailah. Sitting here trippin' over Desiree, I forgot about my girl. In the four years that she's been with me, I've never put anyone before her in my mind. It's for the best that Des stopped this mess. I don't need to be messin' around with some chick. Lemme call my baby.

I walk to the kitchen and take the cordless phone back to the couch. I hit 1 on the speed dial.

"Hello?" Monique's voice is soft and tired.

"It's me. Is she up?"

"Yeah. She shouldn't be, but she is. Hold on. Nailah! Here."

"Hello?" Her voice makes my night.

"Hey, sweetheart."

"Hi, Daddy."

PART II

PART II

CHAPTER 21

HUNTER

Alicia is standing in my doorway, with a short beige dress on that's practically see-through. Why she bothers dressing up when she comes over is a mystery to me, since her clothes just end up in a pile by the bed in a matter of minutes, anyhow. Tonight is no exception. Pulling her into the apartment, I kiss her from the living room, past the kitchen, and into the bedroom before we come up for air. Pushing the straps of her dress to the edges of her shoulders makes the whole thing just fall to the floor, revealing . . . everything, since she didn't bother putting on anything underneath. Her body is calling me collect, and I'm ready to accept the charges.

Wouldn't I just love to hop on this bed and get to doing what we do best, but Alicia is all about the buildup, so I try to enjoy the anticipation as she slides my shirt over my head, rubbing her breasts on me as she does it. I'm ready for her to unzip my jeans, but instead, she throws me onto the bed. "Put on some music." It's the first thing she's said since she walked in the door.

Grabbing the stereo remote from my nightstand, I hit PLAY, only to realize that I still have my CD changer stacked to play all sad songs: Babyface, 112, Jagged Edge. Dealing with Manny over the past couple weeks has been tough, and my social life has been kicking my ass, too. Desiree isn't returning my calls, and I got the blues. Hopefully, this night with Alicia will take my mind to better places.

I watch her naked body as she searches my CD racks for a little mood music. Of all the women I've ever been with, Alicia is definitely the one who seems most comfortable in her skin. When we were together, we'd spend whole days in the crib, with nothing on but a pair of socks. Not like she has anything to be embarrassed about. She turned down Alvin Ailey right before college, and she still has a dancer's body, long and lean. No huge titties or big ol' ass or anything, just a tight package all around. My favorite part is the crease down the middle of her stomach, which she maintains without even doing a single sit-up.

She puts in all three of my Prince *The Hits* CDs and sets the stereo to random shuffle. Good choice. You get a little of everything with that dude. Slow and sexy, fast and freaky, there's a song for whatever you're feeling. "Purple Rain," my favorite Prince song, second only to "Adore," kicks things off, and she starts dancing for me. Not some choreographed Janet Jackson routine, but slow hip swinging and back arching. It's like a private strip club with a free lap dance. As she rolls her body all up on me, I can't wait for her any longer, so I take my jeans off myself. My boxers are sticking straight up like a tent, but it's all good. My body doesn't have a choice but to react when this sexy chick is rubbing her thighs and licking her lips right in front of me.

Finally, she straddles me and pushes my shoulders until I'm horizontal on my mattress. I reach toward my nightstand to grab a condom, but she takes my hand and puts my fingers in her mouth. As she guides my fingers from her neck down the middle of her body until I reach the jackpot, I know I have at least a half hour of foreplay left, so I settle into savoring the moment.

It's a nice view from down here as I touch, tease, and tickle the woman hovering over me. She just got back from visiting her family in Miami yesterday, and I can tell she spent most of her time on the beach. Alicia is almost as obsessed with tanning as those Northeast white girls I used to go to prep school with. Originally, her color is a medium light brown—pretty much passing the brown paper bag test. But she loves getting as dark as she possibly can, and I must admit that the added color does bring out her muscles and cuts even more. When we went to the Bahamas together last year, I got to see her tanning process firsthand. She greased herself up like she was about to enter a bodybuilding contest; then she took the straps of her bikini down so she wouldn't get any tan lines. She would lie by our hotel pool for so long that I swore I could hear her sizzle. Because of her obsession with the sun, her breasts and her ass are always several shades lighter than the rest of her body, which I always tease her about. She claims she's going to start hitting nude beaches to avoid that problem.

I would kill for her to donate a few moments of her time below the belt, but I'm never about coming out and asking a woman for head. Instead, I toss her a wink, hoping that she gets my message. She winks right back and makes her way downward, taking my boxers off with her teeth and then putting in some quality work, I must say. I remember when we first started dating, and Alicia was the most selfish woman in bed I'd ever met. Her motto was that it was better to receive than it was to give. And she had the nerve to be demanding about it. Barking orders during sex: taste me; touch me here; stop touching me there; do it harder; slower; softer, faster, longer; hurry up; take your time; talk to me; don't say anything; look at me; close your eyes. She finally just had to get cussed out. This was real life, not a porno movie, and therefore, I wasn't gonna be taking instructions like she was a damn film director.

Over the course of our relationship, the physical got better, while everything else got worse. Her carnal commands became whispered requests and, at last, evolved into silent understanding. Meanwhile, our incompatibilities outside of the bedroom became clearer and clearer. I'd met her the week I moved back to New York to start medical school, and she was all impressed about that at first. My first year wasn't that hard, and she got to see me all the time while still being able to brag about being with a future MD. But as soon as my second year hit, she got tired of the med school thing real quick. She saw the hours I had to spend studying as "a direct affront" to her and what we had. Her words, not mine. I tried to make as much time for her as I could, cutting down my hours in the lab and even skipping class sometimes to meet on her lunch break. But it wasn't good enough, and she kicked me to the curb a month before my boards. That might have been a blessing in disguise, because all I did was study until the big day came, and my score was better than I even hoped for.

A few weeks after my test, I was feeling on top of the world, getting back into the social scene, enjoying single life for the first time in a year and a half. I ran into Alicia one night at the Kit Kat Club and ended up taking her home with me. That was the beginning of our regularly scheduled booty calls. Perfect timing, considering that I was about to start my rotations at the hospital and didn't really have time to be on the prowl for prospects. But then Alicia went home for vacation, so our little visits stopped for a sec. After my two dates with Desiree, I thought I'd never have Alicia in my bed again, but here we are.

Alicia's jaw must be pretty tired, cuz she's been getting me nice and happy for a while now. This time when I go to reach for the condom, she doesn't protest. When we start getting busy to the sound of Prince's "Erotic City" in the background, I'm beginning to feel better about just about everything. Manny got released from the hospital yesterday, with regained motion from the waist up, and he was in decent spirits when I popped in to say good-bye. I give myself over to flipping Alicia on her back and propping her right leg on my shoulder, telling myself that Manny's not going to benefit by my thinking about him at this exact moment. Alicia's sound effects are making me feel like a sex king. I've always told her, if they had such thing as radio porn shows, she'd be a star.

The music slows down, and I switch to a deep, circular rhythm, closing my eyes in appreciation for how good Alicia feels underneath me. *It's been seven hours and fifteen days, since you took your love away*, Prince's voice sings, all brokenhearted. I can't help but see Desiree in my mind, her gorgeous face on the Brooklyn Bridge at sunset. I guess I'll never know how it feels to kiss her, never mind make love to her. I wonder what she's like in bed. From the playful personality she exhibited during dinner at my crib, I can imagine her being a fun sexual partner. Just laughing a lot, real comfortable. But at the same time, she has a thoughtful, deep way about her. I can picture the two of us doing it, and it being so off the hook that we both just cry afterwards.

This is awful. I'm having sex with one girl and thinking about another. I've never done that before. Suddenly, I just want to be done and for Alicia to be out of my bed. But I can't just stop in the middle of everything, so I maneuver her on top of me so I can lie back while she takes us home. We go through about three more Prince tracks before she has her loud-ass orgasm, and I can finally get my shit off and be through.

It doesn't take long once I get back from the bathroom to realize that something is different. Normally, by the time I return from throwing out the condom, Alicia is getting dressed so I can walk her outside and put her in a cab. Tonight she's snuggled under my covers, giving me this weird puppy dog look.

"Come here, honey," she purrs, pulling back the sheet for me to join her. I'm definitely thrown off by her request, but it might not be so bad since I was feeling too tired to put on clothes and go outside, anyhow. As long as we can just go to sleep, this'll be cool.

I get in beside her, and she's immediately all over me, wrapping herself around my body like a human pretzel. Now I'm not against cuddling. The feel of a warm body through the night is lovely. But tonight is one time when I wish she would use the space that my queen-sized bed offers. Even worse, as soon as she gets situated, she starts talking a mile a minute about her trip. Where she went, who she saw, what she bought. *Damn it, just shut up already.*

It dawns on me after about fifteen minutes straight of her going on and on about her life that she hasn't paused even once to check how I've been recently. Cutting her off in the middle of a story about how she talked her way into the VIP section of a club on South Beach, I ask, "How come you never ask me how things are going at the hospital?"

She gives an annoyed sigh. "I ask you all the time."

"Yeah, maybe a generic question. But nothing specific."

Her voice is rising in anger. Could be because of my

accusation, could also be because she didn't get to finish her South Beach story. "Well, I'm not a damn medical professional, Gregory. How am I supposed to know what to ask?" Weak excuse. It's not like Desiree is a doctor. But she still had me talking about my favorite patient and my biggest frustrations.

Meeting my silence, she presses on to explain. "Plus, I figure you're so tired and stressed when you leave that place, it would be the last thing you'd want to think about." Her tone switches from pissed off to whiny. I can't decide which is worse. "Besides, it's not like you ask *me* about work."

What am I supposed to ask her about? She's a buyer for Barneys. Girls' juniors at that. Is she serious? People are dying at my job. People are dying for bell-bottom jeans at hers. Of course, I can't say that, because she'll label me a hypocrite, which I am, in all honesty. So I just shut my eyes and hope the conversation won't continue.

It's hard to say how many minutes pass before she opens her mouth again. Time can move real fast or real slow when you're lying in bed with your eyes closed. "Gregory, I think we should get back together."

Oh hell, no. She did not just say that. Why would she want to do something like that? And why would she bring it up in the middle of the night? Goodness, her head is right on my chest. I hope she can't feel my heart beating. What do I say? Shit, shit, shit. Robyn told me that messing around with my ex was a bad idea. She just looked at me like I was a damn fool when I told her that we were on the same page, that it was just a physical thing. I wish I could call her right now and ask her what to say.

"Baby, are you sleep?" Alicia asks in a soft, sweet voice that reminds me of how she used to talk when things were good between us. It gives me the perfect excuse not to answer. Just pretend like I didn't hear her statement at all. Maybe she won't have the guts to repeat it in the light of day. Prince sings through the silence. *If I was your girlfriend/I'd be there for you if somebody hurts you/even if that somebody was me.* Sounds tempting. But only when I picture Desiree mouthing the words, and that's the image I see in my head until I fall asleep.

CHAPTER 22

JASON

When I see Big O leaning against the wall on the 2/3 platform at 125th Street, I remember why I hate taking the subway. There's always the risk of running into some-one I don't want to see. Otto Jones, known to folks on the street as Big O, was legendary in Newark when I was coming up. His nickname had nothing to do with his size (especially since he was, and still is, a bony-ass dude), but with how much pull he had on the streets. He linked up with my brother when they were both trying to make names for themselves in the hood, and the two of them were real tight for a while. Had some little niggas work-ing under them, and everybody was making dough. But Jamal decided to get big time, expand his "client base," as he called it. So he left the little nickel-and-dime bag stuff to Big O and started pushing serious weight up and down the Jersey Turnpike. But they stayed cool until Jamal moved to Florida a couple years back. And from the big ol' smile on his face, I guess he's happy to see Jamal's little brother, too.

"What up, Jay!" he shouts before he even reaches where I'm standing. A few women waiting for the train roll their eyes, and men try to look tougher as he jogs past them to reach me. He gives me a pound and pulls me in for a hug, gripping me pretty strong for such a small guy. "How you been, son?"

"Cool, cool," I answer in a softer tone, trying to encourage him to model my volume level. "What about you, Otto?"

His eyes slant a little bit when I use his real name, but I want to send a message from jump. I'm not about the street anymore; the childhood games are over. "I been real good, Jay. What you been doing since you got out?"

He had lowered his voice some since his first greeting, but it still isn't soft enough to prevent nearby onlookers from hearing that I happen to be an ex-con. "I started up a business. Been working hard." *Where the hell is the train?*

"Oh, right. The gym in Secaucus. I heard about that. Yo, I moved my business to Queens. Newark got a little hot after you got picked up, 5-0 sweatin' everybody. But I'll stop by your gym sometime, see what you got goin' on."

I've been trying to keep my cool, but there's no way this clown is gonna be bringing his thug ass into my place of business. Isn't he thirty years old? Still rockin' oversized hip-hop gear and a hat to one side. And still selling. Damn shame. "Honestly, Otto, I'd appreciate if you didn't."

He steps back, shocked by my words, and then comes closer, his voice now soft and threatening. "What, you too fucking good for old friends now?"

"We were never friends." I look him dead in the eyes and suck on the insides of my jaw. This sucka doesn't scare me. I can pick him up and toss him on the third rail with one hand. And if he's packin', he's not trying to go to jail on my account.

He smiles that kind of smile that has nothing to do with being happy or amused. Through a set of gritted teeth, he says, "I was your brother's boy. Any friend of Jamal's should be a friend of yours. Especially since if it wasn't for that hunk of cash your brother left you before he quit town, you'd still be slingin'."

I look around and notice that a small circle of space has cleared around us. No one is trying to get caught in our cross fire. "My brother didn't do me any favors. That was the least that fool could do. And whether he left the dough or not, I wouldn't be caught dead living a sorry-ass life like yours." The train comes barreling through the tunnel midway through my response, and I'm not sure if he heard the end of what I said. I turn my back to him and walk a few train cars down before I step on.

I should've used my car to pick up Nailah instead of taking the damn train. But I wanted to finish this book on the ride. Zadie Smith is really doing her thing with this novel. Plus, Nailah loves the subway. Now I have to stay alert the whole trip in case this jackass wants to try and step to me. He probably won't, though. Even though Jamal is all the way down in Miami, folks are still scared to cross him. I try to put Big O out of my head and concentrate on other things, like seeing my daughter or getting in touch with Desiree. But running into him brings everything back.

It's been ten years since I was known in the hood as Jamal's nerdy kid brother, but it feels like a lifetime ago. I was hardly a nerd, but I guess it's a matter of perspective. First of all, I went to school, even after I turned sixteen and it was legal to drop out. And my grades were okay—mostly Cs, with As in English. I did always love to read, and once one of Jamal's boys spotted me on the bus with a book in my hand, I was forever labeled a scholar. My goody-goody rep was also helped by the fact that while Jamal had a different around-the-way girl in his bed (or his car) every night, I was holding it down with Monique. My brother would tell me that we were blessed with good looks, and it was only right to bless as many women as possible with a piece of the pie. But as much as I loved Jamal, even idolized him at times, he couldn't convince me that Monique shouldn't be my only girl.

It was never my plan to get caught up in Jamal's game. Mo and I had plans of our own. She was two years behind me in school, but she'd been talking about college since we met her freshman year. When I hit twelfth grade, she stayed on me about my applications, making sure I got all the recommendations and checking over my essays. She told me that I should be honest about all my family dirt, because admissions people loved hard-knock life stories. I didn't have a problem with that. If all the Newark heads could know my biz, what did I care if some stiff at NYU knew the deal, too. So I broke it down: my mother's chronic depression, her sending me and Jamal to the States to live with her brother and his wife, Jamal falling in with the wrong people as soon as we got here and living a life a crime, and me eventually following suit if I didn't get into college and out of these streets. Worked like a charm. I got into all my schools, and the whole neighborhood was proud of me, including my brother and his crew. They always respected what I was trying to do.

It all came crashing down when I found out that because my aunt and uncle didn't have official guardianship of me, I was still considered an international student. No financial aid. My uncle felt real bad about it and offered me a spot in his plumbing business. I appreciated his looking out for me, but damn, did I hate that job. I'd come home from snaking drains, smelling like shit, with a couple dollars in my pocket. Meanwhile, my brother had a pimped-out crib, the phat ride, and flashy jewelry, without even having to leave his house. Within the year, I was doing runs for him. He didn't want to bring me in. It took me months to convince him, and he still gave me only "low-risk" tasks. And knowing that Monique would kick me to the curb if she knew what I was doing, I kept plumbing with Uncle Steve. But at least I could afford to buy myself some gear and treat my girl the way she deserved to be treated.

Monique graduated from high school and started at Rutgers, which was far enough away that I could stop working for Uncle Steve and work for Jamal full time. Jamal didn't trust anybody except me, so over time I became his right-hand man. Never doing anything too dangerous but always strapped just in case. Keeping an eye on the dudes working for him. Occasional deliveries. Arranging pickups. That kind of thing. At one point, this new guy came into town, saying he relocated from D.C. and wanted to get linked up in my brother's operation. Jamal told me to have him shadow me for a couple weeks to get a feel for the guy. Well, the new guy turned out to be an undercover cop, and before I knew it, I was facing a seven-year sentence unless I gave the police enough info to take down my brother.

My stop comes up, and I look all around me as I step off the train. No Otto. The entire walk to Monique's, I'm looking over my shoulder, staying on the defensive. I hate Jamal for all this. Maybe it was my choice to get involved in his hustle, but I never thought he'd let me sit in the joint, keeping his secrets. Thank goodness I had some sympathetic people in the system, including the undercover cop who brought me down, and I got out in three for good behavior. The whole time I was there, Jamal never came to visit me once. Never volunteered to trade my life for his. My big brother skipped town and left me with all his demons. I'll never forgive him for that.

I ring Monique's bell, hoping that she'll answer the door with Nailah at her side. I need to see my girl's face to get me out of this mood. Besides, greetings with Monique were always awkward. Sometimes we'd do a hug with all types of space between us. Other times a kiss on the cheek, which is more like putting the sides of our faces near each other. The easiest solution is when she just greets me with Nailah, so I can direct all my focus to our daughter.

Finally, something goes right with me today, and Monique answers the door with Nailah propped on her waist. Big O and Jamal melt away at the sight of Nailah's smile. "Daddy!" she squeals, holding out her arms for me to take her.

"How's my girl doing?" Monique hands her over, a task made more difficult these days since this child is getting big. How is she four years old already? Even now that she's walking, talking, and reading, we still call her "the baby" and hold her in our arms too much for her own good. But she's already spoiled, and habits are hard to break.

Nailah's hair is in small cornrows, with a single white bead on the end of each one. They look nice. Nicer than when I do them; I can't get the braids that small. She's rocking a Jay's Gym T-shirt, which I had made especially for her, and a pair of yellow shorts. I give her a kiss on the forehead and follow Monique into the house.

Monique leaves me in the living room while she packs Nailah's overnight bag. "Nailah!" she shouts. "Come tell Mommy what videos you want to bring to Daddy's house." Nailah obediently trots in the direction of her mother's voice, leaving me to sit back on the couch and wait. It kind of frustrates me that we still have to pack a bag for Nailah when she comes over. I mean, she has her own room at my place, with everything she could want. But this little girl is so particular about her toys and games that she's not willing to leave any of her favorites at my house. They have to travel *with* her. So her Little Mermaid tote bag has her favorite doll (which never changes, a dark brown rag doll that my mother sent from Montserrat), her toy of the moment, and whatever cartoon movies she's currently into.

I glance around the room at the pictures on the wall and on the mantle, like I haven't seen them hundreds of times before. I try not to cringe at the picture of Nailah, Monique, and her husband, Andre. After all, it's his house, and he has every right to display a picture of his wife and stepdaughter. And to be fair to Monique, there's a picture of me holding Nailah as a baby right next to the other photograph. It's an extreme close-up of our profiles. It hadn't been a close-up originally, but Monique brought it to the camera store and zoomed in to hide my prison uniform and the security guard in the background.

I have to smile, as I always do, at the picture of Monique hanging on the wall. It's her high-school yearbook picture, and I still remember when she gave me the wallet-sized one seven years ago. "It's cute, Penny," I'd said teasingly. Everybody at school called her Penny, since she looked almost exactly like Janet Jackson's character on *Good Times*. And even though it was her senior year, her wide eyes and round cheeks made her look so much younger. She hated the nickname almost as much as she hated the fact that I usually called her Mo. "Mo is a boy's name," she'd complain. But to me, it was just the right amount of irony, because there was nothing masculine about her. She was the softest person I'd ever known, not in a pushover way, but in that gentle way that lets you know someone will be a good mother.

Monique and Nailah return to the living room, Nailah dragging her backpack behind her. At the same time, a key turns in the front door, and Andre enters, with a bellowing hello. His smile doesn't fade when he sees me on the couch, and I stand up to give him a pound and a pat on the back, our standard greeting.

"How's it going, Jay? Good to see you. Taking the baby for the night? Be prepared to watch *The Lion King* at least a couple times. She's been in a Simba kind of mood lately. Maybe because Nala kind of sounds like Nailah. I don't know." He puts his hands on his sides contentedly. "How's business? I know I keep saying it, but I gotta get over there sometime. I must have some muscles hidden away somewhere, right? If anyone can help me find them, it would be you," he chuckles.

I make a good-natured comment about how it's more important to work hard than to work out, and no one's mad at him for that. Listening to his hyper ranting and looking at his round face and slight potbelly, it crosses my mind (as it does at least once a month) that Andre's name and appearance are completely mismatched. Andre is the name of a smooth talker, a stylish dude. This guy looks more like a . . . Bert, or a Harold. And I also can't help but wonder (as I do at least once a week) how Monique could have loved me for seven years and love Andre now. We're complete opposites. Look at dude's hair. Keeps it real low to distract attention from his receding hairline. And Monique used to tell me that hair is the sexiest thing on a man's body. I started wearing cornrows because she liked them so much. Her favorite male celebrities are Lenny Kravitz and Maxwell. She's all about Afros, braids, and dreads.

Andre walks past me, gives Nailah five (up high and

down low), and touches Monique's cheek after kissing her hand. Dre never acts too affectionate with Nailah or with Monique around me. He's so considerate that it makes me mad sometimes. I wanted to hate him so much, but I couldn't. Still can't. He loves Monique. Treats her like a queen. Nailah, too. Loves her to death but doesn't try to step on toes. None of that "Nailah, you have two daddies" bullshit. She calls him Dre (which sounds like Jay on her four-year-old tongue, so that can get confusing), and he's okay with that. Even when I first got out and he'd pretty much been the man in her life since she was born, he knew his place, without any battles necessary.

"Honey, I'm gonna get some rest," Andre says softly to Monique. She nods, and he heads down the hallway and up the stairs. "See you soon, Jay," he says over his shoulder.

"He had to go into work today. Can you believe that? On a weekend?" I can believe it. The brother works hard to pay for the roomy house they're living in. Not to mention the tuition bills from when Monique went back to college, and the new tuition now that she's in grad school.

"He's a good man," I answer. She flashes me a heart-felt smile, knowing that it takes a lot for me to say shit like that. "Uh, Mo, before I head out, I needed a little advice about something."

The surprise on her face is clear. Mo and I talk about a lot of things, mostly the baby, sometimes her classes, sometimes my gym, but it's not often that I ask her for advice. "I'm listening," she says, sitting on the La-Z-Boy across from me.

I know Nailah's only four, but I feel like kids absorb everything, so I give Monique our silent motion that signals a kid-free conversation. "Sweetie, why don't you go keep Dre company until Daddy's ready to go?" Nailah runs down the hall, without a second thought, and we can hear her small feet scramble up the stairs. "Be careful!" Monique and I shout at the same time.

It still takes me a while to speak once Nailah leaves, because I don't really know what I want to say. Part of me wants to tell it all: meeting Desiree, becoming friends, developing feelings, making a move, getting rejected. Still, this is Monique sitting in front of me. My first love. My only love, for that matter. A little older, a little heavier, but still perfect in my eyes. But then my eyes drift down to the diamonds on her left ring finger, and I get the strength to broach the subject. "I met someone."

"It must be pretty serious if you're telling me about her." Valid point. Monique and I have never had a single conversation about me and another woman. Even since she married Andre, she hasn't heard about any females, as I never planned on giving her the details of a few meaningless sexual exploits.

"Depends on what you mean by serious." I stop there, continuing to debate the level of detail I should give. "I like her. A lot. But we haven't gotten very far . . . physically. Or verbally, really. There's a lot she doesn't know."

"Such as . . ." Monique prods gently.

"Take your pick. She doesn't know much."

"Jamal?" Monique and I use my brother's name to sum up that entire dark period of my life. I shake my head no. "The baby?" I shake my head again, but this time I can't meet her eyes. What do I look like, telling my child's mother that I haven't told a woman I'm interested in about our daughter?

She sighs but holds back any verbal judgement. "So what do you need advice about? How to tell her?"

"I don't even know if I need to get that far. The girl has some issues. With dudes. It's like she's scared to like me or something. I kissed her"—I look down at the floor before I continue—"and she flipped out. Left my apartment all flustered."

Monique rubs her palms on her jeans, a nervous reaction that I'm familiar with. "Jay, I don't know how to say this, but maybe she just doesn't like you."

I laugh. Because I know that there's no way in hell that Desiree doesn't dig me. A man can feel those things. But I decide to travel a different course with Monique. "It's Desiree Thomas."

Mo jumps out of her chair, with her hand over her mouth in shock. She jogs around the coffee table a little bit before she finally sits back down. "The writer? Are you serious?" Wow. From her reaction, you would think I said I was dating Halle Berry or something.

"Yeah. Now I know you read a lot of magazine articles and stuff, so have you read anything about her? Like her personal life?"

"I've read a few things about her, but she always keeps her romantic life private. But you said she seems to have issues with men? Hmmm . . ." She looks at me for a moment, then looks away, then back at me. "Jay, do you think her novel was a true story? That what happened to her character happened to her? That character in *No More Lies*. Troy. He really did a number on Daphne. He cheated the whole time they were together, made her feel like she was the reason for it, even got physically abusive that one time—"

"I remember." Monique isn't saying anything I haven't thought about. But I can't believe that strong, self-confident Des would let herself be manipulated by a man that way. And if a dude had the nerve to lay a hand on her, there is no question that Desiree would sock the dude right back. "I don't know, Mo. Daphne was naïve, gullible, insecure . . . That's just not Des."

"Well, I'm still not sure what you're asking me, but if

you're wondering whether a beautiful, talented woman is worth ironing out a few kinks, I'd have to say yes. Especially in your case, where women you actually have feelings for come around once—"

"Every ten years." I didn't mean to make her uncomfortable, but she's rubbing her thighs again. I want to put my hands on top of hers, the way I used to when she'd have her nervous reaction, but it's not my place anymore. I call out Nailah's name. It's time to go.

CHAPTER 23

DESIREE

"I kissed someone." Robyn, Lloyd, Kahlila, and I are finishing up a delicious dinner in Little Italy, and I figure I might as well shake things up a little bit.

Robyn almost chokes on her wine. "Someone? You mean a man?"

"Who else would I mean, Robyn?" I ask, with a giggle.

"Shit, I thought maybe you and Imani crossed the line of friendship or something!" Lloyd hits Robyn's arm scoldingly. "Don't hit me! I mean, wouldn't you think *that* was more likely than Desiree hooking up with a guy?"

Suddenly, Robyn and Lloyd are talking over each other in an animated discussion about whether or not I would ever "go gay," and Kahlila is shouting requests for details about the man in question. I look around to see if we're making a scene, but luckily, our noise just blends in with the loud family atmosphere of the restaurant. I eat a mussel from my bowl of frutti di mare, and when they're still chattering away, I put my hand up for silence, which surprisingly works.

"Wow. You're using some of my teacher techniques," Kahlila laughs.

"People, people. Settle down. His name is Jason, and he's Imani's neighbor. Kahli, I mentioned him to you a while back. He's sexy, smart, down-to-earth . . ." I can feel a cheesy smile creeping on my face.

"You sure didn't mention all those qualities before," says Kahli.

"My shady ex-boyfriend's name was Jason. I don't like that name. Jasons lie and Jasons cheat. Is he single?" asks Robyn skeptically.

"He says he is. But he's very mysterious, so I don't know what to believe."

"Mysterious how?" asks Lloyd through a mouthful of lasagna.

"For starters, he keeps a room in his apartment locked at all times. I have no idea what's in there. A few times I've been tempted to just ask him, but Jason's not the type who's easy to confront."

"It's probably nothing" and "That's some sketchy shit" come out of Kahlila's and Robyn's mouths simultaneously. Lloyd chuckles softly.

"So if you don't mind my asking, what made you give in to physical temptation after all this time? Especially with a guy you're not sure you trust," Lloyd asks thoughtfully. He reminds me of my dad sometimes, with his soft questions and mellow demeanor. When we first met him our freshman year at Franklin, he was a brilliant grad student sporting this ill-shapen Afro and some rimless glasses that made him look like a cartoon character. He's come a long way in the past few years, wearing his hair in short twists and moving to funky glasses with black plastic frames, still staying true to his musician-philosopher vibe, but in a much more stylish way. Lloyd and I have never hung out on our own, but I've always really liked him as a person and never understood why Kahlila spent her time in college pining over his roommate, Dave, instead of getting with Lloyd, who was obsessed with her from day one. Then when Lloyd and Robyn became close friends, I couldn't figure out why they didn't pursue any romance, either. But who am I to talk.

"It's funny, because I do trust him. I trust that he respects me, he sees my flaws and still enjoys my company, and he's not trying to do me wrong. I know there are things about him that I don't know, but that's not the reason for my hesitation." It feels so weird to be talking about a man in my life. It's like being transported back to our little dormitory suite, sitting on Kahlila's bed, whispering secrets, and laughing long into the night.

"So what *is* your hesitation, Des?" Kahlila inquires with interest. Funny, the last time I saw her, I'd planned to make Jason part of my master writing plan. Looks like things took a different course.

"My hesitation has nothing to do with him. It's just that it's been five years! It's been so long that I can barely remember how to feel anything for anybody. And . . . I don't know. . . ." I trail off, eating a forkful of pasta.

"You're scared," Robyn states, like it's already a foregone conclusion. "And you should be! Getting hurt is a big risk, and if we're being totally honest, you probably *will* get hurt at the end of all this."

"Robyn!" protest Kahlila and Lloyd at the same time.

"What? It's true! I mean, what are the odds that Desiree's first man out of hibernation turns out to be 'the one'? Still, I think you should go for it. This little celibate siesta is getting ridiculous. I haven't had sex in eight months. Feels like a lifetime. I don't know how you do it," Robyn says, shaking her head in disbelief.

"It's not just about sex," Kahlila reminds Robyn reproachfully. "It sounds like Des is considering a relationship with this guy. That's the real issue here, isn't it?"

I feel kind of silly, being that Jason has never even broached the topic of being with me. Until the moment we kissed, I wasn't even sure if he saw me as more than a buddy. "I don't even know if he wants a relationship, Kahli. But you're right about it not being a sex issue. And Robyn, you're right about my being scared. None of my feelings really make sense."

"Sure, they do," Lloyd offers. "For five years, you've been in total control of your life. You've regulated your feelings; you've prevented people from infiltrating your existence. Suddenly, this guy slips through the cracks, and you're terrified. You've worked so hard to micro-manage every aspect of your life. What if this guy forces you to surrender control?"

"I could've sworn you were getting your doctorate in philosophy, not psychology," criticizes Robyn, which sets her and Lloyd to arguing again. I'm glad for the distraction. It affords a few moments to consider Lloyd's words. From the first day I met Jason, he's refused to let me dictate the course of our interaction. Yes, he's let me into his life, but only because he chose to. Not because I tricked him into it or manipulated his thought process.

Kahlila clears her throat and delivers a forceful "Excuse me!" to Robyn and Lloyd, revealing a snippet of her own teacher instincts. "Desiree, I know it's an adjustment to open yourself up to a guy again. But it's time. I disagree with Robyn. Who says this guy can't be the one? And even if she is right, it doesn't mean that he's going to break your heart. And even if he does . . ."

"Okay, okay. I get it. Give Jason a chance." It's the advice I wanted. Even if I hadn't gotten it, I probably would've called him tomorrow, anyhow, apologizing for my dramatic exit and asking to see him again.

Robyn points out a bit of oregano stuck in Kahlila's teeth, so Kahli heads to the restroom. Despite the heavy meal I just devoured, I'm suddenly feeling lighter than when I sat down, and I cheerily change the focus of conversation to Lloyd. "I'm really glad you came up to New York for dinner tonight, Lloyd. How much longer do you have at Franklin before you can call yourself Dr. Bryant?"

He lets out a contented sigh. "My dissertation is coming along really well. I should be done by the spring." Robyn and I give him a modest round of applause, and his cheeks get a little red.

Since I just allowed everybody to dabble in my business, I decide to turn the nosiness on him. "So are you happy that Kahlila is going to be taking a teaching job near Franklin?"

Robyn bursts out laughing, obviously knowing what I'm getting at. Lloyd joins in as well. "You think you're slick, Desiree."

"What do you mean?" I ask in a fake innocent voice.

Lloyd looks around to make sure Kahlila isn't coming back before he answers. "Seriously, I think it will be great to have Kahlila around to spend time with. But those feelings I used to have for her . . . They're so dead."

"Really?" Robyn looks more surprised than I am. Weird. I figured that with her and Lloyd being so close, she would know if he wasn't interested in Kahli anymore. "You never told me that."

"You never asked. My romantic interest in Kahlila faded when you guys were still in undergrad. Then she went off to Arizona, and I didn't see her for two years. I was kind of afraid tonight when I saw her that everything might come back."

"And . . ." Robyn is really pressing Lloyd on this. I haven't seen her this anxious in a long time.

"And nothing. She's a great person. But she's just a

friend." I nod in understanding, and so does Robyn, wearing a grin on her face as wide as a five-lane highway.

After dinner, Kahlila takes the PATH train to Jersey for drinks with J. T., while Robyn, Lloyd, and I get on the subway uptown. Lloyd gets off at the Port Authority to take the bus back down to school. I try to keep my balance on the train as I hug him good-bye. I notice that Lloyd whispers something in Robyn's ear during their embrace, causing her to giggle like a schoolgirl. Once we find two seats to settle into, I waste no time grilling her.

"What the hell was that about?" I demand, swinging my knees toward hers so I can look her in the eye.

Now Robyn is too chocolate-colored to blush, but her cheeks would definitely be red if they could. "I don't know what you're talking about."

"Bullshit! First, you're cheesing like crazy when Lloyd says he's not in love with Kahli; then you two are sharing sweet nothings before you say good-bye." Just then, the guy selling batteries walks through the subway car, but I've been an honorary New Yorker way too long to let that distract me.

Robyn allows her eyes to follow the vagrant vendor's path for a little while. "I've been thinking that I need to look at the men who are already in my life and start evaluating them as potential suitors."

"Girl, that's like trying to wear some shit with the tags still on that's been hanging in your closet for years. It didn't fit then, and it doesn't fit now."

She laughs. "That's a good one. Write that down. But seriously, maybe I didn't give someone enough of a chance. . . ."

"Ain't no use trying to accessorize the outfit with good intentions," I say as I pull my red notebook out of my bag and jot down the gist of our conversation.

"I hear you, but what if you just thought that the outfit didn't flatter you, but really you were just too biased to recognize that it actually did?"

"I'm lost in the metaphors, love. Are we talking about Lloyd or that ugly-ass cable-knit sweater you used to have in college?"

"Okay, here's the deal." Right then, a man and a woman get on at Seventy-second Street. Not a big deal, except they're both wearing miniskirts. "I've always been attracted to Lloyd."

"Really? Even back when he was a dork?" She has 90 percent of my attention, but I can't help but marvel at how amazing that guy looks in a pair of fishnets. Are the eighties making a comeback? He's making me want to put my hair in a banana clip and throw on some leg warmers.

"Yeah, even then. Actually, confession time: Lloyd and I slept together once the summer after freshman year."

I want to scream, but screaming on the subway is an unwritten violation. Lord knows, if I heard a high-pitched scream on the train, I'd be pulling the emergency brake and getting the hell out of there. Instead, I just sit, with my mouth wide open. Robyn has my undivided attention now, no question.

"It's not that serious. I'd just found out that my Jason had been cheating on me, and Lloyd was feeling all depressed about Kahlila," Robyn explains rationally.

I have so many questions that they're all jamming into each other on their way out. Luckily, she answers them without my having to ask. "It was an amazing night. But we decided to go back to being platonic because we were really both just rebounding. I didn't tell you guys, because I didn't want it to ruin any chance of his being able to get with Kahlila later on. I knew that was who he really wanted."

"But now, five years later, you're hearing that Kahlila is a thing of the past. So what now?"

She slouches in her seat and folds her arms. "I don't know, girl. It still feels like sloppy seconds to me."

"How so? You were the one who had him in the first place, not Kahli."

"I had his dick, Desiree. She had his heart." Several passengers turn our way when they hear that one. It's not often that subway conversation is intriguing enough to turn heads, but a mention of reproductive anatomy usually snags some eavesdroppers.

This is a lot of information for me to take in at once. Therefore, I'm not really in the position to give Robyn any advice yet. But my gut is telling me that she and Lloyd would make a great couple. Their temperaments are very different, but I think they would complement each other.

"One thing I do know," Robyn practically announces to everyone sitting in our vicinity, "is that I sure could use some ass in my life. Like I said before, Des, I don't know how you do it." Oh great. Now all the strangers are looking over at me, trying to figure out what exactly it is that I "do." Robyn always did have a low alcohol tolerance. The third glass of wine might have erased a few of her boundaries.

"I don't know what's gonna happen with this Lloyd thing, but in the meantime, I would love a no-strings-attached booty call to keep me occupied until we get it figured out." She crosses her legs and jiggles her foot impatiently, as if she expects this person to come walking up to her at any moment.

All this talk about sex has me thinking about the feel of Jason's hand sliding around my waist and up my back, and the taste of butter on his lips, left over from the microwave popcorn we'd been eating. But I try to concentrate. "Any prospects?"

"Well, there's a guy at Columbia named Greg who I'm pretty tight with. Good-looking, easy to talk to, all that."

At the sound of the word "Greg," I almost choke on the spit in my own mouth. Over the past few weeks, I had successfully managed to put Hunter out of my head. I'd felt bad at first for ignoring his multiple messages, especially when he left me a message after Aaliyah died, remembering that I said she sang my favorite song. I'd been tempted to call him, just to rap about how life is short and you just never know, but I'd called Kahlila instead, and we reminisced about old times while we played Aaliyah's CDs. Over time, though, Hunter's voice mails stopped, and so did my guilt. As a matter of fact, even though this is the first time I'm seeing Robyn since I met Hunter, he hasn't crossed my mind a single time this evening. "Greg?" I manage to squeak.

"Gregory, yeah. Actually, his name is Hunter. Long story. But we're study buddies and good friends, and I've considered suggesting that we engage in some extracurricular activities." She nudges me playfully, and I force a smile.

"You would actually come out and ask him that?"

"I feel totally comfortable saying whatever I want to Greg. That's not a problem."

My life has gone officially twilight zone on me. If Robyn decides to make Hunter her booty call, I'm gonna have to hear about sex with a guy who most likely wanted to have sex with me. Only not the real me. The me I made up so that I could write a made-up story that's not really all that made up. "So why don't you do it?"

"A few reasons. First, he already has a booty call. He still messes around with his ex-girlfriend." Well, well. I definitely hadn't gotten that impression from Hunter.

I guess he's not the choir boy he painted himself to be. "Second, I don't think he's down for meaningless fun these days, anyhow. He's been pretty depressed lately. A patient of his was seriously injured, a young kid he was really close to."

Oh my God. It can't be Manny. I remember Hunter talking about him. It was the only patient he mentioned by name. But he was working in pediatrics, so I'm sure he knows plenty of kids. This feels so wrong, knowing that I know the guy whom Robyn's talking about, yet I'm keeping it to myself. I feel the truth bubbling in my stomach and threatening to spill out of my mouth when the automated subway lady says in her unnatural professional voice, "One hundred twenty-fifth Street."

"That's my stop," I mumble.

"Okay, sweetie. Tell Imani I said hi," Robyn says, giving me a half hug from her seat. "And keep me posted on your Jason saga."

"You do the same." Although if Robyn and Hunter decide to take their friendship to the next level, that's the last thing I want to hear about.

CHAPTER 24

HUNTER, DESIREE, AND JASON

I haven't been to church in about twenty years, but I might have to go praise the Lord tomorrow morning. When Kevin called to tell me that some of the guys in the med school were heading out, I'd just gotten off a rough shift in the ER and had been looking forward to some sleep. But a voice in my head told me to go. I haven't been out in a long time, and I could use a fun night. Now that I've cut things off with Alicia, I have nothing to occupy my evenings. So I met up with the fellas and took the subway to Jimmy's Uptown right when it was segueing into club mode. I started regretting my decision as soon as I saw that ladies were free while we had to come out of our pockets something serious. Yo, if guys always have to pay more at the club, how come we don't at least get admitted faster than the women? Got us standing outside, with a twenty-dollar bill in our fist, while the chicks just waltz right past the velvet rope.

Scanning the gender-segregated lines, I can tell that it's an upscale crowd. The women, who are outnumbering us about four to one, are wearing that conservative sexy gear, instead of the clothes that look like you could do some business on the street corner once the club lets out. The guys are patiently waiting their turn to be admitted, and as they reach in their wallets for their licenses, they allow their university or office IDs to flash for a prolonged minute, making sure the ladies get a glimpse.

I remember something Alicia had told me once about there being two types of club crowds. The "around-the-way" clubs contain all types of black people, from the thugs and chicken heads right on up. She equated those venues to shopping at Marshalls: you have to go through a lot of crowded racks, but with patience, you'll come across some real good deals. On the other hand, crowds such as this one at Jimmy's, the bougie black folks, are the equivalent to shopping at Benetton, or another boutique-type store. Women see all the choices as soon as they walk in, and everyone is trying to buy the same outfit. She told me this the first time we met at the Kit Kat Club; apparently, Alicia had gotten a bargain when she got me, the unsuspecting medical student, to buy her a drink.

According to Alicia's theory, the bougie spots work to my advantage, being one of the few good-looking brothers up in here. Still, by the time I get inside, I'm almost too annoyed to appreciate the fly faces, bangin' bodies, and hot music. But everything changes when I see Desiree sitting at one of the tables near the now-empty stage. She'd clearly come to see the live music set and was now sitting back, watching the scenery change, with two women and a guy. Can't really tell if the dude is paired up with anyone. I'm about to walk over there and say what, I don't know. But before I can put one foot in front of the next, she glimpses me, practically jumps out of her seat, and heads in my direction.

* * *

Things were looking up for me. The day after I had dinner with my college friends, I called Jason and was welcomed by a very happy voice on the other end. Turns out he had just sent me an e-mail saying that he missed my company and wanted to get together. As tempted as I was to jump in my car, plow through the Lincoln Tunnel, and speed to his apartment, I had decided to be more disciplined about my writing. So I told him that I'd be putting in serious hours at my laptop until the weekend. We spoke every day, though, and with each conversation, I liked him a little more by the time we hung up the phone.

Seeing him today was a little awkward, since we never discussed the kiss that went wrong, or how we were going to interact the next time we met up. There was an uncomfortable hug, and I think he mumbled a compliment. Thank goodness, we brought Imani and Sheila to break the tension, and by the second set of the performance at Jimmy's, Jason's arm was around me, and it felt perfect. The singer was doing a cover of India.Arie's "Ready for Love," and I was starting to think homegirl was sending me a message.

After the performance was over and the DJ started setting up, Imani and Sheila were ready to go, but I convinced them to stay for a while longer. As Imani and Jason got into a serious conversation about the revitalization of Harlem, I started to space out, looking absentmindedly around the club. Oh shit. Oh God, no. Hunter Gregory is not standing twenty feet away, staring me right in my face.

Okay, yes, he is. It's definitely him. Looking better than I remember. I don't know many men who can pull off a light purple button-up shirt, but he's doing it successfully. He kind of reminds me of those men in the Macy's catalogues, modeling the suits, with those smirks on their faces—the smirks that say, "You know you want me. Otherwise, why would you be catalogue shopping for menswear?" Where is my mind right now? I have to keep him away from this table. If he comes over, he's sure to find out that I was a total liar during our two dates and five phone conversations. Not that it really matters, but as bitchy as I can be sometimes, I really hate for people to think badly of me. Plus, the even bigger risk of his coming over is that Jason will find out that I was playing with Hunter's head, which means that I could just as easily be playing with his. And my feelings for Jason are even realer than I want them to be. No, I have to cut Hunter off in his tracks. Do some damage control.

As cool as this evening has been, all I can think about is getting out of here. From the minute I heard Desiree's voice on the other end of my phone the other day, all I've been thinking about is kissing her again. All right, maybe doing more with her than just kissing. But sitting at this table with another couple, pretending to be all interested in the music, holding up my end of the conversation, it's worse than Chinese water torture. Not that I really know what that involves, but it must be pretty shitty.

Imani and Sheila are talking about leaving now that the live music is through, so maybe when they head out, I can push for an early exit as well. Although when Desiree begs them to stay and dance, I start rethinking my plan. It might be fun to get on the dance floor for a little while. I'm not usually the dancing type, but if that's the soonest way I can get to touch this girl's body, then let's get this party started.

I manage to get my focus back once Imani starts talking about Harlem's property values and its changing population, because that's some shit I gotta be passion-ate about. My neighborhood and my money are high pri-orities. Hate to admit it, but Jamal taught me that. But my attention gets sidetracked when Desiree excuses her-self from the table pretty suddenly. I watch her for a while because I'm afraid she might be sick from that calamari she ordered. I'm not down with that squid stuff. But instead of going in the direction of the bathroom, she walks straight over to some pretty boy who looks like he just won the lottery. By the time they hug, I'm not even trying to continue the conversation with Imani any-more. Once she notices that I've checked out of our dis-cussion, she nudges her girl, and they start gathering their things to leave.

"Jason, we're gonna sneak out while Desiree isn't here to stop us. See you soon," says Imani, resting her hand on my shoulder as she rises from her chair.

"All right, ladies. Take care." Saying good-bye requires me to remove my eyes from Desiree and the dude for a moment, but I'm not trying to come off like a jealous boyfriend to Imani.

As soon as the women disappear, I go back to studying the scene. Things have only gotten worse since I turned away. This Tyrese-looking asshole is holding Desiree's hand, looking at her up and down like she's a dessert he's about to take a bite of. Then he twirls her around, most likely giving her some corny-ass line like, "Lemme get a full view of this outfit you got on." Actually, if he says some shit like that, he's probably gay. I didn't think of that. This is probably her gay friend or something. Nope. The way he just scoped her ass when she did her 360 makes it pretty clear that he's straight. Straight-up interested in my girl.

Of course, she's not, in any way, really my girl, which is why I can't roll over there and throw my weight around. I just have to sit here like a punk and wait for her to come back.

By the time I get the back view of Desiree's ensemble, all is forgiven. Somehow, the sight of the strip of exposed skin between her shirt and her pin-striped pants—hanging low enough to reveal the dimples on either side of the crease in her back, just a half inch above an ass that's looking juicy and tight all at the same time—it's enough to make me forget that this is the woman who simply stopped taking my phone calls. Call it weakness. I call it weighing my priorities.

Still, there's no way I'm going to run into this girl and not make her do a little explaining. I'm just about to ask her what I did to get myself cut off so dramatically when my boy Tommy comes over for an introduction. Other than becoming a renowned orthopedic surgeon, Tommy's only goal in life is to be in the presence of beautiful women as often as possible. Being that he's five-foot six, practically engaged to his longtime girlfriend, and obviously stepping on my toes here, there's no way he can think that he has a chance with Desiree. But Tommy is just content to shake a gorgeous girl's hand and see her smile. So I grant his unspoken request.

"Desiree, this is my boy Tommy. We go to school together."

"Pleasure to meet you, Tommy." She smiles and extends her hand, making Tommy's night all in one swoop.

"The pleasure's all mine, love," he says, kissing Desiree's knuckle. I'd forgotten that the guys I came with have been drinking since a few hours ago, and obviously Tommy is feeling the effects. It all seems pretty harmless until I see the look on Desiree's face. Anger and disgust rolled into one facial expression.

"I gotta get back to my friends," she mumbles and begins walking away. As lovely as it is to watch her go, I can't let her leave. I grab her arm as gently as possible, not wanting to get a similar look to the one she gave Tommy. She stops, folding her arms as she turns back to face me. I glance over at her table to see if her friends are taking in the scene, and that's when I notice that only the dude is still sitting there. I guess that answers the question of whom he came with, especially since he's in my grill, like he's ready to come over here and bust my ass. It's a pretty effective stare, and part of me is about to send Desiree back to the table without another word. This dude looks dangerous to me, and it's not the cornrows, the muscles, or the fact that he looks uncomfortable in nice clothes. It's something that he wears on his face, like he's been through some mess in his life that will come to the surface if provoked. But at the same time, if he wanted to start something, he'd be over here and not still sitting in his seat.

"Promise me, you'll see me again. Even for an hour." I'm practically begging, but I'm not even ashamed. Desiree is in my thoughts all the time, even when I have another woman in my bed. It's got to mean something. And if she's seeing the guy sitting over at that table, it's not like I can't win her over. I'm sure I beat him out in every category: height, education, charm. As for looks, yeah, he's got that whole thugged out/pretty boy thing going on, and he's definitely wider than I am, but from the little I know about Desiree, it's not going to come down to the superficial, anyhow.

"Fine. I promise. See you later," she says quickly, practically running back to her date. Whatever. He'd better soak up his time with her tonight, because his days are numbered.

That nigga better be glad as hell that my parole isn't up yet. I can just hear my probation officer now. "Jay, you were doing good. Real good. I didn't think we were gonna have any problems. Then you beat up some guy over a woman who ain't even yours? That's a damn shame." But my PO's imaginary lecture alone wouldn't stop me from getting in the brother's face. What really held me back was the thought of Nailah having to come visit her daddy behind bars. It's one thing to do it during the years when she isn't going to remember anything, but I can't have my baby thinking of her father as a criminal.

At times like this, I wish I drank so I could roll to the bar, order a scotch or something, and let myself mellow out. Instead, I gotta sip on this ginger ale and watch as this cocky son of a bitch grabs Desiree's arm. Finally, she begins making her way back to me. I don't even pretend like I wasn't watching them. And I decide not to pretend like it didn't bother me, either.

She barely sits in her chair before I ask, "Who was that?"

"What?" she says, faking like she's distracted by a person trying to squeeze past our table.

"You heard me." Her eyes open wide at the tone of my voice. But I'm not apologizing.

"I don't know what your problem is, but he's Robyn's good friend." She looks me right in the eye, like she's daring me to challenge her story.

"Who's Robyn?"

"You've heard me talk about her. She's my girl at Columbia Medical School."

"Right, right. So this dude is Robyn's man?" I already know the answer, but I wanna make her say it.

"No," she says, looking down in her lap. "She and Hunter are just friends."

I want to laugh when she says his name. Figures he has a soft-ass name like Hunter. "Well, he obviously wants to get with you." She doesn't say anything to that, which makes me add, "If he hasn't already."

I don't know why that comment makes me so mad. Maybe there's an implication that I'm some easy ho who'll give it up to any guy in a good school and a nice shirt. And I've told Jason before that I haven't let any men into my life in a very long time. So for him to suggest that I've "gotten with" Hunter basically means that he thinks I'm a liar. Maybe this is a fair assessment on his part, being that our initial interaction was based on the lie that Imani was my girlfriend, but it doesn't stop me from being offended.

I can't think of anything harsh enough to say, so I leave the table instead and walk to the other side of the room. I'm tempted to go back over to Hunter and his friend, but that would probably just cement Jason's theory that we've slept together. Not to mention that his boy Tommy is revolting. How dare he kiss any part of my body when he doesn't even know me?

Leaning against the bar, I try to look like I'm having a decent time, without inviting any male attention. A very difficult thing to do. Luckily, I only have to sustain it for a few minutes before Jason is next to me, circling his arm around my waist and whispering in my ear. It's like someone just flipped the ON switch in my body, and I'm tingling all over. "I'm sorry, Des," he whispers. "Let's dance."

The deejay is playing an old-school reggae set when Jason takes my hand and leads me onto the dance floor. We begin dancing far apart, my hand still in his, stepping and swaying to "Murder She Wrote." I would have never been able to imagine Jason comfortably moving to this music, but here he is, crossing one foot over the other, dipping down and coming back up, even twirling me around a couple times. "Check you out doin' your thing. I'm impressed."

He gives a fake look of conceit. "It's in the blood, girl. But you don't know nothin' 'bout that," he teases. I'd forgotten that he's originally from the islands. He must have come to the States pretty young, being that he doesn't even have a hint of an accent. There's so much about his life I want to ask him. But at the same time, if I want to learn more about him, he has to trust me. And I guess, I haven't done too good of a job with that tonight.

"I hate to bring this up again, but there's nothing going on between Hunter and me." He nods in response, but I can't tell what's behind his blank expression. "And there never has been anything, either." The music switches to a slow calypso beat. *Sorry . . . is all that I can say. . . .* Instead of answering me, Jason pulls me closer, and by the end of the song's first verse, our bodies are intertwined, and I can barely think straight.

Watching Desiree and her muscle man get their groove on is like watching a highway accident. You know you should turn your head and keep driving, but you just can't. There are plenty of attractive ladies in this place to talk to, or I could join my boys at the bar. But I can't help but wish I were in that guy's shoes, feeling Desiree's body pressed against me.

"She's a real bitch, huh?" Who knows how long Tommy's been standing next to me, being that he's not on my eye level. I'm too jealous to defend her, so I just shrug my shoulders. "Who's the guy?"

"No idea." I try to sound like I haven't given the question a second thought, but my head is spinning, trying to create a realistic scenario. Maybe he's someone she knows from Jersey. An old boyfriend, even. But now that she's trying to come up in the world, work in the city, get her modeling career going, he'll start to feel like she's too big time for him. He probably does construction when he can get the work, or . . .

"I didn't even get to tell her I liked the book," says Tommy, watching her with an annoyed expression.

"What the hell are you talking about?" This guy is drunker than I thought.

"My girlfriend made me read her book last year. It was actually pretty good," he reluctantly admits, sipping on his Henny and Coke. I still have no idea what he's talking about, but something tells me that Tommy is not the idiot in this conversation.

"So she was in a book? Like a fashion magazine or something?" I'm desperately trying to put the pieces together.

He looks at me like I'm a lunatic. "Okay, that *is* Desiree Thomas, right? Author slash ice queen?"

I stare at Desiree, just catching glimpses of her frame between the mass of bodies on the dance floor. Her back is arched as she slowly moves her hips in some complicated figure eight against her mystery man. I didn't know she had all of that in her. But apparently, I never knew anything about her at all.

CHAPTER 25

JASON

"Jay, I'm pregnant."

Suddenly I'm not sitting on my living-room couch, talking to Monique on the cordless phone. Instead, it's five years ago, and Monique is staring at me with her doe eyes through the prison glass, telling me that she's carrying my child. Now, just as it was then, I can't find the words to respond.

"I wanted to tell you," she presses on, "because . . . well, because it's a major change in our lives. Mine, Andre's, Nailah's, yours."

"Have you told Nailah already?" I try to imagine her reaction. Probably excited, since a lot of the kids in her neighborhood have siblings.

She laughs softly. "I haven't even told Andre yet." Whoa. She's telling me before she tells her husband. At another time, most likely later this evening, I'm going to have to analyze that further. But not right now. Not while Monique is still on the phone, and Desiree is on her way over.

"Why not?" I have to ask that at least.

After what seems like an eternal moment of silence,

she breathes out an "I don't know." Not satisfied with that answer, I know that if I wait long enough, she'll say something else. It takes six seconds. "I'm so happy, of course, and Andre's gonna be . . . You're better with words than I am, Jay. Give me a word that magnifies happy times a thousand."

"Ecstatic?"

"Not happy enough. But you get the point. Anyhow, I guess, I'm holding onto my old life for the last few moments that I can." Nailah is laughing in the background, and I wonder what she's up to.

"Your old life?"

"Yeah, when it was just the two of us . . . and Nailah." Ninety-nine percent of me is sure that she means her and her husband, but that one percent of doubt is making my head spin. I hear Andre's cheery greeting in the distance. "Jay, I gotta go."

"Okay. And Mo?"

"Yeah?"

"Congratulations." I can feel her smile through the phone line, and I try to give one back before I hang up.

Monique is going to be a mother again. And I don't have anything to do with it. What if Nailah doesn't want to spend as much time at my crib when the baby comes, because she'll want to be at home with her little brother or sister? And this is going to strengthen the bond that Mo and Dre already have. But why should I be bothered by that? They're married. This is what married people do. They have kids. The doorbell rings before I can think about it anymore.

The sight of Desiree, with a wide smile on her face, should make me forget about things, but it doesn't. I absentmindedly motion for her to come in, and she takes a seat on the couch, reading the backs of the videos I'd rented for us to watch. It's not until I walk into the kitchen, open the fridge, stare into it, shut it, and return to the couch that she notices something is wrong.

"You seem distracted. You okay?" The sincerity of her question makes me want to tell her the truth about everything. Maybe this is a great opportunity. I'm definitely getting sick of locking Nailah's room every time she comes over. Okay, here we go. "My friend . . . Mo is gonna have a baby."

She gives me a knowing smile before I can further explain. "Awww, and you're sad that things are gonna have to change with you two. No more boys' nights out, huh?"

It's too easy to accept her explanation. Do I really have the energy to clarify her thinking? *No, Mo is my ex-girlfriend who I had a kid with four years ago. But this time she's pregnant by her husband. I'm upset because while I'm falling hard for you, I've never completely let go of the hope that one day Monique, Nailah, and I could be a family.* "Pretty much, yeah."

"I can imagine that it'll feel really weird when my friends start having kids. Being a parent . . . That's like when you fully enter the land of the grown-ups."

Tell me about it. I try to shake off all of my stresses and join her on the couch. She scoots sideways onto my lap and gives me a soft kiss on the mouth. "Don't worry. When Mo has his baby, you can still play with me, okay?" I reposition her so that she's fully facing me, her legs on either side of my waist, and replace her soft kiss with deeper ones. Hearing the tiny sound of pleasure that she makes in response successfully takes my mind away from everything except making that sound come out of her again. The summer dress that she's wearing is spread out like a fan over my legs and hers, and I reach for the hem to pull it over her head. She immediately pulls away.

"I take it that you're tired," she says apologetically, "of just kissing."

Now that's a tough one. On one hand, we've only messed around a few times since that night at the club. I, in no way, feel like it's my right to push things further. But it's not like I haven't been fantasizing about where this could go. Thank goodness, she doesn't wait for me to respond.

"I'm gonna need some time. Before I'm ready." The poor thing looks so uncomfortable having this conversation that I'd say anything to put a smile on her face again.

"Nobody's rushing you, sweetheart." To reinforce my point, I gently move her off of my lap and rise from the couch, standing over her, with my arms folded. "How about we do something to take our minds off . . . the tension?"

"What do you suggest? Getting on your treadmill?" she asks, with a smirk, gathering her hair and bringing it over one shoulder. Looking at her do that gives me an idea.

"How about you let me braid your hair." I stare at her, trying to imagine what Des would look like with cornrows.

"Are you serious?" she asks, with a half-laugh.

"Dead serious. That way we can't even look at each other, and my hands will be occupied so I can't try to have my way with you." Besides, I want to tell her about Jamal, about Nailah, about Monique, about my hopes, my fears. Maybe it will be easier to talk to her when I don't have to see her face.

I run into the bathroom to get a comb, while Desiree places a few cushions on the floor to sit on. She tries to insist on a mirror, but I deny her, saying that she's not allowed to see my work till I'm done. I really just don't want her to be able to angle the mirror on my face as I confess all my sins. I mean, even the priest gives you a screen to hide behind, right?

I run the comb from the middle of her hairline down to the top of her neck, creating a straight middle part. Figure I'll keep it simple with eight braids to the back. They'll look nice, especially since her hair is so long and the braids will hang past her shoulders. She's rambling about her new growth and how she hopes her scalp isn't flaking on me, but her hair feels soft, and her scalp is clean. After a few minutes of talk about tender-headedness and braiding overhand instead of under, we fall into a contented silence.

Once I finish the first braid, I use the remote control to turn on the stereo. Chico DeBarge is singing one of his ballads, and I take it as a sign. This CD came out when I was locked up, and it was like the dude had written all his songs with me in mind. Turns out Chico had spent some time away himself, and that's where he got his motivation. But it's been two years since I got out of that cell, and I still can't get his CD out of my play rotation. I hit STOP to start it from the beginning, and I mentally compose the phrasing of my admission while I weave my fingers in and out of Desiree's hair.

You know I'm free/Out on parole/Just got my papers, honey/I'm really home/So what's going on, suga/How is your life, baby/It's so good to be back . . . The lyrics of "Love Still Good" suddenly have me thinking about the old days with Monique instead of how to tell Desiree the truth about me. I recite the title of Desiree's book over and over again in my head. *No More Lies, No More Lies, No More Lies* . . .

The sound of Desiree giggling interrupts my mental exercise. "Am I tickling you?" Nailah always accuses me of having "tickle fingers" when I braid her hair.

"No, not at all. It feels fine. Very relaxing." That makes

me feel pretty good, being that she was looking so tense earlier. I remember how soothing Monique's hands in my head used to feel, and my mind is somewhere else again that quickly. "I'm just laughing at the words to this song," Desiree adds, with an amused tone.

Her comment snaps me out of my daze right away.

"So this guy thinks he can just come back to his woman after goodness knows how long he's been in jail, and she'll be waiting for him? That's a good one."

"Stop shaking your head," is all I can say. So what now? *Well, Des, it's funny you should mention it, because that exact same thing happened to me and my baby's mother. Oh yeah, I forgot to tell you I have a daughter. And that I have a record.*

"These braids aren't staying braided without something on the ends, Jason." She touches her head to feel the section that I've done so far.

"I have rubber bands."

"Aw, hell no! I'm not breaking off my ends with some rubber bands. When you're finished, I'll run to the corner store and get some coated elastics. You should use those, too. I'll buy you some pink ones. How would you like that?"

"Uh-huh." I try to focus on keeping her hair smooth as I make my way down the braid, and Chico continues to sing my life. *But you found another/And I understand, lover/'Cause I lost my brother/From the war on drugs . . .*

"Honey, what's wrong? You still thinking about your friend and his baby?"

Desiree has never used an affectionate term for me before, and it sounds real nice when she says it. It makes me want to share myself with her, even though I know she's not ready for one of my bigger confessions.

"Des, I lied to you about something." I'm glad I can't see her face, because I'm sure her eyes are getting real squinty and evil right about now.

"I'm listening." All the warmth she had in her voice when she called me honey is long gone.

"Your book. I told you I hadn't read it. But that's not true. I read it before I'd even met you."

She puts her hand on my hands to see how far I have left with the braid I'm working on. I'm guessing she wants to turn around. "Why would you lie about that?" Her tone is a little less cold now. I wonder what she thought I was going to say.

"Just habit, I guess. From the time I was young, I always felt like I had to hide that I loved to read. It still feels strange to tell people." I reach the bottom of the braid, continuing until my fingers can't hold the tiny sections of hair anymore.

Desiree turns to face me as soon as she feels me rest the braid over her shoulder. "Goodness, Jason. We've known each other almost two months now. I'm a freakin' writer, and you don't tell me that you love to read? You're such a dork." She reaches under her butt for one of the cushions and hits me with it.

"Hey, I'm sorry! No need to assault me in my own house." I grab the cushion out of her hands and rest it next to me on the couch. "If it makes you feel any better, I loved your book. Especially the way you used the poems in the story to match what Daphne was going through. That was tight."

She slides from the floor to the couch, moving the cushion so she can sit beside me. From the Kool-Aid smile on her face, I can tell that she likes me more now than she did before, which makes me feel a little guilty. Because I know if I'd told her one of my for-real for-real secrets, she'd be scooting away from me instead of closer. "Thank you. I was really self-conscious about putting my poems into the book. I'd never studied poetry and wasn't sure how good they were."

"Well, they spoke to me." She takes my hand by my four fingers and kisses the palm. Man, this moment is getting way too emotional. I don't deserve all this affection. "So who's your favorite writer?"

She takes my hand away from her mouth, lacing her fingers with mine. "Gloria Naylor."

"Yeah, you like those sad endings, huh? Your book ended all tragic, with the girl by herself. And the chick's husband dies at the end of *Mama Day*, doesn't he?"

"I prefer to call the endings bittersweet, thank you very much. What about you? Who's your favorite?"

"I gotta go with Melville."

She laughs and snorts by accident. The look of embarrassment on her face is pretty funny. "Oh right, cuz *Moby Dick* ends on such a cheery note."

"I hear you, but I read it in eleventh grade, and that was the first book where I really learned to read beyond just the plot. Looking for symbolism and all that."

"Too bad my book doesn't have any symbolism."

"Your book reflects real life and real problems for people our age. That's important. Not every story has to make some great statement about good and evil."

"I just wanted this next novel to be my masterpiece, my *Moby Dick*. And so far it's just not doing it for me." She re-braids the ends of the cornrow I most recently finished.

"Des, you know what Melville said once? It's my favorite quote of all time. He said that life begins at twenty-five. Now look at you. You're not even twenty-five yet, and look at all you've accomplished. How are you gonna beat yourself up for not writing your masterpiece yet? Shit takes time, baby."

She nods, with a begrudging smile, not wanting to admit that I'm right, but knowing that I am. "You're twenty-seven. So your life began two years ago?"

"Yup. I bought this apartment, started my gym. Everything just fell into place." The day before my twenty-fifth birthday, I got out on good behavior. And that's when my new life started. If I look at it that way, maybe I won't ever have to tell Desiree about the years before that. But that doesn't solve the problem of the bedroom door I keep locked whenever she comes over. Because Nailah's the only part of me that carried over from the bad side to the good. She's the only thing that makes my early years bittersweet, instead of plain old sour.

CHAPTER 26

DESIREE

I'm in so far over my head that I might never be able to come up for air. Thinking that I could grab a quick coffee or something with Hunter and be on my way, I agreed to a date when I saw him at Jimmy's Uptown. It was the only thing I could say to get him out of my face. I could feel Jason's eyes on me the whole time we were talking, and I just needed the conversation to be over.

Actually, that's not true. A tiny part of me was excited to see Hunter. He's a handsome guy who's been more than kind to me. And, according to Robyn, he's been pretty down lately. It may be none of my business, but I want to know if things are looking up for him. It's funny. Just a few months ago, I wouldn't think twice about a man's feelings. I guess once my guard started coming down, my whole heartless foundation fell apart.

But once I realized that seeing Hunter was something that gave me excited butterflies, I knew I shouldn't be going. So I dodged his calls for almost three weeks, to no avail. He just kept calling. Eventually, I gave up and was actually looking forward to a friendly outing when he asked if we could do dinner instead of lunch. Nighttime meetings are always more suggestive, but I acquiesced. After all, as soon as our dialogue got underway at the restaurant, I planned to drop the news that I was back with an ex-boyfriend of mine. He'd presume I meant Jason since he saw us dancing at Jimmy's, and everything would be resolved. Project Make-Believe over.

Of course, nothing is ever simple in my life. When we met downtown, Hunter told me we were going to eat in Brooklyn. I thought he just wanted to give me the tour of his borough. Turns out, he's not only introducing me to his old neighborhood. He's introducing me to his mom.

Now I don't realize this until we're standing on the sidewalk in front of a medium-sized apartment building, and Hunter is looking at me with this silly smile on his face. "So Ma volunteered to make us some dinner, okay?"

Holding on to a small hope that he is referring to his Latina girlfriend, I repeat, "Ma?"

But it's too late. He's already rung the bell, and we're being buzzed in. My shock is being replaced by sheer anger. How is he going to introduce me to his mother without telling me? First of all, I'm still rocking the cornrows that Jason did for me yesterday, and I'd decided to dress down in order to match the hairstyle. A Baby Phat cotton tracksuit is not suitable "meet the parents" gear.

More importantly, he's forcing me to lie to this woman. I have to tell his mom that my last name is Whiteman, I work as a secretary, and my ultimate goal in life is to be an actress. It's bad enough to have to keep this going with one of my peers, but I don't want to pretend with a parent!

But whose fault is it that I'm in this predicament? Not Hunter's. He's just a nice guy who wants the girl he's interested in to meet his mom. If I'd been up front with him from the beginning, this would actually be a momentous event. Instead, I feel like I might throw up, and I haven't even eaten yet.

I plaster a smile on my face as we get off on the second landing and walk down the hallway. A young-looking woman with honey brown micro-braids is standing in the doorway of the second apartment on the right. As we step closer, I see that she has Hunter's chiseled nose and narrow face. "Hey, Doc. Who's this pretty girl you bringing in my house, tryin' to show me up?" She laughs a loud, high-pitched laugh, which puts me at ease a little bit. Hunter ignores her question for the time being, kisses her on the cheek, takes my hand, and leads me inside.

"Ma, this is Desiree, the girl you've been hearing me talk about for months." Oh, goodness! Is that true? From the hearty hug that she gives me, I'm guessing it just may be.

"It's really nice to meet you, Mrs. Gregory." The TV is playing an old *Three's Company* rerun, and I practically have to shout over it to be heard.

"Girl, please. Call me Lenora," she instructs as she walks over to the television set and turns down the volume. The TV looks so old that I wonder if it even has a remote control, but the cable box sitting on top proves that it can handle new technology.

I look around the space as she makes her way back over to Hunter and me. Nothing quite matches, but everything seems to go together. The living room boasts everything from antiques to modern pieces, from reproductions of African-American art to family pictures. It looks like she's lived here forever, without the space being dusty or out-of-date. "Your apartment is great. It has a lot of character."

She seems pleased by my compliment, and Hunter can't stop smiling. "You like it? It's in a good location, I guess. Got it from my great aunt in the seventies. Rent controlled. Can't beat it. I'm not letting go of this place. Most people dream about owning a home, right? Not me. Not true New Yorkers. We rent for life!" She laughs, a rich full laugh, not a nervous one, like the one I return. Why am I nervous? Because I want this woman to like me. Not like it matters.

There's an awkward moment when mother and son are just staring at me. "Hunter didn't tell me you wore braids. I'm lovin' them. You do those yourself?"

The last thing I want to think about right now is the bonding experience that Jason and I shared yesterday when he braided my hair. I've been falling for him so quickly, and his admitting that he'd read my book sent me into crush overload. I couldn't believe that I was having a conversation about Melville and Naylor with a guy who looks like he should model men's underwear. "Um, a friend did them for me."

"Well, they look real nice. Y'all ready to eat?" Lenora's tone of voice reminds me of a loving grandmother, even though she barely looks old enough to have a grown son. Her down-home demeanor relaxes me, and I'm suddenly starving. Hunter volunteers to put out the silverware in the "dining room," which is really a corner of the fairly large living room, where a mahogany table sits with four high-backed chairs, each with a different printed cushion to soften the experience for your backside. I follow Lenora into the kitchen to fix the plates.

A greasy pan of delicious-smelling fried chicken sits on the stove, along with a pot of red beans and rice. I start dishing out portions as she hands me the dinner plates, and then she dashes into the refrigerator to pull out a large Tupperware bowl. She talks as she pulls off the lid and adds large spoonfuls of the contents to each plate. "Don't feel like you gotta eat the potato salad. I know people can be picky about whose potato salad they eat. You like mayonnaise? Cuz I ain't really into mayonnaise all that much, so I use a ranch dressing instead. Doc and Jasmine, that's my daughter, they just love it."

"I'm sure I'll like it, too," I assure her as I carry a plate back into the dining room and she carries the other two.

"Aw shit, we forgot drinks," Lenora mutters right as we all sit down to eat, and leaves the table. My parents would never curse in front of company, but for some reason, it makes me feel like family when Lenora does it.

"Desiree, you drink wine coolers? I got Seagrams, a whole bunch of fruity flavors," she shouts from the kitchen.

Wow. I can't remember the last time I had a wine cooler. I think it might have been at a cookout on the first warm Saturday of spring my freshman year. No, that was a Zima. I'd have to go further back in my memory to recall a wine cooler moment. "Sure. Any flavor is fine."

"Ma, you don't have anything better than that?" Hunter shouts in an almost whine. He's been pretty quiet tonight so far. I wonder if he's stepping back to let me sink or swim. This is probably a test to see how well I fit in. But whether I pass or fail is inconsequential. As soon as we get out of here, I'm ending this.

Lenora reenters, balancing an almost full bottle of Alize and three glasses. "You're right, baby. We gotta do it up right." Once the drinks are poured, we say our cheers and get down to eating. I notice that no one prayed, which kind of surprises me. My family doesn't pray at every meal, but we always do when we have people over. It's kind of black people etiquette, I think.

The food is well seasoned without being too salty, and

I ask her if she did anything special to her chicken. As soon as she says that I'm welcome to come over anytime, with or without Hunter, to get a cooking lesson, the guilt sets in. I'm relieved when she changes the subject and starts talking about her job. Turns out she's a secretary at a big financial group downtown. She tells this crazy story about how her boss is having an affair with one of the other secretaries at the job, and the secretary's husband, who also works at the company, knows about it but pretends not to since he's getting it on with this college intern who started at the beginning of the summer.

I'm half mesmerized by the twists and turns of her soap-opera office drama, but I'm also wondering why Hunter doesn't chime in about the fact that I'm a secretary as well. I mean, I'm glad that he doesn't, because I'm not in the mood to have to invent some fictional work experiences, but it seems weird to me.

By the end of the meal, the Alize is hitting us hard. Well, it's definitely hitting me and Lenora. I can't really tell about Hunter, since he's still being all mellow and laid-back. His mom decides to bust out with the old photo albums, and we move to the couch and begin flipping through the pages. Every picture has a story attached to it, and I hear about days as early as when she met Hunter's father on a school trip, and as recently as when Jasmine had her baby. It's fun watching Hunter through the years. The boy never had an awkward stage. He went from an adorable kid to a handsome teenager to a sexy man. I think about my own family photo album and wince at the thought of my eighth-grade class picture, with my bushy, pre-permed hair, my mouth full of braces and rubber bands, and the baby fat I'd yet to shed.

Hunter interrupts by asking his mother about the DVD player that she bought a few weeks ago. I guess she keeps pretty current, after all. I don't even have one yet. She excitedly opens a little door on her TV stand, revealing a small collection of movies. We can't agree on what movie to watch, so we flip through the channels, landing on BET's *Comic View*. A crass female comic is delivering some killer one-liners. I wonder if Hunter feels uncomfortable during the risque jokes, but Lenora is laughing hardest of all. It must be nice to have a parent who you can treat like a friend.

Somewhere during the next routine, I must have drifted off, because Hunter is shaking me as the credits roll. Lenora is going back and forth between the dining table and the kitchen, putting everything away. I tell her that I feel bad for not helping, but she says that she doesn't let guests clean in her house. Hunter says that we should be going, and I begin rambling a bunch of thank-yous and really-appreciate-its. Lenora gives me another heartfelt hug, and I'm sad that I probably won't see her again.

When I look at my watch, I can't believe that it says 11:07. I hope Imani is still up when I go back to her house. Part of me wishes I was going back to Jason's place instead, but another part of me is thinking about what it would be like to spend the rest of the night with Hunter. That's when I know that the Alize isn't completely out of my system yet.

CHAPTER 27

HUNTER

"Doc, you forgot something!" Ma calls after me once we're halfway down the hall.

I jog back to the apartment while Desiree leans against the wall to wait. Knowing my mom, I didn't leave anything behind. She most likely wants to weigh in with her opinion, and I'll admit, I want to hear it.

We step inside, and she closes the door behind us. "What do you think, Ma?"

"I can't help but like her, baby." She looks at me with these proud eyes, like she can't believe I finally picked someone she approves of. Alicia never ranked high on her list—something about her being a prissy, bougie-ass diva. In fact, she actually cheered when I broke it off, once and for all, with Alicia a few weeks back. It wasn't fair to Alicia now that she wanted more, and my heart wasn't in it.

"Neither can I, Ma."

"Well, don't mess the thing up standing in here talking to me. Go on now." She rises on her tiptoes to kiss me on the cheek, opens the door, and practically throws me outside with a hard shove. I try to gain my footing before Desiree turns my way.

"So what did Lenora say about me?"

"She likes you a lot." Desiree beams a 100-watt smile, which makes me feel comfortable pushing the envelope. "How could anyone feel otherwise?"

I'm afraid that her smile will fade once she hears me increase the flirtation level, but it doesn't. Once we make it out into the fresh air, she leans against my shoulder, mumbling something about it being chilly outside. I'm perfectly warm, but if she needs an excuse to touch me, I'm not arguing.

We walk in silence to the subway station, which gives me some time to process where things stand with Desiree. I think I've figured out why she felt the need to lie about who she was. I mean, she's this model type who happens to be some kind of brilliant writer. Just on those two facts alone, she's probably pulling all types of dudes. I'll bet, most of the time she can't even figure out which men like her for what's inside, and which ones are all caught up in the package. So she was testing me, trying to figure out if I would be interested if she weren't the successful young prodigy.

I can't be mad at that. I've thought lots of times about going out and pretending like I wasn't in med school. But I think a small part of me was afraid to find out that a lot of women only like me because of it. Not that I don't have any other positive attributes, but none of the other ones seem to matter.

I'd filled my mom in on the whole story last week. She was cracking up. Thought the whole thing was hilarious. It was her suggestion to bring Desiree to the house. She said that maybe by my opening up and showing her a personal part of my life, Desiree would feel more comfortable doing the same. I figured it couldn't hurt, but I knew I couldn't tell Desiree where we were going ahead of time. She'd cancel the date for sure. So I sprung it on her, hoping that she wouldn't be too pissed off, and she handled it like a trooper.

With the exception of a sleeping old woman, we're the only people in our subway car, so I decide to step up my game, putting my arm around her and pulling her in close. She snuggles on my chest and shoulder willingly, even tracing swirly lines on my leg with her index finger. "Your mom is great. I didn't expect her to be so cool."

"Oh yeah? What did you think my mom would be like?" She shrugs as a response, and I nudge her to respond. But in that split second, though I can't see her closed eyes, I recognize her slightly parted lips as the sign of an unconscious person. How much of that Alize did she and my mom polish off? I held back a little, sipping slowly, because I knew I had to have my wits later when I confronted Desiree about the real her. But for now, I can't bear to disturb her deep, even breathing.

I don't know where Desiree was planning to get off the train, but I need to switch over at Ninety-sixth Street, so I shake her to get off there, too. A bit disoriented, she follows me obediently to the subway platform. But once we walk a few feet, she seems to have shaken off her residue drunkenness. "You taking the 1/9 from here?" I nod. "I'm gonna head up to the street and catch a cab to my girl's house near 125th."

"I'll walk you." I'm not ready for this evening to end. Even though it's gone even better than I imagined it would, I haven't gotten to the bottom of Desiree's many lies, and I can't end the night before I do.

We climb the stairs to Ninety-sixth and Broadway, Desiree tugging the back of my shirt as she walks behind me. On the sidewalk, instead of immediately hailing a taxi, she puts her arms around my waist and rests the side of her head on my chest. I don't know if this is Alize or a sudden change of heart, but she really seems to be feeling me tonight. I'm tempted to allow the charade to play on for just a few more days. Why wreck a perfect evening?

"Thanks for bringing me to your house, Hunter. I had a really, really good time." She pulls back enough to look me in the eyes, and once she bats those eyelashes at me, I'm powerless to do anything except to lean down and kiss her.

Her lips, soft and full, brush against mine, tentatively at first, but with eagerness after that. For a second, I imagine what we must look like—a young couple in a passionate embrace on the streets of New York City— and I wonder if I'm dreaming. But as soon as I feel like I might have to pinch myself to make sure this is real, she pushes me away. Literally. I go backwards a few steps, almost losing my balance. She offers no explanation. Just stands there looking up at the sky, hands on her hips, pacing back and forth on the pavement.

I'm pissed off now. She's taken her little games too far. Bad enough that she hasn't been straight with me from jump. Now she wants to turn me on and off. For what? Just to play with my head? Maybe this is her idea of fun or something. But the jig is up.

"I know who you are, Desiree." I expect her to play innocent and deliver a high-pitched "What are you talking about?" But she just freezes in her tracks and looks at me guiltily. "Why couldn't you just tell me the truth?"

"It's complicated," she says in almost a whisper.

My voice gets louder in response. "I'm an intelligent guy. Try me."

"I'm working on my second book. I was stuck." She pauses and turns away from me. "I wanted to see what it would be like for a guy who had everything to be interested in a girl who was less than perfect."

For a full minute, I'm absolutely speechless. Then, I have so many things to say that I don't know which sentence I want to say first. I settle for, "I was a fucking experiment?"

"Hunter, I'm sorry. I never—"

"What? You never meant to get caught?"

She bites her bottom lip, wringing her hands in fake anguish. Maybe she wasn't lying about wanting to become an actress.

"Hunter, it wasn't supposed to go this far. I never expected you to be someone I really wanted in my life . . . as the real me." Finally, she looks me in the eyes, and for a moment, I want to believe her, forgive her, and move forward, with nothing to hide.

Against my better judgment, I give her a chance to patch things up. "So now that everything's out in the open, you still want to chill with me?"

No answer. What seem like hours pass by. But she doesn't say anything. How long can I wait for a scheming chick to say that she wants to be with me? This is bullshit. I'm out.

CHAPTER 28

DESIREE

How, in just a few short months, did I go from being a prude to a player? It's been over a week since I sent Hunter storming down Ninety-sixth Street, and I feel terrible about it. But I couldn't keep juggling him and Jason the way I was. Hunter is great. His mom is great. But Jason is amazing too. I don't know much about his past, and I couldn't even begin to predict where we're headed. But in the here and now, no one makes me feel more alive than he does. Sometimes I'm afraid that our chemistry just might make the room blow up.

Still, Hunter's facial expression when the truth came out is haunting me. Because that was the first moment that he bore no resemblance to Trevor. The whole time I dated Trevor my freshman year of college, I never ever once saw him look sad or hurt. At first, his upbeat quality was a positive. Always wearing a killer smile, he gave the impression that nothing could bring him down. He had a great sense of humor, and we teased each other a lot. I would get my feelings hurt when he took jokes too far, but he would laugh off all of my stingers. I admired that about him and tried to become less sensitive. But soon his comments weren't funny anymore. He'd insult my body, call me stupid. And he never once seemed sorry for the pain he caused. But Hunter, he showed all three emotions in one tortured stare—sad that I wasn't really into him, hurt that I would lie about it, and sorry that he ever met me.

But I can't ruin a fantastic night with thoughts of what's already over and done. Paula really outdid herself this year with her annual Publisher's Party. Originally intended as a way to connect bigwig publishers and editors with her clients, the event has evolved into *the* soiree to attend in the New York literary scene, especially for people of color. Last year, Imani and I went together, and I spent the evening trying to forge professional relationships without encouraging romantic ones. This year, when Imani told me that she was bringing Sheila, I strongly considered staying home. It's not like I'm looking for a publisher. As a matter of fact, I knew that Random House would be up in my face if I decided to show up, bugging me about when they were going to receive a copy of my manuscript.

Then I got the idea to invite Jason. We'd been spending loads of time together over the past few weeks, doing everything from working out to movies and dinners, including a really fun double date with J. T. and Marisol. We've even been doing some "sustained silent reading." That's what he called it, like we were back in first grade or something. I told him that I hated to read other people's stuff in the face of a deadline, because I'm always scared that I'll subconsciously steal something. But he insisted that reading was the best way to stimulate my own creative juices and loaned me all types of books way outside of my own genre for inspiration. It was during one of these sessions of quiet time that I brought up the party. "It's cocktail attire," I said apologetically, knowing that having to dress up would be Jason's number one objection to going.

"What's that? Like a tuxedo or something?" His eyes were still on the pages of *Song of Solomon*.

"No. More like a suit."

"I'll be there," he said after a pause, without ever looking up from his book.

And that's what's so great about him. There's no guessing about his feelings. No game playing. No need to hold back. I feel confident that I'm the only woman in his life, despite the fact that he definitely has secrets I've yet to learn. And while most of the time I'm completely comfortable in his presence, the idea of going to this party with him gave me the jitters. I went out and bought a new dress for the occasion—a deep purple number with a neckline that plunged down to right above my belly button. I even got a pair of violet stilettos that did things for my calves that I thought only the machine at the gym could. Felt a little stupid on the train coming into the city, I must admit. But it was worth it to see the look on Jason's face when I took off my shawl at his apartment to use the bathroom.

We drove downtown to the party in his Acura. This was the first time I'd actually ridden in his car. On Broadway, a cab dashed into our lane without checking its blind spot, and he put his arm in front of me while he swerved to avoid the cab with his other hand. His protective nature was instinctual, and it reminded me why I have been able to let my guard down with him and no one else in the last five years. He always makes me feel safe, like no one, including him, could ever hurt me.

The way Jason tipped the valet when we parked, adjusted his Armani suit jacket (which I have a sneaking suspicion he bought specifically for the party), and guided me inside with his hand on my back, you'd think he went to events like this every day. He never ceases to amaze me. Walking through the party with him, I almost expected everyone to bow as we passed by. And people *were* doing double takes—maybe because we looked so good, or maybe because no one in this room had ever seen me with a date before, except for Imani and Sheila, who were chatting it up across the room with E. Lynn Harris. I had to smile to myself, remembering Imani's complaints about being compared to him all the time. I'm sure she won't mention that tonight.

Standing next to Jason made me feel like a better package. He elevated me. For a while, we shut the rest of the world out, just staring at each other, smiling, and exchanging silly compliments. That's when we decided that he would stay at my place tonight. "I'm driving you home, right?" he asked, eyeing my cleavage, and then moving back up to my face.

"Uh-huh. And it'll probably be too late for you to drive back into the city," I answered, noticing that he'd bought a suit that was baggier than the traditional fit, appropriating Armani to suit his style.

"Yeah, I think it will be." And then we just stood smiling at each other for a few minutes more. "Oh shit, Des. Is that Colson Whitehead?"

I follow Jason's eyes to one of the bars and see a young black man, about Jason's complexion, with a lot of hair on his head. "Yeah, looks like him."

"Yo, *The Intuitionist* was a crazy-ass book. I gotta go rap with him," he said, and he headed over to the writer excitedly. I watched as he spoke to Colson, gave him a pound, and they settled against the bar for what was to be a long discussion.

I decided to use my alone time to face my editor at Random House. I was barely in speaking range before he started bombarding me with all the questions I knew

I would get. "Your summary of the story was pretty vague, Desiree. Can you give me any more specifics? Paula talked about your maybe needing an extension on the deadline? What's it looking like? We're expecting big things from your sophomore work. Are you ready for the tour? It'll be twice as long as the first one." I was drowning in a sea of insecurity, but then I looked over at Jason, a hundred feet away. He was pointing me out to Colson Whitehead, and our eyes connected for a split second. I could feel Jason's pride in me, and I was suddenly eloquent and powerful.

I soon had my editor and one of his associates completely at ease, and we were sharing a joke when Paula rushed up to us, presumably to rescue me from what she assessed to be a full attack. She seemed very relieved that I didn't need her assistance, but she pulled me away anyhow, under the guise of "author/agent shoptalk." I knew she wanted to gossip.

"Desi, he's gorgeous. Where did you find that one? He's not a writer, is he? Friends with Colson?" She stared at the two of them, not even making an effort to be subtle.

"No, he's not. He's Imani's neighbor." I couldn't even utter those few short sentences without a giddy smile appearing on my face.

Paula let out a tiny squeal. "This is huge. So tell me."

"Tell you what?"

"How you *feel*, honey. I can see it on your face, but I want to hear you say it."

I paused for a second, trying to come up with the perfect way to describe my emotions. But Paula's not only my agent. She's a friend, and I didn't need to rehearse my answer for her. "I'm nicer to everyone I meet. I replay conversations that we had in my mind, trying to recall his exact wording and intonation. I tell pointless stories about him to my friends. When I know I'm going to see him in the very near future, I get this excited flutter in my stomach. And when we're together, I process every iota of his being: his strong hands, the way his left tooth angles slightly toward the one beside it, the way his head bobs when he listens to music." I lower my voice before I continue. "And when he touches me, even just a playful tap or an affectionate arm around me, this tremor just runs through my body, and I pray he can't feel it."

Paula smirked through the champagne glass she was sipping from, and her eyes were mischievous, like she was harboring a tantalizing secret. "What?" I demanded.

She finished her swallow of champagne, took a step closer, and mouthed the words to me. "You're in love." Touching my shoulder like a proud mother, she walked away to join her husband near his photo exhibit on the far wall.

My first reaction was to completely dismiss Paula's theory. How could I, a woman with more than her share of defenses up, manage to fall in love in a matter of months? Ridiculous. But I started thinking about the last time I was in love with someone. I hadn't known Trevor two months before I thought I'd met my soul mate. In the early stages, Trevor was pulling out all the stops: fancy restaurants, expensive gifts, weekend getaways. For a teenager, it all seemed so grown up. That, combined with our sexual chemistry, had me believing that I'd met "the one." I assumed that he insulted me to make me a better person, a person worthy of his company. And the rumors on campus about his sleeping with other girls—those were just lies spread out of jealousy.

And now I'm two months in with Jason. We haven't had one expensive dinner. We've never spent the night together. But all the signs are still there. I guess when I fall, I fall fast and hard. I didn't expect it to be this easy the second time around.

The rest of the party was a blur after my revelation. I joined Jason in kind of a daze, trying to process the idea of my being in love. I decided to pass on the champagne, not wanting to smell unappealing to Jason later on. And besides, when I drank too much last week, I kissed a person whom I was supposed to be getting rid of. I didn't want to make any mistakes this evening.

So now we're on the Turnpike, and my mind is racing with thoughts of what's going to happen when we get to my place. I peel off the thick blanket of silence laying over the car. "There's a gas station when you get off at my exit. It should be open."

"The tank is almost full."

I'm tempted to drop the subject, but later I don't want to regret not handling these practical details. "No, it's just that . . . I don't keep condoms at my house. And I wasn't sure if you had any—"

"Say no more," he says, trying not to break into a grin. I feel the engine rev up a little bit as he increases his speed.

He leaves the engine running as he runs inside the little convenience store at the gas station, and jogs back toward the car with a smile on his face. At the sight of my questioning look, he pats his inside jacket pocket. Except for a few instructions on how to get to my condo, we don't exchange any words for the rest of the ride.

Once we get inside, I don't even bother to turn on the living-room light before I grab him, kick the door shut, and kiss him all the way down the hallway to my bedroom. We leave a clothing trail on the way; his tie, suit jacket, and button-up shirt are all gone by the time we reach my bed. He looked so handsome all night, but I'm happy to see him looking like the real Jason again, in his signature wife-beater. He pulls me on top of him and unzips the back of my dress, pulling so hard that we both hear the seam rip. I laugh and begin to take off his undershirt, but Jason seems upset by it.

"It's not a big deal, honey. I can get it fixed," I mumble, kissing his neck and chest.

He gently lifts me off of him and sits up on the edge of the bed. "Now see, your dress ripping like that was like a wake-up call for me."

My heart is thudding inside my rib cage. "You mean you don't want to do this?"

He chuckles, which calms me down a little. "Are you serious? I've thought about this moment from the time you handed me that hub cap. I fantasized about this moment from the first time you ran on my treadmill. And I've been dying for this moment since the first time we kissed. But if I waited that long, I need everything to be right when we do this." He takes a deep, slow breath. "Baby, I have something I need to tell you."

Panic does not adequately describe what seizes my body. "Oh my God. You have a girlfriend."

"No, I don't. But I do have a girl. A daughter named Nailah. She's four. Just started half-day kindergarten a few days ago." Nailah. I've heard that name before. At the jazz club with Nicole. She asked Jason about a Nailah, whom I presumed to be his girlfriend. But after spending so much time with him, without a woman ever surfacing, I put it out of my head.

"So that's who Nicole was asking about when we were all at B Sharp."

"Yeah. Nicole's done some baby-sitting for me before. Nailah likes her a whole lot."

I never thought I'd feel a rush of relief at the news that the man I'm falling hard for has a child. But here I am, feeling it. Maybe it's because I've known all along that Jason was keeping something from me, something that he wasn't going to share until he fully believed that I was someone to be trusted. And now it's out in the open. "Okay, tell me more."

"More like what?"

"Where does she live? What's your relationship with her? How are things with her mother? Why didn't you tell me before?"

"When she's not with me, Nailah lives in the Bronx, and she's my whole world. Her mother and I are still very close." My eyebrows must rise when he says that, because he follows that up with, "Don't worry. She's married and has another child on the way." I want to ask more about her, like why they broke up in the first place, but I guess we have to take one thing at a time. "And as for why I didn't tell you before, well, I'm not exactly an open book, in case you haven't noticed."

"I can relate," I say with a smile, remembering the locked door in his apartment and imagining the colorful room behind it. "Well, I can't wait to meet her." And it's really true. I'm already picturing how beautiful and smart his daughter must be.

"I've never introduced Nailah to any woman in my life before. But I think you're an excellent exception." I feel a tear welling in my right eye. I really hate how emotional I can be sometimes.

Jason sees the tear rolling down my cheek, wipes it away, and kisses the spot where it had been. Guiding me to lie down on my bed, with my purple dress still half on, he takes my leg and kisses my pinkie toe. He begins to slowly move his way upward, kissing as he goes—sometimes a soft and gentle brush of the lips, other times a flicker of the tongue. My whole body is shaking as he moves up the thigh to my hips, finally pulling the dress over my head and slipping off my sheer black thong. Five years. Five years since I've bared everything to a man. For a moment, I'm paralyzed by the thought. When things ended with Trevor, I'd decided that it was our physical intimacy that had made me the most vulnerable. If it weren't for that, I wouldn't have been able to mistake his lust for love. And if it weren't for our having sex, I wouldn't have experienced the thing that I still can't bear to think about.

My eyes must convey the fear I'm feeling, because Jason takes my hands and holds them. I don't know how long we sit there, staring at each other, holding hands. He waits for my cue to continue, kissing me on my stomach before spending some quality time on each breast, sucking one playfully while he massages the other. Sounds are escaping my mouth now—not any recognizable words, but definitely noises of pleasure. He's breathing heat on my neck, and I'm eagerly anticipating the moment when our lips connect. But right before he places his mouth on mine, he bites his lip and caresses my face with his hands, then proceeds to make his way back down, spreading my legs and making himself comfortable in my center. His tongue is sending me into spasms, and my body explodes for the first time in . . . forever.

I'm ready for the next step, and I unfasten his dress pants and peel off his boxer briefs. I don't know when this man had time to roll on a condom, but when I feel his package, that joint is strapped on. I love the Boy Scout in him. First, he teases me with just the head, then he enters a little more, and I gasp at the feel of the entire length of him. It's been so long that my body is a bit shocked at first. "Are you okay?" he asks, with worry in his voice.

"Mm-hmm. Don't stop." And we don't stop until we're both spent, having changed positions about five or six times, moved from slow to fast, gentle to passionate. I'd thought about turning on my stereo when we first entered the room, but we didn't need it. Our moans and screams made for their own sound track, and the satisfied silence once we're through is the best music we could be listening to.

After holding each other for a long time in a sweaty squeeze, we take trips to the bathroom and finally settle in under the sheets, ready for sleep. I have a lot that I want to say to him, but it's late and I don't want to keep him up. But when I turn over and face him, his eyes are open. "What's on your mind, sweetheart?" His voice is raspy and thick.

"Five years ago, when I stopped dating, I let my friends think that I was planning to swear off men indefinitely. But I never planned for it to go this long. I just wanted to wait until I was ready to trust again. I thought, if someone is deserving of what I can give them, they'll be patient with me through all the tough stuff. I'm ready to be vulnerable with you, Jason. And it doesn't even feel as scary as I thought it would."

"You know what that means. You've gone from being hurt and bitter to being hurt and better."

"Did you make that up?"

"Yup, just made it up on the spot. You want to use it in your book?"

"Yes, please."

"It'll cost you," he says and takes my breath away with a long, deep kiss. I smile, happy to have gotten my feelings off my chest, and I close my eyes to settle into sleep. But thoughts of Jason's daughter are keeping me awake.

He's almost in dreamland when I disturb him with my next question. "Don't be offended by this, but was the pregnancy planned?"

He laughs groggily, his eyes still shut. "Aw, hell no. We were young and stupid."

"So did you guys ever consider . . . not going through with it?" I turn my body away from him, concentrating on the clock at my bedside, not wanting him to see my face.

"Nah. We never did. Monique and I had been together since my junior year of high school, her freshman year. There was too much love between us to not be happy about something we created. I mean, trust me, I do believe in a woman's right to do what's best for her, but not having Nailah would've destroyed us."

I can't answer him, out of fear that my voice will reveal how close I am to crying. I want to tell him at that moment. I want to tell him what I went through, and how it did destroy a part of me, a part that's just now beginning to heal. But my mouth can't form the words.

I think about how to tell him for so long that I must doze off, cuz the next thing I know, Jason's shaking my arm. "So are we legit? You're my woman now, right?"

"I'se yo' woman. And you'se my man."

We giggle, and I tell him that we should make sure we remember the date as our anniversary. I grab the journal next to my bed and use the pen inside its pages to write the exact time and date: 3:29 a.m., September 11, 2001. For the first time in five years, I'm truly happy. I feel free, like today is the beginning of much more joyous times for me. I fall asleep without a care in the world.

CHAPTER 29

JASON

It was all a dream. That's my first thought as I turn over in the morning and throw my arm over what I expect to be Desiree's naked curves. Instead, my hand touches cool, rumpled sheets. My eyes snap open, and I sit up straight. Disappointment turns my stomach. But then I realize that the sheets I'm lying on are light purple. The ones on my bed at home are green. "Thank God," I say out loud, and I lie back down, trying to mentally draw pictures of last night on the ceiling.

I let myself relive a couple of highlights, like when she whispered in my ear, "I can't wait another minute to have you inside of me." The tone of her voice turned me on by itself, never mind what she said. Then when she straddled me, winding her hips and grabbing her hair like she was performing at a reggae concert—damn, that was like an adult video come true. And just when I thought the show couldn't get any better, she flipped it and turned around, giving me a back view that almost made a grown man cry. And did I really tell her about Nailah? Did she finally open up about having been hurt for so long? It's like I've been carrying this bar on my back, with three plates on each side, and I finally got to rest the weight back in the cage.

"Good morning, handsome." Desiree interrupts my video replay of the evening, leaning in the doorway of her bedroom, with her arms folded. She's wearing a long, silky robe with the belt tied loose. I want to pull on that belt until the robe just falls on the floor. "Want something to eat?"

As soon as she's spoken the words, I smell that irresistible odor of salty breakfast meat. I can't remember if she knows I don't eat pork, but right when I'm wondering about it, she says, "It's turkey bacon," like she can read my mind or something. "And eggs and pancakes!" she shouts as she heads back into the kitchen.

The alarm clock on her nightstand says 9:30 exactly. I don't have to be at work till noon, which means that maybe after we eat, I can get another taste of Desiree. I flip on the TV just to get some noise in the room while I look around for my T-shirt and drawers. I'm peering under the bed when I hear, "Leslie, is there an estimate of how many people would have been inside the buildings this morning?" Leslie's voice sounds mad shook when she answers, which isn't too normal for a news reporter, so I take a look at the screen.

What the fuck? One of the World Trade towers has a fucking hole in it. What kind of explosion would have done all that damage? When the cameras pan out, I see a similar black hole in the second building. This must not be the news. But why is there a movie on network TV this early in the morning? No, it can't be a movie. This is the reporter chick I see all the time. After a couple seconds, the shock lessens, and I deduce that somebody must've bombed the place. Didn't this same thing happen a few years back? Only this time, it looks . . . Well, for the people who are above the holes, it looks hopeless.

I finally get my voice enough to shout for Desiree to get in here. She runs in, and all I can do is point at her nineteen-inch box on the dresser. Just then, the reporter gives us the "if you're just joining us" catch-up. We watch taped footage of a plane flying into the second building as the first one already bleeds smoke and fire. I put my hand over my mouth; she puts hers over her eyes. No, this has to be some kind of sick joke. This mess can't be real. But how did they get the hundreds of people to run through the streets, screaming?

Slowly, Desiree takes her hand away, and she stands frozen about three feet from me, her mouth hanging open, her eyes blinking real fast. When they show this guy jumping out of one of the fiery skyscrapers in desperation from about a hundred flights up, she runs into my arms and starts sobbing on my chest. "What's happening to us?" she asks over and over again through her tears. I guide her to the bed, and we sit at the foot, glued to the television. And if this makes me a sucker, whatever, but I'm scared as shit.

For the next half hour, we sit holding each other, listening to the news as they piece together what happened. Watching footage of the Pentagon in flames. Learning of another plane that went down in Pennsylvania. Hearing that all the planes in the whole country have been grounded. Finding out that the terrorists are thought to be of "Middle Eastern descent," and wondering what made them come to that conclusion. I mean, it's not like we don't have some twisted-ass people in our own country.

I haven't said a thing since she walked into the bedroom, but the numbness is wearing off, and I can start to think again. "You know anybody working down there?" I know there ain't a damn person in my life who works in those buildings, but I figure someone who went to a fancy college like Franklin University might know some corporate types. Desiree shakes her head no, staring straight ahead, with a glazed-over look on her face.

After a few more seconds with no sound but the anxious voices on the television, she screams, "Paula!" all of a sudden, making me jump a little bit. "Her office is downtown." She springs into action, dialing numbers, which motivates me to do the same. First, I call work to see what's going on. We open at six in the morning, which means that folks could've fallen off the treadmills, watching those televisions we got posted in every corner. It takes five tries before the connection goes through, but finally, the answering machine picks up. After another several attempts, I get Hakim on the cell, and he tells me they closed up. We'd play tomorrow by ear.

Desiree is still on the phone when I hang up, sniffing and wiping her eyes. "Okay, take care," she says eventually. Turns out Paula took the day off after her party last night. My mind starts turning, thinking about the way fate works, wondering what a businessman could've done differently today to save his life. On the news, we watch this company president say that he was late getting to work this morning because he took his daughter to her first day of kindergarten. His five-year-old is the reason he's not dead right now.

That's when I think of Nailah. And this guilt grabs my throat as it has been a full hour since I first saw that our world has gone crazy, and I haven't thought to call my daughter. I mean, I know she's fine. She's all the way in the Bronx. And it's Tuesday, which means that Monique only has a night class, so they're home together right now. Aw, damn. I just remembered Andre. I know he works somewhere down by the water. I call their house, and Monique answers halfway through the first ring.

"Jason, thank God. I've been calling your apartment and the gym, and nobody's picking up."

"Why didn't you call the cell?"

"I did. Couldn't get through."

"Y'all okay over there?"

"We're . . . you know, we're getting through. Andre called, and everybody who works in Manhattan is on foot, since the subways aren't running. He said the streets are packed with people just walking in silence. Last time we spoke, he was almost in Harlem. So he should be up here within the hour."

"That's good. That's real good. What's Nailah doing?"

"She's in her room with her dolls. I want to go in there, but every time I'm around her, I just start losing it. What world are we gonna have to raise this girl in? And then the baby . . ."

"I know, sweetheart. I know." The word flows outta my mouth like water, and it's not until Monique gets quiet that I realize what I said. I quickly look over at Desiree, but she's talking a mile a minute on her phone and didn't hear me.

"Do you wanna talk to her?" Monique asks me. I'm about to tell her yes, since nothing could bring hope to this day more than the sound of my daughter's voice, when Desiree shouts my name and points to the TV. Monique must be in front of one, too, because she says, "Oh my God" in a whisper. Together the three of us watch one of the towers fall.

I am sitting here on a comfortable bed, next to a beautiful woman, on the phone with the wonderful mother of my child, in a house where a happy, healthy little girl is playing in her room. I am blessed. There are people in that collapsed pile of wreckage who, just a few hours ago, probably felt the same way I do right now. This is some bullshit. This just isn't fair.

"Hey Mo, I'll talk to Nailah later."

"I understand." Her voice is shaky.

"Don't let her watch TV, okay?"

"Jay, give me some credit." The shakiness is gone. I should've known better than to question her judgment as a parent.

"Sorry. I'll talk to you later."

"All right. And Jay, I'm glad you took my advice."

"About what?"

"Don't play dumb with me," she says teasingly. "I can hear her voice."

I don't know what to say. There's been no one since Monique. No one who meant anything. And even though she's married—and pregnant—a part of me still feels like a cheat.

"Times like these, Jay, we need people in our lives. People to hold on to. I'm happy for you. See ya." She hangs up before I can answer. Desiree is looking at me when I put the phone down.

"Is Nailah okay?" I wonder how much she heard after all.

"She's fine."

She tells me that she was checking in with Kahlila, who started her new job teaching in Philadelphia a few days ago. She's in the teachers' room right now, trying to stop crying before her next class starts. Kahlila's from Boston, and her mother had four coworkers on one of the planes, one of whom was like an aunt to her. They were all going on a business trip. I hadn't thought about the people on those planes. I try to imagine their last few moments, but it's too damn scary.

After those first few phone conversations, it's like we suddenly have the urge to call everyone we know. Even if we know they're okay. Just to call. We spend the next three hours on the phone, she on the land line, I on the cell. Sometimes calls go through; sometimes they don't. She calls her parents in Baltimore, who are relieved to report that all of their friends and family who work in Washington, D.C., are safe. Meanwhile, I check in with my mom and pop in Aruba. They have no concept of how big or small New York is, so for all they know, the World Trade Center is down the block from my brownstone. They're relieved to hear from me. They say Jamal had called them about an hour earlier, asking if they'd spoken to me yet. I tell them to let him know I'm fine. Ma pauses, like she wants to convince me to call my brother, but I start giving my exit speech before she can go there. They, as always, end the conversation by asking when I'm bringing their granddaughter down to visit. I usually dodge that question, but when I peek at Desiree next to me, cradling the phone to her ear and biting her fingernails, and then I turn to the devastation on the television, getting out of here with Des and Nailah doesn't seem like a bad idea. If we have the guts to get on a plane.

Once we've finished talking to every single person we know, we drag our feet to the kitchen to see what we can save of the breakfast. I'm so hungry that I eat everything after she reheats it, but she just picks at a piece of toast. After a few minutes of that, she goes back to her bedroom, the television drawing her in like a high-powered magnet. I finish my plate, throw away the leftovers, and wash the dishes. It's not even to score points. It just feels good to be doing something.

She's back under the covers by the time I come back. I get in with her, and she gets comfortable, using me like a human-sized pillow. For the first time, I think to use the remote to see if there's anything else on TV. Damn, Des has got like a hundred channels, but there's no escaping New York City. Maybe a small news story in D.C.,

Pennsylvania, or Boston, but like clockwork, the stations return to those giant buildings crumbling to smoke and ash.

We've now seen the smoke pouring out of the towers enough to watch those images without emotion, but every time they profile an individual person—a twenty-something Indian girl lost in the debris, a pregnant wife whose husband called her from one of the towers after the plane hit, a teenager at a nearby high school whose innocence just got robbed—Desiree starts crying all over again. I can't believe that this is the same woman I met just a couple months ago. Even last night, when we were talking, it seemed like she was about to lose it a couple times. When I saw how shaky she was after hearing about Nailah, I knew she wasn't ready for the rest of my story. In due time. We have bigger issues to think about now, like if it's safe to step outside ever again.

By sunset, we've reached this functional funk, where we go about normal tasks, with this unusual heaviness. Desiree finally feels how hungry she is, being that she hasn't eaten anything all day. I volunteer to go fix her something, but she says that she needs to get away from the TV anyhow.

I spend a few minutes wondering if anyone survived the towers falling. I hope they didn't. One time when I was little and still living in Montserrat with my parents, my brother and I were playing outside, and I got pinned underneath a wooden fence. We were playing some game Jamal invented, an island-ghetto-fabulous version of cops and robbers. He slipped underneath the fence with no problem, but I was chubby back then, and midway through, I couldn't go forward or backward. My brother tried and tried to get me out, but he couldn't. I had to wait there until he ran home and got my dad. It was the worst feeling, being trapped and alone, especially once the sun set. Imagine if you knew no one was ever going to save you.

The phone jolts me out of my thoughts, and Desiree shouts to let the machine pick up. That was a given. I'm not about to answer her phone, especially on a day where it could very likely be a family member calling. But at the sound of the beep, I know it ain't hardly her mom.

"Desiree, it's Hunter. I was calling to make sure you and yours were okay. I tried earlier, but you know . . . The phones were all crazy. My mom works down the street from the towers. She's fine, thank God. Yo, this has me thinking about how fucked up this world is. Nothing is promised, you know what I'm saying? Things with us didn't end very well the other night. I don't know why you did what you did, but it doesn't mean that I didn't feel something special with you. And when we kissed . . . Anyway, give me a call. I want to see you again and clear the air. Bye."

As soon as I hear the word "kiss," I'm collecting my shit. My mind's already trying to figure out a place to stay tonight. It's probably impossible to get back into the city. I call Hakim on his cell. Luckily, he picks up, and I tell him I need to crash. That's why Hakim's my dawg. He doesn't even ask me why. Once I have all my gear on, I walk out into the kitchen. Desiree is flipping a grilled cheese sandwich.

I make sure my voice comes out nice and even when I start talking. "Yo, check your machine. I'm not mad. But I need all or nothing in my life, especially in times like the ones we're livin' in. You're clearly spreading yourself too thin to give me all. Later." I turn around and walk out of her apartment before I can see the look on her face.

CHAPTER 30

HUNTER

Between 9/11 and being hung up over a damn female, there's no way I can concentrate on this medical journal article. It's been a week since Osama Bin Laden went and fucked up every American's false sense of security, and shit has been absolutely unreal. I never thought our world could change so much in so short a time. New York especially. Since when do we smile at police officers? Since when do we look suspiciously at strangers on the subway? Since when do we put American flags in the windows of our high-rise apartments? Since this past Tuesday, I suppose.

School has definitely taken a back burner, and not even the professors or the attendings at the hospital seem to mind. A couple of my classmates lost friends in the towers, and one girl's dad died at the Pentagon. Somehow memorizing ACLS protocol doesn't seem so important when two thousand of your neighbors just got killed. This Indian guy at my school, Anant, kept us busy with escorting people who looked like they could be Middle Eastern on simple errands, like going grocery shopping. The news keeps hyping up the sense of unity that our city is feeling right now, but there's a lot of hate, too. For once, black folks aren't the only victims of racial profiling. Anyone with brown skin, jet-black hair, and an unusual name is susceptible to being cursed at, chased, or worse.

Things are beginning to feel a little bit normal again, though, which makes me feel guilty. I know it doesn't feel normal for the girl in my class without a father anymore. But we can't think about this stuff 24/7. We have lives to live and degrees to earn. So Robyn and I vowed in our first study session post-9/11 that terrorism would not be a topic of conversation. However, that still gives me room to rap with her about my girl problem. I give a couple of sighs, flip the pages loudly, and stare off into space so she can ask me what's wrong. Unfortunately, Robyn seems to be dealing with her own set of problems, biting the cap of her pen and reading the same page of her neuroanatomy book for a half hour.

Looks like I'm not going to get to vent my issues until I ask about hers, so I finally give in. "Everything okay, Robyn?"

She looks over at me like she forgot I was sitting at her kitchen table. "Oh, everything's fine. Just have a lot on my mind."

The dining chair is starting to feel a little hard under my ass, but we'd decided months ago that the kitchen was the best place in our apartments to study. Bright light, no TV, and no soft couch to make us sleepy. But since it looks like we're about to have a conversation that has nothing to do with medicine, I take her hand and drag her to the living room. She's so little that it takes no effort to practically toss her on the couch. "So talk to me," I say as I sit next to her.

She looks in my face, with her eyes all squinted, like she's trying to read if I'm someone who can be trusted.

Obviously satisfied with what she sees, she launches into a hypothetical. "What if you really liked someone and you thought they were the perfect match for you . . ." Wow. So far it sounds just like my problem with Desiree. "But before that person was trying to get with you, they had strong feelings for a close friend of yours?"

No, this definitely isn't my problem. "Break it down one more time?"

"Okay, I'll give you a fake example. Like, say you met a girl who was all that. We'll name her . . . Jane."

"Jane? Is she black? I don't know any black chicks named Jane."

"Fine. We'll name her Shaniqua. Anyhow, Shaniqua is your potential soul mate. But you soon find out that Shaniqua was once in love with Kevin. Or Tommy."

"Which one is it?"

"Good grief! Does that make a damn bit of difference?"

"I mean, I'd respect her more if she was digging Kevin. Tommy's my boy, but he's not too smooth, n'ah mean?"

"Okay, just forget it. Forget I brought it up." She crosses her arms and turns away from me. For a second, I feel like we're a married couple who just had a spat before bedtime.

"No, no, come on, Robyn. I was just messing with you. So did my boy hit it or not?"

After a moment of contemplation, Robyn faces me again. "No, they never slept together. She liked him, but he didn't like her back."

"Why not? I thought you said she was all that."

"Enough! Just answer the question!"

I can barely remember what the question is at this point, but I do my best, being that Robyn is getting heated, and I don't want her kicking me out before I get to tell my own sob story. "If they never hooked up, it doesn't seem like it would be an issue to me."

Robyn looks annoyed by my answer, like I somehow made her dilemma too simple. "But wouldn't you feel like second choice?" With everything that's been going on this past week, I'm shocked that she seems this concerned about a hypothetical question. Obviously, it has some relevance to something that's going on with her, and I'm sure she'll eventually fill me in on it. But in the meantime, I just want to wrap up this conversation so I can figure out if I need to forget about Desiree once and for all.

"Robyn, we're not teenagers anymore. Everybody has a past. You're the one always complaining about the shortage of good men. You can't let something that bruises your ego a little bit prevent you from pursuing something that could be pretty special." Finally, an answer that she seems to like. Her dimple pops out as she gives me an appreciative smile, and she gets up to return to her books in the kitchen.

"Not so fast. It's my turn." I'd decided that I was only telling the Desiree story once, and that Robyn was going to be my audience. I couldn't bring myself to tell my mom that we were just characters in Desiree's new novel, so I said something about her being too busy writing to go out with me anymore. Ma clearly didn't believe a word I said, but she's good about respecting my privacy when I need her to. So she just gave a "That's too bad, Doc," and changed the subject. As for my boys, the story was just too humiliating to share with them. The last thing Tommy needed to hear was that he knew the true identity of my love interest before I did. Robyn was my logical choice for a confidante. She's already seen me cry. What could be worse than that?

"What's up?" she asks, plopping back down on the couch.

So I begin at Kenny's Soul Food Restaurant, head

downtown for sushi, and walk the Brooklyn Bridge. I confess my reservations about dating someone who hasn't finished college. But then I'm won over despite our differences and begin to think that she could be the best thing for me. I even take Robyn to my bedroom with Alicia and describe how Desiree stays on my mind even while another girl lies in my bed. Finally, we head to Jimmy's Uptown, and that's when the shit hits the fan. When I get to the part where Tommy recognizes her to be someone other than the person I thought I knew, her mouth drops to the floor. Her look of absolute shock doesn't disappear even as we go to my mom's house for dinner, and I'm pushed away after a kiss on the sidewalk. She's still paralyzed with surprise as I explain that I've been used to model a character in a book.

As I break down the whole story to Robyn, it occurs to me that it all does kind of sound like a work of fiction. Maybe I shouldn't blame Desiree for trying to use material from her real life. But then I remind myself, that's not what she did. She invented a fake life just for the purposes of writing a story. It would be one thing if we hooked up, and she used parts of what happened in her writing. As long as she changed the names, I wouldn't give a shit. But to straight set me up the way she did? That was wrong. And then for me to go and call her house—that was a straight-up sucker move on my part. Rambling on her answering machine about all types of crap. And to add insult to injury, she hasn't even called me back!

"So I'm still waiting to hear from her" is my last sentence before I shut up and wait for Robyn to respond. I know my story is a lot to take, but she still looks like she saw a ghost or something. Instead of giving her opinion on the subject, she walks out of the living room and down the hallway. I hear her in her bedroom for a moment before she returns, with a photo album in her hand. It's a small, thick book that holds one picture on every page. Robyn doesn't look like she's going to say a single word, so I guess there's nothing left to do but to open it.

On the first page, Robyn is sitting at a desk in what looks to be her dorm room. The background shows that she's in the process of moving in, so I take it to be her first day of college. Yeah, she's definitely a freshman, with her baby face and old-school haircut. The next page displays two pictures: One is of her and another girl in front of some old-as-dirt building on Franklin's campus. The other is Robyn hugging her father, who looks like he's getting ready to leave after helping her get settled.

These pictures are cute and everything, but I'm getting a little impatient. "Uh, what do these have to do with—" But then I stop. Because the next page explains everything. Robyn and the same girl on the previous page are sitting on a twin bed, laughing with none other than Desiree Thomas. I start turning pages in the album like a zombie, just flipping to the next picture, not registering any emotion. Desiree is blazing in at least half of the pictures, looking just as pretty as she does now— maybe a little bit thicker and slightly younger, but still Desiree.

Robyn waits for me to get through the whole book before she speaks. "I had a feeling when you described what your Desiree looked like that she sounded way too much like mine . . . ," she says as she gently takes the album out of my hands. It's like she knows that I'm about to blow.

Sure enough, I'm out of my seat as soon as my hands are free. "What the fuck is this all about?" I practically shout.

"Watch your mouth, Greg. There's no need to be cursing at me." Her voice is calm, but her eyes are panicked.

"I'm not trying to hear any lectures, Robyn. You've been fucking with my head for months!"

"That's not true! I didn't even know that Desiree knew you! This is all news to me." She stands up and puts her hands on my arms.

I lift my arms to shake her off. "You expect me to believe that? It's just coincidence that she chooses me to experiment on?" My mind is running a mile a minute as I try to remember everything I've told Robyn in the past few months. I'll bet that as soon as she left my presence, she'd be on the phone with Desiree, reporting all the details.

"Yes! It's just coincidence."

"Okay, okay." I try to lower my voice, because I'm not the one who's going to come off like the crazy person in all this. I want this girl to admit that she's been playing the shit out of me. And losing my cool is not gonna help. "So I'm supposed to believe that. But it is true that Desiree is a close friend of yours, right?"

"Right." She looks relieved that I'm not yelling anymore, and she sits back down, leaning way back and staring at the ceiling.

"But you've never mentioned her to me before."

"I mentioned her when you said you were dating someone named Desiree. But you told me it wasn't the same person," she reminds me, sitting up straight.

This is true. But still, how could Robyn be completely innocent in all this? "We've been friends for almost a year, and you never told me you had a friend from college who lived in the area, who was a famous writer, none of that."

"Maybe if you ever gave me a chance to speak . . . ," she mumbles under her breath.

"What's that supposed to mean?"

"You're self-centered, Gregory. This conversation started with me asking you for advice. Look where it's gone." Suddenly, Robyn's voice is infused with all the anger that mine had a few minutes ago. "Every time I try to tell you anything, you manipulate the conversation back to you and your problems. Like your situation with Alicia or drama at the hospital . . ."

"Oh, okay. I'm sorry. Next time one of my patients gets hit by a bus, I'll make sure to let you talk about your man troubles first." This is unbelievable. I'm getting attacked when she's the one who was helping her girl run game on me.

"That's not fair, Greg! Of course, I wasn't talking about Manny. I'm talking about us, and the way we interact every day."

"Then why are you even friends with me if you feel like I'm some egotistical maniac?" She doesn't answer. "See, you just kept me around to get info for your shady homegirl!"

"Greg, I'm just as mad as you are right now. Desiree never told me what she was doing. I've been in the dark, just like you. And yes, sometimes I have issues with how self-centered you can be. But you're my boy. We're friends. You can trust me."

I think about it for a second. She sure does look like she's telling the truth. But being naïve and missing obvious signs—that's what got me in trouble in the first place. "Whatever, Robyn. I don't gotta trust a damn person but myself." And with a quick stop in the kitchen to grab my books, I'm out the door.

CHAPTER 31

DESIREE

Imani never comes to Jersey, a place she disdainfully refers to as "the armpit of New York" (which is especially ironic considering that she grew up in Pittsburgh, hardly a mecca of aesthetics and culture). So I feel extra bad that when she decides to venture to Weehawken, my place is a total mess. I hadn't expected any visitors, but I guess Imani could hear the catch in my throat when she called earlier and I told her that everything was okay.

But it's not. And my apartment is a reflection of that. Imani just drops her jacket on the already cluttered couch and shakes her head in pity at the sight of my living room. It's usually a space that I'm proud of: the oak wood entertainment system with the thirty-three-inch TV, the framed jackets of my favorite books on the wall, along with the laminated reviews of *No More Lies* from *Publishers Weekly* and *Black Issues Book Review*. My CD racks spiral almost to the ceiling, and the stereo speakers are mounted up high in the far corners (courtesy of my dad). But today, the CD racks are practically empty, due to the fact that the cases are strewn all over the lavender carpet. I'd been playing sad songs for the past eight days

straight, putting any tune having to do with death or loss
on heavy rotation. My video collection is similarly ransacked, as I've been watching and rewatching tragedies
like *Pearl Harbor* and *Titanic*. Seeing the poor on-screen
actors stuck on the Titanic and on the ship that gets overturned in Pearl Harbor makes me think of the people
who were in the World Trade Center or the Pentagon or
on those planes. And watching those heroines fall in love,
only to lose the men of their dreams, makes me feel a
little better about Jason walking out on me. At least he
lives a short drive away. He could be off fighting the
Japanese or floating lifeless in the ocean.

Imani walks left until she reaches my kitchen, where
dishes are piled sky-high in the sink. When she opens the
dishwasher to load them, she sees that it's already full. So
she turns the on switch and continues across the black-
and-white floor tiles, which are now black and gray from
neglect, down the hallway to my bedroom, where she
can't help but give a sorrowful "Mm, mm, mm" at the
sight. I haven't changed the sheets since Jason slept on
them. His cologne is still detectable on the pillowcase if
I bury my head into it deeply enough and sniff really
hard. I haven't made the bed since then, either, or vacuumed the rug, or removed the dirty pile of laundry from
the corner.

"I'm scared to see the bathroom," Imani mutters, rubbing her fingers across her forehead as if to stave off a
headache.

"The study is clean," I offer as I grab her hand and
drag her to the smaller room where I go to write. Motioning for her to sit in my comfy swivel chair, I slump
into a heap on the floor.

She stares at me for a while with a "whatever are we
going to do with you" expression. "So talk to me

about why you're living in filth and procrastinating on your deadline."

"What makes you think I'm procrastinating?" I retort defensively.

"From the way this room looks, it's obvious that you're not spending a damn bit of time in here." She swivels around to my desk and runs her finger across my laptop, leaving a dark streak behind. "Plus, your computer is ridiculously dusty."

I can hear the whiny tone in my voice as soon as I start talking, and I listen to my pitch getting more and more nasal over the course of my tantrum. "Give me a break, Imani. It's only been two weeks since September eleventh. Who in the world was being productive in the days after that? Then, once I started thawing out from that numbness, I had to devote a few days to trying to patch things up with Jason. I left messages, wrote what I considered to be very touching e-mails, even mailed him a picture of us that Paula sent me from her party. Nothing. So, of course, I had to take another few days to mourn his absence."

Imani rolls her eyes, but in her voice, I detect a hint of empathy. "So that brings you to the present, right? Now you can get back to work."

"Not quite. I was almost at functioning capacity last night, when I got a call from Robyn. She found out that I'd been using Hunter for book research. He accused her of being in on it. Man, did she cuss me out something good." I shiver at the memory of some of the insults she slung at me last night. It would have been easier had she stuck to the typical name-calling for which women are famous: bitch, whore, etc. But instead, she questioned our friendship, calling me a selfish liar whom she, apparently, can never trust again. Ouch.

"You did deserve a cuss-out for that, though."

Leave it to Imani to deliver the tough love, telling me something I already knew.

"No kidding. But now Robyn's not taking my calls, either. And with all this stuff on my mind, how am I supposed to focus on getting this manuscript finished?"

"Okay, Des. Here's what you're gonna do: sit down at the chair and channel all that sadness, fear, disappointment, and passion into your writing."

"Imani, my book's about a lawyer who falls for his secretary. I don't need all those emotions to write that story."

"Well, maybe you need a new story."

My chuckle turns into a snort. "Yeah, right. Write a whole new book in one month."

"It just takes some focus," she answers casually, like we're talking about making the perfect lasagna or something.

"What's this new story supposed to be about?" I know it's a crazy idea to start the book over at this point, but something about the thought is intriguing me a little.

"Why don't you stop fighting the inevitable? I've been with you when you do book signings and meet fans. What's their most popular question?"

"They wanna know what happened to Daphne," I grumble reluctantly.

"So why don't you give the readers what they want and write your sequel?"

"Isn't that just a cop-out? Using the same characters all over again?" The whine in my voice is back.

"There will be new characters and new experiences. Besides, Daphne has done a lot of growing over the past five years." She lifts my chin so that I have to meet her motherly gaze. "Haven't you?"

I'm not trying to get stuck in some Hallmark moment, especially when I finally managed to go several hours on end without weeping. Changing the subject is in order.

"Jason was only in my bed once, but it feels empty without him."

I can tell Imani's patience is wearing thin. "Girl, I like Jason for you, and I'm sorry it didn't work out, but you have no time to be crying in your pillow. Your deadline is one month from now. Get crackin'. And if things get real lonely at night, grab the bullet and go for yours."

"The bullet?"

"You're kidding, right? You go five years without sex, and you don't know about the bullet? It's a girl's best friend. Put the remote control on high—"

"I'm sorry, but did you say remote control?"

"Your birthday's coming up, right? I'll buy you one as an early present. You'll thank me."

I can just picture her and Sheila confidently strutting the aisles of the sex shop, debating which model and make would best suit their prudish friend. "Where is Sheila tonight, anyhow?"

"You know she was in San Francisco on business when flights shut down. So she's still out on the West Coast."

"It's been over a week now, though. She still can't get on a flight?"

"She can, but she's terrified. I mean, she's taken Flight 11 plenty of times. Two days before the attacks, even. She's actually thinking about taking a train. Or I may fly there so I can travel back with her."

"I feel like a total idiot. Here I am bitching about my trivial problems, and Sheila is stuck three thousand miles away from you because the world as we know it has fallen apart. It's crazy, isn't it? We'll never be able to get on planes again without fearing that some crazy assholes could fly us into some building."

"Don't feel bad. You're right. You shouldn't be feeling so sorry for yourself. But I shouldn't, either. We have temporary problems that will resolve themselves. Look,

I'm gonna head back to Harlem before it gets too late. I'm sure Sheila is trying to call me."

"When will you just step into the millennium and get a freakin' cell phone?"

"You know, I didn't think I would ever get one, but after last Tuesday, I can't imagine something awful happening and not being able to reach people quickly." She rises from my ergonomic office chair with a sigh, and pulls me from the floor with a strong right hand. "Do you wanna say a prayer before I go?"

I can feel my eyes getting larger at the sound of her question. This from the woman who has repeatedly said that she's not setting foot in a church until she's allowed to be married in one. "Since when are you religious?"

"You can believe in God without believing in religion. Now bow your head and close your eyes, heifer." I obediently follow her instructions. Still holding my right hand, she takes my left as well and begins her prayer.

"Dear Lord, please keep us and our loved ones safe in these troubled times. Not only safe from physical harm, but safe from living an existence wrapped in fear and anxiety. Allow those people whom we've hurt to forgive us, and allow us to forgive ourselves for mistakes that we've made and missteps that we've taken. Force us to see the joy in every day, and remind us when we feel like we have nothing that we still have more than most. And push us to exceed our own expectations, relying on the strength that You give us, and not the affection of anyone else, to achieve our goals." She finishes with an "amen" that sounds like a question, as if she is awaiting an answer from her congregation.

"Amen."

CHAPTER 32

HUNTER

I've daydreamed more than once about Desiree paying me an unexpected visit at my apartment, standing in my doorway, looking luscious and longing. But when I answer a knock at my door on Thursday evening and Desiree stands before me, all I can feel is disgust. For a second, I give serious thought to slamming the door in her face. Instead, I settle for giving her the ice grill while she gets up the nerve to say something.

"Can I come in?" she asks timidly, obviously not wanting to plead her case in the hallway.

Not altering my facial expression in the least, I take a small step back so she can squeeze past me into the living room. I'm glad she doesn't push her luck and take a seat. She just stands with her hands swinging at her sides, looking at the floor. She can stand there all night before I open my mouth.

It does feel like a quarter to forever before she speaks. Her voice sounds like it could break at any moment and that she could burst into tears. Actually, looking at her more closely, she looks close to the breaking point all over. Her gear is kind of crazy, and the skin around her

eyes is all puffy. I have a feeling that Desiree has been
dealing with more than just the drama with me. "Hunter,
I'm not here to apologize. Not that I don't feel more
sorry than you know. But I'm not going to waste your
time by insisting that you forgive me for stuff that may
very well be unforgivable."

I don't know how to feel about that one. On one
hand, it feels good to hear her acknowledge how jacked
up her whole plot was. But at the same time, she could
just be too lazy to put in the serious work it would take
for me to move past what she did. "So why are you here
then?"

"Robyn." I give a tired sigh at the sound of her name.
Learning that Robyn was in on the whole scheme hurt
more than Desiree's betrayal. I always presumed that
Robyn would be in my corner, that we were boys. Well,
not quite boys, but real good friends.

"Hunter, when I met you at Kenny's, I had no idea
who you were. When you said you went to Columbia, I
wondered if you might know Robyn, but y'all aren't even
the same year in school. I didn't think you would be
tight. Robyn and I haven't been in great touch lately, so
the first time I learned you two were friends is when you
mentioned her on our second date. She never knew
about what was going on. Not until you told her the
other night."

Why I would take a self-proclaimed liar at her word is
beyond me, but I do. More than Desiree's sincerity, I
think what makes me believe her is the fact that Robyn
told the same story. And Robyn has never given me a
reason to distrust her. I've confided in her about my
booty calls, my career fears, and even shared a few embarrassing childhood anecdotes. Never have I heard a
single tale repeated in the greater Columbia community.
Of course, I'd like to think that I've done the same for

her, serving as her sounding board and keeping her secrets. But what she said Tuesday night was still bothering me. I guess I did make our interaction about me and my issues 90 percent of the time. I'll have to do a better job with that.

"That's cool. I'll rap with Robyn and straighten things out."

Desiree looks surprisingly relieved, like when your ears pop hours after you get off a plane, and everything suddenly sounds louder and clearer. "Great." Here is where she should be walking the five feet back to the door and taking her ass home, but she's rooted in place, with an awkward smile on her face. That's when I know that she's only half satisfied. Though she may have said otherwise, Desiree wants to be forgiven. She's hoping to leave having resolved things between me and Robyn, and also between me and her. Witnessing the silly grin and the nervous way she's shifting her weight from one leg to the other, I can't help but remember Tanya Jackson. And thinking back on what went down with Tanya, it's very unlikely that I'll be able to hold a grudge against Desiree.

When I was nine years old, Ma had just gotten her job working as a secretary for the bigwigs downtown, so she signed me up for an afterschool program. It was great for the first week. The boys pretty much spent the hours playing kickball, basketball, and dodgeball, which was fine with me. Anything where I got to run around was a treat. I was never the best shot or the farthest thrower or kicker, but I was always fast. So making friends at the program wasn't a problem.

We were in the middle of a close game of kickball when my mom came to pick me up one day. I wanted to be the one to win the game for my team before I had to leave, and I also wanted to show off a little bit in front of my mother. So I tried to slide into home plate (which was really just a chalk square in the dirt) just as the kid was trying to catch the big, white, bouncy ball to get me out. Our feet got tangled, and my ankle got sprained real bad.

That's how I became friends with Tanya Jackson. We spent those weeks that I couldn't play any sports making papier-mâché animals inside the rec center. As we dipped newspaper in gooey brown paste, we dipped into each other's lives, trading stories about her teenaged brother, who was always picking on her, and my little sister, whom I swore was the most annoying person on the planet. Sometimes we talked about other kids in the afterschool program. *Joanne wears fake Adidas sneakers; TayShawn picks his nose and wipes it on his clothes; Nikia always be asking people for some of their candy, but when she got Sour Patch Kids, she don't ever be sharing.*

One day, when our papier-mâché creations were drying, we went outside to watch a game of dodgeball. Tyrell was trying to act all big and bad, as usual, throwing the ball mad hard and laughing when people complained about how it stung when they got hit. I noticed Tanya giving him a weird look, which I interpreted to be annoyance. Tyrell wasn't one of my favorite people, either, so I was all too glad to share a tidbit. "Ty pretends to be all tough, but he's in my class at school. The other day, his pen leaked and got on his pants, and he started crying, talking about how his momma was gonna tear him up if he stained up his clothes."

Tanya giggled, and even though her teeth were kinda crooked, she looked real cute at that moment. So I smiled my pre-braces crooked-ass teeth right back, and I thought we were sharing a nice little PG-rated moment when Tyrell stopped the game by holding the ball in his hand and pointing over to us. "Look, y'all! Gregory and Tanya sitting in a tree—"

"Shut up, stupid!" I yelled back and hobbled back into the rec center.

The next day, a crowd of kids encircled us as Tyrell confronted me about the story I had told to Tanya about him crying at school. Turns out that Tanya, the little traitor, had a crush on him and had used my story as a way to break the ice and start a conversation. And there I was, about to get my crippled butt kicked because of it. Luckily, Tyrell's bark was worse than his bite, because when he pushed me and I pushed him back, he noticed that my push sent him farther into the throng of onlookers than his had me. Judging that he might not win the fight, he bowed out, mumbling about how he'd get me once my ankle healed.

The next day, Tanya tried to come up in my face, asking what color we should paint the papier-mâché dinosaur, like nothing had happened. I gave her the silent treatment for a while, but it didn't take long before I let her giggles get to me. We were laughing together again by the time my mom came and scooped me that afternoon. That's my problem. It's hard for me to carry a grudge, especially when the person begging my forgiveness is a woman with a pretty smile.

So I can only laugh at my own weakness as I offer Desiree a seat on the couch. It almost seems silly not to. Once we start talking about 9/11, and she asks me about how Manny is doing, it kind of puts my pain into perspective. Talking about Manny makes me think of how supportive Robyn was the day he got hurt, and I want to ask Desiree if she's spoken to her. It feels weird, though, changing the subject after talking about major tragedies, like the World Trade Center or the paralysis of a thirteen-year-old kid. No matter how long you've been talking about it, you feel guilty for not talking about it more. It's as if moving on to a lighter topic signifies that you haven't respected the gravity of the catastrophe, like you're dismissing it. Still, there are only so many clichéd ways to state that life is unpredictable, and most of the time it sucks.

"So have you worked things out with your girl?" I ask at last.

She pauses, looking a bit defeated before forcing a cheerful expression. "Women take time. I'm courting her right now."

"Oh, I see. Making up with Robyn requires bouquets of flowers and heartfelt letters. Meanwhile, I'm taken care of in one visit, huh?"

She looks worried that I'm genuinely offended, and that all the progress we've made in the past half hour could be thrown out the window. But my laugh puts her at ease again. Chilling out with Desiree like this is pretty cool, but I can't say that I feel the same spark I felt in the past. And I don't think it's just because she's looking kinda torn up today. Maybe my obsession with Desiree was more about me than it was about her. She happened to come along at a time when I needed to be swept up in something. Things with Alicia were playing like a scratched-up CD, and I needed a reason to hit STOP.

"Desiree, about that message I left you, talking about the kiss and everything . . ."

"Yeah, about that. Hunter, I think you're incredible. But I have feelings for someone else, and even though that's not really going so well right now—"

"Enough, enough! I get the drift. I don't need a live and in-person pity speech. The fact that you never called me back sent the message loud and clear." She gives a nod of understanding, while I can't help but wonder who this person is that she's feeling. Probably the cat she was dancing with at Jimmy's. I hope she's not one of these successful chicks who fall for the hard-knock-life homies who only serve to bring her down. Maybe I'll get a better sense of who she is once I read her novel.

"So how's your masterpiece coming along?"

She lets out a long sigh—the type that a tired mom might give when being asked about her mischievous toddler. "The good news is that I'm really happy with the story line I have mapped out, and I'm falling head over heels in love with my characters. The bad news is that I had to start all over to make that happen."

"Well, I'd better get to read this book. And I don't wanna wait till it's on the shelves, either."

"That's fine, but anyone who reads the first draft has to give feedback."

"Not a problem. I want an acknowledgement, too."

"Done."

"And 10 percent."

"Now you're pushing it." I watch the beauty come back to her face as we share a laugh. Being friends with her might take some adjustment, but if I could paint papier-mâché with the Benedict Arnold of afterschool programs, I think I can be cool with Desiree.

CHAPTER 33

DESIREE

I know my body. My period lasts five days: one heavy, two medium, one light, one drip. One week after it ends, my breasts swell about half a cup size. My freshman year of college, I used to wear all my low-cut tops during those few days. Two days before the end of my cycle, my chest gets tender, and it hurts when I run, even with a bra on. And on the twenty-eighth night, the cycle repeats itself.

Which is why as I sit on the toilet on the thirtieth morning, staring at the unblemished crotch of my cotton panties, I'm in a mild state of panic.

I know that most people wouldn't view being one day late as cause for alarm, but it does seem like an odd co-incidence. In the five years that I had no chance of get-ting pregnant, I was right on schedule without fail. Now, the first month that I do have sex, the shit just doesn't want to arrive on time.

As I go about my morning routine, I try to rationalize why my body may be off track this month. For the past couple weeks, I haven't been to the gym, which is the longest I've gone without working out in years. Could that disrupt my internal pattern? After I finish brushing my teeth and washing my face, I do a few sit-ups on my bed to try and get the juices flowing.

Over a bowl of cereal, I sit at my kitchen table, reviewing the play-by-play with Jason in my head. That night, I was definitely representin' in the purple cleavage dress, which means it was that time in my cycle when my eggs were just begging to be fertilized. Of course, the obvious counterargument to this line of reasoning is that Jason was shielded in latex before I even had to ask. We were completely responsible. But there is such a thing as a margin of error. Can you always feel when the condom breaks? Or what if the condom sat so long on the gas station shelf that it lost all of its . . . resilience? It's not like we were checking the expiration date on the package or anything.

Still, what are the chances? It's much more likely that I'm a little late than a little pregnant. Although I do believe myself to be one fertile mama. The one time I let myself give in to that "just let me put it in halfway to see how it feels" bullshit my freshman year, I suffered the consequences.

And it's because of that mistake five years ago that I'm standing in the shower, second-guessing my rational side. I stare at my stomach, which suddenly looks more rounded than usual. *Don't be stupid, Des. You just ate breakfast, and your tummy always sticks out right after a meal. Besides, your body wouldn't look any different so early in the pregnancy, anyway.* One thing that *is* noticeable early on is an increased appetite. I almost hyperventilate in the steamy tiled tub as I remember the whole pizza from Papa John's that I had delivered last night. Polished it off in twenty minutes. But it's not like it was a large or anything.

I dry off from the shower, put on a pair of period

panties (positive thinking never hurt anybody), a T-shirt, and shorts. Lying on the bed, I stare at the ceiling, wondering what Jason would say if I told him I was pregnant. What was it he had said about Nailah? That he and Monique loved each other too much not to have her? I doubt he feels that way about me. He wouldn't let an ambiguous message from Hunter scare him away if he were in love.

But it really doesn't matter what he'd say, because I'll be damned if I'd allow him to affect my decision. I made a vow in a clinic on April Fools' Day, 1996, that I would never, ever repeat that experience. I was there by myself, having kept my shame a secret from everyone except Trevor, who responded to the news with the clichéd "And how do I even know it's mine?" He acted like he was doing me a favor by writing me a check and never calling me again. I sat in that waiting room, part of the assembly line of women old and young, white and black, married and single, rich and poor, with our only common bond being an overwhelming sense of regret. Lying on that cold stretcher, with my feet in stirrups, with the sound of that horrible vacuum and the casual conversation of the doctor and nurses mixing together to form an environment of absolute torture. That day is why I promised myself that I would never again give myself to someone whom I couldn't trust. And even though Jason's mad as hell at me right now, I do think I could trust him to be supportive.

God, what would my parents say? *Who is this guy? Oh, he owns a gym. Where did he go to school? He didn't. How did you meet him? He lives in the brownstone next to Imani. How did he get the money for his gym and his house? No idea. And is he ready to be a father? Sure. I mean, he already is. And what's his relationship with that child's mother? He is very close to her. Then why aren't they together? She's married. How long has she been married? Since their daughter was two. And what was Jason doing that he couldn't step up and marry her himself? No idea.*

But they'd eventually soften, especially when they saw their first grandchild. I saw an old picture of Jason, and he was a gorgeous kid. I'm sure a baby boy would be his spitting image. And a girl—well, she'd be light-skinned, with long hair and possibly green eyes. Going through life pretending not to see the hungry looks of men and the angry stares of women. The she-thinks-she's-cutes before she even speaks. Feeling like a modern-day tragic mulatto when she's not even biracial. Yeah, I hope it's a boy.

Lying on my back very still, I lift my T-shirt and put a hand on my stomach, trying to feel a heartbeat. I know it's too early for that, but I'm craving some kind of definitive proof.

Springing from my bed, I grab my keys and wallet from my dresser, mash my feet into a pair of flip-flops, and head out the door. Driving to the grocery store down the street, buying a pregnancy test, and going back home—it all seems to happen outside of me, like I'm watching myself run this errand. I appear calm and composed, but my insides are doing somersaults, which I take as another possible sign of life. Could the baby be kicking already? I know I'm beyond irrational, but that knowledge doesn't stop my crazy thoughts.

Back home in my bathroom, still humid from the shower, I read the box. Says you can take it as early as the day you miss your period. I unwrap everything carefully, like it's a science experiment. That's when I realize I can't pee. My bladder is completely empty. I run warm water from the sink over my hand, a trick I learned at a sixth-grade slumber party. Works like a charm. I squat over the toilet and manage to squeeze a few drops onto the "wand," as it's called on the box. They make it sound like a fairy tale: if you hold the wand and say "presto," you won't be pregnant after all. It's kind of funny how so many things connected to sex are totally unglamorous. Pregnancy tests, used condoms, STDs, pills, diaphragms, vasectomies, the list goes on. I set the wand on the sink and wait.

All at once, I'm eighteen again, more frightened than I've ever been, staring at the plastic stick like it's a crystal ball. Hoping that the test will give me an extension on my innocence. Making deals with God in those few minutes that I will never be irresponsible again. Promising that if I could just be allowed a few more years before I got pregnant, I would be the best mother the world had ever seen.

But today, a month before I turn twenty-four, when I'm financially secure, responsible, and dying for someone to love, the crystal ball says no. *There is no life growing inside of you. You're merely stressed. Stressed out that your book deadline is in three weeks, and your boyfriend left you, and you barely like the person you've become.*

I put the toilet-seat lid down, sit on it, and allow the tears to flow.

CHAPTER 34

JASON

Every once in a while, I'm grateful to own a car in New York. Grocery shopping is one of those times. It's unnatural to have your groceries delivered. And it's not fun to have to cart your food down the sidewalk in one of those wheely things. So even though driving up 125th to Pathmark was a bitch, with mad heads double-parked and several buses threatening to cut my life short, it's nice knowing that I can buy as much as I want without stressing it.

I never write shopping lists. When I see brothers in the supermarket, glancing at their small square of paper, checking off items as they place them in their carts, I can't help but think it's a little gay. It ain't that hard to remember that when you went to make yourself a bowl of cereal, there wasn't any milk. My shopping style is to walk the aisles, pick up the things that I like when they're on sale, and remember the necessities. My stroll is a little crippled today because of how crowded this place is. Usually, I shop on a weekday morning, when I pretty much have the store to myself, sharing it with a few elderly women and the occasional twenty-something female, who's staring at me, most likely wondering why I ain't at work. I never bother trying to explain.

But Sundays are a different story. Everybody's picking up their stash for the week, and everybody has their kids with them. "Ma! Lemme get them Frosted Flakes," begs an overweight kid in the cereal aisle as his mother walks briskly about fifteen feet ahead of him. "Boy, you best pick up them corn flakes and keep walking. That's why you got so much baby fat on you. All that sugar." His mother doesn't even look back as she answers, tending to the toddler riding in the cart she's pushing. Blubber boy is unfazed, picking up the Frosted Flakes *and* the corn flakes, probably scheming to make one last plea at the register.

I smile. Everything changes when you have kids. The food you keep in your crib is different. The way you plan your time is different. The way you see yourself is different. Nailah is what brings me shopping today in the first place. Monique and Andre are taking a trip to visit Dre's family in North Carolina, knowing that this might be their last chance to get away before the baby comes. So I get my girl for an entire week. Between my job and her kindergarten schedule, we weren't gonna have much quality time, so I took the week off. That way, we can hit up the children's museum on the Upper West Side, spend an afternoon in Central Park, and maybe even take a drive down to Six Flags, although I need to check with Mo to see if Nailah might still be too young to really enjoy the amusement park thing.

Figuring that Cinnamon Life is a happy medium between sweet and healthy, I grab a box from the shelf before moving on to the juice section. Lately, I've been buying juice boxes for Nailah so that she can help herself when she's thirsty. Monique and I agree that teaching our daughter independence is key. But sometimes it's so tempting to spoil the hell outta her, especially when I look into her eyes (dark, with long lashes like Monique's, and shaped like mine) as she asks for a new doll or another cookie. But I remember the one thing my mom did for me before she shipped me and my brother to Jersey, and that was to make us self-sufficient. And with my aunt's long hours as a nurse, and my uncle's reluctance to be a father figure, I needed that trait more than anything.

Part of me knows that Nailah will never have to duplicate my childhood. Between Monique, Andre, Mo's parents, Dre's parents, and me, she will never lack the guidance that I missed out on. And that's what I remind myself when I give in to her high-pitched requests, slipping her an extra cookie or surprising her with a brand-new Barbie. Monique shakes her head when she sees me doing it, saying in her gentlest voice, "Stop trying to make up for lost time, Jay." I always brush off her comment, but I know she's right. A lot of my desire to give Nailah the world comes out of the fact that I missed her first two years.

I can count the number of times I saw Nailah while I was locked up. Monique brought her regularly at first, but after a while I told her to stop. I hated it—the guards watching my tears fall on Nailah's blanket, being told that my time with her was up, living in fear that Nailah might one day remember her early days of visiting Daddy in prison. I told myself that my daughter would be okay not knowing me at first, because once I got out, there wouldn't be a day that went by where we wouldn't be together. That was when I was holding out hope that Monique and I would pick up where we left off. I'd already told her to move on, but I couldn't stop my fantasy of the three of us being a family.

Then I found out about Monique's new man. Apparently,

things between her and the corporate brother were getting serious. More than the hurt of losing Monique as my girl, it killed me to think that Andre was getting to play house with my daughter. And while the transition went better than expected once I entered Nailah's life, I still feel guilty about that period of time where Dre got to be more of a dad than I did. Which is why I drop some coloring books into my shopping cart as I pass a kiddie display at the front of the store.

I'm second in line at the register when I realize that I forgot milk and eggs. Shit. Maybe keeping a grocery list isn't so wack after all. I'm huffing and puffing all the way to the refrigerated aisle at the back of the store. My hand is on the 2 percent gallon when I feel someone walk up behind me. "Hi, Jason."

Okay, corny or not, I'm writing out that damn grocery list from now on. Because I had to go and forget two of the main items that I needed, I'm stuck having a conversation with Imani. Not that I don't like the woman, but I've been successfully dodging her since shit with Desiree went bad. "What's goin' on?"

"Not too much," she says cheerily. "Just tryin' to pick up some ingredients for my celebratory dinner with Sheila tonight." She swings the basket of vegetables in her hand, and her dreads swing right along with it.

"What's the occasion?" I feel obligated to ask.

As she explains to me how Sheila just arrived back from the West Coast today, stuck there since September 11th, mostly due to fear, I feel bad about dodging Imani these past couple weeks. She has her own shit to worry about, and getting in my biz with Des is the last thing she's interested in doing. "I'm real glad to hear she's back safe and sound. Tell her I said whassup."

"Will do. So what about you?"

"Oh, I'm just doing some shopping for the week."

"No, that's not what I meant. What about you? When are *you* gonna have a nice reconciliatory dinner with Desiree?"

Guess I jumped the gun, thinking that Imani wasn't gonna butt in. I manage a smile, which surprises me, since her question really pisses me off. This ain't no lovers' spat that me and Des are in. The shit is over. And the way she suggested that we just need to kiss and make up is annoying. "Chill with all that, Imani."

I managed to request a change of subject in a pretty relaxed tone of voice, but she answers me like I just told her to fuck off. "So I take it that means never? You're never gonna get in touch with her?"

You might think you know me, but you don't. Once I'm done with people, I'm done. My own brother betrayed me, and I ain't spoken to him since. If you have my back, I'll do anything for you. But try to play me like a fool, and I ain't stickin' around to let you do it twice. It's what I want to say, but I know that will only bring on more drama. "I think that's between me and her, don't you?"

"Not when she's crying on *my* shoulder about it." The cheery tone she had earlier has been replaced with 100 percent attitude.

Whatever. Clearly, Imani is exaggerating the situation. Desiree wouldn't be shedding any tears over me. She's tough, like I am, and she might be upset that she messed things up, but she ain't boo-hooin' to her girls about it. "She'll be fine."

Imani sets down her basket and puts her hands on her hips. "It took her three hundred pages and five years to 'get over it' the last time a man broke her heart. What makes you think she'll do better this time around?"

Monique's words come floating back to me. *Jay, do you think her novel was a true story?* As usual, Mo's wisdom reveals itself. For a second, I feel myself softening, remembering what happened to Daphne in the story. Remembering the love she felt, the way her man used it to his advantage, and the way he threw her away when they came to a bump in the road. But at the same time, if all that really went down with Des back in college, then she should have learned by now to appreciate a man who's trying to do right by her. She shouldn't have been lying about dude at Jimmy's being Robyn's friend, getting all mad when I suggested that he hit it, when they were clearly messing around the whole time we were getting to know each other. My body tenses up again. "Well, she does have a book deadline coming up. Maybe this will make a good story."

Imani looks at me like she can't believe it's really me she's talking to. "I never thought you were this cold." I think I even see her shudder.

Like I said, you don't know me. "Don't put this shit on my shoulders. I wasn't the one who lied about some other nigga." Hunter. How she gonna like me and be kissing on that bitch-ass herb? It's like Monique choosing Andre after being with me, only worse. At least I respect Andre as a man.

I'm ready for Imani to come back at me something fierce, but instead, she's studying the contents of my shopping cart. Juice boxes, kiddie cereal, and children's books are interspersed with bread, meat, and potatoes. She looks me up and down, like she's seeing me for the first time. "Looks like you haven't been all that honest, either, Jason."

I'm glad she walks away after that, because there really isn't shit I can say. I wonder why Desiree didn't tell Imani that I have a daughter. Maybe she thought Imani already knew, being that she lives right next door. Funny how I never bump into her when I have Nailah with me. But that's beside the point, because what Imani said was true. I told Desiree that I'm a father, but I never told her the full truth about me. I haven't lied, but I haven't been up front, either.

Damn. I'd been doing well keeping Desiree out of my head—putting in extra hours at the gym, reading all the books I'd been putting off because they were too long, and making some changes to the apartment that I'd been meaning to do. I couldn't even chill with Nailah that much because Monique was trying to squeeze in all types of extra time with her before her vacation. So instead, I sat in Nailah's bedroom, painted her book-shelf, and put a couple more shelves on the wall. For a four-year-old, the girl requires mad storage space.

The past two weeks, since I walked out of Desiree's condo, I've really missed the company of my homies from the old hood. When I got out of the joint, I vowed that I wasn't hanging with none of my boys anymore. Some of them were real good people who just got caught up in the game, like I had. But still, I couldn't take any chances. The only exception is Hakim, who used to sell all types of bootleg items when we were teenagers, making some nice change for himself. But he never got caught up in nothing too serious, and he managed to get out of Newark to get an associate's degree. I was all too glad to hire him at the gym. His business skills come from the streets and the books. Still, Hakim can't be knowing all my business. He has a big-ass mouth, and if I told him exactly why I had to sleep on his couch the night I walked out on Desiree, all of my employees would know the next day.

Thinking about Desiree being able to "cry" on Imani's shoulder really makes me kinda jealous. I wish there was someone I could rap with about what's going on in my head. Was I crazy to think this chick could be my soul mate? I wouldn't mind some feedback on that. There were a couple of soul-mate signs, which may have just been odd coincidences. Like the way she keeps a couple of gallons of water in her fridge and fills little water bottles with them to take on the go. Or the way she insists on paying people by giving them money in their hands instead of putting the cash on the table. Or the way she always smiles when she sees little kids being bad. All things I do, too.

I haven't even filled Monique in on what went down. I can't tell her how much I miss Desiree every moment I'm awake. I can't talk about how I'd been dreaming about watching *The Lion King* on the couch with Desiree and Nailah, all cuddled up like a family. That's not stuff Monique needs to hear.

As I slowly push the cart back to the checkout, I wonder if I made the right decision, ignoring Desiree's phone calls. By the time I start stacking my groceries on the conveyor belt, I convince myself that I did. Desiree opened me up too much for my own good. Made me want to bare my soul. Soon I'd be telling her things that no one ever needed to hear about. Putting on muscles in prison so I could fight off guys who had beef with Jamal and wanted to take it out on me. Meeting a dude in the library who seemed to be cool, relieved there was someone I could talk books with, only to have him ask me if I would let him "suck me off" sometime. Being grateful for the glass between me and Monique when I first saw that sparkly diamond ring on her finger, scared that I might break her hand, trying to take it off. Yeah, it's better off that I leave her with the image of who she thinks I am—the guy in the Armani suit, with nothing to hide but his daughter's stash of Barbies.

CHAPTER 35

DESIREE

"Deep condition, Mami?" The woman at the Dominican hair shop, with huge hips and jeans that look like they were painted on her body, stands over me as my neck tilts back awkwardly into the sink.

"Yes, please."

"Five dollar extra," she reminds me, although I come to get my hair washed here once a week, usually by her.

"That's okay," I respond automatically, trying to get comfortable as the water runs through my scalp and a few errant streams hit my ears and eyes.

"Sorry, Mami," my shampoo woman says instinctually before launching into a lightning-fast, animated conversation in Spanish with a younger girl setting hair in one of the styling chairs.

Once she finishes slathering palmfuls of thick beige cream through my hair, she piles the dripping mass on top of my head, surrounds it with a plastic shower cap, and leads me to the hooded dryers. This is the point in the process each week where I marvel at the steps that black women go through for beauty's sake.

Next to me, I notice that the feet in the chair are

swinging in the air, as opposed to being planted firmly on the floor like mine. I look over to see a girl, about four years old, with skin the color of a Dove Bar—the ice cream, not the soap—balancing a head full of hard plastic rollers. She wears a flowered summer dress that reaches her ankles, and sandals on her feet, which display her pink painted toenails. She squints and squirms under the heat. A woman, whom I guess to be her mother, quite the diva herself, walks over to the child, comforting her with assurances of how beautiful she'll look. Tears brim in the little one's eyes.

If you were mine, I'd never make you endure this. You were beautiful before they tugged at your tender scalp and sat you under that instrument of torture. But she's not mine. Mine would be about her age now, a little older. I do that a lot: calculate the age of my would-be child, wondering how my life would be now had I chosen differently. Lately, I've been picturing my son or daughter playing in a big open field with Nailah. I don't know what either child looks like, but I see their bright clothes and little hands.

I've been doing what Imani told me. Every time I feel like this, on the verge of exploding with sadness, I run to my laptop. My novel is making progress. So much so that I managed to send quite a few chapters to Paula, who said the story read so well that she was sure the editors wouldn't mind that it wasn't told from the male point of view, after all. Her renewed faith in me got me a gig at an authors' panel today at Barnes & Noble downtown. Bebe Moore Campbell, Diane McKinney-Whetstone, and me. I know I'm not on their level, but Paula says I pull in the younger demographic. My book is like Dr. Seuss next to their stuff. Actually, I need to stop selling myself short. People can sniff your confidence from a mile away, and if these folks coming to hear us speak today don't hear my excitement about this new project, I can kiss my best-seller dreams good-bye.

I didn't know I was going to do it until I heard the words coming out. Each of us was supposed to give a ten-minute talk about anything related to our experiences as novelists. I usually talk about the process of putting a story together, the importance of writing daily, that kind of thing. But today something else entirely escapes my lips. My voice is composed, and my sentences flow as clearly as spring water, but I only catch fragments of my own story.

"Daphne is based on me—my experiences, my flaws, my fears. . . ."

"My first real boyfriend preyed on my insecurities. Though he never hit me, the way that Troy abused Daphne, I felt emotionally battered by the end of it all."

"Putting my pain to good use was the only thing that kept me sane."

One side of my brain is screaming for me to stop talking. *This is too personal. These strangers don't need to know all your business!* But as I make eye contact with the fifty people in the room, most of whom are women, their understanding nods push me to go on.

Surprisingly, when it's Diane McKinney-Whetstone's turn to speak, she echoes my sentiments, talking about how she relied on her hometown of Philadelphia and her alma mater, the University of Pennsylvania, to shape the events in *Blues Dancing*. Bebe Moore Campbell talks about the same thing—how she often chooses to write about events that affected her personally, like the L.A. riots in *Brothers and Sisters*. I feel a weight being lifted off me, hearing these women whom I admire say that all fiction writers use what they've experienced to shape their stories.

During the Q&A, only two questions are for me. The first is whether I know who's playing Daphne in the movie version of *No More Lies*. Paula told me that when you sell the rights to your book, you pretty much lose any say in what happens after that, so I've tried not to think too much about how the movie will be cast and what changes will be made. I decide to deflect the question with humor. "I don't know who'll play Daphne. Maybe I should take some acting lessons and play her myself!" Good-humored chuckles rise from the crowd.

The second person, one of the few males in the crowd, asks what my new book is about. I'd been so busy telling these people my life story, I forgot to plug the new novel. "It started off as a book from a male point of view. But I realized I wasn't ready for that. I still don't understand men enough to think like them!" Soft laughter. "So I'm rediscovering Daphne, five years later."

"A sequel?" he askes. "In an interview a while back, you said you'd never write one." Wow. Who knew people paid attention to anything I said?

"Well, in that case, we'll call it a companion book instead. There are a lot of new faces, and Daphne is a very different woman this time around." I smile, knowing that Imani would be proud.

A lot of readers have brought their worn and tattered copies of *No More Lies* with them to be signed. I can't believe it's been almost two years since my debut novel went to print. It's never ceased to amaze me how many women still read and reread the story, and watching them clutch their copies like a Bible today just revs me up to finish my sophomore work. I've grown a lot as a writer since my first effort, with my freelance work, and reading so many inspiring classic and contemporary writers. And I've grown a lot as a person too, letting love back into my life and facing my issues.

It's the closest I've gotten to contentment since September 11th as I autograph books for the line of people standing in front of the table where I'm sitting. Wishing I had more time to converse with each person, I'm forced to rush, barely able to get their name and sign my own.

I'm writing the date on the title page of a reader's copy when she says, "I loved your book."

Something about her voice makes me look up. It's soft but really sincere. She's about my age, and she continues talking when we make eye contact. "Especially Daphne. She is so . . . complicated. It makes her real to me. And now that I'm hearing that it's based on your life, I feel like I already know you."

"Thank you. So much." I want to say more, that compliments like hers are the reason I'm still trying to make a career out of what I'm doing. Or that putting my drama on public display seems a lot less scary when you hear that people are feeling you. But I try to convey it all in my smile.

"I can't wait for the next one," she says cheerily.

I'm about to tell her to expect it in bookstores soon, but who knows what my editors will think about my entirely new draft. Better hold my tongue. "To whom should I make this out?" I ask, my pen poised in the air.

"To Nailah. I want my daughter to read this someday." My pen freezes, and my stomach seizes into knots. I know immediately who is standing in front of me, and I'm scared to look at her again. But when I finally get the guts to meet the eyes of Jason's ex, I'm pleasantly surprised by her expression. It's just as friendly as before. Monique's face is soft and familiar, like that of your favorite cousin.

"I know you have a few more books to sign," she says

politely. "Do you want to grab a cup of coffee or something afterward?"

I force out a "sure" before returning to the task at hand, grateful for the distraction. While I'm autographing the last few copies of *No More Lies*, my mind is consumed by what this woman would've come here to talk to me about.

As Monique stands in front of me in line at Starbucks, I finally get a chance to steal a long look at her from the neck down. She is wearing black pants that fit her at the waist and fall loosely down her leg, square-toed black pumps, and a white ribbed turtleneck with a black sweater coat over it. A classic outfit that is truly ageless. Her face has a baby roundness, but her composure is well beyond her years. This is Jason's first love. And from the way she looks at me, with a sad/happy nostalgia for what they once had, I know she still does love him, simply allowing her love to change form. Kind of how you wake up one day and the moon is full. You hadn't noticed it as it grew and grew, but suddenly, there it was. I wonder if she marvels at where she is right now— having coffee with Jason's most recent girlfriend while their child is at kindergarten.

I order a hot chocolate and can barely believe how fast autumn has descended on the city. Seems like just the other day it was summertime, and I couldn't get enough of the iced vanilla chais. Summertime, when Jason's eyes changed shades in the sun and . . .

"Should we do the small talk thing, or do we just jump right in?" Monique speaks our first words since we entered the coffee shop.

"I think I'm a little too uncomfortable for small talk, but I could give it a shot."

"Why are you uncomfortable?" she asks, leaning in closer.

It's such a silly question that I kind of throw my hands to either side of me, as if to say, "Take your pick." I think she's perfectly aware that the question requires no answer, but she looks at me expectantly despite the rhetorical implication. I realize that she simply used the question as a springboard to start the dialogue.

"It's a little awkward sitting here with Jason's ex-girlfriend." I wonder if those were the right words. Did "ex-girlfriend" trivialize what they had? After all, they have a child together. But I didn't want to say "baby's mother," considering the ghetto-fabulous associations that the term has assumed. "First love" suggests that Jason had others, but "only love" sounds so absolute.

"So what did he tell you?" she asks.

"Not much. I know that you and Jason were high-school sweethearts. And I know about Nailah." Saying out loud the few facts that Jason revealed on the last evening we were together brings everything back. The intensity of the night, the shock of the morning, the anger of late afternoon. "Maybe if I hadn't messed everything up, I would've learned more."

She shakes her head gently, which makes me feel relieved. It's a small gesture that assures me she came in peace. And maybe I'm reading too much into it, but I also get the feeling that she doesn't think I'm the only one to blame.

"I was at Jason's last night, picking up Nailah. I asked him how you were doing. He said that you weren't seeing each other anymore and hadn't been for three weeks. When I asked him why, first he was all short with me."

"What did he say exactly?"

She looks embarrassed by the answer she has to give. "In his words, 'We chilled; she cheated; I jetted.'"

His words sting more than a little bit, but Monique presses on before I can fully feel their impact. "But then I bugged him for details, and it became clear to me that while you may not have been completely honest, there was no real cheating involved."

It's tripping me out that Monique actually had a conversation with Jason, defending me, and I can't for the life of me figure out why. "Did you say that to him?"

"I sure did. And that's when he said you were too good for him."

"Excuse me?"

"He said that if you only knew his whole story, you wouldn't be able to handle it. He said you need some preppy guy who's never had a reason not to be proud of himself."

What the hell is Jason talking about? I thought we weren't speaking because I kissed Hunter. Where is this elaborate theory coming from? "I don't know why he said that. I did get distracted for a moment by someone else—a medical student, kind of preppy, I guess. I can't excuse that. But I love Jason. And I never thought I was too good for him." As soon as the sentence comes out, I wonder if I should've confessed that I had fallen in love. I haven't even said those words to Jason. But Monique nods patiently, not appearing surprised by anything I've said. She sips on her decaf Frappuccino, in no hurry to respond. During that period of silence, I have time to replay her words. *If you only knew his whole story* . . .

"Monique, what part of the story don't I know?"

She'd been staring at the people in line at the counter, but my question brings her eyes back to me. "That's why I wanted to talk to you. I want to tell you what he thinks you can't handle."

The idea that Jason put her up to meeting me is just entering my head when she says, "Jay would kill me if he knew I was doing this."

"So why do it?" I feel my defenses coming up. Jason knows me well. Maybe I don't want to know whatever it is he's hiding.

"Because if I tell you, and you don't run, then he won't have to keep inventing reasons to push you away. That's what he's doing, you know."

I think about that. Was the message from Hunter just an excuse? Was it just a matter of time before Jason would have found a reason to jump ship?

"Okay, tell me." I convince myself that I'm ready for anything.

She inhales and exhales deeply, and pushes the now empty plastic cup away from her. "Jason missed Nailah's birth. And her first two years of life."

Oh, I get it. He's a reformed dog. Got cold feet when his girl got pregnant, and headed for the hills. I would've never pegged him . . .

"Because he was in jail."

I had been reaching for my hot chocolate, and I knock it over for a second, spilling a little before righting it again. I'm grateful for the brown pool of liquid on the table, because it gives me something to tend to as I process what Monique just said.

Jason had been in jail. There's no way that's true. This is the guy who picks up litter when he sees it on the street and holds it till he passes a trash can. And he was there for years? "What did he do?" I ask, already making a list of crimes that I would forgive him for, and ones that I wouldn't.

"Selling."

I hadn't gotten to that crime on my mental list yet. I'd

listed murder and assault as definite no-nos. Embezzlement and fraud were acceptable. "Selling what?"

"Drugs, Desiree." She gives me a scolding look, a little upset that I made her say the word.

"I meant which ones specifically." Somehow, marijuana and crack are falling on opposite sides of my list.

She gives a soft, breathy laugh, and I presume she can imagine what I'm trying to rationalize. "It wasn't Tylenol. Not even close."

"And he was guilty? He wasn't framed?"

"Yes and no. Yes, he was guilty of the charges. But it was a setup, intended to get him to sell out his brother."

"Jason's mentioned his brother a few times, but only in a couple of childhood stories." Then I remember something Jason wrote in an e-mail, about him and his brother having a falling out.

"I'm not surprised he didn't tell you anything more recent," answers Monique. "Jay refused to give up any information that might incriminate his brother, but he never expected that Jamal would let him stay locked up like that. Especially once Jamal found out I was pregnant. But Jamal was facing a lot more than a few years in prison. He could've been in there for life. So he skipped town, leaving me with some money to hold for Jason when he got out."

"He thought he could buy Jason's forgiveness."

"No, he knew better than that. But it was the only way he knew to try to make the situation a little better."

I try to imagine Jason behind bars. If I forget about the violence that goes on in prison, it's actually not that hard to picture him in his cell, reading a book. He has such a loner's spirit that I could see his not even minding the isolation. But a brother's betrayal? I know Jason wouldn't take too well to being stabbed in the back.

"So you and Jason were still together when he . . . got arrested?"

"We were. But he got sentenced to seven years. Every time I saw him, he begged and pleaded with me not to wait for him. He even wrote me a letter telling me to move on and find someone better. But I was just a few months pregnant and couldn't imagine being with anyone other than the father of my child. I was really depressed for several months after Jay's trial. I dropped out of college and barely left the house. I was probably about seven months pregnant when one of Jamal's "associates" came to my house with a hundred thousand dollars in cash."

I gasp, and she smiles a little. "Yeah, that was pretty much my reaction. I called one of my friends from college and asked her what I was supposed to do with the money. Her dad worked for an investment firm, and she sent me there. That's where I met Andre."

"I'm sorry?"

"Oh, I figured you knew his name. Andre's my husband."

It's really hard to sit and listen to this story without reacting too much. This must have been what soap operas were like before television was invented: people just sitting around, telling outrageous tales.

"Andre listened to my whole saga, with no judgement in his eyes at all. I brought him to meet Jay so he could run some investment strategies by him. At first, Jay didn't want to have anything to do with Jamal's money. But when Andre told him how Jay's criminal record was gonna make it next to impossible to secure a job once he got out, he gave in, for the sake of our future child's comfort.

"Nailah was born pretty soon after that, and I didn't have time to be moping around the house anymore. Andre was always coming by to check on us, and our relationship gradually started to grow. He helped me get back into school and kept my spirits up.

"Dre was just as thrilled as I was when we heard that Jay might be getting paroled. We were scared that if Jay didn't get to spend any time with Nailah until she was six years old, then their relationship might be damaged forever. The timing of Jay's release actually coincided with our wedding date. Andre and I got married the day after Jason got out. It was actually his twenty-fifth birthday."

I wonder if Jason viewed that as fortunate or devastating. "Did he go? To your wedding?"

"No, he didn't," she answers, sounding saddened by the fact. But she perks up right away, adding, "But the good thing was that we left Nailah with him when we went on our honeymoon."

"That must've been . . . hard." Poor Jason, having to figure out on the spot how to take care of a two-year-old. And the poor little girl, being left with a man she barely knew.

"Tell me about it. She screamed and cried when Dre and I left. It was all I thought about while we were away on our trip. But that was the last time Nailah ever cried at the prospect of spending time with her father."

She seems grateful to have gotten to the end of the story, as am I. At least now that the truth's been told, I can figure out how to deal with it.

I can tell that she's waiting for an answer, so I manage a few words. "Here I was thinking that I had Jason figured out, when I was just scratching the surface."

"Jay is way too complicated to ever figure out fully, but at least now you know what he was so afraid to tell you."

I think about this whole exchange that I've had with Monique, how it is the complete antithesis of the "baby-mama drama" you see on TV all the time. "Monique, why are you trying to fix things between Jason and me?"

She takes her cup from the table and plays with the rim. "I got a happy ending. I want Jay to have his."

After a long pause, she touches my arm. "And I want Daphne to have hers, too."

CHAPTER 36

HUNTER

It all started two days ago, when I was coming into the building after a shift at the hospital. Robyn and Desiree were on their way out, laughing and talking like the old friends that they're supposed to be. Apparently, Desiree had come over for the last stage of the making-up process, and it had gone smoothly.

It was a little awkward seeing both of them together. Of course, we tried to break the tension with a few silly jokes about the situation. Then Desiree asked me how things were at the hospital, and she told me that she was plowing her way through her new book. Once the small talk had run its course, I made my way to the elevator. Robyn called back to me, "Greg, I made some pork chops if you need something to eat later."

I don't know if it was what she said, or the naturally caring way in which she said it, but it got me thinking. Robyn is always looking out for me. Whenever I go to her place and she's fixing something to eat, she always makes me a plate without my ever having to ask. She's even stopped by the hospital a couple times to drop off a sandwich when the cafeteria has been closed. She's done a lot of things for me that don't involve food, but for a guy who is always hungry, the food examples really stand out.

In the elevator on the way up to my apartment, I did a little side-by-side comparison in my head. Desiree is fly, but so is Robyn, just in a smaller package. Desiree scored mad points with Ma, but Robyn actually reminds me of her, which is the highest compliment you can get from me. Desiree is this talented writer, but Robyn's a brainiac, too, making a name for herself in the second-year class by setting the curve on all her exams. The only difference between the two? Robyn's been in my face all along—the perfect match for me—but I just refused to see it.

It's a miracle that she's still single, really. She wants to be treated well, but she's not a diva. Whenever Robyn goes on bad dates and tells me what the dudes did wrong, it's never anything real petty. I always take her side. And whenever I confess something foul that I did regarding women, she tells me off, but she never holds a grudge about it. And while she has a serious side, she can crack jokes with the best of them, always impressing the fellas when she hangs with us at the crib.

I ran these things through my head all last night and during my entire shift today. Luckily, it was my last day on the floor; my evaluation had already been done, and no one seemed to notice that my head was in the clouds. Now I'm finally back home, and I can't wait another minute to talk to Robyn.

Dialing her number at lightning speed, I'm excited to hear her voice after two rings. "Can I stop by?"

She hesitates a minute before saying, "Um, I guess. But I'm leaving in about twenty minutes."

I debate whether I should forget about it. Twenty minutes isn't very long to state my case. At the same time, I can't hold this in any longer. "Okay. I'll be there in a second."

The walk down the steps and through the hall to Robyn's apartment has never seemed longer. When she opens the door and flashes her dimpled smile, I relax for a moment. But my anxiety quickly rises again at the thought of what I'm about to say. "You're nervous," she says as I walk into her apartment.

"You can tell?"

"Of course. It's understandable. Moving from your ER rotation to surgery is scary. Plus, the hours are gonna kill you. Having to be on call every other—"

"That's not what's on my mind, Robyn."

"What's up?"

"It's about you. You and me. Us. Okay, okay, you get that." I can't take my eyes off my shoes as I talk. "When you asked about liking someone who already liked your friend . . ."

"Greg, don't—"

"No, let me finish. I'm not going to lie. Desiree had me sprung, but for all the wrong reasons. Not taking anything away from her. She's a great woman." I finally get the guts to look her in the eyes, but Robyn's expression is harder to read than the ER attending's handwriting.

"Now I don't know why you asked me that hypothetical question. Maybe you subconsciously knew about Desiree. Or maybe y'all are still lying to me, and you knew about her all along." She opens her mouth to protest, but I wave her off. "None of that matters anymore. All that matters is that I'm sorry I didn't listen to you more closely."

"It's really all good, Greg. Don't worry about it."

"Robyn, just let me do this! You're always trying to make my life easier, but I gotta get this out."

She pulls in her lips, like that's the only way she can

get herself to shut up. I don't know how long that'll last, so I talk fast. "I didn't know that relationships were supposed to be so easy. Being with Alicia was a lot of work—adjusting my priorities to keep her from being pissed off, trying not to trigger her insecurities, searching for interests and values we both shared. Since I was caught up in thinking that relationships weren't supposed to be fun, I couldn't recognize that you and I already had all the ingredients for a great one."

I've run out of breath, and when I go to take another one, it sounds like I just finished running a marathon. In a way, I guess I have. It was an uphill battle to get us to this point—me against my own stupidity. "So what do you think? Should we try to do this?" Over the course of my spiel, I've watched Robyn's eyes soften. My gaze moves down to her lips as I wait for her response so that I can finally kiss them.

A knock at the door startles me so much that I jerk back. She just sighs, gives me a strange look, and turns to open the door.

A light-skinned cat, with twists in his hair, is standing in front of her with a big-ass smile on his face. He looks familiar, although I can't figure out where I've seen him before. "Hi, sweetie," he says, looking down at Robyn like he wants to sop her up with a biscuit. He already has her in his arms when he sees me standing behind her.

"Hey man," he says, the smile still on his face as he releases her five-foot frame. "Lloyd. How ya doin'?" He walks into the room and extends his hand.

"I'm cool," I answer as I give him a pound, thinking that if I say that I'm cool, then it might come true. If the tension was thick before he came in, it's suffocating us now. "Greg." *Who is this guy?* He looks like he came uptown straight from SoHo, where he bought his outfit at one of those skateboarder/artist-type stores.

At the same time, we both turn to Robyn. She hasn't said a single word since I confessed my feelings to her. As she looks at him, then at me, I think I know my answer.

Right when I'm about to make as graceful an exit as possible under the circumstances, I hear her voice. "Lloyd, do you mind waiting in the hall for a second? Greg and I were just finishing up a conversation."

"Sure," the dude answers without hesitation, adjusting his glasses. Still smiling. Unbelievable.

She closes the door softly behind him, leaning her back against it. "Lloyd is a friend of mine from college."

A wave of relief flows through me as I realize that I recognized him from Robyn's photo album. They were posing together in a few friendly pics—nothing threatening whatsoever. There's no doubt that my smile matches the one Lloyd was wearing a few minutes ago.

"When we were in school, he was in love with my friend Kahlila," she continues. Why she thinks I need to know all that, I have no idea. "So when he wanted to pursue a relationship with me, I was really skeptical. That's why I asked you for the advice."

Oh. I thought I felt stupid when I realized that Desiree had been using me to write her book. This is ten times worse. "Okay. That explains it then."

I'm ready to be out, but Robyn is still blocking the door and doesn't move when I walk toward it. "Greg, don't think I never thought about it. I've considered it all—from changing our friendship to booty-call status to marrying you once we graduated."

Well. That's an interesting one. I wonder if she's just saying that to make me feel better.

"But you were still on-again, off-again with Alicia; then you were so crazy about Desiree, and we were so good the way we were. So I just decided to let all of those thoughts go."

Part of me wants to protest. *I was never "on-again" with Alicia. It was just sex. And I was crazy about the fake Desiree, not the real one. Plus, if you've thought about spending the rest of your life with me, isn't that an idea that deserves to be tested?*

Another part of me hears my mom throwing advice my way throughout my childhood. Times when I wouldn't want to get up for school. Times when I would procrastinate on a science program application. *The early bird catches the worm, baby. Ya snooze, ya lose.* Or her personal favorite: *Keep sitting on your ass, Hunter Gregory. The world is gonna pass you by.* I sat my ass on Robyn's couch for a whole year and never made a move. So I step aside and let her pass me by as she heads out on her date, probably to some guitar shop in the Village. Yup, life is unpredictable. And most of the time, it sucks.

I'm muttering those same dismal sentiments to my mother on the phone a few minutes later, only to get a loud sucking of teeth in response. "Doc, you're a damn fool. Anybody ever tell you that?"

"Only you, Ma," I answer monotonously, waiting for her explanation.

"Wasn't it just the other day that you was all sad cuz Desiree dumped you?"

"She didn't dump me, Ma. We just agreed to stop seeing each other. And that was weeks ago." I'm beginning to regret calling my mother.

"Uh-huh. Anyway, if this Robyn girl is so wonderful, how come I ain't never heard about her before?"

"I'm sure I've mentioned her. You probably just don't remember."

"Bullshit, Doc. I may pretend like I'm not listening to

you, but I hear every word you say. And I don't forget any of it." I can hear the water running in her kitchen sink. Since I was little, Ma has always waited until she gets a phone call to do the dishes. She says there's nothing more boring than scrubbing pans with no one to talk to.

"Whatever, Ma. If I never talked about Robyn, it wasn't because I didn't think she was a great girl. She's a really good match for me. And I waited too long to tell her that."

"Damn, you're full of yourself. What makes you think that if you told her any earlier, she would've gone out with your sorry butt?"

"She told me that she's thought about being with me before," I answer, getting defensive. Why can't she be like a normal mom and just try to make me feel better?

"But she never brought it up with you, did she?" I'm too tired of her smart comments to even answer. "Doc, every time you called me when you were at Duke, there was some different girl you were dealing with. Then you came back to New York and hooked up with that bougie-ass Alicia. You hadn't even fully washed your hands of her when you brought Desiree home. And now you're all heartbroken cuz of this Robyn girl I ain't never heard of before in my life."

I'm on the verge of getting off the phone when she finally softens her tone a little bit. "Honey, you don't know how to be by yourself. When things ended with your father, I took two years just getting to know me, figuring out what I wanted out of a partner. Of course, then I took up with Jasmine's father, and that didn't go so good, either. But my point is that you can't choose a girlfriend to replace the last one. You gotta be complete on your own. The woman is just the bonus. You get me?"

"Yeah, Ma. I got you."

CHAPTER 37

To:*kahlila@alumni.franklin.edu,*
lloyd@philosophy.franklin.edu,
robyn@med.columbia.edu,
jt_steinway@alumni.franklin.edu,
hunter@med.columbia.edu,
imanigrace@aol.com,
nicole_mckie@yahoo.com
From: *desiree@alumni.franklin.edu*
Time: Tuesday, October 23, 2001 11:30 a.m.
Subject: the grand finale

Message:
reader friends,

thank you so much for reading my chapters over the past few weeks. your feedback has been invaluable. i've made changes to dialogue, characters, and plot development based on what you told me was and wasn't plausible. and thanks for the compliments on the things that did work; i thrived on those to keep writing against this deadline.

i learned a lot over the past few months. the most important thing i realized is that being in love is the best feeling in the entire world, but only when both people feel it, respect it, and cherish it.

attached are the last few paragraphs of *On a Hot Day in Harlem*. after that, it's a little more revision and then off to my agent. enjoy, and thanks again.

des

Daphne wanted to say that she was sorry. That she'd held forever in her hand and carelessly tossed it to the ground. That her interest in the other man was merely a device to keep from falling hopelessly and irrevocably in love with Justin.

Justin. Who shook the dust off emotions inside of her that she had deemed broken from underuse. Who breathed warm air into her cold body, making sweet honey from bitter beeswax.

But when Daphne found her voice, her impassioned plea sounded like a schoolgirl's taunt. "You can't stop loving me, even if you want to."

"You're right," said Justin after a thoughtful pause, and for a moment Daphne's heart soared out of her chest. "I can't keep myself from loving you. But I can stop myself from getting hurt by you again. I can end things on my own terms."

The thought that Justin could be so rational about a feeling that was never about logic or probability almost made her laugh. But before she could dismiss his absurd claim with a lighthearted comeback, he turned and walked down 122nd Street, his broad shoulders growing smaller as the distance between them increased.

Daphne stood rooted in place, scared that if she tried

to take a step forward, she might collapse, the disappointment proving too much to bear. Before she met Justin, Daphne had been restless, sizzling with frustration and insecurity. Justin was an ice cube on the small of her back—shocking at first, making her want to pull away. Then numbing her skin, making her indifferent to any type of feeling. Finally, the relief from the heat began, and she was soothed. But time had passed, and there was nothing left from the three-dimensional square of frozen water. She'd let the moment in time melt away. And as Justin disappeared from view, she could feel the beads of sweat already gathering on her spine.

To: *desiree@alumni.franklin.edu*
From: *imanigrace@aol.com*
Time: Tuesday, October 23, 2001 12:06 p.m.
Subject: bravo, sis

Message:
Desiree,

I'm so proud of you. Hurston wrote *Their Eyes Were Watching God* in six weeks. Check you out, writing your masterpiece in four. I hope you don't regret taking my advice and starting over. This book emotes a great deal more than your lawyer/secretary book ever could. I think you're finally worthy of going on a book tour with yours truly!

Imani

* * *

To: *desiree@alumni.franklin.edu*
From: *kahlila@alumni.franklin.edu*
Time: Tuesday, October 23, 2001 3:19 p.m.
Subject: I'm so sad!

Message:
des,

   are any of your books ever going to have happy endings? i was really rooting for those two. i don't think she fought hard enough for him at the end. he wanted to take her back. he just didn't see enough from her.

   things down here are going okay. guess what happened last week? lloyd called me up to have dinner—with dave and joy! yup, that's right. sitting down to a meal with my first love and his wife. i can't even tell you why i agreed to it, and i wish i could say i was glad i did it, but i'm not. it brought everything back, and seeing how in love they are didn't bring closure but served as a slap in the face, showing me how stupid i was for believing he ever loved me.

   so, des, you can see why i needed the happy ending in your book. they don't happen often enough in real life.

let's talk soon.
love,
kahli

* * *

To: *desiree@alumni.franklin.edu*
From: *robyn@med.columbia.edu*
Time: Tuesday, October 23, 2001 7:54 p.m.
Subject: that was wack.

Message:
Boooo! Hisss! Lloyd's sitting next to me right now, and he seconds my anger. He also says to tell you that you owe him royalties from the line you stole from him, about holding forever in your hand. Anyhow, stop being such a pessimist, and write the damn ending that everyone wants. I mean, if Lloyd and I can get together after five years of pretending like we didn't want to, then Daphne and Justin should be able to work things out.

Send us the new version when it's done. You'll thank us later.
Robyn

To: *desiree@alumni.franklin.edu*
From: *jt_steinway@alumni.franklin.edu*
Time: Wednesday, October 24, 2001 7:05 a.m.
Subject: Are you kidding me?

Message:
Hey Des,

Do people really talk like that? Daphne should just say, "Dude, I'm sorry! The other guy was a big freakin mistake. You're better in every way. Let's have sex." If she'd said that, he probably would've taken her back.

It doesn't look like anything I told you about NBA groupies made its way into your book, but I'll forgive ya. After all, if it wasn't for you, I wouldn't have met Marisol, and that whole thing is going pretty well. I've never dated a basketball fan before, only fans of the players. Hopefully, she's not just in it for the floor seats!

But congrats on getting it done.
J. T.

To: *desiree@alumni.franklin.edu*
From: *nicole_mckie@yahoo.com*
Time: Wednesday, October 24, 2001 10:22 a.m.
Subject: It was really good!

Message:
Dear Desiree,

Thanks sooooo much for including me in your list of readers. I loved the book from beginning to end. Although I did really want Justin and Daphne to get back together. Sorry if this is none of my business, but are Justin and Daphne really you and Jason? Because if they are, then you shouldn't give up on hooking up again. Jason really liked you. Plus, you'd be surprised how things can turn out sometimes. Like my parents are paying for my older brother to come see me perform at a "Women in Jazz" performance at the Apollo during his spring break. See, just when you lose faith completely in people is when they do something unexpected.

C ya,
Nicole

* * *

To: *desiree@alumni.franklin.edu*
From: *hunter@med.columbia.edu*
Time: Wednesday, October 24, 2001 2:49 p.m.
Subject: Impressive.

Message:
   So the guy doesn't get the girl at the end, huh?
I guess you used me as inspiration for your book
after all. ☺
   I loved the whole story. Daphne is a really
strong woman. Not without flaws, but not above
acknowledging them. And growing every day. I
went back and read your first book also. Pretty
good stuff for a secretary/model/actress . . .
   Look, I can tell that you connect really strongly
to your characters, and I hope the sad ending
doesn't mean that things didn't work out with the
person you said you're in love with. If they didn't,
trust me, it wasn't because I was sitting around
sticking pins in my Desiree voodoo doll. Because
when my future wife comes walking into my life,
I only want good karma coming back to me.

Congratulations,
Hunter

CHAPTER 38

JASON

The weatherman said a strong fall breeze, but it feels more like a winter wind. I guess the sudden chill in the air drove all of the regulars away. The playground at Nailah's school is completely abandoned. Usually at this time, right before kindergarten lets out, a few of the parents who have younger kids are pushing the little ones on the swings as they wait for their older children to get dismissed. Today, they must be inside, peeking into Ms. Nieves's room to see what their four-year-olds are up to. I'm tempted to do the same, but it might do me good to have some quiet time before I have to put on a smile for Nailah.

I settle onto a bench next to the jungle gym, zipping up my leather jacket all the way. It's not so cold when you get used to it. I feel like I've been telling myself that a lot lately. My apartment isn't so cold when you get used to it. My bed. My heart. I've had a few weak moments since I drop-kicked Desiree out of my life. Not so weak that I was ready to pick up the phone and call her, but just weak enough that if she had chosen that particular second to hit me up and say she wanted to see me, I

would've been down. But she never did, and I really
think it's for the best. I could just imagine going home
to her doctor mom and counselor dad, giving them my
history. *Yes, sir. Yes, ma'am. I spent my college years behind
bars. It was quite the education.*

The gravel from the sandbox suddenly blows into my
face. My eyes sting like hell, and I take it as a sign to go
inside. First, I have to open my eyes so I can see where
I'm going. But when I finally rub them enough that I
can squint again, I see three silhouettes in front of me.
A mom and her two boys have just walked out of the
school building. She has one by each hand as they reach
behind her to try to smack each other playfully. "Keep
playin'," she warns. "One of you is gonna take it too far,
and it won't be a game anymore." I watch as they reluctantly stop what they were doing, settling for making
faces at one another instead.

After 9/11, Moms gave me my brother's number and
made me promise to save it. "Just in case," she said. I
don't know if she meant just in case of another national
disaster, or just in case she went off her meds and we had
a family emergency on our hands, or just in case I decided one day to bury the hatchet. But I'm grateful that
I have it as I pull out my cell and highlight his name.

It only rings once before I hear his voice. It sounds so
much like mine that it scares me. "Hello."

"Mawly-mawl."

A pause, and then, "Jay? That really you, family?"

"Yeah, it's me."

A sudden change from happily shocked to panicked
concern. "Is everything cool? Mom and Dad? You in
trouble? Big O called a while back talkin' shit. He didn't
come after you, did he?"

Like I'd call him to help me out of any kind of fix.
"Everybody's straight. Just calling . . . to call."

"I heard that." Longer pause. "I don't know where to begin." He sounds older, calmer.

"Begin by telling me you're out of the biz." I hold my breath for his answer.

"Oh, I've been legit since the day I moved down here, Jay. I own a nightclub in South Beach. It's doing real good."

I smile, remembering how much Jamal loved the ladies. "A nightclub or a strip club?"

He laughs, the exact same laugh that I remember. "Man, I'm done with all that. I got a wifey now. She's the real deal. And she ain't puttin' up with me runnin' around on her."

This surprises me more than hearing him say he was outta the game. I wonder what kind of woman could get Jamal to settle down. "What's she do?"

"Lynette does hair. She's a good girl. No crazy ex-boyfriends, no kids, no secrets."

"Everybody has secrets," I remind him.

"You right about that. She thinks that I used to work in real estate," he says and starts cracking up. When he notices that I'm not laughing with him, he stops.

"Yo, how's my niece doing? Is she three years old now?"

"Four," I shoot back, and suddenly my insides are raging. How's he have the nerve to ask about Nailah, a niece he's never even met? I want to throw the phone into a lake and watch the ripples slowly disappear around his sinking voice.

"Is she tall? Or did she get her daddy's height?" He laughs again, but this time it's unnatural. Maybe he sensed the tension in my voice.

"Maybe you should've stuck around to see for yourself how tall she got."

I hear him breathe in and out, real deep. "Well, I

guess we're done with the intro conversation. We at the meat of it now, huh, little brother?"

"*Don't* call me that." I instinctually lower my voice at the sound of my own anger, being that I'm at Nailah's school, and there's no way I'm letting anybody hear me arguing on the phone.

"Jay, I ain't got no kind of excuses for dippin' out on you the way I did. I left my little brother, I mean my younger brother, all book smart and everything. I left him locked up. That shit wasn't easy for me. Wasn't easy at all. And then, when I found out Mo was pregnant, damn, I felt like the world was beating my ass for all the trouble I got us into."

I can feel my eyes getting watery. Must be some grains of sand that I didn't wipe out. "But lemme put it to you like this," he says. "If I had never been around, pullin' you into what I was doin', you would never have ended up in jail. And if I'd never come to Newark and had stayed in Montserrat, I probl'y woulda been straight myself. So I figured, lemme remove myself from this environment. Lemme save myself, and give my brother a chance to do the same."

"You could've helped me get out so I could see my daughter be born."

"That's really what you think, huh Jay? You trust 5-0 so much that you believe if I had walked into the precinct and turned myself in, they woulda just set you free?"

I want to go over it in detail, tell him exactly what had been offered to me in exchange for diming on him. I want to remind him how I refused it. I want to hear him thank me for saving his life. But what's the point? I know Jamal, and I know he's been living with his guilt for the past five years. "Whatever, Mawl. Let's just forget about it."

"You sure?" I don't answer, so he sighs and continues. "So Ma told me Mo got married. That's jacked up, bro."

"Let's not talk about that, either."

"All right, okay. How about you choose the topic."

"I'm actually gonna run. I'm picking up Nailah from school, and she'll be out soon."

I can tell that he's not sure whether to believe me. "You callin' from your phone?"

"My cell, yeah."

"Can I save this number? Use it sometime?" He sounds timid. I don't think I've ever heard him sound that way.

I try to picture Jamal at a church in a tuxedo, marrying this Lynette girl he was talking about. I imagine them having a baby, and the baby getting bigger and bigger. And then I try to picture myself never getting to see any of it. "Yeah, you can use it."

"Easy, Jay."

"Later."

I stare at my phone for a long time once we hang up. So that was it. The first conversation with my brother since the day I felt those cold cuffs on my wrists. I want to tell someone. My mother would be happy to hear about it, but I can't be calling Aruba from my cell phone. Mo is the next logical choice, but she's in class. It'll be the last semester for her for a while. The baby will be here in a few months, and she'll be a full-time mom again. I should start getting used to not being able to talk to her whenever I want.

"Jason."

When Desiree walks up to me at the playground, I'm sure she's surprised by the lack of surprise on my face. It's not that I expected to see her. But one of the first lessons you learn once you get knocked is how to remove all signs of emotion from your face: fear, anger, happiness. This just seems like a good time to use that lesson.

"How'd you know I was here?" My voice comes out even and cool.

"Monique told me you pick up Nailah on Thursdays. She and I had coffee a couple weeks ago."

I'm speechless. I've seen Mo twice, no, three times, in the past week alone. No mention of an encounter with Desiree. Does that mean they didn't get along?

"She's great. Really great." I smile on the inside to hear that. Somehow, Monique's acceptance of her matters.

"Look, can we get together and talk sometime?"

"You're here now."

Desiree seems unwilling to have a conversation at this exact moment, but realizes that she has no choice. "Monique told me some things . . . about you guys. About you. Your past." I don't think I manage to keep my poker face when I hear her say that. I know exactly what it is that Mo decided to fill her in on. There's no anger on my part, though. Just fear. Figures that Monique would know exactly what I was afraid of and force me to face it anyway.

Desiree hugs herself in an attempt to block the cold. Her jean jacket isn't thick enough. "I'll admit. It kind of freaked me out at first. But what freaked me out isn't what you might expect. I wasn't picturing you as some violent criminal or wondering what traumatic experiences you went through in jail. And I wasn't worried about what anyone might think about you."

It always amazes me how well she can anticipate my thoughts. Those are all the things I worried that she wouldn't be able to get over. "So what was it then?"

"What really messed me up was that I thought I loved you, and I never even knew you."

I don't expect the wave of sadness that practically bowls me over.

"But what I realized, Jason, as I've had more time to think, is that I do know you. Not knowing one part of your life doesn't negate all the things I knew to be true about your character.

"When we first started getting to know each other, you were patient and tolerant of my coldness and how . . . sometimes-ish I was. I was carrying a load of baggage myself, and even though I never shared the specifics with you, I felt like you understood the need to handle me with care."

She takes a step toward me, but not a large step. "Here's the thing about baggage. When you're going on a trip, sometimes it's easier to pack light. Less cumbersome, less intimidating to the people coming to pick you up from the airport. But when you have lots of luggage, you're prepared for anything. Rain, shine, dressy, casual. It's all in the bag."

I've never heard the writer in Desiree come out in her speech as much as I am now. "Our baggage just might be what makes us work. Between the two of us, we have enough experience to weather the storms that relationships bring."

I don't agree or disagree, so she gets the nerve to sit down on the bench and keeps talking. "I took a walk yesterday. On the shore. I drove up to Edgewater and just walked along the beach. It was weird. I'd step into the wet sand, making a footprint nice and deep. But as soon as I turned back to see the tracks I'd made, they'd already been washed away. For the life of me, I couldn't make an imprint on that shoreline.

"You told me that my poems spoke to you. I wrote you one after my walk on the beach." She slips her Louis Vuitton backpack off her shoulders. I almost chuckle at the sight of it, remembering the story she told me about the store on Canal Street where she bought it. She said she thought she was in a spy movie when the saleswoman brought her into a back room and showed her a secret stash of knock off designer bags. I was laughing so hard as she recounted her "covert operation" to pay the woman in cash without anyone else seeing. After she removes a folded piece of paper and hands it to me, I open it to find eight typed lines, with no title:

> *As I lie in a gentle embrace with dead space,*
> *tender thoughts of your being meander my mind.*
> *Though you could have been simply another brown face*
> *on a hot day in Harlem, your cool stare chilled my spine.*
>
> *My music's up-tempo, yours is mellow sound;*
> *They create jazz together, and our song becomes whole.*
> *When we parted, you left something behind that I found.*
> *You said good-bye—and tracked footprints on my soul.*

She waits for me to look up before she speaks again. "You left your mark on me, Jason. For the better. You brought me back to the place where I could feel. Even the fact that I could be hurt by you was a good thing. It's better than not feeling at all. On the shore, when I couldn't even find my own footprints, it reminded me of how we left things. It can't be over between us, because I haven't made my imprint yet. I haven't made you better."

Facing my silence still, she adds hurriedly, "Not that you need to be better. It's just—"

"I get it, sweetheart." My voice is gentler than I meant it to be, and the "sweetheart" kind of slipped out.

A strong gust of wind combined with the dismissal of the kindergarten classes make a whirlwind of activity around us. Kids are streaming out of the door with adults at their sides, and I feel a pang of guilt as I see Nailah tentatively walk out of the building. I should've waited for her inside today.

Her expression changes in the blink of an eye when she catches sight of me, and she runs the rest of the way over. I wave to Ms. Nieves, who's monitoring pickup by the school entrance, and I bend down to give Nailah a hug and kiss. Her pink hooded sweatshirt isn't zipped, so I take care of that before I stand up and glance at Desiree, who's looking like she doesn't know what to do with herself.

"Nailah, sweetheart, this is my friend Desiree," I say, turning back to my daughter.

"Hi, beautiful," Desiree says in an adoring voice. Her hands are on her knees as she tries to reach eye level with Nailah.

"Hi," Nailah responds and puts her arms in the air, her nonverbal way of asking to be lifted. I've never seen her do that with a stranger.

Desiree looks equally surprised but scoops her up into her arms with an extra little toss, which makes Nailah giggle. They look at each other, grinning wide. Nailah's lost a tooth since I last saw her. At the same time, they turn to look at me.

It's impossible not to grin right back.

EPILOGUE

ON A HOT DAY IN HARLEM
ACKNOWLEDGMENTS

This novel technically took me a single month to write, but it was five years in the making. I am so grateful to so many people, and I'm glad that my editor gave me some space to give my thanks.

First, my eternal gratitude to those people who kept me standing during the low points: my parents, Kahlila, and Robyn. During those college years, when I'd lost all confidence in myself, you are the ones who built me back up.

I am also indebted to those people whose art inspires me on a daily basis. Imani Grace, your devotion to your writing is so admirable, and it is a constant motivator. But your devotion to your friends is even more impressive, and I couldn't have written this latest one without you. Nicole McKie, you are a rising star. While our crafts are different, our passion for them is not. You remind me of myself when I was your age. Don't let anyone make you believe that you're less than spectacular.

Shout outs to everyone who read the manuscript in its initial stages. Paula, you are the amazingest agent in the world. Your suggestions before and during the creation of this novel were in-

valuable. J. T. Steinway, you kept me laughing along the way and made sure I didn't get too cheesy with my plotlines. Yes, that's right folks. The pro-ballplayer edits books. I only associate with ridiculously multitalented people. Lloyd, I am announcing to the world that I stole a line from you and used it in this novel (although I'm not telling which line). Consider that your payment. And, Hunter Gregory, thank you for the feedback and support, and for your friendship. If I hadn't forgotten my money at Kenny's Soul Food that day, I would have missed out on meeting one of the most phenomenal men in New York. And yes, ladies, he's single.

I have been more honest over the past year about the sources of inspiration for my books. Before that, I had been reluctant to admit that Daphne is a reflection of me. So now that it's out in the open, I should announce that my next book will not be about her. Daphne is way too happy these days. No one wants to read a book without any conflict. Jason, thank you for being Daphne's peace of mind. Every day, you teach me new lessons on literature, life, and love. You and Nailah keep me smiling.

Herman Melville said that life begins at twenty-five. I disagree. Life begins when you decide to start living it. You can't try to regulate your feelings and shut out the hurt. It's only when you let yourself feel that you begin to heal. Hey, that rhymes. Anyway, thanks for reading.

Desiree

Check Out These Other
Dafina Novels

Look For These Other
Dafina Novels

She needed

And the attic was the place to look. Wasn't that where all the detectives she'd seen and read about always went?

Caitlin mounted the stairs, picturing her stepfather up there plotting with his gang of cut-throat murderers.

The room was dark, and she stood ready for something, someone, to jump out at her. But nothing stirred. When she bathed the room in light from the overhead fixture, she spied an old trunk. In it were only old magazines, yellowed with age. But what was that, way down . . . ?

A wooden box. Locked with some kind of weird puzzle. Caitlin fiddled with it and grinned when the lid popped open. Nothing but a bunch of papers inside.

She picked one up, smoothed it out, her eyes getting bigger and bigger. There was her name, written in bold ink. Caitlin Ashley Emerson had hit the jackpot.

ABOUT THE AUTHOR

Heather McCann is thrilled that her first book sale is to Intrigue. Writing a romantic mystery, according to Heather, combines the best of both fields. When asked how she got the idea for *The Master Detective*, she replied, "A devious mind is a rare and wonderful thing. Ideas come from everywhere—chance conversations, newspapers, magazines and meeting strangers. All one has to do is keep a receptive mind and a sense of humor!"

The Master Detective

Heather McCann

Harlequin Books

TORONTO • NEW YORK • LONDON
AMSTERDAM • PARIS • SYDNEY • HAMBURG
STOCKHOLM • ATHENS • TOKYO • MILAN
MADRID • WARSAW • BUDAPEST • AUCKLAND

To the Ladies' Monthly Sewing Circle and
their generous and wise advice and counsel.
And also to Chris, without whose expertise,
Caitlin wouldn't have seen the light of day.

Harlequin Intrigue edition published December 1992

ISBN 0-373-22207-6

THE MASTER DETECTIVE

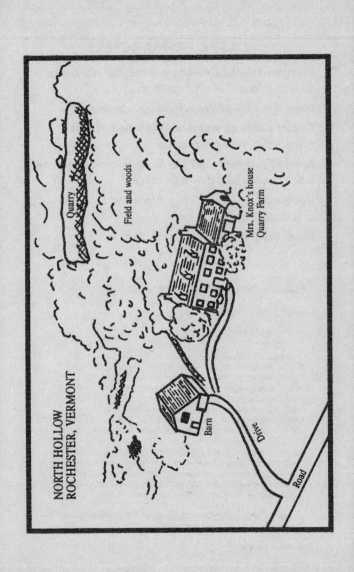

NORTH HOLLOW
ROCHESTER, VERMONT

Quarry

Field and woods

Mrs. Knox's house
Quarry Farm

Barn

Drive

Road

CAST OF CHARACTERS

Margaret Webster—Baby-sitting her niece was turning into a chilling nightmare.

Jake McCall—His real identity was shocking.

Caitlin Ashley Emerson—The little girl was precious . . . and precocious.

Sandy Schuyler—Did she make a deadly mistake when she walked down the aisle?

Robert Schuyler—Loving stepfather . . . or cold-blooded killer?

Madame Zorina—Her predictions always came true.

Chapter One

Seven-year-old Caitlin Ashley Emerson knew a secret nobody else knew. She hitched her long, purple dress up higher as she crept upstairs. The dress was her mom's. Sunglasses, a red felt hat and glittery fairy wings completed her ensemble. It looked as if she was playing dress up, but she wasn't. Caitlin was wearing a disguise. Master detectives did that sometimes.

Her disguise had been thought through carefully. First she'd tried on her mom's red high heels, but the shoes made too much noise. The whole idea was quiet stealth, after all.

She was determined not to get caught. The hard part was getting past the front hall without being seen, and she'd already done that.

She heard soft noises from downstairs and stiffened against the wall, her heart banging against her ribs. Then there was a squeak, like sofa springs shifting, someone getting up and walking across the rug.

Fear filled her inside, making it hard to breathe. She took a deep breath and began humming an old nursery rhyme. Softly, barely a whisper. "'A B C, tumble-down D. Cat's in the cupboard and can't see me.'"

They couldn't see her.

The murmur of adult voices came from the living room, and the sudden sinister sound of footsteps approached. She ducked down and flattened herself against the wall again. As she held her breath, the footsteps stopped, then the front door opened and closed. She let out a breath of relief. Someone had gone out. Her stepfather, no doubt. He'd probably gone out to start the car. Robert and her mom were flying to Florida, and he wouldn't want to miss their plane. A sense of injustice crept over her. It just wasn't *fair*. Why should they get to go to Florida and see Disneyworld, and she couldn't? No, she had to stay behind in this stupid old rented house in Rochester, Vermont, baby-sat by her Aunt Margaret for two whole weeks. Stuck up here on top of North Hollow, which was sort of a small mountain. Her mom had explained all the dumb, grown-up reasons she couldn't go with them. But Caitlin hadn't been fooled. This was all Robert's idea. Maybe her mom was tricked, but Caitlin could see through him. He didn't want her along.

Phooey. She didn't want to go anywhere with him, anyway.

She hitched up her dress again, conscious of a burst of feminine laughter downstairs. Her mom and Aunt Margaret. They were too busy talking to bother looking for her, but she waited, anyway. Master detectives had to be prepared for the unexpected.

Nothing happened. Then, assuming a limp for the benefit of anyone who might be observing her, because that's what master detectives would do, she made her way up the rest of the stairs, only to stumble slightly just as she neared the top.

The murmur of voices from the living room stopped. Her mother came into the hall. "Caitlin, are you all right? What happened?"

She turned as her mother hurried upstairs. "I'm okay. I tripped on my dress, that's all."

"How many times have I told you to be careful when you play dress up? Honestly, that dress is a menace." Sandy slid a comforting arm around her daughter's shoulders and kissed her cheek. "The stairs are steep, honey. You could take quite a tumble. Be careful, and promise me you'll be good for Aunt Margaret while Robert and I are gone."

"Okay."

Her mother gave her another hug. "Robert and I are leaving now. Are you coming out to the car to say goodbye?"

Caitlin frowned and shook her head vehemently underneath the red felt hat. "No."

"Honey, it's only for two weeks. I'll miss you." Caitlin tightened her mouth. Her mother sighed. "I wish you'd try harder to like Robert. He likes you very much."

Only a fool would think Robert really liked her. Grown-ups who liked kids didn't hog all the dessert so no one else could get seconds. And they didn't pinch you when no one was looking.

She looked up at her mother and said, "I don't want to go out to the car, Mom. I'm really busy. . . playing. I'm going to give my Barbie dolls a shampoo."

"All right," Sandy said, giving up at last. "Give me a kiss goodbye. I'll call you from Florida when the plane lands." She straightened Caitlin's fairy wings. "There, that's better. I love you."

Caitlin reached up and slid her arms around her mother's neck, kissing her cheek. "I love you, Mom. Bye."

"Bye, darling." Her mother gave her another kiss and hug and went downstairs. After a few moments the sounds of adult conversation resumed from the living room, and Caitlin breathed a sigh of relief and went down the hall to the little sewing room, which she wasn't supposed to enter. Well, so what? Her Mom wasn't even going to be here. She was going to Florida, leaving Caitlin behind.

She went inside and closed the door quietly, her trained eye missing nothing. Detectives had to notice and remember little details. She looked around, aware of everything. There on the table by the window, together with the blue and white china lamp and the heart-shaped brass box with no peppermint candy in it because she'd eaten the last piece, propped against the alarm clock, was a photograph of herself. It had been taken about six months ago, right after her mother's marriage to Robert. Caitlin had been dressed in jeans and her red Mickey Mouse sweater. She'd been holding a teddy bear. In the picture Robert had his arm around her shoulder, his hand resting on the teddy bear's head. Wind had blown her tawny brown hair, and she was smiling, her two front teeth on the bottom missing.

Thoughtfully, Caitlin sucked on her lower lip. Those two teeth were almost in now, but one of her front teeth on top was missing and the other one was loose. Well, that meant another fifty cents from the Tooth Fairy. And if she kept her room clean for a week or two she'd have enough allowance for more Barbie clothes.

She looked across the room toward the half-open window. At the front walk she could see Robert loading up the trunk of the car. Mr. Perfect. He sure had her mom fooled. A sudden spring breeze blew the curtain in and out. It fluttered into a shaft of weak sunlight, nubby gold threads in the cloth shining all glittery. It was like an omen that everything would be okay, and the master detective would find what she was looking for. Clues.

She bent down and looked under the green-checked sofa. Nothing but little curls of dust up by the wall and the edge of the rag rug. She turned her attention to the closet, but it held nothing but the landlady's winter jackets and suits and a big, bulky parka with a fur collar. She closed the closet door with a sense of disappointment. Where else would a detective look? There had to be *something*.

A small desk stood near the sofa. Working with the skill of a cardsharper, she slid the drawers open silently, one by one. Nothing but sewing magazines and patterns. Carefully she felt the underside of the drawers, just as she'd seen the Bloodhound Gang do it on TV, when they'd investigated the secret of the Martian's curse. Her fingers met only smooth, cold metal. Then, as she felt beneath the middle drawer, she touched something else . . . paper.

She knelt down, her face level with the middle drawer, and she could see it. A small snapshot taped to the bottom of the drawer. Her small fingers worked at the tape, and at last she managed to peel most of it off. The snapshot only tore a little as she pulled it free.

She closed the drawer and looked at it. The top left corner was missing, but that couldn't be helped. She sighed. It wasn't much, just a dumb picture of a man with a mustache, but it was a start. She put the snapshot in the pocket of her dress just as the front door opened downstairs.

There was a short laughing conversation, then thudding feet running up the stairs. Heavy, masculine feet. Heart pounding, she ran to the door and was just closing it behind her when Robert reached the upstairs landing.

His eyes flickered toward the doorknob. He knew she'd been in the little sewing room. She hadn't been quick enough.

He smiled, blue eyes twinkling, pretending he wasn't mad at her. "What are you up to, sweetie? Playing?"

She fixed the sunglasses that were sliding down her nose. "Yes."

He paused a second, glancing again at the door, then said, "Almost forgot the airplane tickets. Your mom would have been furious if we'd gone all the way to Montpelier Airport and had to come back." Half-laughing, he shook his head and went into their bedroom. A few seconds later he came out and went downstairs, calling over his shoulder, "Bye, Cait. See you in a few weeks." Pausing by the front door he went on, "Sandy, it's late. Better shake a leg."

Upstairs, Caitlin turned and went into her bedroom. Kneeling by her bed, she felt around underneath for the hidden shoebox. She put the snapshot inside, then slid the shoebox back underneath the bed and went to give her Barbie dolls a shampoo. Not that they really needed it. It was an ingenious diversion designed to confuse the watchers who might have penetrated her disguise.

DOWN IN THE LIVING ROOM Sandy Schuyler was looking distractedly through her purse. "God, I'd lose my head if it weren't fastened. Where's that key?"

Margaret smiled widely. "You already gave me the front door key, if that's what you're looking for."

Sisters, different as night and day. Margaret Webster's shoulder-length hair was black as a raven's wing, her eyes, green as the sea, while Sandy was fair and blue-eyed. In their twenties, both were energetic and pretty, although Sandy was now pale and thin.

Sandy picked up her purse and walked toward the front door as Margaret opened it. They embraced in a warm hug. "I'm so glad you agreed to watch Caitlin and the house while we're gone," Sandy said. "I really... well, I thought maybe you wouldn't come."

Margaret's green eyes crinkled with warm affection. "Why wouldn't I come when my big sister calls?"

"It's awkward, that's all. Robert and I've only been married six months, and well..." Shrugging, Sandy twisted her purse strap between her thin fingers. "I thought maybe you still had feelings for him. Oh, I know I should have known better." She half laughed and hugged Margaret again. "I've been such a fool. What you and Robert had at one time wasn't love."

"Of course it wasn't, silly," Margaret lied. "Now hurry up and get to the airport or you'll miss the plane. Everything will be just fine here. Don't worry."

Sandy frowned. "Oh, I almost forgot. Since this house is rented, it's full of the landlady's things. Mrs.

Knox left the house as is, when she went to Europe. I told Caitlin not to touch anything that didn't belong to us. Actually, I put the fear of God into her, she's so stubborn. I told her the landlady was a cross between Freddie Kreuger and the Wicked Witch of the West. Lord knows if it's enough to keep her out of the poor woman's belongings." Her mouth quirked into a smile. "Caitlin reminds me of you when we were kids. Always up to something, full of make-believe. I swear, half the time she can't tell the difference between what's real and what isn't. Remember when you were seven and took that swan dive off the shed roof with the towel pinned to your back? You were sure you could fly."

Margaret nodded ruefully. "I broke my ankle and wore a cast half the summer. I missed out on all the swimming, and it itched like crazy."

Outside, a car door slammed. A breeze blew in through the half-opened door, and spring sunlight spilled across the faded Oriental scatter rugs on the wood floor. Sandy glanced at her watch and said, "Oh dear, I'd better go." She leaned over and kissed Margaret's cheek, then dashed down the front porch steps and out to the car.

Margaret waved to Robert from the porch. She didn't want any physical contact with him. "Bye, take care of Sandy."

He glanced up at Margaret, smiling. "See you in a few weeks, Maggie. Take care."

He was the only one who'd ever called her Maggie. For a moment she relived the last time they'd been alone together, that summer night one year ago. She could feel again the warm, humid, night air as they'd

sat in Robert's car, parked outside her Boston apartment house on Marlborough Street. He'd reached for
her. "Maggie, I'm so sorry, but Sandy and I are in
love. It just happened—one of those things. I've asked
her to marry me. Dammit, I didn't want to hurt you,
but there's just no other way. What we had wasn't real.
Someday you'll realize I'm right. There's someone else
for you, darling . . . a better man than I'll ever be."

His handsome face with its heavy eyebrows and
mobile mouth had been drawn and pleading. The roof
light had snapped on as she'd wrenched the door open
and slid out of the car. Running blindly across the
sidewalk and up the steps, she'd prayed she would get
inside before she broke down.

She took a deep breath. Dammit, that terrible night
had happened a year ago. It was over and done with.
A whirlwind romance that had fallen apart. She'd only
dated Robert for a few months before their short-lived
engagement. Then he'd met Sandy at the home of
mutual friends, and that had been that.

She swallowed back a rush of hot tears. She'd
worked hard to change, this past year, letting her
cropped black hair grow until it lay in tangled curls to
her shoulders. She reached up and pushed back her
hair and seemed to hear an echo of his laughing voice.

God, it still hurt so. She wiped her face with the
back of her hand, then waved as their car edged down
the drive. She stood a moment, watching as the car
turned and disappeared down the road.

The view from the house was breathtaking. Huge
twin maples flanked the front walk. Beyond, about
thirty acres of open hayfield sloped down the valley to
distant blue mountains on the far side of the White

River. A hilly patchwork of hayfields and meadows were dotted with black and white cows and sheep. Peaceful. The river glittered in the distance, a silver ribbon winding along the valley floor. Ethereal tendrils of mist floated above the water, quiet and still. Only the caws of blackbirds disturbed the silence. Drawing a deep breath, she relaxed as a sense of serenity and healing washed over her. Life went on. There were other men in the world besides Robert. All she had to do was wait. Sooner or later he would turn up, and she would be drawn to him....

A gentle breeze wafted the fragrance of an immense clump of lilacs that grew by the porch steps.

It was going to be a wonderful two weeks. Laughing softly, Margaret stepped back inside the house and closed the door.

The pine grandfather clock chimed from across the front hall. Eleven o'clock—and somewhere in the house water was running.

She frowned and listened. It sounded as if it was coming from the upstairs bathroom.

It was. Caitlin was calmly shampooing her dolls' hair—and water was overflowing the sink. There must have been at least a half inch of water all over the floor. "I'm shampooing my Barbies," Caitlin said, watching her aunt get down on her knees to mop the floor.

A half dozen dolls in various stages of wet dishabille smiled vacantly at her from the confines of the overflowing sink. "Turn off the faucets, please," Margaret told her niece. "Didn't you notice the water was overflowing? Mrs. Knox owns this house and wouldn't like it if the floor fell apart, which is what happens when it gets soaked.'' She glanced at Caitlin who stared back with heart-shaped sunglasses perched on her head. Her eyes were deceptively innocent.

Caitlin opened her mouth and said calmly, ''I forgot about the water. Anyway, you're not the boss of me. I can do whatever I want.''

Margaret let that remark alone. Time enough to sort out who was in charge of whom around here. First things first. She wrung out another sopping towel in the tub and mopped under the sink. Caitlin got off the toilet seat and stood on the end of the towel. ''How come your hair is black? I mean, Mom's is blond. Did you dye your hair?''

''No, and move your foot, please—no, Caitlin, the one you're standing on the towel with. And don't touch that bottle of shampoo.'' Margaret closed her eyes as the bottle fell on the tile floor.

Caitlin gathered up her dolls and headed for the door, throwing Margaret a challenging look over her fairy wings. ''I'm hungry, and I'm allowed to eat whatever I want, 'specially popsicles.''

''I doubt that,'' Margaret said to her departing back. ''Wait a minute. I'll get this cleaned up, then I'll make us lunch.'' Caitlin shouted something that sounded suspiciously like 'I hate lunch,' and Margaret mopped as fast as she could. Five minutes later she raced to the kitchen and found her niece busy making flour and water paste for glue. The sink, countertops, everything was glop, including Caitlin, who was indignant when Margaret washed her face and hands.

''I like being dirty,'' she said belligerently, making a hideous face.

Margaret finished cleaning Caitlin's face. "Now I can see who you are again." She dropped a kiss on her niece's freckled little nose. "Know what? I love freckles."

"I hate them," Caitlin muttered. "And I hate Robert, too. Why didn't they take me to Florida. It's not *fair.*"

"Because your mom's been sick, and the doctor said she needed plenty of rest and sunshine so she'll get better."

Caitlin put her sunglasses on and said, "Robert's mean. He pinched me."

By this time Margaret was slathering whole-wheat bread with peanut butter and grape jam. She screwed the top back on the peanut butter and said, "I know Robert pretty well, and I don't think he's mean."

"That's because he didn't pinch you. He pinched me," Caitlin said. "I want a popsicle."

"After you have lunch." Margaret gave her a level look. "And I mean it. Lunch first."

"I hate whole-wheat bread. Those weird brown bits are bugs," Caitlin announced, jutting her firm little chin. "I'm not eating any bugs."

"They're not bugs."

"I don't care. I'm not eating it."

Hoping to divert Caitlin's attention long enough for her to forget the brown specks in her sandwich, Margaret picked up a Barbie. The doll was wearing a wedding dress and missing an arm. "What happened to this one?"

Caitlin shrugged her fairy wings. "Her arm got falled off. It's a 'bomination. That's what happens when doctors take parts of you off. Like if you're crazy they take your head off and fix your brain. Then they stick it back on.''

Margaret cleared her throat, then managed to say, ''Where did you hear this?''

''Mrs. Till, the lady who comes to clean the house, was talking on the phone in the kitchen, and I came in to get a drink. I didn't listen on purpose. It's kind of comp'cated. She poured me some milk and kept on talking to this friend of hers named Ruth Ann. She said it was a 'bomination that killed old Mr. Knox after his first wife, Martha, died . . . and he must have been crazy to fall for Polly Knox.'' Caitlin leaned across the table and said confidentially from behind her heart-shaped glasses, '''There's no fool like an old fool.' That's what Mrs. Till said. She said Polly had him roped and tied before he knew what hit him. Polly was Martha Knox's nurse. Martha was sick and old, like Mr. Wendell Knox. She didn't have a 'bomination, just a heart attack what killed her dead.''

''I see,'' Margaret said, trying and failing to get all this straight.

Caitlin took the one-armed Barbie from Margaret's nerveless fingers and inspected it clinically. ''I prob'ly shouldn't play with her until I get her arm stuck back on. Maybe it's in the bathroom. I'm gonna go look.'' She slid off her chair and ran out of the kitchen.

Margaret made a cup of coffee and sat down to catch her breath. Caitlin was a holy terror. Give her an inch and she'd take a mile.

Half-listening for the sounds of water running, Margaret closed her eyes and slipped off her shoes. It had been a whirlwind two days, finishing up everything at the office so she could take a few weeks off and come to Vermont to help Sandy out. Her boss had been understanding, even kidding her about sneaking off to get in some spring skiing.

Fat chance. There wasn't any snow left, and forsythia and lilac were already in bloom. Tulips and daffodils, too. Sandy had picked her up, and once they'd driven over the White River Bridge and turned toward town, it seemed spring had suddenly announced itself. She smiled, remembering one house in particular... about a quarter mile past the bridge. Victorian, white, with spires, a big front porch with a bay window, and of all things, a bright green parrot on a perch in the window. There'd been a woman in the window, feeding the parrot a cracker. She'd had the brightest orange hair. A sign swung in the wind on a post in front of the house: Madame Zorina, Palm Reading, by Appointment Only.

CAITLIN WAS BACK from the bathroom and busily soaking her sandwich in her milk when Margaret opened her eyes and came out of her reverie. "How come I couldn't stay with my dad while Mom and Robert were in Florida?" she wanted to know.

Margaret sighed and fished the pink, mushy remains of lunch out of the glass, in the process spilling most of it. She started mopping up and explained, "Because your dad's in Europe right now." Frank Emerson, Sandy's first husband, owned a small computer company. His dedication to business was the reason their marriage had collapsed. He had had no time for his daughter, either.

Margaret looked across the table at Caitlin who was eyeing the freezer speculatively. She had to smile. It wasn't hard to figure out what was on her niece's mind.

Abruptly, Caitlin said, "How come this house is called Quarry Farm? What does *quarry* mean?"

"A big hole in the ground. Your mom says there's a marble quarry in the field behind the barn."

Caitlin frowned, not looking very interested.

"The quarry in the back field is flooded, honey. It's full of water, at least three hundred feet deep. You're to stay away from it unless I'm with you." Margaret gave her a look, wondering if any of this was getting through. She couldn't read any expression behind those heart-shaped dark glasses.

"I can swim," Caitlin said after a moment. There was something about the innocent tone of her voice that told Margaret her niece wasn't a great swimmer.

"Really."

"Yes." Caitlin looked at her over the top of her glasses. "Do you believe me?"

"Sure, if you say so," Margaret said, smiling blandly and making a mental note to watch her like a hawk around any water.

The front doorbell rang loudly, and Caitlin jumped off her chair and ran down the hall yelling, "I'll get it." Margaret hurried after her in time to see her let in a stout, gray-haired woman carrying a shopping bag of cleaning supplies.

The woman smiled and removed a blue silk scarf from her hair. "Hello, you must be Mrs. Schuyler's sister from Boston. I'm Louisa Till, the housekeeper. I come in and help out once a week."

Margaret shook her hand. "Yes, you have no idea how glad I am to see you."

"Like I say, I come in once a week. Caitlin, honey, stop pokin' at that lace." The housekeeper unbuttoned her cardigan sweater, put down her shopping bag and gently swatted Caitlin away from the fragile lace panels by the front door. "I swear, if there's somethin' somebody doesn't want a child to get at, it's just what they go for. Must be some sort of magnetism. I got five of my own, grown now, thank the Good Lord, but they were all like that, every last one of 'em. Enough to drive a person batty." She turned to Caitlin and said, "Run and play now, that's a good girl."

After mulling this over a moment, Caitlin wandered off to the living room and lifted the piano lid with a crash. Loud discordant banging ensued. "Stop foolin' 'round with Mrs. Knox's piano," Mrs. Till shouted. She looked at Margaret and shook her head. "Lord! Well, I'll be gettin' on with my work. The kitchen floor needs a waxin'." She glanced down the hall toward the living room. The banging hadn't stopped, but had slowed and gentled, clearly becoming some sort of tune.

"I'm practicing," Caitlin yelled belligerently from the piano bench as she launched into scales. "Mom says I have to practice an hour every day."

"Oh, no," Margaret muttered with a groan.

"Maybe I'll vacuum, instead," Louisa said wryly, and turned and bustled off to the kitchen, shopping bag of cleaning things in hand.

Margaret went upstairs to get her purse, after which she pried Caitlin away from the piano and told her to change into jeans and a sweater for a ride to Rochester. She found Louisa vacuuming the back hall, and shouted over the vacuum's roar, "I need to get milk and eggs. Caitlin used the eggs and milk in a 'scientific experiment.'" Louisa rolled her eyes, and Margaret just smiled.

After Caitlin was finally ready, they went to the garage. Robert's little black Fiat Spyder was there—the same car they'd been in when he'd broken off their engagement. They got in, and Margaret coaxed the battery to life. Robert had told her that the battery was weak and the brakes might need adjusting. He was still the same, expecting cars to run without maintenance. Margaret thought it was about time he became more responsible, especially since Caitlin had to ride in his car.

She let out an angry breath of frustration as the engine sputtered and finally caught with a deafening roar. Cautiously she backed down the drive and headed toward town. The dirt road was rutted, narrow and steep, requiring all her concentration. It wasn't until they'd almost reached the bottom of the mountain that she noticed Caitlin was very busy writing something in a notebook. She was humming what sounded like "Twinkle, Twinkle, Little Star," and her head was bent over her work. One small hand held a corner of the notebook while the pencil formed somewhat squiggly words.

It looked like a list of some sort.

Margaret flipped the turn signal and pulled out on Route 100, heading toward town. "What are you writing?" she asked after a moment.

Caitlin gave her a suspicious look, then said firmly, "It's a secret. Very comp'cated. I'm not telling, and you can't make me."

"Who said I was going to make you?"

"Well, you can't, that's all. And you can't be mean to me, either. That's against the law."

Margaret pushed back her hair, and her mouth quirked. "I have no intention of being mean to you. I love you, silly." She looked over at her niece, and the suspicious expression in Caitlin's wide, innocent, blue eyes touched her with a small jolt. Unconsciously she straightened a little.

Caitlin bent her head again, scribbled something, then said, "How do you spell *gold digger*?"

A little shocked over Caitlin's question, Margaret glanced at the notebook, then looked back at the road. They'd reached the center of Rochester. There was a big, white church on the left side of the green. Something was going on . . . a church fair. Cars were everywhere. The green was full of tents and booths. She noticed a popcorn cart, flea-market tables and even a fortune-teller's booth. Maybe Caitlin would enjoy having her fortune told.

"I *said* how do you spell *gold digger*?" Caitlin frowned in annoyance.

The supermarket was just ahead. Margaret pulled the car over to the curb and turned off the engine. "*G-o-l-d d-i-g-g-e-r.* Why do you want to know?"

Quickly Caitlin closed the notebook. "I *told* you, it's a secret. Very comp'cated and *important*."

Chapter Two

In the fortune-teller's tent on the green, Madame Zorina sat alone. She was a fat woman with abundant hair dyed a garish orange. Sometimes she consulted the Ouija, sometimes her pendulum, a glass crystal suspended on a cotton thread. She had great ability with both, but right now she was laying out the Tarot.

She'd shuffled the cards over and over, but they still came out the same. She tried again, sliding the cards together, her rings glittering in the dim, murky light. The Death card came out on top. Death, cloaked and riding a pale horse. She covered it with the Queen of Wands.

Her brother, Vern Boyce, came in with a folding chair. She gathered up the cards and put them away as he began to string a curtain of colored beads across the tent doorway. He whacked a nail crookedly into the tent pole, looped the beads across it and climbed off the chair. He'd been drinking since early morning, and by now he was, as usual, well oiled. He stuffed the hammer in his belt, jerked his head at the beads and snarled, "Yer all set. I'll be back 'round five. I'll be needin' some money."

Madame Zorina reared back from the cloud of bourbon emanating from her swaying brother. Stooped and graying, his face tanned and seamed with wrinkles, he glared at her. "All right," she said grudgingly. "But you lay off that booze. We'd have a chance at getting ahead on some of the bills if you'd stay sober."

He leaned toward her, his rheumy blue eyes blazing like flames. "Mind yer own damn business. I got somethin' goin' that'll mean big money. Somethin' you don' know nothin' about."

"Oh?" she said casually, straightening the paisley cloth covering the card table. There was a crystal ball on the table along with her deck of Tarot cards. "It'd make a nice change if you brought home some honest money."

The air in the tent was strangely golden and murky; sunlight shafted dimly through its canvas sides. A gust of wind rattled the beads, and Vern turned to leave. He hesitated a second, then said, "D'ya see anythin' about me today?" She looked across the table, staring right through him, seeing something past him in her mind. She nodded, and he pulled up the chair and sat down. "Tell me what ya saw. Was it money?"

She shook her head and said slowly, "Your aura is...dull and leaden. Be careful, Vern. I don't know what you're up to, but it's not going to turn out right. I used the pendulum this morning, and I saw terrible black fog enveloping you. It's a warning."

Sweat beads started prickling his face. He stared strangely, hypnotically, mumbling something. "Look, I'm going to get more money than you've ever seen in yer life," he said gruffly. "A real big score. I can't stop now. Ahh nuts, yer bluffin'!"

Madame Zorina stood quite still. "I had visions. I saw things. There was an evil woman—with murder in her heart. And another woman with black hair and green eyes. She was with a child. Their coming will mean terrible trouble."

He lurched out of the chair, tossing it over with a clatter. "I don' know nobody like that. Yer crazy, just like the doctors said."

"Greed means death. Things are not what they seem." Her voice was a low, guttural rasp.

Blindly he began backing away. Sweat ran down his back. "Give up a chance of a lifetime to get big money?" He laughed loudly. "Over my dead body."

IN THE CEREAL AISLE of the supermarket, Caitlin intently examined the back of one brightly colored box. "Hmm, this looks good." Actually, she'd never tried this cereal, and really only wanted the orange yo-yo prize inside. She eyed her aunt thoughtfully, wondering if she knew sugared cereal was supposed to be bad for you. Maybe she didn't know about Mr. Tooth Decay and kids getting hyper on sugared foods.

Margaret turned from inspecting different brands of tea bags and noticed Caitlin stuffing the cereal in the cart on top of the bag of oranges. "Are you allowed to eat that?"

"Sure." Caitlin looked down at her purple sweater and yawned. "Besides, I'm wearing purple. That means I'm the queen and get anything I want."

"No kidding."

"Yes." Caitlin smiled with satisfaction. "I'm gonna be queen all the time and tell everyone what to do. Queens get to sit by kings, and everyone has to bow down to them. I think it's real neat."

Due to Caitlin's missing tooth, all her *s*s sounded like *th*s. Picking up the cereal, Margaret exchanged it for one that looked more nourishing. "Let's try corn flakes, instead."

"I hate corn flakes. Queens don't eat them." Caitlin's eyes shot daggers at the box in question. "I want the one with the yo-yo inside."

"Not today. Even queens don't get their way all the time." Margaret pushed the cart up the aisle toward the dairy section. Caitlin followed, grumbling that it wasn't fair, and that queens did, too, get their way, otherwise what was the point of being queen?

"Maybe it's better just being yourself," Margaret suggested, putting a half gallon of milk and a dozen eggs in the cart.

"I can be myself any old time," Caitlin sniffed. "I want to be somebody else besides."

"Like queen of the world?"

Caitlin didn't smile. Where her wants and desires were concerned she had very little sense of humor.

They went through the checkout, and Margaret only had to tell Caitlin twice to put candy back.

"But why? Mom lets me have candy."

"I'll bet. Once in a blue moon." Margaret pushed the loaded cart through the door and outside. "Look, there's a country fair on the green. Want to go?"

Caitlin grinned, her eyes brimming with excitement.

Margaret put the grocery bags in the backseat of the car and locked it. Then they headed to the green.

"I *love* cotton candy. Can I play all the games?" Caitlin asked as they approached the fair.

"I don't see why not. Which booth do you want to try first?"

"Gosh, I don't know." Caitlin crinkled her nose. "I think I'll try the fishing one, but first I want some cotton candy." She grabbed Margaret's arm and dragged her to the food stand.

Caitlin satisfied her sweet tooth, then played a few games, winning two prizes, a cardboard monkey that jumped up a stick when its string was pulled, and a huge peppermint lollipop. They strolled past the fortune-teller's tent, and Caitlin aimed straight for it. "Let's go in here. I want my fortune told. Does she really know the future?"

Margaret's eyes twinkled as she pushed aside the bead curtain in the booth doorway. "Not really, but it's fun. And it's for a good cause. The church is raising money for a new roof."

The glittering beads rattled shut behind them, and Madame Zorina looked up from her crystal ball. Around her neck she wore a bandanna scarf sewn with gold coins. A black, flowing, glittering gown hung from her ample shoulders. The tent was airless, the lighting dim, yet Margaret realized the fortune-teller was the same woman she'd noticed in the house by the bridge. Her hair was the same odd shade of orange, piled high in mounds and coils, fixed with tortoise-shell pins.

Feeling a little embarrassed, she moved forward and said, "We wanted our fortunes told. Do you use the crystal ball?"

Madame Zorina stared hard at Margaret for a long moment, then said, "I read palms for two dollars. The crystal ball costs more."

"Oooh neat! I want her to read my palm," Caitlin declared, hopping up and down with excitement.

"The lady first," Madame Zorina said, gesturing to the chair across the table. "Then I will read yours."

Margaret sat down and put a five-dollar bill on the table. She took a deep breath and extended her hand, palm up. The fortune-teller's dark, glowing eyes fixed on her hand.

"Your name is...Margaret," Madame Zorina said slowly.

"Why, yes, that's right," Margaret said, staring at the woman, astonished. For some reason she shivered a little. There was something eerie about the way the woman was looking at her.

Behind her chair Caitlin whispered a mystified "Wow, how'd she know that?"

Madame Zorina began tracing a line across Margaret's palm. Her finger trembled slightly, and her breath made a hissing sound. She spoke again in a strange, dull voice. "You have been very unhappy. It is here in your palm. You have loved and lost. But now...another man will enter your life and change it forever."

Caitlin whispered loudly, "What does that mean?"

Madame Zorina raised her strange glowing eyes and said, "It means nothing will be the same. There is more here. I see great danger. Not for you, lady, but for another."

"Oh, really," Margaret laughed, half-embarrassed. She started to get to her feet, but the fortune-teller grasped her wrist, preventing her from standing.

"I was wrong. You are in danger, too," she hissed. "You must be careful. Beware of the silver serpent. The time of danger approaches with the full moon."

Finally Margaret managed to wrest her arm free. "Thank you, I'll be very careful." She stood and told Caitlin they were leaving. "It looks like it might rain. I'd like to get back home before it starts."

"What about my fortune?" Caitlin sat down in the chair. "I don't want to leave yet."

"All right," Margaret said with a sigh.

Madame Zorina took Caitlin's hand and peered into it for a moment. Then she frowned and said, "You are young. There's little here to see." Her voice trembled and her face shone with perspiration.

Caitlin stuck out her hand again. "It's not fair! I paid my money. I should get my fortune."

Reluctantly Madame Zorina looked at her palm again. "You will be a catalyst. You will make the difference between life and death for one whose life hangs in the balance." Abruptly she stopped speaking and dropped Caitlin's hand. Fumbling amid the folds of her black gown, she made the sign of the cross. "Here, take back your money. It's not fitting. Go...go!" She made flapping motions with her hands, all but shooing them out of the tent.

"What happened?" Bewildered, Caitlin stared at Margaret as they stumbled through the curtain. "How come she told us to leave?"

"I don't know." Margaret paused and slid a gentle arm around her niece's shoulders. "Never mind. Let's get something to eat. Aren't you hungry? I am!" She steered them both across the grass toward the hot dog concession stand. She realized that the fortune-teller had been badly frightened. Stark fear had lurked in her eyes. Whatever she'd seen in Caitlin's hand had scared her to death.

Shrugging mentally, Margaret decided not to worry about it. They were at a country church fair to have fun, not to dwell on ridiculous dark warnings from some woman dressed in exotic beads and bangles pretending to foretell the future.

Reaching the concession booth, they bought two hot dogs with the works and two sodas, then wandered over to a nearby maple tree and sat down to eat. Caitlin had trouble disentangling the paper wrapper from her hot dog. Most of the mustard and relish ended up down the front of her bright purple sweater.

"Want some help?" Margaret said offhandedly as another blob of mustard plopped into Caitlin's lap.

"I can do it myself. I'm not a baby!" Caitlin chewed in silence for a while, then burst out with "How come I didn't get my whole fortune! I got cheated! It's not fair!"

Lips curving in a smile, Margaret glanced at her niece. "The fortune-teller gave the money back, so you really got your palm read for free."

"Sure, but you got a whole fortune. I only got half."

"Well, I'm twice as big as you are, so my fortune's bound to be twice as long." Margaret didn't have much hope in Caitlin's buying this feeble argument, and she was right. Her niece looked at her with scorn.

"That's dumb. I got cheated, I know I did. She got to the part where I was going to do something important, and she just stopped! How come she didn't tell me everything?"

"Madame Zorina's pretty old." Margaret screwed up her hot dog wrapper and picked up the napkins Caitlin had strewn all over the grass. "Maybe she was tired and couldn't read any more palms today."

Caitlin gave her an intent look. "Hmm, you're pretty old, and she's got to be even older 'n you. Maybe she took a nap and she's rested up now. Why don't we go back?"

Ignoring the remark about her being "pretty old," Margaret looked across the green toward the fortune-telling booth. "Madame Zorina's gone. Her booth's closed."

"I WANT TO SEE a movie," Caitlin demanded loudly. She yanked Margaret's sleeve. They were walking past the town movie theater just as a matinee was starting.

Margaret looked at the poster by the ticket booth. The movie seemed suitable for kids. "Okay, I guess we can go." She bought tickets, and they went inside. Luckily the show was just starting. Caitlin sauntered down the aisle and picked a row about twenty feet from the screen. She sat down, leaving the end seat for Margaret.

Caitlin crammed some popcorn in her mouth. "The ending's kind of dumb, but I like the part where the spaceship lands in the shopping mall." She chomped another mouthful and looked at two little girls who sat down next to her.

Margaret frowned. "You've already seen it?" Caitlin nodded through a handful of popcorn, and Margaret said exasperatedly, "Why didn't you say so?"

Caitlin shrugged. "I felt like seeing it again."

The little girl next to Caitlin whispered something in hushed conversation. Margaret glanced around the near empty theater deciding they weren't bothering anyone. And after all, it would do Caitlin good to talk to someone her own age. Life had to be lonely for her up on the mountain. There were few close neighbors, let alone any with children.

Margaret settled back in her seat and watched the movie. Every once in a while she caught a word or two of Caitlin's whispered conversation. The other child said her name was Nancy and she had two brothers and a cat called Tiger because of his stripes.

"Where do you live?" the little girl asked between bites of her candy bar.

"In Mrs. Knox's house," Caitlin whispered loudly. "We're renting it. My mom got married to Robert, and we moved here last month."

Nancy stared curiously at Caitlin. "The *Knox* place?" Caitlin nodded and Nancy chewed thoughtfully on her candy bar. "Mrs. Knox married old Wendell for his money, and he died. She got plenty. My mom says she's set for life and she's blowing a mint on that trip to Europe she's taking."

The other little girl, whose name was Kelly, leaned over and said, "Yeah, my mom says Mrs. Knox has more money than a dog has fleas. Is your family rich, too?''

Caitlin shrugged. ''Mom inherited money from some old aunt last year, but Robert's just got his job. He works for some drug company, he sells stuff to doctors and hospitals.'' She frowned and asked in a low voice, ''What's Mrs. Knox like? Is she weird, or what?''

''Kind of stuck-up.'' Kelly unwrapped a chocolate bar. ''Want some?''

''Sure.'' Caitlin broke off a piece and put it in her mouth. She chewed a minute, then turned and said to Margaret, ''I'm thirsty. Can I get a soda and a candy bar?''

All three little girls were looking at her hopefully, so Margaret took a few dollars from her purse and handed it to Caitlin. ''Be sure and come right back.'' Immediately all three girls ran up the aisle, giggling and whispering.

Left alone, Margaret watched the screen without really following the movie. She thought about the bizarre fortune-teller. It was odd that Madame Zorina had known her name. Well, there could be a logical explanation. Maybe the town grapevine was working overtime. People knew everybody's business in a small town like Rochester.

Margaret frowned, remembering that the woman had known about her unhappy love life. But most women had their hearts bruised once or twice by the time they were in their mid-twenties. That had been standard fortune-telling patter. The other things Madame Zorina had said about danger coming with the full moon, false lovers, the silver serpent was non-sense.

Margaret drew a deep breath and let it out again. Madame Zorina should have known better than to scare a small child with talk of death.

The three children came back and pushed past Margaret into the row. "Oh, here's the best part," Caitlin pointed out in a loud voice. Immediately a woman sitting two rows toward the back of the theater told her to be quiet. Caitlin scrunched down in her seat and grumbled, "I only said it was the best part."

The scolding seemed to have an effect; for a short time all three girls watched the movie in comparative silence. Only the crunch of popcorn and slurp of soda interrupted the dim quiet of the theater. But once action erupted on the screen, Caitlin leaned over and began whispering to Nancy and Kelly again. Every once in a while Margaret heard Mrs. Knox's name mentioned, so she tapped Caitlin on the shoulder.

"Stop talking. You're ruining the movie for everyone else."

Caitlin shrugged, stuffing the last of her popcorn in her mouth. "This is the most boringest part, anyway."

"I don't care. Other people want to watch it. Now be quiet."

With a loud sigh, Caitlin settled down in her seat. When the movie ended a few minutes later and the lights came up, Nancy and Kelly ran up the aisle after yelling goodbye. Caitlin walked just ahead of Margaret, balancing a half-empty soda and three candy bars.

"Caitlin," Margaret said as they came out into the street and moved through the straggling crowd. "Gossip isn't nice. You shouldn't have talked about Mrs. Knox to those little girls. How would you like it if people talked about you behind your back?"

Caitlin tossed her head. "I wouldn't care. Besides, I'm going to be a detective or maybe a writer when I grow up. They have to know practically everything, and how can you find out things unless you ask questions?"

Margaret didn't have an answer for that. She unlocked the car and told her niece to get in and fasten her seat belt.

They drove to a nearby station to get gas. There was a car at the self-serve pump. A tall, dark-haired man had just finished and was hooking the nozzle back on the pump. He was handsome in a craggy-faced way, and Margaret felt a little unsettled when he glanced at her. The fortune-teller's prediction floated through her mind. She wouldn't become obsessed over every good-looking man she saw.

When they got back to the farm, Louisa was just leaving. She beeped her horn and drove off down the road. Parking in front of the big red barn Margaret unloaded the groceries.

"Can I play outside for a while?" Caitlin asked, looking at her aunt with puppy eyes.

"Okay." Margaret picked up the last bag and closed the car door. "But don't go far. It looks like it might rain."

The sky to the west was darkening. Rolling clouds topped the mountains in the distance, and a brisk wind had sprung up. It smelled like rain, and the mountains were now indigo, except in their shadowed folds, where they looked almost black.

Deciding she would give Caitlin twenty minutes or so to play outside, Margaret closed the door and went to the kitchen to put away the groceries.

CAITLIN MADE a beeline for the door at the side of the barn. She'd tried it yesterday, and it had been open. Nothing much to see inside but musty old hay and a bunch of rusty tools. But she'd noticed a canoe paddle by the hayloft. That might have interesting possibilities.

The door creaked as she pulled it open. She went inside. In the utter stillness of the barn's dim interior, her footsteps sounded loud. The only light came from dusty windows set high in the barn walls. She hesitated a moment, hearing a soft scurrying sound from a nearby stall. Mice, prob'ly. She wasn't scared of mice. Well, not much, anyway.

Swallowing hard, she looked to the left, toward the hayloft. The paddle was still there. She picked it up and ran back to the door, closing it behind her.

There was a barely perceptible path leading up through the weedy field. Carrying the paddle, Caitlin made her way up the path through the field to the top of the slope. On the other side of the field, surrounded by woods, lay the quarry. Dark green stone lined the steep sides. Birch and pine saplings grew in cracks of the stone, and she could see that the path continued downward, curving around to the south side of the quarry, emerging far below near a large, flat slab of marble.

A small wooden boat was tied up by the large rock. It was perfectly obvious the paddle belonged to the boat. What would be wrong with taking the boat out for a while? It was Mrs. Knox's, and she was in Europe. She wouldn't care, Margaret thought happily.

She shifted the paddle to her left hand and grabbed on to a birch sapling as she made her way, slipping and sliding down the quarry path. She knew she should ask permission to use the boat. But that would be dumb. If she didn't ask, she couldn't be told no.

Wind rustled in the trees as she reached the large rock on the far side. A few raindrops began to fall, but by now she was determined to take the boat out for a ride. She untied the rope and got in, clutching the side of the boat for balance. It wobbled, and she sat down on the seat in the middle and paddled away from the rock.

She grinned. This was really neat, really fun.

She took a look at the far side of the quarry. It seemed a long way away. Leaning over, she peered down into the green water. It was clear and looked about a thousand miles deep. She could see way down past the dripping paddle, where the water changed imperceptibly from green to black.

Caitlin dipped her fingers in. It was cold—and deep. She wondered what kind of fish swam in the quarry. Dolphins? No, they lived in the ocean. Sharks probably... or deep-sea monsters lurking down in the depths. Maybe she'd got her fingers out just in time. What if they surged up and knocked the boat over? She would die, her body sinking down to the bottom... unless sea monsters swallowed people whole.

She was being silly and took a deep, reassuring breath. Sharks lived in the ocean, also. And there would only be small fish, like the ones that nipped her toes last summer in the pond in the town where they used to live before her mom married Robert.

Caitlin paddled some more, and the boat swung out toward the center of the quarry. Overhead, gray clouds massed, their shadows racing over the water. She felt their chill for a few moments before they raced on, leaving sudden shafts of sunlight so brilliant that the shadows cast by the trees lining the walls of the quarry looked black as ink. Imperceptibly the errant raindrops grew harder, and thunder rumbled in the distance.

MARGARET WAS just folding up the last of the grocery bags when the doorbell rang. She went to open the front door and found a tall, dark-haired man standing on the front step. He smiled warmly, and Margaret guessed he was in his early thirties. "I was looking for Robert Schuyler. My name is Jake McCall."

A little shiver of excitement ran down her backbone. He was the same man she'd seen at the gas station. He topped six foot three, with thick black hair brushed back casually from his forehead, tanned skin and a hint of crow's feet at the corners of his gray eyes. Warm appreciation lurked in his smile. Though large and rugged-looking, there was an odd gentleness about him.

Releasing the breath she'd unconsciously been holding, Margaret said, "Robert's away at the moment. Are you a friend of his?"

His gaze flickered from her sneakered feet up her jeans past her fire-brigade-red sweater to her slightly flushed face. "Yes, I'm an old friend. Actually, I'm his former brother-in-law. He was married to my sister, Betsy."

Chapter Three

"Please, come in," she stammered, her mind in a whirl. He held out his hand as she closed the door. As his fingers gripped hers she felt a tingling sensation all the way up her arm. "I'm...well, it's rather complicated. I'm Margaret Webster, Robert's sister-in-law."

They moved into the living room as she explained about Sandy's having married Robert the summer before. Jake nodded and said, "I heard he'd married again. I haven't seen him since...well, in some time." And he sat down in a wing chair.

Margaret sat on a small Hepplewhite settee as the clock in the hall chimed six. She said with a puzzled frown, "I can't get over Robert's having been married before. He never mentioned it. I can't understand why—were he and your sister divorced?"

Jake hesitated for a second. His quick smile faded as he unbuttoned his tweed jacket. "No, my sister died suddenly three years ago. I was out of the country at the time. I'm a civil engineer, and my job sometimes takes me abroad." There was a small silence, then he went on, his voice lower, "Robert was with her when she died."

"I'm so sorry," she said inadequately.

"Betsy had asthma and a heart condition, but medication had kept it under control for years." His voice rasped and he cleared his throat. "My family was in shock when she became ill...and then suddenly died."

Margaret felt very uncomfortable and was caught off guard when Jake asked, "I gather your sister and Robert are happy?"

"Of...course," she stammered, "they couldn't be happier. They've gone to Florida for a couple of weeks." The words just seemed to continue as she added, "Sandy's been sick, some sort of flu. Her doctor suggested rest and warm weather to prevent pneumonia from setting in. I'm taking care of my niece, Sandy's daughter from her first marriage." When he didn't say anything, Margaret added, "Caitlin's seven, and a holy terror."

He studied her for a long moment. "You look like you can handle her."

"Sometimes I'm not so sure," she said. Then, feeling awkward again, she continued, "How did you find out where Sandy and Robert were living?"

"Believe me, it wasn't easy. When I got back from Australia, Robert had sold the house and moved out of town. He and my sister owned a place in Connecticut." Jake shrugged his wide shoulders. "It's pretty involved, and I got lucky. The people who bought the house remembered Robert's saying at the closing that he'd changed jobs. He mentioned a possible move to northern New England. I knew he was crazy about skiing. We'd always talked about it, and he described Rochester, a quiet town west of Rutland where he'd spent some time skiing. I had to come north on business and took a chance he might have ended up here. A few calls downtown at the local realtors, and I hit paydirt."

"I see," she said with a small smile.

"Robert's a great guy. I didn't want to let the family connection drop."

"Yes, he's pretty wonderful," she agreed, the distant, pain-filled expression in her wide green eyes telling Jake she was hiding something.

He'd damn well touched a nerve there, he knew. Her face was pale now, leaving her pensive looking. Her generous mouth was set in a determined line, as if she'd made up her mind about something. But just as quickly as he'd caught her expression of sadness, it was gone, and he wondered if he'd imagined it.

"Do you live in Vermont ordinarily?" He shot her a curious look.

The clock chimed six-fifteen, and she glanced toward the hall with a frown. "No, I live in Boston. Sandy and I grew up in western Massachusetts. This is my first visit to Vermont. It's so quiet and peaceful." Abruptly she rose from the settee. "I'm getting a little nervous. My niece is playing outside, and I really ought to check and see if she's all right. There's a quarry up behind the barn. I told her to stay away from it, but with Caitlin you never know."

"Why don't I go with you?" he suggested easily, getting to his feet.

Margaret was already down the hall. She yanked open the back door and called Caitlin's name. When there was no answer she ran outside, past the red barn with its dark, staring windows, then up through the field, blackberry canes whipping at her jeans.

The wind was rising, gusting, and rain spattered against her face. Thunder roared and crackled beyond the smoky blue of the clouds massed over the mountains.

"Caitlin?" she yelled again and again above the wind. The night was dark and wild, the sky eerily lit with streaks of yellow lightning to the west.

"Caitlin?" Jake McCall's voice boomed behind and to her right. Still no answer. They kept running, plunging through the scrubby undergrowth toward the steep edge of the quarry.

And suddenly there was Caitlin, sitting in a small boat, paddling madly toward the quarry's edge. The boat appeared to be making some headway, although it wobbled furiously from side to side.

"Oh, God," Margaret cried. Cupping her hands around her mouth she yelled, "Caitlin, make for shore. I'm coming!"

Jake came up behind her and caught her arm. "Let me go first. I'll get her."

The last thing she wanted was an argument, and anyway, Jake could probably reach Caitlin sooner. She nodded quickly, following him down the steep path, frantically grabbing saplings to keep from falling. Already he was several yards ahead, running as he neared the bottom of the path. When he reached the flat rock, he dove in and swam out toward Caitlin in the wooden boat, which by now was going around in circles.

Dragging in a shaky breath, Margaret ran the last few yards to the rock. Rain was pouring down in sheets; she could hardly see the boat with Caitlin in it.

Lightning flickered, eerie and blue. Then suddenly the quarry lit up bright as day, and she saw them clearly. Jake had hold of the prow of the boat and was determinedly swimming back toward shore.

Over the rumble of thunder he yelled, "*Sit down*, Caitlin. I'll take you in!"

For once Caitlin did as she was told, although there was a mutinous expression on her face.

When they reached the rock, Margaret helped her out of the boat and hugged her. "My God, I'm glad you're all right!"

Jake climbed up on the rock and tied the boat's mooring line to a sapling. "It was a close call. That's no place to be in a rainstorm."

Caitlin frowned, hunching her small, wet shoulders. "I was only doing Mrs. Knox a favor."

"I'll bet." Margaret grabbed her arm and marched her back up the path to the top of the quarry. "I told you to stay away from this place. What possessed you to come down here?"

"Mrs. Knox left the boat out. I was just going out for a little ride before taking it back to the barn. Mom says to put stuff away when you're through with it, so I thought I'd—"

Margaret hustled her along through the blackberry bushes. "Not another word. I don't want to hear any of it. You're taking a bath and going straight to bed when we get back to the house." She turned her head and called to Jake who was bringing up the rear with the paddle. "Would you lock that up in the barn, please?"

"Sure," he said and headed diagonally through the field toward the barn.

Caitlin was still complaining nonstop. "I can swim, honest. You can ask Mom when she calls. She'll tell you it's okay if I go to the quarry by myself."

By this time they'd reached the back door. Margaret ushered Caitlin inside. "I don't care if your mom says you swim the English Channel every six weeks! You're not to go near that quarry while I'm responsible for you, and that's final!"

A large puddle of water was accumulating around Caitlin's small, sneakered feet. She sneezed. "It's not fair. I never have any fun anymore."

Margaret dragged Caitlin upstairs to the bathroom to take a nice hot bath. Over her niece's objections, she helped her off with her sodden purple sweater. And as she unsnapped the button of Caitlin's jeans, Margaret half listened for the slam of the back door. Jake was taking a long time putting the paddle in the barn.

As if she'd been reading Margaret's mind, Caitlin sneezed again and said suddenly, "Who was that man who pulled me out of the water?"

"A friend of Robert's," Margaret muttered as the back door slammed. Caitlin kicked off her sneakers, then yanked off her socks and threw them in a heap on the floor. Margaret sighed tiredly and said, "Pick up your things and put them in the hamper."

Ignoring this, Caitlin climbed into the tub. "Robert used to know Mrs. Knox, too, a long time ago."

"Where did you hear that?" Margaret remembered Sandy and Robert talking about the landlady. They said they'd only seen the woman once, when they'd signed the rental agreement at the realty office down in Rochester.

"I read a letter he wrote to her. He signed it, 'love.'" Caitlin lay back and began kicking her feet, making violent waves that slopped over the sides of the tub.

"Stop that. Where did you find a letter from Robert to Mrs. Knox?" Margaret stared at her niece, forgetting completely that she'd told her over and over it wasn't nice to pry into other people's affairs.

Sitting up, Caitlin began soaping her rosy-pink belly. "I'm not telling. It's a secret." She threw a sidelong glance at her aunt. "Want to play riddles? I'm really good at it."

Margaret opened the cabinet door and rummaged around for shampoo. "Okay. You start."

"Long neck, crooked thighs, little head and no eyes. What am I?"

Thinking hard, Margaret picked up the shampoo, closed the door and turned back to the tub. Caitlin was scrubbing away at the bottom of her left foot.

She frowned as Margaret knelt by the tub and took the top off the shampoo. "Don't get that stuff in my eyes. It stings. Come on, what am I?"

"I won't, I promise. And I don't know." Margaret poured a little in her hands and began sudsing Caitlin's already wet head.

"A pair of fire tongs! I told you I was good! Want to play again?"

"No, I know when I'm out of my league." After rinsing Caitlin's hair, she helped her out of the tub and toweled her off. "Wrap that around you and get into your pajamas."

Caitlin nodded, then looked up and said, "Know what Nancy said?"

"Nancy?" Margaret's brow furrowed slightly, and then she remembered the little girl in the movie theater. "Okay, I remember her now."

"Her mom says Mrs. Polly Knox has a lot of nerve. After old Wendell Knox died, even before the grass was green on his grave, she had a man move in." Caitlin tilted her head. "How long does it take for grass to get green?"

"I don't know." Margaret leaned down and let the water run out of the tub. "Where did you hear this nonsense?"

"You never listen. I told you, Nancy's mom. She said there was this big scandal. Polly Knox told everyone that the man was her cousin, but nobody believed it. Nancy's mom says Mrs. Knox wouldn't know the truth if it walked up and bit her on the ankle, and that her supposed cousin was shiftless and bone lazy. What's *bone lazy* mean? How can your bones be lazy?"

Margaret sighed with exasperation. "They can't, but they can get tired. Maybe this cousin of Mrs. Knox's was sick, but that's not the point. This is gossip, and you shouldn't listen to it. Whether or not Mrs. Knox's cousin came to stay at her house is none of our business. When Nancy started talking about it you should have changed the subject."

Caitlin looked at her in stubborn silence. Then she burst out, "Mrs. Knox and her cousin fought a lot about money, too." The expression on her face said that she knew this for a fact.

Margaret gave her a long, serious look. "How do you know they did?"

"I'm not telling. Anyhow, it's a secret." Caitlin hitched the towel up under her arms as if that were the end of the discussion.

Unfortunately Margaret knew that Caitlin's enormous bump of curiosity had been aroused as far as Mrs. Knox was concerned. She'd poke her nose into every nook and cranny of the poor woman's life, and nothing would stop her.

Launching into a lecture about leaving other people's things alone, about trust and the violation of privacy, Margaret stopped in mid-sentence and asked, "Do you understand what I mean, Caitlin?"

"No."

"Do you care?"

"No. I *told* you I'm going to be a writer or a detective when I grow up. Writers have to find out stuff."

Margaret gave up. "Go get your pajamas on, then blow-dry your hair. The dryer's in the closet on the middle shelf. You do know how to use it?"

Caitlin nodded and turned toward the door. She took a step, then looked over her shoulder. "Mrs. Knox left her winter coats in the sewing room closet, but the one in her bedroom has lots of uniforms in it. White ones. She used to be a nurse." There was a secretive smile on her face.

Margaret drew a deep breath, emphasizing every word as she spoke. "No more going into her bedroom. It's off-limits."

"Mom told me there was a law passed so you could find out stuff—the Freedom of Information Act." The tone of Caitlin's voice was superior, implying it was too bad her Aunt Margaret was so dumb.

"That law has nothing to do with snooping in that woman's bedroom closet. You stay out of her room, and I mean it!"

Caitlin tossed her head and went to her bedroom while Margaret went downstairs to the kitchen. Jake was at the stove, just turning the gas on under the kettle.

"I hope you don't mind, but after that soaking, I thought we could both do with a hot cup of tea." He grinned, his hair dark and wet with quarry water. In fact, he was wet from head to foot.

Margaret sighed. "I'm sorry. I forgot you were soaked, too. Let me get you a towel from the downstairs bathroom."

His grin widened. "I could use one."

A minute later she was back with a thick blue towel. He took it and scrubbed furiously at his hair, wiping his face and neck as the kettle whistled.

Margaret switched the gas off and got down two mugs. "I can't thank you enough for your help."

"How is Caitlin? No ill effects, I hope." Jake's deep voice held concern.

"No, she's fine. She went off to get her pajamas after lecturing me on the Freedom of Information Act. Honestly, she's only seven, but she'd try the patience of a saint."

He raised an amused eyebrow. "An only child?" She nodded, and he said, "That explains it."

Margaret got out tea bags and poured boiling water in the mugs. "There's cream and sugar on the table, or I can get you lemon if you prefer."

He pulled out a chair for her. "No, this is fine." His hand brushed against her back as she sat down, leaving a trail of warmth. He sat across the table and stirred sugar into his mug of tea. "Does it worry you, staying here alone while your sister's away?"

She shrugged. "At first I didn't give it much thought. But now I realize it's quite a responsibility. This place is full of valuable antiques. I pray that Caitlin doesn't break anything."

His eyes caught and held hers. Gray blue, magnetic, darkly lashed, with those laugh lines at the corners. Nice eyes, direct, honest. They were smiling at her, saying he liked what he saw.

He sipped his tea and lowered the mug. "The landlady must have insurance if she's renting."

"I hope so. She'll need it," Margaret said grimly. She sat back in her chair with a sigh. "The truth is, I'm not concerned so much with what Caitlin breaks. It's everything else she does that worries me. Every time I turn around she's poking her nose into Mrs. Knox's belongings or eavesdropping on conversations. She's even got a notebook she carries around with her, writing down everything she hears. Her excuse is that she's going to be a detective or a writer when she grows up. And they need to know everything. That's where the Freedom of Information Act comes in. She's decided it gives her carte blanche."

He laughed, a relaxed, easygoing laugh that brought a smile to her lips. "What else does Caitlin do?"

"She practices the piano every day for an hour. I'd like to lock it up and throw away the key—she's that bad."

"I remember my piano lessons when I was about that age." He smiled and scrubbed his hair again with the corner of the towel. "The metronome ticking away. Pure torture. I don't know how my teacher stood it. On a good day I'd hit one note in ten. And I didn't have many good days." He leaned back in the chair and went on musingly, "Poor old Mrs. Perkins probably wore earplugs. Either that or she was deaf as a post. Taught piano to generations of kids. A real martinet. Once I hid a grass snake in the piano and sat there, figuring she'd call the lesson off when she found it."

Margaret sat back in her chair, unable to contain the beginnings of a grin. "What happened?"

He shrugged. "Mrs. Perkins had the last laugh. She picked up that snake and threw it into her garden without turning a hair, then kept me practicing scales for an extra half hour. She was really something else. They don't make characters like that anymore."

"I wonder." Margaret ran a thoughtful forefinger up and down the handle of her mug of tea. "I met a woman today who was quite a...character. A fortune-teller down at the church fair on the town green."

"Sounds interesting," he replied with a distinct twinkle in his eyes. "What happened?"

She took a sip of tea. "Caitlin and I saw her sign, Madame Zorina, Famous Psychic—Palms Read for Two Dollars. So, we went inside. Everything seemed fine." She paused a moment in recollection. "No, that's not true. She seemed upset as soon as we entered the tent. Maybe it was my imagination working overtime but she seemed to turn white as a sheet the minute she laid eyes on us. And once she began reading our palms it got worse.''

"What happened?"

"At first she said the usual thing, that I'd meet a tall, dark-haired stranger who would change my life." Margaret threw him a slow, shy, half smile. "I guess you'd qualify."

"Ahh, the plot thickens," he drawled teasingly. "What else did she predict?"

Margaret gave an embarrassed laugh. "Oddly enough, she knew my name and something else about me." She hesitated a second, then explained, "The truth is Robert and I were engaged for a short while before he met my sister. He fell in love with her, and that was that, as they say. It was mainly bruised pride, but at the time..."

There was a little silence, then he said quietly, "It felt like your heart was broken."

She gave an embarrassed shrug, realizing suddenly with a dawning feeling of surprise that she was finally over Robert. He was simply someone she'd loved once. That terrible aching hole in her heart was gone for good, and with its passing she felt a lightness inside. An incredible sense of freedom.

She lifted the mug to her lips and said self-consciously, "I didn't mean to bore you with a rehashing of my love life. It's odd, though. Madame Zorina put her finger on it just like that."

"Probably a lucky guess."

"Two lucky guesses?" she said, trying to sound nonchalant, as if the fortune-teller hadn't actually frightened her.

"What else did she say?" His face was solemn, concerned, with just a trace of a lingering smile in the curve of his mouth.

"There was terrible danger ahead, for me and someone close to me. Something about a snake and a full moon." She shrugged uneasily. "I know it sounds crazy, but there was an eeriness about her I can't explain. Her eyes looked...almost transparent, not just glowing, but lighted from within. Like a Halloween pumpkin." She gave a little shudder and went on. "Maybe it was the tent. It was so dark you could hardly see your hand in front of your face. And while she was telling our fortunes, I...I really believed her."

"She might have a little ESP, but it sounds as if she's just a typical con artist," he said thoughtfully.

Margaret leaned forward. "When she started reading Caitlin's palm she got frightened for some reason and wouldn't tell us what she saw. Her hands were shaking." She drew a breath and said, "Naturally, Caitlin wouldn't leave until she had her fortune told. Finally Madame Zorina gave in. She said Caitlin would be a catalyst and make a difference between life and death in someone's life. Then she gave us back our money and threw us out of the tent. She even made the sign of the cross. I almost felt like Dracula!"

"No trace of fangs from where I sit," he said with a grin, gray-blue eyes dancing. "Madame Zorina's got quite a line in hokum."

She sat back and tugged her sweater down slightly. She wished she'd been more particular about what she'd packed in the way of clothing. The red sweater, although her favorite, soft and warm, was three years old and getting shabby and thin in spots. She tugged at the hem of the sweater again as she noticed Jake's gaze flicker over her shoulders and lower.

"Sorry to be such a mess. I wasn't expecting company. Living way up here, Caitlin and I dress more or less to please ourselves."

His eyes strayed from her creamy smooth face and heavy mane of curly hair to her gently rounded slenderness. "Don't mind me. I don't count as company. Just your garden-variety brother-in-law, once removed." A hint of laughter threaded his deep, husky voice.

Feeling a wave of warmth that had nothing to do with the hot tea she'd been drinking, she fiddled with her teaspoon. The trouble was he didn't look like any garden-variety brother-in-law she'd ever seen. Even one once removed. He was too darned handsome.

Dark, rugged good looks, lean athletic build and an easy, engaging smile, reflected in eyes the color of the evening sky. She drew a deep breath, deciding he was nice enough. He hadn't displayed any wolfish tendencies, although she'd noticed his eyes looking her up and down.

"Vermont's beautiful, isn't it," he commented after a moment. "There's a sense of peace that's indescribable. You went so quiet on me there, I thought maybe you'd fallen asleep."

She smiled and shook her head. "Not asleep, maybe dozing a little, though. The peace of mind creeps up and takes you by surprise. When I first arrived, I was still running at the usual stressed-out level. But after I'd been here a couple of hours I noticed how calm I was. I'd love to find a small place up here when I'm drawing social security."

"Somehow, when the time comes, I doubt you'll have to count on social security for subsistence," he said with a wry grin. "I expect there'll be a long line of men who'll offer you a good deal more than that."

She gave him a level look across the table. "That's supposing I'm in the market for some man to support me, which, I assure you, I'm not."

"A case of once burned, twice shy?"

"Perhaps. I prefer to call it common-sense independence. I like standing on my own two feet. It's something I've been doing a long time. My parents died my last year in college. Except for Sandy, I've been more or less on my own ever since."

"Independence is fine, but living up here on the mountain you'd better make damn sure the car's in working order."

She gave a little laugh. "Now that you mention it . . ."

"What?"

"It's Robert's car. The starter sticks, half the time third gear doesn't work, and the battery's temperamental."

He got up. "I'm pretty good with engines. Why don't I take a look at it for you?"

"That'd be great." She smiled gratefully and went with him to the back door. "It's out by the barn. Here's the key."

"No problem." He pocketed the key and opened the door. Wind blew in droplets of rain. "Be back in a minute." With a flash of a smile he was gone, running toward the barn.

JAKE OPENED the driver's door of the Fiat and leaned
in to pull the hood latch. It jumped in his hand as he
felt the hood pop open. The interior of the car smelled
of wet leather and something else, faint and flow-
ery...like Margaret he thought. Getting in, he tried the
starter. It turned over reluctantly. The dashboard battery light flickered and died—so did the engine.

He tried again, flooring the accelerator. This time
the engine caught, hiccuped once or twice, then settled into a low roar.

The car needed a tune-up, for sure. He pulled the
parking brake. It felt loose. He got out and looked
under the hood, poking around at the plugs.

He pulled one out. Corroded as hell. He put it back.
Just like Robert. Never kept a damn thing in running
order.

He used a handkerchief to wipe grease off his hands
and got back behind the wheel. The engine wasn't
running like a top. If he had tools and parts, he would
replace the plugs and wires himself.

Leaning down, he switched off the engine and
pocketed the key. He sat there a moment longer,
watching rain run down the windshield. His attention
was caught by a shining drop of water running along
the inside seal. A leak. Rain continued dripping,
thudding monotonously on the floor mat on the passenger side.

Something shiny winked at the edge of the mat.

He leaned past the gearshift and pulled back the
mat, his fingertips touching something glittery and
hard. He picked it up. An earring. Little diamond
chips surrounding a red, oval stone. He frowned. It

looked like a ruby set in platinum. Expensive. Maybe Margaret's or her sister's.

He got out and slammed the door. Head ducked low against the rain, he ran back to the house and up the steps. Margaret looked disconcerted when he dropped the earring in her palm and told her where he'd found it.

"Well—it must be Sandy's. It's not mine. I'll tell her you found it when she calls."

"If there are tools in the barn, I'll fix the car. It needs a tune-up, and the brake cable's snapped."

She drew in a deep breath. "I don't want to put you to any trouble. I'll get it fixed at the garage in town."

He smiled at her. "You don't want to drive that car. Especially with Caitlin in it."

He could tell from the firm set of her chin that she hated to ask for favors. Her answer was indirect. "No, I don't want to take a chance and break down."

He grinned. "Tell you what. I'm tired now, but tomorrow I'll fix the car, and we can go out to dinner. How's that?"

Her green eyes met his, looking mildly amused. "If you're suggesting a night out on the town, I accept."

"Great." He turned to leave. "If there's an emergency before I get it tuned up, be careful."

"I will."

She walked him to the front door, and when he reached his car, he glanced back at the house. Shivering, she thought of Madame Zorina and her predictions.

UPSTAIRS, Caitlin peered over the stair banister for a moment, listening. Nothing but the low murmur of voices coming from the kitchen. They would be busy for a while, she thought hopefully. Time to do some more detecting, like Sherlock Holmes. She frowned. Aunt Margaret had said Mrs. Knox's room was off limits. Surely the Freedom of Information Act applied in this case. If a person really needed to find out stuff, then it'd be okay to snoop. It'd practically be their duty to go investigating.

Mrs. Knox's room was just down the hall. Pushing it open, she went inside and looked around. Blue and white wallpaper with flowers on it, a big canopy bed and a dressing table with a mirror.

If there was one thing Caitlin liked, it was mirrors. She went over and sat on the bench in front of the dressing table, looking admiringly at her reflection. She turned her head sideways and glanced at her profile. She practiced a few smiles.

Growing bored, she looked down, noticing there was a drawer in the dressing table. She pulled it open. A tube of lipstick rolled sideways in the drawer, coming to a stop next to a photograph half-hidden by a box of face powder.

This was more like it, she thought happily. Face powder and lipstick! Prying the lid off the box, she discovered to her delight that it contained a fuzzy pink puff. She dabbed some powder on her cheeks and nose, gazing critically in the mirror. Maybe lipstick would look good. She took the top off the tube and leaned close to the mirror, concentrating with all her might as she colored her lips.

It was hard to do. The orchid-pink tube slid sideways off her upper lip, garishly marking her cheek.

Some got on her nose, and she used tissues to get most of it off.

She stared at her reflection and decided she needed another layer of lipstick. There! Now she looked beautiful. Replacing the tube in the drawer, she picked up the photograph. It was boring. Just a woman with blond hair in a pink, frilly blouse. A big tree with lights and decorations could be seen behind the woman, and she held a half-unwrapped box in her hands.

Losing interest, Caitlin dropped the picture back in the drawer and slid off the bench. Just then she heard the sound of the front door closing downstairs. She tiptoed out into the hallway and looked around. No one was upstairs. That meant Aunt Margaret was someplace downstairs. What if she came upstairs? If Aunt Margaret found out she'd been in Mrs. Knox's room, she'd probably be punished. Well, she would say she'd just forgot. That was an excuse that worked pretty well, most of the time.

She went into the bathroom, deciding to blow-dry her hair. Even Sherlock Holmes prob'ly dried his hair once in a while.

As Caitlin had predicted, Aunt Margaret came upstairs, walked into the bathroom, took one look at her face and groaned. "Oh, no! Where'd you get that lipstick? It's all over your face!"

Chapter Four

Caitlin cast a dreamy look at her reflection in the bathroom mirror, admiring the way her mouth glimmered. "It's only a little smeared. I got it practically all off. Aren't I pretty? I look just like Barbie."

Margaret was too busy soaping up a facecloth to answer immediately. But as soon as she began scrubbing, she had plenty to say. "Never mind *Barbie*. How *could* you?" She drew in an angry breath. "I told you over and over to stay away from Mrs. Knox's bedroom. That's where you got the lipstick, isn't it?"

Caitlin eyed her aunt, wondering exactly what tone to take. Even under the diffuse lighting of the bathroom she could detect the flush rising on her aunt's throat, could see the grim line of her mouth. She was real mad.

"I forgot."

Aunt Margaret's mouth got madder looking. Without a word she turned and went down the hall to Mrs. Knox's bedroom. Caitlin took one more look in the mirror, then trailed after her. "I didn't hurt anything."

But Aunt Margaret apparently didn't care that she hadn't broken anything. She was busily cleaning lipstick smears off the top of the dressing table and throwing away littered tissues.

Caitlin yawned and wandered over by the dressing table. It only took a second to pull open the drawer. "Look what I found. A Christmas picture." She held it up, and Aunt Margaret took it from her fingers, barely glancing at it before tossing it back in the drawer. Caitlin picked up the lipstick. "How come Mrs. Knox left this behind when she went away? It's brand new."

"How should I know? She must have more than one lipstick. Maybe she got tired of that shade of pink." Aunt Margaret looked around the room for a moment, then marched Caitlin out into the hall and shut the door firmly behind them. "I'm going to make pizza for supper. Do you think you can behave for half an hour?"

Caitlin looked at her aunt with mild amazement. What was she talking about..."behave." Of course she could do that. "Sure."

Aunt Margaret's reaction was interesting. The look on her face registered frustration, irritation and a sort of hopeless resignation. In Caitlin's experience, grown-ups generally reacted like that, even when you weren't actually breaking anything. She waited for a long, boring lecture.

It didn't come. Instead, Aunt Margaret gave her a thoughtful look, then patted her shoulder. "Okay, I'll put the pizza in the oven. Then we can watch a movie. There're some tapes in the den."

"I know how to run the VCR. Mom lets me."

Another thoughtful look, then Aunt Margaret smiled. "Find a movie you like while I get supper ready."

She turned and went downstairs to the kitchen. Caitlin waited until the coast was clear, then climbed onto the banister and slid downstairs.

Sherlock Holmes was still on the job.

It took only a minute to put *Escape to Witch Mountain* in the VCR and turn it on. Aunt Margaret wouldn't complain about a movie like that, and it was loud enough to cover up what she planned to do. Searching the den prob'ly wouldn't make a lot of noise, but master detectives didn't take unnecessary chances.

Tall bookshelves ran along the far wall of the den. A lot of books with hardly any pictures, Caitlin thought, surveying the brightly colored spines. Still, there might be a clue, something written in invisible ink or in secret code. She smiled in pleasurable anticipation. No problem for Sherlock Holmes, hot on the trail of a master criminal. An open-and-shut case.

She dragged the piano bench over to the bookshelves.

MARGARET SLID the pizza into the oven and closed the door. She savored a minute or two of relative peace and quiet, if one could call the movie sound track floating down the hall from the den soothing.

Placing napkins and plates on the table, Margaret froze when she heard a thump and a sharp cry of pain. That hadn't sounded like a movie. She dropped the napkins on the table and ran to the den.

Sure enough, Caitlin was just picking herself up from the floor. Obviously she'd fallen off the piano bench. She rubbed her small backside. "Ouch."

Margaret helped her up. "Are you okay?"

Caitlin nodded. "Uh-huh. I just fell off the bench."

"I thought you were going to watch a movie."

Caitlin turned away and stuffed something white into her pajama pocket. "I am, in a minute. I was looking for a pencil. For my notebook writing. I broke the point on this one. See?" She turned around and held out her notebook and pencil.

Margaret frowned. Something funny was going on. Caitlin hadn't been holding that pencil a minute ago. No, there'd been something white in her hand. It had looked like a folded piece of paper.

Caitlin was wearing her round-eyed innocent look. Margaret sighed and said, "There's a sharpener in the kitchen. I'll sharpen it for you."

Shrugging, Caitlin flopped on the sofa and began watching the movie. "Okay. Let me know when the pizza's ready. I'm starved."

With a frustrated shake of her head, Margaret went back to the kitchen. What was the point of confronting Caitlin and telling her she knew there'd been something else in her hand? Caitlin would just come up with another story.

At the ring of the oven timer, Margaret took the pizza out and cut it into slices. She had to realize that Caitlin was only seven, insecure and upset with Sandy's being away.

She decided she wouldn't say anything about the mysterious piece of paper. Not right now, anyway.

Margaret ignored the small voice echoing at the back of her mind that suggested Caitlin wasn't an ordinary seven-year-old. Somehow she knew she would live to regret it.

JAKE DROVE down the mountain toward town. Rain was still falling heavily enough to keep the windshield wipers busy and make the narrow road surface dangerously slick. He had to pay close attention to his driving. Not much traffic along the road, not even on the highway.

He was thinking about Margaret—her unconventional beauty. Her hair was that rare true black with a sheen like silk. Its heavy masses framed her smooth face, modeled with precise delicacy. And those eyes...huge smoky and green, black lashed. Tiger eyes. Robert must have been crazy to give her up.

He wasn't aware that he was smiling faintly as he drove past the town green. The church fair was over; the booths and games removed. Every bit of refuse had been picked up, and the grass glowed greenly in the rain-drenched night air. Only the sign remained, flapping wetly in drizzle between two huge maple trees.

In the back of his mind he heard Margaret's voice describing the fortune-teller, Madame Zorina.

On an impulse he pulled the car over by the curb and turned off the engine. There was a second-hand bookstore half a block back. He got out and dashed toward the dimly lit storefront. The bell tinkled as he closed the door behind him, nodding to the woman behind the counter. "Good evening." She smiled and immersed herself once more in her paperback. Clearly a late customer couldn't compare with the exploits of her detective-hero.

Jake was a compulsive book buyer. Back in his apartment in New Haven, he had stacks of books, so many they wouldn't all fit in the shelves. He kept meaning to arrange his books in some kind of order.

He walked down the narrow aisles in the bookstore, knowing he could waste the rest of the evening here. He plucked a copy of *Bleak House* from the shelf and a paperback of Agee's *A Death in the Family,* before he found the Occult shelf. Assorted volumes, including a large, blue *History of Witchcraft,* and another on palmistry and Tarot. Not that he seriously believed Madame Zorina was a real witch, but she'd known Margaret's name. Of course, someone in town could have mentioned that she was taking care of Caitlin.

Carrying the four books, he walked back to the cash register. His footsteps echoed on the dusty floor. Outside, rain was pounding on the windowpane, shining like diamonds. The clerk looked up as he approached. "Find something you like?"

"Just these four." He placed the books on the counter. "You probably don't get many people buying books on witchcraft and palm reading."

Shifting the pile of books, she glanced at their spines. "Not many, but you'd be surprised what interests people."

"I noticed a fortune-telling booth at the fair today," he said pleasantly.

"Oh, Madame Zorina?" The clerk gave him an obscure smile. "What did you think of her? Oh, that's an even five dollars."

"Very impressive, I admit." He got out his wallet.

"Ugly as hell and a real crackpot, but if she told your fortune—" The clerk shrugged. "I'd pay attention if she said not to fly anywhere. Not that I believe everything she says, but there's *something* about her predictions. People laugh, and maybe she does mix in a few whoppers just to make things sound spectacular. But every once in a while she sees things. She read my palm and everything she saw was right on target. She said the man I was seeing wasn't trustworthy, that he really disliked women. I found out Madame Zorina was right. And she told me I would come into money. Not two weeks later my uncle died and left me this place. I've been selling books here ever since."

"It could be a form of mental telepathy."

The clerk shrugged. "Emotional atmosphere, something you can't explain in ordinary terms. Just because you can't see something doesn't mean it's not there. The air we breathe." She rang up the sale and closed the cash register drawer. "Maybe Madame Zorina tunes in on things that are invisible to the rest of us."

He picked up the stack of books and turned to go. "Is she ever wrong about her predictions?"

"Sure." The clerk chuckled. "Last summer she pestered the fire department for weeks. Said she'd had a vision that the town would be hit by a flood. No one paid her any mind, then the volunteer firemen were hit by a flood—one of their hoses sprang about a thousand leaks, flooding out Harvey's barn over in South Hollow."

Jake frowned and shifted the books under his arm. "She sounds like she's off her rocker."

"Who knows. Maybe she is." The clerk picked up her paperback. "But like I said, if she told me not to take any plane rides for a while, I wouldn't get on one for a million bucks."

MARGARET AND CAITLIN ate their pizza in front of the TV. It was eight o'clock when *Escape to Witch Mountain* ended, and Caitlin declared she wasn't a bit sleepy, so Margaret let her stay up and watch another movie.

Sorting through the shelf of video tapes, Margaret found *Dial M for Murder.* She put it in and pushed the Play button. "It's twenty years old and black and white, but it's a classic."

Caitlin rolled her eyes. "It's dumb. I saw it ages ago, and I didn't even like it."

"Too bad." Margaret sat down on the sofa. "Maybe you'd rather go write in your notebook or play with Barbie."

"Maybe I will." Caitlin yawned, suiting her actions to her words and heading toward the stairs. "Good night."

Margaret frowned. There'd been something fake about that wide yawn. She certainly was up to something. Unfortunately with Caitlin the possibilities for mischief were endless. She'd better go up and check on her in a little while just to make sure she hadn't climbed out the window and taken off for the quarry again and another forbidden boat ride. After a moment she called up after Caitlin, "I'll be up to tuck you in bed in a few minutes."

"Okay." Caitlin's voice floated downstairs, then her bedroom door slammed, and Margaret sat and watched the TV with a blank stare. Her mind wandered, and she thought of Sandy and Robert. Most likely they would call tonight, and then she would tell them about Jake McCall's visit. How would Robert react to the news? she wondered. The sudden appearance of an ex-brother-in-law he'd never mentioned. He'd probably told Sandy about his first wife by this time, that she'd died during an asthma attack.

But what if he hadn't?

She got up and pushed the Power button on the VCR, then turned the TV off. Funny, she had a strange, almost superstitious reluctance to tell Sandy and Robert about Jake.

Sandy had gone through so much with her nagging illness. She'd looked so pale and thin, and poor Robert was clearly worried about her health.

Margaret still couldn't make up her mind. Picking up the supper dishes she took them out to the kitchen and mopped up dried grape jam on the floor in front of the refrigerator where Caitlin had dropped it. All the while the thought of Jake McCall hovered in the back of her mind. His strong, lean face alert and compassionate. She sighed as she put the mop away.

She went upstairs to check on Caitlin. Her bedroom door was closed, and when she opened it quietly, her niece was curled under the covers, deep in sleep. Margaret dropped a kiss on her freckled nose and crept out into the hall again, leaving the door slightly open. Caitlin might wake in the night and call out.

She went downstairs and turned off the lights and locked the house up for the night. Then she curled up on the bed with a paperback mystery until after midnight, waiting for a call from Sandy. But the phone never rang. Finally she fell into exhausted sleep, and maybe it was the storm—the wind had strengthened, rattling dead branches off the big sugar maples in the driveway—but when she fell asleep, she began to dream a terrible nightmare.

She'd come home from work and entered her apartment in Boston, walking into the living room. Only somehow, it was Mrs. Knox's living room, with the crewelwork draperies, the piano, the ticking clock. And she was overcome by the most deadly fear she'd ever known. Sandy was sitting on the Hepplewhite settee, only it wasn't her sister at all. It was a big, stuffed doll that looked like Grace Kelly.

The French door was open, the draperies billowing. Someone had just left. She ran through the house calling frantically for Sandy. But each room she went into was empty.

She woke with a start, covered with clammy perspiration, shuddering...and heard Caitlin crying, "Mommy..." Margaret got out of bed and pulled her robe on, then ran down to Caitlin's room. Her niece was sitting up in bed, rubbing her eyes, still sobbing her heart out. "I...I had a bad dream," she gulped as Margaret took her in her arms.

"It's okay, I'm here now. The bad dream's all gone." She rocked Caitlin back and forth, kissing her cheek. "See? Everything's fine now."

Caitlin glared up at her. "How can everything be okay when Mom's still married to Robert? I *hate* him! He's awful, he hogs all the dessert, even when there's enough for me to have seconds. How would you like it if he was your stepfather and pinched you when no one was looking? He's a mean old pig, and I hate him, I'll always hate him! I don't care what Mom says or you say, he *stinks!*'' The rest of her mumbled complaints trailed off in a hiccuping wail.

"Shush, it's okay, I've got you. Nothing's as bad as that, honey." Margaret hugged Caitlin, brushing back her rumpled hair with her lips. "It's probably pizza that gave you bad dreams. You ate too much."

Caitlin shook her head and sniffed. "I like pizza. It's Robert. That's why I have bad dreams, because he's my stepfather and I hate his guts."

Margaret settled herself more comfortably on the bed, nudging something bulky under the blanket with her knee as she pulled Margaret back against her breast and rocked her. "It was the storm, that's all. But the rain sounds lovely on the roof. Hear it pattering? It's like a lullaby. Hush now, darling. Try and go back to sleep."

She kissed Caitlin's forehead and laid her back down among the covers again. She didn't dare get into an argument about Robert again. It was none of her business, anyway, whether Caitlin accepted him as her stepfather or not. That was Sandy's problem, thank God.

Caitlin sniffled once or twice, then fell back to sleep, curled up among the blankets like a cherub. Which only proved appearances were deceptive, Margaret thought tiredly as she crawled carefully off the bed, trying not to wake her again. But her foot caught the edge of the bulky object under the bedspread and knocked it onto the floor.

It was a shoebox, and its contents spilled out onto the rag rug. She glanced up at Caitlin, but her niece's even breathing never faltered. She was dead to the world.

Margaret got down on her knees to gather up everything and put it all back without waking her. All sorts of odds and ends dear to a seven-year-old's heart, she thought wryly. A matchbook, an empty cigarette pack, Ninja Turtle cards, and an outdated itinerary from... She peered at the thin sheet of paper in the dim light from the hallway. A Rutland travel agency— Gateway Tours—for a trip to St. Kitts and Martinique, dated two years ago. A folded letter, probably the white paper Caitlin had been hiding behind her back earlier, and a black and white snapshot of...Robert. He had a mustache in the picture and was standing in front of Mrs. Knox's house! Robert said he'd never seen this house before the real estate agent showed it to them.

She tilted the picture toward the light and looked at it again. The upper left corner was torn, and it was crumpled. Clearly Caitlin had done her best to straighten the creases. Robert was looking slightly away from the camera as if he hadn't known his picture was being taken. The focus was blurred, but the house in the background was definitely Mrs. Knox's and the man was Robert with a mustache.

She tumbled everything back in the shoebox and tucked it carefully under the bedspread by Caitlin's feet. Now was not the time to tackle Caitlin about this. Obviously this was the booty she'd gathered through her ceaseless snooping. If she wanted to find out everything she could about the landlady, nothing would stop her.

Margaret went into the hall and noticed a slight draft from downstairs. A loose shutter began banging against the house, then a dead tree limb thudded onto the roof. She went downstairs, yawning widely. Her mind couldn't stop thinking about the photograph. It must have been taken a while ago. He'd never had a mustache in all the time she'd known him. And why had he pretended he'd never been in this house before they'd rented it? She remembered how he'd been unable to even recall Mrs. Knox's name. He'd turned to Sandy. "You know, darling, Mrs. . . . the owner of the house. . . ."

She reached the bottom step and decided not to think about it anymore. There was a definite draft coming from down the hall. The air was colder, and there was an eerie sensation engulfing her.

Margaret switched on the overhead chandelier. It swayed slightly, crystal droplets tinkling in the stream of wind.

She followed the trail of cold air into the living room and saw that the French door had blown wide open. She closed it tightly and went into the kitchen. The window over the sink yawned wide; cold air blew in and out, knocking over several pots of herbs. Dirt littered the counter and floor.

"Oh, no! What a mess!" She leaned over the sink and closed the window before sweeping up the dirt and remains of the herbs. Then she noticed the cellar door was open, too. Somehow that was the last straw.

Margaret stood at the top of the stairs, shivering in her quilted robe, in a state of near panic. Below, the cellar lay in nightmarish darkness. She tried the light switch on the wall, but the bulb had burned out, and it was set so high in the ceiling it would take a human fly to reach it.

There was a flashlight in the counter drawer, but the batteries were almost dead. She shook it, and the beam brightened; but after only a few seconds it flickered and settled into a dim yellowish glow. Margaret glanced at the kitchen clock. Three a.m. That settled it. No way was she going down those stairs, no matter how many windows were open down there. She heard a slight clinking noise from somewhere in that yawning darkness. A fallen branch hitting a cellar window? Wild horses couldn't drag her down those stairs.

She shut the door tightly, blocking out a mental picture of thieves breaking into the cellar.

Suddenly the shutter stopped banging. All was quiet. She sighed and went back upstairs. Thank God Caitlin had slept through the whole thing. She peeked in the half-open door of her room. Yes, there she was, still sleeping like a baby. She prayed Caitlin would stay that way for the rest of the night and went down the hall to her room.

DOWNSTAIRS IN THE CELLAR the woman who'd tripped over the carton of old whiskey bottles rubbed her ankle, swearing softly. That had been too damned close. If that interfering idiot had come down and found her prowling around, she'd have had a hell of a time explaining what she was doing.

In the dark her eyes were angry, then calculating. She removed a tiny pencil flashlight from her coat pocket and slowly scanned the dimly lit cellar as the gas-fired old furnace kicked on suddenly with a roar.

There was a small door next to the furnace, but the
woman ignored it, knowing it led to an old fruit cellar. She started edging up the stairs. It was unlikely the
door had been left unlocked, but worth a try. She
turned the knob, but it didn't budge. Either she got the
door open, or she would have to try some other means
of getting into the main house.

Luckily the door was old and ill fitting in its frame.
Her plastic credit card worked nicely and edged the
bolt back with only a muted click. She pushed the
door open and found her way to the kitchen. The table and chairs were barely discernible in the dark. She
continued down the hallway, gauging the distance in
the blackness. Using the flashlight sparingly, she took
great care not to allow the beam anywhere near the
windows. The house was quiet, and everyone should
be in bed. She looked at the luminous dial of her
wristwatch—three-thirty. Which gave her plenty of
time to search downstairs.

A subtle gradation of grays and blacks indicated the
white-painted risers of the front staircase. She worked
her way through the living room, dining room, then
the den. She ran the flashlight along the bookshelves
on the far wall. Dozens of paperbacks, some hard-
covers. Books on gardening, art, travel, all aligned
carefully—except for one volume that protruded from
the shelf, by maybe half an inch. A big, red dictionary.

Picking up the book by its spine, she tucked it under her arm and searched carefully in the space where
the book had been. Her fingers found nothing, and
she began pulling other books out, throwing them to
the floor without thought. Soon the shelf was bare.

She ran the flashlight's beam over its surface, cursing softly, "Where the hell is it?" She seemed to sway with a mixture of sheer rage and fear, then took a deep breath to collect her wits. Composing herself, she took a quick look toward the hall to make sure she hadn't wakened anyone when she'd tossed the books on the floor. All was as quiet as a tomb. She gathered up the books and stuck them back on the shelf, but not in the same order. There wasn't time for that. She would take one more encompassing look before she was done. She stretched out a manicured hand and straightened the dictionary, wondering if *he'd* found them, the damn bastard.

Well, there were other, more pressing things to be taken care of, including a cold-blooded murder; but it wouldn't be her first killing—and she suspected it wouldn't be her last.

She walked silently across the worn oriental rug to the front hall, catching a glimpse of her ghostly reflection in the gold-framed mirror on the wall, and laughed softly. Then she opened the door and let herself out of the house.

Chapter Five

In the morning Margaret stood staring at the front doorknob. She felt a jag of fear like a knife in the stomach. The door was unlocked, but she remembered locking it before she went up to bed last night. Someone had been in the house while she and Caitlin had been asleep!

She swallowed hard, studying the hallway. Everything looked normal. But someone had to have been in the house last night.

Really frightened now, she went through the house, room by room, looking for anything missing or out of place. Nothing seemed to have been touched or stolen. Mrs. Knox's silverware still rested in the dining room sideboard. The TV, stereo and VCR were still in the den.

"What are you doing?" Caitlin asked from behind her.

Margaret almost jumped out of her skin. She took a deep breath and turned around. "I put a book down somewhere and can't remember where I left it." Carefully conversational, she went on, "That storm last night was awful, wasn't it? The kitchen window blew open and knocked the plants all over the floor. Honey, you didn't unlock the front door when you came downstairs, did you?" Caitlin was wearing her heart-shaped sunglasses. They waggled from side to side when she said no. "Oh, then I must have done it myself." Margaret gave a smiling shrug. "What do you want for breakfast—cereal or pancakes?"

A HALF HOUR LATER Margaret was washing the breakfast dishes and getting up the courage to go down the cellar stairs to check for broken windows when the phone rang.

A woman's voice said expectantly, "Polly?"

"I'm sorry, Mrs. Knox isn't here."

"Oh . . . well, uh, to whom am I speaking?"

"Margaret Webster. Who is this, please?"

"Where is Mrs. Knox, and when will she be back?" the woman said rudely.

"I don't give out information to strangers," Margaret replied, her voice crisp.

There was a small pause before the caller said, "Well, then I might—thank you very much." The receiver went down with a bang.

Margaret frowned and hung up. What was that all about? She really couldn't think about the caller. There was a more immediate problem on her hands. Should she call the police about the door? And tell them what, exactly. That she'd found it unlocked? They would thank her politely for reporting it and decide she was a nut, the type of hysterical woman who looked under her bed every night.

She put the last dish away just as a horrendous crash erupted from the other side of the house. Caitlin was at it again!

She ran down the hall and caught her niece standing on the edge of a chair, reaching up into the hall closet for something. The chair was teetering back and forth as Margaret dashed up to catch Caitlin before she fell. But the chair skidded and they both tumbled to the floor, landing on several boxes of games and puzzles that had already fallen off the closet shelf. There was an odd creaking sound, and Margaret glanced up in time to see the rest of the shelf come down, as well.

She grabbed Caitlin, shielding her quickly as a glass punch bowl whizzed past, a framed photograph, woolly hats, and lastly, what looked like a partial afghan, with the crochet hook still stuck in it.

Luckily Caitlin was unhurt. The punch bowl and photograph hadn't been so lucky. They lay on the floor, smashed to pieces. Margaret counted to ten and helped her niece up. "Get me a broom, pronto."

"I was only—"

"Never mind what you were doing. I'm trying hard not to spank you, Caitlin. Now go get a broom and dustpan."

Margaret swept up the glass and tried to control her temper while Caitlin stood by, explaining how it hadn't actually been her fault. "I was shooting a paper airplane, and it went up in the closet. So I had to get the chair and climb on it to reach high enough to get it down off the shelf. I didn't want to bother you because I knew you'd get mad."

Margaret leaned on the broom and fixed Caitlin with a fiery green stare. "The whole mess could have been avoided if you'd asked for help." She looked around at the dismal pile of broken glass on the floor—and there was no sign of a paper airplane anywhere. She strongly suspected it had never existed in the first place. "Where's the plane?" she asked accusingly.

Caitlin craned her neck and peered up where the shelf had been, as if she expected to see the fictitious plane still circling, like a tiny jet over a fogbound airport. "Wow, it's gone! Maybe it didn't go into the closet at all. Maybe it flew into the living room, instead."

Margaret gritted her teeth and put the shelf and its contents back up in the closet, then she dumped the shattered remains of the punch bowl and picture glass into the garbage. She went back into the living room to find Caitlin innocently writing in her notebook. "I think it's time we had a talk." But even as she opened her mouth to deliver a stern lecture on privacy and the responsibility of living in someone else's house, she knew it was a mistake. If she admitted to looking through the contents of the shoebox, Caitlin would go underground like a mole and Margaret would have no idea what she was up to. If she hammered away about Mrs. Knox, and how Caitlin shouldn't be snooping into the woman's belongings, inevitably she would say the wrong thing and Caitlin would redouble her efforts to find out all she could about the poor woman.

But it was too late now; she'd already started the lecture. So she droned on, emphasizing the need for honesty. When she ran out of breath and ideas, Caitlin asked, "Do you want to play gin rummy?"

Margaret stared at her, exasperated, feeling at her wits' end. What in the world was she going to do about Caitlin? She was tired of being bamboozled and bullied by a seven-year-old, and blurted out, "What exactly is in that notebook of yours. Don't bother telling me it's a secret. I don't want to hear any more of that nonsense."

Caitlin eyed her warily. "Uh, I told you. I'm gonna be a writer when I grow up, and I've decided I'm gonna write mysteries. So I'm collecting clues and stuff."

"About what mystery in particular?"

Caitlin took a dim view of this line of questioning. Frowning, she pushed the heart-shaped sunglasses back up on her nose, fiddled with the notebook cover and kicked at the leg of the Hepplewhite settee. Finally she said grudgingly, "Okay, I might as well tell you. You're gonna find out, anyway. It's about Mrs. Knox."

"What about Mrs. Knox," Margaret said with dawning horror.

"Well, she's *dead*, of course. Robert killed her. Here, see for yourself." She shoved the open notebook into Margaret's lap.

Margaret stared at the notebook in disbelief. It seemed to be partly in some rudimentary code, appealing no doubt to Caitlin's sense of the dramatic, and all about the probable whereabouts of Mrs. Knox.

Caitlin had written at the top of the page "Caitlin Ashley Emerson" in as fancy a script as she could. Underneath she'd printed a painstaking list:

P. Knox, t.y. ago, w. P.M.!
Psnd? Stbd? Kdnpd?
In Qry???
In lynbyn?
Buryd alve???

Margaret shut the notebook with a decisive snap. "This is ridiculous. The woman's in Europe."

Caitlin smiled. "Ha! That's what Robert wants everyone to think."

"What's your stepfather got to do with this?"

"Everything! He killed her, see?" Caitlin opened the notebook again to the appropriate page and tapped the first item on the list. "Two years ago Mrs. Knox *wasn't* Mrs. Knox. She was Polly Merrill. I know because . . ." She paused and shot Margaret another wary look. "Never mind how I found out. I know, that's all. Her name *was* Polly Merrill. Then she met Wendell Knox. He was rich and he owned this house with his wife, Martha. They were both old, but Martha was real sick. That's their picture that got broke in the closet just now."

"Oh, really," Margaret commented dryly.

"Yeah, well, Polly Merrill was a nurse. Remember, I told you about the uniforms I saw in her closet?" Margaret nodded dumbly, and Caitlin prattled on. "Polly got to be Martha's nurse, and then Martha died. Remember my friend Nancy?" Margaret found herself nodding again. "Well, Nancy said her mom said Polly knew a good thing when she saw it and latched on to Wendell before he knew what hit him. He married her, then he died, too. And that's how Polly got to be rich."

"That still doesn't explain why Robert would want to kill the woman. He doesn't even know her." Margaret shook her head in disgust.

Caitlin chewed on her lip in silence for a moment, then said with an air reminiscent of Sherlock Holmes cluing in the bumbling Dr. Watson to the obvious particulars of their current case, "I happen to have other stuff, proof he knows Polly. Only it's *knew* now, on account of she's prob'ly dead. Even if he didn't stab her or shoot her or anything, he prob'ly locked her up in a dark dungeon full of rats, where she starved to death, or he buried her alive, or something. Maybe he killed her and dumped the body in the quarry after he got her to go for a boat ride. That's why the boat's still there. He didn't feel like putting it away." Caitlin's eyes gleamed behind her sunglasses. "That's proof she's dead. Mrs. Knox would have put the boat away like you're s'posed to, right?"

Margaret took a deep, bottom-of-the-lungs breath. She glanced from Caitlin's stubborn expression to the notebook in her lap and then to the shoebox—that no doubt contained the proof Caitlin was talking about.

Margaret opened her mouth, but nothing came out. She just sat there, shocked and stunned. Caitlin's obsession with Mrs. Knox had obviously gone too far. If only she could talk to Sandy and get help dealing with all this! She cleared her throat, racking her mind for something intelligent to say. "Uh...look, your theory about Polly Knox—none of it would explain Robert's wanting to kill her."

"He's *mean and rotten,* that's why! They prob'ly fought...well, I know for a fact they had fights about money. Never mind how I know, I just do. Robert prob'ly wanted all Polly's money, and she wanted to spend some on her trip to Europe." Caitlin yawned, then said affably, "So he killed her dead."

Margaret stared at her in disbelief. "Because he didn't want her to spend her money on a trip to Europe? Come on, Caitlin! You just don't like Robert. Mrs. Knox would have to leave a will making Robert her heir, before he'd inherit anything." She shook her head. "Not one word of this makes sense. Why am I sitting here arguing about this. I must be crazy."

Snatching back her notebook, Caitlin jumped to her feet in sudden anger. "Okay, don't believe me! I don't care! Robert will get away with the perfect murder, and it'll be all your fault! And he might even hurt Mom to get her money, too. He tells lies all the time! When Mom was so sick he didn't even call the doctor—even though he told her he did." She gulped for breath and rushed on furiously. "It was all a big fat lie! I hid on the stairs and watched him pretend to dial. *He lied, lied, lied all the time, and I hate him!*" Caitlin turned and ran down the hall and upstairs. Seconds later her bedroom door slammed.

Margaret fought the urge to rush after her and talk this out once and for all. But Caitlin was too upset and angry; she would never listen to reason. Her imagination had conjured up this mountain of preposterous accusations and lies about Robert.

Sandy had warned Margaret that Caitlin went overboard at times with her pretending. Taking a deep breath, Margaret wondered if her niece had gone to Sandy with the same ridiculous stories about Robert. And if she had, why hadn't Sandy told her?

Caitlin, Sandy and Robert really needed to talk out their problems. Either that, or Caitlin would drive them all crazy.

DOWN BY THE RIVER in the white Victorian house, Madame Zorina passed her ringed hands over a crystal ball. She was breathing heavily, eyes focused on the swirling clouds within. "Come on, I ain't got all day. Whaddaya see?" Vern Boyce stared across the table, eyes narrowed in resentment.

"I see many things." Madame Zorina breathed deeply. "Children's games, nursery rhymes...'A B C, tumble-down D...'" When she spoke, her breath stirred the black lace draped over her orange hair and made it tremble. "*D* stands for *death*, Vern. That's what I see. It's here in the crystal. *You, terrible danger, death!*"

He flinched, the cords standing out in his neck. "Yer lyin'. There ain't nothin' in that crystal ball. I told ya before, there's big money comin' my way. I ain't doin' nothin' to spoil things." His smirk revealed grimy teeth. "I ain't got time for your nonsense."

"Death will come." Her voice shook with emotion.

Sweat broke out on Vern's brow. He brought his fist down on the table hard, making the crystal ball shake. "Listen to me, old lady. I know something and it means big money."

"No." She shook her head and folded her hands in her lap. "It means *death*."

MARGARET WAS still sitting on the Hepplewhite settee when the hall clock struck noon. She felt unsettled and worried—especially about the unlocked front door. She knew she'd better make lunch before she scared herself to death.

About half an hour later Caitlin came downstairs just as Margaret took open-faced bacon, tomato and cheese sandwiches out of the oven. Sending Margaret a grumpy look, she said, "I don't want to talk about my notebook and Robert anymore. I'm hungry. I want—"

With a smile Margaret went over and gave her a big hug. "Lunch. Okay, I'll feed you, and I promise not to say one word about your notebook. Sit down while I get the milk." She slid the sandwiches on two plates and looked around. Caitlin was standing on the stool by the counter, examining the wall calendar.

"When's the next full moon?" she asked curiously.

Surprised, Margaret walked over and took a look. Finding the tiny full moon, she tapped the calendar. "Here, next Monday. Why?"

Caitlin got down, in the process knocking over the nearby flour and sugar tins. White powder cascaded everywhere, and by the time Margaret got it all cleaned up, Caitlin was halfway through her sandwich. She shot a quick look at her aunt. "Want to know why I asked 'bout the full moon?"

Margaret sat down across the table, the pleasant aroma of toasted tomato and cheese curling up between them. She was afraid to ask.

"Of course, if you don't want to know..." Caitlin mumbled past a mouthful of sandwich.

"Okay," Margaret conceded with a tired sigh. "What's the big deal about the next full moon?"

Caitlin leaned forward, eyes gleaming with excitement. "Madame Zorina, natur'ly. She said it means *danger,* remember? She even knew your name, so she prob'ly knows all kinds of stuff. She said I was a . . . a cantaloupe or something. What did she say I was?"

Margaret groaned mentally, then swallowed hard and said, "A catalyst."

"What's that?" Caitlin demanded.

"An expert at driving me crazy. No, it means you make things happen. At least she got that part right." Margaret managed to catch Caitlin's glass of milk just as she was about to knock it over.

"I've got a neat idea." Caitlin eyed the wall phone. "Why don't we call her up and ask her to tell the rest of my fortune. She prob'ly got over being tired by now."

"I don't think that's such a great idea," Margaret said thinly.

Just then the phone rang, and Caitlin grabbed it, shouting into the receiver rudely, *"Who's this?"* She listened for a second, then handed it to Margaret. "It's for you. Some dumb man."

The dumb man was Jake McCall. She could hear the smile in his deep voice. "Hi, I thought you might like to go out to dinner. That's of course, if you can get someone to stay with Caitlin."

Margaret hesitated. Somehow his voice sounded different over the phone, deeper, more intimate. She found that her hand holding the receiver was trembling slightly. Before she gave in to any second thoughts she said firmly, "Yes, I think I can get someone.'' It would be a relief to get out of the house, even for an hour or so, and Mrs. Till could probably come in for the evening. She'd said she was available most nights for baby-sitting.

Besides, it would be the perfect chance to talk to someone who could be objective about Caitlin's ridiculous obsession about Robert and Mrs. Knox. She turned and glanced over her shoulder at Caitlin who was busy pulling clothes off one of her Barbie dolls. That absorbed pose didn't fool Margaret. Her ears were flapping a mile a minute. She was dying to know what they were talking about.

''How about the inn down in Rochester?'' Jake murmured in her ear. ''They have really good seafood. I could pick you up about seven.''

''I'll have to call Mrs. Till, but if she's busy and can't stay with Caitlin, I could make dinner for us here,'' Margaret suggested. Her cooking was strictly utilitarian, nothing fancy.

He laughed. ''Let's hope your baby-sitter's available. Not to cast aspersions on your cooking, but I have a feeling Caitlin would be underfoot all evening.''

''Exactly.''

He laughed again, and Margaret felt a treacherous weakness in her knees. They talked for a few more moments, then Jake hung up and Margaret turned to see Caitlin watching her. With an effort she brought her mind back from its sidetrack of Jake's lean face, his piercing eyes and rich deep voice.

Caitlin shrugged her shoulders in disgust. ''Dumb love stuff!''

"I sincerely hope so," she agreed gravely, her green eyes laughing. Just then the front doorbell rang. She told Caitlin to stay in the kitchen while she answered it. A tall, stooped man stood on the porch. He had weather-beaten features and wore overalls and an old red and black lumber jacket. He nodded and took off his cap.

"The name's Vern Boyce. I'm Mrs. Knox's handyman. Thought I'd stop by after last night's storm and clean up the yard. Mrs. Knox likes me to keep the place tidy lookin'."

Margaret gave him a curious look. Sandy hadn't mentioned a handyman, and there was something unpleasantly sly about his dark eyes, as if he was secretly laughing at her. "I'm sorry, I don't know anything about a handyman." She went to close the door, and he pushed it open with a large, dirty hand. "What is it?" she asked steadily, every muscle of her body tense. She didn't like the way his narrowed gaze slid past her shoulder into the house. He swayed slightly, and from the strong odor of liquor on his breath, she realized he was very drunk.

"Mrs. Knox'll be real mad. She likes the place kept up nice." He grinned suddenly. "You stayin' here alone? Pretty lady like you? Gets lonely up here on the mountain. I could stop by, keep you company for a while if you like."

Caitlin had appeared in the hallway. That's all Margaret needed. Now she would have to explain drunken men to her. Margaret shoved the door shut quickly, missing the look of consternation on the man's angry face.

Caitlin frowned darkly. "Who was that?"

"Mrs. Knox's handyman." Margaret gave her a reassuring smile. "I said we didn't need him today."

"Oh." Caitlin stared at Margaret's white face for a long moment. "You were scared of him, weren't you?"

For a second Margaret considered denying it, then changed her mind. "Yes, I didn't like him or trust him. If he comes to the door again, don't let him in."

Caitlin nodded cautiously. It was on the tip of Margaret's tongue to ask if she knew if her mom had made arrangements with Mrs. Knox's handyman to keep the yard cleaned up, but Caitlin turned and went off to the kitchen without another word.

Shrugging her shoulders, Margaret watched from the window as Vern Boyce staggered out to his truck and drove off. She drew a sigh of relief and went downstairs to the cellar to look for broken windows while it was still daylight. Maybe she could fit some cardboard in place of any broken panes.

It was surprisingly dark at the foot of the stairs, even though it was barely two o'clock. A carton of empty whiskey bottles stood near one of the columns that held up the kitchen floor overhead. She shivered. It was cold down here, damp.

Several more cartons of bottles were stacked against the far wall. Why hadn't Mrs. Knox thrown them out? And how much did the woman drink?

She ducked under a cobweb and found a broken window. A branch was sticking through the hole in the glass. Carefully she removed the branch and tore a piece of cardboard from a carton. She fitted it over the broken pane. That would have to do for now.

Caitlin clattered down a few steps and looked around. "Wow, look at all the bottles. Do you think she drank all that before Robert killed her?"

Margaret frowned. "I thought we weren't going to talk about that nonsense anymore."

"Well, I forgot," Caitlin muttered offhandedly, wandering down another step or two. Margaret reached out a hand and grabbed her arm.

"No, you don't. This cellar is off-limits. Too many dark corners and glass bottles. Get back upstairs and don't poke that nose of yours down here again." They climbed back upstairs, Caitlin still arguing that dark corners never scared her, she was brave, she would be okay. Margaret didn't buy that argument and firmly locked the door behind them.

MARGARET WAS just fastening her earrings when the doorbell rang and Jake arrived, a little before seven-thirty that evening. With a critical eye she took one last look in the mirror. Her blue dress was an old favorite, falling in swingy folds to just below her knees. Maybe not the latest fashion, but it was comfortable, and she always felt good when she wore it.

She went downstairs and came face-to-face with Caitlin who was coming from the kitchen with a mug of hot chocolate. As she opened her mouth to warn her not to spill it, the contents sloshed over the rim. She closed her eyes, but when she opened them, Caitlin was still there. She prayed for patience. "Take that back to the kitchen and drink it. And bring a damp cloth to mop this up."

By this time Jake had appeared in the living room doorway. His gaze took in her appearance, the graceful line of her figure, the way her black hair shone in the light from the overhead chandelier. He smiled. "Hello."

"Hi, I'll be ready in a minute," she said apologetically. Pushing down a bewildering sense of familiarity and ease, she snatched up her coat and purse. The feeling was so strong her heart was pounding. "I'll be back around ten or so, Mrs. Till."

The housekeeper, whom Margaret had called and asked to baby-sit earlier that afternoon, was leading Caitlin off to the kitchen for a damp cloth as Jake held the front door open.

"Don't you worry, Miss Webster, we'll be just fine." Mrs. Till smiled comfortably and gave Caitlin a nudge down the hall. "Didn't I tell you to drink that in the kitchen? Land sakes, you never listen!"

THE RIDE TO TOWN was fairly short, as they'd decided to eat at the inn, a big, white-pillared establishment with a side terrace for summer dining.

Jake ushered her up the steps and inside. "Heard from Robert and Sandy yet?"

She shook her head no. "They're probably having too much fun, but I'm sure they'll call soon."

They ordered drinks and pea soup as a starter for grilled swordfish. At the small white-draped table Margaret slowly relaxed amid the murmur of conversation, soft laughter and the clink of cutlery.

It was a large room, half-full of diners. A huge fieldstone fireplace took up the middle of one wall. Flanking it were tall, black-glassed windows, which by daylight would reveal a spectacular view of mountain peaks and blue skies. Now the windows revealed a few bright stars and winking candlelight.

"How's your business going?" she asked pleasantly as their drinks arrived.

The waitress left and Jake said, "So-so. I'm involved with a project in downtown Rutland. They're talking massive reconstruction. It means tearing down quite a few buildings." Jake just stared and found himself looking directly into Margaret's eyes. They were extraordinary eyes, green as pools, fringed with thick black lashes.

"I thought you said you were a civil engineer. I didn't know they put up buildings."

He smiled. "Usually we're involved in things like roads, bridges, highways. Sometimes, though, we're called in if there's large-scale demolition."

"Dynamite and blowing up buildings? Sounds like a schoolboy's dream."

"Not quite, but pretty close," he admitted with another smile. "What do you do when you're not taking care of Caitlin?"

"Nothing as exciting as your job. I work for an insurance company in Boston." She gave a half laugh. "At least Caitlin's a change from insurance forms five days a week."

"Has she recovered from her boating adventure?"

She nodded. "I think so—" She looked up as the waitress placed the soup on the table. "As a matter of fact, I wanted to talk to you about something."

The waitress left and Jake glanced across the table at Margaret curiously.

"Caitlin doesn't like Robert. In fact, she seems to despise him." She gave a sad shrug. "I guess it's natural. She hardly sees her real father. And when Sandy married Robert, she probably thought she was losing her mother, too."

"They haven't been married long. Give her time, she'll come around."

"It's not just hurt feelings. Caitlin's making up stories, telling horrible lies about Robert."

"What sort of lies?" he asked, puzzled. She sighed and sat back in her chair. She wore a soft velvet dress of blue with bell-like sleeves and a deep neckline. Her skin was smooth and creamy. Her breasts moved softly beneath the heavy material as she shifted her shoulders. He said gently, "Come on, it's really bothering you. Tell me about it."

Reluctantly she met his gaze. "I'm just about at my wits' end with her. She's convinced Robert has killed the landlady, Mrs. Knox. She's collecting clues, writing her suspicions down in a notebook."

"Sounds serious. Robert might end up behind bars if he's not careful."

"It's not funny," she said, her green eyes wide and hurt.

"Okay," he said gravely. "But I wouldn't worry too much about her detective work. When the landlady returns, Caitlin will realize she was wrong. It's probably just a phase she's going through. Robert and your sister will have to deal with it."

She flicked him a noncommittal glance. Her body was tense, her fingers taut as she gripped her napkin, as if she felt she had to hang on to something. After a long moment she let out a breath. "Something else has me upset. I got up this morning and the front door was unlocked. I locked it last night before we went up to bed. Someone was in the house last night, I'm sure of it."

"Anything missing? Did you call the police?"

"Not that I could see. And I had no real proof, so I didn't call them." Her husky voice trailed off, her eyes brilliant in the candlelight.

"Caitlin might have left it open and forgot to tell you," he suggested quietly.

"I asked her, and she said she hadn't touched the door." She drew a deep breath, smiled ruefully and said, "God, I wish Sandy and Robert were home. I know my sister isn't well, but Robert could certainly handle things."

"Well, they'll be home soon. How'd you meet Robert, anyway?" he asked curiously.

She shrugged. "Downhill skiing, last year. I was at Killington with friends. Trail conditions were awful, wall-to-wall ice. I slid halfway down the mountain on my backside, then hit a tree and panicked. Everyone was back at the lodge. I was cold and scared, and Robert happened along, thank God. Calm and cheerful, he talked me down the rest of the way." She smiled in reminiscence. "I don't think I could have made it without him."

"He's a damn good skier. Rock-climbing, too," Jake said thoughtfully. "He's always been pretty much of a loner."

"He never had much family life. His father died or ran out on the family. His mother remarried when he was ten or so. He's been more or less on his own since he was a teenager." She smiled. "But he turned out all right, even without much of a stable home life."

"A terrific guy," Jake agreed, leaning back in his chair and stretching out his legs.

Margaret noted the smooth play of muscle and the long, lean lines of his body. Intimidating. She frowned and pushed the thought out of her mind. "Yes, charming, and a great sense of humor, too." She glanced at Jake and saw that his eyes were crinkled up in laughter.

"Are . . . you still in love with him?" His voice was quiet, his eyes no longer laughing.

She flushed. "No, I'm not. That's all over now." Her choice of the word *now* was instinctive and revealing. He didn't answer, and she flicked a quick look at him.

He was sipping his wine, gazing back at her almost abstractedly. She couldn't tell what he was thinking, and she picked up her fork and began to eat to cover her confusion. He was a virtual stranger, yet she felt as if she'd known him for years. She'd told him things she wouldn't have told anyone else.

Jake put his wineglass down. "I picked up new plugs for Robert's car. And a brake cable. Won't take me long to install, and I'll change the oil while I'm at it. Make sure the car's in good shape. You don't want to risk a breakdown while you're at the farm with Caitlin."

She nodded, and any constraints on their conversation seemed eased. They talked about Margaret's dream of owning an herb farm. "I love gardening," she admitted with a self-conscious half smile. "I know I'd be good at it."

"If your thumb's as green as your eyes, you're all set," he said quietly.

She spread her hands and smiled, then tilted her head. "What about you? Do you really want to build bridges and roads for the rest of your life?"

"It'll do for now. I have a cabin on the Maine seacoast where I go when the world closes in." His voice was low. "Do you like Maine?"

She nodded. "I haven't been there in years, though."

"We'll have to see what we can do about changing that," he said with a wide smile.

Jake paid the bill and they left the inn. The ride back to North Hollow and Quarry Farm seemed oddly short. Margaret felt so at ease with Jake, drawn to him, as if she'd known him all her life.

As he pulled the car into the driveway and switched off the engine, he turned his head and looked at her. "Stay a minute. There's just one thing…" He reached for her, cupping his hand around her soft cheek.

The thud of her heart sounded like thunder to her ears as her lips met his. Her lips parted, and all individual sensation—the warmth of his body against her breasts, the movements of his lips and tongue and hands, were swallowed up by an overwhelming wave of sheer physical pleasure.

When she went into the house a few minutes later, she could still feel the warm touch of his mouth on hers, like a luminous imprint no observer could miss. She could still feel it as she fell asleep hours later.

Chapter Six

Master detectives didn't need much sleep. They had to be awake practically at dawn, on the trail of evil master criminals. Caitlin's stomach rumbled, reminding her she'd only eaten three cookies, hardly enough to keep Sherlock Holmes going for long.

She'd got up really early. The kitchen clock said seven-thirty, and the sky was just turning a pearly gray outside the window over the sink. She took another cookie from the pantry and popped it in her mouth, chewing as she went back upstairs. Not back to her bedroom, of course. There were important clues to be searched for and found.

The attic, for instance, would be a good place to look. Mrs. Knox kept the attic door locked, but Caitlin had already taken the key, kept ordinarily in a drawer in the hall table. The key lay small and hard in her jeans pocket.

She mounted the stairs to the attic, picturing the master criminal—Robert—plotting in the attic with his evil gang. Master criminals always had a gang of evil cutthroats who sat around waiting for orders to wreak havoc on the innocent and unsuspecting.

Mrs. Knox had prob'ly been unsuspecting before Robert and his gang hit her in the head and heaved her in the quarry, she thought, swallowing the last morsel of cookie.

Sherlock Holmes or the Bloodhound Gang wouldn't be caught off guard like Mrs. Knox, no sir. She glanced around the upper hall, standing motionless for several seconds, ready for anything, even Robert's evil gang. Nothing stirred.

The attic door stood at the end of a short hallway, up two steps. The door was painted white and opened easily when Caitlin inserted the key. She stepped inside. The attic was a big room with an enormous brick chimney in the middle of the floor. Bulky cartons, trunks and rolled-up rugs were piled against one wall. Dusty furniture took up most of the space behind the chimney; and overhead, old clothing was hung from rods laid across exposed beams. Nothing much else to see but shadowy stacks of magazines and old newspapers.

Still, she had to steel herself for a few seconds before walking around the dusty attic. It was dark, hard for even a master detective to really see anything. She noticed a light switch on the wall and flipped it upward. Brilliance flooded down from an overhead light onto the jumble of cartons, old furniture and junk.

A wrought-iron garden chair stood near a tall cupboard with dusty glass doors. Glass objects glinted on the cupboard shelves. They looked like scientific stuff. Certainly, if Robert were a mad scientist trying to take over the world, which Caitlin dimly remembered from extensive comic book reading was their usual sinister aim, this stuff would be just what they'd use.

She looked around and spied an old trunk by the cupboard. Walking over to it, she tried the lock. Success! Opening the trunk, she was disappointed to only find yellowed magazines inside, dated May, 1945. She flipped through the pages, bored. There wasn't much to see. Advertisements for weird-looking cars and cigarettes.

She flipped a few more pages. The ladies in the pictures wore peculiar hairstyles and funny clothes. Dumping the magazines on the floor, she found clothes underneath. They smelled musty, like old perfume. There was a black dress with a lace collar, a fringed shawl. She reached way down, and her groping fingers touched something hard. A small wooden box with a curious design on the front.

The box was locked. The top wouldn't come off, no matter how hard Caitlin tugged. It was some kind of weird puzzle box.

But that wasn't a problem. She was good at puzzles. Master detectives had to be expert at that sort of stuff. You just had to figure out which square to push. Frowning harder, she sat down on the dusty floor and experimented further, pressing first one square of wood, then another.

Nothing happened. The lid wouldn't budge.

She thought a minute, then carefully pressed her fingers against every other square on the front of the box. Nothing. She sighed and thought harder, then tried pressing a different sequence of the squares. One after another—until she heard a tiny muted click and the lid popped up. She grinned and let out a breath she didn't realize she'd been holding.

There was a bunch of old papers in the box. She picked up the one on top, smoothing it out, her eyes getting bigger and bigger as she realized her name was written in bold ink on the worn paper.

JAKE HADN'T FORGOTTEN his promise to give the Fiat a tune-up and arrived just after eight a.m. He climbed the back steps and tapped on the door. "Margaret?"

She opened it, long black hair curling about her face. She wore a vivid blue shirt and jeans and looked delightful. "Hi."

"Thought I'd get started on the Fiat bright and early."

Her face took on a rosy flush and her green eyes smiled at him. "Wonderful, how about coffee?"

"Maybe later. I'd like to get started right away." He gestured toward the barn. "Does Robert keep any tools for the car there? Socket wrenches, screwdrivers?"

"I think so. There's a shelf just to the right by the door. You can't miss it. Right next to a set of old tires."

"I'll find it, no problem." With a wave he turned and crossed the yard to the big red barn. The door creaked as he slid it open. Dust motes swirled up and got in his eyes. Coughing slightly, he brushed a cobweb off his face and looked around. The shelf Margaret had mentioned was just to his right. A toolbox sat on the shelf. He opened it and got lucky when he found socket wrenches to fit the Fiat. The old tires leaning against the wall were probably Robert's, too.

He brushed dust off the sidewalls. The tires were in pretty good condition.

Ten minutes later he had the oil changed and had popped in a new air filter. A new cable for the safety brake lay in a box on the Fiat's front seat. He would install that after he checked the plugs and wires.

"I thought you could use some coffee." Margaret's voice brought him out of the depths of the engine. She smiled and handed him a mug. "How's everything going?"

He sighed. "Okay, I got the oil changed. It was practically sludge. Robert has run the car into the ground. He shouldn't have left this car for you to use."

She brushed a gentle finger across his cheek. "Every time I think about it, I want to scream. Lucky for me you came around." She touched his hair ever so gently. "I've got waffles cooking for Caitlin's breakfast. Got to get back to the kitchen. See you later."

Jake tried to concentrate on replacing the plugs and wires after Margaret left. But thoughts of her haunted him while he worked. He finally kept his mind on the job long enough to complete it, then turned his attention to the brake cable. While he was sliding the jack under the front axle, he noticed the cut on the sidewall of the left front tire.

He touched the cut. It was almost down to the fabric. The tire was fairly new and should still be under warranty. He opened the glove compartment. Robert might have left the sales slip and warranty there. Maybe Jake could get a new tire.

The compartment was a clutter of maps, rubber bands and dusty papers. He sorted through them. No sales slip.

But he did find a wristwatch which he recognized as soon as his fingers touched it. *Betsy's*. He suddenly felt sick to his stomach.

Jake held on to the watch and closed his eyes, rubbing his fingers gently across the leather band. In his mind he could still see Betsy wearing it....

Stunned, he put the watch back in the compartment. He then sat back on the seat, letting in a deep breath. This trip was taking its toll on him. He had to get hold of himself—and thinking of Margaret would help.

Needing something to do with his hands, Jake reached for the maintenance book in the glove compartment, unconsciously skimming the pages. When he went to put the manual back, he noticed a folded piece of paper on his lap, which had to have fallen out of the book. Unfolding the paper, he laughed when he saw that it was a tire sales slip and warranty from a store in Rutland. Great! He would go back to the store and get the tire replaced.

He folded the sales slip and put it in his pocket. As he was finishing attaching the brake cable, a beat-up pickup truck rattled up the drive. A skinny, unshaven man in a red and black lumber jacket got out and went up the back steps to the house.

Jake wiped his hands on a rag and took a step toward the house as the man began yelling and rattling the doorknob.

"Lemme in! I want money, lots of it! If you and Mrs. Knox wanna keep me quiet, you're gonna pay big! Goddamn it, I want what's comin' to me. A hundred thousand!" The man's voice was thick and slurring, and Jake realized the man was drunk and dangerous.

Margaret opened the door a crack. "I don't know what you're talking about. Go away! If you don't, I'm calling the police!"

By this time Jake had walked over and grabbed the drunk by the arm. "Better get on your way. The lady means what she says."

Boyce stumbled backward, shaking off Jake's hand. "Damn it, I want what's mine! They can fool some people, but not me—I want money to keep my mouth shut."

Jake raised his voice. "Call the police, Margaret."

Boyce shook his fist in fury, then stumbled over to his truck and drove off as Jake ran up the back steps. Margaret was standing in the kitchen, already on the phone.

"No, I told you, he was drunk and yelling threats. Restraining order? Yes, I'd appreciate that." She hung up and held her hand against her forehead for a moment. "They're sending an officer to Boyce's house to have a word with him. I can swear out a restraining order if he comes back."

Caitlin came into the kitchen, something small and wriggly in her hand. "Look, a worm! I found a new pet. I'll keep it. Maybe it'll have babies."

Margaret took a deep breath. "Worms need damp earth. They have to stay outside." She firmly ushered Caitlin out the back door. "Put it under the lilac bush. And when you come in, go upstairs and wash your hands."

Caitlin gave a bored shrug and looked up at Jake who smiled at her. "What's a 'straining order?"

"A legal term," he said with a wink. "Better put your worm under that lilac bush." She ran down the steps and around the side of the house, and he turned to Margaret. "Boyce is probably the neighborhood screwball. Once the police talk to him, he'll leave you alone. You don't have to be nervous. If he makes any more trouble, I'll pay him a visit."

"I'm not nervous," she said firmly. "I'm concerned. We're isolated up here, and I'm not taking any chances."

"Well, he's gone, and the police'll take care of things." He glanced at his wristwatch and then kissed her. When they both came up for air, he said ruefully, "I'm running late. I've got to go to Rutland for a new tire. I'll call you when I get back. In the meantime, the car's tuned up, and you shouldn't have any more trouble."

Caitlin came back in, wormless, just as Jake left. After being told twice to wash her hands, she waved them under the dripping faucet and dried them on her shirt. Then she sat down at the kitchen table and said nonchalantly, "What if the bottles in the cellar are that mean old man's? What if he hides in the cellar and drinks?"

"They're not his." Margaret gave her a suspicious look. "And when did you go down into the cellar again? I told you not to."

Caitlin buttered a piece of toast with unnecessary care. "Last night, while you were out with Mr. Mc-Call. I thought I heard a funny noise, like a raccoon was down there. So I went and looked, but there wasn't any raccoon, only a whole lot of bottles." She looked up at Margaret and said, "What if they're really his, and he comes back?"

For a horrifying second a vision of Vern Boyce creeping around the cellar flashed through Margaret's mind, and fright made her voice sharp and angry. "They're not his, and he won't bother us anymore. I called the police."

BUT LATE THAT NIGHT, after darkness had fallen, Vern Boyce returned. He banged on the door with a hard fist, yelling, "You don't scare me none, lady. I know what's comin' to me. Where's Mrs. Knox? I want money, and I want it now!" His rheumy eyes glared at Margaret, who was peering out the window. "Mine! I'm only after what's mine. I could make big trouble if I tol' all I knew. You know wha's goin' on, *fraud.*" He reared back and glared at her. "Zorina says yer nothin' but trouble."

"Go away. Mrs. Knox isn't here, and I don't have any money for you."

Boyce peered blearily at her and spoke in a low, mean snarl. "Zorina says there's terrible black fog comin' to swallow me up. I don' believe it. She ain't always right. I want my money! Hand it over, or I'll come in and get it!"

"Go away! I'm warning you, I'm calling the police!" She swallowed hard. Boyce's face was rigid with fury. His fist went back as if to smash the windowpane.

Then, suddenly, as if in answer to a prayer, headlights appeared down the road and slowed at the end of the driveway. Boyce grinned with satisfaction and said, "Looks like I'm gonna get what I come for!" He wove unsteadily down the back steps and out toward the car. Then, bending at the window by the driver's side, he appeared to hold a brief conversation.

Margaret dashed to the phone and dialed the police with shaking fingers. Oh, God, she thought frantically, if he came back from that car he would break the window and nothing could stop him.

For a moment fear made her legs rubbery, and she had to lean against the wall. Answer, she thought. Behind her the clock chimed eleven-fifteen p.m.

Damn the police! Why didn't they answer? She glanced out the window to see if Boyce was still there. The driveway was empty—the car and Boyce were gone.

Then the telephone line went dead.

VERN BOYCE climbed into the front seat of the car and slammed the door. "Just so's we unnerstan' each other. I want half."

"I said I'd give you half, didn't I?" The driver smiled and started the car, edging it up the track behind the barn. The engine growled softly as the car bounced over the rutted field, the headlights casting a yellow glow in the velvet blackness of night.

"Words come cheap. I don' trust nobody, less'n I see the color of their money." Grinning, Boyce patted his hip.

The driver's gaze moved fractionally downward and to the right. Boyce meant business. He had a *knife.*

It was fixed to his belt in a sheath over his left hip, where he could free it simply by snapping open the single narrow leather strap. In one second the blade could be slipped from the holder and wrapped tightly in his fist. In two seconds it could be jammed deep, slicing soft flesh.

Leaving the headlights on, the driver switched off the engine, and they got out of the car. Boyce turned and said with an uneasy laugh, "Funny place to hide money, up by the quarry."

Smiling reassuringly, the driver walked around the front of the car and joined Boyce on the dirt path. "Better than a bank these days. Negotiable securities, easy to cash, anonymous." The driver shrugged and said, "Can't do better than that."

They were standing at the edge of the headlight's glow. The night was chilly and silent, with only a half moon above. Boyce scowled. "Yeah, but why bury it up here?"

The moon went behind a cloud, hiding the driver's expression. "It's safe. Nobody's around this time of year." Even as the driver spoke, Boyce took the knife out of the sheath and held it in front of him.

They walked up the path into the shadowy darkness, Boyce a few steps ahead of the driver, who leaned down and silently picked up a large, flat rock.

The quarry lay just ahead, black as a grave.

Boyce took two steps and started to turn around, saying in a guttural, gravelly voice, "Ain't we gonna need a shovel? Hey, quit wastin' my time. Where's the money?"

Frowning, with a tense, predatory look on his face, Vern never got his answer as the driver swung the rock overhead, smashing it downward, full force, on his skull. He fell facedown in the weeds, and his knife flew out of his hands, sparkling for a moment in the glimmer of moonlight.

The ground was wet and thick with weeds as the killer leaned down and deliberately smashed Boyce again in the back of the head. The rock made a sickening dull noise as it cracked his skull open.

The killer let out a breath of relief and put the rock down. Boyce was definitely dead.

The only movement was the wind whispering in the trees. It took just a few seconds to roll the body over the edge of the quarry. A moment later the sound of a splash echoed from far below. Then the killer threw the rock and knife after the body and walked back down the path to the car.

Vern Boyce's murder had taken less than five minutes.

MARGARET STOOD in the doorway to Caitlin's room the next morning, frowning. It was time for breakfast, but she wasn't in the bathroom or anywhere upstairs. Where was she?

Ordinarily Caitlin's antics filled her with a blend of frustration, worry, and—once in a while—half-acknowledged amusement. This morning she was not amused. If she knew Caitlin—and she did—she was somewhere in the house, poking her nose into things that were none of her business.

Fuming, Margaret went downstairs. Where was she? "Caitlin?" When she walked into the living room, the French doors to the terrace were standing slightly open.

Immediately she thought of the quarry. Pulling a sweater on as she ran through the field behind the barn, she crashed through tangled weeds and grasses, then up the slope to where the path ended at the steep quarry.

Margaret's mind filled with nightmarish images of Caitlin lying facedown in the water. Oh God, what if it was already too late? No, she told herself. Everything would be all right. She would find her safe and sound.

By the time she looked over the edge of the quarry, Margaret was half out of her mind with fear.

The quiet, black waters lay far below, mirroring the blue Vermont sky and wisps of cloud drifting across it. She could see something floating on the surface, not Caitlin, thank God, but a bundle of old clothes, dark and sodden. Blue denim, red- and black-checked—a lumber jacket.

As if she wasn't really there, Margaret watched as a head gently bobbed up and down in the water as if in slow motion. She became hypnotized by its rocking— and then as reality set in, she found herself wide-eyed and as white as a ghost when she realized what she was staring at. Vern Boyce's body.

Not knowing where she found the strength, Margaret scrambled down the side of the quarry, breathing hard, panting, grabbing handholds of saplings, working her way closer to the body.

She didn't know what she could do. He was *dead*. Her stomach churned, and she fought back a wave of nausea as she reached the flat rock by the water's edge.

He must have fallen from the quarry rim, hitting... No, she wouldn't think about that. He might still be alive. She had to concentrate on trying to save him.

She got down on her knees and tried to grab his leg.
The body bobbed up and down just out of reach in the
lapping water as if he were a creature in a nightmare,
as if she would wake up and find none of this was real.

Over her own gasping, she heard the sounds of birds
twittering in the clump of birches on the far bank. The
buzz of dragonflies and mosquitoes. Even the sweet
scent of lilacs on the morning air. Overhead the sky
was still beautiful. The same wisps of cloud drifted
through the blue; the sun, rising in the east, was a
dazzling gold.

It was only the quarry that was different, full of
death. Her heart beat furiously, and she started shaking, shivering with fear.

Margaret took a deep breath and tried to control her
shaking. Stretching her hand out farther, she managed to grasp his pants leg and pull him toward the
rock. God, he was a big man, heavy. She would never
get his body out of the water.

Her spine seemed to curve in horror as she forced
her hands to grab hold of the soaked jacket, struggling to haul him up on the rock. His head banged
against her left knee leaving a smear of blood. She
swallowed bile and looked away from the bloody head
and the reddish wet streak on her jeans. The body
seemed to be stuck, snagged on some underwater
projection, a branch or a rock. She yanked harder, and
suddenly it broke free and slid upward with a disgusting wet sound that rubbed her nerves raw. She tried
not to hear the noise it made sliding across the rock,
tried not to look at that dead face. The eyes were open,
staring. Quarry water dripped from his mouth.

Oh God, she thought, *I'm going to faint.* But that meant falling into the quarry or onto the body. She really didn't know which would be worse.

She closed her eyes and pulled, eventually managing to get the upper half of his torso onto the rock. Then she huddled there beside the body, unable to move, shuddering.

He was slumped halfway out of the water, his neck bent at an unlikely angle, the head sagging in a position that seemed anatomically wrong. A horrible sticky, bloody place marked the back of the head. Margaret had never seen a dead body before.

In the back of her throat she made a wet choking sound, which quickly grew into retching noises. She was thoroughly sick, vomiting into the water of the quarry. Her throat burned as she sat back on her heels, dizzy, weak and shivering with violent spasms of revulsion. Suddenly, from nowhere, she began to cry, gasping tears of shock and horror, the culmination of all the accumulated stress of the past few days.

CAITLIN WAS in the kitchen when she got back to the house. "Where have you been all this time?" Margaret demanded, wiping tears from her face with the back of her hand. Fat tears still tracked down her cheeks and settled saltily in the corners of her mouth, then dribbled over her chin. She hugged herself, then pulled a tissue from the box by the wall phone, blew her nose and got control of herself. "I said, *where were you?*"

Round-eyed with curiosity, Caitlin stared at her. A guilty look crossed her small, freckled face. "Uh, playing checkers. I'm real good, and I like it when it's my turn all the time. Uh, what's wrong? How come you're crying?''

Obviously Caitlin had been up to her usual tricks, but Margaret didn't have time to go up and check for Mrs. Knox's broken belongings. "Nothing's wrong," she said flatly, thinking this was the understatement of the year. "Go into the dining room and eat your breakfast. I have to make a phone call."

She closed the kitchen door and dialed the police. The line was working again, thank God. She could hear the click of the connection, but inside her head she kept seeing the back of Vern Boyce's head. And she couldn't seem to stop shaking. She drew deep breaths and, with an effort, banished the vision.

After she hung up the phone, she felt better, knowing help was on the way. She looked out the window when the squad car arrived, then told Caitlin there'd been an accident down the road and to go up to her room until the police left. Reluctantly Caitlin climbed the stairs, and when she heard the door close, Margaret went to the back door and let the police in.

The policeman was in uniform, powerfully built, blond, blue-eyed, with the hard, no-nonsense voice of a cop. He had his right hand on the gun at his hip. His eyes were direct, assessing. "Police. You called us?"

She nodded. "Yes, I'm Margaret Webster."

"This your house?"

"Well, no. My sister's renting it for the summer from Mrs. Knox. My sister's away with her husband on a trip. I'm just staying here while they're gone, watching their daughter."

"You say you found a body?"

"Yes, Vern Boyce." She gestured toward the field behind the barn. "In the quarry—he's dead."

The officer nodded again. "I'll take a look." He stepped off the back step and walked away through the field.

She closed the door and leaned against it. Her legs were trembling, and she was still so cold. She willed herself to walk to the counter and pour a cup of coffee. She drank it slowly and managed not to spill any.

A few minutes later she saw the policeman come back from the direction of the quarry. He reached in the open window of the squad car and spoke into the radio. Then he straightened and walked toward the house.

She opened the door and let him in. "He's dead, isn't he?" It wasn't really a question. No one could survive a head wound like that.

He nodded and got out a small notebook. "You have any idea what he was doing up there?"

"No. He was Mrs. Knox's handyman. He came around the other day, and last night... again. He was drunk. Maybe he wandered up there in the dark and fell in. His head—" she cleared her throat "—was badly injured. He wasn't breathing when I found him."

"Why would he be wandering up there in the dark?"

She felt she was losing some important advantage that she couldn't identify. She shrugged. "I don't know. He came around looking for work after that big storm on Wednesday. I sent him away."

The policeman gazed impassively at her, waiting. He didn't say anything, and the seconds stretched out. There was a vaguely uncomfortable silence. "And?"

She shrugged again, helplessly. "Well, he was drunk. I called the police station and reported it. Then last night, when he came back, I tried to call again, but the line was out. He was yelling threats, shouting. Frankly, I had no idea what he wanted."

"And you say Mrs. Knox is . . . ?"

"I'm sorry, I'm not explaining this very well. She's in Europe." She swallowed hard, feeling an overwhelming sense of guilt. Why hadn't she made more of an effort to reach the police last night? If she'd tried again, say fifteen minutes later, maybe the line would have been working. The police would have come by, and Vern Boyce wouldn't have fallen in the quarry.

The policeman nodded. He jotted down a few more words, and said, "His truck's parked down the road a hundred yards or so. Keys still in it. We'll check and see if he ran out of gas, but if not, well, he probably came up here with something definite in mind . . . maybe to use your phone. Did he say anything about running out of gas? Did he ask to use the phone?"

She took a deep breath. "No. He didn't say anything about running out of gas. I *told* you, he was drunk. Nothing he said made sense. He kept talking about money. I didn't have any money for him."

The officer tucked the notepad into his breast pocket and looked out the door. Two police cars were pulling up, and an ambulance. He turned to go. "You'll be available if we need you?" Another question that wasn't really a question, and she nodded stiffly. "If the coroner finds alcohol in his blood, it could well be an accident. Boyce had a pretty good reputation as a drinker."

As Margaret closed the door behind the policeman, Caitlin said from behind her, "I saw a movie once about vampires. Want to know where they chomp you?"

"No, and I thought you were supposed to stay upstairs," Margaret said, briskly walking down the hall. She would do the laundry, vacuum, work her way through the day, and maybe she would forget what was burned into her memory.

"You said I could come down when the policeman left. Right on the neck, that's where they get you. Is that what happened to the man in the quarry?" Her eyes were bright with curiosity.

"No." Margaret eyed her in frustration, weighing how much to say. Clearly, the less said, the better. "It was an accident. He fell in the quarry and drowned." Caitlin's eyes widened and her small mouth fell open, and Margaret quickly said, "I told you it was dangerous. You're not to go anywhere near it unless I'm with you."

Caitlin whipped out her notebook and pencil. She flipped a few pages and asked, "Who drowned?"

Margaret gave up, realizing there was no contest. Caitlin wouldn't be satisfied until she got the whole story out of her. Or thought she had. "Mrs. Knox's handyman."

"Was that who came to the door last night?"

Margaret frowned. "Nobody came to the door last night."

"Yes, they did." Caitlin gave her a long look. "Somebody was yelling and banging on the door. You told him to go away. It was after I went to bed. You were yelling real loud. You woke me up."

"It was just someone on the road who was lost." This sounded like a transparent lie, even to Margaret, and she walked past Caitlin's unblinking stare with the definite feeling that this wasn't the end of it as far as her niece was concerned—not by a long shot.

BY NOON everything in the house shone—the woodwork gleamed, the bathrooms, the piano, the delicately carved legs of the settee in the living room. She vacuumed the floors and rugs, plumped the pillows, dusted, straightened the pictures, washed, dried and folded the laundry.

She was exhausted. All she wanted to do was climb into bed and pull the covers up over her head, but she knew what she would see in her mind's eye—the flat rock, herself pulling Vern Boyce from the quarry. His dead, staring eyes.

Finally she dragged herself to the kitchen and fixed lunch. The hamburgers and fries she cooked were overdone, practically fried to a crisp, but Caitlin ate hers without comment, too intent on her own thoughts to notice what she was eating. Margaret knew she was planning a new assault in her campaign to find out all she could about Vern Boyce's drowning, but hadn't yet figured out the right strategy.

Margaret sat down with a weary sigh and had scarcely swallowed a cup of coffee when the phone rang.

"What's going on up there?" Jake asked peremptorily. "It's all over town that someone's died up at the quarry."

She hesitated. Caitlin seemed engrossed in her French fries, but she was listening to every word. "Yes," she said at last. "Mrs. Knox's handyman, that man who was here, drunk and yelling threats . . . drowned in the quarry."

"Are you and Caitlin all right?"

Her heart thudded. "Yes, we're both fine."

"Look, I'm tied up for the rest of the afternoon, then I'm coming up there. I can make it around six. We could go out to dinner. If you can't get a sitter for Caitlin, we could eat at the house."

"I'm not much of a cook," she admitted.

"Okay, then I'll do the cooking. I'll be there by six."

She hung up with a sense of physical shock. For some reason, her heart, her breath, every nerve seemed painfully alive, aware, racing, anticipating seeing him again.

Chapter Seven

"What about your promise?" Caitlin demanded suddenly. "You said when the car got fixed, you'd take me someplace special."

Margaret sighed, sensing a battle of wills. "You were supposed to clean your room. It looks like a pigpen."

"That's because I'm decorating," Caitlin replied nonchalantly. "It's supposed to look like that."

"If you want to go someplace special, you have to pick up those toys. A pigpen doesn't make it with me." There was no answer from Caitlin who was sitting on the rug, her head bent over a picture she was coloring. Margaret drew a frustrated breath and picked up a magazine, listing various attractions around Vermont. She leafed through it and stopped, her eye caught by one particular article. There was more than one way to skin a cat. She said, "Caitlin, would you like to see how they make maple syrup in a sugar house? All you have to do is clean your room."

"Okay," she said, glancing up. "Only I need some new magic markers. Could we get some while we're out?"

"Maybe." Vaguely Margaret wondered what had happened to the practically new markers she already had.

Caitlin closed her coloring book. "What's a sugar house?"

"A special place, wait and see." Margaret helped her into a sweater, only half listening as Caitlin's head popped up through the neck.

"In olden days people didn't have markers. They wrote with other stuff, like reg'lar pens. Their writing was funny looking. All squiggly." She grinned up at Margaret. "My markers are real neat. Only they got used up in my picture. Especially the blue one. I needed lots of blue."

"Oh." Margaret glanced in the hall mirror. It was an old mirror, and the wavy, silvery glass made her face look bloodless and pale. She fished in her purse for her lipstick.

"It got all used up. The blue one," Caitlin repeated.

"Uh-huh."

"Well, I need more *blue*."

"Fine." Margaret put the lipstick back in her purse. "We'll get more while we're out."

"Because I really need them or I can't finish my picture. Want to see it?"

Margaret started to say yes but thought better of it. Caitlin had the most incredible one-track mind. From ten feet away, her picture looked suspiciously like a large body of water with a stick figure of a man in it, floating facedown.

She propelled Caitlin toward the stairs. "Clean your room. Now." Five minutes later Caitlin came down, saying she was ready to go, her room was all clean. Margaret suspected she'd simply moved everything from one flat surface to another. On the other hand, maybe Caitlin had picked it all up. And pigs could fly, she thought morosely. Well, a little trust once in a while wouldn't hurt. Even with Caitlin.

"Okay, let's go," she told her, and Caitlin jumped down the last stair with a yelp of glee and ran outside to the car. Margaret stood motionless in the doorway for a long moment, wondering just what she'd let herself in for. Then she followed her outside.

Today was probably one of the worst days in her life. Margaret couldn't believe that watching Caitlin was turning into a nightmare. Every time she thought about Vern Boyce, she felt like fainting. Hopefully, taking Caitlin maple sugaring would be relaxing and fun. On second thought, nothing could be calming with her niece.

Margaret took the magazine with her. The list of sugar bush camps was fairly comprehensive; the directions to the nearest—Top O' the Hill Farm—two miles north on Route 100.

They found the farm with no problem. It was off a side road, a fair distance up a steep and rolling hillside. As they drove up, a gray-haired man in overalls was just starting a tractor.

"Everett Davis," he said with a welcoming grin. "You're just in time. I'm heading out to the sugar house. Want a ride?"

Margaret shook his hand and introduced herself and Caitlin. "I should have called first, but we stopped by, hoping you'd be sugaring."

His smile widened. "Sure am, and it so happens I need an expert taster." He reached out a hand and gently tousled Caitlin's hair. "How'd you like to volunteer, young lady?"

"Yes, please," she said happily, and in seconds they were seated in back of the tractor, bumping over a makeshift road through the woods.

"Most places use vacuum tubing. It's quicker," Everett Davis shouted over the engine roar. "But I kinda like the ping of sap droppin' in buckets." Winking at Caitlin, he went on, "Besides, squirrels ate most of the danged tubing first year I tried it."

The road wound upward a quarter mile through the woods until at last they arrived at the sugar house, tucked into a stand of old maples with about forty cords of wood stacked neatly in back. A plume of steam issued from the chimney. They got out, and Everett Davis led them inside.

Caitlin twitched her small nose in delight. It was magic. Everything smelled so good, and she got to sample homemade donuts with maple sprinkles on top. She chewed a second donut and looked at the three flat evaporators that filled most of the sugar house. "We add sap to one side," Everett Davis explained. "And we strain what comes out the other end." He grinned at Caitlin. "How about some cider?"

A large barrel with a tap stood in one corner. Everett gave her a mug and told her to help herself; and shortly Caitlin, her stomach full, was peering out the window, hoping to catch a glimpse of deer.

Margaret sat on a stool and sipped instant coffee made with hot sap directly from the evaporator. It was wonderful, relaxing, and best of all, a world away from Quarry Farm and dead bodies. Smiling gratefully at her host, she said, "This is really special."

"It's a lot of work. I've got five sons and two daughters, and everyone pitches in. I planted some of these maples forty years ago. Those trees are youngsters compared to the big ones. Generally I use a team of Belgian horses to collect the sap. Got four teams, nothin' beats 'em." He grinned. "They stop and go on command and don't tear the woods up like a tractor."

Caitlin peered from the window. Something moved outside in the late afternoon gloom. She squinted harder. A breeze had sprung up. Prob'ly just wind blowing the bushes, she thought with a sigh.

Then it moved again. She saw it this time. A big deer with antlers, and a smaller one . . . no, two more standing in the trees. The smallest just a shadow, a light fawn-colored smudge on the blue-black stand of trees. Suddenly they looked up, ears pricked. Then they were gone, bounding away with a flick of white.

Turning from the window, she sighed happily and said, "I saw *three* deers! Just like Bambi!"

Everett laughed and added more wood to the fire in the stove. "Thought I'd seen one earlier today. A big buck."

"No, there were *three. I saw them!*" Caitlin's face was flushed with triumph, and Margaret's heart gave a queer, painful lurch. Caitlin had her dad's mop of light brown curls and a funny turned-up nose, but her stubbornness reminded Margaret irresistibly of herself at that age.

She got up and looked out the window. "They're gone now."

"I know." Caitlin leaned against the wall, arms crossed, prepared to stand there for the rest of the afternoon. "We can wait till they come back."

"We can't do that, honey," she said with a wry smile. "Mr. Davis has other things to do. We're probably holding him up."

Everett looked up from stoking the fire. "Don't let that worry you. I don't have a set schedule. Take your time."

She glanced at her watch. "Actually, we have to get home soon. But we'd love to buy some maple syrup if you've got some for sale."

Happily, he did. And soon they were driving home laden with maple butter and several jugs of homemade syrup, which, Caitlin informed Margaret, she was going to pour on crackers and eat for dinner.

"Okay, but not for dinner, for dessert," Margaret suggested. She would have left it at that, but Caitlin peppered her with complaints, stating that she hated stuff that was good for her.

"It's not fair," Caitlin said grumpily.

"You'd get sick of sweets if that's all you ate."

"No, I wouldn't."

"Would I lie to you?" Margaret insisted, pulling the Fiat to a stop in front of the barn. She turned off the engine and took out the key.

"People don't always tell the truth." Caitlin opened the car door and got out. She gave Margaret a long look. "Robert doesn't."

Oh, no, not that again, Margaret thought. The telephone incident. She frowned and said, "You must have misunderstood what he was doing. I'm sure he called the doctor."

Caitlin followed her into the house. "He didn't. He's a big, fat liar and *I hate him.*"

Margaret put down her purse, nerving herself for another unpleasant argument, but Caitlin disappeared upstairs, and then the phone rang.

It was Sandy. Margaret breathed a sigh of relief. "You don't know how worried I've been. It's been days—"

"I know, and I'm sorry, really. It's just that it's been so hectic. We've been driving around, seeing the sights—wait, Robert wants to say hello."

"Hi, Maggie." Robert's cheery voice boomed on the other end of the line. "How're you doing? How's Cait?"

"We're both fine."

Dimly Margaret heard Sandy's voice in the background. "Give me back the phone..." The sentence ended on a smothered burst of laughter, and Robert continued, "I've got to hang up. We're at a gas station, and some guy wants to use the phone. Everything's fine, right? Bye, Maggie. We'll give you another call in a couple of days."

"No, wait! Something's—" The phone went dead, cutting off Margaret's barely voiced protest. Lips tightly set, she replaced the receiver. God, it was just like him, to talk for two minutes, if that, and not give her a chance to say anything. Damn Robert.

Still annoyed, she turned and saw a pair of headlights edge up the drive. It was Jake. Unconsciously her breath caught in her throat. Thank God he was here.

When she opened the door, he took one look at her face, told her she looked terrible and took her in his arms.

She managed a small smile and said, "Finding Vern Boyce in the quarry this morning took its toll on me." He held her gently. Expressing sympathy, as a friend, her mind warned. But she was pressed so close to him she couldn't move, and she didn't want to move.

His face against her black hair, he kissed her temple and said, "Is there a drink in this place?"

"Oh, Jake." She put her head on his shoulder and swallowed a curious giggle that bubbled in her throat.

He lifted her face and kissed her for a long time. "Now go get us both a drink."

There was bourbon in a decanter on a tray in the living room. Jake splashed some in a glass, added a little water and handed it to her. Then he poured a drink for himself and gave her an encouraging push toward the settee. "Go on, sit down before you fall down."

The drink really gave her a jolt. She knew she was suffering from some sort of post-stress syndrome, delayed shock. She took a deep breath and said, "I'm not the fainting type."

"You look like your knees are going to fold up. Your face was white as a sheet when you answered the door. Now your face is red." He took the glass away from her and put it on the table. "Now tell me what's upsetting you, besides finding the body."

Her throat stung from the bourbon. She took another breath and pulled herself together. "Vern Boyce showed up here late last night, drunk, demanding money. I didn't let him in, and he got angry, shouting threats, pounding on the door. I kept telling him to go away, but he wouldn't. Then a car came along, and he seemed to know who it was. He went to talk to the driver, and that's the last I saw of him—until I found him in the quarry this morning."

"Did you explain all this to the police?" he asked quietly.

She nodded. "Yes, they said he might have run out of gas. His truck was parked down the road, the keys still in it. The theory is that he stopped here to use the phone, but—"

"But what?"

"He never mentioned wanting to use the phone. He just pounded on the door, yelling things that made no sense." She chewed on her lower lip for a moment, then said with a shrug, "Ranting and raving something about a black fog and how I didn't scare him."

"Sounds like he was paranoid."

She shrugged again. "He was drunk. I was scared half out of my mind. Then I tried calling the police again, but the line was down. When I looked out the window he was gone, and so was the car."

"What time did this happen?" Jake asked, leaning forward.

"I don't know, after ten-thirty." After a moment she added uncertainly, "No, I ran to call the police, and the clock chimed. It was a little after eleven."

Jake was silent for a moment, then said, "And Vern ended up in the quarry."

"But why would he go up there at that time of night?" she asked, puzzled. "It's too cold to go swimming."

"Maybe he went there with one of his drinking pals. They could have gone up there to tie one on." He eyed Margaret somberly. "Come on, you're thinking something. I can practically hear cogs whirling in that brain of yours. What is it?"

She shook her head, frowning. "I was remembering how angry he was. He saw the car and said something about knowing how to get what he wanted, then he left."

"That settles it then," Jake said firmly. "He recognized a pal, had another couple of beers. I bet the police will find an empty six-pack or two tossed in the field. Once they were half-bombed out of their minds, they wouldn't care how cold it was. One of them probably suggested swimming, and off they went. Or maybe the pal took off, and Boyce wandered up to the quarry and fell in. An unfortunate accident."

"I guess so. The police asked a lot of questions."

"That's their job." He gave her a reassuring smile and said, "What about Caitlin? How's she taking all this?"

"In perfect stride. It's just another mystery for the great detective to solve." Margaret shook her head and went on, "I took her off to a sugar house this afternoon, to get her away from here. We both needed it." She gave him a rueful grin. "Lord knows if it did any good."

Jake gazed at Margaret as her shoulders slumped a little, the cloud of black hair tumbling about her pale face, her slim body in a wine-colored wool dress...she was so damn vulnerable.

A muscle in his jaw tightened. He rose to his feet and moved toward her, then stopped himself. From the stairs came the sound of footsteps, and Caitlin ran into the room. She took one look at Margaret and said loudly, "I'm starved, and you forgot to buy my markers. You promised!"

"I'm sorry," Margaret told her. "Next time I go to town, I promise." Caitlin still looked grumpy, and she added hurriedly, "Your mom and Robert called a few minutes ago. They asked how you were and said to give you their love."

Caitlin hunched her shoulders. "How come I didn't get to talk to Mom?"

"They hung up before I could tell you," she explained. "They were in a gas station, someone else wanted to use the phone." She threw Jake an exasperated look. "I think Robert just ran out of change. You'd think he'd get a telephone credit card, but you know how he feels about credit cards. He absolutely refuses to use them."

"Really? I didn't know—" Jake looked slightly puzzled.

"Well, I'm still hungry," Caitlin announced with a heavy frown.

Jake smiled at her. "Lead me to the kitchen. I'm a genius with leftovers. I'll whip us up something good in no time."

Immediately Caitlin's eyes lit up. "Can I help?"

His grin widened. "Sure."

Rushing into the kitchen, Caitlin dragged a stool up to the counter. "I get to stir, and if there are any eggs, I get to break them."

Margaret followed her into the kitchen and wrapped a large green apron around Caitlin's waist. "You're the official assistant chef." She glanced at Jake and added, "I guess eggs are on the menu."

"Omelets," he replied from the depths of the refrigerator. "There's ham in here, tomatoes, lots of good stuff."

In a matter of minutes, he and Caitlin had prepared a fragrant omelet mixture and poured it in a frying pan while Margaret set the table. Caitlin rushed around the kitchen, fetching various ingredients, dropping only two eggs on the floor—accidents Jake dismissed airily with a grin and a wink.

The two chefs tossed a green salad with Jake's secret dressing, and they sat down to eat. Caitlin, face sticky with maple syrup she'd poured on her omelet, exclaimed after two bites, "It's *great!* Want some syrup? It's real good."

"No, thanks," Margaret and Jake said in chorus.

Caitlin gave them a complacent look, chomped down the rest of her omelet, and burped in a vulgar fashion. "'Scuse me. Can I go upstairs now? I wanna play 'Uncle Wiggly.'" Margaret nodded helplessly, and Caitlin dashed upstairs.

"She's really something else," Jake said with a laugh.

Margaret tilted her head and gave him a warm smile. "What amazes me is that she cleaned her plate without an argument. I can never get her to do anything without a pitched battle."

"Knowing how to handle kids isn't all that hard," he said blandly. "Treat 'em like anyone else. Respect their dignity."

"And feed them delicious suppers," she added with a satisfied sigh. "Your secret salad dressing was wonderful."

He leaned back in his chair, chuckling. "Good food, good company...I'll have you eating out of my hand in no time."

"Not so fast. You have Caitlin right where you want her, but I'm older and wiser."

The grooves that ran from his nose to his chiseled mouth deepened as he laughed. He really had a magic touch with a frying pan, she thought. And with small children, too.

She lifted her eyes and looked across the table at Jake. He was reaching for the carafe of wine, and she stared at the width of his broad shoulders and the beautifully coordinated way he moved. He went to top up her glass, and she put her hand over the rim.

"No, no more, please," she said with a smile. "Another drink, and I'll fall asleep right here. I've no head for alcohol."

He smiled back at her in a way that shimmered down to the very soles of her feet. "Dessert? If you have any fresh fruit, we could have—no, on second thought, I'll take care of that...later."

"Oh, no," she pleaded laughingly. "I couldn't eat another bite." She felt tantalized with food and drink and something else she didn't dare analyze—a feeling lovely and wonderful.

He got up and switched on the stereo, and the strains of a French love song wafted on the air. "Come on, a little exercise will clear your head." He took her in his arms, and Margaret gave in to her base desires and wrapped both arms around his shoulders, more or less draping herself on him.

"Jake, I know I'm not much help, but I can hardly stand, let alone dance. That wine—"

"I'll hold us both up," he said with a laugh. "Let's see if a little passive exercise helps."

She followed him perfectly as they swayed gently from side to side. And when she became aware that her head was resting against his neck, her eyes on a level with the pulse that beat just under his jaw, she felt her breath catch in her throat.

There was a certain tension in the way he was holding her, and she straightened away from him, allowing her arms to assume a more normal position. "Don't move," he whispered, kissing her hair.

"You're terrible, plying me with liquor," she accused, laughter burbling in her husky voice. "And irresistible food, and what was worse, I sat here and let you do it. I didn't stand a chance."

"Maybe I poured the wine, but you sat across the table looking at me with those big, green eyes," he teased. "Those lips." He dropped another kiss on her hair and said softly, "I'm the one who didn't stand a chance."

"Is that so?" She laughed up at him, feeling wonderful, exhilarated, and just a little dizzy.

His feet slowed to a stop and his arms tightened, and she was acutely aware of every muscle in the length of his body. "I think we'll take a rain check on dessert. You're in no condition to appreciate the subtleties of my fresh-fruit compote." He leaned down and kissed her again, savoring the feel of her lips, the sweet taste of her mouth.

By some sleight of hand, which was beyond her comprehension, she found herself lying on the settee half on top of him, her face tucked into the curve of his neck. She breathed in the clean scent of soap and slightly musky maleness, a smile curving her lips. She opened her mouth and tasted the tautness of his skin and felt an immediate reaction beneath her.

"God, Margaret, you're beautiful," he groaned, and his hands did something wonderful to her back. The touch of cool, evening air touched her flesh as the zipper of her dress slid down.

Passion raced through her body, rousing her from her dreamy state, and she pulled away slightly. "Jake, I don't know..."

All her old doubts returned with a rush, and she found herself at war with her own inclinations. She wanted to trust her judgment and fall in love. He seemed so...right. But she'd been terribly wrong about Robert, and her intellect told her it could happen again. There were no guarantees in love. What if he didn't feel the same way she did? What if Jake wasn't interested in a long-term relationship?

His hands moved over the satiny skin of her back and then slipped under her own weight to cup her bare breasts, and she could feel the swollen softness tightening into hard nubs pushing against his palms in an involuntary invitation that left her shaken and breathless.

He turned his face and she was drawn into a kiss that left her open and completely vulnerable, a kiss that sent wild emergency signals racing to all the shadowy feminine areas of her body. And when she felt his hands smoothing her hips, sliding slowly on that bit of nylon that covered her under the fallen sides of her dress, she panicked. His hands were pressing her even closer now, and she began to struggle. "No, please...Jake," she pleaded, scrambling up to sit trembling on the edge of the settee. She tugged at her dress, pulling it up over her suddenly chilled shoulders. She fumbled with the zipper and finally got it up. Where were her shoes?

And then the doorbell rang. Jake's smoky gaze met hers and a reluctant grin crept across his face. "Saved by the bell."

She went in her stockinged feet to answer it. A woman was standing on the front porch. She smiled coolly as Margaret opened the door and said in a breathy, slightly flustered voice, "Yes?"

"Ah, I'm Violet Chadwick, a dear friend of Polly Knox's," the woman said, a small smile curving her thin lips. "Polly borrowed a special book of mine a few months ago. I know she's in Europe and it's rather late to be calling, but I tried to telephone you earlier. The line must be out again. This town has terrible phone service." The woman smiled again. "Anyway, I wondered if I might come in and look for that book. It means a great deal to me, and I'm sure Polly wouldn't mind."

Jake came up behind Margaret as she shook her head. "I'm sorry. I can't take responsibility for something like that. You'll have to wait until Mrs. Knox comes back from Europe. I'm really sorry."

Violet Chadwick stiffened. A small woman, she could have been anywhere from thirty to forty, with chiseled lips and glossy black hair. Her eyes were obscured by large, brown-tinted glasses, and she wore a well-cut blue silk suit. She frowned. "I can see you don't quite understand. Really, Polly wouldn't mind."

"Perhaps not," Margaret interrupted sweetly. "The point is, *I* would. I'm sorry, you'll just have to wait. Good night." She closed the door as the woman drew a breath of anger and stalked off the porch toward her car.

Margaret turned to find Jake smiling at her with appreciation. "You handled that with authority. Very impressive." They turned and went back to the living room.

Violet Chadwick got behind the wheel of her car and slammed the door. A rosy splotch spread over her features as she drove off ill-temperedly toward town.

MARGARET CAME UP for air from Jake's teasing kisses. "Who's doing the dishes?"

"You wash, I'll dry," he suggested, nuzzling the side of her neck. "Mmm, you smell delicious." Abruptly the doorbell rang again. For a moment they stood, frozen, staring at each other. Then Jake said, frowning, "Are you expecting anyone else?"

"No." The house was like Grand Central Station, the phone ringing constantly, people banging on the door at all hours of the day and night. Margaret shrugged wearily, and they went back to the front hall. She opened the door.

Madame Zorina stood there, a figure straight out of a Gothic horror movie. She wore a black, hooded cloak that blended with the darkness so that her wrinkled face seemed to float within the dark hood. Over her arm was a basket of vials, bundles of dried herbs and strings of garlic.

"I had to come," she said. "It was my brother you found dead in the quarry. I foretold his death...." She raised a hand to push back her hood, and Margaret saw that she was trembling. Determination and a strange exultation glowed in her eyes.

Margaret opened the door wider. "Why, Madame Zorina, I didn't know...I'm so sorry." Her voice trailed off helplessly. Not knowing what to say, she shook her head and gestured toward Jake. "This is Jake McCall, a friend of mine." He nodded politely but shot Margaret a puzzled glance, obviously startled by the psychic's bizarre appearance.

Madame Zorina stepped into the hallway, her eyes moving quickly, scanning everything. "This house is full of evil. I feel it. Terrible illness, hatred and death. It must be purified," she said finally. "Dark forces are at work. You are in danger, I must weave a circle of protection."

A smile tugged at the corner of Jake's mouth. "Perhaps Madame Zorina would like a drink. I could use one myself."

They moved to the living room, and Jake mixed drinks. He handed the psychic a strong whiskey and water. She drank deeply, then lowered the glass and seemed to get a grip on herself. Settling her bulk into an armchair, she said, "I used my crystal pendulum. It twirls, and the directions it takes indicate answers to questions I put to it. Right means yes, and widdershins, that is, left, means no. Usually." She drew a deep breath and went on, "My brother was a fool."

"Look, madame," Jake said, a faint ghost of suspicion narrowing his eyes, "we're sorry about your brother's death. But it has nothing to do with this house or Margaret. You're wasting your time with all this talk of dark forces."

She drew another deep breath, her eyes fixing him with a glittery, malevolent stare. "You don't believe me. I sense your thoughts, and you're wrong. Dead wrong. You will beg for my help before this is over, and I may not be here to give it."

Jake muttered under his breath, "This is crazy."

Margaret frowned and said, "Madame, why won't you be here? Do you think some harm may come to you, like your brother, Vern?"

"No, certainly not," the psychic retorted, horrified. "I'm well aware of the evil forces my brother tampered with, but my absence will be more mundane. I have reservations for a weekend at Atlantic City. I intend to make a killing at the blackjack tables."

Jake grinned at Margaret conspiratorially. Maybe the psychic was crazy as a loon, but clearly she had her own agenda. And she obviously didn't have any hang-ups about using her so-called powers for monetary gain.

"I don't claim all the answers, but I have powers," Madame Zorina crooned. "You came here by chance, didn't you, Mr. McCall. You find you're linked to Margaret by strange circumstance. Oh, don't bother answering. I know. I've seen this in the Tarot. You both are linked now and for all time, into death and beyond. You had to come. The golden chain that binds you called you here when Margaret needed you."

Madame Zorina rose, her black skirts whirling about her ankles. Jake let out a long breath. It was possible the psychic had some kind of ESP power. He opened his mouth, but before he could speak, Madame Zorina interrupted. "You couldn't save your sister—even if you'd been in this country when she fell ill. Nothing could've altered the events."

Jake turned and spoke to Margaret. There was a look of compassion in his face as he glanced back at the old woman. "I don't know how she knows about Betsy's death, or that I was out of the country then. There has to be a perfectly logical explanation for all this." He leaned down and kissed Margaret's cheek, saying softly, "Let the old girl work her spells and incantations. Humor her. Later on, I'll drive back to town and get my things. You can't continue to stay on in this nut house by yourself . . . with only Caitlin for company."

Margaret sagged against him in relief. There was no point in being coy. She *knew* she wanted him to stay at the house, and what's more, he knew it, too. The look of gratitude in her green eyes told him all he needed to know.

Abruptly Madame Zorina rubbed her hands together. "We must begin at once. Time is short, almost the full moon, the time of greatest danger. Protection must be symbolic. Come, we must turn out the lights and use only candles."

Margaret whispered to Jake, "We might as well. It's the fastest way to get rid of her." He shrugged in agreement and switched off the table lamps. Margaret moved about, lighting several candles. In the eerie, moving light, the moon looked uncanny, shrouded in darkness with only the glow of candlelight.

Outside it was raining again. And gradually, as Margaret watched the old woman's face and glittering stare, the rasp of her voice and soft drumming of the rain on the roof blended into a single low sound. Her cramped legs grew numb as she sat in the middle of the rug with Jake. He was half swearing beneath his breath as Madame Zorina began anointing the windows and doors with liquid from the flask she produced from her basket. She walked backward, dribbling the contents of the flask in a wide circle around the seated pair. She was careful to stay within the unbroken circle.

She said to Margaret, "There are emanations in this house. Lies, menace, evil. Hate. I feel it. The scarlet beast, one who uses the silver tongue of the serpent—he is the Evil One. And he is not alone. There is another who seeks to harm you and the child." Suddenly her eyes darted toward the stairs.

Caitlin was standing there, rubbing her eyes sleepily. "How come you turned off the lights? What are you doing?"

Madame Zorina whirled, and again her inky skirts flared outward. She pointed a clawlike finger at Caitlin. "Don't worry, child. I have said you are the catalyst, and so you shall be. No power on earth can change your destiny. You will save the ones you love."

Chapter Eight

Madame Zorina walked toward Caitlin, holding out a string of garlic like a Hawaiian lei. Margaret ran past her and put her arms around Caitlin. "Please leave her out of this." Turning to Caitlin she said firmly, "You're supposed to be in bed."

The psychic went over to the doorway and began draping the garlic across the lintel. Fascinated, Caitlin couldn't take her eyes off her. "Gosh, she's real neat! And she says I'm gonna save everyone!"

"We don't need to be saved," Margaret muttered, marching her niece toward the stairs. "It's your bedtime. Madame's upset. Her brother just died."

Caitlin scowled. "Nancy's mom says she's schizofrantic. If I had a brother and he died, I'd be schizofrantic, too. How come he died?"

"Her brother was Vern Boyce, the man who drowned in the quarry," Margaret admitted tiredly. "Come on, up you go. Back to bed."

Caitlin's scowl deepened and she stubbornly refused to budge. "I want to stay and watch. How come she's putting all that stinky stuff on the doors?"

"It's garlic. She thinks the house is unhappy and, er, needs to have its bad feelings removed." Margaret hauled her up another stair.

Caitlin's eyes widened. "Like that movie where there were ghosts in the TV and everyone disappeared in a hole in the closet? Wow! Maybe we have ghosts!"

"We don't have any ghosts," Margaret retorted, glancing over her shoulder at Madame Zorina who was fingering her crystal and pointing it at Caitlin with an unnerving fixed stare. She was also mumbling under her breath, reeling off a litany of spells.

"Ackshully, we do have ghosts," Caitlin said complacently. "Madame Zorina's brother's prob'ly a ghost now, and he's real mad because he drowned. The ghosts in that movie were angry. They came right up where they were digging a swimming pool. Maybe her brother's gonna come out of the quarry like that and get us!" She looked up at Margaret, and her expression was just what Margaret expected it would be—excitement and delight overlaid by a thin glaze of fright.

Margaret dropped a kiss on Caitlin's forehead and hugged her tight. "No one's going to get us. Vern Boyce isn't there anymore, honey. The police came and took him away in the ambulance."

"But the quarry could still have lots of skeletons," Caitlin said hopefully. "Mrs. Knox and other people Robert decided to get rid of. That's prob'ly where he hides all the bodies."

She stared at Caitlin, at a complete loss for words, and Jake came to the rescue. "Interesting theory. We'll have to discuss it in the morning. Hang on, I'll give you a piggy-back ride up to bed." He hoisted Caitlin up on his shoulders and took her upstairs before she could protest. Then Margaret heard his voice telling Caitlin he would read her a story if she promised to go right to bed. And of course Caitlin demanded one with a ghost in it. "I don't know any," Jake said, faint amusement evident in his voice.

Margaret leaned against the banister. He sounded so comfortable, so calm. She felt her frazzled nerve ends begin to smooth out. After all, why should she be so uptight? Compared to Vern Boyce, she had little to complain about.

Madame Zorina came into the hall, shrugging into her cloak. "I did what I could, but it may not be enough." Her wrinkled face was lined with worry. "Remember my warning. Beware of the time of the full moon and be careful around water. One more caution—the serpent glides in *deadly* earnest. I have seen him in visions. You will have to defeat him." Then she stamped out of the house, leaving a silence that vibrated.

Jake came downstairs. "My God," he said faintly. "Madame Zorina's really something, isn't she? No doubt flying home on her broomstick."

Margaret straightened away from the banister. "At this point, nothing would surprise me."

He looked out the window as he shrugged into his raincoat. "Nope, there goes her car down the road. No broomstick." He opened the door, and their eyes met. "Forget Madame Zorina's nonsense, and stop worrying about her brother's death. He was drunk and fell in the quarry."

She sighed tiredly. "I guess you're right. I'm worrying about nothing."

They stood in silence for a few seconds, then Jake pulled her into his arms and kissed her long and hard. "Lock the door behind me. I'll be back as soon as I can."

After he'd gone she went back to the living room and switched on the table lamps, then put out the candles, one by one. She got a broom and swept up the neat little piles of herbs Madame Zorina had dribbled on the floor. Then she went to the kitchen and put the kettle on. When the water boiled, she made a mug of tea and sat drinking it with one eye on the kitchen clock, waiting for Jake to return. The tea was scorching hot, but she sipped it absently.

Madame Zorina's voice echoed in her mind. "This house is evil and full of lies."

She stirred the tea and then paused, the spoon dripping unnoticed onto her dress as her mind grappled with that ugly thought. This house, nestled cozily on a mountain, with bucolic hayfields tumbling down to the valley below, was just a simple Vermont farmhouse. Nothing sinister or evil about it . . . except that Vern Boyce had drowned in the quarry. *Stop it,* Margaret told herself. That was just an accident.

Some imp of perversity reminded her Caitlin had talked about lies . . . *Robert's lies.*

Ridiculous, she thought. Believing everything a seven-year-old said was on a par with believing Madame Zorina.

The doorbell rang again, startling her. Margaret jumped and noticed the puddle of tea on her dress. She put the spoon back in the mug and mopped disgustedly at the spot with a napkin. Not much good, but it didn't matter. Jake was back. And she realized for the moment that was all that mattered.

THE LIGHTS FLICKERED as she unlocked the front door. Outside the downpour was deafening, like a solid wall of water beyond the porch. Jake's dark hair was plastered flat to his head; the ends dripped water. The shoulders of his tan trench coat were black with rain. As he shrugged it off, the overhead chandelier chose that moment to flicker ominously again. It was symptomatic of the state of Margaret's nerves that she jumped like a nervous rabbit.

"Maybe a bad bulb," he said, looking up at the chandelier with a frown.

"No, the hall lights dimmed a minute ago, too. I hope we're not in for a power outage." She draped his coat on the umbrella stand.

"So we keep this handy." He grinned and picked up a candle. "Come on, I'll make coffee. Something hot. You're white as a sheet."

Her face was pale and drawn, her eyes huge with exhaustion, and she was shivering. There'd been a chill draft when the front door had been open, but it was closed now, and she was still shaking. The lights flickered again, then went out altogether. Jake fumbled with matches and lit the candle. He smiled at her across the flame. "Ah, let there be light."

"I'm so glad you're staying," she said fervently, moving closer. He slid his free arm around her and they went out to the kitchen. He told her to sit while he made coffee.

He dried his wet head with a dish towel and got down two mugs. His movements in the murky dark-

ness were accompanied with bumps and repressed ex-
clamations. He was limping slightly as he carried the
kettle over to the table and poured hot water into the
mugs.

"I took my shoes off and then kept stubbing my
toe." He grinned apologetically as she glanced at his
stockinged feet.

"We're a matched pair. My shoes are somewhere in
the living room." She warmed herself with the glow of
his smile. The color began to come back into her face.

"I like candlelight. It's romantic, even worth my
clumsiness." His eyes twinkled endearingly, making
her laugh.

She wished she could simply enjoy his company instead of having to worry about bodies, weird psychics
and Caitlin, who spent most of her time making wild
accusations about her stepfather. Robert was a lot of
things, she thought. But he wasn't a criminal or a liar.

Even though she'd already had a cup of tea, the
coffee tasted good. Her mind felt clearer. Robert had
told one lie she knew of. He'd denied ever having been
in this house before renting it, and the snapshot in
Caitlin's shoebox proved that wasn't true.

Her quick smile faded, leaving her pensive looking.
Jake stared at her for a long moment. "Funny, you
look a little like my sister in this light. Betsy had dark
hair, too. Her birthday's next Thursday." He drew a
breath and said, "She would have been twenty-six if
she'd lived."

"It's so sad. She had everything to live for, youth,
a loving husband." Margaret murmured.

"And no money problems. No small thing in this
day and age," he said with a shrug. "Betsy had a hefty

trust fund from her godmother.'' Getting to his feet, he hauled her out of the chair. ''You look all in. Go on up to bed.''

There was another candlestick on the small table by the stairs. He lighted it with his candle, handed it to her, and they went upstairs. ''This bedroom is yours,'' she said, opening the door. ''The bathroom's just down the hall. If you need another blanket, the linen closet's next door.'' She smiled and saw a subtle response in his eyes.

There was a laughing note in his voice as he said, ''I won't need another blanket. I'm pretty warm-blooded.'' His smile turned into a devilish grin.

She reminded herself Caitlin was sleeping not twenty feet down the hall. That is, if she was really asleep. Margaret opened her own bedroom door and placed her candle on the bedside table. Turning, she looked over her shoulder at Jake. ''Good night.''

''You're beautiful,'' he said, watching her flush. He looked as if he was about to say something else, but changed his mind, and instead, just stood looking at her.

I'm falling in love with you, Margaret. The words formed themselves in *her* mind as he watched her with twinkling eyes. Seven words so clear that for a moment she thought he'd said them aloud. She stared at him, overwhelmed. The laughter was gone from his blue-gray eyes now, and she couldn't decide what expression was in its place. All she knew was that she'd heard those wonderful seven words in her head, and there he was, watching her with a gentle and perceptive glint in his eyes.

"I want—" she mumbled helplessly. "I... I don't know what I want." In two swift strides Jake was standing in front of her. He pulled her gently against his chest and slid both arms around her waist. His hands moved gently upward, caressing her back to her shoulders. She could feel the strength of his arms and the warmth of his passion and had just enough time to close her lips shut before his mouth covered hers.

His lips were warm and hard. She denied the sudden unexpected tingling in her own body and clenched her hands at her sides so she couldn't throw both arms around his neck and give herself to his embrace completely. He drew her even closer, his tongue flicking along her full lower lips, teasing into the corners.

She forced herself not to respond, feeling her nails dig into her palms as she stood rock still.

He lifted his mouth from hers, and with his face still close said the seven words aloud. "I'm falling in love with you, Margaret. Think about that tonight while I'm sleeping down the hall in my lonely bed." Then he leaned down and kissed her cheeks, her eyelids and lastly her forehead. "You haunt me, darling, but I can wait until you're ready."

She lifted her arms and ran her open palms across his taut chest, feeling the smooth muscles beneath his shirt. Their eyes met, and she smiled. Somehow it seemed that he moved an inch closer, and her heart lurched at the gentle light she saw there in his eyes.

"Good night, sweetheart," he whispered, pushing her inside her bedroom. "Before I change my mind."

"Good night," she said in a strangled voice as the door closed softly. She undressed by candlelight, pulled a nightgown over her head and crawled into bed. For five long minutes she lay there, staring at the ceiling, listening to rain falling on the roof, fighting the urge to go down the hall and knock on his door.

Finally she admitted it was a losing battle and got out of bed again. She padded barefoot down the hall and knocked softly. "Hi," she said in a small voice as he opened the door. "I...I couldn't sleep. I thought maybe you'd still be up."

He gave her a steady look. "What did you have in mind? Cards?"

"No."

"Then what do you want?" A dimple lurked in his right cheek.

Margaret answered with her eyes, and Jake hesitated only a moment before scooping her up in his arms. "I've been lying in bed staring at the ceiling, and all I see is you," he said thickly, kissing her lingeringly on her mouth. "You're shivering. We'd better get you straight to bed."

She slid her arms around his neck. "I'm getting warmer, but I'm still cold. I think I need drastic treatment."

He grinned broadly, carried her into his room and kicked the door shut. Their laughter and bantering came to a halt as their eyes locked. Jake laid her down gently on the bed. "Are you sure this is what you want?" He still held her in his arms, sliding one hand into her hair. He curved his other hand around her face and caressed her cheek with his thumb.

"Yes, I'm sure," she said hoarsely, not averting her eyes, and intensely aware with every fiber of her body that she wanted him.

He kissed her gently, then lifted his head slightly. "What about Caitlin? Is this going to be awkward for you?"

Margaret shook her head. "No, she's asleep. And the truth is, I wanted you to stay. I was almost afraid to stay alone with her in the house with everything that's happened." Her breath brushed his lips, and she felt sweet, honeyed passion flow through her. Her eyes met his in an intense gaze. "This feels so right...so wonderful, Jake. I need you. I can't think straight when you touch me."

"Sweetheart, what do you think touching you does to me?" He lowered his mouth that remaining fraction of an inch, kissing her deeply as he lay beside her.

She surrendered completely to the spell of his nearness, lost in sensation as he pulled her nightgown off. Afterward, he settled his hands gently on her hips and pulled her against him. "I want to make love, darling."

She let out a long sigh of delight. "So do I." She parted her lips as his grazed hers, his tongue flicking inside her mouth. His hands slid upward, shaping the slimness of her waist, upward...and she felt her breasts swell in anticipation of his touch. Pulling her tongue from his mouth, she kissed his lips, featherlight, slow, just brushing them with hers. Then she sank her head on his warm shoulder, drifting in the tantalizing pull of passion, feeling her naked body against his hard length.

Her eyes closed as his fingers twined in her hair at the back of her neck, caressing, turning her face up to his as he came up between her legs. He was gentle at first, slowly, inexorably moving inside her. Her arms were around him, palms flat on the damp, warm skin of his back. Holding him, aware of every sinewy muscle, every hard plane of his body.

He whispered into her hair, "Oh yes, darling, that feels so good." He pulled her tightly to him as she kissed him, their bodies moved in timeless rhythm.

He was driving her insane with pleasure and longing, and what had been calm and tender erupted into unchained passion. Her mind emptied, and she knew nothing but the explosive heat of his body throbbing into hers.

Afterward they lay together for a long time, not speaking.

He touched her cheek with his fingertips. "That was wonderful. Oh, my darling..."

She smiled, perfectly content. This wasn't just a passing, thrilling sexual encounter. It was something more than the physical act of love. He was all she'd ever dreamed of in a man, all she'd ever wanted. Her eyelids drooped, her breathing deepened, and she slept in his arms.

He lay beside her, not moving, not wanting to disturb the deep sleep into which she'd drifted. She felt so soft. He held her close and brushed her face with his lips. Her skin felt like warm silk.

He gazed down at her in the candlelight's glow. She lay curled within his arm, her body nestled close. Protect and love, for better or worse, until death—

She must have heard his small intake of breath. She opened her eyes, saying, "I'm not asleep." Turning sideways, she drew him closer, sliding her arm over his body.

"What do you say we try that again?" His voice was a throaty whisper, then his lips came down on hers as the candle flame guttered out and the room fell into darkness. Rain drummed softly on the roof, but neither noticed.

Chapter Nine

Warm lips brushed hers. The touch was a butterfly kiss. Margaret drew a deep breath and opened her eyes to find Jake smiling down at her. He leaned over and kissed her again. "Mmm," she breathed, placing her hands on his shoulders, drawing him close. Something sweet and wonderful was exploding inside her, and she kissed him slowly, deeply, unable to find words to explain how she felt.

He rolled over, the light in his eyes asking, demanding, and she smiled up into his intense gaze. He was so close his breath fanned her cheek. "Oh, Jake..." Her voice trailed off in a happy sigh. She reached up to pull him nearer and abruptly froze.

From down the hall Caitlin's voice yelled, *"Maarrgarret!"*

She sat up, the sheet sliding down to uncover her breasts, and Jake's breath caught in a sigh of regret. He groaned and rolled over. "Talk about poor timing."

"Sounds like she's sick." Margaret slipped out of bed and pulled on her nightgown as Caitlin began coughing plaintively. "Maybe after I give her some

medicine, she'll go back to sleep and you and I can do
something more interesting.''

UNFORTUNATELY the rest of Margaret's morning
passed in a blur. Caitlin's throat ached, her nose was
stuffed up and her eyes were red. When Margaret took
her temperature, she had a slight fever.

Jake had just finished taking a shower when she
passed him in the hall outside Caitlin's room. He wore
a white towel around his waist, his naked back was
dark and lean, beaded with droplets of water. Dancing rays of sunlight from the hall window caught in his
wet hair, and she forgot everything but the need to be
in his arms. He bent his head and kissed her. His lips
tasted wet from his shower. He smelled clean and
soapy and faintly masculine. She kissed him back
whole-heartedly.

Caitlin's loud wailing brought her back to reality.
''I've got to give her more cough medicine,'' Margaret sighed. Jake suggested he needed a certain kind
of medicine, and she laughed, ''Maybe later.''

''MARGARET, I'm thirsty!'' Caitlin wailed for the
tenth time that morning. ''I want a popsicle.''

She poked her head around Caitlin's door. ''Okay,
okay, keep your shirt on. You can have a popsicle after you take a spoonful of this syrup.''

Caitlin heaved herself up among the pillows. ''I said
I need a popsicle. Didn't you hear me?'' Another violent heave and she knocked over a pile of comics,
which slid off the bed and onto the floor. Tumbled in
the mess was a small wooden box.

"Yes, I heard you," Margaret said between clenched teeth, bending to pick it all up. With the box in her hands she looked at Caitlin. "Where did you get this? You haven't been in Mrs. Knox's room again, have you?"

"No, you said not to. I found it in the attic, in a trunk with some old clothes."

Margaret tugged at the lid, but the box wouldn't open. "You're not supposed to play in the attic." Curious, she asked, "What's in it?"

"Some dumb old papers. It had my name on it. I'll show you how it works. It's a puzzle box." Caitlin pressed her fingers on the design of wooden inlaid squares. When the lid opened, she took out the papers.

"This isn't your name, honey. It's Great-Aunt Caitlin's." Margaret scanned the papers...and couldn't believe what she saw on one of them. Shaking, she put the other papers back in the box and numbly held on to the one she left out. She forced herself to look at the paper again. It was a business contract with Great-Aunt Caitlin's name on it...and one other signature...that of a nurse, Polly Merrill.

Stunned for a moment, Margaret put it down and picked up the cough syrup.

"How come she has my name?" Caitlin asked suspiciously.

"It's a family name. Your mom named you after Great-Aunt Caitlin. Now open your mouth." Margaret poked a spoonful of cough syrup into her mouth. "I'll get that popsicle for you."

"I can't breathe." Caitlin sniffled loudly. "Am I gonna die?"

"No, you're tougher than this cold. You'll be fine."
Margaret noticed the glass thermometer had slid down
among the blanket folds and reached for it just as
Caitlin sat on it. Caitlin handed her the two pieces and
flopped back on the pillows, managing to look weak
and pathetically helpless.

Margaret sighed. "Now I'll have to find another
thermometer."

"There's another one in the table next to Mom's
bed," Caitlin said in a small voice. "I know because I
was looking in the drawer for something...a pair of
scissors, and it was next to some of Mom's wedding
pictures."

Margaret went down the hall to Sandy and Robert's room to get the thermometer, but her mind was
still on the piece of paper she'd found in her aunt's
box. Things were becoming very bizarre. She just
wanted to block everything out of her mind.

She opened the door to her sister's room and went
to the bedside table drawer. Pulling the drawer open,
Margaret found what she was looking for. Unable to
resist, she took Sandy and Robert's wedding pictures
out and began skimming through them. There was a
snapshot of the two as they left the church. And there,
behind and just to the left was a woman with blond
hair—who looked like the same person in the snapshot in Mrs. Knox's dressing table, which had to be
Mrs. Knox herself. She wore a dark blue suit, pearls
and sparkling earrings in this picture. And she was
staring at Robert with an odd expression on her face.
The earrings...Margaret drew a long breath of shock
and took the picture over to the window where the
light was better. Then she went to Sandy's jewelry case

and took out the earring Jake had found. When she took it back to the window and compared it to the ones Mrs. Knox was wearing in the snapshot, she went numb.

Trying to clear her head in order to think, Margaret started to piece everything together. Jake found an earring in Robert's car, which Margaret assumed was Sandy's. Then the woman in the snapshot—who had to be Mrs. Knox—was wearing the same earring. And to further complicate matters, Caitlin said she'd read a letter from Robert to Mrs. Knox, which he'd signed *love*.

The only logical explanation—and one she just couldn't believe—was that Robert and Mrs. Knox had been lovers! And somehow Robert had ended up renting her house after he'd married Sandy. What a mess....

"Aunt Maarrgarret, where are you? I'm hungry! I want a popsicle!" Caitlin's voice floated querulously down the hall.

Startled, Margaret stuffed the snapshot and earring in her pocket and went back to Caitlin's room. Her niece glared up from behind her comic book. "Where's my popsicle? I need it right now."

"First, young lady, I'm going to take your temperature." Margaret took advantage of Caitlin's open mouth to stick the thermometer inside. After a minute she took it out; it read just under one hundred degrees. "Drink some juice, and I'll go get your popsicle."

Caitlin glared but did as she was told, sitting up to finish the juice while Margaret straightened the bed and smoothed the sheets. And there, sticking out from under the pillow next to her ever-present notebook, was an envelope. Margaret picked it up. It was un-sealed. Inside was a small white pill. She frowned at Caitlin, who flopped back on the pillows and began coughing loudly.

"Where did this come from?" She turned the en-velope over. Nothing was written on it. "Where did you get this?" She stared at Caitlin, determined to get an answer out of her, one way or another.

Caitlin glowered at her. "I found it in the drawer by Mom's bed. I bet Robert was giving her stuff to make her sick. Bugs or something. I hate him! He's mean! He caught me coming out of their room and he twisted my arm, an Indian burn, and said that's what hap-pened to kids who stuck their noses where they didn't belong. He stinks!"

Margaret sighed. "What am I going to do with you? You never should have touched this."

"There's lots more medicine. It's not like that's all there was. Robert was always giving Mom stuff to take. And she kept throwing up. Anyways, it was only one dumb pill." Caitlin made a face. "I only wanted to see what it was, like if he put bugs or worms in it to make her throw up."

"Margaret," Jake called from the foot of the stairs. "The eggs are done. I'll get the morning paper." The front door closed, and he went down the driveway to the mailbox.

Margaret had forgotten that Jake was making breakfast. "This isn't the end of this," she said firmly, waving the envelope with the capsule in it at Caitlin. "I'm going downstairs, but we'll discuss this later." She started downstairs, debating what to do. It was after nine o'clock, Sandy's doctor's office should be open. She ought to call and see if he could fit Caitlin in without an appointment. That would put to rest any fear that she was sick with anything more serious than a cold.

She found the paper in the hall table with emergency numbers written on it and dialed the doctor's number just as Jake came in, shutting the front door behind him.

He eyed her curiously. "Who're you calling?"

"Sandy's doctor," she said. "I'd like him to take a look at Caitlin. Would you get her a popsicle? Grape, if possible."

He nodded, dropped a kiss on her nose and went out to the kitchen. A minute later, flourishing a purple popsicle, he went upstairs.

He knocked on Caitlin's door. "Hi. Heard you were hungry."

"Goody, grape!" Caitlin wriggled with pleasure, ripped off the wrapper, and stuck it in her mouth.

"How about some company?" He sat down on the side of the bed, pushing aside a clutter of games and comics. "Not feeling so good, hmm?"

"Awful." Caitlin sniffed pathetically and eyed him over the popsicle. "And Aunt Margaret's real mad. She won't listen, and it's not fair. It's not my fault."

He gave her an encouraging smile. "She's pretty fair-minded. Just talk to her. It can't be that bad."

"Yes, it is." She munched on the popsicle. "Besides, it's all Robert's fault."

"He's not even here. What's Robert got to do with your aunt's being mad at you?"

"Everything, that's what," she said solemnly. "He kidnapped Mrs. Knox, that's the lady what owns this house. He's got her stuck in a dungeon someplace, prob'ly." She shrugged and wiped her mouth with her pajama sleeve. "Or she's in the quarry. That's where Robert's gang hides the dead bodies."

He opened up the "Uncle Wiggly" game and laid out the board and pieces. He didn't know quite what to say. Caitlin had her mind made up that Robert was some kind of monster. After a moment he said, "Want to go first?" They played a few minutes, Caitlin absentmindedly having taken two turns in a row; and he shook the dice, determined he wasn't going to say anything to encourage her over-lively imagination. "Six." He moved his piece along the board. "Sometimes we get crazy ideas about people we're not sure we like very much."

Caitlin shook the dice and moved her piece. "Five! I'm gonna win." Unfortunately, she landed on "lost in the woods" and had to go back three. Eyeing Jake's piece, two spaces back and gaining fast, she reached for a red card. "Great! I get another turn."

Giving her a serious look he said quietly, "Do you know what I'm talking about, Caitlin?"

Ignoring the board directions to "go back three," she headed for Dr. Possum's house and a sure win. "Of course. Robert's mean and tells lies all the time. Aunt Margaret doesn't believe me, but I know I'm right. He stinks."

"Granted, you don't like him. But why would he kill Mrs. Knox?"

"Because he wanted her money." She sniffled once or twice, then sneezed violently.

He handed her a tissue. "Robert has plenty of money. He doesn't need Mrs. Knox's. Here, mop your nose." She grimaced, but did as she was told. Jake said quietly, "You just resent your stepfather for some reason."

Caitlin paid no attention to this silly remark. She tossed the tissue on the floor. "He tells lies all the time. He puts worms in Mom's medicine so she throws up. And he never called the doctor for her. I know because I saw him pretend to dial, only he didn't." Moving her piece to Dr. Possum's, she beamed. "I won!"

Jake folded up the game board, not sure he'd done the right thing, getting Caitlin to talk about her feelings of resentment toward Robert. She hadn't changed her mind. He hadn't made any headway at all.

Margaret said from the doorway, "The doctor can see you if we go down right away, so get up and put some clothes on, Caitlin. Want me to give you a hand?"

Caitlin glowered. "Is he gonna give me a shot? I'm 'llergic to shots."

"Not that I know of." Margaret sighed tiredly. "Come on, get up and get dressed."

Jake followed Margaret out into the hall. She closed the door and put her fingers to her lips. "Shh, I don't want her to hear. Look what I found under her pillow. Caitlin's sure it's full of worms or bugs, put there by Robert to make Sandy sick."

Jake turned the pill over in his palm. "Robert gets all kinds of samples in his work for that drug firm. He's always in and out of hospitals and doctors' offices." He frowned at Margaret. "Maybe he thought he'd...help Sandy on his own."

She gave an unhappy shrug. "God, I don't know what's going on. Take a look at what else I found." She showed him the snapshot and earring. "Mrs. Knox, that's who the woman in this picture has to be...she's wearing these earrings, the same as the one you found in Robert's car."

Jake's face was expressionless, but the line of his mouth tightened as he compared the earring in his palm with the wedding snapshot. There was a heavy beat of silence.

"I...I don't understand all this. The lies—" Margaret began. "Why didn't he tell anyone he'd been married? The entire time *we* were engaged, he never said a word about having been married to your sister. And he let me—and I'm sure Sandy, too—believe he had no money. You said your sister had a trust fund he inherited when she died. Yet we used to talk about scraping up money to buy a house someday." She swallowed hard.

Jake frowned. "It was a nice amount of money. Hardly something you'd forget."

"He could have made bad investments, been unlucky," Margaret speculated.

"That's a possible explanation, but—"

"Oh my God!" Margaret felt chilled all over.

There was something in her tone of voice that Jake didn't like. "What?"

"Sandy inherited Great-Aunt Caitlin's estate just after they got married. A lot of money." Sarcastically Margaret said, "He doesn't have to worry about charge accounts now."

"I remember you telling me he doesn't have any credit cards—" Jake fished a folded slip of paper out of his wallet. "You're wrong. He charged four tires for the Fiat less than a year ago. I found the charge slip in the glove compartment. See?" He held out the paper.

She looked at it, then stared dumbly at the signature on the bottom. "My God, *she* paid for four new tires!"

"What are you talking about?" Jake snatched the sales slip and scanned the signature on the bottom in disbelief. "I didn't even bother to look at who signed it. I just assumed it was Robert." He gave a low whistle under his breath. "Polly Knox's name is turning up everywhere. Something's going on here."

"I don't understand any of it," Margaret said bitterly. "Robert's got all these secrets...his marriage to your sister, money he's inherited, this affair with Mrs. Knox—" She glared at Jake, daring him to contradict her. "It was an affair. He was her lover and lied about never having seen her before renting this house. Now he's married to Sandy, and Caitlin swears he's giving her pills to make her sick." She shivered, feeling a terrible sense of apprehension. "I'm afraid."

Jake gave a grim sigh. Then he had a thought. "Ask the doctor what the pill really is when you take Caitlin down to see him. If he says the pill's harmless . . . we've laid one ugly suspicion to rest."

"Come back in half an hour." Margaret dropped a quick kiss on Jake's mouth and climbed out of the car. She extricated a still-complaining Caitlin from the back seat and went into the doctor's office. Jake drove two blocks up the street and parked in front of a combination toy, gift shop. Okay, half an hour, he thought, checking his watch. Time enough to pick up something to make Caitlin feel better.

The bell over the door jangled as he entered the shop. He noticed a woman behind the counter, then looked again. It was the same woman who'd stopped by the house last night. Violet Chadwick. "Hello, we met last night," he said politely.

She arched an eyebrow. "Oh, yes, you're..."

"Jake McCall. I was at Mrs. Knox's house last evening."

She smiled briefly. "Can I help you with something?" Her tone was bored, as if she had little time to waste.

He looked around. "I was hoping to find a good game or book for a little girl." The shelves were stacked with all kinds of things. He picked up a Parcheesi game and glanced at the rules on the back. Pretty straightforward. Maybe too simple. Caitlin was one hell of a complicated kid. After more thought, he chose a few books and took both the game and books to the counter. "I'll take these." Smiling, he added, "Nice shop. You must get a lot of business."

She rang up the sale and put the merchandise in a bag without bothering to look up. "We do all right."

He took out his wallet. "Do you work here full-time?"

"No," she muttered. "Only part-time, to keep busy." Her narrowed eyes flicked over him. "Are you a friend of the people renting Polly Knox's house, the Schuylers?"

"Actually, I'm Robert Schuyler's former brother-in-law. He was married to my sister a few years ago."

There was a small silence, then she said hurriedly, "Did you want to include a card? I'm sorry, I should have asked if you wanted this gift wrapped."

"Maybe I'll get a card, but never mind the gift wrap. It'd be off in two seconds." He took his time selecting a card from a nearby rack. "Vermont's lovely. Do you know if they have any hiking trails, waterfalls, that sort of thing?"

"I can't help you. I've only been here a short time. I'm from Connecticut."

He glanced up. "Really? I spent a few years in Connecticut. My sister and brother-in-law owned a house in Fairfield. Ever been to Fairfield?"

"No," she said icily, handing him the change. She banged the register drawer shut.

Shrugging, Jake picked up his package and left the shop. He found a phone booth and made a few business calls, then went back to the doctor's office and parked. Margaret and Caitlin were just coming out. He leaned over and opened the door. "Great timing."

"Yes," she agreed, turning to make sure Caitlin had fastened her seat belt. Jake gave Caitlin the package.

"For you. A get-well present."

"Wow! Thanks! Can I open it, can I?" Caitlin already had the books out of the bag and was tearing the lid off the Parcheesi game.

She seemed much better, almost her old feisty self. But Margaret looked decidedly worried. She glanced at Caitlin, then said quietly to Jake, "She's got the flu, some bug going around town. The doctor says she'll be better in a day or two." Looking quickly into the back seat again, she said, "I asked him about Sandy, and he said he'd only seen her once, that she looked run-down. He prescribed rest and vitamins. I mentioned her nausea—I thought Caitlin might have caught the flu from Sandy—well, he said he and Sandy talked about her vomiting, and in his opinion it was a touch of food poisoning." Margaret swallowed hard. "Jake, I don't know what's going on. He had no idea Sandy had gone to Florida. Why did Robert say the doctor had suggested she take a Florida vacation?"

Jake started up the car and pulled away from the curb. After a moment he reached over and gripped her hand, hard. "Good question, and one I don't know the answer to... like a good many things about Robert. They don't add up."

Margaret drew a deep breath. "There's more. The doctor said he hadn't heard from Sandy since the first visit. He expected her to call back, and she never did. When I asked if she should finish the antibiotics he'd prescribed for her, he didn't know what I was talking about. He'd never prescribed anything for her. So why was that pill in the bedside table?"

Caitlin unsnapped her seat belt and leaned over the front seat. "I know why. Robert put it there, after he put bugs in it to make Mom throw up."

Jake gave Margaret a sideways look. "Did you show him the pill?"

She nodded. "He said it was a barbiturate. There was a code number on it. He said you couldn't mistake it for anything else."

"It could be Robert's, left there accidentally, or something Mrs. Knox left behind. It's her house.

Sandy might even have found it in the medicine cabinet and meant to throw it out.

"I might believe that if there wasn't something else that was extremely disturbing. Finding the wedding snapshot and the pill took over my thoughts for a while, and I forgot to tell you about something." She paused for a breath. "My Great-Aunt Caitlin—who died and left Sandy her estate—hired a nurse for several months before she passed away. I found the nursing contract—actually, Caitlin found it—in a box in the attic with some of Great-Aunt Caitlin's old clothes. Sandy must have stored it up there. Well, the nurse was Polly Knox—only she was Polly Merrill then."

Jake's mouth hardened. "What are you saying? That Polly could have known about the will and that a niece was the heir?" He stopped abruptly. The reality of where his thoughts were leading him was just taking hold. "If Robert discovered from Polly that your aunt was leaving money to one of her nieces he could have originally thought that you were to get the money—and set up your first encounter at Killington where you were skiing."

"I was mentioned in the will. But she changed her bequeaths constantly. It was kind of a game with her. She told me once when I was ten that she'd cut me out of the will if I didn't clean my plate. We were visiting for the weekend, and she fed us lima beans. I couldn't stand them," Margaret said quietly.

"Ugh! I hate lima beans. They make me sick," Caitlin remarked from the back seat.

"Your theory sounds very scary," Margaret went on in a trembling voice. "He could have broken off the engagement when he found out Sandy was the heir, not me. Polly must have gotten another look at the will. Or maybe the will was altered one last time, and Polly didn't discover it until it was too late. Robert had already met me, and we'd gotten engaged."

He gave her a long look, knowing deep inside that this was true. "We need solid proof. And so far all we have is speculation. The earring and Polly Knox's signature on a charge receipt is not enough."

She stared at him. "How do we get more proof, one way or another?"

Jake drew in a ragged breath. "There's only one thing we can do now to make sure Robert isn't trying to kill . . . Sandy." He raked his hand through his hair and said, "I know we haven't mentioned murder out loud, but that's the only conclusion we can come to at this point. And the only way I can think of to get some proof that Robert goes after women with money—and then tries to kill them—is to pay a visit to my sister's doctor in Connecticut." Margaret squeezed his hand, telling him that she understood how hard this was for him. "If we find out there was anything remotely suspicious about Betsy's death . . . I'll ask to have the body exhumed . . . then find Robert and kill him."

Margaret, in a strained and low voice, said, "Sandy will have to be told when she calls next."

"If she calls," Jake said softly, wrapping his arms around Margaret.

AN HOUR LATER they were on their way to Connecticut. Mrs. Till—over Caitlin's strenuously voiced objections—came to the house to baby-sit.

The drive down to Fairfield was tense. Margaret's mind was full of worry and fear. She was half dreading what Betsy's physician might say.

Jake stopped at a gas station near Hartford to call and make sure Dr. Wellstone could see them. By two-thirty they turned off the Interstate onto a local highway. It took them another fifteen minutes to reach the doctor's office.

He was a thin, wiry man, half-balding, and his eyes were bright blue and shrewd. He had a slight limp when he walked. He gave them both a discerning look as they sat down. "I have only fifteen minutes to spare," he said apologetically. "I know you've driven a long way." He raised an eyebrow. "What did you want to know?"

Jake leaned forward in his chair. "Was there anything at all suspicious about Betsy's death? I'll get straight to the point, could she have been...murdered? By some untraceable poison or an injection of air?"

Dr. Wellstone hesitated, then said, "No, her heart gave out. Yes, it was unexpected, but she had a heart murmur."

"She'd had it all her life. You told her the medication was taking care of it, that she didn't have to worry."

Dr. Wellstone picked up a pen and rolled it between his fingers. "True, and under ordinary circumstances, she shouldn't have died." His face grew somber. "Unfortunately she was that one in a million that medical science can't predict."

Jake shook his head. "You didn't perform an autopsy—how can you be sure her death was due to her heart murmur?"

Dr. Wellstone pursed his lips, then put the pen down on his desk blotter. "We didn't perform an autopsy because, frankly, her husband denied us permission. I would have liked to pin down the cause of death more exactly, but with her heart and the asthma attack she suffered that night, well, it didn't seem... necessary. Her husband was with her when she died. He described what happened and called for a nurse immediately. However, it was too late. She was gone."

"All you have is her husband's word about what happened that night." Jake gestured with a despairing hand. "So you really don't know."

"I won't waste your time or mine, arguing. Your sister had a serious medical condition—"

"Which was controlled successfully for years," Jake interrupted grimly.

The buzzer on the desk sounded twice. Jake rose. "Thanks for your time, Dr. Wellstone. It was most informative."

They were both grimly silent on the drive back to Vermont. Jake's face was rigid and flushed with suppressed anger. Margaret was still too stunned to say much. She sat, her hands clenched in her lap. *Naive* was not the word to describe how ignorant she had been about Robert. She'd fallen for his easy charm, flattery... How could she have been so easily deceived?

As for poor Betsy's death—if it had been murder, Margaret had to admit it had been ingenious. She'd died in the hospital, with the best of medical care available, surrounded by doctors and nurses. Then Robert had played the grieving widower—and had sat back and inherited all that lovely money.

Chapter Ten

Luckily there was little traffic on the road by the time they turned off Route 100 onto North Hollow Road. They'd stopped in Rochester to buy cough syrup and markers for Caitlin, who no doubt would still be awake. It was a little after nine o'clock, with the air sweet smelling and fresh from so much rain. Jake squinted as a pair of headlights flashed in the rear-view mirror. Margaret twisted in the seat and took a look. "Someone else on the way home."

"He's not in much of a hurry." Jake glanced in the mirror again and shifted to second. "He could have passed us back there."

The road rose ahead in a series of looping curves, but visibility was good because of the moon and the lack of fog. Jake turned the wheel right. Loose gravel rattled beneath the wheels. "Do you think Sandy's called tonight?" He tried to keep concern out of his voice. Margaret had enough to worry about.

She pushed her hair back tiredly. "I don't know. God knows what I'm going to tell her—" She stopped speaking abruptly as a wash of backlight flooded the car. Coming closer and closer, the car following had turned on its brights.

"Damn." Jake squinted and flipped the mirror up. Absently he checked that his seat belt was fastened. "Got your seat belt on?" Margaret nodded and he went on grimly, "It gets narrower and steeper around the next curve."

Margaret took another quick look out the back window.

"All we need is a jerk tailgating." He tightened his hands on the wheel. The road surface was poor, mostly ruts with patches of thin, hard, finely ground stone toward the crown of the road. He had to ease up on the accelerator for a right curve because he felt the rear end of the car drifting. "Hang on, I don't like this."

Margaret put a hand on the dashboard, bracing herself. She could feel the rear end vibrating as the car slewed sideways toward the black pine trees, spectral against the background of bare rock and earth.

"No place to pull over and let him pass," Jake muttered. "We'll just have to put up with him until we get to the farm."

Suddenly the headlights grew huge in the rearview mirror, and their car was hit from behind, causing it to skate sideways with no control, bouncing off the rusted fencing that edged the shoulder of the road. "My God," Margaret gasped.

Jake threw a furious look in the mirror. The headlights came up again, blinding him, the gap between the cars narrowing to nothing, and he thought of the pivoting tendency of the car's rear end if they got hit again; then the car would automatically go into a skid.

There was an explosive pop as the car's brake lights broke. The car lurched suddenly sideways, and immediately its mass began to dominate its momentum. The fence loomed, grew gigantic in the windshield, then was gone as the car skidded away.

"Hang on!" Jake was trying to control the wheel instinctively now. Left to right the car skidded, wider to the left and again wider to the right. He knew better than to jam on the brakes. He smelled the clutch burning, and the car went into a slow spin. One part of his mind was thinking of how he would wring the neck of the drunk in the other car if they lived long enough for him to get his hands on him; and another part heard the brittle bumping of their tires across the ruts as the car spun in a series of crazy loops, the headlights from behind appearing and reappearing in the windshield. He thought he heard Margaret scream, then they were rammed again, obliquely this time, just behind his door handle. He braked, but it was no good, they were going too fast. The car went straight through the fence with barely any impact. He felt the drag of his seat belt and a moment of weightlessness before the car tilted nosedown and struck something—a boulder, a series of saplings—and struck again, rolling, tumbling, now on its side, now on its roof; and the long sound of raw metal scraping against stone as it slid to a stop. Their speed, momentum, died; the silence was eerie; the moon reflected oddly in the cracked mirror.

"Are you all right?" He grabbed Margaret's shoulders. Her eyes were closed. A streak of blood ran down her cheek. He shook her gently. "Margaret, we've got to get out!'' She stirred; her dazed eyes cleared as they focused on his face.

"My God, what happened?"

He was already unsnapping his seat belt and hers. He pulled her out, stumbling, rolling as they landed. Then he got to his feet and scooped her up in his arms. He looked for the nearest cover, and limped behind a pine tree.

There was a noise, an eerie crackling, and red light glowed all around. The explosion made the ground shake and the trunk of the pine tree tremble against his shoulder. A second explosion rocked the car. The air reeked with the smell of burning gasoline.

His coat had been ripped at the shoulder; he swallowed hard. The shock of the crash was just setting in. The car hadn't met much resistance as it had hit that fence; it had broken away like so much wet paper. Numbly, he held Margaret in his arms and watched the car burn.

"I can stand," she mumbled.

"Sure?" She nodded, and he set her on her feet, keeping a firm arm around her waist. He was just realizing the "accident" had been deliberate. Not a drunk out for a few laughs, recklessly forcing someone off the road. No, they'd been the target of an attempted murder. Nothing showed from the road above. No light, no dim face, no sign of anyone leaning through the gap in the fencing to make sure there were no survivors.

"Can you walk?" He brushed the tumbled hair away from her face. In the fading glow of the fire her face looked pale.

"I'm okay, just shaken up some," she whispered.

"We'd better get moving. Head for the house. It's not that far. We can make it." His breathing was painful, it felt suspiciously like a cracked rib; and a warm wetness was dripping down his hand. "Come on." A light wind sprang up as they climbed back up to the road, and when he glanced down the mountainside, he saw sparks blowing from the burned-out shell of the car. The smell of burning rubber was thick and acrid in his nostrils, coming stronger now.

They limped onward. The woods were silent and peaceful, moonlight sifting through the trees to dapple the road. Yet Jake was aware all the time of a mounting tension. Danger. The word was so clear in his mind, it might have been written in fiery letters against the trees. Whoever had forced them off the road might return.

Ten minutes later they stumbled up the front steps of the farm. When they went inside, Mrs. Till drew a shocked breath. "Land sakes, what happened?"

"We had an accident with the car," Margaret told her. She gave a little laugh. "Believe me, it's a long walk up the mountain." She sank down in a kitchen chair. "Where's Caitlin?"

"She's in bed. I fed her supper. Never mind her." Mrs. Till wiped her hands on her apron. "Let me get you a cup of tea. You both look like you could use it."

Margaret shook her head. "No, you go along home. We'll be fine." Mrs. Till looked skeptical, but listened and left.

The back door closed behind her, and Jake took off his coat, awkwardly easing it past his shoulders. He winced. "God, I'm tired. I could use a drink, and I don't mean tea." He headed slowly to the living room and the whiskey decanter. Margaret pushed him gently onto the settee. "You're in worse shape than I am. I'll get you a drink." She poured it with shaking hands, and he gulped it down. A fire was burning in the fireplace. A log shifted, and a shaft of sparks curled upward.

Jake leaned back and closed his eyes. When he opened them again, she was kneeling in front of him, dabbing at his bleeding left hand with a towel. There was a bowl of pinkish water on the table, a pile of gauze bandages and a pair of scissors.

"I'm glad to see you're conscious again. How do you feel?"

He said slowly, "Like someone who's supposed to be dead at the foot of the mountain. I don't know how you can move."

She grinned. "Women are the stronger sex, didn't you know that?"

"Someone tried damn hard to kill us...." His voice trailed off, and he pounded his fist on his knee. "If this is tied in together with Robert...I'll kill him with my bare hands."

"We can go to the police, tell them everything and have an all-points bulletin put out for him." She got up and went over to the phone on the hall table.

He raked his hair back with his good hand. "Nothing will stand up in court. He'll sue for false arrest, raise hell ... and see to it Sandy meets the same fate as Betsy. An unfortunate accident, brake failure on her car, a fall downstairs. She's in love with him, she'll believe whatever he tells her until it's too late."

"What about Polly Knox? If she's in this with him, when she comes back from Europe the police can question her, maybe she'll break and tell the truth."

He looked at her out of ice-cold eyes. "What if she doesn't come back? What if she's dead?"

Margaret drew in a long breath and stared at him, speechless. Just then there was the dull thud of something falling upstairs. "Caitlin," she said, frowning. "I'll check on her."

Caitlin was examining the contents of her shoebox and looked up guiltily as Margaret came in. She allowed her face to be wiped with a damp washcloth. Margaret's eyes were drawn irresistibly to the shoebox as she straightened the pillows and put a jumble of dominoes back in their box.

"Those things in the shoebox, where did you find them all?" she asked casually.

Caitlin's jaw dropped comically; for once she seemed to be at a loss for words.

"I found it the other night when you had that nightmare. It fell on the floor and I picked up the things that fell out," Margaret went on chattily. "What about that picture of Robert?"

Caitlin shrugged. "I found most of the stuff in the den, but the picture was in the sewing room, under a drawer. He looks dumb in a mustache. How come he said he'd never been in this house before he and Mom rented it? That's the front porch and the big maple tree in the picture. I reco'nize the woodpecker hole in it."

"Never mind about that now," Margaret said evenly. "Where in the den did you find the other things?"

"On the shelf, behind the big red dictionary."

Margaret drew a deep breath and thought hard. Had Polly Knox hidden Robert's picture and other things as evidence? Maybe she was afraid of him, and the snapshot was a crude form of life insurance. She'd cleared off to Europe in one hell of a hurry. What if Caitlin was right and Polly was dead—hadn't Jake just said the same thing, that she'd never gotten to Europe? What if her body had been weighted and thrown in the quarry. Such a handy place for dead bodies....

"I was coloring and then I decided to look for something to read and dropped my crayon behind the books. I was trying to get my crayon out, and there was all this stuff behind the dictionary." Caitlin's face radiated blameless innocence.

Margaret stared at the shoebox. The letter. Maybe that was the evidence they needed to convince the police. "What about the letter? Was it behind the dictionary, too?"

Caitlin nodded. "Yeah, do you want to read it? It's all about fights over money." She dragged the cover off the shoebox and rummaged inside. Handing the letter to Margaret, she added, "See? He signed it 'love,' too."

Margaret scanned the letter quickly.

Dear Polly, everything's going well. I've rented an apartment in Allston, too expensive, but it's suitable for my needs. About the money, call it a loan—with the big payoff down the road. Trust me, that's all I ask. Let's face it, I'm no saint. You of all people ought to know that. But it's what we agreed on. We're a team, and a good one. Don't mess things up now. And honey, if we're talking threats, I can make plenty of my own. Your hands aren't clean. In the meantime, think over what I said. I'm going to Killington on Wednesday. Plan to call you when I get back.

Love, R

Margaret couldn't move. She stared numbly at the letter in her hand, seeing only a blur of white and black. After a moment she drew a long breath and checked the end of the letter again. "It doesn't have Robert's signature on it. It's just signed *R*."

"Yeah, I know. But it's his letter," Caitlin said with a wide yawn. "He always signs notes for Mom like that, with an *R*?"

"But it could be someone else's letter." Margaret looked at Caitlin who yawned again and shook her untidy head.

"Nope. It's gotta be his."

Margaret rose and picked up the shoebox. "I'd like to show this to Jake, the little wooden box, too."

"Sure." Caitlin hunted around among the toys and games and handed over the wooden box. "Just 'member to push the squares backward, every other one. Or it won't open."

Margaret went downstairs to find Jake standing in the front hall. Their eyes met as she came down the last step. Shadows lurked in his. She gestured toward the kitchen. "I've got something to show you. A letter Caitlin found. It's from Robert, at least I think it is. And it's written to Polly Knox. Let's sit down and go over the clues Caitlin's collected. Then we can decide if it's enough proof."

A few minutes later they'd spread everything out on the kitchen table. The earring, the wedding snapshot, Robert's picture on the front porch, the letter. Reading it quickly, Jake said grimly, "There's nothing damning about it on the surface." He drew a harsh breath. "Robert wrote it. I'm sure of it."

Margaret paused in the act of opening the wooden box. "All right, let's just say it's his. Robert had an apartment in Allston. And the letter mentions Killington. Of course that's where Robert met me, on that ski trail."

She was pressing the squares of an inlaid wooden box. As it opened, he asked, "What's that?"

"Some of Great-Aunt Caitlin's bills and papers stored up in the attic. Nothing important, a maintenance agreement for her TV." Margaret went through the papers, one by one. "Another for a VCR, and the contract with Polly Merrill."

Jake's gray-blue eyes darkened. "If we can get Polly to testify against Robert—if she's really in Europe and not dead—we could get him. Call the local travel agency and see if she booked a flight to Europe."

"What about the car? Shouldn't we report the accident first?" Her green eyes were huge and exhausted looking.

He shrugged. "First let's figure out if Polly really went to Europe. The car can wait. It's not going anywhere." He rubbed his aching side and read the letter again while Margaret called the travel agency.

"There's no booking in Polly Knox's name for Europe," Margaret said when she came back. Her voice shook. "Oh, Jake, what are we going to do?"

"We find Robert and Sandy. Where were they staying in Florida?"

"The Surfside Motel, near Orlando. But they've moved on by now. Sandy said they would drive around and stop when they felt like it."

He was silent for several seconds. "Is there a travel guide in the house? The oil companies sell them, with motel listings."

She nodded in relief. "In the den. Sandy looked through it before they left. I don't think they took it with them."

As she found the travel guide and ran her finger down the first page of listings, she said, "This seems so useless. Couldn't we notify the Florida police?

"What do we tell them? There's a possibility Robert killed my sister and is going to murder yours?"

She bit her lip. "It all ties in. Polly was my Great-Aunt Caitlin's nurse and found out what was in her will. She must have told Robert I was the niece who was inheriting everything. Then my aunt changed the will. When Polly found out it was too late. He was already engaged to me and had to break off our relationship to court Sandy."

Jake shook his head. "The police would never believe us. I don't know if our accident tonight is tied in somehow—but it's a damned odd coincidence." He gave a bitter laugh. "Robert probably knows people who'll kill for the price of a drink."

Margaret, shaken, sank down in a chair. "I don't believe this is happening." She was pale; lines of strain showed around her curving mouth.

"Look at this from the point of view of the police. You're the bitterly jealous sister. You lost the man you were in love with, and maybe you wanted to get your hands on her money, too. They might even suspect you if anything happened to Sandy."

"That's crazy," she said dully. "Anyone who knows me..."

He shrugged. "You have two strong motives for murder—jealousy and greed." He gave a mirthless smile. "I'd make the short list, too. Especially after they got through talking to Dr. Wellstone and learned I'd been asking questions, trying to prove Betsy'd been murdered. Presumably I'd be bitter because I hadn't inherited my sister's money."

"But we know Robert's a killer. He was with Betsy when she died—there was no autopsy."

"We *suspect* Robert's a killer, but we're a long way from proving it. All we have are a few pieces of circumstantial evidence. We've got one option now. To get to Florida and convince Sandy she could be married to a cold-blooded killer."

Chapter Eleven

Or Sandy could already be dead, a small voice in the back of Margaret's mind whispered. Fear and anger knotted her stomach, blocking out all thoughts of anything else. Margaret stared at the pages of the travel guide, trying to concentrate. Suddenly she remembered that picture of palm trees on the right-hand page. The motel with two pools.

"Jake, I remember Sandy marking a motel in Lakeland."

"Let's check the location." He spread a large map of Florida out on the table. "If they headed south, they had two choices, the east coast or the west coast. The Everglades rules out anything else."

She let out a silent breath. "Unless he had plans for her that included the Everglades." Miles of saw grass, mangrove swamp and alligators. "For all we know he's already killed her." Her eyes filled with tears.

"Stop it," he said sharply, turning toward her and taking her into his arms. "Margaret," he said softly. His arms were sliding around her waist, holding her close.

There was a noise from the hallway, the unmistakable shuffle of seven-year-old slippered feet. Margaret sighed and turned her head.

Caitlin was standing there with her bathrobe buttoned up all wrong. She had a battered teddy bear under her arm. "I woke up. I had to go to the bathroom." She frowned darkly. "There's no more toilet paper. I called, but you didn't answer."

Margaret went over and put her arm around Caitlin's shoulders. "Okay, go back upstairs. I'll get more toilet paper from the linen closet."

Caitlin's eyes narrowed as she stared at Jake. "Wow! There's blood on your shirt, and it's all torn!"

"And you've got a cold and shouldn't be out of bed," Margaret told her, gently but firmly. "Back to bed."

"But I'm thirsty. I need another..."

"I'll get you a drink," Margaret promised, bending to drop a kiss on Caitlin's rumpled head. "Upstairs now." Deftly, she began walking her upstairs.

Jake's voice floated after them. "I'll just call and report the accident. Better late than never. The police—"

Oh no, Margaret thought wearily. That's all they needed, the magic words: *accident, police.* Sure enough...

Caitlin halted dead in her tracks. They'd made it as far as the landing. "What accident? Is someone else dead?"

"No, Jake's car ran off the road. He's reporting the accident, that's all. Come on, I'll tuck you in." She managed to get Caitlin back in bed, a lengthy process because everything had to be just so.

The window had to be opened another half inch, the vaporizer refilled. And then Caitlin still hadn't gone to the bathroom.

Margaret shook her head and went to refill the toilet paper holder, and after Caitlin came out of the bathroom, it took another ten minutes to settle her in bed. "Good night, honey." Margaret leaned down and gave her a hug and kiss.

Caitlin frowned. "Where are my magic markers? You promised you'd get them for me."

The markers were burned to a cinder at the foot of the mountain, Margaret thought grimly. As they both might have been.

"We'll have to get more tomorrow." She sat down on the side of the bed and took Caitlin's hand. "I've been thinking."

"What?" Caitlin asked suspiciously.

"Well, Jake and I are probably flying to Florida tomorrow. I was going to ask Mrs. Till if she could stay with you for a few days, but I remember she said she was off to Canada day after tomorrow. Which leaves us with a large problem." Margaret drew a breath. "The problem is, who's going to baby-sit you while I'm gone? Your father's in Europe someplace. I can't reach him, and anyway—" She took another breath. "Things are complicated, to say the least."

Caitlin's face set into a mutinous frown. "I wanna come, too. I wanna go to Disneyworld."

"But you're not feeling well," Margaret said, feeling Caitlin's forehead with the back of her hand. "Hmm, your fever's gone."

Magically Caitlin's face beamed with hope. "See, I'm better, and there's nobody to baby-sit." She sighed happily. "So I get to go to Florida, too."

Margaret hesitated, then gave up. "I guess so." Squeezing the small hand in hers. "I'm worried about your mom...and Robert. There might be something...wrong."

Caitlin nodded. "I told you there was. Robert's *mean*. Ackshully, he's a mean old pig, and I hate him." She yawned widely, "But everything's gonna be okay because Madame Zorina says I'm gonna save everyone."

"I hope she's right." Margaret got up and turned out the bedside lamp. "Sleep tight, honey. Sweet dreams."

"'Course she's right. Madame Zorina's magic." Caitlin yawned again and wriggled down under the blankets. "G'night."

When she descended the stairs, Margaret found Jake waiting at the foot. "You look all in," he said, concern in his eyes.

"I am," she agreed, half-laughing. "I can hardly keep up with Caitlin. She's got more energy than a herd of wild horses."

"Then I'll tuck you into bed, and call and get reservations on a flight to Florida tomorrow morning." He slid his arm around her shoulders and walked her back upstairs.

Halting at the top, she looked up into his eyes. "We have to take Caitlin with us. She's feeling better, and Mrs. Till's away. There's no one to leave her with."

"Okay, we'll manage somehow," he said with a wry smile.

With reluctance she crawled into bed and pulled the covers up. She yawned as his arms encircled her body and he laid a gentle kiss on her lips. "Go to sleep. I'll be up in a few minutes." Deftly his fingers unbuttoned her blouse and slipped it off. Her bra followed, then her jeans. He slipped a nightgown over her tired head and tucked her in again. "I'll be back soon."

Those were the last words she heard, and in a few moments she was sound asleep.

In the morning she dragged herself out of bed and took a hot shower, hoping it would bring her back to life. Jake was already downstairs making breakfast, judging from the aroma of coffee and toast wafting up the stairs. She grabbed a salmon wool dress, pumps, stockings, and got dressed. After winding her hair into a neat chignon, she applied lipstick and blusher in a vain attempt to bring color into her pale face and blinked at herself in the mirror. The reality of everything flooded back to her tired mind.

They had to find Robert before he added Sandy to his list of victims.

As she got downstairs the phone was ringing, and she picked it up. It was Violet Chadwick, calling to ask if they'd heard anything from Polly Knox. She said chattily, "By the way, I heard there was a terrible accident up on North Hollow last night. A car burned. The police said it was totalled. You don't happen to know whose car it was?"

Margaret leaned against the doorjamb. "The car belonged to my friend, Jake McCall, and by some miracle we walked away from that accident."

"My, my, how lucky," Violet said worriedly.

"Yes, now about Polly Knox, I haven't heard anything. As a matter of fact, I'll be gone myself for a few days. I'm flying to Florida sometime today."

"Oh, I see—well, I won't keep you," Violet said briskly. "Have a pleasant trip." She hung up with a sharp click.

Margaret sighed and replaced the receiver. Turning, she saw Jake coming from the kitchen. He was scanning the front page of the morning paper.

"They're holding an inquest into Vern Boyce's death next week," he said quietly. At her startled intake of breath, he shook his head. "Don't worry. I talked to the police last night. They know we're going to Florida. That's all cleared. They'd like you to be around for the inquest. As things look now, they're leaning toward accidental death. They found several places on the quarry wall where he hit before entering the water—if he was drunk and fell in."

TWO HOURS LATER they were in the departure lounge at Montpelier Airport, in front of Gate 5 to Orlando, via Boston. Jake was sitting beside Margaret, his thigh just brushing her knee. Her salmon wool skirt was crushed between them. Through the folds of wool she could feel the hard, warm touch of his muscular leg.

Caitlin was sitting on the other side of Margaret, peeling the paper from a stick of grape bubble gum. Popping it into her mouth, she chomped happily.

Margaret reached up and felt her hair with her fingertips. It was sticky. Bubble gum. They'd spent the better part of the last hour on the drive to the airport listening to Caitlin read excerpts from her notebook.... "Robert's a rat, but we're gonna get there just in time to save Mom. Madame Zorina says so. Robert's gonna go straight to jail, and we can all go to Disneyworld." Leaning her folded arms across the back of the front seat so that her nose was right next to Margaret, Caitlin had blown a big bubble, which burst all over Margaret's hair. What a mess!

Margaret got to her feet. "I'm going to the ladies' lounge to try and clean the gum out of my hair! I'll be right back."

Caitlin jumped to her feet. "I have to go to the bathroom, too. And I'm thirsty. Can I get a soda?"

"No, we don't have time. Maybe on the plane," Margaret said as they walked past the gift shop display. The store was full of jugs of maple syrup, books on Vermont, handmade wool afghans, wintry ski posters. Her mind drifted to Jake and herself in a cozy ski lodge, the firelight flickering in a stone fireplace. No, in bed would be even better. Tangled limbs, his warm skin sliding over hers. . . .

"That lady over there keeps staring at us, really hard," Caitlin said idly in between bubbles.

In spite of herself, Margaret paused and looked around. There was no one in sight but a couple of teenagers, a pair of black-robed nuns, and a thin man in a very ugly bow tie. "Come on, we don't have much time," she said shortly, marching on toward the ladies' lounge.

Caitlin hurried to keep up, looking over her shoulder. "Well, she's not there now, but I saw her and she was looking at us, she really was." Caitlin sounded disappointed.

Margaret shouldered open the lounge door. "Oh, come on, it was just some woman watching people pass by. She was probably bored and had nothing better to do."

Caitlin stalked past her indignantly. "I saw her. And she wasn't bored, she was *staring*." She disappeared into the toilet stall and the lock clicked. Margaret walked over to the sink and fumbled in her purse for a comb.

"I notice things like that," Caitlin said from behind the partition. "'Cause when I grow up I'm gonna be a writer. You know, I already told you that."

Inwardly, Margaret heaved a sigh. She tugged the comb through her matted, gummy hair without much success.

"I'm collecting information for a book."

"On what?" Margaret muttered, probing a sore spot on her scalp. Maybe a pair of nail scissors would cut off the worst of the gum.

"It's on murder," Caitlin said happily. The toilet flushed, the door opened, and she came out. "Seeing as I'm practically an eyewitness, sort of."

Margaret shoved the comb back in her purse and swallowed hard. "Let's sincerely hope not."

"What? Oh, yeah, well...I know Mom's gonna be okay, but there's always Mrs. Knox and Vern Boyce." She leaned closer and said in a clear, carrying voice, "It had to be Robert or someone helping him. *An accomplice!*"

And from the far side of the partition came the sound of a flushing toilet, a door opening, footsteps...Margaret turned and glanced quickly at the woman leaving.

It was one of the nuns, and she was eyeing Caitlin with a sort of dreadful fascination. Margaret forced a brief smile as the nun gave her a wintry stare and washed and dried her hands in utter silence.

Caitlin lodged her gum in the corner of her cheek and turned on the water. She soaped her hands. "There's all kinds of evidence. Like Robert didn't get rid of Mrs. Knox's clothes after he kidnapped and killed her. And he left the boat in the quarry. There's the letter and his picture. I wonder if he tortured her first."

Margaret, quite familiar with torture by now, closed her eyes and said wearily, "That's very interesting."

"Sure, he could have cut off her—"

Opening her eyes, Margaret said, "Not one more word!" The nun shook her head in grim disbelief and left.

THEIR FLIGHT LANDED in Orlando about four o'clock. Although it was getting late, the sun was hot and the sky was still a brilliant blue with dollops of ice-cream clouds piled on the horizon.

Margaret stood with Jake at the baggage carousel. The claims area was crammed wall-to-wall with milling people, half of whom were looking for luggage, the other half looking for friends and relatives.

It was a madhouse. She found a vacant chair and sat down tiredly. Caitlin was standing next to a nearby pillar, examining the crowd. Looking for the mysterious woman she'd seen in the airport departure lounge in Montpelier. Caitlin was certain the lady had boarded the plane, and Margaret hadn't been able to convince her the poor woman deserved privacy on her trip to Florida.

Jake piled the bags at Margaret's feet. "Look, I'll give the Surfside Motel in Orlando a call and see if they know where your sister and Robert went. They might have called ahead and made reservations at the next motel."

Blowing a bubble, Caitlin sauntered over. "Let's go to Disneyworld first, because what if they close it down or go on strike and I don't get to go?"

"No, we find your mom and Robert first, then we go to Disneyworld," Margaret told her firmly.

"Phooey." Caitlin sighed and looked around, then grabbed Margaret's shoulder. "I saw her! She's over there, on the other side of the baggage thing. She's right next to the old lady with the black hat." She shook Margaret again. "Aren't you coming with me? We can catch her."

"No," Margaret said flatly. "Leave the poor woman in peace."

Caitlin gave her a look of belligerent contempt. "Great! That's just great. She could be part of Robert's gang, his *accomplice!* She could be planning to kidnap me for all you care!"

Margaret suppressed an impulse to laugh out loud at the thought of a gang member capable of such stupidity. "There isn't any gang. It's just some woman going on vacation."

Jake came back from the phone and car-rental booths. "Ready to go? Come on." He helped her up with one large hand, somehow grabbing Caitlin and their bags, propelling them toward the terminal exit.

It was ninety degrees outside and humid. The warm air struck Margaret's face like a blow, rising from the pavement in stupefying waves. They walked through the parking lot toward the car Jake had rented, a silver-blue Buick Regal.

He bent to unlock the trunk and stow away their bags. Margaret leaned against the front passenger door and tried not to breathe. Her wool skirt was sticking to the backs of her legs.

Caitlin came skipping around the front of the car. "There's something dead between the cars in the next row. I think it's a cat, only it's so squashed you can't tell." Her eyes were round with innocence.

"Oh, God," Margaret said tiredly. "Caitlin, please."

"It prob'ly got runned over. There's a lot of blood. And flies. Flies are crawling all over it."

She felt she was going to throw up. And wouldn't Caitlin love that, she reminded herself. Resolutely, Margaret choked back the remains of the in-flight meal.

Caitlin was saying, "All that blood. The car must have got spattered with it. What if it was Robert's? All we have to do is look for a car with blood all over it."

"Get in the car and be quiet." Margaret yanked open the back door.

But Caitlin still had her pièce de résistance to offer. "It looked like the head came off."

"Enough, young lady," Jake said quietly. "If you open your mouth again, I'll turn you over my knee and whale the living daylights out of you."

That did the trick. Caitlin gave him a reproachful look and climbed in the back seat.

Jake slammed the trunk closed, and they got in and drove off toward the highway. "The Surfside desk clerk said he heard Sandy mention Lakeland as their destination. So we'll head down there," Jake said as he pulled onto the highway. "It's quite a drive. Once we get to Lakeland we'll register at a motel, and I'll see if I can get a line on where they went."

Margaret sighed and leaned her head back on the neck rest. After a moment she put on a pair of sunglasses against the late-afternoon glare and stared out at the shimmering heat rising from the road. She closed her eyes and dozed fitfully. She woke with a sense of panic when the motion of the car stopped.

Jake was looking down at her with a smile. "Wake up, sleepyhead. We're here at the motel."

She sat up and took off the sunglasses. The sun was setting. She rolled down the window and breathed deeply. The sky was blazing red and gold, and there was an ocean breeze to take the edge off the oppressive heat.

Jake got out of the car and stretched, and she flipped down the visor mirror and stared at her reflection. Her mouth was pale, and there were shadows beneath her green eyes. Haunted by Robert? Or by her growing fear that they might not be in time to save Sandy?

They went inside the motel to register. Jake gave her a wry look. "A double and a single?"

"Right," she murmured sweetly.

She dragged a loudly protesting Caitlin away from the soda machine. The coin return was broken, and she'd been playing it like a one-armed bandit and winning. Margaret made her return almost two dollars in nickels and quarters to the desk clerk.

The moment they got to their rooms, Caitlin switched on the TV, found cartoons and turned up the volume loud enough to make the walls shake. Then she sauntered to the bathroom and shut the door.

Margaret marched over and turned off the TV, bumping into Jake who was putting their bags on the bureau. His hands came out and caught her arms, and she found herself held tight to his body. Startled, she looked up into his face. He wore an expression of frustration and lingering desire.

Her body was pressed close to his, her heart racing, her breasts crushed against his jacket. He was very tall, looming over her. There was no room to move, but a single step backward and she bumped into the double bed.

His hands tightened on her arms, and her lips parted. It was a moment lost in time, they might have been alone in the world with a thousand things to say—all about love and passion.

He drew a deep breath, and suddenly his eyes were laughing down into hers. "Guess my timing leaves something to be desired."

She never had a chance to reply because the toilet flushed, water ran in the bathroom sink and the door opened, all in a matter of seconds.

Caitlin came out of the bathroom and looked suspiciously from Margaret's flushed face to Jake's tall, broad back. They were now the width of the bed apart, but she must have had eyes in the back of her head. "Dumb, drippy love stuff," she said disgustedly.

MARGARET WOKE REFRESHED the next morning and got out of bed. She went over to the window and pulled back the curtains, letting in the clear, golden morning light. Her eyes flickered to the palm trees dotting the edge of the parking lot. No sign of a breeze.

It was sunny and hot, just like yesterday. She'd better hurry and dress. Jake had said he wanted to be on the road by nine. It was almost half past eight. Maybe she ought to wake Caitlin. She gazed across the room at the humped blankets on the other bed.

No, she would let her sleep awhile longer. Jake had said he would make a few phone calls this morning and try to track down reservations Sandy and Robert might have made with the large motel chains.

She walked past Caitlin's bed and into the bathroom where she washed her face with bitingly cold water. She felt frustrated, caught in a dangerous spiral from which any activity was better than doing nothing.

She found a road map of Florida in the desk drawer, along with colorful brochures of assorted tourist attractions. She fanned them out on the desktop. Hmm, there seemed to be an inordinate number of alligator farms.

Sighing, she turned to the map. Lakeland. That's where they were now. Tracing her finger along the black line past Disneyworld west from Orlando, she found Lakeland. But where, she wondered helplessly, was Sandy?

"I'm hungry." Caitlin's voice, neglected sounding, startled Margaret. Then the sound of something breaking made her wince. Caitlin had knocked an ashtray off the bedside table as she'd yawned and sat up.

Margaret picked up the pieces. "Give me time to shower and dress and we'll find Jake and go eat." Dumping the glass in the wastebasket, she ignored Caitlin's brooding look of indignation and went into the bathroom.

When she came out and slipped into her clothes and picked up her purse, ready to take Caitlin next door to Jake's room, all the little girl had to say was, "I was ready ages ago. They'll probably be out of pancakes, and that's all I feel like having."

"Good, you're both up." Jake grinned as he came out of his room. "I made more phone calls. No luck with most of the big chains. They must be staying in smaller motels."

Margaret stared at him, unable to block out the thought of Sandy being found dead in a motel bed, Robert the innocent, grief-stricken husband.

"What's the matter?" Caitlin tugged at her hand. "You look real unhappy."

She managed a small smile. "Oh, nothing. Just thinking about your mom."

"Don't worry about Mom. Everything's gonna be okay." Caitlin's voice held determination and unshakable faith in herself and the predictions of Madame Zorina.

"That's right. We'll find Sandy and straighten this out," Jake said, putting his arm around Margaret. He squeezed her shoulder gently. "Okay now?"

She reached up and touched his hand. Then she sighed and said quietly, "Okay."

They went down to the restaurant where Caitlin ate a royal breakfast of pancakes, sausages, fresh orange juice and milk. Margaret picked at her order of toast and scrambled eggs, not really tasting anything. She couldn't help wondering why Jake was so quiet. Every once in a while she caught a glimpse of something in his eyes. Was it worry? He didn't want to frighten Caitlin, of course.

She drew a deep breath, trying to relax. Caitlin looked at her across the table. She wore a milky mustache. "I forgot to bring my Barbie dolls."

"Well, you brought other books and toys," Margaret said encouragingly.

"I could have taken Barbie swimming," Caitlin mumbled through a mouthful of sausage. "She likes swimming. So do I."

Margaret shot a quick glance at Jake. "What do you think? Have we time to let her swim for a half hour or so?"

Pushing back his jacket sleeve, he checked his wristwatch. "If you make it quick. Take her back to the room and change while I settle the bill here." He shrugged. "We'll try and make up time later once we get on the road."

Ten minutes later Caitlin was jumping into the azure waters of the swimming pool. And Margaret sat on a lounger, thinking about Sandy and where she was and if she was all right.

Suddenly Caitlin was standing, dripping on the cement pool surround. "Aren't you going in?"

"No, we don't have time."

"Oh, well I'm kinda cold." Caitlin shivered and hugged the thick towel around herself. Margaret rubbed her back and legs with the towel ends, trying to warm her up.

"There, that better?"

Caitlin's freckled face glowed up at her in the sun-shine. "Uh-huh, I had fun."

Giving her a quick hug, Margaret picked up her clutter of shoes and shirts, and they trailed back to the motel room. Caitlin peeled off her bathing suit and climbed into shorts and a cotton T-shirt while Margaret packed everything into their suitcases.

"Can I go out in the hall? I think I dropped one of my toys." Caitlin was hopping up and down by the half-open door.

Margaret frowned thoughtfully, and hesitated, then said, "All right, but don't go far. I'm almost packed." Even as she spoke she realized she was talking to the air. Caitlin was gone.

Chapter Twelve

Out in the hall Caitlin looked first in one direction, then the other, frowning. She hadn't been fooled, not one bit. Robert's gang had obviously followed them here to Florida. Prob'ly the gang was working in pairs. The woman in the airport terminal had boarded the same plane. She'd been sort of dumb, staring like that. Easy for a master detective to spot. The other one, though. Hmm, maybe the other gang member had been the old lady in the black hat.

Sure. Some really bad guy, bent over and wearing a gray wig. He was prob'ly reporting back to Robert right now, telling him where they were, and that Caitlin had been swimming. Robert wouldn't even believe that she could swim. He always made cracks about how kids got in the way and should keep quiet. Once he'd even said he would cut her tongue off if she stuck it out at him again.

Caitlin hadn't told anyone about that.

The master detective frowned. Anyway, she wasn't scared of old Robert. He was just a big jerk.

She decided to go left, up the wide metal stairs to the second floor. There might be a telephone that the old lady in the black hat would use to call Robert.

Carefully she dropped a small cloth doll near the foot of the stairs, in case Aunt Margaret checked to see if there really was a lost toy. Suddenly, down below, a door slammed. A man came out and walked away, carrying a brown suitcase. Caitlin shrank back into the shadows on the stairs. The cement walls closed in on her. Her heart thudded like drumbeats in a horror movie.

Nothing moved. Nothing stirred. The master detective had escaped detection. Slowly she relaxed. She waited another few seconds, then climbed the remaining stairs to the second floor. It was darker up here. Shadowy corridors stretched off to the left and right. Inky blackness painted the distant end of the hallway. The cloak of darkness beyond the last door was impenetrable. Did light from the overhead fixture seem bright from down there? Could she be seen?

She moved quickly to the left, sliding her body against the wall. A burst of muted sound came from behind the nearest door. A TV. Whoever occupied that room prob'ly wouldn't be opening the door.

The master detective reached in her pocket for a piece of bubble gum. She unwrapped it and took a large bite, chewing slowly, watching the nearest door with suspicion. More noise, clapping and laughter. It sounded like a game show.

She blew a big bubble, popped it and licked it off her cheek, her shrewd glance taking in something else of interest down the hall. A large, gray metal machine in a lighted niche. Every once in a while it made a whirring noise, then a muted kind of a clunk. Clearly this needed further investigation.

She strolled up to it and lifted the lid. Lots of sparkly ice cubes winked up at her. More than anyone would ever need, she thought, idly blowing another bubble.

As she watched, another load of ice cubes fell into the bin from some mechanism in the back. It had little red knobs on the side, and funny dials. She leaned over the edge of the bin and fiddled with the knobs, turning one, then another, wondering what would happen. She twisted one knob too hard.

A whole lot more ice cubes began gushing forth into the bin, making a terrible racket. The knob came off in Caitlin's hand as she jumped back in surprise. There was a loud explosion, and thick, oily smoke curled up from the bottom of the ice machine.

MARGARET CLOSED the suitcase and snapped it tight. One last look around to make sure she had everything.

Suddenly someone knocked on the door. The motel desk clerk was in the hallway with Caitlin by the hand—as if she were some exotic species of chimpanzee. Caitlin was scowling. The desk clerk handed her over and said, "She was running around unattended."

"Thank you, my niece was just looking for a toy she dropped." Margaret was uncomfortably aware of a guilty gleam lurking in Caitlin's eyes.

He shrugged. "She did a job on the ice machine up on the second floor. Damned thing can't be fixed until tomorrow. The manager said he'd appreciate it if you kept the kid under control for the rest of your stay."

Caitlin said loudly, "I didn't do anything. I was just watching it make ice. I wanted to see how it worked."

She came inside, and Margaret closed the door and gave her a long look. "Why did you go upstairs to the second floor?"

Caitlin gave her a perfectly innocent stare. "I was looking for my toy, like I told you. See, I found it." She held up a small cloth doll.

A doll Margaret had never seen her play with before. She gave her another long look and said, "I see."

For some reason Caitlin seemed somewhat subdued as they went out to the car and helped Jake load the suitcases. She climbed in back and got out her notebook and pencil.

Jake got in front beside Margaret and closed his door. He looked over at her. "I found the motel they stayed in two nights ago. They didn't say where they were going, but the desk clerk said Sandy looked well enough. They went out to dinner, then came back early. Robert told the desk clerk Sandy tired easily. They spent the day sailing."

She drew a breath of relief. "That sounds innocent. I mean, maybe we're jumping to conclusions. Maybe there isn't anything to this whole mess—"

He shrugged and pulled the car out onto the highway. "There's one way to find out. We confront Robert, see what he says."

They drove past a shopping center. Across the street a bank sign flashed the temperature. Eighty-nine degrees at 10:47. A typical sweltering Florida day.

She glanced at Jake, wondering why he hadn't turned on the air-conditioning. He grimaced and said, "One little problem with the car. I noticed it yesterday, just as we got to the motel. The air conditioner's on the fritz, so we'll have to suffer for the day."

"I'm hot," Caitlin remarked grumpily from the back seat.

"Too bad," Margaret told her. "We're all hot. You're not the only one."

"Yeah, but all I have is a dinky little window. The front seat has two big windows," she complained, scribbling away in her notebook. In a matter of minutes she'd started some sort of list, humming, a look of dreamy contentment on her face.

Margaret sighed and flipped the visor down against the glare of the sun. She wondered how long it would take to find Robert and Sandy.

Jake leaned over and gripped her hand reassuringly. "Come on, don't think what you're thinking. We'll get there, I promise."

She flashed him a wan smile. "Thanks, I was just wondering how many places we have to check."

"I covered most of the motels at this end of Route 75. If we hit the ones on Route 17 and head for Marcos Island, we should find them. There won't be any more places to look except the Everglades."

And that was one place they didn't even want to think about.

The wind came through the open windows like armloads of hot, dusty grit. The highway stretched to the horizon. Nothing but palm trees, traffic and hot scorching sun. Margaret's skin was moist with perspiration, the dust sticking to it like glue.

Predictably, Caitlin began clamoring for a bag of donuts as they stopped at a gas station to fill the tank. The breakfast had proved to be less than filling.

Margaret looked questioningly at Jake who sighed and gave in. If they were lucky, the donuts would keep her busy for a whole ten minutes. Jake paid for the gas and drove to a nearby donut shop and went inside. When he came out and got back into the car, they jounced out onto the highway again.

Caitlin ate three donut holes and declared there was nothing to see. "I'm not having any fun. This is boring." Her mouth crammed full, she said, "After we find Mom, I'm going to Disneyworld. You promised, right?"

"That's right," Margaret agreed.

"And I'm gonna meet Mickey and Donald."

"Right."

"And go on all the rides as many times as I want."

"Okay," Margaret sighed. Jake shifted in the seat and gave her a sidelong look, and she saw the pained laughter in his blue eyes.

"Heaven help us," he muttered under his breath.

Another half hour or so later they passed two more shopping malls and several motels. Jake and Margaret took turns going into the motels, asking the clerk on duty if they'd had a Mr. and Mrs. Robert Schuyler registered in the past day or two. They had no luck.

They passed another shopping mall, crowded with cars glittering in the sun-drenched air. And a McDonald's restaurant, which Caitlin spotted.

"I need a hamburger and large fries. Besides, I have to go to the bathroom."

It was only twelve-thirty, and they could get out to stretch their legs. Jake turned in, found a parking space, and they went inside.

The lunch crowd was just building, and the air-conditioning must have been broken. It was hotter inside than it was out in the sun. The counter girls sagged over the shining metal counter. "Take your order, sir?"

Jake got ice tea with extra ice for himself and Margaret, and a hamburger, large fries and a milkshake for Caitlin. Margaret tugged on his shirt. "Get catsup for Caitlin's fries. She won't eat them without it."

He looked around and frowned. "Do you want to eat in here? It's hotter than the hinges of hell."

"No," Margaret said, pushing back her damp hair. "The idea of eating anything makes me feel sick, anyway, but the heat in here is unbelievable."

Caitlin returned from the bathroom, and Jake paid for their food. Pushing open the glass door as they went outside was almost a physical shock. Stupefying heat rose off the asphalt.

They got back in the car and Caitlin munched on the hamburger contents separately.

Jake drove slowly around the back of the restaurant to the exit lane, and Caitlin reached over the front seats to turn on the radio. It came on full blast, all but deafening. Margaret grimaced and groped for the volume control numbly and lowered it. Caitlin flopped back into her seat and became totally engrossed in squeezing catsup on her fries.

"Fasten your seat belt," Margaret reminded her, glancing into the back seat. The catsup spurted out of the little plastic pack in Caitlin's hands, dribbling all over the large fries.

She leaned back in the front seat and closed her eyes. The hours passed, and they drove on under the hot sun, stopping at each motel they saw, asking in vain about Mr. and Mrs. Robert Schuyler. Finally it was almost seven. The sun was setting, a glowing ball of orange in the growing dusk. Caitlin was cranky, hot, tired and hungry. They were all exhausted. Clearly, they had to stop for the night.

"Okay, next motel we see," Jake promised. The glittering red neon sign up ahead announced Vacancy. Jake pulled in and parked, and they all went in to register. Caitlin was yawning widely, but declared she was really thirsty. Could she have a soda?

Margaret nodded tiredly and groped in her purse for change. Handing her more than enough, she turned to sign the register as Jake collected their keys and picked up the bags.

They trailed wearily up to their rooms, Caitlin sucking noisily on her drink. Margaret wondered with the half of her tired brain that still functioned, if Caitlin was ingesting too much junk food and caffeine.

Jake unlocked her door and put their bags inside. "Give me time to take a quick shower, then we'll go down to dinner."

She nodded and pushed Caitlin inside, kicking off her shoes. Lord, she was tired. She sighed and told Caitlin to sit on the bed and watch TV for a few minutes. "I'm going to take a shower. I'll be out in a minute."

Caitlin yawned and flopped on the bed, already lost in some car chase on TV. Margaret unzipped her dress and went into the bathroom. She turned on the water and stepped in the tub, letting the cool water run in streams over her exhausted body.

Just as she'd toweled off and pulled a cotton dress over her bra and panties, Caitlin let out an ear-splitting scream. For a wild second her stomach dropped and she didn't know what had happened.

Caitlin was still yelling, and she ran into the bedroom.

"There's someone at the window!" Caitlin's face was white with fright. "A big face with staring eyes. Like a skull! Or a ghost!"

Margaret ran to the window and pulled the curtain shut, completely closing out the growing dark of night. "For heaven's sake, there wasn't anyone. It was your imagination."

"Oh, yes there was. I saw him, or her. I don't know if it was a man or a woman out there, but I saw something out there." Caitlin swallowed hard, shivering with dread. Even master detectives felt fear once in a while. She remembered noises she'd heard outside, just before she'd seen the face. Scraping sounds. No flesh-and-blood person could be out there. It had to be a ghost.

But why would ghosts be following them around, she reminded herself. No, it was Robert's gang. It had to be. Vaguely she wondered how he'd managed to get ghosts to join his gang.

"You saw your own reflection out there." Margaret pulled the curtain to one side and looked out.

There was no one in sight, only the silvery glow of the full moon.

Caitlin glared at her. "I know I saw someone. And we didn't have the light on, either. The moon's out and it's full, just like Madame Zorina said it would be. Danger! We've got to be real careful!"

Margaret ran an exasperated hand through her hair. "Never mind that full moon nonsense. What were you up to at the window?"

"I thought I saw some funny lights," Caitlin said reasonably. "Like a UFO landing. It circled, so I shined my flashlight up at it. I was signaling." She was wearing her best innocent look.

"Where did you get the flashlight?" Which Margaret now saw lying on the floor by the window where Caitlin had dropped it.

"I found it."

"Where?" she said grimly.

"In the lobby while you were getting our room key. I found it by the soda machine, and I thought it would be a good idea if we had one. We might get a hurricane and the electricity could go off. They get hurricanes in Florida all the time," Caitlin said confidingly.

She wasn't sure how to approach this bit of information so she ignored it, turning slowly around and picking up her purse. Just then Jake banged on the door. "Margaret, what's the matter? Let me in. I heard Caitlin yelling."

She opened the door. "Caitlin thought she saw something at the window and screamed. It was only her imagination."

"No, it wasn't. It was a ghost," Caitlin muttered stubbornly.

Margaret sighed and exchanged wry glances with Jake who ruffled the top of Caitlin's head with a large hand. "Nighttime can be scary when you're in a strange place."

"I wasn't scared. Or only a little," Caitlin admitted in a small voice.

"Well, you don't have to be scared," Margaret told her, hugging her tight. "We're here, and we wouldn't let anything happen to you. No matter what."

ENTERING THE RESTAURANT and sitting down to a relaxing meal was wonderful to Margaret. So... normal...soothing, shutting out threatening possibilities like people staring in windows and cold-blooded murder.

Caitlin ordered fried chicken, cole slaw and French fries. Margaret looked determinedly out the window while she dribbled catsup on her fries in long, scarlet ribbons.

Jake suggested they have onion soup, and it came in a small brown bowl with French bread and melted cheese on top. It tasted wonderful.

"Can I have another order of fries?" Caitlin looked at Margaret hopefully. Catsup dripped down the front of her T-shirt like a modern painting done by the splash and splatter method.

"No," Margaret said firmly. "How about a salad?"

"Or dessert? How about an ice-cream sundae?" Jake suggested, getting out the menu again. After some thought, Caitlin ordered a strawberry sundae, and Margaret drank a cup of tea, feeling herself slowly unwind inside.

Jake paid the bill and they left the restaurant. They walked along the narrow flagstone path that circled around behind the motel.

It was dark now. Only the rising moon and the lights from the motel rooms cutting bright coins on the surface of the pool. Everything was deathly still. A few birds twittered, then fell silent and began again almost as if they were watching them stroll along the path.

Margaret decided she wanted to buy a paper. She touched Jake's arm. "Would you take Caitlin back to the room for me? I want to run back and pick up a newspaper. There might be something in it Sandy and Robert would notice. I don't know—an advertisement or tourist attraction. Motel listings, anyway." She handed the key to her room to Jake.

"Don't be long. Caitlin's going to teach me how to play Old Maid. I think I'll need help."

Margaret reached up and kissed the strong line of his jaw. "Five minutes, no longer. Bye."

Exactly seven minutes later she was hurrying along the flagstone path, the evening paper under her arm. Overhead the full moon was riding high over the inky lace of the treetops. She passed alongside the pool. The night wind was picking up. Margaret shivered a little. Across the pool a whispering rustle of branches. Just the wind rustling in the bushes, she thought, staring across the rippling water of the pool. She stood there a second, feeling her heartbeats thud against her side. Silence weighted the air.

Shaking her head, she walked on, hastening her steps. There was no warning. Only a sharp blow against her back, and the flagstones tilted, the palm

trees angled, everything was suddenly sliding sideways until the lights on the horizon were vertical and
she was falling through the air. Weightless. Slow motion. She was falling headfirst into the pool with
someone's arm locked around her neck, one hand
savagely across her mouth to keep her from crying out.

The shock of hitting the water momentarily drove
the breath from her lungs. Down, down, and she was
desperately kicking, clawing her attacker, trying to
fight free.

But she was tired, all but exhausted. Her lungs
dragged for air and found none, only water.

The attacker was murderously determined.

Her fingers scrabbled blindly at the arm tight across
her neck, feeling the soft flesh. Kicking out with her
feet, she pushed off from the bottom of the pool, and
they lifted, rising, shooting upward through the blue-
white world into the air.

The hand covering her mouth slipped free, and she
took a breath, heaving air deep into her lungs, and
they filled, giving her strength and life. Her lungs, her
entire body was suddenly bursting with rage.

She continued struggling, closer now to the pool's
edge. Her attacker must have been using the coping at
the top for leverage, clawing at her face, her hair,
yanking her backward and under the water once more.

Rolling over on top of her, holding her head under,
her attacker's legs were twined tightly around her
body—like snakes. Holding her down. Her vision was
darkening and the last throbbing of life and eternal
night was coming.

She let herself go limp, sagging motionless, no
longer resisting the force of the arm hooked across her

windpipe, the body locked against hers like a lover, slowly windmilling in a dance of death.

Don't move. Don't think.

The pool was darkening, going black. God, she felt cold. To survive she had to move, to fight. But she had no strength to move. Her lungs felt as if they were bursting. She couldn't feel her hands or feet anymore. *This must be what it's like to die.* And oh, God, she'd had a warning. Caitlin had mentioned the full moon. Madame Zorina had told her to be careful around water.

From a great distance she heard voices, laughter, and slowly, carefully, she felt the pressure ease from her windpipe, and she was floating facedown in the water.

She felt numb, nerveless and oh, so sleepy, but knew this feeling was a trap. She had to resist the growing dark, the death-bringing black of night. It was so close, so close now....

She kicked feebly and turned her head to the right. Yes, there was the coping. It seemed so far away, but when she reached out a hand, there it was. She'd reached the edge of the pool.

She clawed and hooked her fingers on the coping, rolling sideways, lifting her head clear of the water. And then breath eased back into her lungs. She gasped for air, gagging and coughing. The pain in her lungs was scalding, like a balled fist driving into her chest.

The voices grew louder now, voices changing, no longer conversational, but yelling, shouting. She couldn't understand what they were saying.

Hands reached down and hauled her out of the water, rolling her over. Life-giving hands pushing in and out on her ribcage.

She realized someone was on his knees, giving her artificial respiration. And somewhere in the back of her exhausted mind came the thought of poor, drowned Vern Boyce. This was what it had been like for him, only he hadn't come back from the dark world of death.

She kept coughing, and vomited rapidly, ignominiously.

"What happened?" the desk clerk asked, handing her a towel. "My God, lady, you almost drowned!"

People were standing, staring down at her, shaking their heads, talking in low voices.

She wiped her face and streaming eyes. God, she felt weak. The damn towel kept sliding out of her nerveless fingers. And she was shuddering uncontrollably. In a whisper worse than a scream she gasped, "Someone pushed me in. Someone was trying to kill me."

The desk clerk helped her to a lounger and covered her with a blanket. He didn't appear to have heard what she'd said. "Look, we'll get you a doctor. Make sure you're all right."

She didn't have the energy to fight with him, she barely had the strength left to wipe her face again with the edge of the blanket.

He chewed nervously on his mustache. "It's motel policy when a thing like this happens, lady. Oh, here comes the doc now."

The doctor was a rather corpulent, sad-looking man with a black bag. He looked into her eyes, down her throat and ears, took her pulse, listened to her lungs and questioned her persistently. Had she had a few drinks with dinner?

"Someone pushed me in and held me under," she said, her voice hoarse and shaking. She pulled the blanket around her. "Someone was trying to kill me."

The doctor gave her a lightning glance and frowned at the desk clerk who shrugged and said it was the first he'd heard of that. The tone of his voice suggested it was a figment of her imagination.

She looked steadily into the doctor's eyes and said, "I didn't have anything to drink. I was going back to my room after dinner, and someone pushed me into the pool and tried to drown me."

His eyes narrowed. "Do you know who it was?"

"No," she admitted helplessly. "I never saw his face."

"You never got a look at this guy's face . . . the person you say pushed you?" By this time the desk clerk wasn't bothering to hide his disbelief.

"No." Her denials seemed to drift away on the night air like smoke—as nebulous as her attacker seemed to be.

"Look, Ms. uh . . ."

"Webster," she supplied tiredly.

"Look, Ms. Webster." He handed her a cup of coffee. "We, that is the management, don't want any trouble. You didn't see who pushed you. You've got no real proof, nothing except your story. I'm not saying you're wrong, only . . . maybe you're mistaken. It was dark, right? And you were hurrying. You could have lost your footing, slipped and fallen in. Maybe you hit your head on the cement coping. Know what, lady? You should be counting your lucky stars and maybe lay off the booze, not run around making wild accusations about someone attacking you."

She looked up at the desk clerk, stunned. How could he be so damned casual about attempted murder? Anger washed over her, leaving her shaky.

If there was one thing she knew, it was that someone had tried to kill her and come damn close. She sipped the coffee, forcing the hot liquid past her bruised throat. It hurt like hell to swallow.

The desk clerk turned to the doctor. "Wouldn't it be better if she went to a hospital?" He meant better for the motel. Attempted murder was bad for business.

The doctor shrugged and put the stethoscope in his black bag. "It might be better if she were admitted. She's suffered a severe shock." He snapped the bag shut. "But it's her decision. I can't force her to go."

They were talking about her almost as if she wasn't there. As if she was an object to be disposed of any way they wished.

She huddled in the damp blanket and stared at the azure water in the swimming pool. It was peaceful, calm and empty—except for the newspaper floating on top of the water. And her shoes bobbing hideously up and down. Her purse must have gone straight to the bottom.

For one terrible moment time ceased, and she was feeling that nauseating blackness, struggling, kicking and clawing; and she knew she was going to die.

She shuddered and turned her head. She couldn't look at the pool. The bright moonlight mocked her. Why hadn't she taken Madame Zorina's warning seriously? Why hadn't she been more careful?

The next few minutes passed in a blur. The desk clerk got the pool scoop and retrieved her shoes and purse. He dumped the sodden newspaper in the trash and put the shoes and purse on the flagstones by her chair. They lay in a puddle at her feet, the water spreading, darkening the stones.

She couldn't seem to stop shaking. Some huge source of physical energy was jerking at her exhausted joints. She spilled the coffee and had to carefully put the cup down on the flagstones by her purse.

It's fear, she thought. Fear was making her shudder and shake. Why on earth had she gone back to buy the paper? She straightened up with difficulty.

"I'm not going to a hospital," she said firmly. "I'm going back to my room."

The mob of curious onlookers was melting away. She wondered exactly how she was going to crawl back to her room. She didn't think she could get to her feet, pick up her belongings and walk that far without falling flat on her face. Especially since there was something very wrong with the way her legs were acting. Her knees were shaking. Crawling, prickling fear was sweeping over her flesh in horrible constant waves.

Chapter Thirteen

Jake, with Caitlin at his heels, pushed past the desk clerk and doctor, took one look at Margaret and said, "My God, what happened?"

"I fell in the pool." She struggled to her feet with Jake's help, knowing it would be wrong to show fear in front of Caitlin. She had to remain cool and calm. She filled her lungs with a shuddering heave, throwing all her energy into control. She managed a weak smile and said, "Come on, let's go back to the room."

Jake picked up her things and they left, Caitlin trotting silently alongside. As soon as they got to the room and the door was shut behind them, Caitlin said, "How'd you fall in? It was Robert's gang, right? Prob'ly the old lady in a black hat. Did she hit you with her cane?"

Jake turned on the TV and told Caitlin to sit down and watch it, then he pushed Margaret toward the bathroom. The wet blanket dropped to the floor as he took her in his arms and held her tight. Kissing her hair, rubbing her back, he whispered hoarsely, "Thank God you're all right. Everything's going to be all right now. You're safe with me." He rocked her tenderly, his arms folding her close.

His face blurred before her eyes. "Someone pushed me, tried to kill me. Oh, Jake, he held my head under. I thought I was going to die." Tears ran down her cheeks, and her hands clutched at his shirt. "I couldn't breathe. I was so scared. I don't know why he let go, maybe people were coming. I thought I heard people talking, then suddenly, he was gone."

Her knees gave out then, and she sagged against him. Her head burrowed into his warm chest, and she sobbed—great heaving sobs of fright and thankfulness.

With a half-muttered curse, he tightened his arms around her, buried his face in her hair and pressed her closer. "I don't know what the hell's going on, but...thank God you're okay. Shush, oh, honey, shhh," he whispered between soft kisses.

Caitlin's raised voice came through the door. "If it was an accident, how come people were saying you thought someone pushed you in? Was it because the moon was full? Madame Zorina said—gosh, I'd better write all this down in my notebook!"

The large hand rubbing Margaret's back went quite still. He drew a deep breath and said quietly, "Do we call the police?"

As quietly as he'd spoken, Caitlin had heard him. "Yeah, we should call the police. I could tell them Madame Zorina said you were in danger when the moon was full, and I could tell them it was that woman following us, or the old lady in the black hat. They're both members of Robert's gang! I could tell them I saw her!'' She seemed to think this was indisputable evidence.

Margaret took a sobbing, hiccuping breath and said between sniffles, ''What do I tell them? Someone pushed my head under and held it there? No, I didn't get a glimpse of his face, and oh, yes, I'd been warned by a fortune-teller to be careful around water while the moon's full? If they take down my statement, which is doubtful after they hear the nonsense Caitlin's spouting, they'll laugh their heads off and tell me to quit drinking.''

Jake rubbed her back, caressing her gently. He whispered soft words of endearment and encouragement. With each one Margaret felt his strength and tenderness working a healing. She clung to him, feeling herself slowly emerging from the hell of life-threatening fear. The warmth of his body thawed her wet, half-frozen body. Then he tipped her head up and kissed her, and the last of her anguish dissipated like a frost in the summer sunlight. She felt light-headed, encircled by love. Shaping her hands to his face, she gave herself up to his kiss. ''Oh, Jake, I love you,'' she whispered against his mouth.

''I know, I love you, too,'' he murmured hoarsely. ''I'm not going to let you out of my sight until this mess is over.'' Kissing her again, he pushed her gently toward the shower. ''Get out of those wet things. I'll bring in your nightgown and put Caitlin to bed.''

She nodded and wiped her wet face with the back of her hand. He gave her a smile of encouragement and left, the door closing with a soft click. She took a hot shower, dried herself off, got into the nightgown Jake put by the sink and climbed into bed.

He got in beside her, leaned over and turned off the light. "I'm staying here with you. Don't tell me no. Just go to sleep." He drew her into his arms, cradling her against him, and she held on with no intention of ever letting go.

"I'm sorry," she whispered. "I never should have gone back for the paper."

"Hush, don't be silly." With one arm supporting her head, he gently smoothed damp tendrils of hair from her cheeks. "Just go to sleep. Things will look better in the morning."

But would they? Somehow she didn't think so. And long after Jake's breathing had become measured and soft with sleep, she lay beside him, gripping the blankets tightly up around her neck.

Her life before the pool incident seemed cloudy, almost surreal. The only reality was that she'd almost died about... she took her arm from beneath the blanket, checked the time on her wristwatch, and saw with grim amusement that it had stopped.

Right now, safe within Jake's arms, she was less frightened than she'd been. Not that the situation was really any better. Her mysterious attacker was still out there somewhere. He could easily try again. It was just that fear seemed unable to stay at the same pitch for very long.

She was safe with Jake beside her. But inside she knew cold, sickening fear remained coiled like a snake, ready to strike her at any moment. But if she could haul herself beyond the shaking horrors, keep the fear lying down the way it was now, maybe she could come up with some constructive thinking.

She lay in Jake's arms, trying not to tremble. And then she thought—what if Caitlin was right and some woman had been following them all this time? Even an old woman with a black hat. That arm around her neck could have been a woman's. But no, the maniacal strength of the attacker's arm had been that of a man.

After a while tears filled her eyes, blotting out the darkened motel room.

MARGARET LAY quietly, huddled in Jake's arms, dreaming. It was starting again, the sickening blow between her shoulder blades, and she was falling. Then her lungs were filling with water, aching. The whole world was blue water, dizzying, endless death.

The murderous arm tightened around her neck, choking off her air supply. In the final seconds she fought, clawing, kicking, but it was too late. Everything was fading, going pitch-black. Everywhere there was nothing but water and the awful gasping pain. She was dying.

She woke all at once, gasping for air, sitting straight up in bed. Her throat was raw with pain, her breathing coming in panicky shallow breaths.

It was almost dawn. Outside it was cool and misty. The sun hadn't had time to bake off the dampness from the night before, and the air was actually breathable. The sun rose, a dazzling gold in a cloudless blue sky.

The pale morning light striking through the curtains shouldn't have struck her with such dread. She struggled awake, caught in the half panic of the dream. She felt infinitely vulnerable. Her horrifying dream had vanished, but reality was far worse.

A tremor shot through her body, and Jake sat up and took her in his arms, holding her tight. "Come on, honey. It's okay, I'm here. I've got you."

She held on to him, light-headed, almost weak with relief. "It seemed so real. Oh, Jake, it was horrible, I was scared to death!"

Crushing her against his chest, he vowed, "No one's ever going to hurt you again. Never." There was a faint catch in his low voice. She nodded, and he gave her a bone-crushing squeeze. "That's my girl."

But her mind was a blur of questions. What if her attacker came back? And most of all—why would someone try and kill her?

With an effort, she took a deep breath and managed a small smile up at Jake. "I'm okay now."

They got up, showered and dressed, and got Caitlin up for breakfast. In the restaurant they sat by the window at a small round table. Margaret drank coffee and tried to act as if she wasn't sitting in a shimmer of fatigue and fear. Jake kept Caitlin busy with a cheery conversation about dolphins and other Florida sea life.

He only had half her attention. Margaret could see Caitlin's brain whirling, sifting through last night's pool incident. She waited, braced for Caitlin to launch into a discussion of Madame Zorina's warning.

"So that's why we have to be careful about pollution and what we dump in the sea. Other creatures live there," Jake explained.

Caitlin nodded and worked her way broodingly through fresh orange juice, scrambled egg and toast with curls of butter. She paused to give Margaret a gimlet-eyed stare.

Was she frightened? Margaret wondered. That was the last thing they wanted, but lying about things wouldn't help. Margaret gave Jake a warning look over Caitlin's head then said quietly, "What's wrong? You're awfully quiet."

A large blob of egg fell off Caitlin's fork and she tidily brushed it off the tablecloth onto the floor. "I'm kinda worried about Mom. Maybe the person who pushed you is gone. What if it was the old lady from the plane and she's gone to meet Robert? Do you think she killed Vern Boyce, too? And besides, how am I gonna save everybody if we're stuck here?" Her voice was a penetrating hiss.

Jake reached over and put his arm around her. "Right after you finish that milk, we're leaving. We're going to find your mom and Robert and everything's going to be fine. I called half the motels in the state, tracking them down. They took the highway we're on now. Finding them is just a matter of time."

But did they have enough time, Margaret wondered.

They finished breakfast, went back to the room, packed and were on the road west, along the route Robert and Sandy had taken, by nine-thirty.

By eleven, Caitlin was hungry again, and they stopped to get her something to eat. This kept her relatively quiet, except for the slurp of soda.

But just after they'd passed through a major highway interchange, Caitlin became abruptly excited, bouncing up and down in the back seat like a jack-in-the-box. "Guess what! There's a car following us!"

Jake's hands froze on the steering wheel. He frowned and looked in the rearview mirror. "Where?"

"Behind us, no..." Caitlin twisted around to look. "I can't see it anymore, but it was there."

Jake kept one eye on the mirror, but he didn't see anything suspicious. Nothing but a white station wagon with Florida plates, a pickup truck, and a looming tractor-trailer. The pickup truck passed them as he slowed deliberately. Then the tractor-trailer with a full load of plywood and finally the station wagon.

Margaret saw him look at the fuel gauge. She leaned over and checked. Two-thirds full. They wouldn't need to stop for gas for hours.

She sighed. They could get gas when the needle dropped to a quarter full. In the meantime they could drive like a bat out of hell. Just drive fast enough, and everything would be all right.

"I spilled my fries," Caitlin said in an aggrieved voice. "Now I can't eat them." Grease and catsup was smeared all over the upholstery. "I want an ice cream," she said loudly. When neither Jake nor Margaret answered, she sighed, got out her pencil and notebook. "After I catch Robert and his gang, I'm gonna write my book and maybe I'll go on TV. My picture'll be in all the papers, too."

Why couldn't she be like other kids, Margaret thought. If Caitlin were average, she would be making lists of license plate numbers and states, or how many cows they passed.

Jake downshifted and braked at a traffic light. They saw a string of motels coming up, and Jake pulled off the highway and checked to see if Sandy and Robert were registered. No luck at the first three motels, nor at the fourth. They drove on underneath the blistering sun.

After a while Jake glanced in the mirror again and thought he saw a silver car. He watched it off and on for a time and decided it was gaining on them slowly but surely. There was another exit down the road about forty yards. He turned off and roared down the exit ramp. In the distance there came the whistle of a train.

Two left turns in succession, then a right, and they were a good two miles past the highway, coming up to a grade crossing. No gates to drop down and block passage over the tracks; nothing more than tired, peeling white crossing signs marked the tracks. The railroad was raised several feet to get above the low and often wet countryside.

The whistle screamed again. Jake braked, slamming his foot too hard, and Caitlin was pitched forward against her seat belt in back. The notebook and pencil went flying.

They stared down the track. The train was whipping toward them. They'd never make it if they tried to beat it across the tracks.

The engineer grinned down at them and waved at Caitlin. Jake pounded on the wheel in frustration while Caitlin poked her head out the side window and waved enthusiastically at the train crew. "Hi," she yelled.

"Will you please sit down," Margaret muttered in a low voice.

The train was long, carrying lumber stacked neatly. Margaret had grown up in rural Massachusetts and had seen enough freight trains to know what went on.

Sometimes the wood on trains like this was stacked so
badly that it would shift and slide off, which meant the
train had to stop while the crew adjusted the load.
Since it wasn't their wood, the crew usually just heaved
it over the side, that being considerably easier than
restacking. But whatever. It meant time. Time while
the train was stopped, blocking the grade crossing.

Oh God, don't let anything fall off that train, she
prayed.

Caitlin plopped down again. "This seat's awful
small," she complained. "And it's hot, too. My legs
are sticking to the plastic. How come they didn't make
the seats bigger?"

"Because the car wasn't built that way," Jake told
her.

Jake looked through the rearview mirror. Nothing
to see but empty road. Right next to the road was a
falling-in, unpainted frame house. It had been years,
he thought, since anyone had put any energy into the
collapsing, gray frame house. The windows were long
gone, the front porch sagged. An old refrigerator and
a broken space heater decorated the doorway.

A few hundred yards to the west were several old
barns and a shed. No one moved near them. No engines droned. No voices broke the hot still air. Tire
marks had worn away the grass in the front yard of the
gray house, but there was no car parked there now.
Deep pine woods ringed the back of the farm.

Beside him, Margaret sighed and lifted the hair off
her neck. She took a deep breath, sucking in the hot,
humid air. If anything, she thought morosely, the train
was slowing, swaying. She tried to figure out if the
wood stacks were shifting.

Jake smiled reassuringly and glanced back into the mirror. He didn't see a car.

Margaret gripped her hands in her lap and prayed. *Don't let that car find us.* Not while the train's blocking the crossing. She looked out the back window and saw weeds in the front yard of a nearby house moving in the hot wind. What if the driver of that car had a gun, she thought. If he drove up, they would be trapped like sitting ducks.

"Seventy-seven freight cars," Caitlin said proudly, writing it down in her notebook. "I counted."

The caboose, a blue one, trundled across the track, and Jake gunned the accelerator and charged across. In the rearview mirror he caught a glimpse of a silver-gray car just coming around the bend in the road near the unpainted frame house.

The wind that came in the window cooled his sweaty forehead. He floored the accelerator, trying not to swerve, trying to ignore the gleaming silver car coming up fast behind them.

When they reached the highway, no one would change lanes to let them on. Jake had to wait, the motor idling, while three cars and a pickup truck whizzed by. Then he pulled into the traffic lane and accelerated. Out of the corner of his eye he saw the silver car pull onto the highway behind him.

Margaret threw a look in the back seat. Caitlin was so busy writing in her notebook she didn't notice what was going on. She wished she could be calm, but she couldn't forget the way her lungs had ached, starving for air during that murderous attack in the pool. The look of the last air bubbles floating upward and hands strangling her...

Jake sighed at the look on her face and said, "Don't think about things we can't control, honey. We'll get there, somehow."

Margaret swallowed a silent sob and stared out the window. There was no way they would make it in time. They had to stop along the way in each and every motel until they found Sandy and Robert. She was sure the silver car would follow along behind, like a huge cat stalking its prey.

Chapter Fourteen

Caitlin was reading a brochure about alligator farms. "It says they eat everything. They've found lots of stuff in their stomachs. Jars of pickles, gold balls...dog collars. It says here one ate a poodle and another got a retriever that went into a canal to fetch a ball for its owner. One time and he was gone, *whump,* ball and all. They taste chewy—sort of like chicken and fish. Alligators, I mean, not dogs." She leaned forward and spoke in Jake's ear. "Could we stop and try a gatorburger?"

He glanced in the rearview mirror and said, "No," almost absentmindedly. He was too busy wondering how many motels they would have to check before they came across Sandy and Robert.

And there was the matter of the silver car following them. He thought of waving down a police car. But he would say someone was following them, and of course there'd be no car around.

They came up to a rest stop. It was a collection of motels and restaurants at an enormous highway interchange. He got out and checked all the motels with no luck. Still no trace of them.

Margaret looked at the map. "This is Route 17, it's a more direct route south. They might have taken it." He nodded, and they turned onto Route 17. They asked in the next three or four motels, but no one had seen or heard of a Mr. and Mrs. Robert Schuyler. They passed a large lake on the left, then the highway traveled past a river flowing quietly westward toward the Gulf of Mexico.

Caitlin didn't seem worried anymore about her lack of gatorburgers. She wasn't even writing in her notebook. She was staring tiredly out the side window at the cloudless sky.

They'd been driving for hours now. Time had ceased. The sun baked away at the landscape, and it was an effort for Jake to exert himself in that fierce light. The dazzle from the highway was blinding. By five o'clock, both the earth and sky seemed absolutely white.

He looked in the mirror again. Dammit, the silver car was there again. He thought they'd lost it at the last motel.

Wearily they continued down the highway. The air in the car was stifling. The gas gauge read one-quarter full. Soon they would have to stop for gas. He began to look for a station and for another fast-food place.

By six o'clock the gas gauge read below one-eighth, and the sun was still beating down on the car. Margaret was wilting in the front seat, and Jake's hands were so wet with sweat he could hardly hold on to the wheel. Thick spongy waves of heat surged through the open windows every time they came to a stoplight.

Jake knew he was watching the mirror more than the road now. The silver-gray car mesmerized him.

The sun glinted off its radiator and darkened windshield. He tried to make out what the driver looked like, if it was a man or a woman, but all he could see was the shape of a human head.

What the hell was he going to do? How could he protect both Margaret and Caitlin? What would happen when the sun went down and it got dark? He had a terrible premonition that that was what the driver of the silver car was waiting for. Once the sun set, he would move in for the kill.

Margaret groaned and wiped her face with the back of her hand. She was so tired and hot. Her bones felt like they were softening, melting in this awful heat. Her eyes felt sore and red in the dazzling glare of the lowering sun. She'd lost track of the white line in the road, lost track of time, the hours they'd been driving.

As the dusk of evening drew on, the temperature became cooler, and Caitlin got tired of the awkward posture she'd had to assume to stare out the window with her seat belt still securely fastened. Once more she got out her notebook and worked on a list. It was about Robert and what the police would do to him once he was arrested.

1. they cold make him eat katerpilers till his stomach bustid.
2. throw him off the highest building in Boston without him wearing a parashoot.
3. take his tonsuls out without anastheetik.

"I'm hungry," Caitlin complained. "If I don't eat soon, I'll probably have to go to the hospital."

"All right," Jake replied grimly. "There's a place up ahead. We'll stop there." They pulled in and Margaret got out and took Caitlin inside. She paid for hamburgers and fries and sodas, then took Caitlin to the bathroom. When Caitlin had finished washing her hands, they went back to the car. Jake opened the door for them. Margaret balanced the tray gingerly as she handed a hamburger and a soda into the back seat.

"Gosh, I'm starved," Caitlin said as she took the food and ripped the wrapping from the hamburger.

Margaret got into the front seat. Jake munched on his hamburger as he started up the car. "Aren't you eating?" he asked.

"No." She shook her head. "I got a hamburger for myself, but now the thought of food makes me feel awful."

"You ought to eat," he told her as they pulled into a nearby gas station. "It won't do Sandy any good if you go hungry." Reluctantly she opened up a hamburger and tried to eat.

"Damn," Jake muttered. A sign said out of gas.

And across the street the silver car waited patiently, its motor idling softly. Margaret could see motes of fog dancing in its headlights. They started up the car again and backtracked to the highway. So did the silver car. Jake got the rented car up to seventy and they roared down the road. The rear lights of the cars going fifty-five materialized so fast he couldn't estimate distances. He dropped back to sixty.

The headlights of the silver car crept closer. It was eight o'clock now and dark as the inside of a tomb. ake was so tired he could hardly drive. Unwillingly he recognized they would have to find another gas station, and right away.

Imperceptibly his foot pressed down harder and the car shot forward. He swung the car inland, away from the coast with its spectacular views of the Gulf of Mexico foaming in the purplish dusk. The highway wound westward again, and they reached Marcos Island.

He didn't see any of the island's beauty. His lean face tightened with fury, a muscle working in his jaw. He stared at the glowing headlights in the mirror for the hundredth time. Robert was connected to that silver car—he would bet his life on it.

They were in deadly danger and Jake couldn't do a thing about it. Sweat prickled his forehead. They needed time to find Sandy. He began to calculate with icy fury just what their chances were. They'd covered all the likely motels and turned up nothing. One more motel to go, the Yacht Club Inn and Restaurant. He would go inside, see if they were registered, then, no matter what, he would drive to the nearest police station and see if the state cops could help. He didn't know what else to do. He had a feeling they'd just about used up the last of their nine lives.

Jake saw the sign for the Yacht Club Inn and pulled off the highway. When they reached the motel and parked the car, Margaret got out. No cars had turned in behind them.

"Is Mom here?" Caitlin yawned and looked around.

"We're going to find out." Margaret helped her out of the back seat. Jake put his arm around Margaret's shoulders and they walked toward the entrance. Water splashed in a stone fountain by an elaborate staircase leading to a terrace for outside dining.

Margaret slowed as she glanced toward the restaurant. "Let's check the restaurant first. If they're registered here, maybe they're still eating."

At the top of the stairs they scanned the seated diners. At first no one seemed to resemble Sandy and Robert, then Margaret saw a blond woman touching her wineglass to that of her companion. She laughed, a low, delicious chuckle, and Margaret grabbed Jake's sleeve. *"That's Sandy, and she's all right!"*

Caitlin darted through the scattered tables. "Mommy!"

Startled, Sandy turned her head and Robert stood up, his attention focused on the man walking behind Margaret.

A grin spread across Sandy's pale face. "Wha...at are you doing here?" Scooping Caitlin into her arms, she glanced at Margaret. "How did you find us?"

"It's a long story." Margaret kissed her. "Are you okay?"

"Robert's taking good care of me..." Sandy's smile faded. "But this bug won't quit."

He put his hand on her shoulder. "Darling, this is Jake McCall." He hesitated, then said with a sheepish grin, "The truth is I was married to Jake's sister some years ago. He's my former brother-in-law."

Sandy stared, but didn't seem to know what to say. Finally she whispered, "You were...married before?"

He squeezed her shoulder. "It was tragic, darling. She died of asthma, a terribly sad thing. Which is why I never told you."

She frowned and put down her wineglass. "Why don't we go back to the room. I . . . I don't know what to say." She got up, pushing her chair back.

Jake said grimly, "We're coming, too. Margaret and I have a few things to discuss with you."

Sandy shrugged and, holding an uncharacteristically subdued Caitlin by the hand, led them down the steps and around the back of the motel to their room.

Robert's face was shiny with sweat, and he had some trouble getting the key in the door lock. Finally it clicked open, and they went inside. Behind them the door didn't quite swing shut.

Sandy switched on the bureau lamp. A brown leather suitcase lay beside it. Robert's probably, Jake thought grimly. He wondered what it contained. Maybe, just maybe there might be some proof in that suitcase they could use.

He took another look at the suitcase. It wasn't locked.

"I'd like to tell you a story about money and murder," Jake said quietly.

Sandy sat down on the bed with a bewildered look on her face. "I don't understand. . . ."

Jake shrugged and put his hand on the suitcase. "Robert inherited a trust fund when my sister died."

Robert's eyes narrowed to blue-white ice chips. "Hey, that was three years ago. What the hell's gotten into you?"

"I'll bet you played the stock market and lost. Or was it real estate that went bust?" Robert's face went red, the line of his mouth grim, and Jake knew his shot had struck home. "What's in the suitcase? Pills you are using to poison Sandy?"

Margaret grabbed Caitlin and dragged her to the bathroom. "Stay in there," she told her. "Don't come out."

"But I want to read my clues." Caitlin took out her notebook and flipped the pages. "I can tell Mom about Madame Zorina and how I'm gonna save everyone."

"Not now!" Margaret hissed. "Stay here and be quiet." She turned around as Jake flipped open the suitcase. Right on top was a plastic bag full of pill bottles.

"My allergy medicine. No big deal." Robert took a step toward the suitcase. Light winked off his snake's head belt buckle.

Jake picked up the plastic bag. The bottles inside rattled eerily in the sudden silence. "Let's have this analyzed. What do you think we'll find . . . barbiturates? Downers, tranquilizers?"

Robert took another step toward the suitcase. His face was angry, his eyes glittered with fury. "The joke's gone far enough. It's not funny."

"Betsy's death wasn't funny. You killed her, you bastard! Then you ran through her money and looked around for another victim." Jake threw the bag of pills back in the suitcase. "You and your girlfriend, Polly Merrill . . . now Mrs. Knox. She saw the old lady's will, and you spent months romancing the wrong niece."

Sandy stared at both men, her face pale. "What's he talking about . . . *girlfriend* . . . *killing? Robert, please . . . what does he mean?*"

"Sandy," Jake tried to say as calmly as possible, "Polly Knox knew who you were before you rented her house." Jake stopped a minute, and then went on,

"Since Mrs. Knox is a nurse—and I use the term loosely—she was employed by your aunt to take care of her before she died. And she did more than nursing. Somehow she got hold of your aunt's will and found out about a niece who would inherit lots of money.

"She only made one mistake," Jake said, shrugging his wide shoulders. "The name of the niece who inherited everything."

"I talked to your doctor in Vermont, Sandy. He never prescribed antibiotics for you," Margaret said.

"No one'll believe any of it." Robert's noisy breathing seemed to fill the room like a rushing wind, yet the silence was so complete the click of the air conditioner coming on was perfectly audible. He flexed his fists.

Sandy moved out of his reach and picked up the phone. "I think . . . I want to call . . ."

Robert twisted his mouth into a parody of a smile. "Honey, you don't believe this, do you? Hey, it's a damn lie. Wait a second, I love you. Listen, Margaret's had it in for me ever since I broke our engagement. She's jealous."

Jake took hold of Robert's arm and shoved him toward the door. "It's over. You're finished." In a blur, pivoting angrily, Robert shrugged off Jake's arm and threw a punch, knocking him backward into the bureau. The lamp crashed over, the shade tilting crazily.

Jake got up, swaying dizzily.

A letter opener lay by the fallen lamp. Robert grabbed it, striking in a blur of speed, swinging the blade in Jake's face. Jake managed to turn partly away from the blow, but the blade tore along the side of his head, drawing blood. He sagged, dazed, dropping to his knees.

Margaret backed away, yelling desperately to Sandy who stood frozen by the end of the bed. "Get the police! For God's sake, Sandy, move!" An icy shiver ran up her spine at the numb, disbelieving look on her sister's face.

Robert lunged forward. "Damn, I should have taken care of you a long time ago!" He took Margaret down, screaming and kicking, a tangle of arms and legs. His lips twisted into a grisly smile. "I'm going to take my time with you and make you suffer first before I kill you!"

Caitlin peered out the crack in the bathroom door, then shrank back in the shadows as a blond-haired woman walked silently through the half-open motel room door... and reached into her purse, pulling out a gun. "It's all right. I'm here, Robert, and I'll blow the head off anyone who tries anything."

Caitlin stared from the darkness of the bathroom. The woman smiled and thumbed two tiny levers on the gun. Caitlin wondered what a master detective would do in a situation like this. Her mother wasn't calling the police, she was still frozen, staring blank-eyed.

Very carefully Caitlin slipped out of the bathroom. The woman didn't see her, her back was turned, and she was focused on Robert who was getting off Margaret.

Robert stood and composed himself. "A nasty car accident is in order. We'll find a deserted side road and set the car on fire. That'll take care of things nicely."

Caitlin crept silently out the motel room door. Outside was a planter with flowers and a large rock. *If anyone's going to save everyone, it's got to be me,* she thought grimly. She picked up the rock and went to look in the window.

Robert was hitting Jake in the face, and her mother was shaking as if she couldn't believe her eyes. The woman with the gun was pointing it at Margaret, lining up the sight.

Caitlin threw the rock as hard as she could; the window smashed and glass flew, hitting the woman. She screamed and dropped the gun. Margaret grabbed it, pointing it with jittery hands at Robert and the woman who was cradling her wrist as if it were broken. "Don't move, I'll shoot!"

"It's okay, Mom, I fixed Robert." Caitlin ran and put her arms around her mother. She stared at the blond woman; somehow she looked familiar. Then she put two and two together. Wow, Mrs. Knox wasn't dead after all! Robert hadn't killed her and thrown her in the quarry.

Robert glared at Polly. "This is your fault, dammit! Didn't you see the kid at your back?"

She winced as if he'd struck her. "You got us into this mess with your greed. First it was Wanda Marshall you had to marry six years ago. 'A little extra digitalis would take care of her bad heart,' you said. 'The doctors won't suspect a thing.' I was satisfied with her money. But no, you had to get your hands on Betsy McCall's money. The law of averages caught up with us. 'Just one more,' you said. So you married this one, and now my wrist is broken and look what it got us—jail!"

Robert glared furiously, sweat gleaming on his handsome face. "You lying bitch, who killed Martha

Knox? And that fool husband of hers? You're the one who injected a syringeful of air into the old geezer.''

Beside herself with anger and pain, Polly raged on. ''I married you nine years ago for better or worse. We didn't need all this money. I went along with what you wanted because I loved you.''

''Shut up,'' he snarled. ''Your hands are as bloody as mine. You couldn't just pay off Vern Boyce. No, you had to kill him. So why didn't you finish off Margaret in the pool? It should have been a piece of cake.'' He noticed Margaret's hands holding the gun were shaking, and he grinned.

''One wrong move and I'll shoot,'' Margaret said weakly.

Robert moved toward her. He was less than eight feet away. ''Looks like you'd better say your prayers.''

The snake's eyes glittered at his waist, and Margaret shuddered. Madame Zorina's warning about the silver serpent.

Chapter Fifteen

She pulled the trigger. Nothing happened. She pulled it again. Still nothing. Dazed and bloody, Jake struggled to his feet, realizing she'd forgotten to jack a bullet into the chamber. "Margaret, pump a bullet into the chamber!"

She bit her lip and fumbled desperately with the gun, then squeezed off a shot just as Robert laughed . . . and lunged at her like a demon from hell.

The sound of the shot filled the room. It echoed off the walls and reverberated in the windows. Robert went down, groaning, a wet red stain spreading down his trouser leg.

"Wow!" Caitlin was round-eyed. She took out her pencil and began scribbling in her notebook.

Margaret couldn't move. She'd actually fired a gun. She felt sick to her stomach, but kept the gun pointed at Robert and Polly.

Behind her Sandy hung up the phone. "The police are on the way. They'll be here any minute."

Carefully Jake removed the gun from Margaret's trembling fingers. "Let me hold that, Annie Oakley.

I'll keep an eye on them." He put an arm around her. "Okay?"

She nodded numbly, staring at the blond woman. There was something about her. And then she knew. Polly Knox was Violet Chadwick! The same woman who'd come to the house in Vermont, saying she was an old friend.

She'd worn dark makeup to disguise the contours of her face, dark glasses and a wig. High heels had added height.

"Why didn't you drown last night?" Polly hissed. "You and your sister were fools to think Robert ever loved you. He's mine!" Her voice dripped venom.

Jake jerked the gun at her. "That's enough. You can tell your story to the police."

"I should have climbed down the mountain and put a bullet through you when I had the chance," Polly snarled. "Stirring up trouble, asking questions. Like Vern Boyce, nosing around once too often, blackmailing me. You should have ended up like him. Dead."

Margaret shivered and turned her face into Jake's shoulder. He kissed her hair. "It's okay now. It's all over."

JAKE SHOOK HIS HEAD, watching the police load Robert and Polly into the back of a cruiser. Polly had had a bout of wild hysterics as they handcuffed her. She was calm now, but her eyes were wild, her mouth creased with hate.

"Vern Boyce really must have been putting the arm on her," he said with a tired sigh. "He must have had suspicions about Wendell Knox's death, then recognized Polly Knox in town at the toy shop when she was supposed to be in Europe. He blackmailed her, but she wouldn't play that game."

Margaret leaned on his shoulder. "And with his drinking, he was bound to let something slip. She had to get rid of him."

"Caitlin was right all along." He bent down and kissed her hair. "Polly followed us on the plane, and when you were alone by the pool, she tried to kill you."

"I managed to fight her off until she heard people coming and let me go, thinking I was dead." Margaret shuddered a little.

He dropped another kiss on her hair and held her close. "Thank God, you weren't."

With the departure of the police, things were still in an uproar. Sandy's room was cordoned off, the scene of a crime. Jake led Sandy, Caitlin, and Margaret back to the main lobby and rented a couple of rooms for the night.

Sandy sat in a chair in an alcove just off the lobby. She turned as Margaret came in. She was calm, but her face was smudged with tears. Margaret sat down and gave her a cup of coffee. "Compliments of the management. Don't worry about Caitlin. She's safe and sound with Jake. There's a game room next door."

Sandy smiled. "He seems very nice. Thank him for me, will you? Caitlin—"

"Is having the time of her life, making up rules as she goes. Don't worry," Margaret said.

"How could I have been so blind?" Tears glittered in Sandy's eyes. "All that time...everything was a *lie.*"

"He was an expert, a pathological liar, smooth as silk." Margaret shrugged sadly. "He fooled a lot of women, including me."

"You saved my life," Sandy whispered, her voice breaking. She drew a shaky breath and wiped her cheeks with the back of her hand. "My God, he poisoned me for months. I kept getting weaker and weaker...I never guessed."

Margaret reached over and hugged her for a long time. "Hush, it's all over now. He can't hurt you anymore."

At last Sandy smiled a little. "I still don't know how you and Jake figured out what Robert and Polly Knox were up to. Caitlin said something about...a fortune-teller and a full moon and a snake." She looked puzzled. "What sent you down here just in time? Straight out of the blue like that? Was it Jake? Did he know or suspect Robert?"

Margaret's lips quirked into a grin. She shook her head. "You'll never believe me."

"Try me."

"It was Caitlin and a fortune-teller up in Rochester. Somehow the woman had real powers, and she tuned in on Caitlin."

"You're right. I don't believe it." Sandy shook her head.

"I'll let Caitlin fill you in on the details, especially the part where she's the heroine."

"Which, knowing my daughter, is the most important part." Sandy sighed and shook her head. "She's something else, my Caitlin."

"She's a darling. I wouldn't change a hair on her head." Margaret hugged Sandy once more. "But am

I ever glad she's yours, not mine. She's—'' She searched for the words, but Sandy merely smiled and found them for her.

"Enough to drive a person straight up a wall."

A HALF HOUR LATER Margaret tucked Caitlin in for the night. "I wish I'd hit her in the head and killed her dead," Caitlin remarked. "Mrs. Knox was really wicked, wasn't she?" Margaret nodded, and Caitlin went on with another yawn, "She was going to kill you, just like Madame Zorina said. And I saved everyone."

"That's right." Margaret brushed the hair off her niece's forehead and dropped a kiss on her nose. "Thank you, honey."

Caitlin frowned and hitched herself up in bed. "One thing Madame Zorina was wrong about. She said a snake was gonna get you, a silver one. But there wasn't any snake."

Margaret nodded. "Madame Zorina was right about that, too. Robert was wearing a belt with a silver buckle, shaped like a snake's head."

"Oh, yeah, I 'member I saw it." In a lurid flash Caitlin saw it again in her mind. Robert holding his bleeding leg, the light winking off his green-eyed belt buckle. "Wow!" She thought a minute, then gave Margaret a shrewd look. "So now we can go to Disneyworld. Mom's in the shower, but she said the police will want to talk to us for a few days. And if she's busy, then you and Jake can take me, right?"

"Okay, it's a deal," Margaret promised with a broad smile. "Know something funny?"

"What?" Caitlin asked sleepily.

"Your Mom says I was a lot like you when I was seven."

"Did you save people from getting killed by bad guys?"

Margaret shook her head. "Not quite. But I jumped off a shed roof, pretending I was Superman. I wore a towel on my back." She grinned. "I really thought I could fly."

Caitlin considered this for a second, then frowned. "You couldn't fly?"

"No, I broke my ankle and couldn't swim for a whole summer. But you know what?"

"What?" Caitlin looked puzzled.

"In a way you were Superman tonight. You were flying."

"Ackshully, I'm a master detective." Caitlin corrected her with a sleepy yawn.

"Yes, you are, and I love you very much." Margaret hugged her tight, kissed her and turned off the light. As she left the room, Jake took her in his arms.

He cocked a quizzical eyebrow down at her. "What was that all about?"

She grinned and shook her head. "Superman was just having a chat with the great master detective."

"You've got me completely confused. Superman? I don't know…"

"It's a long story, part of my checkered past involving a shed roof, a towel and my unshakable belief that I could fly."

His eyes crinkled with laughter. "I see. In that case, how would Superman like to move in with me? We could get married."

"My apartment's bigger, so you're moving in with me. Besides, I'm not sure I want to go to Australia." She reached up and brushed his lips with hers. "I like Boston. It's got swan boats, the Bruins and the Celtics. I forgot to tell you, when I bleed, it's Celtic green. I'm a fanatic basketball fan. They don't play basketball in Australia, do they?"

"I don't know." A gleam warmed his gray-blue eyes. "I only know I love you to distraction, from the first moment we met. You opened the door, and I was a goner."

"Actually, Caitlin opened the door."

The corners of his mouth turned up. "I stand corrected."

"That's okay, Caitlin's enough to confuse anyone." She smiled up at him. "Now where are we going to live?"

"I don't know," he admitted with an irresistible crooked grin. "I've got a place in New Haven where I hang my hat, and a cabin in Maine. We can find a place to put you."

Her toes curled and her heart melted and she knew she'd live anywhere as long as he was there, too.

"Want to guess what I like?" he teased.

"No, you tell me," she said, softly kissing his lean jaw.

"Look at this!" Margaret exclaimed three months later as she was sorting through replies to their wedding invitations. There was a large postcard with a picture of an Atlantic City casino among the small white envelopes.

Jake snatched it out of her fingers and turned it over, whistling in surprise. "Of all people, our favorite fortune-teller, the one and only Madame Zorina!"

Margaret slid her arms around him and kissed his mouth. "What does she say?"

He took time out for another kiss, then read the card aloud.

Dear Margaret and Jake,

Naturally you are getting married. Didn't I tell you your fates were entwined? Relieved all is well and that terrible threat has been removed. So, Robert Schuyler was the serpent, just as I foretold! And that woman, striking the night of the full moon, trying to drown you! I read the entire account in the newspapers. Caitlin, of course, saved your lives, it all happened as I said it would. The little girl is headed for great things. Sorry to say I will not be able to attend your wedding. I have been barred from the Atlantic City casinos. Apparently they resented my winning so much of their money! I plan to be in Las Vegas for the next few weeks, and after that, Monte Carlo! My aura is bright and the moon is in Saturn. I read the Tarot, and the cards looked very promising. Adding them all, I got a total of sixty-six, and the card ruling my sign was the Wheel of Fortune! My good luck continues! I shall let nature and the Fates take their course.

                    Affectionately, Madame Zorina.

Jake plucked the card from her fingers and read it. "Well, looks like she won the jackpot."

Sliding her arms about him, Margaret kissed him on the mouth. "Mmm, know what I think?" she said, slightly light-headed from his closeness.

"What?" Jake's arms tightened around her, and the postcard fell to the floor.

After an interval she laid her head on his shoulder and smiled. "We're the ones who hit the jackpot." Her breath caught in her throat at the look of love she saw in his eyes. Then further discussion of Madame Zorina and jackpots became nonessential as Margaret gave herself up to the delights of Jake's warm, crushing embrace; and the glow of love surrounded them both like a golden halo.

ROMANCE IS A YEARLONG EVENT!

Celebrate the most romantic day of the year with MY VALENTINE! (February)

CRYSTAL CREEK
When you come for a visit Texas-style, you won't want to leave! (March)

Celebrate the joy, excitement and adjustment that comes with being JUST MARRIED! (April)

Go back in time and discover the West as it was meant to be . . . UNTAMED—Maverick Hearts! (July)

LINGERING SHADOWS
New York Times bestselling author Penny Jordan brings you her latest blockbuster. Don't miss it! (August)

BACK BY POPULAR DEMAND!!!
Calloway Corners, involving stories of four sisters coping with family, business and romance! (September)

FRIENDS, FAMILIES, LOVERS
Join us for these heartwarming love stories that evoke memories of family and friends. (October)

Capture the magic and romance of Christmas past with HARLEQUIN HISTORICAL CHRISTMAS STORIES! (November)

WATCH FOR FURTHER DETAILS IN ALL HARLEQUIN BOOKS!

CALEND

HARLEQUIN

AMERICAN ✦ ROMANCE ®

Happy Holidays

A Calendar of Romance

What better way to conclude American Romance's yearlong celebration than with four very special books that celebrate the joy and magic of Christmas and Hanukkah, on sale now!

Be sure to complete your Calendar of Romance collection with the following titles:

#421—*Happy New Year, Darling*
#429—*Flannery's Rainbow*
#437—*Cinderella Mom*
#445—*Home Free*
#455—*Sand Man*
#461—*Count Your Blessings*

#425—*Valentine Hearts and Flowers*
#433—*A Man for Easter*
#441—*Daddy's Girl*
#449—*Opposing Camps*
#457—*Under His Spell*

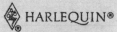

HAPPY VALENTINE'S DAY

James Rafferty had only forty-eight hours, and he wanted to make the most of them.... Helen Emerson had never had a Valentine's Day like this before!

Celebrate this special day for lovers, with a very special book from American Romance!

#473   ONE MORE VALENTINE
by Anne Stuart

Next month, Anne Stuart and American Romance have a delightful Valentine's Day surprise in store just for you. All the passion, drama—even a touch of mystery—you expect from this award-winning author.

Don't miss American Romance
#473   ONE MORE VALENTINE!

Also look for Anne Stuart's short story, "Saints Alive," in Harlequin's MY VALENTINE 1993 collection.

HARVAL

Praise for
Devour

"Wow! This is one heck of a book! Reading it, I felt so many emotions, I didn't even know where to begin for my review. Mostly, though, I felt excited and exhilarated that this author had gotten this book so right. . . . Ms. Morel is a wonderful storyteller. *Devour* kept me on the edge of my seat from page one. Paranormal lovers everywhere will love this addition to their library." —Romance Readers at Heart

"Interesting . . . intriguing." —*Romantic Times*

"Ms. Morel's story should have a broad range of appeal, with elements of urban fantasy, horror, and romance all skillfully intertwined." —Huntress Book Reviews

"Exciting. . . . Melina Morel provides a fast-paced story that werewolf fans will want to read." —*Midwest Book Review*

Also by Melina Morel

Devour

PREY

Melina Morel

A SIGNET ECLIPSE BOOK

SIGNET ECLIPSE
Published by New American Library, a division of
Penguin Group (USA) Inc., 375 Hudson Street,
New York, New York 10014, USA
Penguin Group (Canada), 90 Eglinton Avenue East, Suite 700, Toronto,
Ontario M4P 2Y3, Canada (a division of Pearson Penguin Canada Inc.)
Penguin Books Ltd., 80 Strand, London WC2R 0RL, England
Penguin Ireland, 25 St. Stephen's Green, Dublin 2,
Ireland (a division of Penguin Books Ltd.)
Penguin Group (Australia), 250 Camberwell Road, Camberwell, Victoria 3124,
Australia (a division of Pearson Australia Group Pty. Ltd.)
Penguin Books India Pvt. Ltd., 11 Community Centre, Panchsheel Park,
New Delhi - 110 017, India
Penguin Group (NZ), 67 Apollo Drive, Rosedale, North Shore 0632,
New Zealand (a division of Pearson New Zealand Ltd.)
Penguin Books (South Africa) (Pty.) Ltd., 24 Sturdee Avenue,
Rosebank, Johannesburg 2196, South Africa

Penguin Books Ltd., Registered Offices:
80 Strand, London WC2R 0RL, England

First published by Signet Eclipse, an imprint of New American Library,
a division of Penguin Group (USA) Inc.

First Printing, September 2008
10 9 8 7 6 5 4 3 2 1

To Laura Cifelli.
Thank you.

ACKNOWLEDGMENTS

A big thank-you to the staff at the Denise Marcil Literary Agency: Denise Marcil, Maura Kye-Casella, and Katie Kotchman. Thank you to Lindsay Nouis of NAL. And a special thank-you to the multitalented artist Mabelyn Arteaga, who created my beautiful Web site at www.melinamorel.com.

Chapter One

When Pavel Federov and his assistant arrived on the scene, they found the fearful parents huddled with the police, everybody looking cold and scared in the light of the police cruiser's headlights. A small child, abducted by a stranger, was out there in the woods, taken from her bedroom in the middle of the night. When her parents discovered her missing, they saw the open window, the overturned furniture, and they called the police. One of the policemen called in Metro Investigations as special consultants.

"Pavel, glad to see you. Ivan, how ya doin'?"

The policeman greeted his acquaintances and got down to business, explaining what had happened, introducing them to the parents, and telling them the facts of the case.

"When was the last time you saw Yvonne?" Pavel asked gently. The mother looked as if she were in shock.

"At seven," she said, struggling to hold back tears. "We read her a story and put her to bed." She raised her eyes and looked up at the tall man with the accent and said, "Please bring my baby back. She's only . . ." At that point the woman leaned against her husband's chest and burst into sobs, too distraught to continue, terrified at what might be happening to her child in the hands of a stranger.

Pavel nodded as the man tried to comfort his wife. "And when did you realize she was gone?" he asked the husband.

"Two hours ago. We saw the open window, the chair on the floor, the blanket missing from the bed, and no Yvonne. We checked the house, put on the lights outside, and then called the police."

Pavel turned to the cop. "Did your guys lift any prints from the window ledge or the furniture?"

"Yeah," he said. "Come over here. Give Mr. and Mrs. Croft some space."

Pavel and Ivan looked concerned. They knew the cop had nothing good to tell them.

Several feet from the parents, Sergeant Murray said, "The guy's prints were in the system. Sex offender. Two months out of jail. He just did time for an attack on a kid in Rochester. She survived but just barely. I want the son of a bitch. I want him tonight before he hurts this one."

"If he hasn't already," Pavel said grimly. "All right. What can you give us to work with?"

"We found footprints leading from the house to the street. It's been raining and the ground is kind of wet. The prints continued into the trees, and the woods are so overgrown, it's sort of hard to make out anything, especially in the dark."

"Did you call in the dogs?"

"We don't have any dogs. The town cut the budget. But we called to the police department in the next town over. They're bringing them in. But not until tomorrow."

"Too late," Pavel said in disgust. "All right, Ivan and I will go into the woods and see what we can find. If he's on foot, he might know his way around, but in the dark, he's liable to get lost anyway. Okay. Ivan, are you with me?"

"Right behind you, boss."

Pavel turned to the sobbing woman before he and his assistant headed into the trees. "If she's there, I'll find her," he said quietly. "I won't give up till I do."

"Thank you," she said tremulously. "We'll be right here

waiting. As long as it takes," she whispered through her tears.

Making their way into the woods that surrounded the rural upstate town, Pavel and Ivan quickly disappeared from view, even with the headlights flaring into the trees. They had done tracking assignments before, but never with the urgency of this one. Somewhere in this tangle of trees and undergrowth was a terrified child in the hands of a predator. That thought alone made the men focus like lasers.

Walking slowly enough to get their bearings in the dense darkness, Pavel and his assistant crept through a tangle of new growth and paused. "Do you hear it?" he asked.

"It's a child," Ivan said. "She's crying. Not close by, either."

"Can you pick up a scent? I'm getting the smell of tobacco. And sweat."

"He's sweating from fear."

"Then let's make sure the sick bastard has plenty to sweat about. Let's go!" said Pavel.

With that, both men disappeared, and in their places stood two dark cats the size of panthers, lifting their heads to take in the scents on the night air, a mixture of trees, animals and humans. Then they reared back on their haunches and sprang into action, hurtling through the tangle of trees in the darkness, paws pounding on the forest floor, scattering bits of earth beneath them as they ran, homing in on the man's scent.

Half a mile ahead of them in the dark, a skinny, middle-aged man dropped the sobbing child he had stolen and sat down, exhausted. Out of shape and fearful of being spotted with his victim, he had run from the house as fast as he could, but now, wheezing and lost, he had to rest. The child stood watching him for a moment; then she turned and started running as fast as she could.

"Oh, shit!" In a second her captor was after her, shouting for her to come back while she moved silently in the trees, hiding behind a large pine tree as he staggered toward her, panting and gasping.

In the telepathic language of werecats, Pavel ordered Ivan to see to the child as they closed in on the pair, their paws thundering in the night as they raced toward the kidnapper. "I'll take care of him. You make sure the baby's safe," he said.

Hurtling toward his target, Pavel reached him before Ivan could seize the child. With a mighty leap, the panther-cat hurled him to the ground and bit him as they thrashed on the forest floor. The man shrieked with pain, helpless in the grip of the big cat.

Pavel had to force himself not to kill. He tamped down the killer in him while he flung the human against a tree, where he collapsed into a heap and lay facedown on the ground, whimpering with fright.

Satisfied that the kidnapper wasn't going anyplace, Pavel shape-shifted out of sight of his prey and returned to human form in the black pants and commando sweater of his company. As a werecat of the northern regions, he had been granted the gift of returning fully clothed by a god. Tonight, he was glad he had it.

"Ivan? Did you find the child?"

"Right here, boss. Pavel, meet Yvonne. And now we're going to take her home."

When Pavel and his assistant had the kidnapper handcuffed and on his feet, they called in the capture to Sergeant Murray, who relayed the news to the parents, who wept with relief. They had been preparing themselves for tragedy; now they were beside themselves with joy. In that dark forest, where death and danger lurked, those strangers had just given them back their child.

"What do we owe you, mister?" the father asked. "We want to thank you properly. You've just saved our family."

He shook his head. "The police will get a bill. All you have to do is take the little one home and keep her safe."

After he said goodbye to them, Pavel turned to Sergeant Murray and said, "The criminal is a lunatic as well as a pervert. While we were bringing him in, he kept screaming about being attacked by cats. Can you believe it?"

"Lots of strange things out in those woods, Pavel. You never know," the sergeant said with a wink. As a fellow werecat, he knew the score.

The long drive back to Manhattan seemed almost carefree compared to the gloom of the ride upstate. New York's only all-werecat security force had had a success tonight, and both men were glad things turned out well.

Later, when Pavel returned to his apartment and checked his voice mail, he found a message sent from half a world away by a shaman of his clan. From several time zones to the east came the raspy voice speaking slowly and deliberately, with the formality of another era.

"Beware the false ones who swear to uphold our traditions yet seek comfort with our enemies. They will cause turmoil. Even now chaos brews in the city of the Horseman, and the leader stumbles. All will be left in disarray."

If he hadn't known the reputation of the shaman who had left that message, Pavel Federov would have rejected it as nonsense, but the old man had foreseen too many things that turned out to be true. The only problem was, his predictions were often so hazy that until they materialized, nobody knew what he meant.

Pavel was a Russian Blue werecat, a member of an ancient group that had originated in the icy regions of the North. His residence might be New York, but geography meant nothing. His heart beat for his clan. And this intimation of disaster unsettled him.

Pondering the consequences of this strange message, Pavel took out his cell phone again and punched in the number of his cousin Vladimir, who kept odd hours. It was well past four in the morning.

"It's Pavel," he said when Vladimir answered. "I've just

received a call from the shaman. Sounds like something is going on in St. Petersburg. He used a phrase: 'The leader stumbles.' Do you have any idea what that could mean?"

"It could mean someone's in trouble. Someone important. Maybe even a human."

"Do you think it's political?"

"Hard to tell. People rise and fall from power. Maybe that's what he means. There are some who might say that the Hierarch of our clan stumbled when he married that flashy wife of his."

"Good point," Pavel said drily. "He had no business marrying outside the clan. And he did it anyway. I still can't believe it."

"I can see how he fell for her. Bella is a beauty."

"He's a fool. Those damned Siberian Forest cats are poison. He'll come to regret it, but by then it will be too late."

"Such cynicism. No wonder you're not married."

Pavel gave the phone a cold glance. His cousin was being tactless, but not intentionally. Sometimes people just forgot.

As if Vladimir had quickly realized his gaffe, he said, "Sorry, Pavel. I didn't mean it like that."

"I know. Well, call me if you hear anything. I'll do the same."

The clan might be anxious over nothing, the Russian decided. Talk, gossip, rumors. Sometimes he felt that people needed some kind of threat to liven up their dull lives. Not in his case.

No. Pavel's surveillance company had enough jobs to keep his whole staff occupied. Industrial projects, cheating spouses, computer crime, and even VIP bodyguard details. Just this past week, he had sent a man to infiltrate a network of crooked Wall Streeters. This evening they had helped rescue a child. Two weeks earlier they had nailed an embezzler at a bank.

That was small potatoes. Recently Metro had followed the vice president of a multinational corporation who was selling the secret formula of its leading sports drink for cash. Pavel's man got the whole thing down on video, and the veep was last seen calling his lawyer from jail.

This vocation paid well, Metro Enterprises provided employment for a handful of fellow werecats whose unusual skills made them invaluable to Pavel, and it eased the problems of citizens in need of a helping hand with their personal or corporate dilemmas, but it left Pavel with an emptiness that even large amounts of money couldn't fill. Vladimir had it right. He was a hopeless cynic who had seen too much crime, treachery, and plain stupidity to have the slightest faith left in anyone's better nature.

But, he reflected sadly, if Natalya were still alive, he wouldn't give a damn. The whole world could go off the rails, and he'd still find something to smile about if she were there. It was his tragedy that she wasn't.

Chapter Two

"Marc? There's so much static in this connection, I can barely hear you. Where are you calling from?"

"I'm at the warehouse. We've got trouble. Somebody's been going through our stock."

"Are you serious?" Vivian Roussel rose from her seat, cell phone in hand. The first thing that came to mind was the expensive porcelain they had just purchased. "What did they take? Any of the really pricey pieces?"

"I'm still trying to find out if they managed to steal anything. It's like they were going through the place and just targeting the paintings. None of the smaller boxes were opened. They don't seem to have bothered with those rare porcelains."

"You're sure?"

"Yes. They moved the paintings around. I've got our invoices here, and I'm checking to see if anything's gone missing."

"What do you think?"

"So far, so good. But it's too early to tell what's been taken."

"I'll meet you there," Viv said. "Give me forty-five minutes."

In all the years that they had been in business, nobody had ever broken into their shop or their warehouse. As Viv put the closed sign in the window and grabbed her coat, bag and keys, she felt violated in a strange way. In her very special circle, she and Marc were admired and respected, aristocrats of their species. Nobody had ever dared to harm them or even threaten them, especially not another werecat of their clan. Princely descendants of one of the legendary females of their kind, their clan held them in high esteem. The perpetrators must have been human, Viv decided angrily. That sort was so brazen.

"What about our security system?" she asked when she arrived at the warehouse to find her brother examining their property.

"They disabled it, so they had to be pros," Marc said glumly. "And I'd love to know just what they expected to find."

"Maybe they have us confused with somebody else. Our Russian imports don't have a provenance from the Winter Palace. Our pieces are unique and expensive, but it's not as though we have a cache of emeralds and diamonds on the premises."

"We wish," he said with a wry smile. "Well, I'm going to call the Leader and tell him the news."

The Leader, John Sinclair, was the head of Marc and Viv's werecat clan, the Maine Coon cats, and he was not pleased by the phone call.

"When you call attention to yourselves, these things happen. Human greed. Envy. Don't call the police. Handle it in house."

"But the police—"

"You handle it yourselves," he repeated in a near growl. "Meanwhile, tighten up the security. I'll send you information about whom to contact. I know a firm that's very good and very discreet. No police."

He might as well have said it was their own fault.

"Well," Viv said, once her brother relayed his conversation with their Leader, "I'm sorry we didn't invest in better protection. Obviously our system has flaws." She looked annoyed. "He told you not to involve the NYPD?"

"You know how he is about outsiders. If it involves our clan, we take care of it, although I think this is just a normal break-in. Nothing related to us as werecats, I hope."

"All right. How do we do this?"

"We have to find a better security agency." Marc raised his shoulders and his hands in a gesture of defeat. "I'll be choosier next time."

"Well, we'd better get somebody down here fast. We can't leave it like this. Who knows what will disappear if anybody finds out the place is unguarded."

"I'm on it," he said. "We have to show Sinclair we can protect our business."

"Pavel here. How's the weather up north?"

"Fine. If you like snow," the voice on the other end replied. "September, and they're already sweeping the stuff off the sidewalks. But you didn't call me from New York to chat about the climate. What's going on?"

"Here? Not much. The usual. I'm more interested in what's happening in Petersburg."

"Well, let's see. . . . Prices are out of control. You can't even buy a small apartment without a ton of money. Traffic is a nightmare. Nationalist demonstrations are popping up all over the place. We're living the wild and wonderful world of post communism."

"That's not what I mean, Yuri," he said with a grin. "I'm interested in news of the clan." Pavel waited. Then he asked, "Nothing?"

"Nothing much. The Hierarch and his company are in negotiations with foreign investors to drill for oil in a remote area of Siberia. Things are moving very slowly. There's talk about the government banning foreigners from the oil fields in the name of national interests. It's all iffy at the moment."

"Anything else? Any talk of trouble within the clan?"

"No," Yuri replied. "Just lots of gossip about the Hierarch's gorgeous wife. Madame Bella Danilov appeared at an exclusive reception for members of St. Petersburg's business elite. Madame Danilov opened a new boutique on Nevsky Prospeckt. Very busy lady," he said drily.

"Yes, isn't she?"

"Well, the members don't like her, but she seems to make him happy. A few members wanted him to step down but he refused. He told them if he could overcome an ancient prejudice, so should they."

"Bella must practice witchcraft. No Russian Blue cat before him would ever have considered mating with a Siberian Forest cat."

"Well, new times, new rules. But this doesn't make the clan happy," Yuri said seriously.

"Anybody unhappy enough to cause real trouble over this?"

"No," he said firmly. "The Hierarch is a popular leader. We may grumble about his lousy choice of a mate, but he's been good for us. He takes care of his own, and bottom line, that's what counts."

"Glad to hear it," Pavel said. "If I get back home for a visit, we can get together."

"Great. Hope to see you in the New Year. Oh," Yuri said almost as an afterthought, "this isn't clan-related, but it's big news here—the government and the Church have recently announced that the famous icon of the Virgin of Saratov was stolen sometime in the last three months. All efforts are being made to track it down. The usual."

Pavel reacted in shock. This was a national treasure, the holy icon Russians credited with sparing the city of Saratov from extermination by Tsar Ivan the Terrible back in the sixteenth century. Believers prayed to the virgin for protection against enemies of the motherland and for protection in battle. Werecat or not, Pavel had prayed to the Virgin of Saratov when he was a Special Ops soldier in the Chechen war, and he felt a devotion to her that had outlasted his combat duty.

"This is disgraceful," he exclaimed. "Who the hell would do such a thing?"

"Nobody knows. They questioned all the monks who live at the shrine, and they claim the icon was hanging in the church one day and gone the next. Workmen had been doing some repairs around the time of the theft, but they just vanished like smoke when the icon went missing. Nobody can find them."

"Naturally," Pavel said with disgust. "Keep me posted on this."

"Of course," Yuri promised.

Pavel put the phone back in his pocket and felt revolted. If the only thing concerning the brethren back home was the Hierarch's new bride, perhaps the shaman's worries were groundless. When was it news that a man, even one who led the Russian Blue werecats, had fallen in love with the wrong woman?

Pavel remembered nights as a young boy, when his old babushka used to retell the legends of their clan, of celebrated battles involving the Russian Blue cats and their fierce enemies, the Siberian Forest cats, of how the Siberians kidnapped and killed other clans' kittens and sacrificed them to their evil god, Moroz the Dread.

At that point, Grandma would piously cross herself and glance at the icons, then put her arms around Pavel and hug him. "Never, never let yourself be seduced by the Siberians," she would say. "Even now, the evil creatures still worship Moroz."

After that scare, she would make a hot glass of tea and talk of other things, but Pavel could never quite get over the uneasiness he felt regarding Siberians. He wondered if perhaps the Hierarch's babushka had neglected this talk. If so, it was a damn shame.

With all the upheavals of recent years, had people become

so totally callous that they would dare to steal a miracle-working icon wrapped in centuries of their country's history?

The thieves had to be humans of the lowest level, he thought with disdain. Werecats had more respect for sacred things.

Chapter Three

"Marc, I'd like to order another enameled tea service in the *boyar* style," Viv said. She sat at her desk in the office of Old Muscovy, their antiques shop, and scrolled through her inventory on the laptop. Then she suddenly rose to her feet in surprise as her eyes focused on a tall gentleman at the door, waiting to be buzzed in.

"What's the matter?" Marc asked. Then he turned to see what had startled Viv. In an instant he hit the release button for the door and rushed over to greet the Leader himself. "He doesn't look happy," Marc muttered to his sister just before he opened the door.

He wasn't. Tall, trim, and already going gray at the temples, the Leader nodded to the Roussels and exchanged formalities, letting Marc take his coat and allowing Viv to serve him tea. Then he said, "You know how much I've always liked you two, but lately you've been pushing the envelope. You did an interview on TV, and that probably attracted the burglar." He gave them a significant glance and let that sink in. "This business is fine, but keep your distance from the humans. You let the humans into your affairs, and it always bites you in the ass. Once they start digging, it could affect the whole clan. I felt I had to let you know how seriously I take this incident, in case you were still thinking of calling in the police."

"I can't understand why we were broken into in the first place," Marc replied. "It's never happened before. What did they expect to find? We don't carry appliances or other things that crooks can turn into quick cash."

Viv looked at the Leader and said, "Do you think they could have gotten our warehouse confused with another one? Maybe someplace where they store other kinds of goods? I can't imagine most thieves wanting Russian paintings and art objects. Besides, after I checked all the articles against our inventory, they were all there. It's very odd."

"Maybe we're making too much of this. People get broken into every day. Stores get robbed. It happens. We do business in a big city. Eight million people and not all of them are honest." Marc looked hopefully at Sinclair as he spoke.

The Leader nodded. "Well, this time, it could just be a random breaking and entering, but whatever it is, it stays within the clan. You're lucky nothing was taken. Have it investigated, and if it appears to be directed against you specifically as werecats, I'll put my Special Squad on it. But we probably won't have to go that far."

Sinclair's blue eyes rested on Viv for a second, and he gave her the kind of smile few werecats ever received from him. Even John Sinclair had a soft spot for one of the clan's aristocrats, a direct descendant of a werecat demigoddess. Viv glanced at him with her large amber eyes, and for a nanosecond, Marc could swear that the Leader nearly purred.

"I've made inquiries," Sinclair said. "Mac Dugan has worked with a security firm on the approved list. He'll give you their contact information. I was in the neighborhood, so I thought I'd look in on you." He glanced directly at Viv. "You're coming to the monthly meeting, I hope."

Viv didn't miss the tone of voice or the way his eyes caressed her. She nodded. "Oh, yes. I'll be there."

"Good," he said. Then with that resolved, the Leader said he had an appointment and left.

"Now *that* was a dominance display," Viv murmured. "Me boss, you underlings. He doesn't usually come calling."

Marc gave her a smile. "But it looks as if you're one underling he really likes."

"I'm not the kind of woman who likes taking orders. Our Leader is the iron-fist-in-the-velvet-glove type. Things have to be his way."

"He's the boss," Marc said with a shrug. "Be happy he likes you. That never hurts."

"You're right," she said with a lingering glance at the door. "We just have to be thankful we didn't lose anything and get on with it."

Marc nodded. Then he said, "By the way, did you receive an e-mail from Bella Danilov? I got one this afternoon. She wanted to know if we were pleased with the condition of the goods upon arrival."

"No," Viv said. "She probably just sent it to you. She seemed to like you."

Marc looked unexpectedly startled. He shook his head. "No," he said. "She was just a friendly person. And she's married to a very rich man."

"She didn't seem all that friendly to me. And I swear she's one of the werefolk. Maybe another cat. Or even a fox. I picked up on her pheromones and found them a little off, but that could be from the strong perfume she uses. She struck me as favoring her human side over the were side. And she treated me like a nonentity."

"Well, she wasn't that bad. She took us out to lunch at a nice restaurant and picked up the tab. Great place for Russian cuisine."

"True. But she was such a phony all the same. Any woman who has a cell phone encrusted with diamonds is screaming for attention. 'Look at me. I'm filthy rich!' "

Marc chuckled. "She's a spoiled darling," he said. "But

she did sell us a nice assortment of paintings, and she did help us get them through customs with a minimum of hassle, so for that, I'm grateful."

"Yes. It could have been much worse. I've had some pretty awful experiences with customs in the East. Madame Danilov certainly helped us there."

"So you see," Marc said, "even Bella Danilov has her good points."

"One or two," Viv conceded drily.

"You know, Mac already sent me the info on the company he's used. He gave me their number. Says they're very dependable. Let's hope that break-in was a one-shot deal," said Marc.

"I hope you're right. We have a lot of inventory tied up in that warehouse."

Both Roussels looked pensive. They felt shaken at being targeted since their high status in the werecat community had always prevented that, and they didn't like the idea that perhaps humans had managed to circumvent their security. The whole episode was unsettling.

As if reading her mind, Marc said, "I'll bet the burglars were human."

Viv shrugged. "That could lead to other problems," she said with a sigh.

Pavel's cousin Vladimir was a former Russian military man who worked as a houseman for a very wealthy and reclusive gentleman named Ian Morgan, an investor and collector of beautiful artworks. The fact that Mr. Morgan was also a vampire did nothing to diminish the respect Vladimir felt for him. Mr. Morgan, in turn, had nothing but admiration for the loyalty of werecats. They got along quite well.

"The art world is talking about the theft of the Virgin of Saratov," Ian noted one evening as he glanced up from the newspaper. "It's one of Russia's most venerated icons. What sort of crook would steal something like that when he couldn't possibly fence it?"

"One without shame or brains," Vladimir said grimly.

"People have lost all sense of tradition. They break into churches, into museums and seize national treasures. Then they try to sell them on the black market to sleazy millionaires. Disgusting."

Vladimir nodded. Then boldly, he asked, "Sir, has anyone ever approached you with something like that?"

Ian glanced up. "Yes," he said. "About thirty years ago, with an offer of magnificent Greek vases taken from an excavation in Bulgaria." He smiled. "I got in touch with Interpol and had the satisfaction of seeing the thief sent to jail. The head of antiquities in one of the Bulgarian museums turned up dead on the streets of the capital shortly after."

"Very good, sir."

"If I hear anything about the icon, I'll contact the police," he promised.

"If Pavel can help you, please let him know, too. With him it's personal. He credits the Virgin of Saratov with keeping him alive during the fighting in Chechnya."

"Vladimir, I had no idea you werecats held those beliefs. I thought . . ."

"We're eclectic in our belief systems, sir. We embrace many concepts."

Well, Ian reflected, *live and learn.* For an icon so steeped in Russian history, even the Russian Blue werecats were prepared to come to her rescue. Impressive.

Chapter Four

Monthly meetings on the estate of their Leader were a tradition among the Maine Coon cats. Sometimes the Leader invited the local members of the clan; sometimes he requested the presence of those who lived out of state. Clan business headed the agenda, and werecats with sharp eyes could often tell who the rising stars were by noting the seating arrangements. Protocal was rigid, and the dress code required human form.

Viv had driven out to the estate in the Jersey suburbs, been buzzed though the gates by security, and, dressed in an elegant black dress and silver jewelry, entered the foyer and headed to the ballroom where the meeting was about to begin. She smiled a greeting at various acquaintances as she accepted a glass of chardonnay from a waiter and strolled around, making conversation with serious-looking werecats from New Jersey and Connecticut. Suddenly the lights flashed, signaling it was time for the presentation.

To her surprise, the Leader motioned to her to sit up front, making Viv wonder if she was going to be held up as a bad example. She wished she had been able to persuade Marc to attend this time. She actually felt a little uneasy.

With everyone's attention on him, the Leader went to the podium and responded graciously as the audience, in regulation human form, applauded. White teeth flashing, he wel-

comed them and said, "With the vast array of technology at
the disposal of humans and werefolk alike, life under the
radar is becoming harder and harder to maintain. I'm going
to show you a clip from a documentary broadcast last month
to illustrate that."

Lights went dim as he turned on a large flat-screen TV.
Immediately several humans appeared, swearing they had
seen large jungle cats prowling the farming communities of
the Midwest, killing livestock at will and causing chaos in
the neighborhood. Gasps arose from several members of the
audience as the next footage showed what the humans called
a large black panther sauntering across a woodland clearing.
The feral beast that had terrorized miles of farmland was one
of them. In the next clip, he was dead.

"There, ladies and gentlemen. You see for yourselves
what happens when one of our brethren chooses to go feral,
when he throws off all restraints and allows the humans to
find him. He went on a killing spree over four counties. This
led to his execution by the local police and to numerous articles in the tabloids. We must never attract this level of attention."

"Leader?" A stocky werecat with a clothing store in the
Bronx raised his hand.

"Yes?"

"Does anyone know what made him go feral?"

"His wife claimed he was under stress at work and he
chose this way to attack his problems."

Another hand went up. "Did the humans realize he was
one of us?"

"According to our people in law enforcement, they believed he was simply a panther who had escaped from a cir-
cus or a private zoo. But the point is, any kind of behavior
that makes the humans take notice is deadly for us. We exist
on our own terms. We don't intermingle any more than necessary. This is our strength. Those who abandon this princi-

ple always come to grief." He looked grim. Viv had a horrible feeling he was looking right at her.

After the presentation, the Leader motioned to Viv and
took her hand as he escorted her to his study, the inner sanc-
tum where major decisions were made. She hoped she didn't
seem as nervous as she felt.

"Viv," he said as he directed her to take a seat, "we have
to talk."

This sounds bad. She wondered what he was going to tell
her.

When they were seated on the same sofa, he looked at her
with unusual interest and said, "It's werecats like you and
Marc who are the hope of our clan." He paused as he saw the
questioning look in her eye. "You have the DNA of the
greatest werecat who ever was, the demigoddess Krasivaya.
And yet you show no sign of wanting to pass on this gift.
You're shirking your duty to your clan."

"Oh," said Viv, feeling flustered. "Well, I haven't yet
found the male I want for the father of my children. Krasivaya's genes deserve someone special." *Mind your own
business*, she thought angrily. *My genes, my mate. Not your
problem.*

Before Viv could react, the Leader shape-shifted,
prompting a matching reflex in her. Nose to nose on the carpet, the two large Maine Coon cats, one silvery with white
boots, the other black and brown, faced each other down,
looking like shaggy mountain lions ready to tangle.

"Did you forget that I can read your mind when I wish? I
am your leader. Don't be flippant with me."

Viv fought down the growl in her throat. She backed off
and took a submissive posture while the Leader let loose
with a series of growls and hisses that made her fur stand on
end. Then, satisfied with the effect, he shape-shifted once
again and returned to the sofa, a well-dressed executive in an
Armani suit.

Thanks to a favor granted by a minor woodland god thousands of years ago, the werecats of the North enjoyed the gift of returning to their clothed forms when shapeshifting. Otherwise their ancestors would have frozen to death on the tundra.

"You can't waste your gift," he said quietly. "Choose a mate."

Fixing her with a wicked gleam in his light blue eyes, the Leader made her heart do a little flip when he leaned over and kissed her, gently, tenderly, caressing her as he deepened the kiss. She hadn't ever thought of him like that, and frankly, it stunned her.

To her distress, he picked up on that and said, "Think about it now."

"This is too sudden for me to process. You've been married for so many years. . . ."

"And now I'm a widower. I have to think of the clan, Viv, and so do you. We could have wonderful children."

Viv fought to block him out of her thoughts—a gift she rarely had to use since so few werecats could do what he did. She simply nodded. Nothing seemed real right now as she struggled to clear her brain.

"I want a mate I can be proud of," he said as he kissed her again. "I think you do, too."

Viv felt as if her world had gone upside down. Her Leader wanted her for her famous DNA, as if she were some kind of fruit fly in a lab. Because he was a widower, there was no impediment to his marriage with her, and he was such a snob, of course he would want offspring from the most distinguished werecat line of them all.

She had no desire to be the first lady of the Maine Coon cats. She liked her life as it was. John Sinclair was handsome, rich, and powerful, but she wanted love. It was her bad luck that she hadn't yet found it, and she didn't believe an estate with armed guards and an unlimited allowance would be where she'd discover it. Besides, she had heard gossip from some of the other werecat women about his active love life while his wife was still alive. And, of course, there was the story about the mistress he kept in a Park Avenue condo. She wasn't going to be his trophy wife and put up with a harem.

I have to tell Marc, she decided. *He was right about the Leader's interest.*

Still shaken by Sinclair's actions, Viv got through the rest of the evening as best she could and headed to the parking area with a group of werecats she knew from the city. She had barely driven three blocks when a big SUV careened around the corner and stopped just short of crashing into her car.

Viv's seat belt was the only thing that prevented her from injury as she slammed on her brakes and lurched forward. It didn't activate the air bags, but the force of the jolt took her breath away. Stunned from the inpact, she watched as two big men threw open the door of the SUV and ran toward her.

Something about their demeanor alarmed Viv. The looks on their faces suggested they were not simply good citizens coming to the aid of someone in distress; they seemed ready to attack. Whatever their intent was, it wasn't inspired by kindness or concern for her safety. They rushed the car, making a grab for the door handle, which was still locked. They screamed threats at her, beating on the hood, ready to drag her out of the car.

Pulling herself out of her stupor, Viv reversed so quickly she stunned them, forcing them to leap out of her way. Then gunning the engine and blaring the horn, she headed straight toward them, making them scurry back to the SUV, throw open the doors, and jump inside, peeling away so fast they were out of sight before she could catch her breath. Her hands tightened on the steering wheel as she watched them go; then she hit the horn in sheer fury.

By the time three of her brother's friends reached her and jumped out of their vehicles to ask if she were all right, the would-be assailants were long gone.

Hank, Joey, and Pat—all buddies of Marc's who went to Yankees games with him—insisted on taking her back to the Leader's home to let him know what happened. With his mania for keeping clan problems in house, they figured he could deal with it since the would-be carjackers were operating in his own neighborhood.

"Viv, were you hurt? Did you recognize them? How many were there?" the Leader demanded.

"I'm okay. There were two. They pretended they were going to crash into my car to make me stop, and then they jumped out and ran toward me. They were going to pull my door open and grab me, so I backed up as quickly as I could and pretended I was going to run them down. That's when they took off."

"Quick thinking," he said with approval.

"I considered going werecat when I saw them rushing the car, but I decided to save that for my last resort."

"Good. You kept your head."

"Leader, I can drive Viv's car home, and Pat and Joey can take mine. We'll make sure she gets home safely."

"No," he said possessively. "I'll drive her myself. My driver can follow, and you three can follow us. That way, if anybody tries something, we'll be prepared to handle it."

"Really, you don't have to do this," Viv protested. "The men will get me home safely."

"Nonsense. We take care of our own," he insisted, with a meaningful glance at Viv.

Hank, Pat, and Joey looked impressed. This was out of character for Sinclair. They knew he thought Viv was special. Every werecat of the Maine Coon cat clan felt Krasivaya's descendants were bluebloods, but their leader had never paid anyone a compliment like this.

"All right," he said. "Let's get the cars."

Once home, Viv thanked her friends, and then she greeted the doorman in the brightly lit lobby of her building on the Palisades and told him to be on the lookout for anything strange. It would take the men so long to get home that she almost felt guilty about letting them escort her like this. One BMW, one Mercedes, and two big SUVs leading up the rear. Really, such a fuss.

It would be something to joke about later on when everything was safe and two large men weren't trying to jump her.

I don't think I'm going to tell Marc about this right now, Viv thought upon reflection as she put the key in her lock and entered her apartment. *He'll just get upset.*

She got the surprise of her life when she pushed the button on her answering machine.

Chapter Five

"Viv, it's Marc. Pick up if you're there. Stay home tonight if you haven't gone out yet. I tried to reach you on your cell. You didn't answer. I also tried Sinclair's estate. Two men tried to jump me when I went to get my car, but I'm okay. I'm home now."

"My God," she exclaimed. What was going on? Had somebody declared war on the Maine Coon cat sept—or just them?

What was wrong? She and Marc had been in business for more than a decade and had never before had this kind of trouble. Had they managed to offend somebody powerful, somebody who would hold a grudge, somebody who could pay thugs to harm them? It was surreal.

Reaching for the telephone, Viv dialed her brother's number and was relieved to hear his voice. He was safe.

"Hi," she said. "I just got your message. Something similar happened to me when I left the meeting tonight. Two males tried to carjack me. I nearly ran them down, and then Hank, Pat, Joey, and the Leader escorted me home."

"Shit."

"Yes, my thoughts exactly," she said grimly. "But I escaped them. How about you? Did they hurt you?"

"No. They tried to grab me from behind, but I saw something in the side-view mirror as I was approaching the car, and I reacted. They lost the element of surprise and I let them have it with a few good kicks. I think I scared them more than they scared me."

"You're sure you're okay?"

"I'm fine. What about you?"

"I'm all right. Not a scratch."

"Good."

"Did they try to grab you near the shop?" Viv asked, concerned.

"No. I knew I wasn't going to the meeting tonight, so I dropped by a restaurant to pick up something to eat. I was coming out of there when they made their move."

"Then they must have trailed you from the shop."

"That's what I think," he said. "They know where we work. They know where our warehouse is. . . ."

The silence that followed was not a happy sort. The Roussels both felt threatened and hunted.

"I caught their scent," said Viv. "They were some kind of werefolk, but in all the excitement, I couldn't really decide which kind. We need protection. We need somebody really good, and we need them fast. Let's call that firm Mac and the Leader like. Do you have their number?"

"I have it on my desk."

"Well, we can't do anything tonight, but please give them a call tomorrow, explain what's been happening, and ask them to pay us a visit as soon as they can. This can't be random. First the warehouse and now us. And none of it makes sense to me. We don't deal in Fabergé eggs, for heaven's sake. I can't believe somebody is trying this hard to harass us and steal from us." She paused and asked, "Did you activate your alarm system when you got home?"

"You bet I did," Marc replied. "I hope you did the same."

"Absolutely. I also spoke to the concierge before I came upstairs. I told him to watch for anything suspicious."

"Good."

"And I'm going to take out my gun."

"Be careful of that," her brother said. "You haven't practiced in a while."

"I remember how to use it," she replied.

"Maybe we ought to transform tonight," he suggested. "If anybody manages to break in, all they'll see is a cat."

"If anyone breaks in, they'll think they've disturbed a tiger," Viv said forcefully.

"Well, good night. Be careful," he added.

"You, too," she said.

When Viv hung up her house phone, she kicked off her shoes and lay across her bed, wondering how this drama had begun. What had they done? Their shop, the Old Muscovy, had traded in Russian and Eastern European art and artifacts for a dozen years without ever having problems like these. The worst thing that had ever happened was the time a car jumped the sidewalk and crashed into their front door. Luckily nobody was hurt, the insurance covered the damages, and they were back in business right away. Nobody had ever burgled them or tried to abduct them before.

And, Viv thought, if one of the recent episodes could be attributed to the risks of life in the big city, two made that highly unlikely. No. They were under attack. But why? And who was behind it?

None of it made sense, any more than the decision by her Leader to see her as a possible mate. He was an authoritarian snob who wanted an alliance with Krasivaya's descendant so he could claim bragging rights about a trophy wife. She hadn't liked the way things were headed ever since he had assumed command last year after an election that some considered flawed. A few members were investigating that.

The previous Leader was an easygoing gentleman with a charming sense of humor and a fondness for caviar. This one had an obsession with secrecy, staying under the radar, staying out of the news. Rumors said that he'd been CIA in his previous job, so that made sense. But it didn't sit well with

Viv. Fortunately clan rules stated clearly and without any ambiguity that a female could choose her mate. If he tried to overrule her on that essential point and force her into the kind of alliance he wanted, she'd remind him she cherished her freedom. She'd fight to uphold it if she had to. With that in mind, she carefully placed her Beretta on the night table and lay back against the pillows, absolutely worn-out.

Pavel's secretary was trained to take down information and pass it on to her boss so he could decide who could best cover each particular case. Pavel took over from there, interviewed the client, and assigned a man to the case. In certain situations, he did the fieldwork himself, depending on the importance of the job. A call from an unknown party like Marc Roussel would ordinarily have rated the services of his number-two man, but the fact that Mr. Roussel cited a friend of his as a reference and worked as an importer of Russian art and artifacts aroused Pavel's curiosity. Moreover, he had heard about the Old Muscovy from other émigrés, and found himself interested.

Pavel surprised Marc by calling back within the hour and setting up a meeting.

"Would you be able to come to the shop?" Marc asked. "My sister works here, too, and I don't want to leave her alone right now in case those guys come back."

"I can be there by two o'clock. Is that all right?"

"Great. Ah, we buzz people in for security concerns. What do you look like, Mr. Federov?"

"Tall, dark hair, green eyes. I'm wearing a black leather jacket and black pants today."

"Okay, we'll be waiting for you."

"See you later."

When Marc ended the call and clicked his cell phone shut, Viv looked hopefully at her brother. "What did he sound like?"

"Slavic."

"You mean he's not American?"

"With a name like Pavel Federov?"

"He could be second generation."

"This one isn't. His English is fluent, but accented. He sounds businesslike."

"Well, if the Leader and Mac both use him, he has to be a real pro."

"Mac used his company last year when he suspected one of his employees was tapping the till. Federov caught the thief in two days."

"Very efficient."

"Dugan said he was thorough. Military man in Russia before he emigrated. And the Leader must think he's good," he reminded her.

Viv nodded, picturing some short, squat fellow with a buzz cut and a grim expression. What she saw when Pavel Federov arrived at the shop was something else entirely.

Chapter Six

The buzzer sent a zap of electricity into Viv's consciousness as she sat in the back room, going over accounts. With a glance at the clock, she ventured into the showroom, where she saw Marc opening the door to a tall man in black, a six footer who looked as sleek as a panther and just as lethal. This former military man was a tribute to physical fitness, Viv thought. He probably trained every day.

"Hello, Mr. Roussel," the visitor said politely with a firm handshake. "Pavel Federov, from Metro Investigations."

"Glad to meet you. There's my sister, Vivian. She and I own Old Muscovy together. Viv, come say hello to Mr. Federov."

"How do you do?" Viv said with a smile that was warmer than intended. This man was very, very attractive. Those green eyes of his recalled pure mountain streams in scenic landscapes. Then she saw a jagged scar on the hand he extended to her, and she remembered that mountain streams sometimes existed in turbulent, war-torn areas, too.

"Mr. Roussel, Miss Roussel," Pavel said as they all sat down for a conference amid the memorabilia of old Russia, "I have to interview you to determine how Metro Investigations can best serve you, so I'm going to ask some questions. Please don't feel offended. Now, first of all, do you have any known enemies?"

"No," they answered in unison.

Pavel smiled. "Let me rephrase that. Has either of you been involved in any recent disputes with a business associate or a personal acquaintance?"

"We're highly regarded," said Viv. "We try to cultivate good relationships with customers."

"Has anyone accused you of any wrongdoing, perhaps not keeping a promise, maybe even complaining of cheating them? I have to ask this." Pavel looked at his clients calmly. They seemed affronted.

"We have a reputation for fair dealing, Mr. Federov," Marc said. "There's never been any serious complaint lodged against us."

"I don't mean to imply it. I'm just trying to find a motive for the attacks you mentioned when you called us. It's possible you've angered someone. I'd like to find out who it is. Think carefully. Have you had any unhappy customers lately?"

Pavel watched as the clients glanced at each other, and then shrugged.

"Last month a woman in Brooklyn called to complain that our deliveryman took longer than he should have to bring her the cabinet she ordered, but there was a car crash on the route, and he was held up in traffic," said Viv. "She was very unpleasant about it. But I think she was just venting."

"Anything else?"

Marc shook his head. "Nothing comes to mind. We're very customer-friendly."

Pavel tried another area. "What about personal relationships?"

Viv glanced at him. "What are you implying?"

"An angry boyfriend?"

"I'm not seeing anyone at the moment," Viv said.

Pavel found that amazing. This woman was young, attractive, blessed with a face and form that could turn heads.

Her lovely chestnut hair reminded him of Natalya's, a melancholy thought.

"What about former boyfriends? Any hard feelings upon breaking up?"

Viv shook her head. "The men I dated were usually so involved with their work that I think they barely noticed I was gone."

Pavel doubted that.

Viv gave him an amused glance and said, "It's true. People are very self-involved in this town."

"What about you, Mr. Roussel?" Pavel asked, turning his attention to the brother. "Have you been involved with anyone who might harbor a grudge over a breakup?"

There was a pause. Vivian Roussel glanced at her brother in a way that Pavel found interesting.

When Marc failed to respond, Pavel asked politely if he could think of any lady who might be angry at him.

"Tell him," Viv suggested with an expression that suggested a few possibilities.

Pavel raised an eyebrow.

"Oh, come on, Viv. They don't hate me," Marc protested. "Marion, Jill, or Lilly would never stoop to something like this."

"All three spent quite a lot of time reviling you when the relationships broke up. But they were all quite nice," she said. "Wonderful women, really."

"They were all a little overwrought at the time," he protested mildly. "Their anger got the better of them."

"Yes. I suppose so."

Pavel's expression remained professional.

Roussel looked distinctly embarrassed. "They're not angry with me anymore," he said. "They've recovered."

"Were they so bitter that they might consider hiring people to inflict punishment on you?"

"No," Marc said. "I can't see them doing that. It's one thing to hate me and another to spend money on hating me.

And they're not the kind of people who would even know where to find someone in that sort of business. Besides, they've all found new boyfriends and they're happy."

"You may underestimate the fury of a woman scorned," Pavel replied.

"It would be out of character for these women to hire people to break into our warehouse or threaten us," Viv said. "I think they've moved on. And I can't believe they pose a danger to us. I always got on well with them. They wouldn't want to harm *me*."

"You're certain of that?" Pavel inquired. "They might just hate you for being part of the Roussel family. In emotional moments, people sometimes fail to make distinctions."

"Believe me, Mr. Federov, I was friends with all of them," Viv said firmly.

"Yes," Marc said. "I know they've spoken to Viv on several occasions. They're not a danger to us."

Pavel nodded and chose not to comment.

"If you're sure that these women wouldn't have wished to harm you, try to think of a reason a business associate would have."

"We really can't," Viv replied. "We've been trying to figure it out ourselves, and we always run into a brick wall."

Pavel wasn't used to this. Generally the clients had a long list of possible suspects all made out and ready for him to investigate. These two must be angels, he thought wryly. And he knew that was a lie. Angels did not exist in business.

Somebody, somewhere wanted something from them. All he had to do was find the who, the what, and the why. How hard would that be?

"I think I'd better begin with the women," he said.

Chapter Seven

Before Pavel left the Old Muscovy, he had asked for and been given a tour of the premises, observed the large collection of Russian artifacts, from polished nineteenth-century silver to early-twentieth-century porcelain to charming paintings, and he concluded that there was nothing that ought to have put the Roussels at risk for kidnapping or worse. It was an upscale shop, but highly specialized, and they didn't have a large inventory of precious stones or any million-dollar items. No, Pavel decided, the motive for the break-in and the rest had to be personal. He would treat it as such. He would also have to see their homes.

His new clients left him with a mixed impression. Marc Roussel was a nice guy, friendly and cooperative, but apparently something of a ladies' man. Vivian was beautiful and alluring, but he wondered if she could be concealing something about her own past. A woman as beautiful as that without a husband or lover? Hard to believe. Then again, with that kind of beauty and a successful business to her credit, she might just scare off a lot of men. She knew her worth, he thought with a smile. She might not want to waste her time on a man who didn't.

Pavel looked over his notes from the meeting with the Roussels as he sat in his office. A sixth sense told him there was something missing, something essential to understanding these people. He drummed his fingers on the top of his desk. What small clue had they given him to make him think this?

Closing his eyes, Pavel thought back on his visit to the Old Muscovy. Russian memorabilia filled the place. Lacquered boxes, porcelain tea services and figurines, silver teaspoons, and elegant enamel work nestled beside the amber necklaces, earrings, and pendants displayed in glass cases. Paintings of the forests, peasants, and aristocracy of old Russia decorated the walls. All to be expected in a shop like that. What was the odd note?

With a start, he remembered. The cats. He saw representations of American cats at strange places in the shop, and not of random cats, but of the breed known as Maine Coon cats.

These had attracted his attention because he first thought the Roussels had acquired porcelain images of the detested Siberian Forest cats, but upon closer inspection he had realized the figurines were not Russian at all. They represented the famous American cats, who were known for their stately bearing and their bravery in confronting their enemies.

Vivian Roussel had a certain elegance, a sensual allure, and a magnificent head of hair. Her brother was a good-looking guy with striking hazel eyes. Both looked like the epitome of WASP America. Could it be that these two belonged to the sept of Maine Coon cats, one of the oldest and most distinguished native breeds in their country?

Warily, Pavel wondered if his clients had gotten themselves in trouble with other werecreatures. If so, he had to tread carefully, for the clans might retaliate if certain boundaries had been crossed. Perhaps he had wandered into an interclan war.

Pavel always preferred to work for humans. They seemed much less complicated than werecats, who always had some drama in the background. That his highly developed senses couldn't detect their true nature could mean that they were

powerful creatures with the ability to block their pheromones, just as he sometimes could.

The friend who had recommended his firm was a werecat. Even that didn't prove the Roussels were, but it pointed
in that direction. He was probably going to uncover something connected with a castoff lover. Werecats were notori-
ous for their affairs, and from Pavel's point of view, personal
animosity always provided a much more vicious motive
than mere business differences. Jilted werecats were dangerous beasts.

Damn, he thought, these two werecats probably hid more
than they revealed, for instance, the reality of their origin.
Naturally they wouldn't admit it to a stranger; nobody
would. But Pavel was willing to bet anything he was right
about them. Apart from the cat totems in their shop, which
would allow another werecat of their sept to connect with
them, there was the matter of their eyes. Vivian's large
amber eyes were not of a shade ever seen in humans. Marc's
hazel eyes were equally distinctive. Only cats possessed
eyes like those.

Chapter Eight

"Gentlemen, we have a couple of new clients," Pavel announced at his staff meeting the next day. "Marc and Vivian Roussel, owners of a shop called the Old Muscovy. Someone broke into their warehouse recently, and a few days later unknown assailants tried to attack them. I interviewed the Roussels yesterday and accepted the case. We will have to install surveillance equipment at their shop and apartments, plant GPS monitors on their vehicles, and assign them codes with which to contact us in an emergency."

"Do they have any ideas about who is doing this?" asked Ivan, his number-two man.

"They claim they don't."

"Do we believe them?"

"Yes, at this time. One more thing, I believe our new clients are brother werecats, of an American breed."

"They're always the worst," Ivan lamented.

"These two seem to be honest and genuinely frightened by their situation. We will do our best to help them."

Vivian couldn't get Pavel Federov out of her mind. Never mind the fact that the man was tall, dark, and handsome. It was something else, those gorgeous green eyes that hinted of depths that she had never encountered before in anyone, human or werecat. He was just the most attractive male she had ever met in person. And she had met lots of good-looking men, having been a model shortly after college.

Those were strange days, Viv thought. "Discovered" when she accompanied a friend to a cattle call for extras in a film, Viv took a chance and called the number on the business card of a woman who had claimed to be a scout for a modeling agency. It turned out to be true, and Viv made a good impression. The agency loved her exotic eyes and beautiful hair, and this chance encounter led to employment for a few years until Viv decided she liked eating more than she liked posing for clothing catalogues or shampoo ads. Werecats prized their independence, and it rankled that her handlers were so inflexible about what she could and could not do. One day when a photographer sniped at her for a two-pound weight gain, Viv put down her foot, said good-bye, and walked out of the studio, never to return.

However, true to her Maine heritage, Viv had prudently invested her significant earnings and decided to go into business with her brother, who had a degree in Russian studies and a great love of Russian art. So that was how Old Muscovy was born.

With the fall of communism and a great influx of Russians into New York, the shop became fashionable with both émigrés and interior decorators, and business prospered. Life was good. Until this.

At Viv's second meeting with Pavel Federov, she listened attentively as he outlined his plans for her protection and Marc's. Their warehouse, shop, and apartments were to be guarded by strategically placed audio and video cameras. These would be monitored by his team, 24/7. In addition to that, their vehicles would be monitored by GPS, and they themselves would be provided with a small device the size of a dime that could be used to call for help in an emergency if they found themselves in trouble away from their home, shop, or vehicle.

"This sounds very comprehensive," Viv said with approval. "You seem to have covered all the bases."

"We try to be thorough," Pavel replied. "But there is one more thing. In view of the attempted carjacking, I would suggest bodyguards. These people failed once, but they may try again. And until we know exactly who they are and what they want, we should make it as difficult as possible."

"Ah, I don't know if I want to go with bodyguards," Marc demurred. "I mean, how will it look to customers if they suddenly see Mr. Muscle hanging around the shop? It might look as if we're expecting trouble. Besides, several shop owners on the block pay for a security guard to make the rounds. He checks all our stores, and he's dependable."

"We try to cultivate a pleasant image," Viv added. "With older clients, we sometimes offer tea while we discuss business. We try to be as gracious as possible. The sudden appearance of bodyguards might make customers think it's dangerous to visit."

"Including large, vicious types who are trying to harm you," Pavel replied.

"Pavel, with all the safeguards you've mentioned, I think you have us covered."

"We will have you under surveillance on video," he pointed out. "We will be able to follow your cars. But if somebody grabs you and throws you into the back of a minivan, it will take time to rescue you. Even *if* you're able to activate the emergency panic button," he said quietly. "Bodyguards will be there on the front line, stopping any aggression."

Viv and Marc glanced at each other.

"My men can be very discreet," Pavel said. "They are trained in all the latest methods of defense, but they can also be as low-key as you wish."

"I don't know if I want someone tagging along with me all the time," Marc said, still looking doubtful.

"It's in your best interest."

Marc shook his head. "I'll agree to all the other measures, but I'll have to think about the idea of a bodyguard."

After Marc stood up, indicating the meeting was at an end, Pavel turned to the sister and said, "Vivian, even if your brother doesn't think a bodyguard is necessary, you, as a woman, are more vulnerable. You told me you were nearly carjacked at night. If they had been successful, we might not even be having this talk."

"Are you trying to frighten me, Pavel?" she asked with a smile.

"I'm trying to make you appreciate the danger you're in. There's a difference."

As Marc went to the front of the store to greet a client, Pavel stood talking with Viv, admiring her beautiful long chestnut hair and her glorious amber eyes rimmed by impossibly long, dark lashes. She was the loveliest woman he'd met in a long time, and there was nothing flirtatious about her. He found that delightful.

When Vivian smiled, she meant it. She didn't seem to need to play games. That, too, reminded him of Natalya, and he remembered bitterly how optimistic and how full of life his fiancée had been before her brutal and chaotic slaughter.

Pavel worried Vivian didn't take her predicament seriously enough, and there was nothing he could do to impose bodyguards on her if she chose not to accept them.

Damn stubborn woman. She had to be a werecat, he decided. Independent to a fault. And if she could hide her true nature so well, she had to be a very high level member of her clan. Only the most skillful werefolk had that power.

She was an attractive mystery Pavel couldn't wait to solve. And she exuded the most delicious scent, he thought, the kind of scent that befuddled a man's brain.

Chapter Nine

St. Petersburg, Russia

"He's coming out of the restaurant. Get ready. The wife is about five paces behind him, talking to an acquaintance." The young man spoke hurriedly into a cell phone headset, communicating with an accomplice across the street. His voice reflected his edginess as he zeroed in on the target.

"Where is his car?" asked his partner on the opposite side of Nevsky Prospeckt with his hand on a Beretta.

"It's about three meters down the street. The driver is stuck behind our guy."

"I'm going in. Tell the others to follow."

As Dimitri Danilov, Hierarch of the Russian Blue werecats and business tycoon, sauntered through the ornate front door of the Novaya Avrora restaurant, accompanied by two bodyguards, three young thugs in identical black leather jackets, black slacks, and dark sunglasses burst out of nearby cars and raced toward him, opening fire before the Hierarch or the bodyguards could even react.

"Bella! I'm hit!" The Hierarch felt something whistle past his ears at first, then sensed a terrible pain, followed by a large patch of blood beginning to stain the front of his light cashmere coat. He staggered and then suddenly collapsed to his knees, dead before he hit the sidewalk.

As people screeched and stampeded back into the shelter of nearby buildings or simply ran as far from the gunshots as they could manage, a striking blond woman sobbed and fought with a man who was holding her back from running out onto the sidewalk to the mortally wounded Hierarch.

"Goddamn you! I pay your salary! Let me go to my husband," she screamed.

As Bella Danilov watched from behind the door, the three gangsters fired several more shots at the bodies on the ground and then jumped into a getaway car that peeled away with tires screeching and horns blaring. Other drivers moved out of the way in fright and saw the gangsters make a dangerous U-turn and head off for parts unknown.

"Oh, Dimitri! *Dorogai!* My life is over, too!"

Bursting out onto the bloodied sidewalk, Bella Danilov threw off her bodyguard and sank, sobbing, to the sidewalk, where her murdered husband lay.

Cradling him in her arms, Bella rocked back and forth, keening a heartbreaking lament as she did, staring with unseeing eyes at the two other corpses beside him, his slain bodyguards.

While her anxious surviving minder used his cell phone to call the police, Bella knelt there wailing and vowing vengeance as several citizens slithered out from the shops where they had taken refuge and discreetly snapped photos with their cell phones, which they hoped to sell to the news services.

"Pavel! Are you there? Pick up the phone!" Vladimir's hand trembled as he punched in his cousin's number and kept glancing up at the TV screen. Horrific images, taken by a German tourist on Nevsky Prospeckt with a video camera, flashed across the screen, while a veteran CNN reporter warned viewers in a hushed voice-over that these pictures were not suitable for children.

"Vlad, it's six a.m.," Pavel said at last. "What's so important?"

"Turn on CNN. Quickly! It's the Hierarch. He's been assassinated."

For a moment, Pavel felt stunned. Then he leaped out of bed and grabbed the remote. "What channel?"

"CNN. Hurry."

The thirty-two-inch flat-panel TV came to life with a revolting shot of the sidewalk in front of the Novaya Avrora restaurant and the three bodies lying there, with a sobbing woman cradling one of them in her arms and wailing.

"Shit! They murdered him. That's what the shaman's message foretold. The leader stumbles."

"Who do you think is behind it?"

"Any number of people, starting with jealous clansmen and leading all the way up to the higher echelons of business and politics," Pavel replied. "Anyone that rich and that successful attracts powerful enemies."

"What a disaster for the clan," Vladimir lamented. "Dimitri Danilov was the best Hierarch in a long time. A man of talent and vision."

Pavel nodded. "Yes. I wonder if his brother will take over now. He'd be the direct successor."

"There might be some opposition to Boris as Hierarch. He's not as gifted as his brother. Or as popular."

"But he's the same blood, and in the midst of a disaster like this, I think the brethren will be swayed by the desire for continuity."

Vladimir sighed. "We can't even attend the funeral. The twelve-hour rule won't give us enough time to get over there and get to the cemetery. He was killed several hours ago. It will take time to get plane tickets, fly to St. Petersburg—hoping we don't encounter delays—get to a hotel, and reach the cemetery in time."

"I know. But of course, they can't postpone the burial."

Both werecats understood the custom and the necessity

for it. If a werecat was not interred within twelve hours of death, the body would change from human to cat form, thereby shocking any viewers who expected to pay their respects to a man or woman they knew as a fellow human. For the good of the brethren, werecats' bodies went to special morticians familiar with the requirements. Memorial services followed the next day with a closed coffin, and the burial took place quickly. Secrecy was paramount in these matters.

"Bella had better luck than her husband," Pavel commented thoughtfully. "Three men gunned down on the main boulevard of St. Petersburg, and she escapes death."

"The news said she paused to speak to a friend when the Hierarch and the guards exited the restaurant. Then her bodyguard grabbed her at the first sounds of gunfire and prevented her from rushing to her husband."

"Saved by a stroke of fate," Pavel replied. "She's a very fortunate woman."

"Well, I think that puts an end to Bella Danilov's interference in the affairs of the Russian Blue werecats. Ambitious as she is, no member of a foreign clan could ever take over the leadership."

"True," Pavel agreed. "But I still don't think it's the last we've heard of the lady."

"I hope you're wrong," said Vlad. "She's a Siberian. What role could she possibly play in our clan now?"

Pavel didn't know. But that didn't mean he felt she was out of the picture either.

"You're right," he agreed. "I'm too cynical for my own good."

Chapter Ten

After a few weeks of calm had passed, Viv relaxed a little and began to think that perhaps she and Marc had been a victim of a bizarre set of circumstances. It was a bit much altogether, but maybe there was no real plot against her and her brother. She really wanted to believe that. And Pavel Federov made her feel secure with all the high-tech surveillance equipment.

Everything connected with the recent string of events had been so bizarre. Viv was also glad she hadn't heard from the Leader. Perhaps he was too busy with his mistress to get back to her. Or maybe he was scouting some other werecat female with good genes. She hoped so. John Sinclair was just too controlling for her.

Marc sat talking in the back of the shop with a customer who wanted to order a porcelain tea service, while Viv stood at the window looking out onto the street. All was peaceful.

The usual Upper East Side passersby sauntered along the sidewalk: young mothers with stylish baby carriages and nice coats, young men with jeans and peacoats and long mufflers. October brought out the wool coats and gloves. Down the street a vendor already had his pretzel stand hot and ready, while a radio announcer had just warned of temperatures dropping to the midthirties tonight.

Viv wore a soft cashmere sweater dress with a low-slung

belt and a trendy pair of high-heeled Italian boots. The rust-colored dress brought out the chestnut tones in her long hair and flattered the amber in her eyes.

"Ah," she exclaimed. Coming down the street was Hank, Marc's buddy from the association, the one who'd driven her home the night she was threatened.

She buzzed him in as he stopped at their front door and greeted her with a wide smile.

"Viv," he exclaimed with pleasure as he opened the door and stepped inside. "You look beautiful. You know, I was worried about you, so I just had to come down here to see if you were okay."

"That's so thoughtful," she said with a smile. "But it's really not necessary. Nothing has happened since that night."

"Well, good," he said. "How's Marc? Everything okay with him, too?"

"Couldn't be better. He's in the back, talking with a client. Would you like to see him when he's done?"

Hank looked into her eyes and smiled. "He's not the reason I stopped by."

Viv appeared taken by surprise. The ink on Hank's divorce papers was barely dry, and he was giving her the look he used on every pretty woman. The kind of look a kid had when he saw a display of candy. Red males were all like that, she recalled. Marc was a prime example, she thought in amusement.

"Would you like to see the new musical that just opened at the Winter Garden?" he asked.

"Yes. But how would you get tickets? One of my friends tried, and they told her the first available seats were for March."

"Not if you have the right connections," Hank said with a gleam in his eye. "Two orchestra seats for Saturday night," he declared proudly. "With dinner to follow."

Viv hesitated. She really did want to see this musical,

which was the hottest thing on Broadway, but she wasn't certain that going there with Hank would be a good idea. He appeared so eager to get out and play the field after his acrimonious divorce from Brenda that she wondered if it might be a bit too soon.

From sad experience, Viv knew that male werecats had hormonal issues at times like these, and she didn't want to get entangled in a minefield of bruised male ego. On the other hand, maybe Hank would turn out to be different from what she expected. He had come to her rescue, and he seemed genuinely concerned for her safety. Marc always spoke highly of him. And if they clicked, she might find a mate who would be more congenial than her snobbish Leader.

With a few misgivings, Viv said, "Thank you. That sounds lovely."

"You know, if you take the bus into Manhattan, I'll pick you up here and take you to the theater. Then after dinner, I'll drive you home. We won't need two cars."

"Or I could drive in, leave my car at the parking garage, meet you at the theater, have dinner, and you could take me back to the garage so I could drive home."

That way, she would have control over the situation and not leave Hank too many loopholes. That worked.

"Really, Viv, with what's been happening, I'd feel more comfortable driving you back to Jersey. I'd worry about you going home by yourself late at night."

"I have a security specialist who fitted the car with a GPS device. In it, I'm under their watchful eye. It's actually safer."

"But you'd still be alone. You're better off with a male in the car."

Well, maybe Hank had a point, Viv thought. He wasn't leering. He seemed concerned. She didn't want to drive home after midnight by herself if she didn't have to, especially not right now.

"All right," she agreed. "Pick me up here at five o'clock when we close. We could have dinner before the show."

"Fine," he said. "That works, too."

"It was nice of you to think of me," she said.

"Viv, if you only knew how often I think of you," he said with a smile.

Oh, she thought. This would be interesting.

Chapter Eleven

"Vivian, it's Pavel. Just checking to see if all is well."

"Everything's fine," she said. "No trouble anywhere. In fact it's a lovely day."

"Glad to hear it."

This was not like Pavel to call clients in the middle of the day to chitchat, but Vivian brought out something in him that even he didn't understand. Normally he viewed customers as people who merited the very best service he could provide, but he believed in keeping a professional distance. Since he had met Vivian Roussel, he found himself thinking of her in ways that were not work-related, and this troubled him; but it didn't prevent him from making the phone call. He was fascinated by the idea that she might be one of his own kind.

"My monitors indicate no suspicious activity near your homes or your shop," he said. "Your brother is in the warehouse right now. He's inspecting the stock."

"Oh, yes. He said he wanted to check on things."

"He doesn't have to be anxious now. The video monitor is giving us a good picture, so you don't have to worry," Pavel assured her.

"I'm glad to hear it. We actually feel quite safe since we signed up with you."

"Good. But don't relax your guard," he said. "We still

haven't discovered who's behind your recent problems, but we will."

There was a slight pause on the other end. Then Viv said, "If you'd like to stop by and keep us updated, that would be fine. We're here every day but Sunday."

Pavel smiled. "You know, I think that would be a good idea." He was tempted to ask, "Are you doing anything after work today?" but it was a Saturday and he knew women took it badly if men asked them out on such short notice. Even though Vivian had told him she wasn't dating anyone, he didn't want to give the impression that he thought he could just call up and arrange a meeting like that. She would feel insulted.

Sometimes Pavel secretly read the American women's magazines to try to gain a better understanding of female psychology, and they all gave the same message: "Never lower yourself to accept a date for the same evening. Only a woman with severe self-esteem issues would do that." This beautiful woman didn't have any of those.

Instead, he said, "Could you pencil me into your appointment calendar for a Monday meeting? Perhaps we could discuss whatever we've learned over lunch."

That was the kind of thing a professional woman could accept: concern for the progress of a mutual endeavor. Nobody could fault him for that. It was modern and enlightened. *Dear God,* Pavel thought. It sounded like such a blatant ploy; she would see through him as if he were wrapped in cellophane.

He could swear Viv's voice had a smile in it when she said, "Mondays are usually slow. I'm sure I can get away for an hour, and you could tell me what's going on so far. Why don't you call me around ten o'clock Monday morning, and I can let you know the best time for lunch? How is that?"

"Yes," he agreed. "Sounds fine. I'll call you then."

"See you Monday," she said with a trace of genuine warmth in her voice. She sounded delighted.

Pavel was smiling. No, he wasn't smiling. He was grinning. He hadn't felt so happy in a long time, and it felt wonderful.

Why he should feel so damned pleased was a mystery, but he knew it was due to his desire to spend time with Vivian Roussel. That woman possessed something beyond the usual sort of feminine charms. It was something deeper than beauty, something that resonated in his soul.

He barely knew her and he found her incredibly enticing. What might it deepen into if he really connected with her? Pavel wasn't a creature who loved the superficial; he wanted to find his soul mate. If he was very lucky, this gorgeous woman might turn out to be the one.

Or, he thought gloomily, perhaps he was reacting mindlessly to the first woman who managed to push his buttons since he had lost Natalya.

Whatever inspired this frame of mind ought to be explored, he decided. He did not want to spend the rest of his life pursuing trivial affairs. He wanted a family, a home, and a real purpose in life once again. Maybe—if he was extremely fortunate—this chestnut-haired beauty with the lovely amber eyes might prove to be what he needed.

Pavel felt duty-bound to find out. The fact she probably belonged to a prestigious clan of American werecats was an impediment—but not one he wished to dwell on at the moment. His hormones were telling him things his brain didn't want to know.

When Marc returned to the shop, Viv nearly didn't hear him come in. She gave a start when she realized there was somebody in the back.

"Marc?"

"Yes."

"Oh! How did you get in without me seeing you?"

"The back door," he explained. "I glanced in the window, didn't see you, and wanted to know if everything was okay."

"You went round the back to sneak up on a possible intruder? Are you out of your mind?"

"I guess I just got carried away. Anyway, they have the place under surveillance, so I guess we're safe." Her brother gave her a grin. "I went to the warehouse to bring back another piece to go with the ormolu vases in case the client who asked about them wants the whole set. It might give him an idea."

"Good. Sometimes that works. Oh," she said as an afterthought, "I'm going to dinner and the theater tonight with Hank."

Marc reacted as if he didn't quite believe what he'd just heard. "Hank? The guy you once referred to as Mr. Studcat?"

"One and the same."

"Are you feeling well? I mean, I think he's great, but that's because we do guy things together. . . ."

"Like chase women, drink too much, and go to baseball games in a group with other studcats."

"That just about sums it up."

"Well, he asked me to a musical I'm dying to see, and since he was concerned enough to escort me home the night of the meeting, perhaps there's more to him than his 'cat on the prowl' persona."

Marc gave a laugh that was loaded with wicked undertones. "You and Hank. Damn, I never would have thought it."

Viv gave him an uncompromising stare. "Calm down. This is one evening. I'll go out with Hank to see if this is something I could pursue. Or not."

"Sure. And you said you never date divorced men."

"Oh, come on! He was concerned about me, and now he's asked me out. Don't start ordering the wedding invitations. It's just a first date."

"Whatever you say. You're a grown-up. You have a right to be happy." Marc was grinning with delight at the hope that she might actually end up with an old buddy of his. Viv knew he could picture them all hosting Super Bowl parties together, heading up to Vermont for skiing, buying season tickets for baseball games together. Just the kinds of things a good brother-in-law would want to do. Werecat males loved sporting events and were often good amateur athletes themselves. Marc had run track in college.

Of course, first she would have to marry Hank and develop a passion for sports. But, stranger things had happened.

"Did you drive in today?"

"No, I took the bus. Hank's going to pick me up later. He'll take me home."

"Well, good work, Viv. I always knew you two would click one day."

"Marc! You're really getting ahead of yourself. You've always told me Hank is a great guy, so now I'm going to find out. End of story."

"It's still a good move." He smiled. "I wonder what the Leader would think about it. Sounds like he has his eye on you, too."

Something like annoyance flickered over her face for a second. "He should remember the rule about females having free choice over mates," she said. "It's one I take very seriously, and I mean it. No male will ever force me into a marriage I don't want."

Marc nodded. Then he said, "I just want you to be happy, Viv. You pick whoever you want and I'll back you up. Just don't go out of your way to bust Sinclair's balls."

"I won't rub his nose in it," Viv said quietly. "But it will be my choice, and he'd better get used to it or he'll find out who he's dealing with."

Chapter Twelve

Viv knew things weren't going the way she planned when Hank told her over drinks that he'd been crazy about her since they were in high school. Not what she wanted to hear since Brenda, his former wife, had worn his ring since sophomore year.

"Oh, you had so many girls running after you, I doubt you noticed me."

"Sure, I did. I was dying to see you shape-shift. Man, I used to fantasize about that: what you'd look like au naturel. Would you be one of those cute calicos or maybe a brown-and-white tabby? Or even a blonde?"

"Silver tabby," she replied as she lifted a glass of wine to her lips.

"I know," he said with a wicked smile. "I saw you."

Viv nearly rose from her seat. "When?"

"When you were at summer camp with my cousin. I hid and watched you shape-shift. I thought that was the sexiest thing ever. Man, all that pretty silver fur. And those cute little white boots. My tongue was hanging out."

"You Peeping Tom!" she exclaimed. "That's disgusting."

"Teenage hormones, babe," he said with a grin. "Couldn't help myself."

Damn it, Vivian, you let your guard down for once in your life and you end up with this . . . studcat. No wonder Brenda dumped him. She took a deep sip of wine and glanced at her watch. It was going to be a long evening. Teenage werecat voyeur!

"Well, count yourself lucky," she said. "That was your first and last glimpse of the real me."

"Sure," he said with a wink. "Whatever you say."

Despite Hank's presence, the play was fantastic. She decided to take it as a reward for putting up with him. He strutted as they headed back to the parking garage, pleased that he'd scored a coup with the tickets. Now he had further plans.

"Let's go to a club I know down in SoHo. It's too early to call it a night."

"No, I'm really tired. I loved the play, but I'm falling asleep."

Viv could hear the clicking of her heels on the concrete floor of the garage as she hurried to Hank's car. She always hated entering these places at night, with or without an escort, especially now. Glancing nervously around as Hank strolled beside her, Viv felt the small pendant around her neck and liked the security it provided.

"You just want to go home?" he asked in disbelief.

"Yes. I'm exhausted."

Viv heard the click of the remote. Hank opened her door and watched her seat herself before he closed it and went around to his side. "Okay," he said. "Back to New Jersey. But I think you're making a mistake. We could have a good time here tonight."

At about the same time Hank's silver Lexus pulled out of its space, a black Mercedes did the same. It paused, then followed them down the lane, onto the exit ramp, and waited behind them as Hank handed in his ticket to the man at the booth. Viv glanced in her side-view mirror, saw the car, and thought nothing of it. Lots of cars were leaving New York at this time.

"I wonder how the bridge traffic is right now," Viv said.

"Put on the radio. They'll probably have an update."

As they drove in and out of traffic, heading for the Henry Hudson Parkway and the George Washington Bridge, Viv caught a glimpse of the Mercedes that had been behind them before.

Her heart skipped a beat. It was the same one. With the same two men in dark coats.

"I think we're being followed," she said.

"And what makes you think that?"

"Because the men who were in line behind us at the garage are behind us again."

"Probably a coincidence. How many people do you think are heading across the Hudson right now? Thousands. And sometimes they take the same path."

"This is true." She tried to sound convinced.

Hank drove silently now, but it was an uncomfortable silence. Viv could see him glancing furtively in the rearview mirror.

"Are they still there?" she asked.

"Yes."

"Try changing lanes," she advised.

"Okay."

He put on the directional and moved into the fast lane. So did the Mercedes.

"This is feeling a little strange," Hank said. "Have you and Marc gotten yourselves into anything that might draw the wrong kind of attention?"

"If you mean illegal, no," Viv replied. "We run an honest business."

"Then why are two guys tailing us?" Hank seemed worried now. His face lost its usual smile; he glanced back into the mirror from time to time, swearing as he observed the Mercedes behind him, staying doggedly with him.

"I'm going to alert our security service," Viv said as they

headed across the George Washington Bridge. "With any luck they can meet us when we arrive home."

"Call 'em now," Hank said with a shrug. "Our friends in the Mercedes are sticking to us like glue."

Viv pressed the button on her pendant and activated a light. "Hello, Miss Roussel," a voice said. "How can we help you?"

"I'm in a car heading for the GW, and there's another car behind me that's been with me since I left the parking garage in the city. It looks suspicious."

"We have you on our screen. What is your destination?"

"My apartment building in Fort Lee. There's a twenty-four-hour concierge in the lobby. I'll be safe once I arrive home."

"You're not driving your own car, are you?"

"No. I'm with a friend. I'm using my security pendant in his car."

"We have your address. We'll have a man sent to your apartment to meet your when you get there."

"I'm almost home," she said nervously.

"We're very quick," the voice replied.

"That's really high-tech," Hank said in admiration after Viv terminated her conversation. "Do you think they'll be waiting for us when we get there?"

"I hope so," she said. "Rather than those men in back of us. Whoever they are," she added.

This evening she had hoped to enjoy was beginning to look like a nightmare.

Chapter Thirteen

While Vivian was out with Hank, Marc Roussel drove his car back to the parking garage of his Upper East Side town house, gingerly removed a covered, medium-sized rectangular object from the trunk, buzzed himself through the security door, and took the elevator upstairs to his foyer. His heart thumped each step of the way, setting his nerves on edge, making him sweat even though it was the middle of October and the temperature had lingered at fifty-eight degrees all day.

When he told Viv earlier he was going to the warehouse, he was telling the truth, but he hadn't yet made his discovery. Once inside the storage depot, Marc had begun to go through each object in the place, searching for anything that could have triggered the persecution they were now experiencing. What the hell did they have? He was convinced it had to be spectacular, yet to the best of his knowledge, they had purchased nothing so extraordinary that men would hunt them for it. Maybe someone else knew something they didn't. It wasn't a feeling that gave him any comfort, so he drove to the warehouse, determined to inspect everything, even if it took days.

After three hours, Marc lifted a seventeenth-century mirror and gave a start. He didn't remember purchasing this. It was almost hidden behind a larger mirror, and when he examined it, he noticed something odd. On the reverse, almost as if it had been superimposed on the original backing, was a second backing. This was extremely strange. Why would it require two?

Marc was surprised and a little nervous. His first thoughts involved the smuggling of controlled substances. Had somebody placed a box behind the mirror and filled the interior with contraband drugs? Maybe he had a million dollars' worth of coke inside this thing. That would explain all the weird attacks. Somebody had stashed their haul in his warehouse somehow, and they wanted the goods back. Shit!

Gingerly, he examined the mirror and its gilded frame, looking carefully for any traces of white powder. Nothing. Then he felt all around the back of the mirror. Solid wood. Puzzled, Marc then turned his attention to the second backing, carefully feeling the edges with his fingers. What he found startled him.

"Can't be," he murmured. "Not possible."

Torn between growing fear and unbearable curiosity, the antiquarian sat down and popped out the top strip of the second backing until he got a better look at what lay inside. It looked like wood.

"This is like one of those matryoshka dolls," he muttered. Layer upon layer of hidden surprises. Then, frustrated by the task of getting out the piece of wood, Marc lifted the mirror upside down and began to shake it gently. Glints of gold shone in the dim light as the hidden panel within slowly revealed itself, hinting at sublime beauty. When he saw what he had in his hands, Marc trembled with awe and dread.

I'm dead, he thought. *It's all over. These guys—whoever they are—have got to be from the Russian mob. They'll kill us both.*

When he could stop shaking, Marc gingerly slid the painting back inside its hiding place. With his heart pounding, he took the "mirror" and a candelabrum, loaded them into his car and drove off.

As he headed home, plunged into gloom, he realized all his moves must have been recorded on the new video monitors. Marc just hoped his actions had been hidden by the large armoire next to the chair he sat in while he inspected the work. Why hadn't he thought of the damned cameras before? Oh, he was fucked. He had to get hold of Viv and tell her not to go home tonight, to go to a hotel until they could decide how to handle this. The whole thing was too much for them, probably too much for their new security team as well. Hell, maybe those guys were part of the plot? Who could tell? They were Russians, foreigners. Maybe even part of the mob. He hadn't located the source of the trouble until Metro Investigations had gone into the warehouse and wired it. But they only went in because of the earlier break-in and the attempted kidnappings.

Marc's mind was racing so fast, he felt almost irrational. Why did he have to get involved with Russian antiques? he wondered. He could have done something else, maybe gotten a job with the State Department, with some start-up company doing business with the new Russia, anything but this. And Viv was in danger, too. Things couldn't get any worse than this.

When he entered his town house, Marc turned off his alarm, then reset it, placed the mirror and its concealed treasure on a table, and took out his cell phone, punching in his sister's number. Nothing. Her phone was probably turned off since she and Hank were going to the theater.

Trying hard to sound as normal as possible, Marc left a voice mail message instructing her not to return to her apartment but to go to a hotel in Manhattan and call him when she checked in. Something had come up, and it was of the utmost importance *not* to go home.

He hoped she would listen to him.

Chapter Fourteen

"Do you really think your guys will be waiting when we get to your apartment?" Hank asked as he drove nervously while glancing into the rearview mirror. "Whoever's following us is not letting up. I've changed lanes. He keeps pace with me. Are you sure you're not mixed up in something weird?"

"This is the only weird thing *I* know about," Viv replied. "Marc and I are honest. We haven't cheated anybody, and we haven't played fast and loose with the law. I can't imagine why these people are trying to scare us."

"Do you think it's the mob?" he asked seriously.

"Why should the mob want anything from us? That's crazy."

"Well, who else? The feds?"

Viv shook her head as Hank left the bridge and turned into the local lanes, heading for her apartment. She prayed Pavel Federov's men would be there, although she didn't see how they could get there soon enough to be of help right now. Maybe if she and Hank drove straight into the parking garage beneath her apartment complex, they would be safe. Then again, the Mercedes might just do the same.

"Hank, I'm so sorry I got you involved in this. They want me, not you."

"Well, they aren't getting you," he said.

Viv could have kissed him. Despite all the studcat nonsense, Hank was a stand-up guy who wasn't going to fail to protect her. She was grateful for that, even if she did feel horribly guilty for putting him at risk just for being in her company.

When the Lexus entered the parking garage, the Mercedes did the same. Hank drove slowly down the rows of cars, ostensibly looking for a space. When his pursuers slowed behind him at a corner, he put the pedal to the floor and the Lexus shot forward straight out the exit and unfortunately into the side of another vehicle.

Air bags inflated, Viv screamed, and Hank was momentarily incapacitated. Suddenly doors flew open, men with guns appeared and screamed commands at them, and strong hands grabbed Viv and pulled her from the car.

Reeling from the shock of the crash, Viv staggered as she tried to stand up and fight off her attackers. On the other side, Hank jumped out of the car and attempted to tackle the kidnappers, but to Viv's horror, one of the thugs raised a handgun, fired three times, and sent Hank sprawling on the driveway, blood spattering his cashmere overcoat.

"Oh, my God! No!"

Viv shrieked in fear as she watched him try to crawl toward his assailant and grab him. The man turned back to his victim and fired again, putting an end to Hank's efforts.

"Cold-blooded cowards!" she screamed as a stocky character in a sweater and stocking cap took hold of her as she fought back, kicking and punching as best she could.

"Shit, lady! Behave yourself or I'll have to beat you down!"

By way of response, Viv doubled over and sank her teeth into his hand, eliciting a scream and a string of curse words from her abductor. He raised his hand and backhanded her viciously, sending her staggering across the driveway, straight into the arms of his partner.

"Come on! Let's get out of here. Somebody must have called the cops by now. Move it!"

Unseen helpers jumped into the vehicle that had blocked

their escape, taking off with a screech of tires, while two men dragged Viv toward the Mercedes, threw her into the trunk, and roared out of there like they were on fire. In the light of the driveway, a body lay inert, blood puddling around it—Hank, gunned down by Viv's kidnappers.

Frightened and desperate in the trunk of the car, Viv pressed the security device around her neck and spoke frantically into the receiver telling Metro their men never showed up and she was now being kidnapped in the trunk of a black Mercedes.

"We have you on the screen," the voice responded. "You're on Route Four."

"Get me out of this trunk," she whispered frantically, "before these two men kill me. I think they just murdered my friend. They shot him several times and he didn't get up. Help me!"

"Our men just missed you at your apartment. They are now in pursuit," the dispatcher told her with professional composure. "Try to remain calm."

Viv closed her eyes and had to work hard to remain focused. "Remain calm." Yes. Right now she didn't dare do anything else if she wanted to survive, but she felt raw fear tearing at her entrails as she curled into a fetal position and rocked back and forth with sheer frustration. Hank was probably dead because of her, and she shouldn't even have accepted the invitation that had cost him his life. And now she was at the mercy of men who might kill *her*. Why? This violence didn't make any sense. Had they confused her with someone else?

And, as her sharp senses became aware of the odors in the car, she noted with shock that she could detect the scent of a werecat, maybe more than one. The males who had abducted her must be werefolk.

The idea of being manhandled so disrespectfully by another werecat really stunned her. These bastards couldn't be from her own clan. And yet whom could she have angered enough to do this to her?

"We've never lost a client yet," the dispatcher said, and there was sympathy and compassion in his voice. "We're not going to start now."

"Please," she said through clenched teeth. "Just get me out of here before they park the car and kill me! I'm really frightened."

"Viv, if your phone is on, call me."

Marc listened, swore, and pressed END once more. Damn, she was out of contact, wherever she was. Hank wasn't responding to his phone either, and that was odd because the guy was always tuned in.

There had to be a good reason he couldn't reach them. They were probably still in the theater.

The more Marc thought about the possibilities, the more convinced he was of doom. The only thing to do was call Metro Investigations and see if they had Viv in their sights. They had all that high-tech equipment. They could find her.

When he got the call center, Marc was astonished to hear where they located her—in the trunk of a Mercedes heading down Route Four.

For a second he couldn't believe he had heard them correctly. Then he recovered and asked in a tight voice, "Is my sister all right? Do you even know if she's alive?"

"Mr. Roussel, I'm going to pass you over to Mr. Federov. Please stay on the line."

As Marc collapsed into a chair, his mind in chaos, he heard a click and then: "Mr. Roussel, Federov here. We have an ongoing abduction in progress. The gentleman who drove your sister home to her apartment has been shot and Vivian has been kidnapped. We're tracking the car right now."

Marc felt so disoriented he could barely think rationally. Hank had been shot. Was he going to survive? Who would want to harm *him*? Or Viv?

"How are you tracking them?" Marc asked when he regained his composure.

"GPS. Vivian has a pendant with a microchip. She's been in contact with us."

"That means she's still alive."

"Yes. She spoke with the call center. She's scared but otherwise unharmed."

"How long will that last? I mean when they get to wherever they're going . . ."

"We'll be right behind them," Pavel said quietly. "I've alerted our special-action team about the kidnapping, and they're on their way. Three SUVs are tracking her. Would you like the police brought into this?"

"No. Not as long as you can get Viv back yourself." Marc shook his head as he stared at the telephone. He couldn't believe this was happening. If Metro couldn't cut it, then fuck the Leader and call the cops. But he had to give them a chance first.

"I have to be there," he said. "Viv's my only sister."

"I would advise you to stay where you are, Mr. Roussel. We don't know if they have others waiting to abduct you, too."

"Then send one of your guys to come get me so I can join you in New Jersey. Your men have weapons permits, right?"

"Yes."

"Then I'll be fine. Just get me over there."

He thought he heard the sound of a sigh. Then Pavel said, "All right. My man Ivan will be at your town house in fifteen minutes. He'll give you the password "gulfstream" to identify himself. Be ready."

"Don't worry."

These things didn't happen to people like him and Viv. It was madness. But flustered as he was, Marc did one final thing before he got ready to leave home and rush across the Hudson to find his sister. He pulled down the folding attic stairs, went up to the attic with the treasure from the warehouse and stashed it behind some boxes. Then he nervously tossed a cloth cover over it and went to the foyer to wait for Ivan.

Chapter Fifteen

Inside the trunk of the Mercedes, Viv struggled to keep calm and tried to gauge her chances of survival. She was convinced the kidnappers were werecats since their pheromones gave them away. That meant she was dealing with another clan, obviously hostile to her own, or merely angry with her. She was certain she had no personal enemies who would want to harm her. The antiques crowd was more likely to use their tongues as weapons rather than hire thugs to settle scores; besides, the only other antiquarians she knew were humans.

Vivian tried hard to concentrate on something that might be useful. She knew most cars had a device that would allow you to pop the trunk from the inside, but because they were traveling at perhaps eighty miles an hour on one of the busiest highways in the area, she wasn't going to attempt using it right now. Too dangerous. Besides, everything was dark and she wasn't even sure if she could locate the mechanism.

There was only one option open to her, she felt, and that was the ultimate life-in-danger-pull-out-all-the-stops last resort. It might briefly confuse her abductors, but it would also pose problems for her rescuers, if there were any. And if Pavel Federov was as good as his reputation, he would have his whole staff working overtime on this one.

*   *   *

Pavel's worst nightmare was the classic hostage situation with crazed gunmen threatening vulnerable captives. If you couldn't neutralize the enemy, they might kill their victims, but in a rescue attempt, overzealous action might precipitate a disaster. This was what had happened in Moscow at the time of the theater takeover by terrorist gunmen, and Pavel had lost Natalya, the love of his life.

Now he himself was about to relive that grim night on a different continent, with a client he cared about far more than he ought to.

Pavel turned to his driver as they sped down the highway after the Mercedes. "I wish she had agreed to a bodyguard."

"So do I. It would have made things a lot easier."

Viv tried very hard to remember every lesson in survival she had ever learned. Her grandfather had told her things she tried to recall now as she lay on the floor of a car trunk, headed toward an unknown and frightening destination. The surreal quality of her situation almost disoriented her.

At that moment, Viv felt a change in the movement of the car. They were slowing down. She felt a gentle bump as the vehicle went onto another kind of driving surface and seemed to glide toward a nearby destination. They had arrived.

She concentrated very hard, erasing the sounds coming from the outside, thinking only of what she had to do. "Give me the power," she murmured. "Make me strong."

A few minutes later, the driver parked the car in the driveway of a house on a residential street, opened the door, and got out, followed by his accomplice. Both men were armed and ready to deal with any outburst as they approached the trunk.

"Go ahead," said the driver. "Let her out."

With a glance at his partner, the second man clicked the

remote and lifted the trunk door. In disbelief he stared first
at the empty trunk, then at his partner.

"She's not there," he stammered. In the darkness, all he
could see was a kind of fur rug. No woman.

As the two men wondered aloud what had happened to
their passenger, arguing with each other about her disappearance, the pile of fur began to stir. Around the corner, the
first signs of flashing lights approached.

Suddenly the driver screamed in terror as a large, shaggy
cat the size of a puma leaped out of the trunk straight at him,
knocked him to the ground, and tore his throat out. Dumbfounded, his partner lost control of his bladder, changed into
a long-haired cat the size of a bobcat, and began running
down the driveway, turning back to see the animal finish
with his partner and pause before heading straight toward
him.

Frightened out of his wits, the werecat ran as fast as he
could, stumbling in the dark, colliding with a lawn ornament
as he scurried away like a frantic crab, trying to outrun whatever was after him. The female was a fuckin' weretiger,
maybe a werelion, he thought in the grip of hysteria. She
was huge. And they hadn't even realized she was one of
them. Why couldn't he get her scent? He lost his balance
when he collided with a row of brick pavers and fell across
the drive and under the shaggy paws of his pursuer.

Terrified feline screams ripped through the dark autumn
night as the beast seized his throat and shook him like a rat,
tearing a hole in his neck, biting the jugular, chomping down
several times to make sure the prey was dead.

When the cat lay still, the larger furry cat with a magnificent plumed tail and white paws watched him for any sign
of life. Satisfied that he was no longer a threat, the animal
turned around and walked slowly up the driveway and
around the back of the house. If any further attackers arrived, she had to be ready.

                       *   *   *

Sounds of three high-powered vehicles roared into the area, followed by Pavel in one car and Marc and Ivan trailing in another. The special-action team pulled up and quickly blocked the entrance to the driveway while the others took up positions and immediately noticed something lying across the far end of the long drive: a body dressed in a black coat with a dark stream of liquid emerging from beneath it.

"Get the lights over here," called the man in charge. "I think we have a fatality."

"Male or female?"

"Male."

"Holy shit! Look at the damage. Whoever got him tore him up good. His throat's been ripped out."

While two men examined the bleeding corpse at their feet, two others headed down the drive, where a smaller form lay on the grass.

"One more up here. He's dead. He hasn't got a throat anymore. And he's a big cat."

While the team fanned out around the back of the house, Marc arrived right behind Pavel, shocked at the sight in the driveway.

Werecats, he thought nervously as he looked at the two corpses. *The first one didn't have time to shape-shift.*

"There's nobody in the car. We found it with the trunk open. We searched it after we found these two with their throats ripped out."

Marc looked pasty in the blinding light of the car headlights. He glanced quickly at the corpses and then averted his eyes. "We have to find Viv," he said.

"Stay right here, Mr. Roussel," Pavel's driver directed. "We're going to look for your sister. You get back in the car. We have weapons in case the kidnappers had help."

"Then give me one," he said. "I'm a hunter. I know how to shoot, and I can help you if you need an extra hand."

Pavel turned to his driver. "If our client escaped from her

captors, she might be hiding in the backyard. It's dark. She could be trying to take shelter behind trees or behind some shrubs. Warn the men. After what she's been through, I wouldn't want her to get shot by our side."

Nodding, he called out, "Vivian Roussel, if you are in the area, make yourself known. My team is on the premises. The kidnappers are dead. We want you to show yourself if you are able. Just tell us if you cannot walk."

Pavel started to approach the entrance of the house. As he did, he heard a soft voice calling his name. Glancing down, he saw her. Viv was half concealed, kneeling behind a shrub, seemingly in shock. She stared at him, dazed. Her clothing looked ragged from the struggle.

"Are you all right?" he asked as he ran to her and helped her to her feet. "Marc," he called over his shoulder, "your sister is here. She's alive."

"Viv? Are you okay?" Marc pushed his way past the special-action squad. "Did they hurt you? Are you really all right?"

"I think Hank is dead," she said before she sank into Pavel's arms and passed out.

Chapter Sixteen

Marc remained at Viv's side as Pavel tried to question her about her kidnapping and the presence of other werecats in the area. Still dazed by the ordeal, she told him she and a friend had gone to the theater in New York, noticed a car following them all the way home, and then fallen prey to the kidnappers in a blocked driveway. She had no recollection of an animal of any kind. And she had no idea why there were two dead bodies in the driveway of this house, which she had never seen before.

"Mr. Federov, my sister is overwhelmed by her ordeal. I'm sure she would agree to questioning in a day or so, but right now I think she needs to see a doctor."

Everyone looked quite harsh in the bright light of the headlights. Pavel saw the futility of getting any useful information out of this traumatized woman, so he turned to Marc and said, "Fine. But she has to answer some questions in a day or so. I know she's the victim here, but we have to get to the bottom of it."

"Of course. And Metro will have to guard her so nobody else can get to her," Marc said. He looked at Pavel. "I'll take her home with me. We'll call her doctor and help her calm down so you can question her."

"Sure," Pavel said. "But she's pretty shaken up right now. It may take a few days."

When Viv was in the car with Marc and Pavel, she said, "Did Hank survive?"

"My men arrived just after the attack. They called the doctor whose name appeared on a medical bracelet he wore. He met them at a local hospital."

"But did he survive?"

"The last report by my man said he was still in surgery."

A sigh floated out as Viv sank back against the leather seat of Pavel's car. "Then he's alive."

"Just barely. They said he lost a lot of blood."

"I have to see him," Viv said.

Marc turned around from the passenger seat and stared at his sister. "I don't think you're in any condition to do that right now. You ought to have a doctor look at you."

"I was driven around in a trunk, but I wasn't shot. If Hank hadn't been with me tonight, he wouldn't be in the hospital right now. I have to see him. You know it's important. I can help him."

"There will be doctors and nurses there," Pavel said. "He'll be unconscious after the operation and he won't even know you're there."

"It doesn't matter," she said. "If he's alive, I can still help him."

Marc looked back at her. "I'll go see him. I think you should go home."

"Mr. Federov, take us to the hospital. It's important. You can guard me there as well as any other place."

"Then if you see your friend, will you go home?"

"Yes."

"Okay. We're on our way."

At the hospital, they found Brenda, Hank's ex-wife, who was sitting vigil beside his bed. She had been crying, and her eyes were red and blotchy when she spotted Viv and Marc at the door.

"How did you get in?" she asked in surprise. "They're only letting in family right now."

Marc walked up to Brenda and gave her a hug. Viv did the same. They glanced toward the door, where Pavel stood just inside. "A friend pulled some strings," Marc said.

Brenda pointed toward Hank, who looked near death, after his surgery. Tubes ran from his body to a rack near his bed. Monitors kept track of his pulse and his breathing. Then she looked at Viv and said, "Somebody told me he had given you a ride home when you were attacked."

"Yes. After they shot Hank, they threw me into the trunk of a car. I ended up someplace in Bergen County."

"What happened to the guys who did it?"

Viv shook her head as she looked sorrowfully at the man on the bed.

"What does that mean?" Brenda demanded.

"They're dead and I have no idea what happened. I must have blacked out, because the first thing I knew, I was hiding in the bushes of this house, and people were calling my name. It's just bizarre. I'm still trying to take it all in." Even though Brenda was a member of Viv's clan, she didn't want to give out details in such a public place.

"How come you and Hank were together in the first place?" Brenda asked with an edge to her voice.

Pavel listened carefully. He wondered, too. For a woman who claimed she wasn't dating anyone, this must have been considered a date by at least one of the parties.

"Hank asked me to go see a play I had wanted to see. It was just two friends getting together."

"I didn't think you were the kind of woman who would try to take over my husband like that," Brenda said, struggling with tears and anger. "I mean, we just recently split up. Did you ever go out with him *before* we divorced?" she demanded as her voice rose shrilly, overwhelmed by emotion.

Pavel moved into the room and positioned himself so that he could grab Viv if Brenda made a move to attack her. A catfight was the last thing he needed tonight. Both women were exhausted but keyed-up, and Pavel knew the ferocity of werecat women.

"Brenda, I know you're devastated by this, but believe me, there was nothing going on between Hank and me."

"Then why did you come straight here?"

"Because I feel horrified that he got shot, and I wanted to see how he was."

"Well, look at how well he's doing," Brenda sobbed. "Look at what happened to him. If he hadn't taken you out, he'd be fine." She covered her mouth with her hand and sobbed hysterically, shaking all over, and she glared at Vivian. "He has two children. And now they're going to grow up without their father. All because of you!"

"Brenda, would you like to come outside and maybe have a cup of coffee and tell me what the doctors said?" Marc tried to distract her from possibly hitting his sister. And as an old friend, he really did want to hear the prognosis. Two werecat doctors with hospital privileges here had worked on Hank, so he was in good hands. One of Pavel's guys had rushed him to the hospital and called the number on Hank's medical-alert bracelet.

"All right," she agreed, still sobbing. "Just for a minute. I don't want to leave him alone too long."

After the sound of footsteps faded into silence down the hall, Viv walked closer to the bed and gently took Hank's hand in hers.

Pavel gave her a questioning glance. She gestured to him to stay.

Then, as the Russian watched, Vivian Roussel began to chant softly in a language he didn't understand at first. In his mind, he recalled something similar from ages ago, something so old that it seemed to come from a place and a time nobody could even remember. From the ancestors.

Not caring that she had an audience, Viv continued her chanting and spread her arms out wide, encompassing

Hank's inert form as she invoked a force Pavel could only guess at. Indicating the four corners of the room, he knew she was calling on help from the four corners of the universe, asking the elements for help, begging the spirits to rally round this wounded creature.

Suddenly it clicked. Years ago, as a child, Pavel had witnessed a shaman performing a similar ceremony in the lands of the far North. This woman was one, too.

Silently he watched her conclude her prayers and then bow her head as she stood by the bedside and made another sweeping gesture before turning and sinking into the nearest chair.

"Are you all right?" he asked.

"Yes."

Pavel glanced at Hank. "Is *he* going to be all right?"

She looked up at him with a serious expression in those lovely amber eyes. "Yes. His recovery will go well."

Then as he watched, Vivian's head sank forward and she fell fast asleep.

Chapter Seventeen

"I think we all need to talk," Marc said quietly as he, Pavel, and Vivian left the hospital after keeping vigil with Brenda at Hank's bedside.

"Yes, and I don't think we should wait until tomorrow," Pavel replied.

"Then let's go to Marc's place. It's the closest one. Do you have your men watching it?" Viv glanced up at the Russian and silently hoped he would say they were.

"The entrance and exit are being monitored. So far, so good."

"All right," she said. "Then we can talk there."

When the three of them reached Marc's town house, Pavel drove into the garage, parked the car, and after making sure they were not followed, let Marc lead them through the security gate and into the elevator. Nobody said anything as the elevator lifted them to the foyer. Everybody felt drained. It was after four in the morning.

Once inside the town house, Marc turned to Pavel and said, "I think I know why these people are after us."

Vivian stared uneasily at her brother. "What's going on?" she asked.

"You and Pavel stay right there. I have to show you something."

As she and the Russian seated themselves on the sofa,

Viv glanced at him and realized he was studying her. Those light green eyes rested somberly on her face.

"I have to ask you some questions, too," he said.

"All right."

"How did a large man and a big cat end up dead in that driveway when you escaped unscathed—from whatever killed them?"

"I don't remember anything between being driven around in that trunk till the moment you found me on the porch. I don't know whose house it is or who my kidnappers were. It's a blank."

"Did they drug you?"

"No. There was no time. They grabbed me. I tried to fight them off, but I failed. They tossed me into the trunk of their car and hit the gas. I managed to activate that pendant and get in touch with your men. Nobody stuck me with a needle or held a cloth to my face."

"While you were in the car, did you hear sounds of an animal in the area? From what I saw of the wounds, those men had their throats ripped out by a beast."

Viv shook her head. "I'm sorry, "she said. "I must have blacked out. I just don't remember anything. It must be what they call post-traumatic stress."

Pavel's eyes narrowed. "You may be telling me the truth. But you're not telling me everything," he said.

"Pavel, I've been kidnapped. Our warehouse has been burgled. My brother and I both feel like we're running on borrowed time at the moment. Why shouldn't I tell you the truth?"

As Pavel was about to reply, Marc came back into the living room with a large antique mirror in his hands.

"Pavel, I want you to look at this."

The Russian rose from the sofa and watched as the antiquarian placed the large rectangular item on a chair. Then he saw him turn it upside down and slide something out, very slowly, very carefully. When it had emerged, Marc allowed Vivian and their guest a good look.

At first glance, Pavel went rigid, then snapped to attention and devoured the painting with his eyes as if he couldn't believe what he was seeing. Viv stared at his reaction, and then took a closer look at the very old icon before her. Magnificent. The detailing of the golden halos on the Madonna and child were gorgeous. Their painted robes glittered in the light. Expressive eyes looked out at the onlooker with tender compassion.

"This is the Virgin of Saratov," the Russian said at last. "She never left her place in that monastery—except for one brief time—until she was stolen three months ago. You'd better be able to give me a damn good explanation of how she ended up here." A warning glittered in his expressive eyes. His jaw clenched as he faced them.

"I found her in the warehouse this afternoon," Marc said. "I left on a lunch break to go back there and find out what we had that was so attractive to these guys. I started checking all the paintings against our invoices, and I found this disguised in the backing for a mirror. I had no record of it. We had bought one mirror, not two."

"Somebody must have planted it before we left Russia," Viv said with disgust. "That has to be why they broke into the warehouse. Whoever planted it wanted it back, and when they couldn't find it, they decided to kidnap us to see if *we* knew where it went."

She sat down again, plainly overwhelmed, her face drained of all color.

Pavel studied his two clients. He didn't know whether to believe them or not. The fact that they had one of Russia's holiest icons in their possession stunned him. The entire country was searching for it. The highest levels of the Russian government were involved in getting it back. And here it was in the apartment of an American antiques dealer who might or might not be a werecat. Hell, he *was* a werecat; so was Viv. But they didn't want to admit it.

"You have to tell me exactly how you think you acquired it," Pavel said in a stern tone.

"But we don't know."

"Then tell me what happened on your last buying trip. Or the previous one. It had to come from somewhere. When were you last in Russia?" he demanded.

"About two and a half months ago."

"The Virgin of Saratov was stolen about three months ago, according to a friend of mine. The government delayed announcing the theft because of its significance. Do you have any idea of how important she is to believers?"

Viv nodded. "She's supposed to have protected the city of Saratov from Ivan the Terrible. They had resisted him, and his usual policy was to slaughter everybody in town when that happened. Instead, the tsar allowed the people to keep their lives, but he took a huge ransom. When he went back to Moscow, the people celebrated their deliverance by building a special chapel to house the icon they credited with sparing their city."

"Khorosho," Pavel said with a nod. "You've studied your history. Then you know that Orthodox believers venerate the Virgin of Saratov," he said. "They feel that if she could protect a rich town from the tsar, she could accomplish anything."

Viv glanced at him. "I saw the medallion you wear. You must be devoted to her, too."

"I am," he said simply. "And now we have to protect this lady until we can return her to her homeland."

Marc gave him a gloomy look. "I think we're dead if anybody finds out we have it."

"Not if we manage to act faster than your pursuers. And," Pavel added as he turned to Viv and looked her directly in the eye, "you'll have to start telling me the truth."

Chapter Eighteen

"Let's backtrack. It's late and we're all exhausted. Make me understand what happened the last time you went to Russia on a buying expedition. I have to know the truth about how the icon came into your possession."

"First I'm going to make coffee," Marc said. "I can barely keep my eyes open. Would you like some? Or anything else?"

While Marc went to the kitchen to prepare coffee for everybody, Pavel sat studying the icon, almost afraid to find any damage. This was a national treasure, the focus of prayers for millions of believers. He had a duty to get her home safely; and with the attacks on his clients, he knew he faced a daunting battle. Who had taken the Virgin? And for what purpose? Was a cartel behind this? Or was it the work of one lunatic?

"Vivian," he said at last, "when you and your brother were in Russia the last time, where did you go?"

"Moscow and St. Petersburg. We usually work with a variety of dealers."

"Are these the same each time?"

"We generally visit people we've dealt with before, but occasionally we go to a new man, based on references from our previous contacts. It depends."

Pavel opened his hands in an expansive gesture. "Depends on what?"

"On what we're looking for. Sometimes we search for things that we already have a market for. Samovars are very popular." She smiled. "I know it's sort of a cliché, but people like Russian samovars. You can't imagine how many upscale émigrés get emotional when they talk about sitting in Babushka's kitchen in her tiny apartment, with the samovar on the table. It's a sentimental favorite."

He nodded. "What else do people want?"

"Paintings. Still lifes are admired, especially nineteenth-century oils. We generally don't deal in icons. Eighteenth- and nineteenth-century portraits are popular, as well as silver and ormolu articles. Lately there's been an interest in twentieth-century art, but that's not really our area of expertise, although Marc collects early-twentieth-century posters. I prefer more romantic genres."

"Perhaps an elegant Vrubel in blues and violets."

She smiled. "I actually have one in my apartment. It's one of my favorites."

"He had a wonderful style, but he was quite mad," Pavel said.

Vivian glanced at him in surprise. "Did you study art in Russia?"

Pavel shook his head. "No. I once loved a woman who was an artist."

He didn't want to deal with the question he saw in Viv's eyes, so he asked, "Do your Russian dealers specialize in specific areas, for instance paintings, art objects, or silver, or do they offer a variety of things?"

"Well, Kornilov in Moscow is our source for the best silver. We also use a couple of others. For paintings, we have a whole range of people. Sometimes we buy privately from people selling family heirlooms. We try to give them a fair price." Viv added, "I think it's sad when that happens. We don't cheat anybody."

After going through their list of contacts in Moscow and St. Petersburg, Pavel found none who set off alarms. He would check them with his own sources later, but for the moment, everything seemed normal. And then Marc mentioned a name that surprised him.

"We also bought some things from Bella Danilov. She's a businesswoman who seems to dabble in lots of things. She's the one who owns the new boutique Boyarina."

Pavel glanced at Marc and Viv. "She was just in the news lately. Did you hear what happened?"

"Yes. It was on TV. Her husband was shot outside a restaurant in St. Petersburg, right in front of her, but the bodyguard managed to save her. We were shocked."

"Did you ever meet Mr. Danilov?" he asked.

"No. I heard about him from our contacts. He was quite a heavy hitter in financial circles. People said he was very smart—and crazy about his wife."

Pavel looked carefully at Vivian. "What was your impression of Mrs. Danilov?"

"Pretentious. Sorry," she apologized. "It's tragic that she lost her husband that way, but I found her a bit much. I have to be honest."

"I thought she was nice," Marc said. "She was quite a charmer."

"Yes. If she was dealing with a man," Viv said.

Pavel found that amusing. "Did you purchase anything from her?"

"Several paintings, mostly nineteenth-century genre scenes. And a few silver objects."

"And everything arrived in good shape?"

"Yes. No problems. We purchased from four dealers on that trip, and everything came home in one piece."

"If you don't mind, I'd like copies of the invoices from that trip. I'd also like to go through your warehouse. And," Pavel said with emphasis, "I'm going to try to find a safe hiding place for the icon while I make inquiries about returning it."

"This could be dangerous," Marc reflected. "The fact that we have it looks suspicious. We might be charged with stealing it." He hated to think of the Leader's reaction to the headlines that kind of thing would generate.

"What about the men who attacked me?" Viv asked. "I can't imagine that this is going to stop because those two are dead. We need to find out who is behind this, or we'll never be safe."

"One thing at a time," Pavel replied. "I'm going to assign a bodyguard now. You would agree this time, I think."

"Yes. I don't want to go through a second abduction."

"Good. Then I'm going to get in touch with an associate of mine and ask him to store the icon. Do I have your permission?"

"If he can assure its safety, that would be wonderful," Viv said. "We have no claim to it, and we'd like to see it go back home where it belongs."

"Fine." Pavel turned to glance out the window and grimaced. It was almost dawn. Damn.

Taking out his cell phone, he punched in Vladimir's number and glanced at his watch. He hoped there was still time.

Chapter Nineteen

"Morgan residence. Vladimir speaking."

"It's Pavel. Something's come up and I need to speak with Mr. Morgan."

"Trouble?" Vlad asked instinctively.

"Yes."

"The timing is not good," Vlad reminded him. "He's about to turn in."

"I know. I'm sorry it's inconvenient, but when he learns what I want, I think he'll be glad he took the call."

"Hold, please. I'll ask him."

When Ian Morgan heard Vladimir's cousin was on the phone with something important, his curiosity got the better of him, and he accepted the call.

"Very mysterious, sir," Vladimir whispered. "I have no idea what Pavel wants."

Ian was in his predaylight state, a time when he began to feel sleepy and craved repose. Vladimir observed the expression on his face change from mild interest to something else as he spoke with Pavel.

"Is it radioactive or toxic, by any chance?" Vladimir heard Ian inquire.

Pavel must have assured him it was not, because he nodded and said, "Fine. You may store it in the vault here. And we'll have a meeting later to discuss the reason for this."

As Vladimir watched intently, his boss said, "Yes. Bring it over as soon as possible. I will not be available at the moment, but your cousin can put it in the vault. We'll speak tomorrow night. Goodbye."

"Sir, shall I wait for Pavel?"

"Yes. He ought to be here within the hour. Let him in and put away this object he's so anxious to shelter."

"Very kind of you to help him, sir."

"Pavel has proved his value to me on several occasions," Ian said as he headed for the stairs leading to the basement and his daytime bedroom, a windowless room that had the look of a very luxurious bomb shelter. "I can return the favor."

Pavel left Viv at Marc's town house, after advising them to get some sleep, which was exactly what he was planning to do. Last night had rattled everyone, and before Pavel interviewed them again, he wanted to take care of more pressing business: the storage of the Saratov icon.

He called for Metro's armor-plated Hummer and asked two of his best men to accompany him on the trip across town. Getting out the Hummer was always a bad sign; it meant trouble. His subordinates noted that and proceeded accordingly.

The Russian wrapped the mirror with the false backing in an old comforter to cushion it on the journey, and when Pavel entered the vehicle with his cargo, his men appeared surprised.

"You taking home your laundry, boss?" one of them joked.

He smiled. "Not precisely. I have to drop off a package."

They didn't feel obliged to comment after that, and turned the radio to a techno-rock channel, which filled the vehicle with the kind of noise that made conversation unnecessary.

After arriving at Ian Morgan's town house, Pavel rang the

bell, was observed by Vladimir on the closed-circuit TV, and then buzzed into the garage. While his men waited in the garage, Pavel and Vladimir walked down the corridor to a flight of stairs leading to a subbasement, where a steel door guarded the outer entrance to the vault.

"No outsider is authorized to enter," Vladimir said. "Stay here."

"*You* may go inside?"

"Only into the foyer. Mr. Morgan is the only one with total access."

"Very astute on his part. I'd do the same."

Vlad nodded. "Me, too," he said. "Now please hand me this very important object and I'll take it into the first area. Tonight, he'll come and carry it into the vault."

"Vladimir," Pavel said, "what I'm holding is priceless beyond belief. Nothing must happen to it here."

"Please don't tell me it's nuclear."

"No. Nothing like that." He gave his cousin a sharp look. "It's nothing sinister."

"I'm sorry," Vladimir said. "You're being so mysterious."

"You have no idea how serious this is. You don't want to know. But you have my word that it won't explode."

"Mr. Morgan may feel he has the right to examine this package—since he's sheltering it."

Pavel nodded. "Yes. I will speak with him and tell him what I'm asking him to store. I'm relying on his sense of honor not to disclose the contents to anyone."

"Not even to me?"

"To nobody. Even looking at it could place you in danger. The less you know, the better."

Pavel glanced at his cousin to emphasize the point, and he noticed a look of bewilderment in Vlad's eyes. "Just don't try to find out what it is," he said in a kinder tone. "There are some secrets that are better left unknown."

Vlad took the wrapped package, expressed surprise at the

weight of it, and unlocked the steel door before him. "I'll be back up in a minute," he said. "Wait there."

While Pavel did, he heard a sound like a heavy bolt being slid into position, then the echo of footsteps as his cousin descended into the underground vault. Then very quickly, the footsteps came back up the stairs, the sound of a bolt grated again, and Vlad was standing before him and turning his key in the lock.

"Mr. Morgan will go there tonight and put it away. Right now, it's in a storage bin under video observation."

"Thank you."

"I hope people aren't going to try to kill you for whatever you've just entrusted to us."

Pavel clapped his cousin on the back and nodded grimly. "Me, too," he said.

Chapter Twenty

As attractive as he found Vivian Roussel, Pavel still suspected that her version of the events the previous evening wasn't quite accurate. While it was true that she had been kidnapped and thrown into the trunk of a car, the claim that she had blacked out at the time her abductors were themselves attacked and killed left Pavel with doubts. It was a werecat trait to be devious. They were complicated beings, unlikely to reveal themselves to strangers—even if those strangers were paid to protect them. He would have to take another approach.

When he called her cell phone, Viv answered on the second ring. She sounded better than he would have imagined after such an ordeal.

"How are you?" he asked. "And my asking isn't just a polite formality."

"I'm good. Marc and I are still trying to figure out who would have wanted to do this to us, but aside from that, we're recovering."

"May I come over there to speak with you?"

"Of course. When?"

"Within the hour."

He sensed a slight hesitation. Then she said, "All right."

"Oh, another thing . . ."

"Yes?"

"Any word about your friend?"

"As a matter of fact, Hank's condition is improving. His doctors can't believe how well he's coming along."

"Glad to hear it. You must have remarkable gifts," he said, then added, "Goodbye," and pressed the button to end the call.

An American werecat, a shaman, a beautiful woman. And that gorgeous auburn hair. Pavel tapped his fingers on his desk and thought about his client. Very attractive. Very feminine. Yet she must have been the one to kill the two werecats who had kidnapped her. And what a job she had done. Exactly as his old teacher would have instructed: aim for the throat. Take them out fast. Get out of there.

Since this was done while Viv exhibited feline form, no court would be able to charge her with anything. She was a hostage defending her life, in any case. The event never made its way to a police blotter, and those two bodies, both in cat form after twelve hours, went into a landfill. The fact that they turned out to be Siberian Forest cats bothered him. Why were Siberians involved in a kidnapping in New Jersey?

While Pavel reflected on Vivian's abilities, he felt an unexpected jealousy about this man Hank, who now lay in a hospital bed. Pavel saw how Hank's ex-wife had reacted when she spotted Vivian in the room.

It had nothing to do with the case, Pavel reminded himself. It could be nothing more than what she said: two old friends going to see a show because they wanted to. Then why had this Brenda react with such emotion? From what Pavel could tell, he and Marc both thought she might have slapped Viv if given a chance. And he knew there were plenty of high-status female werecats who were bold and passionate; stories of their love affairs were the stuff of legend. Was Viv one of these sirens?

You are a jackass, he thought. *You barely know Vivian Roussel, yet you spend time wondering about her love life.*

*Get over it. You have a job to do. If she wants you to believe
she has no man in her life, it's her business.*

Pavel knew he could get a date any night of the week, and
he often had, but so far it was just a distraction. Since Natalya's death he hadn't found a woman who moved him
enough to wonder about her, speculate about whether she
really liked him, and allow her to occupy his thoughts while
he worked. Until Vivian.

We men are such idiots, he thought with wry amusement.
*If women knew the hold they have over us, we'd be totally at
their mercy.*

"I'm happy to be alive after last night," Vivian said after
Pavel arrived at Marc's and sat down for tea. "I look upon
this is as a kind of celebration. Marc is in his study with the
computer, keeping up with overseas orders."

While Viv acted as the gracious hostess, Pavel questioned
her again about the kidnapping and refused to accept her
claim that she remembered nothing. He found her worry-
ingly attractive, yet this stubborn denial grated on him. He
knew she was concealing the truth.

"Think. You can recall everything that happened up until
the time they opened the trunk to pull you out. Then it all
went blank. I don't believe you."

She shot him a look of anger. "People sometimes go
through trauma and find it so distressing that it disappears
from their memory. It's a fact."

"Yes. But not in this case, I think. I've known people who
fought in wars, killed the enemy in horrible ways, saw their
friends killed, and remembered every revolting detail."

"And they sometimes suffer breakdowns."

"Yes. Unfortunately."

"And others blank it out to spare themselves the pain of
remembering."

"True. But I think you're tough enough to have total recall. You're no weakling."

Viv merely looked at him and gave a small, feline smile. "I do have a strong will. But that rattled me."

"Of course it did. It would have shaken anyone. But you survived, and your armed kidnappers didn't. That leads me to believe you either killed them yourself or had someone— or something—available to do it for you."

Viv took a sip of tea and placed her Russian-style filigree-encrusted tea glass on the table. "I'm not certain you would understand."

"Try me. I've lived through things that might astonish you."

"Unless you and I have certain things in common," she said quietly, "you might find it difficult to credit."

Pavel looked serious. "We're dealing with an enemy who was brazen enough to steal one of his country's most cherished religious treasures. He respects nothing. He fears neither God nor man. This is the kind of person who attacked you. We need the truth in order to protect you," he said as he fixed her with a steady look from his beautiful green eyes. "It's the only thing that will help now."

Viv studied him carefully. She seemed to be weighing the pros and cons of her actions at this point.

Finally she said, "I thought there was something about you that makes you like me and Marc. It's only a guess, but I've rarely been wrong about these suspicions. It's the eyes that give it away. And the pheromones," she said as she looked straight at him.

He looked back at her and said, "If you agree to be truthful with me, I'll show you if your suspicions are correct."

"Fine," Viv replied. "You go first."

Chapter Twenty-one

"All right," Pavel said evenly. "I find it easier to deal with people if I know their true natures. I'm sure you feel the same."

"Agreed." Viv studied Pavel carefully and asked, "Would you like to go into another room if it would make you feel more comfortable . . . ?"

"That's not necessary. Unless you'd prefer it."

"I can handle it," Viv promised.

Pavel gave her a look that sent green flames straight into her soul. His mouth relaxed into a smile. Then he disappeared, and in his place stood a magnificent silver-tipped dark gray cat, about the size of a panther, his muscles rippling as he moved, his light green eyes staring straight at Viv.

Her mouth opened in a stunned O as she watched him. Though his human form was impressive, this splendid animal took her breath away. The silvery tips of his fur gave him an aura of such majesty as he advanced toward her that Viv was speechless with admiration for this creature of the dense and snowy forests. He looked like a prince of the jungle.

Pavel took advantage of her fascination and sat down beside her, allowing Viv to stroke his fur, a magnificent beast favoring her with his display of trust. Overwhelmed, she sank to her knees on the carpet to run her hands over his sleek fur and touch those hard muscles.

He pushed against her, willing her to recall what she was supposed to do. His paws clasped her leg as a hint of her obligation. He pressed against her and fixed his eyes on hers.

"All right, *koshka*," Viv said. "I'll carry out my part of the agreement."

She stood up and moved away, and then she turned around, and within seconds, a large Maine Coon cat the size of a puma emerged and strode majestically toward him, her silvery tabby markings creating a halo around her as she swished her long plumed tail at Pavel, her amber eyes large and beautiful as she saw the delighted gleam in his eye.

She was magnificent, all feline grace with splendid muscles that would allow her to hold her own with any of the big cats, a tribute to the gods who created her, a vision in silvery stripes.

Imperiously she walked with the sensuous movements of a lioness as she flaunted her form and her beauty before his hungry eyes. In the international language of cats, and using telepathy, he asked if she had always had the ability to shape-shift.

"Since I was very young. My mother taught me. She taught Marc, too."

"Did she also teach you about the ancient religion of the shamans?"

"No. That came from my grandfather, who learned it from *his* grandfather. My education is still unfinished, but I mastered enough to help those in need."

"Like Hank?"

"Yes."

The large Maine Coon cat strolled across the room, giving the Russian a good view of her well-muscled form. Beautiful. So much larger than the females of his own breed, so elegant, so glamorous, such color, such silky fur. What a gorgeous creature.

"You lunged at those men when they opened the trunk, didn't you? Then you killed them."

"Like rodents," Viv replied. "They would have tortured me to learn what they wanted. And I didn't know anything. Filthy werecat thugs. Siberians."

"You're sure?"

"I can generally sense other werefolk in my vicinity. And my kidnappers were werecats with a strong, harsh scent. Siberian Forest cats, the worst of the worst."

He processed that. "Did you know about me?" he asked as he moved closer to Viv and nuzzled her provocatively. She raised her head and rubbed it against him, responding to his caress.

"I wondered about you," she admitted. "Marc and I thought you might be one of the werefolk. Sometimes I could detect your scent, sometimes not. The eyes were the giveaway. Of course, my brother was afraid you might be something else."

"What?" he asked in surprise.

"We were actually concerned you might be a Siberian. You know, I have the ability to sense other werecats, but it's difficult to know the clan until they shift. You were hard to detect," she said. "You can disguise your pheromones most of the time."

Viv could see that Pavel was irritated by the remark about the Siberians. He must hate them. "Don't insult me like that," he said as he growled again, his green eyes flashing emerald fire. "I'm nothing like that breed."

"Then you Russian Blues hold yourselves apart from them?"

"Most of us do. It's bad to get involved with them. We stick to our own kind—with some sorry exceptions. Dimitri Danilov, our Hierarch, married one."

"No wonder I found her so repellent," Viv said. "Our clan has its rules, and they're very specific. No interbreeding. It's considered déclassé."

"What if *you* found yourself attracted to a cat from another clan?" he said, moving closer.

"Not likely," she said quickly. Too quickly, he observed. Those nimble paws moved back and forth as Viv tried to distance herself while he blocked her exit with his body.

"All clans have their own taboos," he conceded. "Sometimes I think it's absurd. But it makes us what we are." As he spoke, he looked into Viv's amber eyes with a longing that belied his words.

"I would never let Siberians close to me," said Viv. "The old legends don't lie."

"Yes," he said firmly. "Never let your guard down with them. And remember, some of them still practice blood sacrifice."

Viv flashed her eyes in disgust. "I'm not afraid of Siberians. My ancestor Krasivaya battled them aeons ago and always prevailed. We can defeat them again."

As Pavel moved closer to Viv to test the limits of her devotion to clan rules, Marc walked into the living room, saw the two huge felines, and stopped short.

"Oh, sorry," he said as he made a quick retreat. He wasn't about to ask what he had just walked in on.

Chapter Twenty-two

After they decided to be honest with one another, all three participants now felt they had established a greater degree of understanding, and if Pavel had admired Vivian in her human form, he was reduced to a state of sheer lust for her in feline shape. What a breathtaking animal. She made all Russian Blue females look feeble in comparison. He didn't know if it was the fantastic long, silvery tabby fur or her commanding presence, but once he saw Viv au naturel, he was captivated. Descended from a demigoddess, she looked like one herself.

With all this motivation to protect her, Pavel increased the video monitors, added bodyguards, and advised Viv to consider staying at Marc's until they could track down the thugs who were behind the attacks.

"How long do you think that will be?"

"Hard to tell. My men just called me to say they identified the thugs who threw you into that car."

"Who are they?"

"Small-time werecat punks who hire out as muscle. We're going to pay a visit to some of their friends and see if they can persuade them to answer a few questions."

"Do you think they will?"

"I think a few of them are likely to talk if they think it will help them avoid having the police look too closely at *them*."

"Our clan doesn't like to bring the police in to clan matters," Viv said pointedly.

"Don't worry. The cops won't come calling on you. We're only going to use that line to scare the Siberians. Of course, if they don't help us, there are always ways to make their lives miserable." He gave her a wicked smile.

"What about the two *dead* Siberians?"

"You know about the twelve hour rule. We waited, examined them for any clues they might give, and then two dead cats went into a landfill near Newark. No laws were broken."

"You're sure they were just low-level thugs?"

"The very bottom of the food chain."

She looked puzzled. "You don't think they tried to kidnap me because of the painting?"

"I think they tried kidnapping you as a quick way to raise some cash. You had a business. Your brother would pay to get you back. This type of hoodlum isn't a deep thinker. He's primitive.These two were not the sort who would know anything about art."

"Then you really don't think the kidnapping was connected with the painting."

Pavel shrugged. "I don't believe they're smart enough for that. But we're not letting down our guard, either." Then he glanced at his watch. "This evening I have an appointment with a gentleman who agreed to help us. With the, ah, hidden object. This afternoon I'm going to investigate some Russian angles."

Viv glanced at him.

"They have to be my countrymen," he said with a shrug. "The icon came from Russia, and unless some other ethnic gang of criminals was motivated to grab it, the thieves were Russians, too, especially given the significance of it to our people. If some gang from a raggedy-ass breakaway republic had stolen it, they'd be trying to blackmail the government into paying to get it back. That hasn't happened, so I don't think it's political."

"What could these people want?

"We don't know yet. That's what my crew is trying to find out." He hesitated, then said, "Viv, when you were inside Bella Danilov's shop, did you happen to notice if there were any mirrors like the one we just discovered?"

She tried to recall, but couldn't. "I remember lots of silver, some great paintings, but no mirrors. You know, I didn't like her, but I have to say she was a good businesswoman. She had all the paperwork in order and made sure everything arrived safe and sound. I'd suspect her the least."

"Well, glad to hear that," he said. "I'd hate to think the wife of our Hierarch was capable of such evil. Even if she is a Siberian Forest cat."

Viv raised her eyebrows. "I had no idea. Your Hierarch liked to live on the edge," she murmured. Then she shook her head. "From what I saw, Bella Danilov would be more likely to try to steal a shipment of Jimmy Choo shoes or designer dresses," said Viv. "I can't picture her going after something as dangerous as that object. It's just too risky."

Pavel noted that neither one of them wished to refer to the stolen icon by name. It was as if they were fearful of letting the secret out to some spy lurking in the woodwork.

"Good luck," Viv said as she let him slide his arm around her and give her a kiss before leaving. "Hope your friend can help us solve our problem." She gave him a glance that mingled irony and amazement as she said, "You know, Pavel, before I met you, I had never given the Russian Blues a thought. Frankly they seemed so . . . unimpressive compared with our own kind. And of course, there was the ancient taboo."

"And now, *dorogaya*?" he inquired with a raised eyebrow.

Viv fixed him with the full impact of her gorgeous amber eyes. *"Koshka,"* she murmured, "words don't do you justice."

When Pavel reached the vampire's town house that evening, Vladimir let him in and asked him to follow him upstairs to the salon.

"Any further trouble?" Vlad inquired as he led the way.

"Not yet," Pavel replied. Then with a smile, he added, "Mademoiselle Marais is here again, isn't she? I can smell her perfume. Spicy, like carnations."

"Yes. She's visiting. There's some talk of hunting in Canada, and she stopped by on her way up there."

Pavel knew Catherine Marais hunted werewolves for the feared but low-profile *Institut Scientifique* of Geneva; her reputation was such that any werecreature with a brain knew of her and treated her with respect. Mademoiselle Marais was one of the most deadly of modern werewolf trackers; she and her partner, Paul DuJardin, were the rock stars of their profession.

"I met her briefly once before," Pavel said with a smile, recalling a brunette beauty with a sexy voice.

"Thank God she doesn't feel compelled to pursue creatures other than those lupine scum," Vladimir replied. "Or I'd have to look for another job."

When the Russians reached the salon, Pavel shook his host's extended hand and Vladimir receded into the background, and then left the room. Ian Morgan introduced his beautiful mistress, who graciously recalled meeting Pavel on her last visit.

Without standing on ceremony Ian invited Pavel to have a drink and offered vodka. Ian abstained of course, but Catherine poured Pavel a glass and took one herself. An iced crystal bowl containing beluga caviar and lemon slices stood on a table, mother-of-pearl spoons beside the bowl. Small rounds of toast completed the setup.

"I've studied what you left," Ian announced. "It's magnificent. And authentic."

"Are you certain?"

"Absolutely. It has all the traits of the most refined masters of the art."

Catherine spooned some caviar onto a piece of toast and ate it, listening intently to the conversation.

"I brought it to you for two reasons, Mr. Morgan. The first, for your security system. The second, for your expertise in the art world. Now I'm going to ask for your help in returning it to its country."

Catherine Marais glanced at her lover and asked, "Should I leave you gentlemen to discuss business?"

"No," Ian said. "Please stay. I think you might be able to help us here."

Catherine smiled. "If I can."

Revealing information about the Virgin of Saratov made Pavel profoundly nervous. He didn't even want to tell Vladimir. He and the Roussels were so anxious to keep its presence a secret they were using euphemisms when referring to it among themselves. Now Morgan's mistress was about to find out. He wasn't certain this was a good idea, and he must have appeared uneasy because the vampire said, "Catherine is a woman of many secrets herself. She will understand the need for discretion. And she has valuable contacts who may assist us."

"What is this mysterious thing that's causing you such concern?" she asked lightly.

Pavel felt as if he were putting his head on the block as he replied, "The icon of the Virgin of Saratov."

"The one the Russians have been searching for since it was stolen from the monastery three months ago?"

"Precisely."

She turned to face Ian. "Darling, I've known you for a long time and have never had reason to doubt you, but I have to ask how it ended up in your home."

Pavel refilled his vodka cup and drank. "Mademoiselle, it's a long story."

"We have all night," she said with a steady look at them both. "Let me hear it."

Chapter Twenty-three

The vampire and his partner felt inclined to help Pavel since he wasn't trying to sell the treasure on the black market or make a profit. He and his clients merely wished to send it back home, where it belonged, and Ian wanted to do the same thing. Catherine's contacts might be able to facilitate the transfer.

"But first, I would like to see this legendary icon," she said.

Ian led them down to the vault, allowed them into the waiting area, disappeared down the inner stairs, and returned with the icon, its glints of gold smoldering in the haloes of the virgin and child and in the pattern of their garments. Catherine's eyes moistened as she beheld four centuries of devotion before her, and respectfully, she crossed herself.

"We have to get it back to them," she said simply. "I'll do whatever I can."

Now that he had secured powerful allies in his quest to return the icon, Pavel turned his attention to contacts back home, sending coded messages to a Moscow-based investigator he relied on for his skill in operating under the radar. He needed information on several people, he told him, all dealers in Russian antiques, and he named them. He needed to know if any of them had run afoul of the law, who their clients were,

if they had any known gangster associates, and if they had
ever had dealings with stolen church treasures. It was quite a
list, but Pavel knew his man could find out the dirt, if there
was any, and get back to him in a reasonable amount of time.

Time was truly of the essence here, because unless he
knew who was involved in the theft, the Roussels were still
at the mercy of unknown criminals, and Pavel preferred to
know his enemy, the better to deal with them. Viv had to be
protected at all costs.

To try to facilitate things, Pavel returned to his headquarters, where he switched on the video feed at Marc Roussel's
place and glanced up at the screen occasionally as he delved
into his computerized files. There he searched the database for
Russian mobsters, with subgroups of Georgians, Chechens,
Armenians, and others. He focused on criminal specialties—
extortion, murder for hire, grand larceny, kidnapping—all the
while trying to find something that would lead him to the
criminal brazen enough to have stolen the Virgin of Saratov.
The list was daunting and time-consuming.

The one group he discounted was the gang of incompe-
tents who had kidnapped Viv. He learned that they called
themselves the Rasputnikatz and were a minor league New
York version of a midlevel Russian gang. Their rep was for
quick and easy. Going after the Virgin of Saratov would have
required a criminal mastermind, and Pavel didn't believe that
all the Rasputnikatz combined could have come up with an
IQ higher than ten. Only fools would have been unprepared
for a fight when they opened that trunk. And since Viv and
Marc were able to disguise their natures so well, those Siberians would never even have suspected they were dealing with
a high-ranking werecat who would certainly outsmart them.

St. Petersburg

Danilov Enterprises had arranged a news conference, and a
spokesman for the company, looking appropriately grim,

faced a crowd of local and foreign reporters. Clearing his throat, he glanced around the room and announced the disappearance of Boris Danilov, the brother of the late Dimitri Danilov, and his successor as CEO of the family business.

"Do you suspect foul play?"

"Are any government agencies going to get involved in searching for him?"

"Please, gentlemen. One question at a time. You, sir," the spokesman said.

The reporter from St. Petersburg's largest daily newspaper repeated the question about foul play and asked if the firm's recent venture into Siberian oil could have attracted the animosity of a rival.

"There are lots of companies scrambling for drilling rights. They attempt to conquer their rivals with lawsuits, not murder."

"Sir, when was the last time Mr. Danilov was in contact with his business associates or his family?"

"Three days ago. When he failed to respond to cell phone calls on his private number despite repeated attempts to reach him, we decided to call in the authorities."

"After his brother's assassination, you have to be worried about his fate, of course," said a young woman in a fur-trimmed coat, "but isn't it the usual thing to receive a ransom demand in cases like these? Have you heard from anybody claiming to have kidnapped him?"

"No," the spokesman said tersely. "As of today, there have been no ransom notes. I've called this press conference to let the public know what we know, and to ask for your help in trying to locate our CEO. His family is devastated and in seclusion. We want your help in uncovering any useful information."

"Are you afraid this may affect shares of your stock?" a reporter from the financial newspaper asked.

The spokesman looked pained. He replied, "Our company is quite solid, as you know, and it will survive. We do not wish to be the object of rumors, which is why I've invited you here. We want the public to know that although Mr. Danilov has gone missing, there is no evidence that he has been harmed."

"At this point." That came from the back of the room.

"Yes. So, ladies and gentlemen, thank you for your time. I must get back to my office."

"Sir!"

"Yes?" He paused to take a final question from a young blonde in the front.

"I heard that Bella Danilov disappeared on the way to an appointment at a beauty salon yesterday. Any truth in that report?"

"Sadly, yes." And he quickly hurried off and took the elevator upstairs, leaving several of the reporters wondering what else he had forgotten to mention.

Chapter Twenty-four

"Bella, I don't know if this is a good idea. If our bargaining partners find out we're staging a hoax, our reputation will be ruined. Even my wife doesn't know where I am."

Boris Danilov stood at the window of a dacha on the outskirts of Moscow and toyed with a snifter of brandy as he glanced out over the snowy landscape. At his side stood Bella, his sister-in-law.

"Trust me, it's a good idea. If negotiations break down with the oil talks, Danilov Enterprises loses the chance to compete for the contract, but we get five million dollars under the table. We know we wouldn't have been able to undertake the project without a lot of upgrading, but they don't know it and they're desperate to buy us off. So we'll disappear for a week or so, lose the contract, and make money, anyway."

"Dimitri wouldn't have done this. He'd say it was a cheap stunt."

"He's dead," she snapped. "You have to be more aggressive. We're swimming with sharks here. You have to be the biggest and the best."

The new CEO took a sip of brandy and set the snifter down on a table near the window. He had a sneaking suspicion he might actually be out of his depth, and it unsettled him.

Dimitri's death had left him the de facto Hierarch of the Russian Blue werecats, but he never thought he'd ever assume the leadership. A subordinate all his life, he was sometimes a resentful one as he saw his brother rise to the top, knowing Dimitri was the one everybody admired and fawned over. Truthfully, he felt incapable of supplanting his clever older brother, the genius who had created an empire in such a brief period of time.

The day Dimitri had been gunned down in broad daylight on Nevsky Prospeckt had changed Boris's life forever. Now he wondered why he ever listened to Bella and her grandiose new plans for making millions. They already had plenty of money. Had it helped Dimitri? Could he spend it in the cemetery? Why not leave well enough alone?

Everything the old werecats said about these Siberian Forest cats was turning out to be so true. They were con artists, deceivers, scam artists; the list of unflattering qualities could go on and on. And he had stupidly brought this one into the heart of the family business. That was how clever *he* was.

Boris took another sip of brandy and wished he were back home with his wife and kids, instead of here with this witch. His chance remark about the lack of security in the old monastery church where the icon of the Virgin of Saratov reposed had given Bella the unholy idea that it could be easily stolen. She had put out feelers to shady contacts in the international art world and come up with a prospective buyer. At this point, Boris was terrified at being implicated, especially since Bella prodded him to use his ties to corrupt customs officials to get the icon out of the country, no questions asked. When he had balked, she'd threatened to go to the state prosecutor with details of dozens of his illicit business deals—like importing and selling drugs—if he backed out. Boris was screwed. Werecat loyalty meant nothing to her. Worse than that, he had racked up bills he couldn't pay, so he had put his tail between his legs and said he'd do it. To keep her claws in him, Bella had offered him a cut of the deal. Twenty million divided by two. Now all they had to do was retrieve the icon where underlings had stashed it and complete the transaction with the buyer.

"We'll go to New York and lie low until our time for negotiations expires," she said. "A private jet will take us there tomorrow. While we kill time, we'll take care of the *artistic matter*," she said with deliberate emphasis. "We'll pick up our money for the art transaction and then head home. We'll attribute our disappearance to threats by terrorists who will be implicated in Dimitri's death. That always works. My contacts in the State Security Services will swear we were in protective custody at an undisclosed location overseas, and upon returning, we will be full of gratitude to the FSB, our wonderful security services."

"You've already bribed them?"

"Of course. Two hundred thousand euros each, and they'll produce a file on our case backing up our story. They're dependable."

"We're so lucky to have such friends," he said with irony.

"This will make you rich. You're the new Hierarch. Start acting like one."

Bella turned away in annoyance and walked to the opposite side of the room, close to the eighteenth-century porcelain fireplace, which heated the salon. He could see the disdain in her manner, and he resented her for it.

"I have my own thoughts about this," he said.

"Good. Let's hope they're valuable. I always thought you must have learned something worthwhile during your time at the London School of Economics."

Boris didn't even bother to reply. He felt like saying, "At least I didn't get my education in a whorehouse," but why start a boring fight? He was just too tired.

"I'm going to bed. Wake me when we have to leave for the airport."

As he closed the door behind him, Boris felt as if he was walking into a black hole.

* * *

In the salon of the dacha, Bella paced up and down, occasionally shaking her beautiful, long blond hair as she did whenever she was agitated. Trying to work with Boris was like attempting to gather worms. He was always going in all directions at once, unable to make a decision and stick with it.

She had originally been taken with his tall, blond good looks—the man had the appearance of a male model. Dimitri had been shorter, although not by much, and a lot smarter; he had looked like a handsome and successful entrepreneur, which he was, right down to the Armani suits and Italian shoes. If Dimitri had lost half his brain, he still would have been sharper than his younger brother, but they had gotten on well, and Dimitri had never left Boris out of things.

Boris's only talent was as a gofer, and his usual job was to escort important out-of-town visitors to the nightclubs and the best restaurants in the city while they carried out deals with his brother. The only deals *Boris* made involved things like hash and cocaine.

Always on the alert for leggy blondes, he had discovered Bella in an overpriced nightclub in St. Petersburg, drinking with friends of his. With him as an escort, she had met and seduced Dimitri, shocked his clan by becoming engaged to him, and finally married him in a wedding that was outrageously costly even by the standards of Russia's billionaires.

And now poor Dimitri was dead, and all that remained of the inner circle of Danilov Enterprises was Boris and Bella. At last Boris had found his true calling: he was a puppet.

Exhausted from the stress of dealing with the new Hierarch, Bella shape-shifted and became a beautiful cat the size of a lynx as she searched out a warm place near the porcelain stove, then sank down and drifted into a deep and dreamless slumber, preparing for her trip to New York.

Chapter Twenty-five

Viv had gotten the visit she had been dreading. The Leader arrived at her home, looking concerned, and told her she ought to stay at a secure location while Metro carried out its work.

"You know I care for you, Viv," he said. "If you wish, I'll assign the Special Squad to work on this."

Viv felt worried, mostly over the matter of the mysterious icon—which she had no intention of discussing with John Sinclair or anyone else. Werecats took care of their own problems. The Special Squad generally dealt with security for the Leader. She didn't want to get involved with them and put herself in his debt.

"That's very flattering, but Metro will handle it."

"I've called you twice since the night you were kidnapped. You've avoided me."

"I didn't want to talk about it," she said.

He reached out and cupped her chin in his hand. Before he could kiss her, Viv moved away.

His eyes sent daggers at her. Coldly, the Leader grabbed her arm and pressed her against his chest before she could pull away. "Don't treat me as if I were nothing. I offered you the highest rank in our community. Think about it. And what were you doing out on the town with Hank? Do you think he could offer you something better?"

She pushed away and looked at him in amazement. "You're not offering me the highest position. *You* occupy it. And what I was doing with Hank is none of your business. Leader, I'm tired, and I have no ambition to be your wife. Please go home. Thank you for the honor, but I can't accept."

"You want to waste the inheritance from your ancestor on such an ordinary werecat? Think about your offspring."

"Believe me, I've thought about it," she said. "And I don't want a domineering father for them."

Angrily the Leader shape-shifted, with Viv following. Two large, shaggy cats the size of mountain lions stood almost nose to nose, eyeing each other, waiting for the other to make the first move. They began to circle each other, slowly, deliberately. Then the Leader lunged for Viv, grabbing her by the scruff of the neck, holding her down. Nimbly she flipped over and threw him off, sending him crashing into the sofa. With fury in his eyes, he leaped at her, holding her down once more.

"You're mine," he said telepathically as he crushed her beneath his weight, biting her neck to restrain her. He was going to mate now with her consent or without it.

"We choose our mates!" Viv replied. She felt a flow of adrenaline and let him have it as she bumped him off her back and slashed him with flying claws. Then she jumped on *him* and bit his ear, making him screech with pain and back off, wounded and stunned.

"Leader or no Leader, nobody takes me unless I say so," she flung at him. "It's my right. And you should remember who I am."

Glaring at the silvery beauty in front of him, the Leader was almost panting from the combat. He was older than she was, and not used to rejection. Werecat females made him more offers than he could handle. Nobody turned him down.

"I want you, Viv," he said. "Perhaps this isn't a good time. But we'll discuss this again when you're feeling . . .

more yourself. You've just been through a trauma. I understand."

What part of "not interested" don't you understand? The thought came to her mind before she could filter it out. He looked wounded.

"This is not a good idea," she said. "I know I have a gift I should pass on to my clan, but I must choose my mate, and in my own time, I will. Krasivaya's bloodline will not die out."

The Leader shape-shifted, looking regal and disappointed. Viv shifted and then checked to see if she had left lasting damage; she hadn't. But she had made her point.

"Don't reject something worthwhile for both of us," he said as he walked to the door and let himself out. "It would be a good alliance for our clan. It would take us to new heights."

After she shut the door, Viv did three things. She bolted all her locks, called downstairs to the guard from Metro to make sure the Leader's car had left with him in it, and then called Marc to tell him she was having her bodyguard bring her to his town house. She no longer felt safe. Worse than that, she had the distinct feeling she was dealing with a madman.

Pavel paid Viv and Marc an unexpected visit that evening to bring them dinner from a favorite restaurant and share the results of his initial findings, via his man in St. Petersburg.

Marc provided a good white wine to go with the chicken dish, and Pavel noticed a subtle change in his clients as they ate. Both appeared tense.

"I learned that two of your Russian suppliers have had some trouble with the police," he said.

"Stolen property?"

"No. Failing to secure the proper permits for some of their exports."

"Do you think it might be them?"

Pavel shook his head. "They're legitimate dealers. They claimed they didn't keep up-to-date with customs regulations. My investigator believed them. It happens all the time."

"That's two. What about the others?"

"Your samovar merchant seems to be a paragon of virtue by modern standards, except for his link to the wife of a well-known gangster. He's her favorite purveyor of nineteenth-century antiques. She and the husband are renovating an old palace in the Arbat district in Moscow, and this guy has the job of locating decorative objects to give it the proper ambience."

"Does she have him scouting sixteenth-century icons?"

"No. Too expensive."

"All right," she said. "What about the widow of your late Hierarch?"

"My man is still looking into her business dealings. With her it's difficult because she has a superior security system that makes things complicated."

"He's hacking into her computer?"

Pavel glanced at her with humor in his green eyes. "He's making every effort to investigate her," he said blandly.

Marc had been enjoying his food when he happened to hear something on the kitchen TV that caught his interest. Rising from the table, he walked quickly into the kitchen and turned up the volume. "Pavel," he called, "come in here. You might want to hear this."

The Russian went in, followed by Vivian. What they saw was startling. In the foyer of Danilov Enterprises was a man in a well-cut suit announcing the disappearance of the new CEO, Boris Danilov.

Pavel was caught by surprise. It had to be the first announcement, otherwise he or a New York member of the clan would have seen it. If Vladimir had spotted it, he would have called in the news. Then the American broadcaster added that the widow of the late CEO Dimitri Danilow was said to be missing as well. Some suspected foul play.

"Are the Danilovs under attack, too?" Viv asked.

Pavel threw up his hands in a gesture of bewilderment. He couldn't figure out who would profit by the removal of both brothers. The Hierarch had been involved in negotiations for oil rights in a contested area of Siberia. His assassination made room for his younger brother to replace him. The negotiations resumed, but the business empire Dimitri had created would undoubtedly flounder and then perish under the leadership of Boris, whom nobody respected.

Boris's assumption of the title of Hierarch had been given to him by default, since he was the Hierarch's kin, but clansmen in Russia and in America had doubts about his capabilities. Hushed rumors circulated about requests for him to step down if a worthy successor could be found.

Following the assassination, Boris's detested sister-in-law, Bella, let it be known that the new Hierarch was suffering from the trauma of his brother's murder and would energetically take charge once he had recovered from the aftershock. Within the clan, few believed Boris could do it.

That Siberian lost her meal ticket when the smart one was killed, and now she wants to take over the dumb one and keep him under her thumb. Pavel remembered that cynical remark and wondered if the speaker had been closer to the truth than he thought.

Echoing his thoughts, Viv looked at Pavel and asked, "Do you think Bella could inherit the Danilov empire if both brothers were out of the way?"

"There's a board of directors she'd have to deal with. I don't think they'd let her in."

Viv smiled. "If she's as devious and underhanded as I think she is, she probably got her husband to make out a will naming her his heir. He might have given her a huge interest in the business and sidestepped his brother."

"No. The Hierarch was enamored of her, but he wouldn't

have cut Boris out of his will. Family was everything to him."

"You never know," Marc said as he studied the photo of Bella now on the screen. "She's very attractive. And I'll bet her powers of persuasion would make you forget about anything but pleasing her."

"The Hierarch loved her, but he wasn't a fool," Pavel said defensively.

"But you say the brother is."

The Russian glanced at Viv. "And?"

"She might have been able to exert more control over *him*. If she's still alive," Viv added.

Chapter Twenty-six

"Viv, how are you? It's Hank. I'm out of bed and walking. Well, a little."

"Oh, I'm so relieved to hear you're recovering. Marc and I went to visit you in the hospital after they rescued me that night. I prayed for you."

"Well, it worked. My doctor says I'm healing nicely and ought to be back home before long."

"Did they transfer you to a place familiar with our people?" she asked. Werecats could experience recuperative powers that would astonish regular doctors. They preferred to be with their own kind.

"Yes. A private place in Brooklyn. It's very nice."

Viv smiled. "Is Brenda visiting you there?"

"Just about every day. She brings the kids. And the hospital's going to release me soon."

"Terrific. You know, I've wanted to thank you for trying to save me when they attacked us. You were very brave. I'll never forget it."

Hank paused. "I'm sorry I didn't protect you better, Viv," he said. "How are you? I heard they tossed you into the trunk of a car and drove you around New Jersey."

"They did," she said ruefully.

"What happened when you arrived at their destination? Did they try to hold you hostage?"

"Ah, they didn't get the chance. Something intervened and killed them."

Hank could picture the scene. Viv had gone werecat and those guys were killed right after they'd popped that trunk. Werecats knew what they were capable of when faced with death. A blueblood like Viv would defend herself ferociously, especially if she faced death at the hands of inferiors. Pride would make her ruthless.

"Well," she said cheerfully, "I hear you and Brenda are going to patch things up. I always hoped you would."

He laughed. "Yes," he said. "After getting shot and seeing how devoted she was at the hospital, I thought maybe we should try again. I love my kids and I want to be with them every day. Too bad it took a brush with death to show me what's really important."

"I'm so glad you've reconciled." Viv meant that from the bottom of her heart. She was glad Brenda was getting her husband back, and grateful she would be spared having to make up excuses why she couldn't go out with him.

"And, Viv," he said quietly, "I was semiconscious when you came in. I was pretty much out of it, but I knew what you were doing. I think those spirits all came to my rescue. Until that moment, I didn't realize you had the gift."

"I don't talk about it very often," she admitted.

"It's good to keep the ancient traditions alive," Hank said simply. "And I thank you for it."

"'Bye, Hank. Stay healthy," she said softly.

"Will do."

Years ago, her grandfather had started her education in the ancient wisdom of the werecats, teaching her some of his repertory of healing spells, showing her how to call upon the old gods to come to her aid in times of danger, and instilling in her the memory that she was a direct descendant of Krasivaya, the werecat Venus.

This beautiful creature had ruled a great Northern kingdom thousands of years ago when all the werecat clans fought for supremacy in the frozen lands of forest and tundra. Leading her clan with skill in battle and shrewdness at all times, Krasivaya could take on the size of a modern tiger as she battled rivals for land or influence. Some of her fiercest wars brought her tribe into conflict with the clan known as the Siberian Forest cats, a bloodthirsty collection of hunters and warriors who practiced infant sacrifice and killed their rivals' kittens on an altar to their god, Moroz the Dread.

In a legendary feat of daring, Krasivaya had once led an assault that destroyed Moroz's main sacrificial altar, overrunning the Siberians' stronghold and rescuing a terrified band of kittens, stolen from several clans, who were awaiting death at the hands of the Forest cats. That exploit cemented alliances with six other werecat clans and established her own people as protectors and liberators. Even today, in the memories of many werecats, the name Krasivaya evoked feelings of respect and awe. In her own lifetime, she was treated as a demigoddess and invoked as a guardian of the helpless.

As Viv sat by her grandfather, listening to the ancient legends of her people, Grandpa emphasized her heritage and her responsibility to help those in need, to recognize the world as a place where good and evil do constant battle, and to try to support what is right.

"As you go through life, you will find yourself forced to make choices," he had once said after spending the afternoon instructing Viv in the practices of the shaman. "Always let yourself be guided by your head *and* your heart, never letting one or the other dominate your thinking. Be rational, be kind, and be true to the essence of your being. You have the gift to shape-shift. Use it well, and use your abilities to improve your world, to protect those who depend on you. One day, you may be called upon to imitate Krasivaya," he had said very softly. "Don't fail us."

The memory of that conversation always evoked powerful feelings of respect and duty in Vivian. Lately Grandpa's words came to echo in her dreams as she pondered the cause of the recent disruptions in her life. Why, after years of completely normal business dealings with the Russians, had this problem surfaced? And why did the fact that Bella Danilov turned out to be a Siberian make her so uneasy?

Pavel's clan distrusted them, too. In the back of every cat's mind was the collective memory of the Forest cats' ugly past and the fear that, given half a chance, they might revert to it again. The death of the Russian Blues' Hierarch, the disappearance of his brother and heir, the weird possibility that Bella Danilov might have had something to do with planting the stolen icon in the Roussels' warehouse—all these things left Viv remembering Grandpa's advice.

Use your head and your heart. Logic and emotion. Don't get swayed by either, but take both into account.

Well, right now her head told her to be very suspicious of Bella, and her heart told her to embrace Pavel Federov.

She would trust her instincts on that.

Chapter Twenty-seven

"Yuri, we heard the news that both Bella and Boris have gone missing. What's happening up there?"

On his end, Yuri sighed. Pavel knew last names were unimportant here. Every werecat of the Russian Blue clan was intensely interested in the fate of only one Boris or Bella at the moment. It was the only topic of conversation right now.

"We think we may have lost our new Hierarch. Everybody is concerned," he said.

"Is there any possibility he isn't dead?"

"Sure. There's always that. But why the disappearing act? If they have to send out an official announcement to discuss the rumors, then they're expecting the worst. I think Danilov Enterprises knows exactly what happened and is hiding the truth."

"What's their motive?"

"Who knows? Maybe they don't want the stockholders to think the business is unstable."

"With a dead CEO and a missing replacement? That doesn't exactly inspire confidence. And it's odd that Bella vanished at the same time."

"The clan is in meltdown over this," Yuri said, and Pavel could hear the stress level in his voice. "We're under attack, and we don't know what's behind it. We would suspect

Bella, of course, since she's missing, too, but they say she and Boris have been fighting like hell lately, so I don't think they're in collusion. They really do hate each other. Now some of the clan want to call an election and choose a replacement Hierarch."

"If he returns and finds himself dumped, he'll never forgive us. We don't need that kind of turmoil—two angry Hierarchs claiming the title and the rest of the clan with divided loyalties. What a mess."

"Well, with all the uproar, I don't think any of our guys really wants to give his job away until we know more."

"I hope you're right." Pavel smiled. Yuri was an older werecat with old-school ideas. The younger members were more prone to action. He hoped the youthful faction didn't act hastily and remove the missing Hierarch from his position, since that might trigger clan warfare.

Before he said goodbye, Pavel asked one more question. "Has anybody heard anything about the missing icon? Any suspects in the theft?"

"Nothing, aside from a plea by the patriarch of Moscow and the president to return it to its place in the monastery. There aren't even any names being bandied around, aside from the usual ethnic minorities they blame for everything that's gone wrong."

"Very strange no ransom demands have been made, if that's the case." Pavel didn't really think there would be a ransom; more likely it was destined for a rich American collector. But he didn't wish to say so right now.

"Yes," Yuri agreed. "Maybe the thief just wanted it for himself."

That didn't make much sense either since whoever had sent it across the Atlantic to stash it in the Roussels' warehouse was trying to keep it safe until the right moment arose. That break-in had to have been an attempted repossession that somehow failed. Why? Had the thieves been too incompetent to find it there? Hadn't they had enough time, the right instructions, or the correct invoice?

"Well, thanks, Yuri. I'll keep in touch."

"Goodbye Pavel. Stay well," Yuri added with emphasis.

Damn, thought Pavel. Theft, he understood, but it was always caused by motive. Greed stood out as a headliner, second only to spite. But lately many treasured religious objects had been stolen around the world for the private collections of the superrich. If a man had everything money could buy, what was left to satisfy his lust for possession, except something so rare, so valuable that it would be unique in all the world? He knew this wasn't political. It was all about some greedy billionaire wanting one of Russia's greatest treasures for his own. That was why it had ended up hidden in the Roussels' warehouse, and although the Saratov Madonna was safe at the moment, that didn't necessarily mean she was free from danger. Until Pavel knew she was back in her homeland, he wouldn't feel he could rest. And he wouldn't feel Viv and Marc were secure, either, a thought that was just as troubling.

At least he didn't have to worry about the Madonna for the time being. Deep under the streets of Manhattan, carefully hidden away in one of the most secure private vaults in the city, she remained out of harm's way—thanks to an aristocratic vampire with a passion for art.

Chapter Twenty-eight

Viv was out of circulation while Pavel and his men tried to protect her, and inactivity was grating on her nerves. She was a woman used to freedom of movement, and this kind of confinement exasperated her. The only thing that served to distract her from her frustration with her own situation was news from a member of her own clan, the wife of one of the Leader's Special Squad.

Although Viv was under protective surveillance by Metro Investigations, she could receive calls on her cell phone. Pavel's experts had diverted the signal so that anyone tracking it would have been surprised to find it coming from Minsk. One afternoon, Sarah Jenkins reached her in tears, sobbing out her story over the phone.

"Viv, it was horrible. I think he's gone crazy. He—he attacked me!"

"Sarah. Who attacked you?" Viv asked in alarm. "Are you all right?"

"No," she sobbed. "I'm so upset. And I can't tell my husband. I don't know what to do."

Viv listened to the nearly hysterical sobbing, wondering what had happened and who had harmed her. When Sarah seemed a little calmer, she said, "Please, go back to the beginning. Tell me who attacked you."

There was a long pause, with the sound of stifled sobs, and then the woman said, "The Leader!"

"What?"

"It's true! He stopped by the house when my husband was out, and I thought he wanted to speak to him, so I let him in. All of a sudden he started acting strange and then he grabbed me, went werecat, and . . . he raped me. And two days after this happened to me, my friend Charla called me to tell me he did it to her. He's insane."

"You didn't tell your husband? What about Charla?"

"We were both too afraid. It's his word against ours, and he's the Leader."

Viv felt so outraged, she wanted to kill. She had managed to fight off Sinclair, but this young woman hadn't. It was an outrageous abuse of his power. She thought of Krasivaya, and she could imagine the punishment her ancestor would wish for this evil werecat.

"We have to take action. First, you must tell your husband."

"No!" she protested. "I'm too afraid.".

"Sarah, we have to remove John Sinclair from his position. If not, he'll keep doing this. Your husband is on his Special Squad. He and his men can get close enough to him to take him into custody. We'll have a trial in front of the clan, and we'll remove him."

"No!" she wailed. "I can't. Charla is afraid, too. They'll think we encouraged him. And he'll lie and say we did."

"Then what do you want to do?"

"I don't know," she sobbed. "I'm frightened."

Viv struggled to find the right words. "All right. You've told me, and I believe you. I will have someone shadow Sinclair, keeping track of his movements, gathering evidence. If we can find enough to charge him with one more crime, will you come forward and testify against him?"

Sarah hesitated. Then she said, "Yes. But don't let him harm anyone else."

"If we track him, we can prevent that. But it would be better if you and Charla came forward right now." Viv heard what sounded like sobs again. She said gently, "Please think about it."

"Yes," Sarah replied. Then she clicked off, sounding too scared to say anything else.

Viv struggled with the desire to go werecat, race off to Sinclair's home, and tear him apart. After her own experiences with him, she had no doubt Sarah was speaking the truth. But according to the rules of her clan, such an accusation demanded a trial. Trials required witnesses. Those women were so frightened, they were in no shape to think about facing him in a werecat court. Yet. And Viv was hampered by her own problems right now.

This wretched excuse for a Leader had dared to use his position to prey on vulnerable females? He had dared to try to pressure *her* to accept him as her mate? Never in the history of her clan had such a Leader existed. Viv swore by the blood that ran in her veins that she would remove this evil beast as soon as she could. She wanted this other business to end so she could pursue that.

"Can't we go back to the Old Muscovy?" she asked Pavel when he came to visit her and Marc at her brother's town house. "Send the bodyguards over. They can stay with us all day."

"I have to get out of here," Marc said. "I need a break. We both do. We may end up at each other's throats."

Pavel gave them a bleak look. "You understand how dangerous your situation is. Vivian survived a kidnapping. You were both attacked on the street. You may attract more of the same."

"With surveillance cameras and bodyguards, your men can be there if anything happens. I'm willing—we're both willing—to give it a try."

Pavel didn't appear to be pleased with the idea, but he

agreed. "All right," he said. "We can guard you at the shop. But you still have to be in a safe place at night."

"A safe and separate place," Marc added.

The Russian hesitated. He glanced at Viv. "I have a good location where I can hide you," he said. "It's secure. There is a room with steel panels that slide into place at the first suggestion of a break-in."

"Sounds very high-tech."

"It is. It's my apartment, and I had it designed by an expert."

Viv looked at Pavel. After her recent conversation, she felt cautious.

"Strictly on the up-and-up," he said. "Because of the sensitivity of this case, it's the most secure facility I can think of. You can lock yourself in each night if you wish."

"I think I'll feel safe enough knowing you're there."

Marc looked thoughtful. "You'll have to guarantee her safety," he said.

Pavel nodded. "Of course."

"Where are we going?" Boris glanced out the windows of the Mercedes and failed to recognize the area as their driver sped along the highway leading from Kennedy Airport to New York City.

"An apartment I have in Manhattan," Bella replied. "I bought it—Dimitri and I bought it, actually—under the name of one of our companies. It has good security and nobody has ever bothered us there. Very anonymous."

"New York is a world financial capital. Don't you think they read the news? People might recognize us."

Bella flung him a look of sheer annoyance. "Boris," she said with an edge, "have you seen the contents of American newspapers? All they care about is blond starlets. We're unknown. The only danger here is from Russian expats, so we'll avoid them."

"How long do you think it will take?" he asked.

"If we fail to negotiate for five days, we'll lose the chance to secure the Siberian oil contract. We will stay here for a week and work on that other matter. By that time, I'm hoping to settle both things and walk away with a fortune in dollars."

Boris sneered. "I still think you should have negotiated for British pounds sterling. Or euros."

Bella snapped at him. "I agreed to dollars because that was what he offered. The end result would have been the same in any currency you wanted."

"The euro or the pound would have been better in the long run. Both currencies are climbing right now."

Bella found this lecture quite irritating, coming from a man whose expertise revolved around knowing which nightclubs were trendy. And he dared complain about *her* efforts? As least she could generate money.

"Then, damn it, Boris, you can try your hand at negotiating next time!"

This irritating creature's only function was to give legitimacy to her plans for the future of Danilov Enterprises, because while a Danilov remained in charge, the board of directors wouldn't be able to remove her.

Boris, the new Hierarch of the Russian Blues and the new CEO of Danilov Enterprises, was now her reluctant partner, and he would remain one as long as necessary. With his constant need for money to maintain his lavish lifestyle and assuage his fear of jail, he would tell nobody about their deal with the oil contract.

As for the other matter, he was so eaten up by anxiety that she was afraid he might have a heart attack if things didn't start to sort themselves out quickly. The sooner they made contact with their buyer, the better they would both feel.

Bella could only marvel at Boris's lack of aptitude. She actually pitied his clan and was grateful that she had been born to a werecat sept that had a strong sense of self. These Russian Blues needed her to take charge of them because if they looked to this new Hierarch for guidance, they would all go straight to ruin.

Chapter Twenty-nine

The Danilovs had barely settled in at Bella's Manhattan condo when she picked up her cell phone and made a call that led to a shouting match with the person on the other end.

Insults flowed from Bella's mouth, followed by a rapid-fire series of threats, more shouting, and finally an ultimatum to "Get it or else you'll end up in the river."

"Trouble?" Boris asked.

"Yes. But only a minor inconvenience."

"In connection with?

"That other matter," she snapped at him.

"Ah, your minions botched the job."

Bella appeared to be considering if she ought to admit the truth. Then she shrugged and simply said, "Yes."

She thought Boris looked ready to reproach her, so to cut him off, she added, "We will recover it. It's only a matter of time. So far they haven't been able to find it."

"How far along are they with the plan?" he asked.

"They broke into the warehouse where the icon was hidden, but they couldn't locate it. Meanwhile the owners changed their security system and hired some competent help. Our idiots lost two men so far, and now they're whining about 'additional risks.' They're getting cold feet."

"What if the Roussels spotted the icon first and hid it?"

"No. It was camouflaged pretty well. They aren't smart enough to discover it. Nobody could have," she said flatly.

"So what do we do now?" he asked.

"We have a morale-raising meeting with our helpers and light a fire under them. We don't want to stay here any longer than we have to."

Boris agreed with that. He wanted to get home as quickly as he could. "I'm going to call Marina and tell her I'm safe. She shouldn't have to worry."

He almost thought Bella was going to forbid the phone call to his wife, but he could see she briefly considered the idea and then rejected it.

"Make it brief. Just tell her you're all right and you're involved in an important business deal. You don't want her holding news conferences and attracting more attention than this needs, all right?"

Boris nodded and took out his cell phone with the international connection. He should never have allowed this witch to blackmail him into going along with this scheme. If it hadn't been for the money, he wouldn't have agreed, but Marina was nagging him to buy a bigger house, and he needed a dramatic increase in funds in order to please his wife. When would he ever learn?

He felt disgusted with himself, ashamed he'd betrayed his brother and his clan, and he cringed at the idea of replacing Dimitri as Hierarch. He wasn't worthy. He was a fake, a puppet whose strings were pulled by an amoral bitch for whom nothing was out of bounds. Uneasily he felt he'd made a deal with the devil.

On Marc and Viv's first day back at the Old Muscovy, two large men planted themselves on the premises and surveyed the scene from front to back, the one watching a video monitor in the back room, the other keeping an eye on things in the showroom. Trying not to think too much about her recent troubles, Viv found it difficult to concentrate on her work.

Around one in the afternoon she heard the buzzer ring. Hoping to see Pavel, she glanced toward the door and was taken aback when Bella Danilov stood in the entrance, waving cheerfully. Bella gave her a thousand-watt smile, showing beautiful white teeth, and pointed toward the handle. Viv couldn't believe her eyes. Walking toward the door, she buzzed her visitor in and greeted her.

"Hello, Vivian. I'm so glad to have caught you at the shop. How are you?" That low-pitched voice with the Russian accent overflowed with charm and warmth.

Viv could scarcely believe her eyes. Or ears. "I'm fine. How are you, Mrs. Danilov? I'd like to extend my condolences," she added quickly. "Marc and I were both shocked when we heard about Mr. Danilov's death. There was some speculation you had been harmed, too. It was all over the news."

"Thank you. It was so difficult for me, for all of us who loved Dimitri." There was the trace of a soulful sigh. "But life goes on, doesn't it? Even in the midst of such a loss as his. And of course, nobody understands how very hard it is to deal with this."

Viv flashed her bodyguard a significant glance; he took one look at her and understood. Then he moved closer so he could eavesdrop on the conversation.

"Such a tragedy," Viv said, hoping she sounded sympathetic. "Will you be staying in New York for a while?"

"For the time being. I had to get away from the scene of so much misery. I needed some breathing room," Bella declared, exhaling another tiny sigh.

"Well, I certainly hope you find it here. You've been through so much."

Viv hoped she didn't sound too false. She felt sorry for any widow, but somehow Bella Danilov seemed as if she could recover quite well from whatever fate dealt her. And all the rumors in the werecat community about foul play were wrong. Leave it to her to land on her feet.

"You're probably wondering why I called," Bella said.

"Well, I am surprised to see you. Can Marc and I help you in any way?"

"I was just checking some of my deliveries to the States, and I wondered if there were any irregularities with your shipment. Did everything arrive properly?"

"Yes. In perfect order. Nothing damaged."

"That's wonderful. Did you check it all?"

"Of course. Everything is there."

"Mmmmnn," Bella murmured thoughtfully. "You know, I'm taking a great risk in letting anyone know I'm in the country, but I think I can trust you to be discreet. After what happened in St. Petersburg, I need to recover, and I thought I could do that here."

"Of course I won't broadcast it," Viv assured her. "Is there anything Marc and I can do?"

"Oh, no, but thank your for offering. I was just thinking that since I was in the city, it would be nice to visit your shop. I've heard such good things about it."

Now, of all the things that Bella Danilov could have wanted to do on a secret visit to New York, this was the least likely activity Viv could imagine. Back in St. Petersburg, Bella had treated her as if she were part of the furniture; it made no sense for her to drop in for an impromptu visit and act as if they were old friends.

"Well," Viv said graciously, "since you're here, let me give you the grand tour. And would you like a cup of tea?"

"That would be lovely," Bella answered, looking like a happy schoolgirl as she removed her coat and draped it over a chair. "Do you have Darjeeling, by any chance?"

Chapter Thirty

As soon as he saw Bella Danilov walk into the shop, Pavel's man in the back punched in his boss's cell phone number to alert him to her presence at the Old Muscovy. He was as startled as Viv.

"Watch her carefully. Don't let Miss Roussel leave with her—under any circumstances. I'll have somebody trail her when she goes." Pavel paused, then said, "She must be wearing a coat, right?"

His employee said, "Of course. It's cold out there."

"Then get to it and plant a tracking device on it if possible, and don't let Miss Roussel leave. I don't care what you have to do or what you have to tell her. Just keep her in the shop."

"Right."

Pavel found this impromptu visit very suspicious. He had kept his St. Petersburg and Moscow operatives busy checking out the businessmen Viv and Marc had purchased from recently, and so far nothing suspicious had turned up. Not one of them had been involved in anything dealing with medieval icons. One had sold Marc a mirror dating from 1829, and that was the only mirror on any of his invoices. They still didn't know who had planted the icon in the undocumented one.

While Pavel was sitting at a panel of monitors watching

Bella Danilov and Viv, he noticed something "off" about Bella's demeanor. She was smiling and cheerful in the phony manner he recalled from footage on the nightly news, but something in her expression gave her away. She was carefully observing everything in that shop, as if she were taking inventory.

Bella had gone missing from Russia at the same time as her brother-in-law, but the financial newspapers were concentrating on the disappearance of the CEO, and she was merely the wife of the former one. The tabloids felt free to dwell on Bella's escaping death that day on the Nevsky and vanishing around the same time as Boris. There were a few opinions in one newspaper that her disappearance seemed a little too suspicious right after her husband's murder, and misguided references were even made to a possible "close relationship" to Boris, but those vanished after protests by lawyers from Danilov Enterprises. That line of speculation ceased after a few days anyway when her story was replaced by a gory murder/suicide among the moneyed set. But suspicions had been planted.

Dimitri Danilov's death had shocked the Russian Blues deeply, and the clan closed ranks behind his brother, even if there were some who had reservations. But the combination of bad judgment, assassination, Bella's prominence, and the rise of a sadly inferior new Hierarch disturbed them. Perhaps their clan was suffering from some curse arising from a transgression far in the past, unknown to anyone in the present day, something that could ruin them, little by little. Werecat readers of the tabloids were starting to wonder about their first family.

When Bella returned to the condo, she was surprised to find that Boris had left without a note or a message on her cell phone. This displeased her. Left to his own devices, Boris was likely to go out drinking, and right now, that could lead to spilled secrets.

"Stupid ass," Bella muttered as she opened and shut doors, searching frantically for him. He had left. He was someplace in New York City, probably drunk and drawing too much attention to himself.

Bella knew Vivian Roussel had been amazed to see her, but from her manner, that was all. She didn't flinch or look especially nervous or give any indication of any emotion except the normal surprise of seeing an acquaintance from thousands of miles away suddenly pop up in her boutique. Normal reaction. Discovering her response was the only reason Bella had risked the scouting expedition.

Bella's nerves buzzed with tension, but she felt relieved that the Roussels were fortunately still in the dark.

But where had the mirror gone? Bella had hoped that she might find it displayed in the Old Muscovy. That was a long shot, of course, but stranger things had happened. Her helpers had searched the warehouse and missed it, so that had to mean that somebody else had taken it, and since only the Roussels had access to the place, they must have removed it, simply accepting it as an attractive decorative item. No doubt they had it in one of their homes by now—if they hadn't already sold it. Bella had checked out the contents of their boutique, and she knew it wasn't there.

Her incompetent American help had botched the job when they'd kidnapped Vivian. Now they would have to try again, but this time, she would turn to people whom she could trust. Through her network of clan members, she knew she could find allies whom she could count on to do whatever she required if the price was right.

Shit. It was as if she had to pay a special nuisance tax to get the job done, what with the bribes at the airport, the payments to the goons, and now the need to hire more muscle. All she did lately was pay, pay, pay.

Bella could hardly wait to collect her own little bonanza. She hated being paymaster to the world!

Chapter Thirty-one

As soon as Bella Danilov left the Old Muscovy, one of Pavel's men tracked her to a chic condo in Manhattan, a charming but out-of-the-way place in a building that served as a low-profile sanctuary for visiting movie stars or others who wanted an elegant but discreet shelter.

The concierge was as taciturn as he ought to be, but when he saw a handsome cat walk into the lobby, he accepted his visitor as an amusing distraction. The cat explored a while, eventually slipping into the elevator with a couple of tenants who found him adorable. Domestic cat form was the preferred mode for werecats undercover. They tended to super-size for harder work—or play.

Once the tenants had gotten off at their floor, Pavel's man shape-shifted into human form and followed the signal from the device planted in Bella's coat. Third floor, apartment 3D. At the sound of footsteps approaching, he sauntered back down the hall as a couple got out of the elevator and headed to an apartment at the far end. Casually pushing open the door to the emergency staircase, he descended to the first level and went out a rear exit that brought him out onto the sidewalk. He couldn't wait to get back to Metro to tell the boss he had just found Bella's hideaway.

* * *

That evening, Pavel sat nervously in his own kitchen, watching Vivian prepare a meal. She had turned down his offer to order out, and had insisted on cooking, in an effort to do something useful while she was accepting his hospitality. One of Manhattan's finest grocery stores had supplied the ingredients and Viv was carefully preparing a salad with a variety of greens. Tilapia à la provençale was to follow, accompanied by a good wine and a fruit course for dessert. Pavel tried to help, but his offers were waved aside.

"I do know how to cook," he said as he sipped a glass of mineral water. "I had to learn in the Special Forces."

"But did you have anything edible to practice on? I heard that in Special Ops, you learn how to survive on roast grasshoppers and things like that."

"Well, yes. You have to go on survival training. But where I was, it was too cold for grasshoppers. We shot and ate whatever was available."

Viv glanced at him in curiosity. "What was the most exotic thing you ate?"

Pavel reflected as he poured himself a glass of mineral water. He shrugged. "Well, *you* might consider it exotic. A sable."

"A sable? Seriously?"

"It was him or nothing. And he kept several of us from starving."

She shuddered as she tore up more greens. "I wish you hadn't told me that. I'll never be able to look at a sable coat the same way."

Pavel gave a thin smile. "Me, either," he said.

After dinner, which turned out well, Pavel made Russian-style tea and told Viv what his man had learned about Bella.

"She's keeping a low profile, staying at a very elegant apartment she may own, off the beaten tourist track."

"Is she alone?"

"My man trailed her to the apartment building via the signal from the GPS device we planted in her coat while she paid you a visit. We don't yet know if she has a companion, but we will. One of our female operatives will bug the place when she shows up as the cleaning lady."

"If she's staying with a man, then maybe they were both involved in getting rid of her husband or stealing the icon, or both."

"We don't have any proof of either crime."

"Yet."

"Right. And we have to keep that in mind."

"Have your men finished checking all the antiques dealers we worked with?"

"Yes. They didn't find any hint of impropriety in their dealings with clients."

"And Bella?"

Pavel grinned. "Well, that's quite a story. Arrived from somewhere in central Russia back in the midnineties, took several jobs that used her computer skills, made it her business to become indispensable to her male bosses, caused a divorce in one instance, and ended up working for the Hierarch after his brother met her in a club and introduced her."

"Bella knows how to make friends."

"Bella's friendships took her from hand-me-downs to sables. There are thousands of girls like her: all driven to escape their shabby backgrounds and make new lives with the richest men they can find. Postcommunist economics."

"Do you think her marriage to your Hierarch was all about the money and nothing else?"

Pavel shrugged. "He was crazy about her. She appeared affectionate with him. But who knows? One thing for certain: as his wife, she could have anything she wanted anytime she wanted it." He looked serious. "For that reason, I don't think she would have killed him—or had him killed."

"Then," Viv said, "what do you think was behind the assassination?"

Pavel took a sip of tea, and he shook his head. "My suspicion is a business rival. The Hierarch was engaged in a bid for oil rights. And he wasn't the only one."

"Maybe somebody got tired of negotiating and hired an assassin to improve his chances."

He nodded. "It's possible. These days, stories like that fill the newspapers. The business climate is dangerous. The whole damn country is dangerous."

"Would your Hierarch have had anything to do with stealing the icon?"

"No!" Pavel exclaimed. "He was a person who respected tradition and the faith of Orthodox believers. He loved our history. In fact, he paid quite a bit of money recently to have one of Petersburg's old palaces restored. The man would never have stolen such a treasure. He was probably the biggest werecat philanthropist in the country."

Viv glanced at Pavel and said, "All right, he was an honorable person. What about the younger brother?"

"Oh," he said dismissively, "Boris is a lightweight. He might be lured into all kinds of trouble. But he wouldn't have the cunning or the ability to get involved in such a dangerous scheme."

"You never know. He did manage to become your Hierarch, didn't he?"

Viv knew she had rattled Pavel, as if she had forced him to confront the impossible. She said, "Why don't you make a few calls to Russia and see if he's turned up there—or anyplace else?"

"I will," he promised. "In fact I'll do it right now."

Chapter Thirty-two

"Yuri, Pavel here. Any new information about the Danilovs?"

Pavel heard something that sounded like a curse, and then his contact said, "According to a source whose cousin works as a maid in Boris Danilov's home, Marina Danilov was hysterical when her husband disappeared, going around the house moaning that they'd probably killed him just like they'd killed his brother, scaring the kids, and smashing things. Very dramatic."

"Marina used to be a bad actress in trashy movies. Are you surprised she'd carry on like that?"

"No. But this is the interesting part. After receiving a phone call yesterday, she pulled herself together and went out shopping and dining with her best friends. She went from several days of full-blown hysteria to 'Let's do lunch.'"

"She knows he's safe," Pavel said. "The gravy train rolls on."

"Sure. Our source couldn't believe the change in her."

"Okay. Thanks, Yuri. Again, sorry I ruined your sleep."

"I'll return the favor sometime soon. Good night."

When he hit the END button and folded the cell phone, Pavel looked at Vivian. "After getting a phone call, the new Hierarch's wife went from weepy to happy. Boris is safe."

"Good. But where is he?"

"Maybe in New York with his sister-in-law."

Viv considered that. "How are we going to find him?"

"If he's with her, Bella is going to want to keep him on a short leash. He's a drinker. He's indiscreet. She wouldn't trust him on his own."

"Same apartment?"

"I'd bet on it. Once the new cleaning lady places those bugs, we'll know for sure."

"In the meantime, let's go exploring."

Pavel shook his head. "*I'll* check on it. You stay here. Remember, you're in my apartment because it's the safest place in the city right now."

Viv gave him a disdainful glance. "I'm a werecat, descended from Krasivaya. Your Hierarch doesn't scare me. I've dealt with worse," she reminded him. Pavel and Viv were standing nose to nose. He irritated her by smiling. "I'm serious!"

Pavel nodded. "So am I."

"You're an accomplished security expert, so I'll be perfectly safe with you," Viv pointed out.

"Sorry. You're not pushing my buttons. I don't think it would be a good idea for you to roam around the city right now."

"Let's do it in small-cat form. Who'd be suspicious of a couple of cats? If things get rough, we can always supersize."

Pavel's green eyes narrowed with amusement. "What I would like to do with you as a cat is something quite different," he said with a seductive growl.

Viv's glare turned to a smile. She'd had the same thought. "I think we ought to keep our minds on the objective here and not get sidetracked." She felt a strong urge to shapeshift, which she tried to ignore. Her desire to mate was unbearable.

Pavel smiled back, all kinds of sensual thoughts tumbling through his mind, by the expression in his eyes. Viv found him so attractive, she had a hard time behaving. Nobody had appealed to her in years the way Pavel did, even though he was from a foreign clan. The taboo was fierce—which made him all the more enticing. Thoughts of the Leader's reaction made sweat start beading on her forehead. That might be even more dangerous than facing the icon thieves right now.

"*Dorogaya*," he said softly, "I don't want to see you harmed. That's what you're paying me for. I'll take the chances."

"But if Boris is the heavy drinker you say he is, we could probably track him to a bar and grab him."

Pavel looked dubious. "I doubt Bella would allow him that much freedom."

"She left her little hideout to come see me. He could find his way to the nearest bar if he wanted."

"There's no guarantee he'd be that predictable."

"Does he know the city?"

"I don't think so."

"Then he might do what any stranger would do if he wanted a drink: ask the concierge where the closest bar is."

"Possibly."

"If he gets restless, he's going to want a drink," Viv pointed out. "And if he's staying with the widow Danilov, he's going to require lots of alcohol. Believe me."

"All right," Pavel said. "Then we'll start staking out the bars. I'll put someone on it."

"And what will we do?" she asked.

For a moment, Pavel simply gave her the sexiest smile that had ever registered on her radar. He put his arm around her waist and drew her close. "Let's do this," he said and softly kissed her mouth.

Viv's best intentions of honoring the ancient taboos collapsed in the time it took to put her arms around his neck and kiss him back. She leaned into him as he hugged her tighter, and she startled him by the warmth of her response. She wanted him, and she wanted him right now.

Viv's hands caressed his chest as she sought out buttons to undo, and then realized he was wearing a T-shirt. Undaunted, she slipped her hand under it and felt him react to her touch and pull her closer to him.

Pavel kissed her as he slowly undid the pearl buttons of her silk blouse, and then continued to kiss her as he pulled it out of her skirt and up and over her head as he flung it into the air.

"I hope you don't do this with all your clients," she murmured as she came up for breath.

"First time," he replied, cutting off the conversation with more kisses.

"This breaks all the rules," she whispered as Pavel released her briefly. She stood staring at him, torn between her desire and her fear of the Leader's retribution—if he ever found out. She wrapped her arms around Pavel as he picked her up and carried her into his bedroom.

"Vivian, I won't force you to do anything you feel is wrong," he said as they both landed on his bed. He leaned over her as they stretched out, and he nuzzled her neck, pushing away her long hair and trailing kisses down her throat and into the lovely valley between her breasts.

Viv smiled into his eyes and caressed his hair. Then she said seriously, "I have to warn you, our Leader thinks I should be his mate."

The Russian gave her an amused smile. "I can understand that."

"No, it's not humorous," she said. "I've told him very forcefully I don't wish it. If he knew about this, he would attack you, Pavel," she said seriously. "I've just learned there's a bad situation in my clan. I haven't even told Marc yet. Our Leader is out of control. He's raped two of our females. My clan will have bring him to trial. I've already promised to have him put under surveillance to build a case."

Pavel looked serious. This surprised him, but he would offer help if she wanted it.

"I claim the right of all Maine Coon cats to choose their mates," Viv said without hesitation. "And if possible, I'd like Metro to help me keep watch on our Leader so we can prevent him from harming anyone else."

"Agreed. Now I think we shouldn't talk so much," he murmured. "Our kind is always so much more natural when they just act on their instincts—don't you agreee?"

Pavel sat up briefly and took off his clothing, then removed the rest of Vivian's and slid under the covers with her.

"I'd say that's a good idea," she whispered as she covered his mouth with kisses.

Chapter Thirty-three

The next day Viv and Marc were back at work under the watchful eye of Metro's men, Viv took her brother aside and told him what she'd heard about the Leader. He was shaken. And then he revealed he'd heard some unsettling things a few weeks earlier about Sinclair's newest ideas about security. He was evidently preparing for some kind of dictatorship. Hank was worried, too.

"We have to stop him," Viv said. "I'm having Pavel assign men to track him so we can gather evidence. You could network with some of the members you trust and set up a special meeting for an impeachment. One of the females will testify if someone else will. She's frightened to do it alone. I'll testify that he tried to rape me."

"We have to make sure we have enough support. This has never happened before in the clan. Members might hesitate."

"Our clan has never before had a criminal for a Leader," she replied. "And we can't keep this one. We have to depose him."

Marc nodded gloomily. The proud Maine Coon cat clan was being undermined by a vicious megalomaniac, and right now he and Viv had to contend with their own problems with the Siberians. They felt caught in a vise.

In his town house that night, Marc felt secure enough to suggest to his bodyguard that he wanted to get out. He was used to a social life, and he felt like a prisoner under house arrest. Nobody had tried to kidnap him since the large guys with the muscles had taken up their position at the shop. He was willing to bet the enemy had given up.

"Mr. Federov wants you in our sight," his new bodyguard told him.

"I'd like to attend a gallery opening. You can come, too. They sent two tickets."

"I think it would be smarter to stay home."

"I have to get out. This is driving me crazy. It won't be hard to guard me. We'll be in the same room."

The bodyguard gave him a disapproving look.

"It won't be a problem. It's casual."

"I'll have to check with headquarters," the bodyguard replied.

After some discussion, the bodyguard André closed his cell phone and told Marc they could go. Another guard would meet them near the location.

The gallery opening was a pretty lively affair, with a group of A-list types and their hangers-on, followed by the definite B-list groupies and a mix of others of indeterminate status, most of them dressed in black and all of them interested in the refreshments.

One of the city's chichi caterers provided stylish fare that mingled low-calorie count with creative uses of color. Marc sampled the sushi appreciatively. He recognized a few business acquaintances and greeted several pretty blondes who were networking among the art. He noticed that André refrained from eating or drinking and kept a discreet lookout.

While the guests were circulating, admiring the art or eyeing one another, Marc felt there was something odd about a few of them. Nothing he could put his finger on, but he could feel that he wasn't the only werecat in the room.

"André," he said, "there are other members of the brotherhood here."

André knew what he meant. It was werecat slang for their own kind.

"Which clan?"

"Don't know. But I don't think they're our people."

"I think we ought to make it an early evening, Mr. Roussel. Say your goodbyes to the hosts and let's leave. Be very natural. No rush. But we have to go."

Marc ate another piece of sushi and sauntered over to the artist who had invited him to the party. He praised his work, expressed his regrets, and explained he had an early-morning meeting with clients.

"Nice and easy," André instructed him. "Get your coat and move out the door like there's no rush. When we get onto the sidewalk, we make a quick right turn and hop into the car, which will be waiting for us."

As Marc and his guard exited the party, they were aware of two men who noted their departure and headed across the room to leave right after them.

"You know, I don't want to sound paranoid, but I think we're being followed."

André pulled a walkie-talkie out of his pocket and said, "Bring the car around. We've got company."

As Marc and his guard picked up their pace and headed in the direction of the SUV that drove toward them, André gave Marc a push and shouted, "Run!" as their pursuers broke into a trot and tried to overtake them.

Three loud bangs filled the air as somebody fired at them. André let out a howl of pain as one of the bullets found a target, but he drew his own weapon and ordered Marc to run faster as the waiting SUV approached, headlights blinding them.

When the vehicle pulled over and screeched to a stop, André, even in his weakened state, could see there was something wrong. His partner was gone and a stranger was at the wheel.

"Siberians," he said as he gritted his teeth with pain and

grabbed Marc. "Don't go in. Come on, we have to make a run for it. Now!"

As the driver of the SUV shouted to his associates, Marc and André ran into a dark parking garage and hid. With the two pursuers nearby, Marc made a decision, shape-shifted, raced out in big-cat form the size of a puma, and lunged at them from behind. He inflicted enough damage to buy time, and then took off through the lot with André, even though the guard was clearly in trouble. He lurched painfully on a wounded leg.

Marc shape-shifted again as they ran for their lives, not stopping for breath until they reached a dimly lit bar located on a sidestreet, somewhere in SoHo. A few patrons glanced at the newcomers, then went back to their drinks as the two visitors slid into a booth.

"I chewed those two up pretty well," Marc said with satisfaction. Then he glanced at his companion and saw even in the murky light that he was grimacing in pain.

"I need a doctor," said André. "Fast. I'm calling for backup."

Chapter Thirty-four

When Pavel recovered from their lovemaking a few hours later, he and Viv were curled up in big-cat form in his bed, with him nestled against her magnificent silvery fur and savoring the moment. He nuzzled her affectionately and then hopped off the bed and shape-shifted, disappearing into the hall.

Viv stretched out to full length, languid and very pleased with their first mating. She relived their passionate lovemaking in both human and feline form. Then she stood up, shook herself, and leaped down from the bed and onto the thick carpet where she shape-shifted and picked up her scattered clothing.

As a werecat, Viv felt the same urges an ordinary cat would feel. The desire to mate was strong. As a woman, she felt she had been a little too carried away by passion, and now she wondered how things would develop from here. She wanted this man, even if he was a stranger and from a different clan. He made love in a way that thrilled her.

"You make me very happy," he said as he met Viv in the hall and gave her a look that sent a spiral of lust straight to her core.

"I could say the same."

"Then," he said as he gently lifted her chin and kissed her, "we should take it as a sign that this is a special relationship that ought to be nurtured."

She didn't know if it was anything more than sheer lust that attracted her so strongly to this gorgeous Russian, but she was more than willing to find out. No male, werecat or human, had ever moved her the way he had. It was as if he was the other half she had been missing for so many years.

The mood was shattered when a phone call came in from Metro's call center. Viv heard him ask, "Where are they now?"

There was an explosion of Russian that sounded very angry, and then she heard, "Get back out on the street and search for the attackers. Send two others to case the area. I'm coming, too. I'll go to the bar and get them."

When he hit the END button and flipped the cell phone closed, Viv glanced at him. "Trouble?" she inquired.

"Your brother and his bodyguard went to a gallery opening in SoHo earlier tonight, and they were spotted by the enemy. André was shot and wounded. Marc tangled with them."

Viv rose from the chair and looked stunned. "Where are they now? Is Marc all right?"

Pavel gave a nod. "They're holed up in a small bar in SoHo for the moment. My man was supposed to pick them up, but while he was waiting, he was carjacked and knocked unconscious. Marc and his guard ran for it. Metro's call center just got a call from them asking for help. Marc's okay."

"I don't want those filthy animals to get their paws on my brother."

"We won't let them. I'm ordering my men to cover the area and look for werecats while I go to the bar to get André and your brother. Marc's tracking device will take us to him in case he and Andre have to leave before I reach them."

"Well, I'm not staying here while Marc is in trouble. I'll go with you."

Pavel looked at her very seriously. "That's a bad idea. I don't want to have to worry about you while I'm hunting. It's safer for you here."

"Marc is my brother. I'm not going to sit here without doing something to help him."

"Dorogaya," he said patiently, "if Marc had listened to his bodyguard, they wouldn't be in this mess. I don't want the same thing to happen to you."

Viv shook her head. "I can spot him before you can. It's better if I go with you."

"We're dealing with scum. I wouldn't want any woman I know to fall into their hands, least of all, one I care for."

"Well, I survived an encounter with them before and I came out on top," she said stubbornly. "They ended up in a landfill and I'm still here."

"This is not a good idea."

"Do you have a better one?" she replied.

En route to SoHo, Pavel contacted a doctor who worked for Metro, another werecat, and told him to get ready because he was bringing in a wounded employee. He also called two of his men who were patrolling the area and ordered them to meet him at the bar.

Both cars converged on the dark sidestreet within minutes of each other. Viv and Pavel and two tall men in black entered, drew a few bored glances, and looked around the room. It was small, with very bad lighting, a good hiding place.

"There they are," said Viv as she finally spotted her brother.

Pavel and one of his men lifted André to his feet and helped him out while Marc threw forty dollars on the table to cover the drinks they had to order to stay. They were out of there before anybody had a chance to look twice.

"Pavel!" Viv took his arm.

Standing in front of the two cars were three tough-looking young guys grinning at them, waiting to start something.

"Hey, babe," said one punk, indicating Viv, "you want to add me to your to-do list?"

Pavel tilted his chin in the direction of the cars, and the others helped load André in. "Get him to the doctor," he ordered. "I'll handle this." As the SUV pulled away, carrying André to the clinic, he walked over to the three jerks and said, "Excuse me. I don't think I heard what you said to the lady. Maybe you'd like to say it to me." His eyes gleamed with evil intent. He was itching to go werecat. Viv could smell it in his scent.

"Hey, man, I don't swing that way," one of the punks said with a laugh. They all looked at Viv, who had stayed behind, not wanting to leave Pavel. They couldn't believe she hadn't gotten out of there.

"I think these guys need manners one-oh-one," she said with a glance at Pavel. "Agreed?"

"Right."

As the three street punks started toward them, intending damage, they saw their prey disappear behind the SUV. Bewildered, they looked at one another stupidly and saw something strange walk from around the back of the vehicle and stand facing them, teeth bared, just waiting to lunge. Two big cats, about the size of panthers, one dark silvery gray, the other shaggy.

"Oh, shit! Oh, shit!"

The three young guys practically trampled one another in their rush to get out of there.

"Man, it's that bad weed you bought," one of them screamed as he ran down the street, the sound of big sneakers pounding on the pavement. "Now I'm seeing tigers. I hope they get your ass!"

Viv glanced after them and gave Pavel a swat with her paw. "I thought they were the Siberians who tried to grab Marc. Did you know they were just stupid humans?"

"Thought they might be the bad guys," he said. "Looked dumb enough to be rogue werecats."

"Males," Viv said. "Let's shift and go get Marc."

Chapter Thirty-five

"Marc, I know you're used to an active social life, but until we get the piece back to its owners, I think it's the safer for you to avoid going out at night."

Pavel looked serious. His operative André looked abashed. Two days after his injury, he was back at work, due to the doctor's care and the amazing recuperative powers of werefolk. If the wound wasn't life-threatening, a few days would generally heal it.

"Well, when is that going to happen?" Marc demanded. "We've handed it over to your contact for safekeeping. When are the Russians going to come take it home?"

"As soon as the transfer can be arranged. I think you can appreciate the need for secrecy. The highest levels of diplomacy are involved in this."

"They'd better kick it into high gear," he said. "Otherwise neither one of us is going to survive."

"You and Vivian will be all right during the day with my men on the premises. At night, just stay put for maybe the next thirty-six hours. This will be over before you know it."

Marc nodded. "That's what I'm afraid of." And he gave Viv a look that was full of foreboding.

Since his trip to New York, Boris had found distraction by dining anonymously at various restaurants, as long as they had a good bar. Bella tended to want to shop, but she was strong-willed enough to forgo that ultimate pleasure in order to keep a low profile.

She felt flustered and furious by the fact that all her elaborate plans for stealing the treasure had imploded before she got to New York. As a woman who had reached the top by resolute scheming, Bella could barely cope with the wreckage of her most audacious plot yet. She had taken huge risks, used Boris's contacts to arrange for the theft and transport of Russia's most cherished icon, lined up a buyer, and now because of some stupid, anonymous underling, it was—momentarily—out of her grasp.

"Damn!"

The sound of the telephone jolted her out of her gloomy reflections. Bella walked to the table and picked up the phone, wondering who might be calling her. So few people had this number.

"Mrs. Danilov?"

"Yes. Who is this?"

"A friend."

"Then why don't you tell me your name?" she replied, about to hang up.

"Stay on the phone," he said. "You don't really know me, but I know quite a bit about you."

"So does anyone who reads the newspapers."

"I have someone here who is very close to you."

Bella felt a momentary frisson. She stiffened.

"Don't you want to know who?"

"There is nobody in New York who is close to me," she said. And she hung up.

Bella had scarcely had time to cross the room to get her cigarettes when the phone rang again. She forced herself to ignore it. It continued to ring. She lit a cigarette. The ringing began to drive her wild.

"Who the hell is this?" she demanded as she grabbed the phone and shouted into the receiver.

"You may call me Bill," he said. "I have somebody here who wants to talk to you. Here he is."

"Bella, be polite to these people," Boris said. "They're serious players. They snatched me off the street, and they want what they think we have."

"Why did you have to go roaming around the bars? This is what happens."

"I think they're your people," he said nervously.

"Why?"

"They know about the, uh, transport of that object we're all concerned about."

"And?"

"It looks as if they want a cut of the action."

Bella hung her head, shook it, and then started to swear so fiercely, she feared she was becoming hysterical with rage.

"Let me talk to the one who calls himself Bill," she said abruptly.

"Yes?" he replied.

"Who are you?" she demanded.

"A member of your own clan. We think what you did was very daring, but apt to create trouble for the entire clan if you get caught."

Bella took a drag of her cigarette. What else could go wrong with this plan? Perhaps those Roussels had broken the mirror containing the icon, and *she* was about to inherit seven years of bad luck.

"So you want me to call it off?"

"No, actually we want you to go ahead. We simply would like a chance to participate."

"Not on your life. I took all the risks. I should take the profits."

"Yes," said Bill, "but we're holding somebody who also has an interest in the success of the plan. Since the death of his brother, he's become an important man. How would it look if he were to die and leave a note behind—which would end up on the front page of the tabloids—blaming you for the assassination of your husband and the theft of a national treasure? Very bad for business, right?"

"Boris is not going to kill himself," she said impatiently. "And I didn't kill Dimitri."

"Whatever you say," Bill replied cheerfully. "But we will stage the suicide, write the note, and send it to all the papers. Then you can sit back and watch the fallout."

Bella clenched her teeth in sheer frustration. "How did you grab him? In a bar?"

"Yes. We had a very pretty young woman start up a conversation with him, and when he was about to follow her outside, we pushed him into a car and brought him along with us. He's become quite talkative."

"He's a fool," Bella sneered.

"Yes, but he's also a Hierarch. You'd do well to keep that in mind. He's not exactly fond of you."

At that, Bella kept quiet. Boris might be a dupe who could be manipulated by his constant need for cash, but deep down, his dislike of her might make him willing to do or say things that would come back to haunt her. She still needed his cooperation, and now she had to figure out a way to deal with this new disaster. They said they were members of her clan, so they must have had some tie to the New York Siberians who were supposed to retrieve the icon from the warehouse and return it to her. Were they working together?

"All right," she said wearily. "What do you want from us?"

Chapter Thirty-six

"Pavel," Viv said, "how long do you think it's going to take to get the object shipped back to its country?"

"Catherine Marais is holding talks with key people. They're making plans."

"Good. By the way," she said quietly, "have you managed to find out what John Sinclair is up to?"

"One of my men is shadowing him, hacking into his computer, making inquiries about his friends. So far we've uncovered lots of offshore banking, debts at casinos in Las Vegas and Atlantic City, fights with his mistress, and expensive presents for her. Busy fellow."

"What about our women?"

"Right now he seems to be concerned about the relationship in New York. He's not molesting any females from your clan. And by the way," he said with a smile, "the girlfriend is a Turkish Angora."

Viv's eyes flashed. "That hypocrite! On top of everything else."

"We also learned that he left the CIA under something of a cloud. He engineered a disaster in Bosnia and never regained the confidence of his bosses. They kicked him to the curb after that." Pavel glanced at Viv. "How did he manage to take control of your clan?"

"Clever packaging. Good spin doctors. We were foolish."

Viv and Pavel sat in his state-of-the-art kitchen, drinking a glass of wine after they had finished dinner. He had cooked, and Viv couldn't believe how good the meal was. The man had many talents. And he was so sexy he ought to come wrapped in asbestos. Every time she looked into those beautiful green eyes, she wanted to shape-shift and mate like wildcats.

"How is your employee?" she asked. "The one who was injured when they stole his SUV the night Marc nearly got kidnapped."

"He's recovering."

"Any idea who was behind it?"

Pavel looked at her with those dark-fringed green eyes, and Viv felt her muscles contract. She struggled against the desire to shapeshift.

"It has to be Bella. André recognized his attackers as Siberians he interviewed right after you were kidnapped. At the time, we thought they were just bottom-feeders. Now it looks like she hired them. Of all the antiques dealers you visited, she's the only one who dropped in to case your shop after the icon went missing. You said she treated you like a poor relation in St. Petersburg, and now she wants to be your new best friend. I watched the video of her in your shop. She poked around every corner, looking for something. She has to suspect you have what she stole."

Viv nodded. "That had to be the reason for the visit."

"And when we tapped her phone, we discovered her missing brother-in-law's in New York, too. Very interesting situation."

Viv smiled. "Then you still have a Hierarch."

"Unfortunately he's now in the hands of some members of Bella's clan who want a share of the action. We heard this on the audiotape. They're threatening his life as well as her reputation if she fails to cooperate, so I think Bella's going to make the right decision and cut them in."

"But that doesn't mean a thing since we have the icon and she doesn't."

"Yes," Pavel said, "but maybe these guys don't realize that."

Viv nodded. "But if Bella's hustling them, they'll probably kill her. And your new Hierarch."

"Good riddance to her."

"But what about your Hierarch?"

"Since he's the only we have at the moment, as stupid as he is, we'll have to protect him."

"Even if he helped steal the Virgin of Saratov?"

Pavel shook his head. "If he did such a thing, it would make him subject to the full penalties of our law. He would forfeit all claims to our loyalty. Do you understand what she means to our country? This is a powerful protector of the people. Werecat as I am, I believe she saved me from death several times during my combat service. No Russian Blue in the world would serve a Hierarch who disgraced us like that."

Viv stared down into her wineglass. "How dangerous was it in Chechnya?"

"I don't like to talk about it. It was bad for us and bad for them. Insanity on both sides. I came close to having my head blown off by bombs on several occasions. A wall collapsed right over me and left me standing in the outline of a blown-out window. A member of my unit shot a sniper who had me in his sights because one of their bombs lit up the area and took away his cover. Not good memories."

"And you lost the love of your life."

"Yes. That happened in a theater in Moscow, but it was the war that caused her death." Pavel suddenly looked much older and exhausted. "I nearly went mad with grief. I resigned my commission and retired to a monastery just to be alone. Then, after six months, I got in touch with Vladimir and asked him if he thought I might find work in America."

"And you did."

"Yes. I began by working as a security specialist for an agency, and then I moved up and finally opened my own. We don't do bounty hunting or anything like that. We stick pretty much to high-tech surveillance. Or low-tech if that's what the situation calls for. We do bodyguard assignments from time to time. I've done special assignments for Mr. Morgan, so I've come to know him. Very fine man."

"And the werewolf hunter?"

"Mademoiselle Catherine Marais is very professional, very competent. She and her partner are feared by werewolves all over the world." Pavel smiled. "Did you know that she and her partner took down the last Montfort werewolf?"

"Impressive. She must be an expert."

"The best."

"Ah," said Viv with a wicked smile, "it sounds as though you're quite an admirer of this French huntress. Perhaps there's more to this than you'd like to tell me."

To Viv's amusement, Pavel looked genuinely disconcerted. "No," he exclaimed, "I have no relationship with this lady. She's a business acquaintance," he said as he gave Viv a seductive smile and leaned over the counter to kiss her softly on the lips. The kiss lingered, causing Viv's temperature to rise as she responded. She returned the kiss.

They straightened up, and Pavel walked around to Vivian and took her in his arms. "You're the only woman I'm interested in," he said as he lowered his mouth to hers and kissed her fiercely. "I think you're more than enough to keep me busy." He kissed her again, then again.

"Oh, *koshka,*" Viv murmured, as she ran her hands over his chest, "we could be busy forever."

"All right," he said as he pulled her closer to him and led her into the bedroom. Pavel felt her warm, yielding body against his, and he whispered, "Why don't we begin right now?" And his kiss lingered on her lips. "I love you. You're such a seductive creature. And your human form is enchanting," he murmured as he sank down onto the bed and took her in his arms.

Viv caressed him tenderly as they kissed. Then she became more aggressive and ended up on top of him, with her long chestnut hair undone and falling over him as they embraced and thrashed around in their excitement.

Pavel managed to undress her and himself as they kept kissing, and neither one of them knew how they didn't fall off the bed and onto the floor with all the rolling around.

He felt Viv's legs open and wrap themselves around him as she clung to him. He could feel the rapid beating of her heart as he positioned himself on top of her and kissed her neck, her breasts, her mouth.

When he entered her, Viv uttered a cry of passion that made him want to please her, possess her, fill her with such satisfaction that she would never even want another male in her life.

"Oh, *koshka*," she whispered as they rocked with the force of their lovemaking. "Don't stop! Don't even think about stopping. Oh, Pavel!" She breathed as she flung her arms around him. Her words died in a gasp of pleasure so intense she thought she'd die.

When they were exhausted and lying entangled on the expensive sheets, Viv snuggled up to her lover and kissed him lightly on the cheek. "I think they were wrong when the old lawgivers forbade us to mate with other clans," she murmured. "I wouldn't have known what I was missing."

"So I've helped you see another side of the law," he said sleepily as he rested his head on her breasts and lounged happily beside her. "Very good."

"Perhaps we ought to rethink some of the old notions," she said lazily. "Times change. People change."

But somewhere deep in her soul, she feared she would pay a heavy price for this forbidden pleasure. She couldn't even bear to think of Sinclair's reaction.

Chapter Thirty-seven

Bella Danilov experienced such hatred that she had trouble maintaining her human form. This stupidity affected her at such a primal level that she longed to go werecat and chew him up. Damn Boris! She should have known he'd screw up and leave her open to this kind of blackmail. These New York Siberians could murder him for all she cared. Oh, shit! His death would be bad for her, so she had to keep him alive. With all the likely rumors circulating about Dimitri's death, the last thing she needed was to have a second dead Hierarch in her vicinity.

Damn, she thought. *Of all the things I could have done, why did I have to get involved with this?* That was naturally a rhetorical question; she knew why she had chosen to steal the Saratov icon and ship it to the United States. She wanted to make millions.

Someone help me, she thought as she reached for her cigarettes and selected another one from the pack. *All this bad luck started with Dimitri's death. And now I have to make sure this fool stays alive. What a curse.*

As one of the American presidents once said, "Life is not fair." Didn't she know it.

Catherine Marais had been in touch with the Russians and she arranged for a top-level diplomat to view the icon so he could verify its authenticity. He agreed to the conditions: blindfold until he arrived at the location, then no attempt to determine where he was. Catherine would vouch for his safety. Determined to bring the icon home and restore it to its rightful place, he would have agreed to almost anything to get a look at it. Pressure from the public and from the Kremlin combined to make a powerful incentive for risk.

That night as Vladimir drove across town with Catherine, two of Pavel's men trailed them, keeping watch for any unwanted company. They were in touch with Catherine by cell phone, using earpieces for greater mobility. When the gentleman, a Mr. Lubov, met the car at the appointed place, he got in and Catherine handed him a blindfold and a pair of dark glasses to go over it.

"I'm sorry for the inconvenience," she said apologetically, "but the person who has been entrusted with the icon had nothing to do with its disappearance and doesn't want visitors because of it."

"I understand, mademoiselle. Believe me, as soon as we have the painting, that's the last he'll have to worry about it. But are you certain it is the Saratov madonna?"

"Oh, yes. How it came to be in the United States is a mystery, but it is definitely the stolen icon."

"You have no idea how precious she is to my country. Since the days of Ivan the Terrible, she's been regarded as a protector of the nation. Now I hope I can bring her home."

"You will, Mr. Lubov, as soon as you can guarantee the arrangements."

When Vladimir, who had finally been brought into the secret the day before, drove his passengers into the underground garage of Ian's town house, he and Catherine led their blindfolded guest into the area of the vaults, where Ian was waiting for them.

"You may remove the blindfold," he said quietly. "I hope your trip wasn't too uncomfortable, sir."

The diplomat shook his head as he pulled off the dark

glasses and the black cloth. He blinked as his eyes became accustomed to the light again. "I'm fine. Now I believe you have something you'd like me to see."

"Wait here and I'll bring it to you."

The Russian nodded and glanced around the bare room, at his two companions, and at the steel doors that closed behind the man's back. Catherine and Vladimir stood next to him, all three of them anxious for the next step.

When Ian emerged with a rectangular object covered with a dark cloth, the Russian stood immobile as his eyes went right to it. He stood a little straighter and he drew in a sharp breath as he watched his host remove the cloth. "My God!"

Dumbfounded, Lubov stared at the icon. He gingerly stretched out his hand and touched it, unable to disguise his emotion at the sight of the resplendent Madonna. "This is the Virgin of Saratov," the diplomat said in awe. "My God, I can't believe it. I was so afraid it would be a hoax."

"Are you certain?"

Lubov nodded. "Yes. When I was a child, my grandmother's brother was a monk at the monastery there. Stalin was so desperate during the war that he actually permitted a few old men to keep it open so they could pray for the war effort. He knew the importance of the Virgin of Saratov."

"So you saw the icon there?"

"Oh, yes. My old uncle was devoted to the Madonna, and he used to hold me up so I could get a good look."

He turned to Catherine and said, "This is no forgery. Back in the days of Peter the Great, a Swedish army fought the tsar, and he ordered the monks of that time to bring him the icon so he could take it with him in battle. It received a bullet wound, and if you look carefully, you will see the spot in the wood where the Swedish bullet grazed it. Not many people know this. The monks did, and they told me the story."

All eyes went to the icon, and with Lubov pointing the bullet damage out, they discovered it.

"Then," said Ian, "let us make arrangements for her return."

In a shabby apartment in Queens, Boris Danilov sat nervously between a couple of members of Bella's clan who appeared to be waiting for somebody or something. He glanced around the room and wondered if they lived here or simply used it as a place of business, since the apartment seemed like a sad time capsule of the seventies, all orange accents and shag carpets. Poverty and bad taste had left it adrift in the era of love-ins and disco boots while the rest of the world had moved on.

"Are we waiting for someone?" Boris asked. "Will it take long? I'd like to be on my way, if I can."

"You go when we say so," one of his abductors said.

"Fine. Just let me know," he said.

Boris considered shape-shifting and trying to leap out the window, but although he'd heard some remarkable stories of cats surviving leaps from upper floors, he felt he had too much to lose to attempt it himself. He wasn't completely desperate yet. That was about to happen, but so far he had managed to hold himself together. These thugs needed him and Bella for their plans. Of course, they didn't seem to realize that the icon had gone missing. He considered telling them that, but hesitated. He didn't know what Bella had revealed, and he didn't want to say anything to contradict her.

"Do I know the person who's coming?" Boris inquired.

"Maybe."

After two more hours of this, the Hierarch heard footsteps in the hall, and then the sound of a key turning a lock. He looked expectantly toward the door and then rose as he saw three men walk into the room. Actually two large men dragged a third into the room and plopped him down on the floor.

"Take a good look at him. He worked for you."

Boris did that, but with all the bruises and the swelling, it was hard to make out his features.

"Sorry. I don't know him."

The larger of the two thugs snorted. "He's the one who made the arrangements for the icon to go missing. We've been questioning him."

"What have you done to him?"

"Had a conversation. He doesn't like to say much."

Boris looked at the man on the floor and felt a stab of fear in his heart. He had never seen anyone beaten like this before, and he didn't want these maniacs to get started on *him*.

"What did you want him to tell you?" Boris asked.

"How he managed to hide the icon in that damned warehouse without letting us find it."

"How did you know it was there?"

The big guy gave a nasty laugh that had nothing humorous in it. "Because he betrayed you as soon as he could. Only he didn't know that the contact he had was my brother, who naturally told me. Small world."

Boris marveled at the level of evil in the universe. Betrayed and sold out at every turn, he sincerely wished something good might happen right now. Anything, however small, just to restore his faith in the possibility of hope.

"Oh, damn," said the thug from the sofa. "I think he just croaked." And all the others leaped at their victim to try frantically to revive him.

Thank you, gods, Boris thought. *Thank you.* The secret had died with the man. At this point, Boris wanted to put as much distance between himself and the Virgin of Saratov as possible.

He wanted to forget about the whole crazy scheme.

Chapter Thirty-eight

Pavel's wiretaps revealed that Bella was now having problems with her Manhattan helpers. The audiotapes confirmed that she had been guilty of stealing something important enough to interest other felons, even if there was as of yet no hard evidence to connect her with the theft of the icon, since she and the others refused to refer to it by name. Still, it would have been too far-fetched to think it was anything else.

It bothered Pavel that Bella had been at the scene of the Hierarch's assassination and had survived. It just seemed too convenient for her to have eluded death when three men in her company had been shot down just meters from where she stood. True, the video on CNN showed a frantic Bella screaming and demanding to go to her husband's side, but something about the scent rang false.

I'm a cynic, Pavel thought. Perhaps she *had* tried to get out there as soon as the firing started. But still, she had stayed inside the door of the restaurant, a sensible precaution. Yes, her bodyguard had been holding her back. Yes, she had shown extreme emotion on camera when she had flung herself over her husband on the sidewalk, but for an instant, for a split second, Bella had exhibited the kind of attention to detail that Pavel remembered from the war. A fleeting trace of checking the scene flickered in her eyes.

Were they all dead? Any sign of life? And then full-scale operatic grief, shown round the world on the news.

Damn, he thought. *She could have planned this.* And if she had planned it, she had arranged for the assassination with one of the many freelance shooters for hire doing a lucrative business in removing people's enemies these days.

Now, if Bella had orchestrated Dimitri's death, was Boris her coconspirator? Pavel hated to think so. Boris was their Hierarch now, a man to whom the Russian Blues owed their allegiance. He was most likely Bella's partner in the theft of the icon, but could he have actually conspired in the death of his own brother?

Pavel knew that if he had proof of Bella's involvement in the assassination, she would face retribution for it. Even if she escaped punishment for the theft, she wouldn't escape payback for the murder.

With that in mind, he dialed a telephone number in St. Petersburg and smiled when a tired voice said, "Yes?"

"It's Pavel. How are things?"

"The same. How can I help you?"

"Any word on the killing?"

There was no need to specify which killing. For the Russian Blues there was only one that counted at the moment.

"Rumors," he said. "Speculation. Some of the brethren learned that a group of gangsters was celebrating at a nightclub two days after the murder. They got really wasted and bragged to some female talent that they just made a fortune for five minutes' work."

"Did she ask what that entailed?"

Pavel's friend laughed. "They were drunk, but not that drunk. The girl didn't try to find out too much since she already knew their reputations, and she didn't want them coming after her. But she said they were toasting somebody named Bella." He let that sink in.

"None of that is illegal. And Russia is full of women

named Bella. They'd claim Bella is a girlfriend, and who could say she wasn't? We need something stronger."

"That's all I have so far. The girl knows a lot of shady guys who come to that place to celebrate successful jobs. They wear shoulder holsters and ankle holsters, and they throw money around like there's no tomorrow. She's spotted lots of gang-related tattoos and heard the slang they use. They're our own homegrown mafia."

"Well, we need more than a girl's suspicions. If she can provide you with names or a snitch, we might be able to do something. I'd like to see our leader's killer pay for the crime."

"So would we all. And believe me, we're keeping our ears open. Some of the brethren have an idea that there might be a way to connect Bella Danilov to it, but it will take a while. Interviews, talks, negotiations."

Pavel took this to mean the Russian Blues back home were going to track down the suspects, interrogate them in a way that would make the old KGB proud, and force them to rat out their accomplices. No holds barred.

"Dimitri was a good man and a great Hierarch," Pavel said. "He deserves to be avenged."

"He will be," replied his friend. "Just as soon as we can pinpoint the culprits."

"Good hunting," Pavel said. "Meanwhile, I'll be keeping watch in my territory."

"Keep us posted."

"I will," he replied.

Pavel hadn't told his contact about Bella's New York sojourn, because he knew that the only way to keep information secure was to put a lid on it. When the time came, he would alert the brethren. If there were any moles among the Russian Blues, he wasn't going to make it easy for them.

What he needed to do now was to try to destabilize the relationship between Bella and her brother-in-law. From what he knew about Boris, he was the subordinate here.

Dimitri Danilov had been keeping him around because he was his brother, and werecats would never throw out a sibling, no matter how stupid and useless, unless there was a serious reason.

Lack of character and an excessive love of booze weren't enough for Boris to get kicked to the curb, but now that he was the new Hierarch, the Russian Blues needed a leader, not a drunk with a dependency on a power-crazed Siberian Forest cat. From the mood of his brethren back home, Pavel wondered if some of them might be thinking of a coup.

Wishing to drive a wedge between the Siberian and her puppet, Pavel reflected on what he knew about his new Hierarch. Boris was really just a handsome guy who looked good in his designer wardrobe, who was the designated host for visiting dignitaries, who kept visitors entertained while Dimitri made the deals. He was an empty suit.

What else? Oh, he had married Marina, a skinny blonde with surgically enhanced breasts and lips who made a ten second splash in the movie business with a B film called *Vixens of Voronezh*.

Pavel had seen the flick while on R and R during the war when he and guys from his unit had gotten drunk after an especially bad week, gone to a dilapidated cinema in the boonies, brought some liquid refreshment with them, and laughed themselves silly at the film. They probably couldn't have sat through it if they had been sober. Now he cringed at the thought that Marina was the first lady of the Russian Blues.

Boris Danilov appeared to dote on her, Pavel remembered. He'd had two children with her. Perhaps she could become a source of worry for the new Hierarch as he hid out in Manhattan, so far away from home. She wasn't the hausfrau type, and Pavel would bet anything that if she were offered a chance to have a good time, she'd take it.

He'd make it his business to try to arrange it.

Chapter Thirty-nine

When Boris's Siberian captors released him on the condition that they were now partners who wanted a cut of the money from the icon deal, and returned him to his apartment, he was badly shaken, especially after seeing the battered were-cat they had questioned.

"These people are savages," he said. "They have no respect for life. They'll kill us."

"They are thugs," Bella said. "They can be outsmarted. If the one who hid the icon is dead, then the others don't know where it is. Since we don't know where it is, either, they can't hold us responsible for that, so we're safe."

After digesting that, Boris said, "Okay. So what are we going to do when our contact meets us, expecting to receive the icon?"

Bella looked annoyed. "I'll think of something," she said.

"You're not going to create a fake, are you? There's no way we could pull it off. I say we just give up on the whole thing. It's getting too complicated. Let's just stay here until we've missed the deadline for the oil deal, go home with our cover story, and collect the millions."

"There's too much money involved not to keep going with this," she said.

Boris shook his head. "All I want to do is go home to Marina and the kids. You do whatever you want."

Bella reacted with a burst of anger, swishing her long tawny hair around as she faced him. "Don't be a chicken-shit! We're in this together. You can't bail now. We go home when we sell the icon and the FSB holds a news conference with us to announce that they were hiding us from terrorists, the threat was neutralized, and they've saved our lives. You're up to your ass in this."

"We've gambled and lost. We can't get our hands on the icon. The Roussels don't seem to have it either. Maybe the crooks you hired stole it and are selling it on eBay."

"Shit, I hope not!"

"I just want to go home."

"You can't! Right now I would suggest that you don't even contact Marina. We have to be off the radar for now. We need to plan."

Boris shook his head. "I need a drink," he said. "You can plan all you want. Have fun." And with that, Boris retreated to the kitchen, fighting the urge to go werecat.

In his office, Pavel was speaking with Mademoiselle Marais. Catherine had set in motion the mechanism for re-turning the icon, and Pavel was going to provide security for the site of the transfer. Since he knew her contacts were far-flung and varied, he had a favor to ask, as part of this oper-ation. He wasn't sure if she'd say yes.

"We believe Bella Danilov and her brother-in-law were behind the theft of the icon. And they shouldn't get off un-punished."

"I agree. But since we have the icon and they don't, I think it makes it difficult to pin the blame on them."

Pavel smiled. "I'm not speaking of the law courts. I'm speaking of some other kind of punishment."

Catherine leaned forward. "I'm listening," she said. "What do you have in mind?"

"I want to divide and conquer, and Boris is the weak link

in this duo. Let's make him so fearful and anxious that he can barely think straight."

"You sound like my partner, Paul," she said with a smile. "What's the plan?"

"He has to feel humiliated that this Siberian is calling the shots. She has no real standing in his clan. She's just a sister-in-law. He's the Hierarch. From bugging her apartment we know he wants to go back home to his wife, and now Bella is telling him he shouldn't even contact her. Marina is a bimbo, and Boris probably figures if he's gone long enough, she'll start dating rock musicians and leave him in the lurch. I think we should encourage him in this belief."

"And?"

Pavel looked at Catherine and smiled. "You have many contacts among the jet set. What I'm going to suggest is luring Marina Danilov away to Europe with an invitation to some luxurious getaway where she'll be out of touch with Boris and everyone else for a week or so. Would you be able to arrange this?"

Catherine laughed. "I'm not a travel agent," she said. Then she tilted her head back and appeared to think about it. Pavel hoped she had some ideas.

"What is this woman like?"

"Before she married Boris Danilov, she was an actress in low-budget movies."

"Cultural level?"

Pavel reflected. "She seems to enjoy nightclubs and cosmetic surgery. And she's a woman people notice: pretty face, blond hair, big bosom."

Catherine nodded. "I know an aging director with a villa near Nice. He's going to invite some people to stay with him while his fans hold a retrospective. The local cinema will run some of his old movies, and he's hosting a few parties to celebrate the event. Gilbert hasn't made a movie in ten years, but he's considered an icon of film noir. He owes me a favor. Maybe he'd consider inviting Marina Danilov to his celebration if I asked."

"If we can get her out of St. Petersburg, we'll send her a message allegedly from Boris telling her not to contact him for his safety and hers. She'll have a good time in Nice and probably forget about him for a week or so. That's all we need."

"And meanwhile poor Boris will be unstrung, thinking the love of his life has probably run off with a boyfriend."

"Exactly."

"Psychological warfare," Catherine murmured. "Sometimes it's crueler than a knife."

"We'll save the knives for later," Pavel said with a smile.

Chapter Forty

Pavel paid a visit to one of the cubicles in Metro's communications room and said to Ivan, his best hacker, "I'm going to give you an assignment. I want you to get into Marina Danilov's computer and relay a message from her husband. Only we're going to create it. Understand?"

"Okay. What would you like me to say?"

"First go into her computer and read through her old e-mails to see if there are any from him. Then mimic his style. He's going to tell her to go on vacation to get out of town while things are still unsettled. She'll receive an invitation from a famous European director to attend a film festival. It's all arranged. All she has to do is go there, enjoy herself, and stay put until she hears from him again."

"This is true?"

"Yes. We're working on the invitation right now, so find her e-mail address, find his, and let her know how much her husband worries about her."

"I'll start now."

Pavel smiled at the thought of the effect that Marina's disappearance would have on their Hierarch. From their bugging of Bella's apartment, they already knew that Boris was on edge and Bella's nerves were fraying. This should rachet the tension up a notch and provide fuel for further fights, if not plain hysteria.

With a wife like that, a man had to be watchful. If Boris got sufficiently worried, he might even bolt and head for home despite Bella's warning, and before he reached the airport, Pavel's guys would grab him and grill him. At least that was what they were hoping.

When Pavel took Viv home to his apartment, he noticed she seemed sad or at least very tired. He feared all the recent disruptions had taken a toll.

"Things will be better soon," he said as he watched her prepare dinner.

Viv nodded, but her lovely face never lost its melancholy expression.

Pavel looked at her carefully. "Have I made you unhappy?" he asked.

"No. On the contrary," she said with a smile, "I've enjoyed being with you."

"You don't have to stop," he said quietly.

"Ah, but that's the tricky part."

"Why?"

Viv said ruefully, "Because of the old taboos. Because I'm going to try to organize the impeachment of my Leader, and I may find myself facing a fight with members who don't believe the charges and find it suspicious that I'm relying on the help of someone who isn't even a Maine Coon cat. Old prejudices die hard."

"If you take on this fight, you're going to need someone who has your back. I'll help you dig up enough information to convince your clan that your Leader must go. And I never run from a fight. I have no hidden agenda. I would be faithful to you, and I would fight for you if it came to that."

Viv held out her arms and took Pavel into a warm embrace. "How I want to be with you," she whispered as they clung to each other." She raised her face and let him kiss her tenderly as they stood there in the kitchen, surrounded by so much granite and steel. His kiss deepened and she pulled him closer. Their tongues tangled.

"Would your brother object?" Pavel asked as he gently released her from his arms.

"Actually, I don't think so. You two would get along well, as long as you enjoyed going to baseball games in the summer and skiing in the winter. Marc is pretty easygoing."

"Baseball is a mystery to me," Pavel admitted. "But I'm willing to sit through a few games if it makes me better company. I used to ski when I was younger. I enjoy it. I even had mountain-survival training in my younger days."

Viv smiled at him. "Good," she said. "And, of course, you have talents that make me very happy." A wicked glint in her amber eyes let him know which ones they were.

"Would you like to practice these other skills with me after dinner? I believe you should always keep current," he teased as he stroked the outline of her full mouth and kissed her once or twice again. He held her close and felt her heart beating against his.

From the expression in her eyes, Viv liked the idea. She snuggled up against his chest and murmured that she could keep practicing forever if she had to. It would be delightful.

When they had finished dinner, had a glass of Rémy Martin afterward, and settled into a comfortable sofa to snuggle, Pavel glanced down at Viv and saw something strange. She appeared to be in a trance, staring at the windows into the black night. He gently whispered to her and kissed the top of her head, her cheek, her neck, but nothing seemed to bring her out of it.

Alarmed, Pavel spoke to her quietly, asking her if she was all right.

"Yes."

"What are you doing?"

"Listening to the universe," she said softly.

If he hadn't seen her perform an incantation at the bedside of her wounded clansman, Pavel probably would have made a joke, but he knew this woman had a shaman's gifts, so he simply watched and waited.

After a long silence, Viv seemed to come out of her reverie. She nestled against him and said with a sigh, "We're surrounded by enemies, even ones we don't know about yet. Bella is not the only one who's a danger to us. And she herself is at risk."

"That's true. My clan thinks she killed her husband. And she has to be the reason the icon went missing."

Viv nodded. "In my vision I saw her in the center of a jungle. This often symbolizes a complicated life full of lies, deception, and corruption."

"Any hunters aiming at her?" he inquired.

Viv shook her head. "It was murky. But for some reason I didn't feel she was in danger from the Russian Blues. There are others who have it in for her. I can't really understand it."

Pavel knew from past experience that a shaman sometimes had to spend time trying to interpret what his dreamlike trance meant. They were often allegorical or simply so full of subtle clues that their meaning could be open to several readings.

"But it showed her to be in trouble," he prompted Viv.

"Oh, yes. She's up to her neck, and it won't be easy for her to extricate herself."

"We'll do everything we can to add to her problems," Pavel promised cheerfully. "Now shall we take this discussion to a more intimate level, *dorogaya*?"

"Let's make love like wildcats," Viv said, wrapping her arms around him. "No holds barred."

"Who ever said Maine Coon cats were conservative?" Pavel mused as he watched his lady transform to something the size of a panther.

"Come on, *koshka*," she prompted him."What are you waiting for?"

Pavel took in that silvery fur and those entrancing amber eyes, and he shape-shifted in record time, leaping like a mountain lion on the attack.

So many taboos went by the wayside that evening, it left them both breathless.

Chapter Forty-one

Boris looked at his Palm Treo and grimaced. He pushed some more buttons and gave up, angrily stuffing it into a pocket.

"What's the matter? What are you doing?" Bella asked.

"Trying to get Marina by e-mail."

Bella rounded on him. "What is the matter with you? Someone could trace you. Let it be. She'll be fine. You've already told her you're all right. Point made."

"I love my wife," Boris said.

"Good. You'll see her in a few more days. You can bring her a gift from New York."

"But you don't understand. Marina gets antsy. She'll start going out with her friends if I'm not there."

Bella glared at him. "And?"

"And a lot of her friends are single women who want to meet rich men at trendy nightclubs. They drink too much, and then hit the sack with any guy who'll buy a jeroboam of champagne and talk about romance."

"If I recall, you used to spend most of your time in trendy clubs chasing girls."

"Exactly. This is why I'm worried. She has two small children at home. She shouldn't be doing this."

Bella looked bored. Russian Blues had a different take on these things, she decided. With her clan, a night's escapades meant maybe a bad hangover and some raunchy memories; there was none of this angst that afflicted Boris. Siberians were too adaptable for that. What they did on the prowl stayed out there. They were born cynics.

"Marina was a movie actress when you met her. She needs more out of life than being stuck at home with the kids. Did you ever consider that?"

"She knew when she married me that she would give up her career if we had children. It wasn't as though she was a serious actress who had trained for years."

"Ummm," Bella murmured. "*Vixens of Vorenezh* wasn't exactly *War and Peace*. She played a supernatural slut."

Boris turned red and appeared ready to go werecat, but then gave up on the idea. He wasn't going to respond to provocation.

"Don't try to get in touch with anyone," Bella ordered. "The e-mail's not secure. Marina loves you and will be happy to see you when you get home. She's smart enough to appreciate the danger you might be in, especially after Dimitri's death. She would want you to be safe."

Bella thought Marina was so self-centered, she wouldn't give a damn if Boris vanished from the face of the earth as long as he left her enough money to have a good time. But she tried to focus on a theme that would appeal to her brother-in-law.

"Did she ever tell you she loved me?" he asked pathetically. He looked absolutely vulnerable, a disgusting thing for a Hierarch.

Bella looked him in the eye and said with total authority, "She once told me you were the love of her life."

That worked. Boris seemed to grow taller, and he lost the dejected "woe is me" look she hated so much. The handsome blond Hierarch had returned.

He was so gullible. She thought once again that the wrong man died that day on the Nevsky. His brother would never have allowed her to have such a hold on him. In fact, she was the one who had always been on edge, always trying hard to please Dimitri, always watchful if he spoke too long to an attractive female at a party. Even though people thought she'd kept Dimitri enthralled with some wicked sexual shenanigans, they didn't know the reality of her marriage. Bella had never wanted to lose him. There was nobody else who could keep her in such style.

Catherine Marais had been in touch with the Russians, and she wanted them to hurry up and decide on final arrangements for the pickup. Dealing with them was like walking through a maze.

"What's taking so long?" Ian asked as he and his partner sat in his living room, looking out onto Manhattan at night. "They're not having second thoughts, are they?"

"No. From what I can tell, Mr. Lubov has to clear this with some higher-up, who probably has to contact *his* boss, who may even have to get in touch with the Kremlin. Since it's such a hush-hush deal, this has to mean their secret service will be involved. The FSB always complicates things."

"You know," he said seriously, "I could just teleport the icon over to St. Petersburg. It would get there faster."

Catherine laughed and wrapped her arm around his neck. "I love your sense of humor," she said as she kissed him.

"I'm not joking."

"Darling, you can't do that. I only wish you could. They would arrest you and hold you for interrogation. You would be dust as soon as the sun came up. I don't want to lose you."

Ian smiled. "I love to hear you say that. It makes me feel so cherished."

"Oh, you are," she murmured as she covered his mouth with kisses and let him caress her with that extraordinarily sensual touch he possessed. "You are the dearest thing in the world to me. *Je t'aime à folie.*"

Ian moved his hand along her thigh, and Catherine gave a cry as he touched her intimately. Her body bucked, and she responded by kissing him passionately as he stroked her, arousing her to such a pitch that she began tearing off her clothing so they could become even closer.

"I need you, darling," he whispered as he helped her out of her clothes. "You're the only one I want. Nourish me, Catherine."

She was lying almost beneath him, listening to the beating of his heart. Ian's mouth moved gently along her body, kissing tender parts and nearly making her go out of her mind with lust. Then she felt his fangs.

"Give me what I live for, darling," he said softly as he nuzzled her with the merest trace of those incisors.

In reply, Catherine reached up and brought his mouth down to her throat.

"Quench your thirst," she breathed.

Chapter Forty-two

At Old Muscovy, Marc glanced up from checking sales figures on the computer and looked through the doorway of the
office and across the long expanse of room to where Viv
stood chatting with one of their bodyguards. All seemed
normal.

Two customers were meandering around the displays of
paintings and old silver, talking in quiet tones, speculating
about where they could hang one of the canvases in their
apartment. Marc hoped they'd buy it, although he read a lot
of hesitancy in their body language.

That was a werecat gift, reading humans. It often helped
when he was trying to close a deal, being able to gauge just
how much a client wanted an item. If Marc sensed there was
a strong enough desire for a particular painting or bibelot,
he'd gently push to make the sale, but if not, he'd let them
think it over. Sometimes that worked, too.

Right now, Marc was wondering about another werecat
and his motives. Pavel Federov had certainly helped him and
Viv. Since Pavel had posted his operatives in the shop and on
bodyguard duty, neither Marc nor his sister had been ha-
rassed. This was fine. What worried Marc was the affection
that seemed to be growing between Viv and the Russian.

He wanted Viv to find a mate, but so far, her romantic history was a series of dead ends. Well, he had to admit his was

a bit spotty, as well. Cat genes didn't exactly lend themselves to fidelity and happily ever after. Divorce was rife among their kind. Werecats liked to be on the prowl, literally and figuratively; they generally didn't make good spouses, although there were notable exceptions.

But they knew enough to stay within the limits of their sept. An adventure with a foreign cat was acceptable for a male, but not an admired female like Viv, and now she seemed to have fallen in love with this Russian Blue. Not a good idea, especially since she was a high-ranking member of the clan with a duty to pass on her heritage. With the news about the Hierarch about to burst into the open shortly, he didn't want her to create waves of her own. The Leader was quite capable of turning that into a bombshell to deflect attention from his own case.

Marc had nothing against Russian Blues; he believed they were fine cats, with an impressive history of their own. But he didn't want Viv to get sidetracked by one and become an object of gossip in the community. And with recent developments, he worried about the clan's reaction. How many scandals could they take?

He hated to think that Viv might find this foreign werecat so attractive that she'd consider anything long-term. He could close his eyes to an affair. He couldn't hold her to a higher standard than he followed. But the idea of anything more enduring than a short-lived love affair made him uneasy, especially in view of the circumstances.

Viv was his only sister and he'd told her he'd support her in her choice of mate.

But he hadn't counted on this!

"Boss, I hacked into Marina Danilov's e-mail and blocked all mail to and from the Hierarch. She just received a message from me telling her to pack her things and find a nice place to go for a week or so while he's off the radar. Don't try to communicate with him during this time."

"Good. Now I'll have to get our contact in her house to report back to see if she's going to listen."

"Is Catherine Marais taking care of that invitation?"

"Yes. The French director is sending her a flattering letter, asking her to join him and his friends for the mini film festival."

"You think she'll take the bait?"

"Ivan," Pavel said patiently, "this is the kind of woman who still calls herself an actress even though nobody's asked her to make a film in years. Believe me, she'll be delighted to go. Besides, the south of France is a hell of a lot warmer than St. Petersburg right now. Who wouldn't trade ice and snow for palm trees and flowers?"

"Okay. Hope she goes for it. If I were a woman, I'd be a little nervous about flying hundreds of miles to stay with some old guy I've never met."

Pavel knew he had a point. However, Mrs. Danilov would probably check into one of Nice's luxury hotels for the length of the film festival and experience a lovely vacation on the Riviera, with sunburn the only danger on her horizon.

"Marina will come to no harm in Nice unless it's self-inflicted," he said wryly. "And besides, I think the possibility of connecting with a big shot in the French film industry will outweigh any other considerations."

"Still," Ivan said, "I can't believe she'd be that flighty."

Pavel gave him a thin smile, "She's not exactly a genius. And with the husband telling her to go have fun, do you think she'd turn down something like this?"

Next day, word came in from St. Petersburg that Marina Danilov was heading for Nice with a pile of Louis Vuitton suitcases and lots of suntan lotion. She was also confiding to her friends that this was the opportunity of a lifetime to revive her movie career. She was ready. All the Russian Blues had to do was sit back and let nature take its course.

Chapter Forty-three

The lavishness of Ian Morgan's town house always reminded Pavel of the Winter Palace back home. But he noticed that as Vladimir escorted him upstairs for his appointment with Mademoiselle Marais, his expression was distinctly chilly. Pavel glanced at him in surprise.

"What's the matter?" he inquired. "Is something wrong?"

"Oh, nothing. Except that you wouldn't tell me what you had the night you brought in the *object* for safekeeping. You wounded me deeply, you know."

"I'm sorry. I didn't mean to offend you. I just thought it was too dangerous to involve you at that point."

"We're cousins. We're members of the same clan. I also revere the icon."

"Then you wouldn't want me to do anything to put her at risk," he said.

"Of course not. But you could have told me. I would be glad to defend her, too."

"I'm sorry. The need for secrecy was so great, I felt I couldn't reveal the truth at that time, but I'll keep your offer in mind."

Upstairs in the living room, Pavel joined Catherine. Their relationship was strictly professional.

"I think the Russians have finally gotten their act together," she said after greeting him. "And now they're ready to finalize plans to take her home."

"I would guess that the Federal Security Service is going to take charge," Pavel said. "It's natural for the FSB in matters of national concern."

"A group of recycled KGB thugs," Catherine said with distaste.

"Probably," he acknowledged. "But at least the Saratov Madonna will be back where she belongs."

"Too bad she has to travel with them. But we hope they take better care of her now."

"Definitely. Now," he said as Vladimir appeared with a tea service, placed it on a table in front of Catherine, and left the room, "let's go over the plans."

After careful discussion, Pavel and Catherine fine-tuned their strategy. The Russians would meet with Mademoiselle Marais at a restaurant agreed upon by both parties. She could pick a companion to accompany her to the meeting. The Russians would send two men from the Russian UN mission, who would present their credentials and take delivery of the icon. They would be gone before anyone even noticed them.

"You look as though you have some qualms," Catherine said.

Pavel nodded. "This is quite a different case," he said. "But if you recall, that émigré journalist who met with Russian contacts in London at a restaurant didn't live too long afterward. Don't eat or drink a thing while you're there. I don't trust anybody from the state security services. You shouldn't either."

"Will you be nearby?"

"Of course, mademoiselle. I'll have you under surveillance all the while. And someone I trust will accompany you to the meeting."

"I've handled werewolves, you know. I think I can handle these Russians."

He nodded. "My people respect you very much. And we wish to hear about your exploits for years to come."

"Did you ever encounter any werewolves over there?" she asked curiously.

"Once. An old one was terrorizing a Moscow suburb and several werecats died during its attacks. They asked me to hunt it, and although I felt underqualified, I knew I had to help my own."

"What happened?"

Pavel shrugged. "I prepared silver bullets, put myself in its vicinity late at night, and had to walk through the park a few times to attract its attention. Then I found it. He lunged at me, and I stood my ground and fired. It was one of the scariest moments of my life. I fired away, and he suddenly sank to the ground and went into a spasm."

"Did he play possum?" Catherine asked with professional curiosity.

"Yes. I had been warned about this, so I shot him two more times before I checked the body. By the time I observed him, he was really dead."

"You were lucky. Some inexperienced hunters fall victim to their ruses."

Pavel nodded. "I wasn't taking needless chances. But I'm happy to say I got my werewolf." He gave Catherine a thin smile. "It was also the last time I ever tried. I leave them to the experts now."

She looked at him and nodded. Then she said quietly, "I'll take your advice about the security service too. Just in case."

On his way out, Pavel stopped at the door to speak to Vladimir. He felt bad that his cousin was angry with him for not being let into the loop earlier, and he wanted to make amends.

"Vladimir, I know how loyal you are to Mr. Morgan. If I were to ask you to help me in the transfer of the, ah, object, would you be willing to play a part?" Pavel looked intently at his cousin and tried to gauge his reaction.

Vladimir appeared quite startled. "You want *me* to help?"

"Yes. Mademoiselle Marais will be the one to go to the meeting place, and she will take a companion with her. The Russian secret service is involved, and I would feel better if she had someone at her side who is absolutely loyal— someone she and I trust unreservedly. You would be the best choice on both counts."

"I'd be honored," he replied. "I have the greatest respect for Mademoiselle Marais. And the other lady," he added.

"Good." Pavel gave his cousin a slap on the back and said, "I'll be in touch. It will be soon."

And when Vladimir showed him out, Pavel felt he had atoned for his past slight. Catherine would be in safe hands, and he would have a trusted man on the spot.

The delivery ought to go perfectly.

Chapter Forty-four

The chilly silence in Bella's apartment was broken by the abrupt ringing of the telephone. She gestured for Boris is answer it.

Boris grimaced, but he picked it up and said, "Yes?"

Bella observed him. It had to be those men who had snatched him off the street and phoned her before. She wondered what else they had in mind. Boris appeared to be listening intently. Then she heard him say, "Here she is."

Bella flung her long blond hair over her shoulder and said, "Yes?" as she took the phone.

"It's Bill. I'll be brief. We know you don't have the object and the werecat who hid it is dead. But today I have an update for you."

"Oh, yes?" she said, wondering where this was going. It didn't sound good.

"We just learned that the object is going to be handed over to our countrymen very shortly."

Bella had to stop herself from going werecat. All the trouble she had taken to steal the icon, have it shipped out of Russia, and hidden in the warehouse of some American customers so that she could easily access it by a second theft, and this Neanderthal told her this! He had just flushed all her hopes of financial gain down the toilet.

"Shit!" she exclaimed. "Who managed to find it? The

Roussels never knew about it! They're clueless. Otherwise that woman would have fainted when I showed up."

The voice on the other end seemed to laugh. "It's bizarre. My contacts inside the Russian mission told me one of their highest officials was allowed to see the object by the person who had it. He confirmed it was the real article, and then the person who had it made arrangements with him to send it home. All very mysterious and altruistic. And no names mentioned."

"What is his angle?"

"Oddly enough, he doesn't have one. He just wants to give it back."

Bella paused. "He can't be a rogue Siberian. We'd ask for millions."

The voice seemed to sigh. "I know it's difficult for people like us to imagine," he said, "but all he wants to do is return it. Very strange."

Bella amost snarled. Then she said, "What are we going to do now? It's out of our hands, literally."

"Don't be so sure about that."

Bella listened, almost holding her breath. "Do you have any ideas?" she finally asked.

"One or two," he replied. "Do you still have the customer who wants it?"

"Absolutely."

"You didn't inform him of the little glitch in your plans—as you didn't inform *me*?" he said pointedly.

Bella thought about making some sort of apology and then rejected that idea. "I hoped we could locate it," she said rather lamely. "But at least now we know where it's going."

"Yes, and it will be accompanied by the security service," he said, "but if all goes well, we can intercept it before it reaches them."

Bella thought her caller was crazy. "Somehow I think that will be unlikely. Who has the thing?"

"We don't know."

"What do you plan on doing to snatch it? Conjure it out of the air?"

"No," he said evenly. "I have another idea."

Bella shook her head in disbelief. She saw Boris glumly watching her.

"How do you know all this anyway?" she persisted.

"A mole. A little mole who likes expensive clothing and can't afford it on her meager salary. So she moonlights. She has access to private codes and secure lines, and she's always on the lookout for things that might be of interest to her friends."

Bella gave a disdainful sniff. Some little snoop who would sell out her own country for cash. Good.

"Now," her caller continued, "what about the buyers? Have you set up a meeting yet?"

"No. I couldn't, for obvious reasons."

"You realize I'm only letting you in on this because you've already done the groundwork. We split fifty-fifty, and I'll be there when the deal goes down."

Bella's tone reflected her outrage. "Oh, no! I took all the original risks!"

"Very enterprising," he commented. "It's still fifty-fifty. Or we'll just have to keep it around a bit longer and find somebody ourselves."

"That will take time."

"Exactly. That's why it's in our best interest to take advantage of the present opportunity. Fifty-fifty."

Boris appeared to take notice of the conversation now. He looked alarmed.

"Seventy-thirty," Bella persisted.

"Not possible. I have expenses, too."

"You're ruining me."

"Oh, I doubt that. You're quite the wealthy widow now. You must be worth millions in hard currency."

"Everybody always assumes that, but it's not true. Dim-

itri kept me on a short leash. I need the money! I have a partner. He needs his cut."

"Tell him the bad news then, *dushka*," he said with a
laugh. "It's fifty-fifty or it's nothing. You think it over and
make the right choice. See you."

"Wait! Don't hang up!"

But he was gone.

Bella snarled as she practically smashed the phone down
into its cradle. She felt her skin prickle, as if she wanted to
shift. The sensation roiled her innards.

"What did he say?" Boris asked nervously.

Bella gave him a disgusted glare. "He claims someone
has the missing object in his possession and wants to return
it to the motherland."

"How did that happen?"

"How should I know? The important thing is, this bastard,
the one who calls himself Bill, says he can intercept the object before it reaches the Russians. Once he has it, he wants
us to go ahead with our little business deal. But he wants his
cut. Half the money," Bella said in disgust.

Boris looked genuinely ill. "We need that money. I was
counting on it."

"I kept trying to reduce his demands, but he refused to
back down. We left it up in the air."

Bella glanced away. She was so sick of the whole disaster right now; she wished she had never thought of trying to
sell the holy Virgin of Saratov. Maybe the miracle working
went both ways. The Madonna helped the pure of heart who
appealed to her for mercy. And maybe she damned thieves
who tried to take her away from her rightful place in that
chapel where she stayed to help her admirers.

Either way, Bella was feeling pretty well screwed. She
even fleetingly toyed with the idea of invoking the powers of
her clan's ancient god, Moroz the Dread. But he was so
scary and dangerous that she flinched from it. Besides, the
most effective way to get his attention and his help was to

sacrifice the offspring of a rival clan, and she didn't know of any local werecats with kittens. Rules were rules. Although . . .

Bella roused herself from her despondency and looked at the Hierarch. "We'll go ahead with the plan," she said. "Half a loaf is better than nothing at all."

Boris didn't look pleased, but he kept his thoughts to himself. Sometimes Bella tried to exchange messages with him telepathically, but gave up when she couldn't connect. It didn't surprise her; sometimes she wondered if he had any thoughts at all.

Chapter Forty-five

"Hello. Any word from your partners?" Vivian asked Pavel as he stopped by the shop to confer with his men. They gave him a muted greeting from across the room. Marc saw him and nodded briefly.

"Everything is falling into place. We expect to have the object back in the proper hands very shortly."

"Ah," Viv said with relief. Then she looked up into his beautiful green eyes and asked, "Will it be dangerous?"

Pavel laughed. "No," he said. "Catherine Marais is handling the transfer at a restaurant. The Russians are sending their representatives. After they present their credentials, it ought to take all of three minutes for them to be out the door and away, and probably off to Kennedy Airport for the trip back home."

"This should be a huge coup for the government," Viv said.

"I'm not sure how they'll handle it, but there will certainly be lots of press coverage, with a fair amount of garbage ladled out to readers about how the government worked against all odds to recover it and restore it to the nation."

"Do you think they'll suspect this Frenchwoman of having anything to do with taking it? I wouldn't want her to have any problems because of this. She's doing us a favor."

Pavel reached over and took Viv's hand. "I wouldn't either. Therefore I'm monitoring the entire transaction by video camera as well as positioning my guys all around the perimeter. And a friend of mine who works with one of the government agencies in this country is keeping an eye on it, too. The fact that the object surfaced here interests his group."

"Does Mademoiselle Marais know about them?" Viv asked.

"Yes. It's added protection for her, too."

"Well, I imagine Bella Danilov will have a fit when she opens up a paper and reads that it's back home, safe and sound."

"When the missing Danilovs hop a plane back to St. Petersburg, we'll try to have a group of government types waiting to speak to them," said Pavel. "Bella can make up any lie she wants, but answering questions from the police is going to shake her up. If I know them, they'll find something to pin on her, starting with an investigation into her husband's murder. Bella could probably be charged with any number of crimes, especially regarding the business laws. So could her brother-in-law. If she's controlling him, he's a fool, and he'll most likely be deposed by his clan in the end."

"This is wonderful news," Viv said with a smile. "Of course, with Bella out of the way and the object safely restored to its people, the case will be closed. Then I'll have to turn my full attention to the problem within my own clan."

"I'm already helping with that," he reminded her with a kiss. Clan infighting could be vicious; that was a given. With so many werecats of varying opinions, it might be difficult to convince them their Leader was a criminal. But Pavel would support Viv, even if she were subjected to threats and verbal attacks. He never wanted to leave her.

"I love you, *dushka*," he said softly, looking at her very carefully. Having Viv in his apartment was one of the best things that had happened to him in years. He wanted to continue.

She looked up at Pavel and said softly, "I like being with you. I like cooking for you, and going to bed with you, and waking up with you. You make me feel as though I've met the other part of me that was missing for so long. I love you, Pavel."

He looked at her tenderly and lowered his face to hers. "Kiss me," he said softly.

Viv gave him a kiss that nearly rocked him back on his feet. One of the bodyguards saw this and smiled. Marc looked gloomy and turned away.

"I love you, too, Viv," he said. "I want you to stay with me. I don't want to lose you."

"When this is wrapped up, we'll have to have a long talk," she said. "There are so many things we should discuss."

"Yes," he agreed. "And we'll have to speak to Marc, as well."

Viv remained silent. She looked down. She had seen Marc's expression when Pavel kissed her.

"That might not go smoothly," she said. "This morning he reminded me of the old restrictions on interclan relationships."

Pavel nodded. "It's not something to be taken lightly," he agreed. "But we can work things out." The set expression on her face worried him. Maybe he had been too optimistic.

Viv nodded and then gave him a quick kiss, which made him very happy. She caressed his face tenderly as he looked into her eyes and caused her heart to skip a beat.

"I can't wait for the moment Catherine Marais hands the object over," he said with a smile. "That will be the start of our future."

For the first time in years, Pavel began to see the promise of a life with a woman he loved. It was long overdue. All those years of mourning were coming to an end. Not that he would ever forget Natalya—never. But he had finally given himself permission to love again, and the joy of that decision reverberated in his soul.

As Viv clung to Pavel, her body throbbed with desire, but uneasily she recalled the Leader's strange behavior. He had made his wishes plain, and even rebuffed, he was quite capable of ruthlessly coming after her to attack her in an unguarded moment. They had to impeach him and restore the clan's rule of law.

Chapter Forty-six

As Marc watched Viv and Pavel exchange kisses, he had to turn away from the sight. Damn it, even though he'd tried to be open-minded, he couldn't bring himself to accept such a flouting of the rules. Their sept respected and admired Viv. She shouldn't do this, especially right now. He decided he had to speak to Pavel.

And he didn't look forward to it.

As Pavel said goodbye to Viv and stepped toward the door, Marc put on his coat and intercepted him, asking if he could talk with him privately. The Russian nodded and almost seemed to expect it.

"I thought we might go out for a drink," Marc said as Viv watched grimly from the other side of the room. She sent daggers at him as she saw him leave with Pavel, obviously guessing what the topic of conversation would be.

"See you later, Viv," he said quietly.

Marc knew Pavel's own clan had its rules about interclan relationships, and Pavel had to understand Marc's worries, but the idea of having to speak to the other man about this delicate matter left Marc feeling awkward. The Russian was a great guy. But he wasn't of their sept.

"Pavel," he said after they had gone to a bar where Marc knew the owner and was allowed to use a private room for his meeting, "I believe in plain speaking, so I'll come straight to the point. I'm worried about what's been happening between you and Viv."

With an icy glance, Pavel turned and gave Marc his full attention. Out of respect for Viv, he forced himself to be polite, even though he felt the American was overstepping the bounds. Both men then shape-shifted into big-cat size and circled each other, wary and alert. Tails were twitching, whiskers bristling. Two irate males the size of panthers prepared for trouble, their growls low and frightening.

"I have the greatest respect for Vivian. She's an amazing female, and I hope to have a long-term relationship with her," Pavel let Marc know for starters.

"You understand the rules. Your clan observes them, too. The whole disaster with Bella Danilov shows what happens when one of our people forgets them."

"Vivian is not Bella," Pavel said, managing to convey a growl even in telepathy.

"Exactly. But the situation with the Leader of our clan might bring down more trouble than Viv deserves. We're going to try to bring him to justice. I don't want the clan saying she's doing it because of a foreign lover."

"She's doing it for your clan," Pavel replied, giving Marc a harsh look. "He's a thief, a lunatic, and a rapist." The growl got louder. "I love her. I want to be with her."

Marc fluffed out his fur, making himself look huge. "I know that. I've told her I would support her in her choice of a mate. But I never imagined she might choose one outside the clan. This is unheard-of," Marc growled. "I love Viv, too. I don't want her to suffer from the effects of a scandal, which *will* happen if you don't back off."

The dark silver Russian moved closer, invading Marc's space. Hisses came his way and he responded in kind. Both animals vied for dominance. "If your Leader threatens Viv or tries to harm her, we'll deal with it together. I'm not afraid of a fight." His green eyes gleamed with animal ferocity. "Vivian is no child. And you're not her father. If she and I wish to pursue a relationship, it is not for you to put obstacles in our path. My intentions are honorable. I will never harm her."

"Our brethren don't approve of these relationships," Marc hissed. "We are what we are, and we should stay that way. I have no quarrel with you. I'm grateful for the help you've given us. But I have to tell you how I feel about this affair with Viv.'"

"All right," Pavel said with growl, "you've told me."

"And?"

"And I will tell you that I have no intention of disappearing from Viv's life. I love her. I want to be with her. And I don't want to be your enemy."

Marc gave a low growl. "Russian," he said, "I would like to be your friend. I have nothing against you. But I can't allow you to harm my sister with this forbidden love."

The big gray cat flexed his muscles, and they rippled like silk beneath his fur. The shaggy red cat matched him and let out a low warning growl. Tensions heightened. Heads lowered. Lips curled back to reveal powerful teeth.

"I've seen some of my brothers ruined by these unions," Marc said. "I won't allow it to happen to her. I admit, I've indulged, but I've always broken those relationships off."

Pavel looked so determined, Marc thought he might even leap at him, but the Russian stayed put, and they both circled each other, sizing each other up for of a fight.

"My intentions are honorable. I don't want you to think that I'm a mindless predator. I can offer her a fine home. All I want is a chance to try to make a life with a mate I love. Isn't happiness a right for all creatures?"

"Yes. But Viv has always been loved and respected by our clan. This may cause them to expel her. I don't know if she could deal with that. She's a descendant of the greatest werecat that ever lived, a blueblood of our race."

"I think you worry that this might make your clan censure you, as well."

"I'm thinking of Viv, not me. I'm a male and can handle anything they throw at me. She's a female," Marc said grimly. "What if it's only her senses that are in an uproar, and she becomes rational once she realizes how her actions are received? And right now members of our clan are looking to her to lead them in the fight against our Leader. Don't take her away from us right now."

To Marc's surprise, Pavel merely growled a few times and then let his anger dissipate. That broke the tension as he took a step back and looked at the other cat, staring at him without flinching, his eyes as fierce as ever.

"I was truly in love only once before," Pavel said telepathically, "and I lost her when she was murdered. I thought it was a sign I shouldn't look for happiness again because I didn't deserve it. Then I met Viv and I felt restored to life. Do you ever think I would ever allow someone to snatch this gift away from me? If anyone tried, I would fight for her."

Pavel's quiet determination rattled Marc, since the shaggy cat had never felt this emotion for any of his past loves. He almost envied the Russian for his depth of feeling. Now he could feel the scent of a powerful male force pouring out of his body, the scent of his willingness to die protecting his chosen female. This was elemental and fierce, the sign of a male who would give no quarter.

Marc knew Viv had a duty to the clan to pass on Krasivaya's DNA, and her life would be complicated enough by fighting to remove the Leader without this extra drama. Marc would stand by Viv if it came to a clash with the clan in a battle over impeachment. But the thought of a complete rupture with the clan over her choice of mate disturbed him. He couldn't bear to see her lose her rightful place in their world.

"I will fight for her," Pavel said again, as he made no effort to hide the growl in his throat. "You must know this."

"Good," Marc replied with a growl of his own. "You may have to."

Chapter Forty-seven

After Marc shape-shifted and returned from his talk with Pavel, Viv was waiting for him. The first thing she did was ask him to step into the office, and when he did, she let him know the full extent of her fury. She was so enraged, she was fighting an urge to shape-shift and go werecat.

"You tried to talk him out of seeing me, didn't you? You have nerve interfering with us. You've fooled around with every female who took your fancy, and I've never once objected to any of your little playmates. Just because Pavel isn't from our clan, you feel you can set the rules now? Well, think again! I love him and I will be his mate, no matter how many voices are raised against us. If I have to defy the entire clan to be happy, I will."

"Viv, this is a step toward self-destruction."

"No, it's a step toward independence. Never has any member of my own clan made me feel so complete. If we have to, Pavel and I will start our own clan, made up of all the werecats who had to flee their own septs to be happy. And don't worry. I'm sure if you make it known how much you disapprove and how disgusted you are, you'll become a martyr to werecat family values."

"That's unfair, Viv. All I want to do is prevent you from making a terrible mistake. You're my sister. Do you think I would ever want to see you unhappy?"

"Right now, I'm not so sure," she replied. Viv glanced around and said angrily, "I've looked all over, and never found a man I've wanted more. Pavel is the one. He's good, he's smart, and he cares for me. It's not a ploy. It's the truth. We would both like to become part of each other's lives."

"Viv," Marc said, "remember your heritage. You're descended from one of the greatest werecats who ever lived, and right now, you're acting like some silly little alley cat."

For an instant, Viv stood absolutely still. Then the corners of her mouth began to turn up in a smile full of irony, and she simply looked at Marc.

"When did they make *you* the Ultimate Arbiter of the werecat code?" she demanded.

Flicking him a disdainful glance, she turned on her heel and sauntered out of the office, leaving Marc scarlet with embarrassment.

Regardless of his romantic problems, Pavel still had work to do. Back at his office, he picked up his cell phone and punched in the number of his friend back in St. Petersburg to check on the investigation there.

"Any word on the boys who were toasting Bella?" he said as someone answered.

"It's going slowly," Yuri replied.

"How so?"

"We've paid visits to two of them. They were somewhat reluctant to offer any news, but we worked on them. Oh, and by the way, they're human."

"Did you manage to persuade them that it's in their best interest to cooperate?"

"Yes, but it took a lot of effort," Yuri said. There was a pause, then what sounded like a sigh. "I doubt they will ever cooperate with anyone again."

Shit. The brethren must have beaten them to a pulp, Pavel thought. He shook his head.

"Well, what about the rest of them?"

"We're pursuing that. I'll send you a report of what we have so far, via our usual method. I think you'll find it unsettling."

"Don't let the brethren act like hooligans," Pavel warned. "If it gets out of control, the reverberations could be dangerous. Stay focused."

"I hear you. I'll send you the report right now." And Pavel heard the sound of the phone shutting off.

Leaning back in his chair, Pavel shut his eyes for a moment. With all the uproar in the Russian Blue clan at the moment, he didn't want the brethren to go on a rampage. It would be too conspicuous. He wanted to avenge their Hierarch as much as anyone, but he wanted to do it carefully, and make sure he had the right criminals. Sloppiness only created more trouble.

When the fax machine finally stopped whirring and spat out the last piece of paper into the tray, Pavel reached for the report and clicked the mouse on his computer to a special software program that was capable of decoding what his St. Petersburg colleague had just sent. He scanned the report, created a file, and then fed it into the program he had produced last year to handle ultrasensitive information.

Yuri began by saying a few of the brethren had gone to the nightclub where the suspected hit men had been partying. They'd started talking with the hit men, bought them drinks, and then kidnapped them, threw them into a van, and took them to a place where they could question them at leisure.

Pavel allowed himself a grim smile. He knew what that involved.

At first, the two fiercely denied they had ever participated in any kind of assassination. They said they had heard about the murder of Dimitri Danilov, but so had everyone who listened to the news. They were innocent. After some of the more intensive methods of interrogation, one of them finally cracked and confessed to being there. He was a drug addict and feeling the affects of withdrawal, but in the opinion of the brethren, he was telling the truth.

Pavel wondered about that. He read on. The second assassin tried to kill his colleague when he heard him begin to talk. Now that could be a sign the druggie was on the level.

Yuri stated that the criminals were questioned about this Bella they had been toasting, and they looked blank. Turns out she was the wife one of them had just divorced, and they were celebrating the divorce as well as the killing.

Damn, thought Pavel. He knew it had been too good to be true. Bella Danilov was too clever to use a bunch of garrulous lowlifes like that. She would have been smart enough to deal through a few layers of middlemen and have the shooters on a plane out of town an hour later. And he doubted she would have used humans. Too unreliable.

Then he suddenly read something that made him stop and read it again.

Before they died, these scum claimed they had met with a tall blond man who used to party in some of the same clubs they frequented. One night, while they were drinking, he complained about having trouble with somebody from work and wondered what it would take to get rid of him. After a few more drinks, they offered to do it for ten thousand dollars each. Four of them. He put together the plan, the idea that they should all dress alike in order to confuse any witnesses, and he kept in touch with them to track the victim's movements that day. While the Hierarch was dining at the Novaya Avrora, the blond man called in the final orders, and they rushed the Hierarch as he left the restaurant.

Pavel read the last line and flung the paper across the room in disgust.

When we showed them a picture of Dimitri Danilov surrounded by his top exectives at a company function this year, they looked hard at the photo and picked out Boris. The bastard contracted the murder of his own brother.

Chapter Forty-eight

"These werecats who grabbed you after they failed to steal the icon are called the Rasputnikatz?" Bella said. "I don't know any Siberian gangs at home who use this name."

Boris shrugged. "Manhattan branch. They found out about the icon and killed the guy who was supposed to get it back. They questioned him very harshly. They're bastards."

"What do they look like?"

"Like gangsters. Black leather jackets. Gold chains. Prison tattoos. You've seen their kind at home."

Bella had trouble remaining calm. She was starting to twitch the way she often did before she shifted. All her hard work was coming undone, her schemes had been derailed, and Boris had managed to involve them with a bunch of gangster werecats who had viciously insinuated themselves into their plot. She cursed their vile luck.

Then, as Bella paced the living room, she noticed that Boris had resumed his old "woe is me" demeanor, wringing his hands as he sat on the sofa, staring at the pattern in the carpet.

"You've caused us no end of trouble," she said bitterly. "All my plans are falling apart."

"Oh, that," he replied.

"Yes, *that*. What else are you moping about?"

Boris raised his light blue eyes and said, "Marina. I can't reach her."

"Boris! What are you trying to do to us? It's too dangerous to get in touch with her."

Bella was struggling with her fury. Suddenly she lost control and shifted, forcing Boris to do the same, both supersizing, the furious Siberian now larger than Boris. He was the size of an African serval to her puma size.

"I just wanted to hear her voice. I wasn't going to give away any information," he said telepathically as he moved away from Bella and her claws.

"Just making the call would give you away if anyone wanted to track you. You can't do this."

"What if she thinks I'm dead?"

"Look," Bella growled, "you've already spoken to her. You told her you were fine. She knows you'll be gone for a little bit. She won't become unhinged if you don't call her, because you've already prepared her. Don't be so possessive!" she hissed, flicking her tail in anger.

Bella moved toward Boris and fluffed up her fur, looking even bigger. He lowered his head and backed away. He could smell the aggression in her. Suddenly, Bella lunged forward and flew at him, rolling over the carpets in a pent-up rage she could no longer suppress. Both cats crashed into the furniture, then leaped to their feet, snarling, eyeing each other with anger, wild and hissing fiercely. Boris tried to hit her while ducking her angry claws. He actually got in a few good shots, making Bella even angrier. He raked her ear two or three times before she forced him down. She didn't expect that from him. To her intense shock, he had managed to hurt her.

"I'm going out," Bella announced as she startled him by shifting again. "I have to get some air. This place is choking me." She stroked her ear. The bastard had really hurt her!

Boris shifted, too, and then gave her plenty of room. He

could see the anger in her eyes, even though he felt pleased she hadn't been able to best him this time.

"Don't try calling Marina," she warned him as she paused at the door. "I'll know."

By way of reply, Boris turned his back on her and walked into the kitchen as Bella put on her coat and slammed her way out the door.

Once outside the apartment, Bella caught a cab and headed for Central Park on a glorious late-fall afternoon. Comfortable in a cashmere coat and used to colder temperatures, Bella strolled with a purpose, searching for something, undaunted by stories of muggers. She was a Siberian Forest cat on a mission; let one of those lowlifes try anything with her, and he'd find out what trouble looked like.

Walking relentlessly, searching for the right spot, the pretty blonde attracted a few admiring glances, but responded to none.

Finally, after serious consideration, Bella found what she was looking for, a secluded area with several birch trees forming a cozy mini grove.

Now all she needed was one more piece of the plan, but that part, the most essential detail, might be tricky if not impossible to locate. However, Bella took a risk and decided to make do with what she had at hand. It was a departure from the time-honored protocol of her clan, but she hoped the desperate circumstances might make it acceptable.

Scouting the area, Bella had located a colony of feral cats nearby. They lolled in the autumn sun, lazy and uninspired, two females with three kittens underfoot. A big male sprawled next to the females, his eyes little slits of contentment while one of the queens groomed him. She had found her prey.

A few other passersby crossed her path and went on their way again, bits of their conversation trailing off as they disappeared from view as Bella contemplated her choice.

Three kittens, but she needed only one. Which would be the right one?

She knew what she was attempting was wrong. These were ordinary cats, not noble werecats. What she intended required a werecat kitten, but too desperate right now to think straight, Bella convinced herself that she could fool an ancient god by substituting this second-rate life-form. She had bamboozled many a human, so maybe her talents as a deceiver would work here, too. Damn it, she felt frantic enough to try.

Chapter Forty-nine

As the little colony looked up at the woman standing over them, one of the females was the first to suspect something odd. She rose slowly on her haunches and began moving away, glancing nervously at the interloper. The other cats, guided by instinct, followed her lead, until all that remained was one calico tabby kitten, staring up into the stalker's eyes and mewing in panic, as if it knew it was in the presence of sheer evil.

"You're the one," Bella said. She reached down, grabbed the kitten as it tried to run to its mother, and shoved it into the depths of her coat pocket, where it promptly released the contents of its bladder in fright.

"Shit!" Bella yelped as she felt the wet spot. The thing had pissed on her six hundred dollar coat! Then as she saw the other cats watching her in alarm, she made shooing sounds at them, took a fake run at them, and saw them scatter in fear. She had what she needed. She was pleased.

Walking back to the stand of birches, Bella carefully created a makeshift altar, forming a circle of stones beneath the trees. She placed a small pile of leaves in the center, looked around with extreme vigilance, saw nobody in the area, and willed herself to shape-shift as the kitten fell from her coat and ended up stunned on the ground.

Like a tiger seizing its prey, Bella, now a splendid, larger-than-life Siberian Forest cat, leaped at the small ball of fluff, fastening her razor-sharp teeth around its neck and flung it back and forth in her grasp while her powerful jaws chomped down again and again, penetrating its neck and jugular, splattering the birch leaves with a stream of warm blood.

It was done.

Assuming the supine position required for the worship of Moroz the Dread, the Siberian cat extended a paw over her victim and silently offered it to the grim master of the forests and tundra, begging for his help. To the fearsome lord of the Siberian werecats, she said that she wanted to finish the job that had brought her to New York, and get back home without any further trouble from the gang that had forced its way into her business. She hoped Moroz found the sacrifice adequate from his wretched and lowly servant, unworthy as she was to address him.

That completed, Bella looked nervously around, shape-shifted once again, and scattered more leaves on the small corpse she had left behind. It was over.

Vivian knew she would be safe as soon as the icon returned to its homeland, ruining the hopes of any thieves who might want to make off with it. Pavel and his team were setting up the final plans for the handing over of the painting, and very shortly there wouldn't be any reason for her to spend the night in his protective custody. The thought distressed her.

Pavel reached out to her, took her hand in his, and kissed it as they sat in his granite and stainless-steel kitchen, with its wonderful view of the city lights. He stroked her cheek with his hand.

"Why so serious? Did Marc give you a lecture, too?" he asked gently.

"Oh, yes. He thinks that it's not right for us to want to be together, that we're practically causing a cosmic collapse if we think about anything more than a fling."

"Hasn't he ever been in love?"

"All the time," she said. "But he thinks I ought to follow the rules."

Pavel gave a shrug. "I don't think he has any right to criticize you. Or me," he added mildly. "Since the Leader of your clan has gone astray, the members ought to concentrate on *his* flaws and keep their noses out of your affairs. Your transgression is mild in comparison."

Viv looked at him and nodded. Then she said, "Back in the early days of our history, wars were numerous and nobody could trust the members of another clan. I could almost understand why they forbade the clans to mate with outsiders. Now it's not the same. We don't always have to be at one another's throats."

"Really?" He lifted an eyebrow and gave her a smile that went straight to her heart.

Viv glanced at him. "Yes. Why? Don't you believe it?"

Pavel looked into her eyes with his beautiful green orbs, and said, "I don't think the clans are as ready for harmony as you seem to think. I love you, Viv, but other Maine Coon cats might want to kill me for it. And Siberians should always be kept at a distance."

"You almost sound as if you might agree with Marc."

Pavel shook his head. "I'm a realist. I've fought humans, werecats, and werewolves in my time. Our sense of 'us' and 'them' seems to interfere with all our plans for building bridges. We find it hard to accept outsiders as our equals."

"Marc is predicting a dire future for me if we choose to start a life together. He thinks I'll be cast out of my clan. But it's *my* future we're talking about here, not his, and this has to be my choice and mine alone." She wrapped her arms around Pavel and kissed his cheek, his nose, his mouth.

"And mine, too. I want to play a part in your life. And I want to make you happy. Whatever your brother thinks of

Russian Blues, we are a loyal breed and good parents. If we make a commitment, we honor it." He kissed her and pulled her close to his chest.

Viv smiled at him. "Then we're both talking about the same thing here. Long-term and serious."

"Oh, yes, on both counts. But," he said quietly, "I think we might have to straighten out your clan's leadership before moving forward with our plans."

Viv looked pensive. "Not 'we,'" she said. "'I.' No outsiders allowed."

"Well," he said as he pulled her close to him, "if your clan ever needs help, just remember you have allies. All you have to do is give the word, and I'll have your back. And if we have to, we'll write a few new rules of our own."

"Thank you," she whispered as she kissed him. "It may come to that."

Chapter Fifty

"Have the Rasputnikatz called?" Bella inquired when she returned to the apartment, took off her damaged coat, and hung it up. Mentally she made a note to find a dry cleaner tomorrow.

"Yes, they did," Boris said. "Bill sounded very pleased with himself. I think he's delusional, and if they go through with this plan, we'll get ourselves killed by the Federal Security Service."

"We're in the United States. They're not going to cause an international incident on American soil. Besides, we have contacts in the FSB who will help us."

"That's a fantasy," he said. "If they find out what we've done, they'll abandon us for fear of being implicated themselves. They won't mind lying and being paid to say we were hiding out from terrorists, but this crosses the line."

"They have no evidence we had anything to do with the theft. If they manage to grab these Rasputnikatz, we'll deny ever knowing them. You're the respected CEO of a mighty profitable enterprise. Who are they going to believe?"

"They'll sell us out in a heartbeat."

"They can say whatever they want. They're just not credible. We're temporarily staying in New York while the FSB investigates the assassination of your brother. That's quite reasonable. So far, the police haven't caught the shooters, and we're living in fear we'll be next. All very normal. And," she said pointedly, "we're not the ones who have the icon, are we?"

At that, Boris seemed to relax a little. "Still, I can't wait to get back home."

"Yes. And when we do, you will meet with your board of directors and present them with your strategy for moving forward."

"They'll be upset that we lost the Siberian contract," he said.

"We'll explain that we had no choice but to disappear after the assassination, for fear we'd be killed by the ones who killed Dimitri. There are murders all the time. Nobody would hang around if he felt in danger right now. It would be stupid."

"Agreed."

Bella paused. Then she turned to Boris and said, "Well, what did Bill want?"

"Oh, he said the officials at the mission were going to finalize plans for picking up the object at a restaurant. It's going to be tomorrow or the day after. They're still fighting over who's going to have the honor of actually handling it and taking it home."

"And the Rasputnikatz think they can thwart the government's efforts?"

Boris gave a shrug. "They claim they have inside help, and they feel their plans are foolproof."

"Well, in forty-eight hours, we'll either hear from them saying they've got the goods, or we'll see them being arrested on the local TV." Then she said thoughtfully, "But if the Rasputnikatz can actually pull it off, our deal will go forward, and we'll have what we want."

"They're crazy," Boris replied. "And they scare me." He could feel the hair on his arms stand up, the human version of fluffing up his fur.

Bella darted him a scornful glance. Boris had few talents

in life other than knowing how to make himself look attractive in his impressive designer wardrobe and take clients out drinking. Eliminate the fine clothing, and he was merely a fool who needed a handler to keep him out of trouble. And give him his orders.

"They're only second-rate gangsters," she said as she opened a pack of cigarettes and lit up. "We're more than a match for them."

Chapter Fifty-one

That night, something odd filtered through the apartment—
a kind of breeze that ruffled the draperies in Bella's room
even though the windows were closed and locked. While she
slumbered under exquisite sheets, with her head on a lace-
trimmed down pillow, a presence began to make itself
known, quietly at first, then louder until perfume bottles
were falling from the dresser and porcelain statues sailed
across the room. A crash signaled that Bella had a visitor.

Terrified, she woke with a gasp and sat up in bed, staring
wildly into the darkness while the noise continued. Now a
stench filled the room, choking her as she jumped out of
bed, wondering what was happening.

"Boris! Come here!"

"He can't hear you, and he can't help you," said an unnerving voice. The strange voice seemed close to her ear,
terrorizing her as she staggered in the dark, frantically
searching for the light switch.

Bella cried out in pain as something with teeth grabbed
her by the ankle and nipped her. She screamed as she
crashed against the wall, running her hands all over it as she
tried to find the lights.

More of the toothy things began ripping at her nightgown, and then Bella tripped on the furniture, disoriented by
the darkness and the pain at her feet. She kicked violently as

the teeth sank into her ankles, and when she finally found the switch and turned on the lights, she shrieked as she beheld the sight in her bedroom.

Before her sat a great silver cat the size of a panther, with blazing fiery eyes and ferocious, jagged teeth. The creature surveyed her with an evil expression. Running around the floor at her feet were the ugliest creatures Bella had ever seen—the minions of Moroz—a cross between badgers and weasels with sharp claws and teeth and weird, deep-set red eyes, dark-furred beings that attacked in packs like piranhas. With fangs bared and eyes alight, they watched her.

At the sight of them, Bella screamed and jumped onto the nearest chair, while the creatures leaped at her, trying to bite.

"You know why I'm here," the huge silver cat stated as he glared at her with those fiery eyes.

"No, I don't," Bella replied as she tried frantically to defend herself against one of his minions.

"You called me this afternoon."

Bella stared at him, petrified with fear.

"No," she stammered.

"Yes. Are you so stupid you really don't remember?"

"Lord Moroz! Is it you?"

Despite her fear of those sharp-toothed beasts on the floor, Bella flung herself on the carpet in full submission as Moroz twitched his tail, and they backed off. She prostrated herself before him, shaking with terror, calling on him to forgive her failure to recognize him.

Moroz the Dread sat there, mesmerizing her with his fiery eyes, his expression filled with contempt. His tail twitched with ill-diguised fury.

"Moroz the Dread, lord and master of the forests and tundra, I beg you to forgive me for the annoyance I may have caused you."

"You are pathetic," he said by way of reply. "You have lived a reckless life, abandoning yourself to a frantic pursuit of money and power, trampling on anybody who got in your way, never sparing a thought for your clan."

"Yes, I have done this," Bella whispered, still afraid to raise her face from the floor.

"But you cannot possibly hope to cheat the lord of the forests and tundra by offering him an insulting sacrifice. That is a sin like no other."

Oh, no! Bella thought. *He knew!*

"Oh, yes, he knew. Do you think Moroz is too far away to see the difference between a werecat kitten and an ordinary alley cat?" He flicked his majestic tail, and blinding light flashed around the room, stunning her.

"No," she managed to whisper. Now Bella was so scared she could barely speak. Her throat closed up, and she felt herself hyperventilating with terror.

"Of course he isn't. Moroz saw all of it. He saw your attempt to cheat him and your brazen disrespect for him."

"Oh, no, my lord. There was never any disrespect," she stammered. "Never!"

"You knew this sacrifice was wrong, even as you offered it."

"Please forgive me," she pleaded. "I was so desperate to present you with an offering, and all I could find was a common kitten."

"Nobody has tried to do that in centuries," he said grimly. "They would have been too fearful of my wrath."

"Tell me what I can do to earn your pardon," she pleaded. "I'll do it."

The enormous silver cat just stared at her with contempt. A few of his minions glared at Bella and chilled her with the sound of their growling, and then they began moving so close that she trembled. They gave off a stench that came from the depths of hell itself.

"Please let me make amends," she begged, looking fearfully over her shoulder.

"You can't do anything," he said coldly. "You are a disappointment to me. You are worthless to your clan. All you think of is yourself, never giving any of your brethren a second thought, not even your own wretched family, who desperately need your help."

"Lord Moroz! I have been undone by nerves. Forgive me for that."

He eyed her frostily.

"What can I do to atone for my deception?" she pleaded. "There must be something. . . ."

Moroz the Dread studied her with contempt as he noted her fearful posture, her alarm. Bella tried hard not to tremble, but her scent conveyed her panic. He sensed the terror it betrayed. It oozed out of her pores, adding another note to the odor in the room.

"You are doomed," he said cruelly. "You have insulted me, and you can never make up for that. Your life will be ruined by being linked to Boris until death claims one or the other. He will be your guarantee, and you will be his, bound in mutual disgust but forced to protect the other against your enemies. Inseparable in your wretchedness. Doomed to live and die like castoffs. This is my curse."

Then the great silver master of the forests and the tundra flicked his magnificent tail, and his minions scampered to him. Together in a blinding flash of light, they leaped at her, and she screamed with such terror that Boris finally came stumbling into the corridor to bang on her door and ask if she was all right.

Her heart raced as she sat up in bed and gasped for breath. She screamed and screamed, begging for help as Boris opened the door, looking as if he expected to find an intruder in with her. Bella kept it up as he switched on the light and stared at her. She clutched at the covers, hysterical with fear, eyes wide with terror.

"What's wrong? Was somebody trying to break in? Why are you screaming like that?"

Bella sobbed as she jumped out of bed and threw herself

into his arms, startling Boris into speechlessness. He squirmed uncomfortably.

"Moroz came to visit me," she sobbed. "He cursed me. I'm doomed."

He relaxed. "You were having a nightmare," he said patiently. "That's all it was. There's nobody here."

"You don't understand. He was here. He had his minions with him. They bit me and chased me around the room."

Boris looked at her and through bleary eyes asked, "Where did they bite you? Where are the marks?"

"On my feet and ankles. Look." And she lifted up the hem of her nightgown to show her feet. Bella saw his eyes widen as he beheld the bites and scratches. He froze.

"Maybe you should see a doctor," he stammered, uncertain of what had really happened.

Bella stared at her ankles. She stared at Boris. Suddenly she glanced around the room, afraid to find the vicious creatures who had attacked her. They were gone.

"Go to bed," he insisted. "You had a nightmare and it frightened you. We're both a little bit on edge right now. Get some sleep."

Bella stared wildly around her room. They had been there, and yet there was no trace of anything out of the ordinary. Lord Moroz had come and gone as stealthily as smoke and had placed a curse on her, all because of one mistake. One small transgression.

She felt the weight of her sin as she looked somberly at Boris, the albatross around her neck. Bound to him until death removed one or the other. What a fate.

"Good night," she said abruptly.

Boris nodded as he turned and walked off. "Sleep well."

Chapter Fifty-two

In the elegant Morgan town house the next day, Catherine Marais put down her phone and felt a weight slide off her shoulders. At last the Russians had worked out whatever kinks had prevented them from making the final arrangements for the handing over of the icon. It was on.

She called Pavel immediately. She couldn't keep the delight out of her voice as she announced the good news. "Tomorrow at one thirty. We meet them at the restaurant you suggested. They had no objections. It will be Vladimir and me, and two Russians from the mission."

"Will you recognize them?"

"I doubt it. The only two I've met won't be the chosen ones."

"They'll probably send two agents of the FSB," Pavel said.

"I don't care who they are. As long as we can hand them the package and be on our way, I'm fine. From that point on, it's their job to get the lady back home."

"I'll start on the preparations for the visit. I know the owner. He'll give us access to the place after closing tonight so we can wire it for video. He'll let us know where he'll seat you so we can get a good look at what goes on during the meeting."

"It should take no time at all. The less people know about

what's actually happening, the better. We're going to make it quick and be out of there before anybody knows we're gone."

"Good. I'll call Vladimir and give him his instructions."

"Which are?"

Pavel grinned and said, "Keep his eye on you at all times, and don't let the Russians near you once you hand over the object."

"You're not very trusting, are you?"

"I'm alive because of that habit," he said with a smile in his voice. "But truthfully, I don't think they'll pose a problem for you. You're giving them the thing that the whole country wants returned, and they'll probably get a service citation for carrying it back."

"I can't wait for it to be over," Catherine said with a sigh. "This has kept me in New York longer than I planned, and my partner is e-mailing me to catch the next plane and hurry up to Canada."

"Ah, you're hunting again."

"Yes. Another one of those creatures is on a rampage, creating problems in Halifax. They're trying to keep it quiet, because, well, you know how people get when they hear the word 'werewolf.' Sheer hysteria."

"Who called you in?"

She laughed. "The local government."

"Really?"

"Yes. It's all very hush-hush. I mean, they can't say they're hiring us, but they realize they need more expertise than they have up there, so we got the call. They contacted the *Institut Scientifique,* and we said we'd come take a look. Paul's been there by himself, but he's getting impatient. I can't wait to join him."

"After tomorrow you'll be on your way north then," Pavel said.

"I've already bought my ticket," Catherine replied.

Chapter Fifty-three

The phone rang, and Boris looked at it with grim loathing. Bella flicked him an impatient look. "What's the matter? Answer it."

Reluctantly he did, and the expression on his face reflected his visceral distaste. It was Bill of the Rasputnikatz.

"What's going on?" Boris asked, worried about the answer.

"We have to have a talk. Not on the phone. It could be bugged."

"Okay. Where?"

"Be outside the apartment in ten minutes and you'll see a black BMW waiting. They'll flash the lights. You get in. Okay?"

"Got it."

"Don't make us wait. We don't like that." And then Boris heard a click.

"I have to meet them," he said nervously. "This might not be a good idea. I don't know where they plan on taking me, and I don't trust them after last time."

"Like it or not, we're partners now," Bella snapped. "So go to the meeting and find out what they want. It may be important. And they need you, so they won't harm you," she said firmly. "At least not yet."

With that happy thought in mind, Boris Danilov stood

outside the apartment building in the late-autumn chill ten minutes later, wearing a black cashmere coat and scarf, and wondering if Bill's gang would be punctual. To prepare for the meeting, he'd had a few shots of vodka, but it hadn't helped. He felt himself shaking slightly and couldn't tell whether it was from the cold or from fear. A late-night chat with these guys wasn't what anybody would welcome. They were unevolved werecats, very low-class, not his normal kinds of associates.

Just when Boris hoped Bill had changed his mind, he saw a black BMW pull up to the curb and flash its lights. They were there to collect him.

Dragging his heels, Boris walked over to the car, opened the door, and got in the passenger seat. Bill was at the wheel with two unknowns in the backseat.

"Put on your seat belt. It's the law here."

Boris almost burst out laughing. This was the gang that was going to heist the Virgin of Saratov under the noses of the Russians, and they were lecturing him on *seat belts.*

"If we get stopped and the cops see you're not buckled up, we get a ticket and we get ID'd. We'd rather not take the chance."

"Okay," Boris said. "I understand. Now where are we going?"

"You'll find out when we get there," Bill replied with his usual disdain. "Relax and enjoy the trip."

Even if Boris had been stone-cold sober, he wouldn't have been able to keep track of their route. There were so many twists, turns, and bridge crossings, that he figured Bill must have spent his youth watching spy movies. Nobody could have figured out where the hell they were going in the dark. Boris fell asleep for a while, and then he awakened to the movement of the car slowing down as it entered a garage. A door rattled closed after them and Bill ordered him to get out. He found himself in a small garage, most likely attached to a private home.

"Follow me," the leader ordered, and he took out a key and unlocked a door to a hallway that led to a staircase.

The group went upstairs and Boris realized they were in an ordinary house. It was nothing fancy, not the kind of place that might belong to a crime lord, so he figured it was the home of an underling.

"Sit down," Bill ordered after Boris had removed his coat and scarf. "We have a lot to talk about."

Boris didn't share that opinion, but he couldn't say so. He sat at the kitchen table and faced Bill, who looked quite serious, not a comforting sight. He was a big guy with scars and a short fuse. It was hard to believe he was a werecat; he looked more like a pit bull.

"Tomorrow's the big day." When Boris didn't react, Bill shot him a look of pure annoyance. "Can't you guess? What the hell do you think you're here for?"

Boris was about to reply he didn't have a clue, but he caught himself. That might sound flippant, and Bill could react viciously. "Something to do with the object we're interested in?" he offered, hoping he was right.

"Bingo! The man has a brain after all." Bill glanced around at his henchmen, and they all laughed at the joke.

"You're really going to try to take it away from the Russians, who will have their secret service officers on the case."

Bill grinned with genuine amusement. "Right again."

Now Boris was glad he had made his will. If these maniacs got him killed, Marina and the kids would have an inheritance to live on, and his children would go on to make successful lives for themselves. He didn't want to dwell on the fun that Marina would have pissing away millions on drugs, booze, and boyfriends.

"You look worried," Bill observed.

"Oh, I was just thinking of how those guys will probably

kill anybody who tries to take the icon from them. They're trained for that kind of thing."

Boris couldn't understand why the Rasputnikatz were grinning and chortling as if they were in on the biggest joke in the world and he was the only one in the room who didn't know the punch line. His sharp nose was overwhelmed by the scent of contentment seeping from their pores. He knew his own scent was reflecting something quite different.

Finally Bill got up and clapped him on the back. "Let's drink to our success," he said.

"Sure."

One of the gang handed him a bottle of vodka and a couple of glasses. He set them down on the table and poured Boris a drink. "To success tomorrow."

Boris waited till Bill had a glass in his hand, too, and joined him in knocking back the vodka. "To tomorrow."

Then Bill sat down again and leaned slightly forward, as if he were about to share a secret. Boris did the same, wondering if Bill was going to reveal this suicidal and ridiculous plan. Crazy as it was, it would have one virtue: all the Rasputnikatz would undoubtedly be mowed down by the Russians as they attempted to snatch the icon. With any luck, he and Bella could flee once these insane werecats were out of the picture and then claim to know nothing about any icon.

"You know," Bill said as he gave Boris an amused glance, "I have the feeling you don't quite understand what we have in mind."

"Well, you didn't actually tell me any of the details, only that you were going to snatch the icon from the Russians who were going to pick it up." Boris tried not to look as nervous as he felt.

"You worry too much. For one thing there won't be any contact with the guys who are assigned to get the icon."

Now Boris was truly startled. "But how will you steal it then?"

"Brains," Bill said with a grin. "We're going to beat them to the rendezvous, flash our IDs, say, 'Thank you for returning our icon to the motherland,' and be out of there in three minutes. By the time the real diplomats show up, we'll be on our way out of Manhattan. Once we have the icon under wraps, that uppity bitch will set up the meeting with her client and we'll make money."

Boris knew that his expression must have reflected his utter shock because the Rasputnikatz were all laughing and poking one another in the ribs.

"Okay," he said. "But why did you bring me all the way over here to tell me? I don't understand."

Bill grinned and poured him another shot of vodka. "Because I'm saving the best part for last."

Now Boris noticed the gangsters were really knocking themselves out, roaring with laughter as if he was the funniest thing they'd ever seen. He didn't get it. He looked much better than they did.

Bill leaned forward and said cheerfully, "You and my second-in-command are going to go into that restaurant and pick up the goods. Nobody knows you here. We'll even give you a disguise. But you're in on this just as much as we are, and this is our guarantee you won't betray us. Agreed?"

By way of reply, Boris rose to his feet, took one step away from the table, and collapsed. He was doomed.

Chapter Fifty-four

Waiting for a phone call from Boris, or for some indication that he was still alive, Bella paced the living room and kept glancing at the clock. He had left hours ago and still hadn't returned. She hadn't a clue as to what was going on, and that made her anxious, since she needed Boris at her side when she returned to Russia to carry out her plans for Danilov Enterprises.

Bella hated uncertainty. Ever since the day Dimitri had died, she had been fearful of the unknown. She needed to feel in control; she had to dominate the scene. When chance made this impossible, Bella's nervous system went on a kind of panic alert: her imagination ran wild and her breathing became shallow. Right now she stood in front of the mirror, frantically studying her pale face, convinced she was about to faint or have a heart attack. She felt so unstable she nearly shape-shifted against her will. Nerves again.

She poured herself a glass of wine. Rummaging in her handbag, she found her tranquilizers and swallowed one with some cool white wine. She had to calm down. She had been through worse than Boris's disappearance. It was just that she didn't trust him, and she hated to have him out of her sight for long. When he was left to his own devices and surrounded by these rapacious Rasputnikatz, there was no telling what idiocy he might commit. He might try to work out a separate deal with them and kick her aside.

Hierarch of the Russian Blues! Hah! He was merely a front man who needed a puppeteer to pull his strings. Now that Dimitri was gone, Boris would need *her,* even if he didn't realize it. Shit, Moroz was right. They did need each other: Boris to know what to do, and Bella to have a finger in the pie.

Why did Dimitri have to die? And why did fate spare her at that terrible moment if not to propel her even higher? She had a destiny. She was born to rise to the top and to see others pushed aside to make way for her. Perhaps that was the reason for Dimitri's death.

Bella sighed. She missed him. It was such a trial, shepherding his inept brother.

Boris was a classic case of a "dutifully resentful personality," a mentor had once told her. He feared to make overt moves against those above him, but he was treacherous and sneaky. He would bide his time, slithering along like a snake, always keeping his head down until it was time to strike. Was Boris hatching some kind of plot with those Rasputnikatz? If he was, he'd better rethink that alliance because Bella wouldn't become anyone's scapegoat. Not for those creatures.

Pavel and Vivian were curled up on the sofa in his apartment, listening to the music of a jazz ensemble and kissing slowly and languidly, as if they had all the time in the world. She caressed him tenderly as she snuggled against his chest.

"Tomorrow's the big day," Viv murmured as Pavel kissed his way down her neck, nuzzling her like a contented panther. They were in human form, but the urge to shape-shift was strong. Viv's pheromones were on "sex-receptive" right now.

"By this time tomorrow night, the icon will be in the

hands of the Russians and probably on her way back to Moscow."

"Will you accompany her?"

"I haven't been asked to, although I'd say yes if I was. Right now, I'm operating behind the scenes, and perhaps that's where I ought to stay."

"Have you lost your devotion to the Madonna of Saratov?" Viv asked in surprise.

"No. When I see the welcome reception on TV, I'll have the pleasure of knowing I helped make it happen. She belongs to the nation again."

"That's a nice thought. I'm so glad we discovered the icon before the thieves did. Evil creatures should never get their hands on a sacred treasure."

Pavel kissed her softly on the lips. "I agree," he said. "But I'll relax only after Catherine Marais and Vladimir hand her over to the Russians tomorrow afternoon. At that point we'll be able to say we've done our job. Mission accomplished."

Viv sighed and cuddled against him, happy to feel those strong muscles wrapped around her, her own guardian angel. No man she had ever met had made her feel the way she felt with him. Not only was Pavel handsome and very smart, but he had a charm about him that practically made her purr.

Even with the hostility from Marc, he hadn't gone ballistic or made an ugly scene or insulted him. He simply listened and decided to do what he wanted. Viv liked that. He could wipe the floor with just about anybody who came at him, but he preferred to use his brains. In a world that seemed to wallow in violence and provocation, she found it a welcome relief to be lying in the arms of a very strong man who spoke softly and meant what he said. Of all the werecats she knew, only Pavel was that disciplined.

"You're not expecting any glitches, are you?" she asked.

"No. Catherine and Vladimir will be under constant surveillance, and the restaurant will be carefully guarded. All the Russians have to do is show up, produce their IDs, and pick up the icon. All our people have to do is hand it over and leave. Very straightforward and uncomplicated."

Viv nodded. Then she smiled seductively and purred in his ear, "Oh, *koshka*, let's not think about that tonight. Let's concentrate on the two of us."

Pavel had no problem with that idea. He took Viv in his arms and kissed her as she slid beneath him and slipped her hands beneath his shirt.

"Let's make love like savage predators who rule the jungle and challenge their enemies to defy them," she whispered as she nipped his ear.

"Where does this wild streak come from *dushka*? You always seem like such a lady," he said as he slipped off her blouse and her bra. "You take my breath away."

Viv took his face in her hands and smiled as they kissed. "And I'm only just beginning."

She let him kiss her ear, her neck, her throat, and send a delicious trail of warm kisses down her breasts. Viv sighed as he caressed her and slipped his hand under her skirt and into the waist of her silky pants. Her stomach contracted as he explored the region to the south and then gently probed the moist lips.

"Oh," she whispered as she felt a quiver. "Oh, Pavel!" Her head went back as she felt a shock that made her hips buck. "Don't stop. Oh, keep going." Viv wrapped herself tightly against him and kissed him passionately as he kept up his probing, making her breath come in ragged spurts. Then he kissed her again and paused to undress as Viv tried to help him out of his clothing as fast as she could.

"Hurry up," she said, wanting him in her arms right now. "I want to make love all night."

Pavel smiled at her with those fascinating amber eyes. He thought that was the best idea he'd heard in a long time. He wouldn't disappoint.

Chapter Fifty-five

"Is it safe to stay here until it's time to go to the restaurant?"
Boris looked at the Rasputnikatz and then at the clock. Ten
in the morning. He had the look of a corpse. They had forced
him into an incriminating role, and now he felt as if his life
was over. They would never pull this off.

"Yeah. Nobody will bother us. We've got everything we
need: diplomatic license plates, ID badges, good suits,
driver. We're good to go."

"My hair looks fake," Boris complained. "I won't fool
anybody with this wig."

Bill flicked him an unsympathetic glance. "Do you want
me to call the girl back? She's downstairs having coffee."

"Yes. Maybe she can make it look more natural. It looks
all wrong, and it will draw attention. You don't want that, do
you?"

Bill called downstairs and a cranky young blonde with a
tight T-shirt and big boobs came plodding up to see what he
wanted. Bill pointed at Boris's hair. She gave him a bored
look and said, "What?"

"It doesn't look right," Boris said. "It looks fake."

She placed hands on hips and glared at him. "I'm a professional makeup artist. I've worked on everybody. You hair
looks fine."

"No, it doesn't."

"Who the hell are you to tell me how to do my job?"

"Well I'm your client, and I'm telling you it looks like crap."

Boris found the whole experience surrealistic. Here he was, the Hierarch of the Russian Blue werecats, arguing with one of Bill's girlfriends about the wig she had given him. He shouldn't be here. He should be thousands of miles away, back in his own home, back in his office, surrounded by people who treated him with respect and deference. Dealing with these overseas werecats must be punishment for all his recent sins, he thought. They were so overwhelmingly low-class.

The blonde walked around him and took another look. She made a little pout and went to get her bag of brushes and combs. Boris looked at Bill and nodded as if to say, "See. She finally realizes she made a mess."

When she returned, she pulled off his wig, placed it on a fake head, and got busy with brushes and gel. Then she took out a can of blond spray and applied a couple of streaks. When she plopped the wig back on his head, Boris had to admit it looked better. A little too trendy, but better. He wondered if any diplomat in the world walked around looking like this. He doubted it.

"Oh, we got this for you, too," Bill said, with a nod to the girl. He handed her a small package that appeared to contain some dead hairy thing. When she ripped open the wrapping, Boris wondered what on earth it was and where it was supposed to go.

"He doesn't look the type for a mustache," she said. She eyed the thing as if it might bite her.

"Glue it on him. We want him disguised."

While Boris protested, the makeup artist, a female gang member named Donna, got out some sticky substance, smeared it over his upper lip, and smacked the hairy thing down on top of it.

"It makes him look silly," Donna said with a smirk.

"Then trim it a little," Bill ordered.

Boris could have wept with humiliation. All his life, he had been admired for his sense of style. He had been recently listed in the "best dressed" section of a St. Petersburg men's magazine. These two had just reduced him to clown status.

Bill surveyed the new work and gave a nod of approval. The Hierarch looked like a middle-aged man who was desperately trying to hang on to his youth with fake highlights and a macho mustache.

"Okay," said Bill. "Now run through the routine."

Boris darted him a look.

"Tell me what you do at the restaurant," Bill prompted.

"Valery and I go in, ask the headwaiter for Mademoiselle Marais, get shown to the table, show her our IDs, and ask for the bag. She hands it over. We leave. The car is waiting outside to take us back to you."

"Right."

"And why won't the real diplomats be there?" Boris inquired.

"Because my guys will have a little fender bender with their big car, and while you're taking charge of the icon, they'll be standing in the middle of the street screaming at my men, demanding to see a policeman and making a scene. It'll set them back about ten or fifteen minutes, enough time for us to be in and out before they ever show up."

Boris asked for a shot of vodka. Bill produced a bottle and a glass. "You shouldn't drink so early in the day. You'll rot your liver if you make it a habit."

Boris ignored that remark. "Can I go back to my apartment after we get the icon?" he asked. Boris wasn't at all convinced he'd survive the day, but he felt he had to inquire.

"Sure. But we keep the icon until Bella calls her clients and sets up the appointment. We all go to the meeting, and we split the money on the spot."

"Fine."

Bill grinned and cheerfully slapped him on the back. "Don't look so down in the mouth. It will all work out."

Boris nodded. "Yes," he said. "Of course." And he gulped down a second shot of vodka with a look so grim it startled the makeup girl.

She gave Bill a significant glance. "Nerves," she said with a shrug.

Several hours later, Boris felt oddly calm as he watched the urban landscape whiz by the car windows. A few stiff drinks had helped him achieve this state, but more than that, he had simply accepted his fate as punishment for his sins and was prepared to pay the price. He had reached the end of his rope. In an hour he would most likely be dead and un-mourned by everyone except his children. If he was lucky, Marina would shed a few tears for the man who had loved her to distraction. Bella would simply be annoyed that he had managed to cause her more trouble.

The idea of Bella facing a snag in her plans actually gave Boris a shred of comfort. If he died as a result of this mo-ronic scheme, it would mean that Bella would be unable to carry out her intentions of selling the icon and making mil-lions. Instead, she would be grilled by the police in two countries, and she'd have to spend a fortune on legal fees.

Chapter Fifty-six

"We'll give you a signal when they arrive," Pavel said.

Catherine and Vladimir nodded and saw the headwaiter walk to the front of the house. Everybody felt prepared for action. From upstairs at his station, Pavel sent her a message on her microphone, just checking to see if all was well. Carmeras outside monitored the entrance, and his men were positioned front and back.

"You're coming in fine. Can you hear me all right?"

"Perfect," he said. "And I have you on the monitor."

In the crowded restaurant, diners were discussing business deals, many of them executives who worked in the neighboring offices. Out-of-town clients enjoyed the elegant ambience. The owner surveyed the scene, keeping an eye on things, with an occasional glance toward Catherine and Vladimir.

"Are you nervous?" Catherine asked her new partner. She thought he seemed grim.

"A little. Nobody looks forward to an interview with the FSB. They're just the KGB in new packaging."

"Well, they're not going to be here very long. Hang on. You're doing well."

Vladimir smiled, but he didn't look convinced.

As Catherine glanced toward the door, she saw the owner give the prearranged signal.

Two fairly tall men—one with highlighted brown hair and a mustache and one with blond hair—entered, paused to say something to the headwaiter, looked inside the room, and followed him across the crowded dining room straight to Catherine's table.

"Showtime," she murmured to Vladimir and Pavel. "Here they come."

"Mademoiselle," the headwaiter said politely as they arrived, "your guests."

Catherine smiled but didn't extend her hand, a precaution Pavel had suggested. She thought that reeked of paranoia, but since he was Russian and she wasn't, she decided to go along with him. Vladimir extended a cordial greeting in English.

"You have something to show us," Catherine prompted the Russian who appeared to be in charge. She saw him look flustered and then nod as he reached into his breast pocket and took out an ID from the Russian mission to the UN, identifying him as Ruslan Dvorsky. The other Russian nervously responded in kind, reached in and fished out his ID. Roman Vladimirov.

"So," Ruslan said, looking eagerly at Catherine, "do you have what you said you have?"

"Yes." And she reached underneath the table and pulled out a rectangular package neatly done up in bubble wrap and nestled inside a tote bag bearing the logo of a New York boutique. "Part of the wrap is loose so you can look inside to verify the contents," she said.

He did. The second man looked. They nodded almost in unison and then rose to say goodbye.

"On behalf of Orthodox believers everywhere, we thank you," he said. That done, both men turned and made their exit, vanishing out the front door and onto the sidewalk, where a car with diplomatic license plates waited. Mission accomplished.

"We saw it and heard it," said a voice close to her ear. That was Pavel on the microphone. "It's a wrap."

"May we leave?" Vladimir asked.

"Yes. Let's go home."

They had only gone three blocks when Catherine received a frantic call from her contact at the Russian mission. "Our men were involved in an accident en route to the meeting. Stay where you are. They will arrive, but later than planned."

When Catherine heard that, she had all she could do not to scream. "Too late," she replied. "Someone already took delivery at the restaurant. Ruslan Dvorsky and Roman Vladimirov arrived to pick it up." She gritted her teeth as she listened to the sound of a gasp on the other end. She could predict what he was going to say.

"We have nobody by those names at the mission. What did they look like?"

"Tall. One was blond. The other one had brown hair with highlights and a mustache."

A stream of indecipherable Russian curse words poured out like a torrent. "You have given our national treasure away to a couple of confidence men," he screamed.

Then the line went dead, and Catherine felt as if some leaden substance had entered her soul. "We've been had," she said to Vladimir. "I've just handed the Virgin of Saratov over to unknown parties. The Russians have no idea who those men are."

She thought he might crash the car, he seemed so stunned. "I have to call Pavel," she said. "He recorded the whole thing. At least we have the men on video."

"But *they* have the icon."

Catherine cursed herself for the whole sorry mess. She ought to have seen it coming. She felt a bitter taste in her throat when she entered Ian's town house and climbed the stairs to the salon. As soon as she sat down, she took out her cell phone and punched in Pavel's number. She got him on the first ring.

"Federov here."

"Can you get over here as soon as possible and bring your equipment? We have a disaster of biblical proportions on our hands."

"What are you talking about? What's happened?"

"Those two Russians were fakes. I just handed the package over to two con artists. The Russians from the mission called to tell me their men would be delayed."

"Are you at Mr. Morgan's house?"

"Yes."

"Stay there. I'll be over as fast as I can."

Chapter Fifty-seven

Before Pavel headed to the meeting at Ian's town house, he placed a call to a werecat friend in an ultrasecret American government agency dealing with international trafficking. This theft required an immediate and forceful response. If they didn't capture the icon right now, they might never get a second chance. Pavel would never forgive himself if the Virgin of Saratov disappeared with a bunch of crooks.

"You had that painting in your hands and you bungled the repatriation? Pavel, what's the world coming to?" his friend Tony marveled. "I thought you gave master classes on this stuff."

"I can do without the sarcasm. I need your help. I have the whole transaction down on tape. You can see the two Russians at the restaurant. Maybe they're in your system because of an earlier theft."

"Okay. I have to tell you, you'll have the Russians from the UN on your back over this. They'll think you engineered the whole thing and you've got the goods stashed in your bedroom. These people are very paranoid."

"I know that. This why I'm reporting the theft to you, and I want your help. The two people who met the fake officials had no idea they weren't dealing with the men who were supposed to receive the painting. We acted in good faith."

Pavel sensed a pause. Then Tony said, "If those guys

showed up with official ID and diplomatic plates on the car, that has to mean they had help."

"But who could have known about the exchange? It was a top-level secret."

"Secret until they had to go through the mechanics of setting it up. Staff had to know. That's what I'm going to suggest to the Russians when I meet with them. Time for them to put the screws on the staff."

"I'm going to talk to the two people who handed over the painting. I'll try to find out if they noticed anything odd about the two ringers."

"Okay," Tony said. "I'll get in contact with the Russians and suggest a joint effort to locate the goods, starting with an investigation of whoever had anything to do with it. Since it's such a big deal, they may cooperate. Their president won't be happy if they fail."

"Let me know what you find out," said Pavel.

"Okay. Now you take a real good look at that video and tell me what you come up with. I'd like to nail these guys, too. Okay?"

"I'll talk to my people and review the video. We'll start today."

As the big black car with diplomatic plates pulled away from the restaurant, the two "envoys" who had just leaped into the backseat exhaled and sank into the soft comfort of leather seats. They had done it, grabbed the icon without so much as laying a hand on anyone. Nice and easy.

Valery immediately took out his cell phone and punched in his boss's number. "It's with me," he said. "Everybody's fine."

"Good," came the reply. "Now drive to your second stop and get into the car they're holding for you."

"Okay. See you in a few."

Boris failed to share Valery's euphoria. While grateful they hadn't been arrested, he still feared retribution over the theft, and he didn't put any faith in Bill's promise that he could go once the icon was in the hands of the gang.

Pulling into a body shop in Brooklyn, the two thieves and their driver got out and turned the car and its plates over to the owner. The stolen vehicle would be cannibalized for parts, and the plates would be melted down and disposed of by this afternoon.

On the way back to wherever their trip had originated, Valery held on to the packaged icon as if it were his baby. He was nervous to let go of it, because the leader of the pack had scared him before he left by threatening to cut off his balls if the painting arrived damaged.

Boris sank down into the backseat as far as he could and wished he were home with Marina and the children and far from all these lowlifes, including Bella. That greedy, vicious, treacherous bitch cat had ruined all the lives she touched. The worse thing was that he couldn't see a way to get rid of her; they were accomplices in this, stuck with each other. What a partnership from hell.

The thought of seeing Marina again brought the only glimmer of hope. Even though he might be forced to include Bella in his plans for governing as Hierarch—if the Russian Blues didn't impeach or depose him—Marina would be his refuge and his sanctuary. Even Bella couldn't take that away from him.

Who was he kidding? His whole life was crap. All of it. Deep down Boris knew he had the moral sense of an earthworm, the brains of a gnat, and the luck of an albatross. He wondered uneasily if the Virgin of Saratov could forgive a miserable werecat who had kidnapped her and committed even greater sins.

To Boris's great relief, the Rasputnikatz released him a block away from his apartment after a stop at Bill's place, where he had peeled off the mustache and wig, returned the dark suit they had given him for the caper, and resigned himself to a high-pitched grilling from Bella. Boris felt so exhausted, he barely cared. All he wanted to do was sleep. Or get so drunk he put himself in a coma. His werecat nature stirred in him. He wished to escape, but sadly he had no place to go, except back to Bella. He couldn't even manage a growl.

"Where the hell were you?" Bella exclaimed as she ran to the door when she heard a key in the lock. "I thought they might have killed you."

"I'm fine. I just want to sleep."

Bella wasn't about to give up. "What did you do while you were with them?"

"Nothing. Don't bother me. Just let me go to sleep."

Worriedly she looked into his bloodshot eyes. "Did they give you drugs?"

"No. Just vodka. I'm fine. But right now I need some rest. We can talk later."

"What about the thing?" she demanded, afraid to name it even in her apartment, out of fear of detection.

"Our friends have it. They'll call you." And he walked off into his bedroom, wishing he could sleep for a week.

Bella stared after him, amazed. "They have it?" she repeated. "You mean . . ." She could scarcely believe it. "How?"

"I picked it up at a restaurant," he said. "Happy? I did what you wanted. Now get the hell out of my way."

And with that, Boris slammed the door in her face, too exhausted for further discussion.

Chapter Fifty-eight

Before heading for his meeting with Catherine and Vladimir, Pavel made a quick call to his office and spoke with the man on duty the previous night who was responsible for keeping tabs on Bella and Boris. Anything suspicious?

"She was in all night. He left the apartment around nine and got into a car with some unknowns. One of our guys tried to follow him, but the driver took such a crazy route, we lost him. We don't know where he is right now."

"Did you happen to get the tag number on the car?"

"Yeah. We wrote it down."

"And?"

"Belongs to some woman from Queens. No rap sheet on her."

"Maybe Boris has a girlfriend here," Pavel speculated. "All right. Keep watching them. Let me know if anything strange happens."

"Boss? We have a problem."

"Yes?"

"We lost the audio feed into the apartment. Maybe it came loose. We'll need to reconnect it."

"We'll use Margot for that. Bella's let her in to clean the apartment before. She doesn't suspect her."

"Okay."

Shit, Pavel thought. *What was Boris doing last night?*

Given his reputation, he was probably tomcatting around Manhattan. But right now, Pavel wanted all his time accounted for. According to the criminals captured in St. Petersburg by Pavel's associates, Boris had arranged for his brother's murder. He was more dangerous than he appeared.

This corrupt Hierarch already had blood on his hands, so what would prevent him from committing a robbery half the country would consider sacrilegious? He had no shame; neither did Bella. It made for a frightening combination.

Vladimir looked so despondent when he opened the door that Pavel felt sorry he had involved his cousin in the affair. He should have used one of his own men. It would have been smarter. Now poor Vladimir, one of the most loyal men Pavel knew, would never cease to reproach himself for letting down the Saratov Madonna.

Catherine Marais looked as if she wanted to kill someone. Usually so composed, Catherine seethed with fury at being duped.

"Did you bring the video?" she asked as Pavel entered the room.

"Yes. It's all here. We can take a look at them from start to finish."

"The Russians know what happened. Lubov called me to warn me his men had been delayed—about five minutes after those two fakes walked off with the icon. I had to tell him we'd handed it over. I thought he'd have a coronary."

"Did you speak with them after they calmed down?"

"Yes. He called back later and explained what had happened to his emissaries. Somebody hit their car at an intersection, and they spent half an hour in a shouting match before the cops came and took down the information. By the time a squad car showed up, the man who caused the accident had escaped on foot, leaving behind a stolen car and no ID. At that point, they figured it was a setup, and they called Lubov."

"The thieves had it all planned," Pavel said in disgust as he looked at Catherine. "This means somebody at the UN mission had a hand in it. They've got a traitor in their midst."

"They know that, too," said Vladimir. "And right now you can imagine the grilling they're putting their staff through."

Pavel had memories of special police agents interrogating captured guerrillas in the war. Very grim.

"Do you think they'll be able to root out the scorpion in their bosom?" Pavel asked.

"Depends on how much pain he can take," Vladimir replied with a cold smile.

"All right," Catherine said. "Let's look at the video."

First came the shot of the two Russians getting out of the car. Next they entered the restaurant, spoke with the headwaiter, and walked to the table where Catherine and Vladimir awaited them. They introduced themselves, produced their identification, and took possession of the package. In the last shot, they made their way out of the crowded room, exited the restaurant, got into their waiting car, and drove off.

"Vladimir, do you think they were really Russian? Could they have been Chechens, Georgians, Ukrainians, anything?"

"Russians," he replied. "They spoke English, but I can tell a Russian when I see one. And one guy wore a hairpiece."

Catherine nodded. "Oh, yes. Not bad, but still not good enough to fool anyone."

"What about the mustache?" Pavel asked.

"I don't know," Vladimir said. "That may have been real."

"And his partner? Was that his own hair, do you think?"

"Yes," they answered in unison.

"All right, then let's take another look at these two. Try to remember if they had anything odd about them—besides the hair."

They watched the video so many times it made them bleary-eyed. Darkness began to fall.

"Mademoiselle, I have to go downstairs to assist Mr. Morgan," Vladimir said softly as he rose to leave the room.

"Yes, of course." She looked upset at the thought of having to tell her lover that they had just had a major disaster.

"I've been in contact with a friend of mine who works for the government," Pavel said. "He's interested in recovering the icon. We'll work together."

"Russian or American?" she asked.

"American. But of course the Russians want it back just as much, if not more."

"Both countries will be after it. If we're lucky, they'll be able to take it back. Meanwhile, it's out there someplace in the five boroughs, in the company of scum."

"If it's still in New York, that would be the best thing for all of us," Pavel said. "If they manage to ship it out of the area, it's gone for good."

"Do you think your friend will have alerted the border crossings and the airports?"

"Yes. That would be his first move. When I leave, I'm going to e-mail the video to him so he can take a look at it and analyze it to see if he can find a match to somebody already in his file. I'll do the same with the Russians."

Catherine had never looked so disgusted. "We'll get them," she said. "And when we do, I'll make sure I'm available to testify at their trial, no matter where I am or what I'm working on. Now it's personal."

Chapter Fifty-nine

Pavel decided it was time to start preying on Boris's weaknesses: his love for Marina and his hatred for Bella. The moment had come to call in the services of their covert photographer in Nice, who had been charged with filming Marina at play.

"What are you doing at the laptop?" Viv asked as Pavel sat there with a look of intense concentration on his face.

"Sending a message to a friend. I'd like him to send us the videos he took of Boris's wife. The Hierarch is crazy about her and incredibly jealous. And Marina isn't above flirting and more. With her partying in the south of France, I'm hoping he took wonderful footage of Marina in some compromising positions."

"Footage that will, of course, be forwarded to her husband."

"Naturally."

Viv grinned. "That's pretty underhanded," she said with admiration. "I love the way technology lends itself to such a worthy cause." She put her arms around Pavel and leaned against his back as he sat at the computer. She gave his cheek a soft little nuzzle as she glanced down at the screen. Her pheromones sent a seductive message to his senses.

"We believe he killed his brother," Pavel said. He enjoyed

the caress and kissed her hand. "We're planning on making him frantic over his whorish wife."

"Boris killed his brother?" She looked shocked. "No. He's too soft. I'd put my money on Bella."

"Our sources in St. Petersburg have tracked down the shooters. They claim he hired them."

"They could be lying."

"Maybe," said Pavel, "but they picked him out of a photo of Danilov personnel and said he had hired them specifically to assassinate Dimitri. Claimed to be an angry coworker."

"Could they be wrong?"

"Of course. But if they were, why would they all out pick the same man from a group photo?"

"You know how people are. You give them something to look at, and if one of them says, 'This is the one,' then a lot of the others will agree."

"In separate rooms at the same time?" Pavel asked. "There was no chance of discussion here."

"Incredible," said Viv with a shake of her head. "What's the motive? A takeover?"

"Who knows? He was in Dimitri's shadow all his life. Maybe he got a case of ambition late in his career and decided to take a risk."

Viv looked shocked. "Are you going to the police with this?"

"Not until we get the icon back. Nobody's going to grab Boris until we do. Some of our guys back home have the shooters under wraps. When the time comes, they'll notify the police. Or decide to take care of it in-house."

"Aren't you worried they might escape?"

Viv was taken aback when she saw the flicker of a smile on Pavel's face. "Not where we have them," he said as he looked her in the eye.

* * *

Bella heard a knock on the door of her condo and looked perplexed. She wasn't expecting company. "Get the door, will you? I don't know who it is. I didn't invite anybody."

Bella gestured toward Boris as if he were her lackey. He gave a disgusted look, but he complied, although her tendency to let her human side take over really irritated him. She was a damn diva.

When he unbolted several locks, he opened it and seemed startled. It was Margot, the cleaning lady, standing there beside a trolley loaded with mops, dusters, polish, sponges, and cleaners.

"Hello," she said with a smile. "It's that time again." Margot gave them both a cheerful look and said apologetically, "One of my other customers is away, so I thought I might move you up. If it's a problem, I'll come back on the regular day."

Bella flicked a glance over the living room with its untidy piles of magazines and a few of Boris's bottles, and said, "Fine. The place is a mess. Men are such pigs. It needs a cleaning."

And Margot closed the door behind her and got to work.

About an hour later, Boris sat at his laptop, engrossed in surfing the Web, scanning for stories about Danilov Enterprises, Dimitri, himself, or any progress in the murder investigation. So far, so good. Nothing but unsuccessful inquiries into the assassination. No suspects, no motive, except for the usual business ones. The group who had been negotiating for oil rights with the Danilovs had ended talks, citing their agreement. Fine.

Their contacts in the FSB were doing their job, claiming the investigation was ongoing and they couldn't comment. They dropped hints of terrorist activity behind the assassination and added enough bureaucratic jargon to make it sound serious. To Russian readers familiar with the pattern, it meant the Danilovs were in so tight with the government that nobody was going to find out the truth until it was convenient.

Boris was grateful he was as yet unknown in New York. He still shook with fright whenever he remembered how his knees had trembled as he and that idiot had walked into the restaurant and taken home the icon. How he had managed not to faint at the table was a miracle.

The woman waiting for him was European, but when he realized her companion was a werecat, he nearly threw up, fearing discovery. His sensitive nose recognized the scent, and he panicked at the thought that he might be Russian. It didn't mean he would recognize Boris, especially under that wig and mustache, but it had been enough to rattle him. For some reason, Boris hadn't expected a werecat. Maybe another European or more likely an American. That would have made him feel better.

He couldn't wait to hand over this bad-luck icon to the client Bella had found, hop on a plane, and go home. Yet every step of the way, he had encountered another roadblock. Bella had brought him nothing but misfortune.

He hated this Siberian bitch cat, who had ruined his life, turned him into a thief, and separated him from his wife. He hated her enough to wish her dead. To his shame, he also knew he would never have the guts to get rid of her, either, because he was in too deep.

As he gloomily checked his e-mail, he suddenly found he had a message from Marina. With a delighted cry, he clicked a few times and brought it up.

Chapter Sixty

Pavel picked up his cell phone and heard Tony's voice, his werecat contact in federal law enforcement. Right now, it seemed harsher than usual.

"This Boris must be a real asshole to get mixed up with this crowd. The leader is a lunatic."

"Who are we talking about?"

"Some gang of raggedy-ass morons from Russia who call themselves the Rasputnikatz. They claim to be descended from an illegitimate son of Rasputin."

Pavel frowned. "I seriously doubt he was a werecat."

"Their usual area of expertise is theft, but on a much smaller scale. They send women out as shoplifters. They boost truckloads of small appliances. They steal whatever isn't nailed down—with a few minor sidelines, like dealing dope and smuggling contraband cigarettes. This recent caper is a whole new enterprise for them."

"How did you manage to dig up so much information in such a sort time?"

"I had my guys trace the license plates of the car they used to pick up Boris the night before they stole the icon. Some girl who sleeps with the leader of the pack owns it. She says he asked to borrow her car, and she let him. She claims he told her he was having car trouble, and she doesn't know anything about any icons."

"Of course."

"So we threatened her with aiding and abetting criminals in an international theft of national treasures, and after we revived her, she said she'd give up anybody we wanted as long as she didn't have to do time."

"She isn't afraid of this guy?"

"She is, but she's much more worried about being in jail for a few decades. Besides, we promised that if she rats out her sweetheart, *he'll* be so old when he gets out of prison, he won't even remember he had a girlfriend."

"Good work. So are you going to round them up and bring them in?"

"Hell, no! We're going to let them make plans with their comrades from St. Petersburg to unload the icon. Bella made the original contacts, and we still don't know who the buyer is, so we have to play along and let them handle it. We'll grab them all the night they make the sale."

"Good." Pavel paused. "Have you been in contact with the authorities in St. Petersburg?"

"Not yet. We want to be able to hand them a rock-solid case so they can prosecute these two. We have an interest in somebody they have. We can do a deal here. Everybody wins."

"Understood."

"I'm keeping tabs on their apartment," Pavel added.

"Under the aegis of this agency with regard to homeland-security issues," Tony informed him. "We operate under the radar. Top secret clearance. We stay out of the news. I'm deputizing you as a special field assistant."

Pavel nodded. "Good," he said.

One way or another, Bella and Boris were going down.

As soon as Boris spotted the e-mail from Marina, he clicked on it, expecting to see pictures of her posing with the children in one of the opulent rooms of their St. Petersburg apartment. Instead, he was stunned to find himself opening a video showing Marina and some unidentified men frolicking in a fountain in some tropical land. His wife wasn't wearing much more than a sopping-wet T-shirt, and she was laughing uproariously at her own inability to get out of the water. To his horror, she was acting like a drunken slut.

There were more videos. In one, Marina stood on the deck of some yacht while a scenic landscape of palm trees and flowers filled the background. Next to her, an elderly degenerate playfully removed the top of her bikini while she laughed and laughed, flashing her cosmetically enhanced boobs at the camera.

Boris tuned red with anger at the memory of the bill from the plastic surgeon. Those things had cost him a fortune. And there she was flaunting them in front of strangers. Who were these fucking morons?

Only a feeling a sheer nausea prevented Boris from viewing the whole collection. What he had just seen filled him with such disgust, he wanted to kill somebody. Here he was, in hiding, abused by thugs, at the beck and call of that bitch cat while his adored wife—who should have been taking care of the children back home—was cavorting at a beach resort. He was so angry, he replayed the videos, searching the background for signs that might give a clue as to her whereabouts.

As Boris scanned the screen, he saw the French tricolor waving in the breeze. The slut was kicking up her heels on the fucking French Riviera while he was languishing in Manhattan, risking his life and liberty for Bella's stupid schemes.

This filled him with such righteous anger, Boris did something unusual. He got up and kicked the nearest object he could find, which happened to be a wastepaper basket. It sailed across the room, crashed into a cabinet, and rolled noisily into the corner, where it lay on its side. He kicked it two or three more times, just to vent his fury and hear the unholy racket it made as it hit the furniture, the walls, the tables. His skin prickled, coaxing him with the desire to go werecat. His scent turned dark and musky.

"What the hell is going on here?" Bella ran into the room, nervously darting her eyes around. "What's all that noise?"

"Nothing," he replied, sitting down once more, feeling pleased he had scared her.

"What do you mean nothing? I heard enough noise to wake the dead. What's wrong with you?"

He looked at Bella as if he barely knew her. "Nothing that a few drinks and a new wife wouldn't cure," he said.

Now she looked really bewildered. Then she glanced at the computer screen and saw the video of Marina in a pool, half naked.

"Shit! Where is she, and who is she with? I don't recognize any of those people."

"Me neither. But then, I'm just the poor, stupid husband who lives to get screwed by devious little whores who waste his money."

Even Bella, as selfish as she was, appeared to hear the bitterness in his voice. She glanced at him, not knowing what to say.

"Don't think too much about it," she said finally. "You need to focus right now."

"No! *You* need to focus. I'm as focused as I'm ever going to be. And when I get home, I'm going to be done with all of you," he shouted. "I'm taking my children and going away. We'll go live in England. Or Switzerland. I'll never let her get her dirty hands on them. I'll save the videos and use them as evidence at the divorce trial."

He was still ranting when Bella shrugged and vanished from the room, saying something about him having to work out his problems by himself.

Chapter Sixty-one

That night, Viv and her lover were entwined on the sofa, looking out over the city at night, its millions of lights spread out beneath the window in a breathtaking panorama. Pavel kissed her and Viv nestled against him in delight.

"I always feel safe with you," she said with a sigh. "You make me feel nothing bad will happen to me as long as I'm near you."

"Glad to hear that. Of course, I'd prefer to hear that you shiver with lust when you see me and that you can't wait to hold me in your arms and make love like a wildcat. But 'safe' is very flattering."

She burst out laughing as she slid under him and put her arms around him, caressing him beneath his shirt, nipping playfully at his ear as he drew her into his embrace.

"I don't care what Marc says," Pavel said. "We're meant to be together. And I'm not going to let you get away."

"Promise."

Pavel kissed her gently on the tip of her nose. "I promise. Come hell or high water, it's going to be you and me. Anybody who has a problem with that doesn't have to stay around and watch."

"Make love to me," she said as she threw her arms around him. "Make love as if tonight was the last night on earth and you and I had to make it last forever."

Pavel smiled. He picked Viv up and carried her into the bedroom, where they quickly undressed and dived under the covers.

As Viv ran her fingers through his hair, Pavel kissed his way down her neck. He took her hands in his as she lay stretched on the bed beneath him and held her possessively while he lowered his mouth to her breast and slowly, gently sucked the hard pink nipple.

The sensation raced from her breast to her groin as Viv gave a little cry and quivered as he did the same to her other breast.

"So sensitive," he murmured. "So delicate."

"Oh, *koshka*," she whispered. "Don't stop."

He smiled and then kissed her again on the mouth, exploring her with his tongue, tangling with hers, pleasing her and exciting her at the same time. "Viv, I want you so much."

"I'm yours. There's nobody else I want," she whispered as she opened her long legs and wrapped them around him.

Without missing a beat, Pavel raised himself over her and then pressed into her, entering her quickly, in a steady cadence of love and lust. They tried to outdo themselves, both of them covered with sweat as they mated again and again, obsessed with giving and getting a climax of such intensity that they could feel their hearts pounding in their ears, threatening to burst from their feverish lovemaking.

When Pavel gave a cry of total release and collapsed completely spent in her arms, sated and incapable of moving a muscle, Viv clung to him in passionate possession.

They belonged to each other; nobody was ever going to separate them in *this* lifetime.

In the monitoring command post at Metro Investigations, the man on duty felt his attention drawn to the screen showing the living room at Bella's condo. This view was courtesy of Margot, the cleaning lady, who had also hooked up the audio feed. Right now things were heating up. It looked as if Bella and Boris were about to kill each other.

"What the hell are you doing?" Bella asked. "Where do you think you're going with those suitcases?"

"To the airport. I'm going back to St. Petersburg tonight."

Bella reacted as if he had hit her. "That's insane! What do you plan on doing there?"

"I'm going to file for divorce and take my children out of the country."

"Stop this. You're upset over those pictures, and you don't know what you're doing. All we need is maybe another day, and we can conclude our business and go home. Don't break down now."

"You can conclude any business you want. I don't give a damn what you do any more."

Bella looked frantically around, as if to summon up some argument that might pacify him.

"Are you drunk?" she demanded.

"No. For once I'm absolutely sober."

"Well, I don't think there's a flight to St. Petersburg until tomorrow," she said.

"You're wrong. I just checked on the Internet."

Bella threw herself in his way, blocking his path to the door. "Stop it!" she shouted, savagely pushing him out of the way. " I'm not going to let you fuck this up and spoil my plans. Millions of dollars are riding on it!"

"Fuck the millions of dollars, and fuck you, too, you bitch! I'm sick of being your stooge. I'm going home to the only people who love me. And I'm taking them so far away from you and from Danilov Enterprises that nobody will ever find me again."

As Boris took hold of her arm and threw Bella against the wall, she grabbed an umbrella from the porcelain stand near the door and whaled away at him, screaming abuse as he tried to defend himself.

With a shout of rage, Boris turned into a werecat the size

of an African serval. He sprung at Bella and knocked her to the ground. She shifted into a cat the size of a puma and responded by grabbing him by the scruff of the neck and flinging him against the marble floor, nearly braining him. She let him have it three or four times until he was out cold. Then she vented her rage by circling him, hissing and spitting with fury as he lay there before her. Incensed, she leaped at him and batted him furiously with her paws, her anger consuming her now.

Staggering a little from her effort, Bella shifted once more, gasping from the effort of the fight. Then, reeling across the living room, she sank down onto a sofa and reached for her cell phone.

Her face contorted with stress, Bella punched in a number and said breathlessly, "Get over here and help me. I've just knocked out the Hierarch and prevented him from leaving the country. But he's going to wake up, and when he does, he'll be hard to control."

Someone on the other end must have said something to pacify her, because the man in the monitoring station saw Bella nod her head emphatically, shut off the phone, and go into the next room to get belts and sashes to use as a makeshift restraint until reinforcements could arrive.

Chapter Sixty-two

"Boss, I'm on the monitor here, and I just saw one hell of a fight between the Danilovs. They went werecat, and now she's shifted back and tying him up with belts. I think one of her helpers is on his way over."

Pavel smiled as he heard the message. Confrontations between suspects were always a good thing. With werecats, they were always so close to the edge, it made fights inevitable.

"Keep watching. Call me if things heat up again."

"Right."

Viv cuddled close to Pavel as she draped an arm around him and nuzzled his ear. "Trouble?"

"No. Good news. The Danilovs were just beating each other up. He lost."

For a moment, she went silent, and then she began to rock with laughter. "*She* beat up your Hierarch? Are you serious?"

"That's what my man said, and he watched it on our monitor. They shifted and went at it."

"She's either a lot tougher than I thought, or your Hierarch is very weak."

"Exactly."

"You Russian Blues need a new one."

"Oh, he won't be holding the title much longer, not after we charge him with murder—and theft of state treasures."

"Any contenders among the Russian Blues back home?"

Pavel smiled at her and pillowed his head on her bosom. "You know how things are in any organization. One falls, another rises. I imagine we'll have many claimants for the job. Even as we speak, I can predict that at least four or five ambitious werecats are scheming to replace Boris."

"Are overseas werecats eligible?"

Pavel glanced at Viv and nestled closer to her.

"I haven't checked the rules lately, but the Hierarch has always been chosen from members who live in Russia."

"Too bad. I think you would be a great Hierarch."

At that, Pavel burst out laughing and then gave Viv a passionate kiss. "You American girls have such odd ideas," he said. "They wouldn't consider me."

"Why not?"

"I've lived overseas for several years, and I'm going to announce my engagement to an American of a different clan. If that's all right with you," he said as he looked tenderly into her eyes.

Viv climbed on top of Pavel, kissing him all over and caressing him with abandon.

"I'm all for it," she said between kisses as she turned her attention to very tender parts.

He yelped. "Do that again. Oh, yes. More."

"I'm not really a traditionalist," Viv said as she slid her fingers around his organ and heard him utter a muffled sound of either pleasure or alarm. "We don't have to make a stop at Tiffany."

"Whatever you like is fine with me," he said in a smothered voice, closing his eyes in anticipation.

"Good."

Viv caressed him sweetly and then bent her head to his chest and left a trail of hot kisses all the way down to his belly. She laughed with delight as she saw his stomach muscles contract and felt a sudden growth somewhere else.

"*Malenkaya*, you're torturing me," he pleaded. "Put me out of my misery."

She smiled and proceeded to do just that.

"What took you so long?" Bella demanded as Bill and his driver showed up and she buzzed them into the apartment.

"Traffic. Where is he?"

Bella jerked her chin in the direction of the next room, and the two thugs in black leather jackets went in to investigate. There on the floor lay the Hierarch of the Russian Blues, in human form, securely tied up.

"What the hell are you trying to do?" Bill demanded by way of greeting. "You know you can't go home right now. Not until our business is done."

"I'm through with everything," Boris said, moving and twisting desperately.

"No, you're not. We still need you."

"I went into the restaurant and got you the icon. That's enough. I did my part."

"You did a good job so far, Hierarch. Now stay strong. Don't break down."

Boris writhed in fury. "I just want to go home!"

"You can't go home until everything is done. You and Bella have to return together and let your FSB contacts hold a press conference to claim you were in a safe location overseas while they pursued terrorists who were attempting to attack Danilov Enterprises and the state. Then there will be a news blackout for state security reasons and the matter gets dropped. We go on with our lives. Danilov Enterprises continues to flourish under your leadership." He glanced at Bella as he said this.

"Fuck the company. I just want to go home and see my children," Boris replied.

"You will. But not right now," Bill said patiently. "Certain things have to happen."

"He's hung up about his wife," Bella explained. "The bitch sent him some provocative videos from where she's vacationing, and they pushed him over the edge. She's flashing her tits at everyone on the Riviera, and he's upset."

"What a great wife," Bill said. "If she were mine, I'd beat her black-and-blue when she got home. Why doesn't he just do that?"

"He loves her," Bella replied dismissively.

Boris continued to twist and struggle with his restraints as his captors looked away, trying to decide how best to handle him. Bill gave a scornful glance at the distressed Hierarch and bragged, "Rasputnikatz kick ass. You should try acting like us for a change. You'd be a better Hierarch for your clan."

Boris had settled down a little. He appeared calmer and his breathing had become normal. The others took that as a sign he was returning to his senses. Bella even bent down and said, "I see you're becoming more rational. Good. Just focus on our goal and you'll get through this."

Boris looked up at her and nodded. Then as Bella relaxed, he shape-shifted, burst out of the restraints, and made a surprise grab for her arm, knocking her off balance and throwing her to the floor. Frantically he headed for the closed door, trying to crash it open with his weight, but the door stayed in place. He butted it furiously, taking out his frustration on the unyielding wood.

Immediately Bella and the Rasputnikatz shifted and went after him. Bill was shocked by the bulk Bella achieved when she supersized; at puma size, she looked like a shaggy mammoth compared to her brother-in-law. Boris was far less impressive at serval size. Even Bill was bigger, with his shaggy Siberian coat. Without it, he and Boris would have been fairly well matched.

"You're not leaving," Bella growled telepathically as she

seized the skin around Boris's neck and flung him toward the Rasputnikatz. They grabbed him with quick paws and sent him sprawling over the polished floor. Boris clawed at his opponents and tried to bite Bella, who responded with a nasty swat, raking his face with her own sharp claws. She gave him a couple of good bites, too, hissing furiously as she did.

Hisses, growls, and the smell of anger filled the air, and Bill's subordinate shifted into human form once again and took a small package from the pocket of his jacket. As Bill and Bella fought to restrain their prey, sinking teeth into haunches and limbs, producing feline screams that reverberated on the walls of the marble foyer, the driver unwrapped a tranquilizing dart, approached the combatants, and at the first opportunity, shoved it into Boris's unprotected flank. Then he did it two more times.

The other two cats kept a grip on their prey as Boris slowly lost his will to fight and relaxed his muscles, even as they held him in their jaws. When his head wobbled to the side and his eyes closed, they released him and backed off, rising to their feet and surveying their quarry.

Shape-shifting, Bella and Bill struggled to catch their breath. For spite, Bella took aim at the drugged Hierarch and kicked him viciously in the side.

"Don't hurt him any more than you have to," Bill said, as he pulled her away. "You don't want him to have to go see a doctor who will ask embarrassing questions. Keep the punishment psychological. "

"Get him out of here," she said. "Do you have a place to keep him until we need him to go to the meeting with the client? He has to be implicated in this, too. It's the best way to keep him under my thumb."

"In my basement," Bill said.

"He has to be restrained. Otherwise he'll try to run."

"Steel cage. Strong enough to hold a five-hundred-pound

tiger. The Hierarch won't be that big in his wildest fantasy. I can't belive the Russian Blues picked such a runt."

"He acquired the position by default. They might unseat him, but he'll still be CEO of Danilov Enterprises—which is why he's still useful. I need him cooperative and living in fear of blackmail."

Bill nodded. "All right," he said. "Semyon and I will wrap him in a rug, take him down on the elevator, and load him into my minivan."

"You drive a minivan?"

"It was the first car in the driveway," Bill said. "But lucky for us it was there. Easier to transport him."

"What if he wakes while you're driving?"

"Then I trank him again. Believe me, Semyon just gave him enough to put him to sleep until tomorrow afternoon. It won't be a problem."

"Take him straight to that cage," Bella ordered.

"Of course. Do you think I want to take chances? Now we need you to call downstairs to the concierge and let him know two men are going to be crossing the lobby with an Oriental rug that needs repairs. Can he open the door for us?"

"Why do you need me to do that?"

Bill looked at her with his heavy-lidded eyes. "Because otherwise he might think we've just stolen it, and he might call the cops."

"All right." Bella made the call. Then she directed Semyon to Boris's room, where a suitable carpet lay, and watched Bill and his driver roll the unconscious werecat inside it.

"Give me something to tie it with," Bill directed.

Bella produced some nylon cord, which did the trick. Then with the Hierarch bundled neatly inside the Persian carpet, she opened the door and watched the two men carry him down the hall and into the elevator.

"Keep him safe," she said. Then she went back inside and

poured herself a good stiff drink. Just as soon as she returned to Russia, she was going to find a trustworthy Siberian hit man, give him the address of these Manhattan thugs, and tell him to eliminate them. She would use blackmail as leverage over Boris, but she wanted nobody to be able to get that kind of hold over *her*.

Chapter Sixty-three

Pavel had his favorite fed on the phone just as soon as his monitor called in the news. "Bella's helper is taking Boris back to his place. Can your men track them? One of my guys put a device on the car while the Rasputnikatz were inside Bella's condo. They're ready to hit the road."

"Okay. We'll trail them and find out where the Siberians are taking him. We had to put the girl we picked up in a safe house until this is over. She's been spilling her guts in hopes of cutting a deal. No loyalty at all."

"Good. We'll keep monitoring the widow Danilov. You can have your guys keep tabs on the others. Bella's the one who will get the call from the person who wants the goods, so we won't let up on her. Audio, video, the works."

"Okay. Hope we can do the takedown soon."

"Then you'll alert the Russians?"

"Yes. And we can make a deal with them."

Viv and Marc had their disagreements over Pavel, but at work all went as smoothly as usual. Neither wanted to air their family problems before the customers, and frankly, neither one wanted to prolong the unpleasantness that arose after bitter words concerning Viv's choice of mate.

She knew Marc wasn't happy; he knew Viv would never change her mind. They left it at that and concentrated on business. With the icon in the hands of the crooks, Pavel had removed the bodyguards, since the Roussels weren't likely to be threatened by anyone now. Life was nearly normal.

The night after Pavel's man had seen the fight between Boris and Bella, Viv said goodbye to her brother and headed for the subway to catch the train to Pavel's apartment. Wrapping her muffler tighter to keep out the November chill, Viv walked briskly to the subway entrance, descended the dirty stairs along with a wave of others, caught a train, and arrived at her stop in good time. With her heightened senses reeling from the odor of fuel, stale air, and the occasional puddle of urine on the floors, Viv never noticed or caught the scent of two men hurrying along behind her. They were about five paces in back of her as she walked quickly up the stairs.

After a stop at a grocery store, Viv continued on her way, and as she reached a construction site, two pairs of hands shot out in the darkness and grabbed her, pulling her behind the tall wooden fence that hid them from view. Before she had a chance to fight back, Viv was overpowered, drugged with a chloroform-soaked handkerchief, and carried into the backseat of an SUV with dark windows waiting just inside the fence. Her attackers settled her in, threw a comforter over her for concealment, then pushed open the gate to the site and drove off as quickly as they could, merging into the early-evening traffic.

"Is she all right?" the passenger asked nervously as the driver headed toward New Jersey. "I mean, this is Viv. She's important to the clan. She's practically royalty."

"And it was the Leader who gave the order to bring her in without a struggle. She'll be fine. She'll just have a headache when she wakes up."

"What's going on with him? I've started hearing rumors. . . ."

The driver nodded grimly. "People like to speculate," he said. "What you have to remember is—he's still the Leader. And we're in the Special Squad, so we take his orders."

"But," the man said as he glanced back at Viv's drugged form, "this just isn't right, and I don't like being part of it."

"I didn't hear that," the driver said as he entered the lane of traffic that would take him out of Manhattan's busy traffic and onto the Henry Hudson Parkway and across the bridge to New Jersey. "You're loyal, I'm loyal, and that's what counts. I can't believe he intends to harm Viv. She's too important."

"Then why have her knocked out?" he persisted.

"Let's just concentrate on getting her to New Jersey safely," the driver said. He didn't sound as though he really had an answer.

As Marc was closing up for the night, he suddenly remembered something he'd wanted to ask Viv about the Fabergé picture frames they'd just gotten in from Moscow. He thought she'd put the pieces on display, but he couldn't locate them. Maybe she could tell him where they were before tomorrow. A customer was coming in to see them first thing in the morning.

He punched in her cell phone number and was surprised when his call went straight to voice mail. Maybe she was in the subway and there was no signal. He snapped the phone shut and put it inside his pocket. He'd try again later.

After Marc closed the shop and went home, he decided Viv had had enough time to reach Pavel's apartment, so he called again. He was directed to leave a message.

As he prepared dinner, he felt vaguely uneasy. Viv normally had her phone on unless she was in a situation where she would be requested to shut it off, but since she was only going to Pavel's, it should be turned on. And there was no response to either of his messages.

Don't jump to conclusions, he told himself. There was probably nothing wrong. Their lives were back on track now, the thieves who wanted the icon had it, and nobody would have any interest in them.

As children, Marc and Viv had shared the ability to communicate telepathically in werecat form. Occasionally it carried over into human form. Right now he was trying as hard as he could to make her call him back, and getting no results.

He didn't want to call Pavel's number. He disliked the whole idea of that relationship, and didn't want to call there as if it was perfectly acceptable that his sister, who ranked high in her own clan, was living with him.

At around eight thirty, Marc heard his phone ring, quickly answered it, and was startled to hear Pavel's voice.

"Marc, I got in late and thought I'd find Viv here. Was she detained at work? I can't reach her on her cell phone."

When Viv woke up, she had a violent headache, a sense of disorientation, and no idea where she was. Opening her eyes, she looked around the area and determined she was lying on an elaborately carved bed in a room decorated in spectacular country house traditional, the kind of decor you would find in the more expensive magazines: lots of lush fabrics, with luxurious window treatments and fancy fringe on everything. It was beautiful. But who owned it and how had she arrived here? The last thing she remembered was exiting the subway and walking past that construction site.

Viv tried to sit up, but couldn't quite manage on the first attempt. She forced herself to try again, and after a struggle, she got herself to a seated position, then perched on the side of the bed, wondering if she had enough strength to put her feet on the floor and walk.

Making an effort, she stood on shaky legs and went to the mirror, studying her reflection, trying to determine if she had been injured. Nothing seemed amiss. No cuts or bruises. She was fully dressed in the skirt and sweater she had worn when she'd left the shop, and her clothing hadn't been torn. The only strange thing was her eyes. The pupils were so dilated they looked huge.

She had been drugged and kidnapped.

Frightened now, Viv staggered to the door and tried to open it, but found it locked. She flung open a closet door and saw her coat and handbag inside, but upon opening the bag, she realized her cell phone was missing. She checked her coat pockets. Nothing.

Quickly, she went to the window and peered out into the darkness, trying to get her bearings, hoping she might recognize something, some landmark, anything to give her an idea where she was. The entire area seemed dark, except for lights that illuminated an elegantly landscaped lawn, with a big semicircular driveway and a fence at a distance from the house. A lone figure stood outside in the cold, keeping watch.

As soon as she saw the driveway and the fence, she felt the bottom drop out of her stomach. This mansion belonged to John Sinclair, Leader of the Maine Coon cat clan, her rejected suitor.

Chapter Sixty-four

As soon as Marc and Pavel realized Viv was missing, they joined forces to try to locate her. She could be anywhere. Pavel called some of his men and had them take Viv's subway route. Marc tried to think what she had said a few hours before she left. Something about going shopping for dinner. One of Pavel's men checked all the grocery stores on the way between the subway exit and Pavel's apartment. One grocer remembered a tall lady who matched Viv's description.

"She got as far as that store, at least," said Marc. "Something happened between there and your place."

"I've got the Hummer outside. Let's go check that area. I've got Ivan monitoring incoming calls and signals from tracking devices. If she still has her pendant, she can call us on that. Meanwhile, keep calling her number."

In John Sinclair's mansion, Viv was beginning to regain her equilibrium. She had already tried to open the windows and found them securely locked. She ransacked the room, hunting for anything she could use as a weapon, and discovered her nail file in her bag in the closet. Small, but made of steel, it might be her only hope right now. She placed it in the pocket of her skirt.

Just as she began to hope she might still discover a way

out of the room, she heard footsteps outside the door and it opened, revealing Sinclair and the two members of his Special Squad who had kidnapped her.

"Viv, how are you recovering? I hope you're all right."

"I've been better," she said with fury in her eyes. "And I'd like to leave."

"I'm sorry. Not possible at the moment. First we have to settle some things. For the good of the clan."

"That would be best served by releasing me."

"I'm sorry," Sinclair replied. "Please come downstairs with me. I'd like to speak to you in my office. I have some papers I'd like you to sign."

That didn't sound good, but it would at least give her a chance to move around, she thought. Besides, after her recent experiences with Sinclair, she didn't want a private conference in this bedroom. Too dangerous, especially in her weakened state.

Viv gave his companions a frosty stare. "How did I get here?" she demanded. "The last thing I recall was walking from the subway. It doesn't go all the way to New Jersey."

"I'm sorry, Viv," one of the men said, looking embarrassed. "The Leader wanted to see you and—"

"They did what I asked," Sinclair interrupted. "Now please come with me."

Viv looked at him with contempt and said, "If you expect me to change my mind about marriage, I'll give you the answer right here. Pavel Federov is my mate. And that won't change—except for the actual wedding ceremony." She looked sternly at his aides, Joseph and Matthew, and said, "I invoked my right to choose my mate and he tried to overrule me. You know the rules of our clan just as I do. What he wants it illegal. He's been on a rampage, raping the females of our clan. Two of them contacted me to tell me. And, Matthew, if you think I'm lying, call up Sarah and ask her what he did to *her*."

The Leader turned red with anger and reached for Viv as

they descended the staircase. As he did, she brought back her elbow and gave him a vicious jab in the stomach. That broke his grip on her, and she picked up speed and raced down the stairs and toward the door, adrenaline flowing in her veins.

Locked. In desperation, Viv struggled with the lock and couldn't open it. She looked back at the men. Instead of running after her, Matthew was demanding to know what the Leader had done to his wife, and his expression was furious. Joseph attempted to prevent both men from coming to blows. Rebellion had begun.

Running down the corridor, Viv searched desperately for a telephone, and locating one, she frantically punched in Pavel's number. By this time, the Leader had reached the foyer, still arguing with his subordinates, and shouting for them to get Viv. She heard Pavel's voice, started to tell him where she was, and before she could say more than "I've been kidnapped," John Sinclair broke away from Matthew's grip and grabbed the phone from her hands. In a rage, he smashed it down into its cradle, and ripped the cord out of the wall, his eyes glittering with fury.

"Look at him!" Viv shouted. "He's insane. He wants to force me into a marriage, and he wants to handpick the females for a harem. Matthew, I know you're a good man. If you don't believe me, call Sarah and ask her. Don't be afraid of him."

"Don't listen to her," Sinclair shouted. "Your loyalty is to me!"

"Never in the history of our clan has any leader attempted to subvert our rules and harm our members. Think about it."

Caught between their oath to the Leader and their respect for Viv, the men hesitated.

"You have a choice," she said. "Either you can listen to a corrupt tyrant, or you can call Sarah and ask for verification of what I've said. How long will it take for her to get here?"

Matthew looked down at the floor for a moment as if he

were trying to derive some help from the intricate parquet pattern, and he finally said, "Joseph, I think we should listen to Viv. It won't take long. And then we'll know the truth."

"Thank you," said Viv as she looked the men in the eye. Sinclair looked ready to kill.

"Marc, I lost her! Damn it." Pavel pressed a few buttons and Ivan was on the phone. "Viv just got a call through but it was cut off. Here's the number. Find the address. Now!"

Marc and Pavel sat in the vehicle while Metro's best hacker did his magic halfway across town. In minutes Pavel's phone rang again. "Unlisted New Jersey number," Ivan reported. "But we managed to locate it." And he gave them the owner's name and address.

"Shit! I never thought he'd do something like this. We've got to get Viv out of there. I think he's gone crazy," Marc said, badly shaken.

"I have a helicopter. That will get us out there fast. But is there someplace where we can land?"

"John Sinclair has the biggest lawn in New Jersey," Marc replied. "It's a huge estate."

"Does he have guards, guard animals, electrified wires on the perimeter?"

"Probably all three," Marc said. "The Leader is very concerned about safety issues. And, Pavel," he said, "this is a clan matter. I think I ought to call people and let them know what's going on."

"Fine with me. But we're getting there first. We're allies now. Call your brethren and tell them to get over there as fast as they can. We'll meet them."

Chapter Sixty-five

Pavel, Marc, and three of Pavel's best operatives boarded the helicopter and took off from a helipad near the Hudson River. They were prepared for a commando raid.

Marc had called his friends Hank, Pat, and Joey to let them know there was a critical hostage situation at the Leader's home involving Viv, and they offered their support.

"The Leader must have gone mad," Marc said. "He's the one who's preventing her from leaving. This means clan war. There's no going back."

There was a pause. Then Marc heard Hank say, "If it's Viv's word against his, I'd take her side any day. We'll meet you there."

Marc turned to Pavel as the helicopter rose over the river and soared into the starry winter sky. "They're in."

Viv, Sinclair, Joseph, and Matthew sat in an uneasy silence in one of the salons in the front of the mansion while they waited for Sarah. The Leader restlessly smoked one cigarette after the other, his eyes narrowing as he glared at Viv in a chair near the fireplace. She ignored him and looked out the window, hoping to see headlights coming up the driveway.

"As the Leader of this clan, I have a right, a duty," he corrected himself, "to see to the welfare of our clan, now and in the future."

Viv turned to him and said, "You had a duty to protect your clan. Instead you harmed it." The hatred she felt for this corrupt and evil creature roiled in her stomach, spreading through her entire body. She felt the desire to shape-shift and attack with fang and claw. She tamped it down. That would come later.

"This must be my wife." Matthew saw headlights as a car rolled up the long driveway and parked outside the front door.

Viv noticed the sweat already forming on the Leader's brow. He took a long drag on his cigarette as he watched his subordinate go to the door, unlock it, and let Sarah enter. Now his hand was trembling. Viv wondered if he was considering shape-shifting.

Obviously nervous, and suspecting why she had been summoned, Sarah walked into the room, glanced around, and recoiled as she saw John Sinclair about to come toward her.

"Sarah," he said kindly, "what sort of stories are you telling about me? Haven't I always been good to you?"

Turning away in revulsion, Sarah looked at Viv. "Did you tell Matthew what I told you?"

"I told him you would have to tell him yourself. Don't be afraid. Just tell the truth."

Matthew looked fearful as his small wife sank down onto a sofa and said, "I can't. I'm too ashamed."

"Sarah. Please. It's not just you. It's others, too. If he's not stopped, he'll destroy our laws and then our clan."

Sinclair took advantage of the female's hesitation and seemed to grow more confident. "Viv is trying to fabricate something and drag you into it," he said as he crossed the room and stood before Sarah. "Don't let her."

Eyes wide with fear, Sarah looked at Viv, then at Matthew. "Get him away from me," she pleaded.

At that, her husband said to her, "Sarah, if you tell the truth, I will never hold it against you. I love you."

As Matthew's mate opened her mouth to speak, the Leader whirled around and said hastily as if he were trying to concoct a story on the spot, "She forced herself on me and I was flattered. Look at her—young, attractive, always flirting with me when I looked her way. She offered herself like an appetizer and, yes, I took the bait. You should keep an eye on her, Matthew. She's such a—"

Matthew went werecat. Viv and Sarah jumped up and got out of the way as Matthew hurled himself on his Leader and sent him crashing to the floor. Sinclair flung down his cigarette and responded in kind. He shifted quickly, his larger-form panther size to Matthew's smaller lynx size. Both animals snarled, clawed, and bit, trying to kill the other. The floor looked like a mass of rolling fur.

In all the uproar, nobody noticed the lit cigarette roll under the damask sofa, hidden by the heavy fringe that went down to the carpeted floor. Out of sight, it slowly began to smolder.

Sinclair inflicted serious damage on his opponent as they battled, but Matthew was too stubborn to give up. With a snarl, he flipped the other cat and clamped his jaws on his flank, making him screech with pain. Seeing her husband in trouble, Sarah shifted and attacked her former Leader, the two medium-sized cats turning the tables on him and chasing him up the staircase.

While the three werecats took their battle to the upper floor, Viv heard a noise outside that brought her running to the door. A helicopter was landing on the lawn, men were pouring out, and she heard familiar voices calling to her.

Joseph walked out onto the porch with her, and seeing the invasion, he called to other members of the Special Squad to let the visitors pass. They hesitated, but since there were only two of them on the lawn and they were clearly outnumbered, they stood down.

Viv flung herself into Pavel's arms as he ran to her, and then hugged her brother. "I didn't think you'd be able to find me. I'm so glad to see you."

"Where's Sinclair?" Pavel demanded furiously.

Chapter Sixty-six

"Keep everybody out of the house," Pavel ordered. "I'm going upstairs. Viv, Marc, tell your clansmen to stay outside."

"We're going with you," she said. "This is our problem, not yours. I can't let you take charge."

"She's right," Marc said. "Give me a weapon. I know how to use a nine millimeter."

Pavel knew how clan rules were. It would cause an uproar among his own clan if they resorted to outside help in such a serious internal matter. "All right," he agreed. "I'm here as backup. It's your party."

Guided by the screeching coming from the second floor, they made their way up the stairs as the rest left the house, Pavel's men staying close to the helicopter, the Leader's Special Squad watching nervously on the lawn.

Sounds of a furious fight led them to a bedroom, where the Leader was tangling with the female, having already killed the male. Matthew now lay sprawled on the carpet, his neck spurting blood. Desperately the female clawed, bit, and growled, trying to kill the larger cat.

Marc took aim and fired about three inches from the Leader, forcing him to flinch, releasing his grip on Sarah as he did. With a desperate last burst of energy, the smaller cat flung herself on him again. This time, she succeeded in sinking her sharp teeth into his jugular, scoring a direct hit.

As Viv watched, she saw the wounded Leader shapeshift, drag himself to a nightstand, and pull open a drawer. Then, with a determination that shocked her, he took out a Beretta, faced them, and with blood splashing out of his wound, he raised it to his head.

"Fuck you all," he managed, nearly choking on his own blood. "Viv . . . bitch . . . I'm in charge. . . . Going out my way . . . Still the Leader . . ." Then he concentrated his remaining energy, and looking pale but still defiant, he squeezed the trigger. Blood and brains splattered the room in a shower of gore.

Pavel and Marc rushed to help Sarah, but she had gone limp. When they turned her over, they understood how badly she was injured. Blood poured from a wound in her chest, where the Leader had managed to tear open the skin, and now the lynxlike cat was dying.

"Let's get her out of here," Viv said. "Do you have any kind of first-aid supplies in the chopper?"

"Some."

"Then we have to use them. Come on."

As the group carried the wounded female down the hall, their senses were flooded with the odor of smoke rising from the ground floor. When they reached the staircase, they froze. The first floor was engulfed in roaring flames, and flames were licking their way up the stairs. In the distance they could hear shouts from their friends, muffled by the sounds of the fire.

"Do you know another way down?" Pavel asked.

"No. We've been here before, but never upstairs. That was off-limits."

Viv stopped, looked at the devastation below, and suddenly went still. As Marc and Pavel stared at her, she closed her eyes and said in a language from the beginning of time,

"Gods of the forest and the tundra, help us. Krasivaya, my ancestor, help us. Come to our aid and guide us out of here."

Pavel had seen Viv summon the gods at Hank's bedside. He prayed they would listen to this shaman again. He added his own prayer—to the Virgin of Saratov.

"Krasivaya, help us," Viv repeated, more forcefully. "Take us from this house of death! Great Mother who protected her people, help your children now!"

Just as Pavel turned around and made a decision to try to get them out to the roof, where his men could use a ladder or even the chopper to rescue them, Marc let out a shout and grabbed his arm. "Come on! We can make it down the stairs."

Stunned, the Russian turned back to see Viv descending the grand staircase as the flames rolled back in her path like some fiery tide, allowing her free passage.

With a cat's fear of fire, Marc and Pavel flinched for a split second and then followed Viv to freedom, through a corridor of safety and straight out the front door, where Pavel's team was already revving up the chopper, prepared for an aerial rescue. As they laid Sarah's limp form on the lawn, she reached up to stroke Viv's hand and quietly breathed her last.

Hank, Pat, and Joey arrived in separate SUVs and watched in amazement as the mansion burned out of control, flames swirling through it as it turned into an inferno, with flames swirling up into the dark sky like a beacon from hell. They were relieved to see Viv standing on the lawn next to her brother and the strangers. They wondered where the helicopter had come from.

After questioning the remaining members of the Special Squad on the premises, the werecats drove home, shaken by the death of the Leader and the fact that he had raped some of the females and tried to force Viv into an unwanted marriage. From a distance the sound of fire sirens shrilled through the night, and the werecats dispersed before they were forced to deal with any inconvenient questions.

Viv and Marc returned to Manhattan on the company helicopter and went to Pavel's apartment to talk. It was early morning, but they were so keyed up from what they had just lived though that nobody thought of sleep. First they had to come to terms with what had happened.

"Viv," Pavel said grimly, "did he attack you?"

"No. He tried once before, but I fought him off. But tonight, while we were outside on the lawn, Joseph told me that Sinclair was setting up video cameras in his bedroom to film something later." She looked at him and locked eyes.

Marc's head went up. "That sick fuck. I can imagine what *that* was all about."

"Well, he never had the chance. And if he had tried, I would have stabbed him, straight to the heart. I had a steel nail file in my pocket, just in case. Or I would have killed him cat-style."

"What will your clan do now?" Pavel asked. "Do your laws cover this?"

"We'll have to convene a special meeting," Marc said. "Tell everybody what took place last night: Viv's kidnapping, Matthew's death, Sarah's death. The previous attack on Sarah. At least Sinclair is out of the picture, and we can try to elect someone normal to replace him."

"And change his rules," Viv added. "He was absolutely paranoid. And cruel. The Special Squad was subjected to what amounted to torture if they disobeyed him. We have to disband the group and reconstitute it along different lines. No cult of the Leader this time. Back to our roots. We'll need a big overhaul," Viv said, glancing at Pavel as she took his hand and held it. "A restructuring that might even accept a mixed marriage."

"Yes," Marc agreed. "We have to have a better system so that nobody can seize control the way Sinclair did. He was more dangerous than we ever suspected. And we were all guilty for having let him get that far."

Pavel spread his hands in a sympathetic gesture. "We all suffer from the need to rally around the strong man and delude ourselves into thinking he knows more than we do. Just remember the mistake and don't repeat it," he said softly.

An hour later, Pavel called one of his men to give Marc a ride back to his apartment, and he and Viv were alone, so grateful to have each other after what might have happened just a short while ago. They could still smell the trace of smoke on their clothing.

He took her in his arms and drew her very close to him. "*Malenkaya*, I am so grateful I didn't lose you tonight. The gods kept you safe."

Viv pressed her head against his chest and said with a sigh, "I wish we had all survived the night. Sarah, Matthew . . ." Her voice faltered.

"I would have killed Sinclair myself if he had survived," Pavel said flatly. "He was lucky he was able to do it himself. Alpha male till the end."

"You make me feel so cherished," Viv said softly, as she looked up and gently kissed his face. "I never want to lose you."

Pavel's mouth found hers and he kissed her tenderly, pulling her closer and deepening his kiss as she responded passionately, wrapping him in her arms and clinging to him as if she never wanted to let him go. "You never will," he said.

With that, Pavel and Viv staggered into the bedroom. She sprawled on his bed as he sat down and undressed quickly, eager to posses her. Viv practically ripped off her clothing in return, and when they had peeled off anything that would stand in their way, Viv climbed on top of him and let her long, silky tresses fall across his face and chest, arousing him with his need for her. After what she had just been through, all she wanted was Pavel in her arms, his strength surrounding her, his love enveloping her.

Pavel seized her, kissed her passionately, and took hold of her as she slid herself underneath him. With a gasp, he entered her, and Viv cried out as she and Pavel rocked and writhed in total passion as they both tried to give each other as much pleasure as anyone could stand and still survive. After their brush with death, all they wanted to do was hurl themselves into the passion of living. They mated with such force that Pavel feared he may have hurt her.

Viv gasped as she and her lover collapsed in a sweaty pile of arms and legs, wrapping themselves in each other's embrace. "I love you and I know you wouldn't hurt me. You've always been tender with me, even when we lose our minds and mate like wildcats. It's the thing I love most about you. That and your gorgeous body," she teased.

"Darling Vivian," he murmured. "We're going to make each other very happy for years to come." And he kissed her with such sweetness that it brought tears to her eyes.

Chapter Sixty-seven

Boris's fight with his sister-in-law had resulted in his incarceration inside a formidable steel cage in Bill's basement, big enough to accommodate a tiger. Since Boris's big cat form was only as large as a serval, he had plenty of space. But he would have preferred more luxurious quarters.

Boris knew they wanted him to change back so they could use him for the meeting with the client who wanted the icon; therefore he stubbornly maintained his werecat persona, angering his captors.

"Look at him," one of the lower-ranking associates sniffed disdainfully, "the Hierarch of the Russian Blues. No pride at all."

"He'll see reason sooner or later. Or he'll starve." And with that, Bill led his henchmen upstairs while the Hierarch languished in his cell, miserable and lonely.

Once Bill and the Siberians left, Boris surveyed the room and found nothing helpful. The dampness of the room chilled him and the mold-covered cement walls depressed him. He thought of his present accommodations as a sort of werecat gulag.

How had things turned out so badly for a Hierarch of the Russian Blues? he wondered. A Hierarch commanded respect and reverence. None of them had ever sunk as low as himself, a gofer for a status-crazed, corrupt, utterly crooked

Siberian Forest cat. This is where his misdeeds had led him, and truthfully he knew Bella was merely a distorted reflection of himself, just as evil and just as worthless, simply more vicious. Two of a kind when you came right down to it.

Curling into a large but depressed ball of fur, Boris quietly sought out the oblivion of sleep.

Bella reached out with ill grace and yanked the phone off the hook the next morning as the shrill ringing woke her up. "Yes?" she asked, sounding like a bear being rousted out of hibernation.

"This is Lev," the voice said. "I believe you remember me—and our agreement?"

At those magic words, Bella sat up in bed, leaped to her feet, and became all attention. "Yes. Of course. How are you?"

"A little tired of waiting. I heard through the grapevine that a certain something went missing. Is everything all right?"

"Yes. Fine. We have the merchandise," she assured him. "All we have to do is set up a time and a place for delivery."

"Good. And the payment will be in cash as we agreed."

"Ah, excellent."

Bella nearly shimmied with the excitement of gaining those millions. Then she remembered her deal with the damned Rasputnikatz, and she frowned at the idea of sharing.

"I will be able to meet with you on Thursday night. Is that acceptable?" Lev asked.

"Of course. Name the place."

Lev paused as if considering several possibilities. Then he suggested a hotel in the area of a well-known New Jersey outlet center, with a large parking garage. They would rendezvous in a suite there. When they arrived, they were to ask at the desk for Mr. Morris, and someone would come downstairs and escort them up.

"How many will there be?" he asked.

"Myself, possibly my brother-in-law, and another gentleman."

"All right. I'll have my people there as well. You will bring up the item, we will inspect it, and then if all is satisfactory, we will proceed to payment."

"Fine," said Bella. "What time should we arrive?"

"Eight o'clock."

"We'll be there."

"And don't keep me waiting," Lev said. "Time is money."

"Exactly."

When Bella hung up the phone, she raised her arms high above her head in a delighted victory sign and even did a little dance to express the joy she felt. Millions were within her grasp. Life was good—even if her uncooperative brother-in-law had gone werecat and lay caged in a cellar in the outer boroughs. Trust him to pull a stunt like that just when she needed him.

Chapter Sixty-eight

An employee notified Pavel as soon as Bella got the call that they'd all been waiting for. Things were gathering momentum.

"Tony," he said as he phoned his friend in law enforcement, "it looks as though the deal will go down on Thursday night at a hotel in New Jersey. The contact called Bella to make the arrangements."

"Okay. Who's going to be there?"

"Bella, her brother-in-law, and probably Bill of the Rasputnikatz."

"And on the other team?"

"The buyer and some associates."

"Then we should count on at least six to eight of them, with some of them armed and dangerous."

"Definitely. And I'm going with you. I'll take my best crew." Pavel suddenly sensed a hesitation. He asked, "Are you still there?"

"I don't know about outside help. I think we should keep this federal," Tony said.

"How many Russian speakers do you have on your team?"

"None."

"Then you need us. Remember, we're your associates. We go to the party together."

"You and your men all have weapons permits for New Jersey?"

"We've got the paper. We're good to go."

"You take orders from me. None of the Wild West stuff that got those Blackwater guards in trouble."

"My men are disciplined. We'll be under your command."

"Okay. I'll put you in as interpreters. Do you know who Bella is meeting?"

"Sorry. All we know is the client has to be rich. She's expecting a big payout."

Tony paused. Then he said, "What do you think he wants with the goods? Private collection all for himself?"

"Who knows? These people have so much money they think they can buy anything, break any law. They live in their own expensive little worlds."

"Well, after Thursday, he'll be living as a guest of the state."

Pavel laughed. "He may turn out to be just some greedy little tycoon with a yen for priceless art. In that case, he'll be scared to death when you lock him up. By the time the cell door closes on him, he'll offer up anything he can think of to make you happy."

"My favorite kind of prisoner," Tony said with a laugh.

At Old Muscovy, Marc and Viv found themselves back on the same side once more, and still seething over Viv's kidnapping.

"Sinclair was much more disturbed than we ever suspected," Viv said. "We should have seen the signs, but people who knew what was happening were afraid to talk."

"He managed to hide so many things. If it hadn't been for the attacks on you and Sarah, we probably never would have realized how vicious he was. I've sent out a notice to all the brethren to attend a meeting so we can let them know what happened and start choosing a new Leader. Hank,

Joey, and Pat will give their testimony and so will Joseph, who was privy to a lot of Sinclair's actions. He secretly taped him while he was throwing away clan money in the casinos in Atlantic City and Las Vegas and taking his mistress on vacations at our expense. And other things," he said with disgust.

"I'll be at the meeting, too. I'll tell them what Sinclair did to me and Sarah. Charla, another female, will testify, too, if she's needed. And since Pavel and I are mates and have no intention of breaking up, they may decide to expel me."

Marc shook his head. "Then we'd lose the best of our clan," he said quietly. "I don't think anyone would be willing to do that. I'm sorry I acted like the 'defender of were-cat family values,' as you put it. You're right. It's none of my business, and I'll support you when you announce your choice of mate. After what we just went through, I can't imagine a better brother-in-law."

"Thank you. It means a lot to me."

He nodded. "It's just the two of us, Viv. You're my family. I can't afford to lose you. And if Pavel can adapt to American sports and split a season baseball ticket, he'll fit right in," Marc said with a wink.

Well, Viv thought gratefully, peace had been negotiated and life was back in sync.

Chapter Sixty-nine

A good takedown meant meticulous planning from start to finish. So with that in mind, Pavel and two of his associates met with Tony and one of his men, drove across the Hudson and down Route 3, and then headed for the hotel where Bella was due to rendezvous with her client.

While Pavel's men entered the hotel and cased the place, on the pretext of looking for a suitable venue for a conference with available rooms for out-of-town visitors, Pavel and Tony checked out the large parking garage located nearby, several floors high and open on the sides. Then they surveyed the entrances and exits of both hotel and garage.

After lunch the group gathered at Tony's office in a large building in downtown Manhattan and plotted strategy. The agency was so far under the radar that, although it had the highest security clearance, its personnel was mostly were-cat, its offices were obscure, and its purpose largely unknown. The office door carried the sign NORTH TRADING COMPANY.

Knowing that the mysterious buyer would be staying at the hotel under the name of Morris, federal agents were to enter, present warrants, get the room number, and prevent the desk clerks from making any phone calls upstairs while Tony, Pavel, and another agent would go to the room, burst in, and make the arrests. A backup team would be waiting outside, ready to go in if needed. Agents in the lobby would secure it, while a van containing another contingent would be in front, waiting to herd the thieves in for the ride to jail.

"We'll send an agent in there as a member of the cleaning staff. He'll find out whatever he can about Mr. Morris before we show up. Bug the room if possible," Tony announced.

"Do you think they might put up a fight?" one of his men asked.

"With a few million dollars in play? Sure," Tony said.

"Bella and her brother-in-law went at it the other night in the apartment. He was going to leave and go back to Russia. She managed to knock him out and tie him up before she called her associates and they took him away," Pavel said. "She's pretty frisky."

"What does this woman look like? Brunhilde?" one of the feds asked.

"No. Medium height, slim build. Very attractive," Pavel said with a smile.

Tony shook his head in amusement. "Boris must be a wimp."

"That's his rep, but according to my sources, Boris was the brains behind the assassination," Pavel said.

"No shit?" Tony looked astonished.

"I've been making inquiries back home. My people are planning to take the information to the federal prosecutor after we get Boris in custody. If the brethren don't change their minds and kill him themselves."

"What's the motive behind the assassination? Taking over the Danilov empire?"

"I don't know. Before that, Boris never showed any signs of initiative in anything. Then he goes nuts and orders a hit on Dimitri. Nobody can figure it out."

"He'll be a good bargaining chip with the Russians," Tony said. "I told you we have an interest in a case over there right now."

Pavel nodded. "Now, from my knowledge of Boris's character, if there's going to be any violence during the take-down, I doubt he will provide it. Bella might get hysterical and try to resist arrest, and their buyer will probably have armed bodyguards. Bella's thugs will definitely be packing. Prepare for it."

"Kevlar for everybody," Tony said.

In the basement of Bill's house in Queens, Boris still languished in his cage in feline form, moping and practically inert. One of the Rasputnikatz looked in on him from time to time, trying to figure out how to get him to shape-shift back into human form.

"Hey, you," he said, banging his hand on the cage, "are you going to stay like that forever?"

Boris got up and turned his back on his visitor as he moved away and settled down toward the back of the cage. That pissed off the Rasputnikat, who then opened the cage and shape-shifted himself, surprising Boris.

The shaggy Siberian stalked into the steel enclosure, swaggering a little as he headed straight for Boris, who was actually larger, but sleeker, the size of a well-muscled serval. The stocky Siberian stupidly advanced toward the prisoner, who backed up and snarled at the intruder, hissing with a ferocity he hadn't previously displayed. The visitor seemed unaware of the change.

"What's the matter?" the Siberian asked in the telepathic language of its kind. "Scared to be in the same cage with the big boys?"

"Fuck you. Get out of here."

"Make me."

Quivering with pent-up rage, the big cat sprang at the intruder and knocked him right out of the cage. As the Rasputnikat went flying across the room, Boris leaped after him, attacking him with fangs and claws, setting off an uproar of earsplitting screams and hisses, yowls of pain and fury, while the sounds of falling objects added their own distinct notes as the big cats crashed into furniture and knocked over anything in their path. Bits of fur floated in the air as the cats tried to kill each other, two wild animals bent on murder.

Upstairs Bill heard the racket and came racing down to the cellar. He nearly collided with the large cats, then shape-shifted to try to enforce order, biting and clawing at both until they yielded and stopped fighting.

Limping off to the side, Boris flopped down on the floor and began to shape-shift, ending up in human form and looking as if he'd been beaten up. The Siberian did the same, while Bill watched in disgust.

"Look at you," he said with a sneer. "Brawling like some street cat. My boy nearly tore you up."

Boris glanced over at the winded Siberian. "I think you've got it wrong, pussy. I just kicked the crap out of him."

"Well, you got lucky," Bill said in embarrassment as he glanced at his whipped henchman. The guy was practically wheezing; he also sported a black eye and a few facial abrasions for good measure.

"Whatever you say."

"Look," Bill said, "you're acting like a fool. All you have to do is cooperate with us for the next couple of days, and we all make some money and you go home. Be strong."

"Go get me something to eat," Boris said. He glanced at the Rasputnikat still sitting on the floor, stunned and shaking his head. "And tell fur ball over there to treat the Hierarch of the Russian Blues with more respect. Or the next time, I'll tear out his throat. He knows I can do it. And if he ever again treats me so disrespectfully, I will."

The two Rasputnikatz stared at him as if they were seeing him for the first time as Boris turned his back on them and walked out of that cellar as if he were John Wayne.

Chapter Seventy

Pavel and Viv went out for dinner at a little restaurant in lower Manhattan the night before the takedown, and Pavel just wanted to relax and enjoy Viv's company. Everything had been planned. He and his team had gone over contingency plans. Now all he had to do was wait.

"It's tomorrow, isn't it?" she asked as they nibbled sushi appetizers. "I want to be there."

"Sorry. It's a private party. Top secret."

"You're going to be there."

"*Malenkaya*, I'm the official interpreter."

"Very clever."

"They need Russian speakers for this one. They don't have them."

"How many of your men will be there?"

"A few."

"All official interpreters?" she asked with fine irony.

"Yes."

"The wonderful world of law enforcement. Very interesting."

Pavel took her hand and kissed it. "It's top secret. We're dealing with werecats in the federal system who are in such deep cover that even the highest branches of security don't know about them."

"I still want to be there," she said.

"Sorry."

"Bella Danilov nearly got me killed when her henchmen kidnapped me. They shot up one of my friends. She's broken every law on two continents. I want to see her taken down."

"You'll have to sit this one out."

Viv glared at him with fire in her beautiful amber eyes. "This is important to me," she said. "I want to be part of it."

"You're a civilian. The feds won't allow it."

"So are you, and they want you there."

"I told you why." Pavel gave Viv a smile that sent a little shiver of desire down her spine. "You're too precious to me to want to see you in harm's way. I'd never forgive myself if you got hurt."

"Then let me watch from a distance."

He shook his head as he gave her another high-voltage smile. "Darling," he said quietly, "there are places that are too risky for the woman I love. I went through a terrible loss once. I won't live through a second one."

Viv shook her head. "I'm going to be around for a good long while, *koshka*," she said. "I'm not going away."

Bella felt a rush of relief when Boris called to say he had shape-shifted back into human form and he was ready to play his part.

Surprised at the about-face, she said, "Good. I'm glad you've come to your senses. When this is over, we'll catch a plane for home and be back in St. Petersburg giving a press conference."

"You think so?" he said.

"Sure. This is the last thing we'll do before sending the money to the Caymans."

"I have to keep the Rasputnikatz company until tomorrow evening. I'll see you then."

"How are you getting along?" she asked curiously.

"Couldn't be better. I kicked the shit out of one of them before." And with that, Boris hung up.

What was wrong with him all of a sudden? He didn't seem like himself. Was he joking about beating up one of the Rasputnikatz? They all seemed tougher than he was. Hell, *she* had beaten him up.

He's obsessed with that stupid bitch, Bella thought. That had to be it. The fool was deep in the throes of a meltdown over the extramarital escapades of the vixen he'd married. *Get a grip,* she thought, rather uncharitably. *The world is full of sluts with big boobs. Move on.*

Russian Blues, she thought with contempt. *So idealistic and moronic.*

Chapter Seventy-one

Viv and Pavel finished dinner. Then they took a leisurely route home, enjoying the lights of the city on the early November evening. When they reached his apartment, he drove his SUV into the building's garage, and he and Viv took the elevator upstairs, where they kissed all the way till they reached their floor.

"You're very sexy tonight, *dushka*," he murmured as he pushed aside her long auburn tresses and kissed his way down her throat. "Such an adorable, tough, distracting female."

Viv laughed as he wrapped his arms around her and drew her close to him as he fiddled with the key and finally succeeded in opening his apartment door. They practically fell inside, laughing and caressing.

Suddenly Pavel scooped her up in his arms and carried her into the bedroom, although she was still wearing her overcoat. Viv kissed him fiercely as she struggled to take off her coat with some help from Pavel, and they broke apart only to fling off their clothing before pulling the comforter off the bed and sliding under the covers.

"Ah, I've been waiting for this moment ever since dinner," Viv said. "You're my dessert."

"What a delightful thought," Pavel said. "Nobody's ever called me that."

"You are. And I'm about to sink my teeth into your gorgeous, firm flesh and cover you with kisses."

"Sounds exciting."

Viv climbed on top of him and made Pavel utter a sound that was a cross between a growl and a sigh. "How is that?" she asked as she caressed him. "Does that please you?"

"Oh, yes. Do whatever makes you happy," he teased.

She smiled. "I'm going to do what makes *you* happy, *koshka*."

"Ah, even better."

As Viv slid herself along his magnificent, well-muscled body, Pavel sighed and took her thick hair in his hands as she found the place she wanted to visit. He felt a soft tongue create little circles on his belly as he clenched his muscles involuntarily; then he gasped as she followed that up by blowing on the wet skin. Viv nearly yelped as his hands gripped her hair in a reflex that almost pulled out the roots.

"Sorry," he said. "Keep going."

"Behave yourself. I won't look good if you tear out my hair in the throes of passion."

"I'd love you just as much," he whispered as she lowered her face to his nether regions and began to stroke him with her tongue, making Pavel nearly jump out of his skin as she kept on licking, caressing him, leaving a wet trail down the shaft and working her way up to the tip. He could barely talk as she nearly brought him to a release so fierce, he could hardly breathe or concentrate on anything but the desire to finish.

With the swift movement of a cat, Pavel seized Viv and flipped her over so that she was beneath him. As she wrapped herself around him and brought her knees up, he plunged deep inside her, half incoherent with lust as the two of them joined together in a passionate union that sent covers sliding off the bed and both of them gasping and moaning as they rocked back and forth, Pavel thrusting deeper and deeper inside her as Viv groaned with the force of her response. When they had climaxed, they broke apart and lay next to each other, chests heaving, eyes glazed, so worn out they couldn't even speak.

After their breathing returned to normal, Pavel took Viv in his arms and buried his face in her bosom. "Ah, *malenkayav,*" he whispered. "So beautiful, so ferocious. My passionate, elegant mate."

Viv caressed him with one hand as she lay snuggled against him on her side. "Koshka, there's nobody else I've ever wanted the way I want you. No member of my own clan ever appealed to me like this. I used to think I was cursed," she said sadly. "Then after the gods parted the flames for us and allowed us to pass unscathed, I knew we were meant to be together. If it wasn't so, we never would have survived. I believe they blessed us at that moment," she said softly.

They nestled together, tired and feeling a delicious sense of completion. Viv sighed.

"I have to ask you something," she said as last. "And it's important."

"Yes?"

"I know you were in love with a woman who was killed during a botched rescue in that theater. I know it took you a long time to come to terms with it. Will that cast any shadows over us?"

Pavel shook his head. "I love you, Viv. I loved her. I can't change that. Natalya will always be part of my past. But I let go of that when I fell in love with you. No ghost will ever stand in your way, *dushka*. You're the here and now, my future and my life. There is nobody else."

Viv snuggled against him and kissed him tenderly. "I'm glad you said that, Pavel. Otherwise, I would always wonder."

"Darling," he murmured as he nuzzled her cheek, "you will never have to wonder about anything. You're my one and only."

Sinking into a deep sleep later, after making love two or

three more times, Viv felt happier than she had in years. She had a lover she truly desired, a future ahead, and no doubts about his affection.

Life was beautiful. And then she thought of tomorrow night. She was going to be there. And he was going to be furious.

Chapter Seventy-two

With several agents in place at the targeted hotel bugging "Mr. Morris's" room, checking guest lists, and setting up for the evening's raid, Pavel and Tony assembled their troops, assigned locations, ordered vehicles, and got the weapons ready. It was going down that evening.

"Will we notify the Russians when we make the bust?" Pavel asked.

"Yeah," Tony said. "But only after these guys are in cuffs and being processed. I'm not letting anybody try to muscle their way in on my collar. And we have to set the time and place for the exchange."

"Good."

"Bella's appointment is for eight o'clock. We'll get there ahead of the pack, monitor the guests, and nab them at the time they're exchanging cash for art."

Pavel nodded. "And we'll have the pleasure of sending the Virgin of Saratov back to her homeland, where she belongs."

"Bella and Boris are going back to the motherland along with her. Let the Russians deal with them. And if it's true Boris engineered Dimitri's murder, they'll put him away for so long, he'll be an old man before he gets out."

"If he survives long enough to get old," Pavel said.

* * *

In Bill's home, Boris woke up late and sent one of the Rasputnikatz to look through a selection of designer suits stashed in the basement so he could show up for the meeting in style. He didn't plan on returning to the apartment, and he knew Bill wouldn't approve a little premeeting shopping on his own. Fortunately for him, his larcenous host had hijacked a bunch of Armani suits last week and had a nice variety on hand.

"Try these on." The Siberian he'd beaten up presented him with an offering of four suits and hung them in the closet. "Bill said he had shirts and ties, too."

Boris nodded and waited.

"Do you need anything else, Hierarch?"

"Not at the moment. I'm going to try them on." He gave the Rasputnikat a dismissive glance and watched him leave.

As soon as the door was closed, Boris inspected the Armanis and opted for a sharp-looking dark charcoal pinstripe. After he had dressed, he looked at himself critically in the mirror and tried on the others. Two were an excellent fit; two looked just okay. Boris decided on a navy pinstripe with a blue shirt with French cuffs, gold-striped tie, and gold paisley pocket handkerchief.

The old Boris had returned, stylish, handsome, and ready for the party. All he had to do was get through tonight, and he could be on his way home with millions in the offshore accounts and a new lease on life. This New York detention would be behind him, and he would be free to take the children and find a suitable home somewhere in Europe, far away from Bella, Marina, and business. It was all he longed for.

In her apartment, Bella made a few phone calls to wrap up her stay in Manhattan and then began packing her bags. She and Boris had seats on a private jet flying out of JFK shortly after midnight. She was heading home in style, with millions in her bank accounts. Once home, Bella planned on taking over a few more companies, and under her tutelage, Boris could learn to cast his net wide, turning Danilov Enterprises into the biggest conglomerate in Russia. With her as his closest adviser.

At around six o'clock, Viv said goodbye to Marc at Old Muscovy, and instead of taking the subway to the apartment she now shared with Pavel, she hailed a cab two blocks from the antiques shop and told the driver to take her to her apartment in New Jersey. Once there, she changed into jeans, a turtleneck, and sneakers, put on a down jacket and gloves, and descended to the garage to get her car.

From her home to the point of rendezvous took no time at all, and by seven thirty, Viv had arrived at the hotel's parking garage, entered, and found an empty space on the second level. Switching off the engine, she sat in the dark car and prepared to settle in for a solitary vigil.

With the engine off, the car gradually cooled, and Viv sound herself shivering as the cold night air seeped into the vehicle as she waited. Glancing at her watch from time to time, she could just barely make out the numbers, but she thought it must be close to eight.

Come on, she thought fiercely as she watched in disgust as an occasional BMW or Mercedes pulled into the garage and cruised the levels, searching for a space. One car looked like a possibility, but at second glance it contained three young women, not the one Viv expected.

Damn it. What was with these Russians? They had a business deal to conclude, illegal millions to collect. What made them so slow?

Just as she was about to resign herself to the fact that perhaps Bella and company had arrived earlier and were already inside the hotel, a silver SUV made its way up the incline leading to the second level and slowed down as it looked for a space. With the engine purring, it roamed to the next level and resumed its hunt. In the passenger seat Viv saw Boris Danilov, whom she recognized from pictures.

Viv's heart jumped as she heard them stop the car one level above, heard doors opening, and then heard the sounds of them slamming, followed by the horn as somebody clicked the remote and locked up.

Russian voices filled the air, becoming louder in the chilly night air as three men in overcoats came down the ramp. As Viv slunk down in her seat, she heard the voices and footsteps grow fainter. Daring a glance, she lifted herself up to look out the window, and she could see that one of the men carried a kind of portfolio. She fought a desire to go werecat.

With her heart beating wildly, she saw a second car ascend the ramp and search for a space. Behind the wheel sat Bella Danilov, dressed warmly in mink.

As Bella drove closer, Viv dipped her head until the car passed by. A minute later, she heard the familiar sounds of parking, a door opening and being slammed shut, and then the door being locked with a remote.

She must be running late, Viv decided. Sharp, clicking footsteps made their way down the ramp, as Bella hurried to catch up with her henchmen. The sound of Russian curses floated by as the woman hastened to her appointment, and then the footsteps grew faint and faded away into the night.

Okay, Viv thought. *The players are all lining up. Where are Pavel and the feds?*

In the lobby, one of Pavel's men sat with a drink in his hand, looking like a businessman trying to pick up a female guest with the ID tag from the convention of Realtors going on in the ballroom. As he leaned close to the young woman, they both noted the arrival of Bella and her party coming through the glass entrance doors.

The young brunette bent forward, her long hair hiding both their faces as Bella's group passed by, heading toward the reception desk. "It's on," she said quietly into a mini-microphone hidden in her neckline. "Showtime." And with the flick of a wrist, Pavel's man snapped a photo of the group, sending it up to his boss and Tony on the second floor.

"We give them time to go inside, we listen to them make the exchange, and then we go in." Tony looked around at his team stationed in the room located directly opposite the one "Mr. Morris" had booked and he said, "Any questions?"

"How soon do they seal off the lobby?" Pavel asked.

"Right about now." There was the crackle of a walkie-talkie, and a voice rasped the message that the SWAT team had taken control of the perimeter, and one of the Russians who had accompanied Bella's group was under arrest and being taken out to the van.

The men fell silent as they heard voices from across the hall, the sound of knocking, and then another Russian voice greeting Bella and her companions and inviting them inside.

"What's he saying?" Tony asked softly.

" 'Welcome. Delighted to see you. Is that the merchandise?' "

And then the door closed.

Chapter Seventy-three

"Madame Danilov, delighted to see you again," said the shortest man in the room as he greeted Bella with a kiss on the hand. "Always a pleasure to do business with you."

"The pleasure is all mine," she said with a high-voltage smile as she greeted the bald billionaire. "These are my associates: Boris Danilov, my brother-in-law, and Bill Sirpsky, the head of the Rasputnikatz here in New York. Gentlemen, this is Lev Patritsky. I'm sure you've heard his name many times." She glanced at the two other men in the room, big guys with looks mean enough to melt steel. "And his associates."

The large men gave curt nods in the manner of thugs who didn't put much stock in social niceties. Breaking legs and arms probably came more naturally to them than polite conversation.

Bella turned to her henchmen and cut her eyes to the portfolio Bill carried. "Show him," she said.

Bill was about to reach in and remove the icon when Lev intercepted it and took the bag himself. With nervous hands, he lifted the Virgin of Saratov out of her packaging and held it up so he could get a good luck. In his eyes, Bella saw such relief that she thought he might cry with emotion.

"Stepan," he said to the smaller of the two musclemen, "take a good look."

As Lev Patritsky held it up, Stepan studied it with attention so close, Bella wondered if he was going to whip out a
large magnifying glass and go over it inch by inch.

"My art expert," Lev explained as he glanced at Bella and
her group. "He grew up in the town it came from. He's
looked at it for years."

Stepan gazed at the medieval icon while the rest of the
party watched breathlessly. His eyes roved over the details
of the painting, studying, examining. Then with a curt nod,
he said, "*Da,* it's genuine. Look. This is the mark that the
Swedish bullets made in the seventeenth century. It's authentic. And here is a small chip in the gold that I remember, too."

"Okay," Patritsky said as he expelled his breath in a
whoosh of relief. "We can do business. Here is the money."

As he spoke, he snapped his fingers and the larger of the
two assistants stepped up to Bella and presented her with a
metal briefcase. He placed it on a table, flipped it open, and
said, "It's all there in bundles of hundreds. Please count it.
We don't mind."

Across the hall, Pavel quietly translated the words, " 'It's
all there in bundles of hundreds. Please count it,' " and nodded to Tony. "The deal's gone down. The money's on the
table. Let's go."

Lining up, weapons in hand, the team exited the hotel
room and gathered in the hall on both sides of "Mr. Morris's" room. Tony banged loudly on the door. "Open up. Federal officers."

In the space of a second, they could hear shouts, the
sound of things crashing and men screaming at one another.
Bella's voice rang out, shrill with fury, cursing everybody
and blaming Patritsky for screwing up.

Two of the feds attacked the door with a wooden ram
made for such moments and popped it open. Inside the
room, everybody was scrambling, the bodyguards with guns

drawn, Patritsky screaming at them, Bella frantically trying to scoop up bundles of hundred-dollar bills from the floor. Only Boris seemed oddly still, as if he'd been turned to stone, watching it all with dull, tired eyes, too stunned to move.

"Hands in the air! Get 'em up. Put your weapons on the table. You, don't make any sudden moves, or we drop you," Tony shouted.

Outnumbered by a group of men wearing federal police vests and armed with shotguns, the Russians let themselves be grabbed, frisked, and ordered to stand with their hands against the walls and their feet spread wide apart. Several policemen helped them energetically, and Patritsky shouted his protests at the treatment.

"Shut up and hold that pose. We're not done with you," Tony snapped.

"This is where all your stupid ideas have got us!" Boris flung at his sister-in-law as an officer shoved him up against the wall to frisk him. "You trouble-making bitch. You've ruined my whole family."

"Oh, go fuck yourself! You're such an asshole your own brother wanted to let you go. You don't believe me? Well, he told me shortly before he died that he was going to put you in charge of human resources at one of his holdings in Siberia because you were too incompetent for St. Petersburg!"

At that, Boris became unhinged and he lunged at her. Two of Pavel's men grabbed him and pushed him up against the wall again, kicking his feet apart to keep him off balance.

"You gold-digging slut!" he shouted as little bits of spittle sprayed her in the face. "My brother thought he was so fucking clever. He was always the smart one, the go-getter, the fair-haired boy who could do whatever he wanted while I had to stay in the background and be content with the crumbs that fell off his plate. Well, I want you to know that he's not around anymore because *I* was the one who had him removed. Me! Stupid Boris. Boris the jerk. Boris, whose wife he screwed when he sent him on business overseas!"

All the Russians went dead quiet and just stared at the outraged Hierarch. Patritsky's jaw dropped. Bill appeared stunned. Even the stolid musclemen looked shocked.

Then Bella broke loose and leaped on Boris, hurling him to the floor. She sank her teeth into his neck and held on even while Tony and two of his men tried to pry her off. While they struggled to pull them apart, Boris shrieked and thrashed around on the rug, beating at her with a hatred that he unleashed like a flood. He punched her in the face, the body, the chest. He bit her like an animal, trying to tear her flesh.

"You had my husband killed because he screwed your wife?" Bella screamed as she fought back. She grabbed his hair and banged his head on the floor as federal agents tried to pull her off him. "Everybody screwed that slut! You stupid, motherfucking bastard!"

Suddenly as they rolled around the floor and landed behind a couch, Bella stopped screaming curses at Boris. He went stone silent as well. Suddenly animal sounds filled the air, making everybody's blood freeze. Before the feds or Pavel's men could get a look at what happened, a large, shaggy cat emerged, a beast the size of a panther with blood dripping from its fangs.

"Damn it!" Tony said. "She shifted."

"Take a look." Pavel stepped around behind the sofa. "She got him good."

Boris lay inert on the rug in big-cat form, his face and throat savaged by the larger one, his eyes staring at the ceiling but seeing nothing. Blood gushed from his jugular, pouring bright red stains onto his dark fur and the beige carpet.

As the humans in the room stood around, unnerved, wondering how the hell a woman could have done that, and where had those two beasts had come from, Pavel watched the large cat walk away from the living room and into the next room, where the door to the balcony was cracked open just a bit. He was right behind her.

Earlier, Patritsky had left the door to the balcony slightly ajar in order to bring in some cool air. Now the large tawny beast walked to that door, and as Pavel followed it, the animal pushed open the door, creating an exit for itself to the balcony.

Tony and the other werecats in the room froze as the animal jumped up onto the outside railing and leaped two stories to the grass below. In an instant Pavel shape-shifted and followed her, leaping into a tall fir tree to break his fall and then jumping down to the ground and racing after her, hitting speeds that would have qualified him for the Olympics. The feds ignored questions from their prisoners and started herding them down to the vans. Later, the agents would erase their prisoners' memories of those beasts.

Chapter Seventy-four

Winded by her leap from the second-floor balcony, the shaggy Siberian got up from the ground and began running toward the parking garage with Pavel right behind her in the form of a sleek and speedy cat the size of a panther. Men guarding the approaches to the hotel never spotted the animals because the big cats took a roundabout route that hugged the shadows of the bushes. Thick landscaping provided cover in the night, and the cops got the call to be on the lookout for two big cats only after Bella and Pavel had already bypassed them while they waited for the team to arrive with the perps.

Realizing she was being followed, Bella hunkered down just outside the parking garage and leaped in from the side, putting herself in there before the other cat could do the same. Its fur standing up from sheer nerves, the large Siberian stalked the aisles, searching for the car. In the harsh fluorescent lighting, it looked even bigger than it was, its fur making it huge. Blood stained its coat and whiskers, even its paws. Low growls rose from its throat as it sought escape.

Jolted to full alert, Viv caught sight of the cat, and suddenly she felt her heart race. That had to be Bella. She must have escaped from the hotel and then come here to find her car. Where were Pavel and his men? Did they realize she had shape-shifted? At the sight of the blood, she wondered if

Bella had attacked Pavel. Was he still alive? Frightening thoughts poured into Viv's mind as she watched the blood-stained creature pace the aisles.

If nobody stopped her, Bella Danilov would flee the country and live out her life in luxury, enjoying the profits from her crimes. Viv was outraged at the thought. She was glad she had disobeyed Pavel; right now she might be the only one able to take her down.

As silently as she could, Viv got out of her car and shape-shifted. Bella had already started up the ramp to the next level, but Viv was right after her, a large, very angry cat the size of a mountain lion.

With muscles twitching from concentration, Viv stalked her prey like a stealthy beast of the jungle, and then as the Siberian paused and turned around, alerted by some sixth sense, Viv crouched and leaped, her adrenaline in overdrive.

Feline screams pierced the air. Bella went sprawling on the hard floor of the garage as Viv crashed down on her, biting with all the force she could command. The Siberian screamed with pain and tried to bite back but only succeeded in getting a mouthful of Viv's thick fur as both big cats spun around like dervishes, raising a cloud of dust from the dirty cement floor. Roaring with fury, they leaped to their feet and attacked each other, ready to kill.

Viv chomped down on Bella's sensitive tail as the other cat tried to tear her face, causing such agony to her spine that they could hear the noise even outside the garage.

"You're going to jail," Viv told her by means of the telepathy their kind used. She bit Bella's ear and tore off a chunk as the other werecat shrieked and tried to use her claws.

"I'll kill you!" Bella screeched as Viv sank sharp teeth into her cheek, ripping off a few whiskers. But she was the one who was bleeding. She whipped around, trying to bite her attacker in the neck and sever her spine. Viv made a lunge for her and flipped her over before she could do any damage.

Pavel's roar echoed from a distance, and both cats jumped in surprise. Bella then seized the opportunity to claw at Viv's face and sink teeth into her shoulder.

Enraged, Viv let out a roar that terrified her opponent, and suddenly she morphed into a cat the size of a tiger, furry and furious as she took hold of Bella and grabbed her by the neck. Violently, she swung her from side to side as easily as if she were a toy.

The wounded Siberian moaned in pain as her much larger enemy took a few steps back and flung her headfirst into a concrete wall, bouncing her off the side of a car and picking her up again to throw her against the grille of another one before she was done.

Utterly spent, the Siberian lay on the ground, panting from pain and exhaustion, looking at Viv as if she expected the coup de grâce. "Kill me and get it over with," she said telepathically. "I'd rather die here than face prison in Russia."

"Too late," Viv replied. "You're out of options."

By the time Pavel, still in werecat form, reached the scene of the fight, Viv was standing with one paw on Bella's head, holding her down. To her lover's amazement, she was the size of a tiger.

As Pavel approached and shape-shifted, Viv turned to him and began to morph into human form. "She's yours. I caught her trying to escape," she said as she sensibly kept her foot on the Siberian's neck.

"Thanks for listening to me," he said. "It's nice to think that you're safe and sound at home."

"If I were, I wouldn't be able to present you with this damaged trophy, darling. It's all yours."

She felt her foot pushed aside as Bella shape-shifted and rolled over on the cement floor, sobbing in distress. She had lost everything she worked for: husband, money, reputation. She was ruined and battered, utterly destroyed.

Viv stepped aside and flicked her a disgusted glance.

"You're lucky Viv didn't do to you what you did to Boris," Pavel said. "He's dead. You'll be as good as new in a few hours."

"The bastard murdered his own brother. If it hadn't been for him, I'd never be in this mess."

Bella groaned as Pavel helped her to her feet while several of his men and the feds entered the garage with weapons drawn. They stopped as they heard voices and shouted, "Federal officers! Come down and show yourselves."

"It's Pavel. Vivian Roussel is here with me. We captured Bella Danilov."

"Pavel, it's Ivan. You're all right?"

"We're fine. Stay there. We're bringing in the prisoner."

Chapter Seventy-five

Several months later

"Pavel! Come in here. It's CNN. You have to see this!"

Walking into the bedroom, Pavel glanced at Viv, who was pointing to the large TV screen on the wall. "Oh."

"Sit down," she said as she reached for him and pulled him down on the bed beside her. There on the TV was a clip from the inauguration of the new chapel of the Virgin of Saratov.

Gorgeously robed priests led a procession around the newly refurbished church, swinging censers of incense as they moved. A choir chanted hymns in the background. At the head of the procession was one of the highest-ranking churchmen in the country and behind him walked representatives of the government, all coming together to give thanks for the recovery and reinstallation of the icon, back home in a renovated church—with a million dollars' worth of security equipment installed.

"I can't believe how beautiful it is," Viv said as she stared at the TV screen. "Those colors are magnificent. Are those the original paintings on the columns?"

"Yes, restored and looking like new. The artists did a fantastic job. They were still working on it when we finished our part."

"Now nobody can get in there and steal the icon."

"Not even a cat can get near it without setting off alarms," he said with a smile. "Once they place it in its niche in the iconostasis, it activates a signal that will send an alarm if it's ever moved, even a fraction of an inch. Once that signal goes out, metal doors slide into place and isolate whoever is in the chapel. The police will receive the alarm, as well as the new security station, and with all that racket, half the town will know something's up, as well as the head of the FSB via a private hookup. I think we've covered all the angles."

"I missed you while you and your crew were over there. I was proud that they asked you to do the job, and I knew that you felt it was your duty, but I am so glad that you're home."

"So am I, darling. This is where I live now, and you're part of my life." Pavel kissed Viv tenderly on the mouth and sank down onto the bed with her. "I missed you so much I declined the offer to attend the official ceremonies. I couldn't wait to get back to you."

She smiled into his green eyes. "Tell me what happened to Bella."

"There's something of a mystery about her fate, but from what Tony said, Madame Danilov arrived in St. Petersburg escorted by him and a subordinate, and sometime during the transfer by helicopter to a prison on the outskirts of the city, she suddenly threw herself out of an open door at a thousand feet, and fell to her death in the Gulf of Finland. The Russians searched. They never found the body."

Viv's eyes met his. "Did Madame Danilov happen to have an all-werecat escort by any chance?"

"Yes," he said mildly.

"And now nobody will ever know what she really was. The secret is safe. Tell me, do you think your werecat secret agent friend ever actually planned to turn her over to the Russians?"

"I think he planned to go through the motions to facilitate

the deal he wanted. The man he traded Bella for was human."

Viv shook her head in wry appreciation of the werecat capacity for treachery. "Well, Bella got just what she deserved. No tears for her. But what about Boris? How did they repatriate the body? You told me he died as a big cat."

"They got in touch with his wife, who was vacationing in France, and gave her the sad news. Her reaction was 'Cremate the remains and ship them home.' She contacted the funeral parlor and put it all on her credit card. He's headed home in a small urn, and she's still tanning in Nice and spending his money."

Viv shook her head. She couldn't even bring herself to comment.

"Umm," Pavel said as he kissed the hollow of Viv's throat while she wrapped her arms around him and languidly caressed him. "There's one thing I have to ask."

"Yes?" Viv said as she kissed him along his jaw and finished up with his mouth.

He pulled apart from her kiss and said, "How did you manage to turn into something the size of a tiger? When I saw you and Bella going at it, I thought something else had joined the hunt. You never became that large before."

"Ah," she said with a smile, "you noticed."

"Noticed? It's difficult to miss a gorgeous creature the size of a tiger!"

Viv laughed. "I have many secrets, *koshka*, and I may reveal them someday. These talents go back a long way, back to the time of my ancestor Krasivaya, when our survival depended on our skill in battle and in the magic we could use against our enemies."

"My clan can supersize, but we can't reach those proportions. It's never been documented."

"Aeons ago, in the time of the ancestors, Krasivaya fought a battle against the evil Siberian Forest cats. At that time, she had rescued one of the lesser gods of the forests whom the Siberians had displaced from his sanctuary. To show his gratitude, this ancient forest god gave her the gift of supertransformation. Instead of becoming the larger size allowed to members of her clan, she and all her descendants could call on their shaman powers to increase their size in cases where the battle required it."

"And that night in the parking garage, you needed it."

"Definitely. It was the only means I had to prevent Bella from getting away. I was so afraid something had happened to you during the takedown that I called on all my strength to deal with her and stop her at that moment."

Pavel smiled. "I was glad you did. If you had listened to me and stayed home, we would still be looking for Bella."

"Ah, so you like it when I show some initiative," she said as she wrapped her arms around him.

"In some cases," he said with a grin.

"What about now?" Viv teased as she caressed Pavel with a hand that wandered all over his superb form, stroking, gliding, demonstrating various ways to arouse him.

"Oh, yes. Keep going."

"*Koshka*, you are the most wonderful cat I've ever known," Viv murmured as she started undressing him. She pushed back the coverlet and slid it down the bed. "Let me demonstrate just how far my affection goes."

He wrapped an arm around her as she kissed him, slipping her tongue in and out of his mouth, swirling it around, kissing his neck, his chest, his lips.

Viv tore off her remaining clothes and nestled down under the covers with him. She wrapped her arms and legs around him and kissed him tenderly, playfully nipping at his ear. Pavel had a sharp intake of breath and responded with a kiss that made the little rosebuds on her breasts harden.

"Darling," Viv whispered. Then she shape-shifted and turned into a striking feline beauty the size of a mountain lion. She prodded Pavel with her paw, and he shape-shifted in turn, changing into a sleek gray cat the size of a panther.

With low, throaty sounds, they seized each other and let their instincts take over, ready to celebrate their bond.

There was hardly an object standing in the apartment when they were through.

Also Available
from
Melina Morel

DEVOUR

A werewolf...
A vampire...
And the woman who wants them both.

The dashing Pierre du Montfort is a werewolf who's
never had trouble hiding his cursed heritage. But now
with his dark secret about to be unleashed, he's willing
to do anything—and savage anyone—in order to
stay alive.

Beautiful and intrepid werewolf hunter Catherine Marais
has no qualms about her destiny. Nothing will stop her
from destroying the last Montfort werewolf. Not even Ian
Morgan—the 200-year-old vampire whose electrifying
touch could tempt Catherine to indulge in a forbidden
darkness from which she may never return...

"Release me at once, Viking," Tala commanded.

"Lady," Edon warned her, his patience dwindling fast. "Speak to me again in that tone of voice, and I will have no choice but to teach you to respect the man you see before you."

"Strike me and I will kill you with my bare hands, Viking." Tala gulped, struggling for her breath.

"And how will you do that, hmm?" Edon taunted her. "With what weapon will you slay me, woman? Your viper's tongue?"

Edon used his head as a pointer, nodding to her bared breasts—exposed in the beam of moonlight that spilled into the chamber from the open portal.

"The only success you have had thus far is in baring your breast. Continue the show. I shall enjoy seeing what other charms your struggles reveal."

Dear Reader,

A pagan princess and a Christian warrior must form an alliance if either of their people are to survive in RITA Award nominee Elizabeth Mayne's *Lady of the Lake*. Forced to surrender her heritage and marry Edon, the man responsible for her father's death, Princess Tala fights her feelings for her new husband, afraid that she will let down her guard and reveal a secret that could tear their gentle truce apart. Don't miss this intriguing tale.

Cally and the Sheriff, by Cassandra Austin, is a lively Western about a Kansas sheriff who falls head over heels for the feisty young woman he's sworn to protect, even though she wants nothing to do with him. And in Judith Stacy's *The Marriage Mishap*, two people who've just met, wake up in bed together and discover they have gotten married.

In our fourth title for the month, *Lord Sin* by Catherine Archer, a rakish nobleman and a vicar's daughter, whose lack of fortune and social position make her completely unsuitable, agree to a marriage of convenience, and discover love.

Whatever your tastes in reading, we hope you enjoy all of our books, available wherever Harlequin Historicals are sold.

Sincerely,

Tracy Farrell
Senior Editor

Please address questions and book requests to:
Harlequin Reader Service
U.S.: 3010 Walden Ave., P.O. Box 1325, Buffalo, NY 14269
Canadian: P.O. Box 609, Fort Erie, Ont. L2A 5X3

Elizabeth Mayne

LADY OF THE LAKE

Harlequin Books

TORONTO • NEW YORK • LONDON
AMSTERDAM • PARIS • SYDNEY • HAMBURG
STOCKHOLM • ATHENS • TOKYO • MILAN
MADRID • WARSAW • BUDAPEST • AUCKLAND

ISBN 0-373-28980-4

LADY OF THE LAKE

Copyright © 1997 by M. Kaye Garcia

This edition published by arrangement with Harlequin Books S.A.

® and TM are trademarks of the publisher. Trademarks indicated with
® are registered in the United States Patent and Trademark Office, the
Canadian Trade Marks Office and in other countries.

Printed in U.S.A.

Books by Elizabeth Mayne

ELIZABETH MAYNE

is a native San Antonian, who knew by the age of eleven how to spin a good yarn, according to every teacher she ever faced. She's spent the last twenty years making up for all her transgressions on the opposite side of the teacher's desk, and the last five working exclusively with troubled children. She particularly loves an ethnic hero and married one of her own eighteen years ago. But it wasn't until their youngest, a daughter, was two years old, that life calmed down enough for this writer to fulfill the dream she'd always had of becoming a novelist.

With love,
Delores Maynard Cherveny

Chapter One

Summer, 889 A.D.
Eleventh year of the reign of
Alfred of Wessex
Mercia

Silently, the atheling of Leam, Venn ap Griffin, followed his sister up a trail to the Seven Sisters and their overlook of the Avon Valley. The standing stones thrust up from the earth at the edge of the forest. Neither Venn nor Tala could read the ogham symbols etched upon the stones, though both were well versed in the Latin of the abbeys and the court of their cousin and guardian, King Alfred.

Venn cupped his hands together and boosted Tala to the topmost ledge. She lay down on the hot, sun-heated stone and drew her mantle across her fiery hair to hide it from sight. Far below, the forest ended at the confluence of the shrinking Avon and the positively dusty Leam.

This time of year the Leam should be running deep and fast, feeding the river Avon. But no rain had fallen since Beltane, the first of May. The gods were unhappy, the earth in turmoil. Spirits old and new warred against one another for who would dominate the world of men. The people were confused, not knowing who to beseech for relief from the bitter drought.

"Tell me, little brother, what price did you ask for Taliesin the White at Warwick's market?" Tala broke their silence when she was settled on the flat stone.

"He is a worthy horse, full of spirit and courage. I asked a hundred gold marks, but one Dane wanted to steal him from me for twenty and six pitiful sacks of last year's moldy grain."

"Six sacks of grain is a lot." Tala studied Venn's profile as he intently scanned their parched, dry valley.

"Knowing Vikings, it could have been six sacks of stones," Venn replied scornfully. "I did not want to be cheated and was wary of making any trade for fear of coming up the loser."

"Ah, I see." Tala nodded. Venn prized the white horse and really did not want to sell him.

"It won't be a problem. I can take Taliesin farther afield to graze."

"Strong horses like oats and grass," Tala replied. "So do cows and sheep. They care not for oak leaves and dried-up ferns. We can't keep them if the drought continues."

"I know how to make the drought end," Venn answered.

Tala cut a sharp look at his set profile. Venn was just a boy, too easily influenced by the old ones in Arden Wood. "I don't want you listening to Tegwin's babbling. He speaks nonsense, Venn. Do not credit his far-fetched predictions as truth."

"That's men's business," the lad argued peremptorily. "And no concern of a woman."

"I beg your pardon." Tala responded with a scowl that effectively squelched her little brother's high-and-mighty attitude. "You will do as I say, Venn ap Griffin!"

"Yes, yes," the boy said, dismissing her concern with an impatient wave of his hand.

"Look to this side of the river Avon, Tala. That is what I brought you here to see."

Between the sluggish river and the dried-up course of the Leam, a dozen Vikings labored, guiding oxen and plow, cutting furrows in the earth. Pairs of them stripped the bark from logs gleaned from the felled trees. Others tended a huge brush fire, burning drought-dry leaves and limbs.

The smoke from the hot fire was acrid with the scent of tannin. The black plume rose straight up to the sky, then flattened like an other worldly goshawk soaring in flight.

Venn eased himself up beside Tala on the hot stone. He didn't bother covering his head. His brown hair, tanned skin, leather jerkin and breeks all blended into the neutral colors of the rocks. Only the vivid gold and red in Tala's hair and the glittering torque at her slender throat needed to be hidden in this landscape.

Tala gave the valley a cursory inspection, from the high stockade dominating Warkwick Hill to the distant slopes at the limits of the fertile valley. Two ancient Roman roads bisected it, Fosse Way and Watling Street. Warwick controlled the crossroads and the bridge over the Avon River. Every scrap of land not covered by Arden Wood was taken up by fields planted by Viking usurpers.

In truth, the forest shrank by the day because Vikings constantly slashed and burned trees to till new fields, and yesterday's oaks became the grazing pens of the next herd of cattle.

Near the fields stood their longhouses, each one spawning countless other wattle-and-daub outbuildings. They multiplied like poisonous fungi on the trunks of the sacred oaks in the wet years.

Tala saw much difference between the land today and what she had seen on the first of May. Not a drop of rain had fallen in two months, so the earth was drier, browner, the river Avon lower, its current slower. "What am I supposed to see, little brother?"

"They felled the oaks on this side of the Leam." Venn pointed to the new cut.

"No!" she whispered. "They can't. Watling Street, on the high ground north of the Avon, is the border. They can't cut into our grove. It's against two kings' laws."

"What heed do Danes pay to Wessex law? I see no man of King Alfred's ordering the Vikings to keep to their side of Watling Street," Venn sneered. "They will not stop until they reach the sea at Glamorgan."

"Curse Embla!" Tala made a fist of her hand and slammed it against the stone. "She must be stopped! She has to be stopped."

"Who will stop her? Not you. Nor I."

Tala couldn't go so far as to sit up, thereby exposing herself to the view of the Vikings working on both sides of the river. With all her heart she desired to protect this brother of hers from all the dangers that surrounded him.

"I can and I will—somehow!" she vowed.

"Wheest!" Venn whispered. Riders galloped out of the woods on Fosse Way.

"Don't *'wheest'* me," Tala scolded, quieting all the same.

"Embla has taken on more airs," Venn remarked, mindful of Tala's long-standing hatred for her rival. "Now wherever she rides she makes a Viking boy carry her colors on a staff before her." He slipped his bow off his shoulder and pulled an arrow from his quiver. "I've half a mind to pierce her silks."

"Wait," Tala said, putting a stilling hand on Venn's wrist as he fitted the notch into the bowstring. Fosse Way passed close beneath them, along the valley of the Avon. Only the height of the oaks prevented the brother and sister from being spotted by Embla Silver Throat and her party

of warriors as they galloped up the rise. "Let's see who it
is she rides out to greet. Look, there are many riders coming. Where do you suppose they hail from?"

"East Anglia, by the color of the dust on their horses,"
Venn whispered, cautious now, for sound could travel easily over the trees.

They listened to the clop of the iron shoes of the oncoming horses. Embla and her guard rode out to meet the
newcomers. Her standard refused to spread out in the still,
dusty air. The day's ferocious heat battered down cloth the
same way it hammered people into exhausted lethargy.
Sweat prickled Tala's scalp and ran between her breasts.
She twisted her head, straining to hear the greetings the
Vikings exchanged.

"By the gold offerings at the bottom of the sacred
Leam!" Venn whistled. "Look at the size of that wagon
train! More settlers for sure, Tala."

Appalled, Tala counted the wagons following the crush
or riders. Behind the vanguard came a clutch of beasts of
burden, pulling sleds piled with chests and bundles. When
they ran out of oxen and horses, thralls pulled the remaining sleds. Tala had never seen the like in her life! Not
even King Alfred brought such a massive train on his annual progress to the frontier.

Next at the hilltop appeared a jewel-bright chaise draped
in shimmering silks. It was borne on the shoulders of a
dozen sweating thralls. Women peeked out from behind
the cloths. Jewels on their heads and throats sparkled in
the dazzling sun.

Embla's party of six riders came to a halt before the
kingly procession. The oncoming Vikings had cast off
their cloaks to accommodate the day's grilling heat, pre-
senting an almost dazzling spectacle of sun-bronzed arms
and sweaty, glistening chests.

Even Embla had shed the ermine-edged cloak that she
sported day and night as a badge of her rank—niece mar-

riage to the king of the Danelaw. But she hadn't sacrificed her plumed helmet to the heat.

As the two parties met on the open road, Embla drew her sword and clanged it against her polished shield. The words of her greeting were lost in the clamor of five other swords striking bronze.

Embla dismounted, as did the foremost rider from the east. The newcomer put out his hand in greeting. Embla clasped his arm in a familiar Viking greeting, then, wonder of wonders, put her knee to the ground, removed her helm and actually bowed her golden head before the man.

"Who is he?" Venn demanded, shocked to see proud Embla Silver Throat bow down before any man. "A king, do you suppose?"

Just as astonished, Tala shook her own head. "I don't know." Her eyes were riveted on the tall, dark-haired man towering over Embla. Bands of gold encircled his bare upper arms. Two glittering, bejeweled brooches held a cloth mantle fastened to the leather braces bisecting his powerful chest. He was as dark as Embla was fair, and his skin gleamed as though it were made of polished golden oak. "He is no one that I recall seeing at King Guthrum's court."

At his side walked a man darker than precious ebony, wrapped from head to toe in bleached linen that swept the dust on Fosse Way beneath his feet.

Tala lifted her hand to her brow and pressed against it, unable to fathom what her eyes beheld. She whispered to Venn, "Could they be Romans?" Her jaw sagged further, nearly touching the stone beneath her chest, and her blood quickened as she returned her attention to the uncommonly handsome man dressed in Viking trappings. "Who is he?"

"Let's go find out." Venn quickly put his arrow away and shouldered his bow. He slid down from the stone and put a hand up to catch Tala as she dropped beside him.

Just as curious, Tala nodded as she refitted her girdle to hold her short mantle close to her body. "Let's! I'll race you to King Offa's oak."

Chapter Two

Their passage out of the forest was silent and swift. Neither disturbed so much as a twig, for it was fence month—the time when does dropped their fawns. Both Tala and Venn respected all of the forest creatures and demanded their people do the same.

The short run took them to the very edge of the Leam, where a stand of silver beeches had broken the last time the river flooded, some three summers ago. The bleached trunks spanned the dry river. Only a few remaining puddles wet the caked bottom.

Tala skipped across the natural bridge and stopped at the base of a massive, ancient oak where their grandfather Offa had rested on the day of his coronation. Fed by an artesian river, the oak's gnarled and twisted trunk supported the largest canopy to be found on a living tree beyond the Black Lake's forest. Consequently King Offa's oak shaded a goodly portion of Watling Street.

Nimble as a squirrel after a hoard of acorns, Tala shinnied up the tree and took her favorite position high above the road. Venn climbed up behind her. She could hear his lungs bellowing softly, the wheeze a reminder that he'd been deathly ill this winter past.

Tala spared a look at his face and found it damp with

sweat. Pale blotches tempered the blush on his smooth cheeks. He settled on the limb adjacent to her and calmed himself. The sound of many horses approaching brought her attention back to the business at hand—spying on Embla Silver Throat.

A pair of greyhounds ran into the clearing, preceding the travelers. They paused beneath the great oak to sniff, jump and bark. Tala cast a quick spell that made them sit abruptly and whine in confusion, wondering where their prey had gone off to.

"As you can see, my lord Edon," Embla boasted proudly as she rode into the shade of King Offa's oak, "I've cleared the land south of Warwick to this river. The soil is agreeable here, as along the Avon. My best man, Asgart, and his thanes have applied for tenancy of the new bottomland. This time next year the valley to the south ridge will be plowed and planted. Oats and wheat and hops grow well here."

"I see you have been most ambitious," Jarl Edon Halfdansson replied, complimenting his nephew's wife. All around him were signs of prosperity, save here by the Leam. He remembered the river as a wild stream, free-flowing and full. Now it had not enough water in its muddy bottom to quench the thirst of his horse.

Edon drew back on Titan's reins, halting the black stallion in the cool shade of the oak. It was a blessing to have the hot sun off his head. He ran his forearm across his brow and squinted at the hill fort still some good five leagues to the west.

From the top of the last rise, the Avon valley had looked incredibly fertile and productive. On closer inspection, each field showed the effects of long-term drought. The heads of grain were small. The rich black earth was cracked and parched.

"How long has it been since the last rain?" Edon asked in concern. This drought was not an isolated problem.

Fields in the land of the Franks were in worse shape. This was the third year of unexplainable drought.

"Too long, curse Loki's hide," Embla grumbled. "We've done everything we know of to gather clouds in the sky. We have made sacrifices to Freya, cast spells onto the winds for the four dwarfs. Nothing brings us rain."

She shifted in her saddle and cast a hateful look at the woods beyond the dry river. Lifting her golden, muscled arm, she pointed as she spoke. "There is the root of all our troubles, my lord Edon."

"How so?" Edon saw no malice in the woods nor felt any evil emanating from it. But he was not a superstitious man who gave credence to spells or omens.

"The headwaters of the Leam lay deep in that woodland. A witch has cursed the river and caused it to dry up as you see it now. Her charms are scattered all about yonder oaks. 'Tis that evil incarnate that drives away every cloud that gathers in the sky."

"And would this witch be known to Guthrum by the name of Tala ap Griffin?" Edon asked, his tone as dry as the summer day. Venn cut a sharp glance at his sister. Tala only motioned for him to remain still.

"Aye," Embla assented. "That's the one. Should she ever dare to cross the river onto my land, I'll cut her into seven pieces and trap her soul inside a sealed jar."

Edon changed his focus from the harmless woodland to his nephew's wife. A tall, robust woman, Embla of the Silver Throat made a strong impression upon him. Her full breasts were barely concealed by her cotton tunic. Thick loops of corn-colored hair crowned her altogether elegant head. Despite her pleasing form, she was not an appealing woman. Her voice was strained and strident. Her mouth thinned to a grim, downward curve at each corner. Edon preferred women who at least tried to look pleasant tempered.

A finely crafted necklace of chased silver and amber was

the only ornament she wore. Even though her breasts joggled freely, there was naught else feminine in Embla's demeanor. She carried a shield and wore a helmet and leathern armor strapped to her forearms and legs. Edon could see that Embla considered herself a warrior first and last.

"Wait here," he commanded.

He turned his stallion and galloped back up the dusty hill to intercept his train of possessions. The curtains of the chaise parted and Lady Eloya peered at him inquiringly, her kohl-lined eyes as exotic as her perfumes.

"Is it much farther, my lord Wolf?" Lady Eloya spoke to him in his own tongue, giving Edon a title of awe and rank.

"Not long," Edon murmured in her native tongue, Persian. He put his hand forward to part the curtain more so that he could see into the dark and cool interior of the chaise. "How fares Rebecca?"

"She is bearing up, my lord, as all women must. The babe waits to present himself in good order. Allah wills it so," Lady Eloya promised.

"I will do what I can to speed this infernal procession to Warwick, my ladies. You will be comfortable there." Edon let the silk curtain fall and motioned to Rashid to stay close to the ladies' caravan.

A woman of unique sensibilities, Rebecca of Hebron had refused Edon's Persian physician's assistance this morning when the water of her belly broke and the birth of her child appeared to be their next order of business. Edon had offered to delay their journey to Warwick to accommodate the laboring woman, but Rebecca had decried that suggestion, too. She wanted no part of sitting idle on the open road and insisted the gentle movement of the chaise would soothe both her and the babe. Still, Edon ordered Lady Eloya's husband, Rashid, to remain close in case his vast skills became necessary.

Edon nodded to the bearers, who immediately lifted the chaise again, then began their steady, measured walk behind the hundred horses of Edon's entourage.

More slaves pulled the sleds carrying Edon's menagerie to Warwick. Horses and oxen could not be coaxed into the harnesses dragging the cages bearing Edon's lion, crocodile and wolfhound. So men did what domesticated animals would not.

The wolfhound's soulful eyes were as deeply intense and beautiful as Lady Eloya's—if not more so to Edon. The black that outlined Sarina's eyes was natural. She gave a mournful howl, unhappy in her whelping cage, crying out to Edon astride his horse. He monitored the sled's slow progress down the dusty slope.

Caging the wolfhound was necessary. Without it, Sarina would surely have run off into the woods and reverted to the wild. Edon treasured the dog too much to risk losing her.

"Be patient, my lovely," Edon crooned to the wolfhound, as much in love with her as he was with this land he had dreamed of returning to for so many years. "We are almost home, I promise you."

Finally Edon watched his guards and the drovers pass beneath the ample shade of the great oak. He let the dust raised by a herd of woolly sheep and nimble goats settle before taking up his wineskin and removing the stopper.

Edon lifted his head and tilted the wineskin to his mouth. It was then his eyes located the spies in the oak's leafy canopy. Both the boy and the girl held themselves as still as the dying Gaul's statue on the colonnade in Rome. Leaves fluttered about them, stirred by a hot breeze fueled by the parched land.

When Edon had quenched his thirst, he lowered the wineskin and plugged it. He did not lower his eyes.

"So! You dare to spy on me, do you?" It had been a good dozen years since he'd spoken the odd language of

the Britons, but Edon was certain he was understood, for
the boy reacted by reaching for the knife at his belt.

"Don't even think to try something so foolish, boy,"
Edon cautioned. "I will have skinned you from ear to ear
before you could strike one single blow."

Venn stilled his hand, convinced the stranger's words
were truth. A more menacing soul Venn had never laid
eyes upon. Tala's quick gasp assured him his sister felt the
same tremor of fearful respect.

"I do not take kindly to spies and sneaks. You have
until sunset to present yourselves to me at Warwick, state
your names and tell me who your thane and your father
is."

Edon gathered the reins in his left hand, preparing to
follow his large train of people, baggage and animals to
their new home at Warwick.

"Do not make me come looking for either of you. I
never forget a face or forgive a slight." He made his voice
soft and low when he spoke again for the spies' ears alone.
"One word of advice to the both of you. Bathe before you
present yourselves at my court. I can smell you from
twenty feet away. Don't risk insulting me again."

He put his heels to Titan's sides and galloped out from
under the oak without looking back.

Venn dropped out of the tree and stood on Fosse Way,
shaking his raised fist at the rider's back as he rode away.
"Come back, you dirty Viking, and I'll show you who
stinks!"

Tala joined him and grabbed Venn's fist, yanking him
behind the wide trunk of the oak, out of sight from those
who traveled the road.

"Be quiet!" she commanded. "Don't you ever do anything like that again, brother! If he did come back, he
would cut you into pieces!" Though her voice was soft,
she was obviously furious at Venn's foolhardy words. To

taunt a Viking jarl couldn't be borne. Tala would not tolerate such an act of stupidity again.

Venn reached for his bow. "I'll show him!"

"You'll do nothing!" She cuffed his ears stoutly, then pushed him roughly back to the beech-tree bridge. Venn resisted the thrust of her hand as she herded him back to safety.

Tala proved how deeply upset the stranger's discovery and words had made her when she prepared to beat any hint of rebellion out of her younger brother. "Don't try me, Venn ap Griffin. Defy me and I'll take a strap to your hide and wear you out!"

She gripped his narrow shoulders and shook him hard, then yanked him to her breasts, as if her arms smothering him could protect him from all danger. Her fingers spread into his dark hair and she whispered, "Never do that again! Never risk your life to provoke a jarl. Do you hear me? Have you forgotten our father and all of our kinsmen who had died at the end of Viking swords?"

"No!" Venn's voice came to her muffled by the press of her breasts against his face. He was only a boy. Boys who taunted Vikings were not likely to live to become men. That fear justified Tala's anger, and Venn well knew it.

Pushing him to arms length, Tala stared into his clear blue eyes. "Venn, I promise you, someday you will take your rightful place as a prince in this world," she said earnestly. "The Vikings will fear and respect you. But today, brother, you are a boy and vulnerable. Time and King Alfred are on our side."

"King Alfred does nothing for us, Tala. Every day more Vikings sail their long ships to our shores. Alfred does nothing to send them away. No, even when they land their ships in Wessex he merely shows them Watling Street and invites them to go and find the Danelaw. But they come here to Leam to set up their farms. They don't go to Anglia or York—''

"I am aware of that." Tala cut off his protests. "But Alfred can't strike the Vikings down just because you don't like it when their ships land on Britain's shores. The kings have both signed a peace treaty. We must rely on their law to protect us. King Alfred promises me so.''

Venn shook his head. "What good are words on parchment? Or treaties with out enemies? A king must act.''

"Nay, we must give Alfred's law a chance to work. Do as I say—return to the lake and your lessons with Selwyn. See that the girls have done their chores. I will be there anon.''

"Where do you go?" Venn demanded.

Tala shook her loosened braid back onto her shoulders. "Why, to Warwick...to present myself to the new jarl as he commanded. But you will not come, and do not think to disobey my command." Tala delivered orders easily. At twenty she wielded complete authority over her siblings and their retainers.

Venn knew better than to question her, but he itched to strike out at the arrogant Viking who had taunted them in their own language. Venn would never admit it to his sister, but he was fascinated by the wondrous equipage in the new lord's entourage and his cages of strange and curious animals.

Too smart to argue, he cast a disdainful glance at her. The two simple clothes that covered Tala's torso were belted at her waist by a leather girdle. Embla Silver Throat would mock Tala if she went to Warwick thus attired. "You are not dressed to go to court," he reminded her.

That remark reminded Tala of the stranger's challenge about bathing. The jarl's insult had stung her to the core of her femininity. She knew herself to be beautiful, an unattainable woman desired by men of two kings' courts. Telling color swept into her cheeks.

"See, that is what I mean, little Venn. A grown man is skilled in the art of verbal baiting. He could not tell we were in the trees by our scent," she said purposefully. "Not unless he has the nose of a wolf."

"Fear not, I will go to Warwick via the village at Wootten and bathe at Mother Wren's before I change into robe and crown. All will be well."

Jarl Edon Halfdansson was disappointed by the appearance of Warwick upon his arrival. He'd bought Warwick Hill itself ten years ago from its last owner, a minor atheling of the old house of Leam. There was much to be disappointed over. Edon's nephew, Embla's husband, was missing, and the castle Edon had ordered constructed over the past decade was far from completed.

Warwick offered little respite from the scorching sun. The barest hint of a breeze wafted against the stone walls of the fortress and promptly died. A tremendous heat had built up, inside the great stone keep, and which remained steamier than the catacombs beneath Rome. Not one open shutter allowed air to move from chamber to chamber or floor to floor.

Oh, there were windows and openings, shutters and doors aplenty as per Edon's construction plans. But Embla had thought it best to bolt the shutters and keep the entrances securely barred. She claimed there was no other way to protect from thieving Mercian thralls the treasures he'd had shipped to Warwick in the intervening years.

Edon didn't care much for Embla's disdainful dismal of his plans and orders. Nor had the woman the vision to see that Edon's well-planned, thick stone walls should have made the vast keep cool in spite of such intense heat— provided the windows and doors were open. Instead, the handsome structure had the appeal of a brick kiln sealed to fire pottery.

Edon was aware of his attendants' reactions to Warwick.

Eli rolled his eyes each time he looked at the steamy green
forest, nor could Rashid hide his own awe of the great
woods blanketing acres and acres of land. Eloya and Rebecca were near to fainting from the unaccountable heat.
They had, in desperation, taken over the bathhouse.

"Tell me," Edon said easily, putting aside the goblet of
watered wine his niece had provided him from her own
stores. "When was the last you saw your husband? He has
been missing seven moons now, Guthrum said."

"Eleven moons," Embla corrected. Her thick fingers
tightened on the handle of her short sword. Were she a
man that gesture would have made Edon wary. Were he
less of a Viking, he might have taken insult. "Too long,
my lord Edon. I have given up hope of ever seeing Harald
Jorgensson alive again."

"Surely not." Edon lifted a hand, inviting her to sit and
rest, but Embla ignored it. "You are a Dane's wife," he
continued. "Your man could be on the high seas. He could
this moment be turning his long ship into the north wind
or trading for jewels and furs that will please you. Eleven
months is nothing. I myself have been on voyages exceed-
ing three years duration."

"Forgive me for reminding you, Jarl Edon, but the Avon
has no outlet to the sea," Embla replied.

"Ah, but long ships do traverse the other rivers. The
Severn and the Trent both have access to salt water."

"Not good access from deep inland, Jarl Edon. Weirs
prevent even the most stalwart of long ships safe passage.
No, my Harald has not gone exploring. I know what has
happened to him—he was murdered by the druids. Else he
remains a captive in the dungeon of the keep on Black
Lake."

"If you think him a captive, why have you not assaulted
this keep?"

"No one can reach the lake in the heart of Arden
Wood," Embla told him. "The druids have strewn charms

all through the forest, disguising the trails. The witch has cast terrible spells that turn even my bravest warriors into terrified madmen. No, my Harald has been murdered, Jarl Edon. I know it, and none can convince me otherwise.''

Edon made a rumbling noise in his throat as he considered her words. ''So my brother Guthrum has informed me, but he said there was no proof to that charge. Harald's body has not been found. Is that true?''

''Aye.'' Embla's jaw tightened. ''Harald disappeared the night of the great druid sacrifice to their god Lugh, August 1.''

''I had not realized there were druids still practicing in these isles,'' Edon mused absently. ''How curious...and here I thought the Romans put them all to the sword.''

''The savages exist,'' Embla said intractably.

She turned her back to Edon, and for an unguarded moment she glared at his entourage. His wagons, sleds and carts filled the entire ward of her utterly inadequate wooden palisade. In Constantinople, where Edon had spent seven years as Guthrum's hostage-emissary, such a structure intended for defense would have been torched the moment it was erected, just to prove how useless it was.

''Are you absolutely certain of the date of Harald's disappearance?'' Edon asked. ''It was at Lammas?''

Embla grasped the wood stakes and tilted her chin, exposing a long throat and wondrous white teeth as she laughed scornfully. ''Why wouldn't I be certain? You haven't lived here for years as I have done. It was August 1, the feast of Lughnasa. The night the druids sacrifice a living man to their gods of the lakes and rivers.''

''Granted, it has been years since I last lived in Warwick, Lady Embla,'' Edon said smoothly, ''but I remember the people well. They are for the most part a breed of peaceful, simple farmers.''

Embla snorted. ''They are cannibals. Men are put to death over their Beltane fires. Infants are slaughtered and their bones thrown beneath the foundations of their houses.''

"That uncivilized, are they?" Edon remarked with a raised brow. "How amazingly similar we are then. Vikings leave their newborns outside to weather the elements the first night of their lives. By Byzantine and Roman standards we are both barbarians, are we not?"

Embla checked herself. Her blue eyes hardened in judgment of the Viking jarl before her. She thought him a lazy wretch, a weakling softened by the pampered life of a courtier. He was of no use to a woman determined to amass her own inviolate wealth.

Thank Odin, Guthrum had provided her adequate warning of the jarl's arrival. She'd wished Edon Halfdansson dead many times over the years of her tenancy in Warwick.

Now that she saw him in the flesh for the first time, Embla gave the pampered Wolf of Warwick one sennight in his home shire, certain he wouldn't last that long before he hightailed it to a retreat in Anglia.

She raised a brow, inquiring archly, "Does our home wine not suit your palate?"

Edon wasn't so easily baited. "I saw no grapevines thriving in your arid fields."

"How observant you are, Lord Edon." Embla's tone changed smoothly, and she smiled as she pointed south over the spikes of the wood palisade. "Crowland Abbey was fortuitously placed, as was another monastery in Evesham. Both were pitiful places where monks wore out their knees endlessly in prayer. Their vines were well established. Their cellars were also quite full. It was nothing to dispatch the monks to their Christian hell and relieve them of their surplus."

Edon sampled another taste of the unpalatable wine and deliberately changed the subject. "So who is it that you believe murdered my nephew?"

Embla turned to face him. Her fingers clasped the hilt

of her sword again. "The druid, Tegwin." She straightened, as if refusing to grant Edon dominance over her, despite his height.

He set the cup aside. "What happened to the wine cellar I ordered my nephew to construct? Every casket I've brought with me will sour in this heat if it is not properly sheltered from the heat and the sun."

Embla held a firm check on her simmering temper. She looked toward the fields, which she believed showed her best efforts very clearly. This hideous stone castle of Edon's had no value or importance. The fertile land wrested from the hands of the lazy Leamurian farmers held the true worth of Warwick.

"I have altered some of your plans, Lord Edon. Owing to the bedrock here at the summit of the hill, it was necessary to place one or two of your requested conveniences elsewhere. Now that you have quenched your thirst, shall I give you a tour?"

"By all means," Edon agreed, eager to inspect every inch of his property.

The stone keep was primitive and crude to Edon's eye. But then he was accustomed to the splendors of Constantinople, that gem of cities bustling with artisans, philosophers and scholars.

In time, Edon knew, his own hand would change and alter what was begun here in Warwick. For this was now his home. He was finished with roaming the world, doing his brother's—King Guthrum's—bidding. Now, at the age of one score and nine, Edon intended to establish his own court and turn Warwick into a seat of learning to rival Byzantium.

The two-storied square keep was only the beginning of what he planned to build.

Embla proudly took him to her longhouse first. The building was completely roofed with luxuriant thatch. Its pitch was so high that no smoke from the cooking fires stung Edon's eyes. A raised vent in the center let the smoke rise and allowed a beam of bright daylight inside.

The largest part was used as a hall for feasts and the daily meals. "My chamber is here to the east of the hall, my lord, but if you prefer my services in your keep, I shall move at your convenience."

"That won't be necessary," Edon replied.

Looking around him he saw many thralls at their labors. Women made bread and tended the meat roasting on spits over the open fires. Edon had grown up in surroundings similar to this, as most Vikings did. Farmsteads were the backbone of Viking economy and culture. Embla's longhouse was no different than any of a thousand like it Edon had inspected in his travels.

He thought fondly of the palaces at Rome and Alexandria. With their courtyards and splendid gardens, there was beauty everywhere a man looked. Given time, Warwick would become such a place.

He returned his attention to the woman, whose walk so reminded him of a proud man's strut. Edon put out his hand to touch the carved bone handle of her dagger, which her fingers had flown to so often during their conversation. "This is a curious piece. Who made it?"

At the interest in her prized weapons, Embla offered a genuine smile, the first Edon noted. She proudly unsheathed the dagger and laid it in his hand, expecting his admiration. "Falkirk is my carver. He is good with bone and ivory. This is the goddess Freya hunting a boar."

"An ambitious work." Edon tested the weight and balance of the blade, but was truly enamored of the skill of the bone carving, the attention to detail and the beauty of the craftsmanship. This carver knew what he was about. "It is a worthy weapon. I trust you have little need to use it for defense."

"Humph," Embla scoffed. "Few are foolish enough to challenge me."

"So I have heard." Edon smiled and handed her back her knife, offering his own blade for her inspection. "Mine is more modest, but possibly more deadly in the tempering of the Damascus steel. That is what counts where weapons are concerned, is it not?" His smile faded from his lips. "It is far better to never need to have to unsheath one's weapon in the first place."

The jarl left Embla with those cryptic words. He walked to the well and took a dipper in his hand to quench his thirst.

Asgart, Embla's best man, threw the bucket in the well and drew up a fresh supply after Edon had drunk his fill. Suddenly, the soldier gave with a shout and leaned over the rim. Before his eyes, the water level dropped ten feet.

Asgart's cry of alarm brought everyone in the ward running to the well. The gathering crowd watched the water inch slowly back up the stones that lined the well. It foamed and swirled, a brackish, foul brine. The stench that arose was foul enough to make a strong man stagger.

"The well has been poisoned!" Asgard shouted. He threw the dipper and the bucket to the ground. Edon took a step back because of the stink. Sulfur wasn't a pleasant smell, though the water he'd just drunk had been sweet and pure.

Embla ran to his side and waved her hand across the rising water, smelling the sulfur-tainted air. Fear and alarm darkened her fair cheeks.

"The well has been cursed!" she announced. "The witch has cast another spell upon us!"

Furious, she turned on Asgart, her hand clenching the hilt of her sword. "Damn you, Asgart, bring me that woman! Double your patrols. Find the witch before she causes any more harm. Bring her to me! She will pay for poisoning my well!"

"As you command." Her captain saluted by striking his fist to his chest. Before Asgart could call his soldiers to him and comply with Embla's orders, Edon stepped forward and laid his hand on the captain's arm.

"There is no need to send out a search party."

"But..." Asgart sputtered.

"Keep your men here and go about your usual business," Edon commanded, taking charge of his land and defense of his property. "That was rather presumptuous of my niece to make such a command. I am here now. My men will see to the shire's defense when necessary, Embla Silver Throat."

Both the captain and the woman were stunned by Edon's contradictory order. Only Embla spoke out against it.

"What? You don't know what goes on here," she sputtered.

"I know enough to realize that wells fail during droughts, and it doesn't take witchcraft to accomplish that," Edon replied sternly. "Send your people back to their work."

"Get back to work!" she shouted at the thralls who had come to see what was happening. Edon found it hard to decide which frightened the people more, their mistress or their superstitions. In either case, the poor slaves backed away in alarm.

He didn't believe in such nonsense as wells being cursed by witches. He was astute enough to see that Embla and her people did.

Edon sent one of his captains into the keep to see if the well inside had also been affected. He was met by a servant Lady Eloya had sent running from the bathhouse, to ask what had happened to the water. The sluices in the bathhouse had suddenly gone dry. Rig returned, reporting that the same rotten-egg smell affected the water well in the keep.

Edon gave his head a firm shake, regretting the bad luck

of that. "Then we will have to cart water from the river below the palisade. This is quite unacceptable."

Rig stood beside him as the others moved away. "These people are very superstitious, Lord Edon," he said quietly.

With a meaningful glance at the retreating form of his niece by marriage, Edon said, "That they are, Rig. Let us hope that we can educate them somewhat over time. Shall we adjourn to the keep?"

Chapter Three

The day's heat refused to dissipate until the sun sank within a handspan of the horizon. A soft breeze off the river gently cooled Tala ap Griffin on her walk to the top of Warwick Hill. The fine red glow of the setting sun made it easy for her to slip unnoticed through Warwick's open gates and approach the stalwart keep. Her hair and her mother's scarlet cloak simply melted into the vibrant colors of the dwindling light, making any spell for invisibility redundant. She had no need to cloak herself magically when the dwindling light accomplished all. Inside the wood palisade, a commotion drew the curious to the fortress's communal well.

Curiously, most of the Vikings had gone inside their huts and houses. It was the time of day when their noses led them to steaming pots and fragrant haunches of sizzling venison and pork. Those that lingered in the ward paid no attention to her as she quietly approached the keep and slipped inside.

No dogs barked a warning, no shouts broke the stillness that had come over the land when the cooling breeze lifted off the river. Nothing living took any notice of Tala ap Griffin until she reached the topmost step inside the fortress and came face-to-face with a wolf.

Distracted by the beauty of the setting sun, Edon turned his attention from his crowded table to the wide window aperture gracing his hall. Sundown had come.

He noted the time somberly as he sighed deeply. Come the rising, he would have to go looking for the spies in the oak. He could not allow his authority to be challenged, not even by Warwick's curious children, else he would not be respected in his own shire.

Sarina's throaty growl brought Edon's attention back to the present. At the top of the stairs stood a woman in an exquisite white gown, sheltered by the increasing shadows and a long, flowing scarlet cape. She held herself so completely still in the increasing darkness that Edon almost believed the beautiful woman was an apparition—a vision solely in his mind. He caught his breath, thinking that she could have stood there forever unnoticed by everyone in his hall.

Only Sarina inched toward her, her hackles lifting, her growl a soft warning to Edon's sharp ears. The woman had eyes for only one thing—the wolfhound coming to the end of her leash.

Edon inhaled deeply of the charged air in his hall and discerned that curiosity was the overriding emotion exchanged between the woman and the wolfhound.

Smiling a welcome for the beautiful woman, Edon came to his feet, lifting one hand to Sarina in a command to halt. Edon's motion alerted Embla. She started and looked around, then lunged to her feet, upsetting the balance of intrigue between the woman, the wolfhound and Edon.

"Seize her!" Embla shouted.

The newcomer was obviously not a welcome sight to any of Embla's guards. All six of her Vikings lurched to their feet, bumping their neighbors' elbows as they drew swords from their scabbards. Embla moved hastily, tipping her goblet and spilling wine across the table.

"Seize her, I said!" the Viking woman screamed.

Edon's hand clamped onto his niece's wrist, slamming her sword back home where it belonged. "You overstep yourself, wife of Harald Jorgensson. We are in my hall, at my board. Here the rules of hospitality are more sacred than all the gods in Asgard."

Tala tore her gaze from the wolf to the black-haired Viking jarl. He spoke without raising his voice, but the authority in his command fixed Embla to marble. Tala had never seen or heard the woman crossed before. Her eyes glowed with venom; her body tightened like a snake poised to strike.

Embla found her voice, recovering as she spun around and confronted the jarl in a shrill voice. "You would allow a Mercian witch to enter your hall? A witch who has tainted Warwick's wells? She's come to gloat! She will curse you and steal your soul, suck the breath from your mouth and blood from your heart. Banish her, Lord Edon. You know not what evil you allow."

"My word, all of that?" Edon undercut Embla's venom, halving it with an amused chuckle as his gaze returned to the beautiful lady. He envisioned that lovely mouth sucking the breath from his mouth and found the idea appealing.

Sarina crept closer, sniffing at the woman's trailing scarlet mantle, lifting her nose as Edon did, searching the wind for the newcomer's scent. Edon considered the lady's face and white throat and the firm press of her lush bosom against an elegantly crafted tunic.

Two gilded brooches held the separate cloths fastened at her shoulders. A fine gold girdle rested at the peaks of her hipbones, bringing the sheer white linen to a narrow tuck that widened across her hips and fell in graceful folds to her ankles. A jeweled diadem circled her brow and held a wealth of flaming curls away from her face.

Thus far, Embla's vitriolic attack had only made the stranger smile. And a beautiful smile that was, Edon thought, full of promise and mystery. He allowed his gaze to linger a moment longer on the lovely oval of her face before turning to Embla's restive guards and commanding them to put down their arms.

"The lady bears no weapons on her person. Sit down and be civil, else you will be evicted from my hall. Rig, bring my visitor to the table and make her welcome. Eloya was wise enough to order a setting prepared for her."

"I will not eat of the same food that is served to a Mercian," Embla hissed bitterly.

"Then you will likely starve before our eyes in this hall tonight, Lady Embla. If it so pains you, you may leave and sup in your own hall." Edon dismissed her, satisfied that Rig had moved to the newcomer's side and no harm would befall the beautiful lady should Embla choose to leave in anger.

"I see that blood means nothing to you," the Viking woman sneered.

"On the contrary, wife of my nephew," Edon said with telling candor. "Blood means everything to me."

Embla blanched. Her pale lips tightened and her chin jutted out in fury. Edon saw no gain in allowing Embla to think she retained any power now that he'd returned to his shire.

He was not ready to condemn her for the murder of his nephew, but he had his suspicions. So did his brother, Guthrum. Nor would Edon tolerate any direct challenge from her. Best she learn that now.

"Will we be killed in our beds?" Rebecca murmured fearfully from the near side of the table.

"No, we will not," Edon said resolutely.

Theo turned to distract Rebecca from the commotion of Embla's exit with her six foul-tempered guards. The newborn's mewling became a soft undercurrent punctuating Sarina's throaty growl.

The growling continued until Embla was gone from sight.

Edon realized that it was Harald's wife the wolfhound took such great exception to, not the Mercian newcomer. He started to settle back into his chair, then realized that the newcomer had yet to take a seat. She had paused to greet Sarina and to speak to the two thralls manning the wine casket. Granted, they were only children that Eloya had selected from the compound, but Edon took umbrage that the woman chose to acknowledge anyone before she had made proper abeyance to him.

Blind Theo turned from soothing his wife and small son, chuckling, "So it begins, Lord Wolf."

Ever quick to sense any change in Edon's mercurial temper, Lady Eloya cast a knowing smile his direction. Then she did the unthinkable, speaking out in her clear contralto, in well-practiced Saxon. "Princess, Lord Edon feels ignored."

Tala turned about so quickly she startled the thralls. Another blotch of wine splattered on the unvarnished floor. Sarina rose to her feet and ambled to the stain, sniffing it noisily.

As she gave ground to the wolfhound, Tala found herself the censure of all eyes. She didn't know which was worse—standing still for a wolf to come close enough to devour her or confronting the dark Viking's unfathomable eyes. Frissons of heat skittered over her neck, pebbling the skin on her arms as she turned around to face him. It was the same feeling that had overcome her that afternoon when he'd spied her in King Offa's oak.

"Why did you call me 'princess'?" She addressed the women at the table, not knowing which of the ladies present had spoken to her.

A very beautiful lady at the far end of the boards deigned to reply. "Because Lord Edon's oracle, my husband, Theo the Greek, told us we would have a true princess dine at our table our first night in Warwick. We are in Warwick and you are the only visitor that has come to the hall.''

"Ergo, you are the princess." Edon finished the theorem with simple logic. He saw no reason to add the dictum that the gold torque encircling her neck also proved the theorem valid. He came to Rig's side and took hold of the woman's hand. Her fingers were warm and moist, pale against his sun-browned skin.

"I am honored to be given such rank," Tala replied. She dipped in a proper bow of respect to the lord and all of his guests at the table. "Forgive my interruption of your meal, but I was ordered to present myself at sunset."

Edon blinked in surprise. This beauty standing before him was the bare-limbed nymph in the oak? He shook his head in denial. "You are not the girl I saw hiding in the oak."

"And you said you never forgot a face." She delighted him with a playful smile. "'Haps I should have disobeyed your command and tested your memory, as well as your eyes."

Edon looked closer, admiring the neatly tamed curls held by a net to her diadem. Her fair skin was kissed by the sun, warm and glowing. Wispy red curls escaped at her temple and brow.

"I did not command that you come alone," Edon responded tersely. He felt slightly chilled at the idea of her facing Embla's animosity unprotected.

"I did not say I came alone." Tala chose her words carefully. "It is no matter at the present. You have ample swordsmen and warriors at your table to protect many ladies, be they princesses or not."

Edon deliberately let his gaze move to the empty stairs. "Then summon the boy. He will sup with us as well."

"What boy? I know no boys, lord."

So she would spar words with him, would she? Did she

think his eyes were as sightless as Theo's? Edon motioned to Rig. "Have you discovered the princess's name?"

A handsome smile lightened the planes of Rig's lean cheeks. "Indeed I have, Edon. May I present Tala ap Griffin? Princess, this wolf in fine clothing is Edon Halfdansson, Jarl of Warwick."

The dancing amber lights in the princess's eyes dimmed slightly, as if she'd suddenly recalled a sobering thought. She removed her hand from Edon's. "You are brother to Guthrum and son of Halfdan, late king of the Danelaw?"

"Guilty as charged," Edon answered. He drew back the seat beside his own and placing his hand firmly at the small of her back, guided her to it. She stiffened at his touch, declining to take the seat immediately. By doing so, she wrested control of his hall from his hand. If she would not sit, he could not. If he did not sit, the food would grow cold and no one could eat.

"What ill do you bear my late father?" Edon asked, playing her game momentarily. The top of her head barely reached his shoulder. His hand warmed to the sweet curve at the small of her back. "Halfdan has been gone to Asgard a score and five years. You are not old enough to have been ravished by him, and I know for a fact he did not venture this far south of the security of York."

"Perhaps I am not from the south," Tala countered.

"Ah, but you are, Princess. You are a royal Leamurian. The torque at your throat proclaims you that. Embla bears you great ill and openly calls you a witch. Has she reasons for her animosity, valid ones?" Edon asked silkily.

He allowed his hand to move slowly up the delightful curve of her spine, enjoying the way she pressed back into his hand, seeking a distance he wouldn't allow. He smiled deliberately, as if to ask *who is in control now?*

"Embla Silver Throat is well-known for her malice." Tala couldn't take her eyes from his. "She spreads it about her indifferently, sparing no one."

"She empowers you with the cunning of a witch."

Tala's laugh at that bald charge echoed into the high ceiling of Edon's hall. "Aye, so she does."

"You do not deny the charge?"

"To what purpose? Vikings are known for their stupidity and superstitious ways. Both run hand in hand with brute force. Embla has mastered all there is to learn of that."

"Now you try to provoke me. Sit down, Tala ap Griffin. The food grows cold and others in this chamber want to have their bellies filled before the moon rises. Mind the insults you levy, lest you find there are no stupid Vikings at my table."

That the warning bore a truth was as evident as the deep cleft in the jarl of Warwick's handsome chin. Tala gave in to his command and took the seat beside him. Sitting allowed her some measure of relief, as he removed his possessive hand. But the imprint remained like a brand from a hot iron, tormenting her.

A servant hastily cleared away Embla's spilled goblet, whisking clean linen and gold plate in its place before Tala. She squirmed on the hard chair, tearing her gaze from Eden's face to look at the people at his table. Her palms grazed the lovely carved wood at her hips as she adjusted the chair closer to the table.

Edon watched her fingers unconsciously caress the carved wolf heads and wondered what the stroke of those same fingers would do to his own flesh. He watched as she gave in to a moment of curiosity, studying the various personages at his table. That allowed Edon more time to enjoy the pure curve of her cheek and the symmetry of a perfect nose above lips so sweetly red and full he imagined she'd consumed a handful of berries prior to coming to his hall.

Her gown was in no way unattractive, with its classic lines, but it was not something constructed just for her.

The bright kirtles and fitted silk gowns his ladies favored would better suit her strong coloring and lush figure.

She wore not a trace of perfume, neither oil of attar nor the modest scents of herbal soaps. That appealed to him deeply, for he loved the scent of a woman. That was the richest perfume of all.

The food was served and the meal commenced, during which Edon introduced her to his guests and friends. As ladies were wont to do, she and Eloya struck up a fast friendship, asking about the gowns each was wearing, the source of the rich cloths. The princess seemed very pleased to learn that Eloya and two of her ladies were skilled with needle and thread. Warwickshire needed more such talents.

Amused, Edon and his men let the conversation drift along those lines while they ate their fill. When asked where she had come by her jewelry, Tala ap Griffin became quite animated in her speech, praising the talents of her craftsmen. Her goldsmiths were all Celts trained in Erin who traveled the ancient trade route from Dublin to Anglesey. They, like every goldsmith in the land, congregated in the great trade center of Chester, which used to be Tala's home.

It wasn't all that long before amber eyes turned fully to Edon, catching him in his most thorough inspection. A soft auburn brow rose in an arch. "Am I to be devoured, sir? Like the mutton on your platter?"

Edon moved his shoulder closer to hers and lowered his voice so that she alone could hear his words. "You are not the sprite I spied in the tree."

"What makes you think so?" Tala asked.

Edon considered his answer with care, because it was not his way to give in to an instant attraction. Women surrendered at his beck and call, not vice versa. This woman had a seductive, enchanting power about her that spoke volumes to the barbarian inside him. He wanted to conquer her, take her to his bed in the next chamber and pull her beneath him.

It was a strong and powerful urge, fueled by the fact that he had the consent of two kings to compel her into marriage. Both kings knew of the ancient taboo prohibiting the marriage of the princess of Leam, the Celtic equivalent of Rome's Vestal Virgins. Edon acknowledged only that she was lovely and highly desirable, not the untouchable woman he'd been led to expect, a woman whose allure would be somehow both sacred and profane.

"The sprite in the oak tree was all impulse and curiosity, while tonight you are a mysterious princess deliberately choosing each word and action. You are the kind of woman to be tasted again and again, one delicious bite at a time."

Tala inhaled sharply and drew back enough that the flambeaux illuminated his dark face fully. The jarl was overpowering this close. Her heart racketed in her chest, making it difficult to draw a full breath. He was a wickedly attractive man, handsome and earthy. His black hair spread back from his head like a lion's mane, full of curls and waves.

His brow was wide but his jaw wider, and unlike many of his peers, his cheeks were sleekly shaved. He did not allow even a mustache to grow upon his upper lip, to spoil the deep curves of his expressive mouth. Her gaze fled from them to the brilliant blue of his eyes, so dark they almost seemed as black as his hair. The Romans had a word for a man like him: *satyr.*

"I see that you are a man of vast appetites," she said carefully, with a telling glance at the table before them. "Many ladies grace your table, one suckling a newly born son. Do not look at me with such hungry eyes. I am not your next conquest, I promise you, Lord Viking. I am here because it suits my purpose to meet and address you."

Edon smiled and took the pitcher of wine from the trembling hands of the young thrall so that he could have the pleasure of refilling the princess's goblet himself. "And what purpose is that, princess?"

Tala moistened her lips and told herself to be bold. No timid heart would secure Venn's future.

"Petitions have been sent and recorded by the king of the Danelaw and the king of Wessex. Twenty of my thanes and more than a hundred freeholders and their families and thralls have been maimed, enslaved or murdered by your agent, Embla Silver Throat, since the kings signed the Treaty of Wedmore."

"Is that so?" Edon set the pitcher aside. He knew the facts and was here to set the record straight. Like any woman, the princess exaggerated to prove her point.

"Aye, it is," Tala continued, gaining confidence by the moment. He was not as intimidating as she'd first believed. She lifted the gold goblet full of wine, drank its delicious contents and said clearly, "I was sent word from Winchester that Jarl Harald would be replaced by another."

"Were you?" Edon smiled.

He would choke on that smile in a moment, Tala thought, smiling in tandem. "My cousin, King Alfred, assures me the wergild due me is to be paid in full."

"Did he?" Edon remarked, casting not a single glance at any of the gold on his table. The silly fool mistakenly thought a wergild was paid to her. She was wrong. It was a penalty tax—paid to the king.

"Yes, it is so. I am happy to see this evidence of your wealth spread so generously on your board. Suffice it to say the wergild for hundreds of slain and captured Leamurians will beggar Warwick to redeem it. At long last Guthrum and Alfred's treaty brings justice to my people."

Undaunted, Edon smiled for the bold lady's enjoyment. "I, too, am glad that you so willingly and openly expose your trump hand, Tala ap Griffin. You are not the only flea in the ear of kings. I come fresh from court with orders of my own to enforce on the land called Warwick.''

"My land," Tala declared forcefully. "Viking land ends at Watling Street, well above the Avon. Every scrap of earth between the Severn and the river Trent belongs to the kingdom of Leam, from Weedon Bec to Loytcoyt. The rivers, the forests of Arden and Cannock and all the creatures in them are mine to harvest, not yours.

"Furthermore, I want this fortress razed and the bridge cleared of obstruction. I order my thanes and thralls released from the enslavement imposed upon them by King Guthrum's agent, Embla Silver Throat.

"Secondly, I want your freeholders to take their cattle and their wives and concubines and children to the other side of Watling Street, where you belong. Do that and I will rescind the death warrant sworn against Embla Silver Throat by Alfred of Wessex. He is my kinsman and will listen to me.''

Edon sighed. His raised his palm, commanded her to silence. "I am here to end the bickering and enforce the peace of two kings. The disputed land known as Warwick has become a troublesome shire. Both kings wish to see their realms well peopled by men of war, men of God and men of work. They tire of women who squabble like children behind their backs.''

"Squabble like children?" Tala took exception to that odious description. "I squabble with no one. Your king claims it is a matter of law, not heredity, that proves title and ownership. To that end we Leamurians have put our efforts into drafting laws of ownership sanctioned by our king, Alfred. I do not engage in useless bickering.''

"Are you saying Embla Silver Throat does?" Edon asked.

"Embla Silver Throat engages in murder and mayhem, slaughtering any who oppose her or stand in her way.''

"How is it then that she has not slaughtered you, Tala ap Griffin?"

"Because I am never so foolish as to try to face her alone. I choose to call her to task before the court of kings."

"But you came here to my hall—alone," Edon reminded her.

"You assume that."

"Very well." Edon gave her that point. She was crafty and smart, adept in using the arts of the diplomat. Her endless petitions to Guthrum proved those facts. "May I tell you that my duty is to enforce all the terms of the Treaty of Wedmore, to which you have already referred?"

"You cannot enforce what you will not respect." Tala's eyes narrowed cautiously. "I will not listen to arguments that put my people at fault, when they are the victims of Embla's vast greed and ungoverned cruelty. Every day she burns more of my forest."

"There will be no more burning of the woodlands," Edon said with quiet authority. "Such fires put us all at risk in times of drought. I have ordered them stopped."

"Will you also move your people behind the agreed boundary of Watling Street?"

"That I cannot do," Edon replied.

"Well, you shall, else there will be no end to—"

"Hear me out, Princess." Edon stopped her tirade. "This is not an eyre. This is my supper table. Here we dine pleasantly and converse upon ideas to stimulate thought and creativity. You will save your complaints for the judgment of my court when it is convened."

"How convenient Viking law is," Tala replied, without holding back her scorn. "I have not risked my life coming here merely for the civility of your board."

"You came because I commanded you to come."

"No." Tala assured him. "I came to state my terms and

demand reparations. The sooner made, the sooner we'll have done with one another.''

Edon very deliberately shook his head. He cast a look across the table to Rig, who had quietly returned to his seat after searching outside for the boy Edon had told him to go and look for. A jerk of Rig's head told Edon the boy had not been found.

"Very well, lady.'' Edon sighed and leaned back against the cushions of his high-backed chair. "You have given me your terms. Now I must give you the terms of two kings. Tala ap Griffin, I present to you Nels of Athelney, King Guthrum's confessor.''

A man directly across the table from Tala rose to his feet and bowed deeply from the waist. Tala blinked at him, not certain if she had seen him before. He seemed rather familiar, dressed in a brown woolen tunic with a broadsword belted to his hips. As strong as any man at the jarl's table, he befitted the sword.

"Princess Tala, it has been a very long time coming, but I am most pleased to make your acquaintance,'' said Nels of Athelney. She was nearly a legend in King Alfred's court—a reminder of the days of Camelot and Arthurian epic, closely tied in the minds of Alfred's subjects to the Lady of the Lake and mystical Avalon.

"Tell the princess your purpose for being here, Bishop Nels,'' Edon prompted.

"Simply put, my lord Wolf, I am charged with the duty of seeing that all persons residing in Warwickshire are baptized Christians...with a sword at their throat if necessary.''

"You may have noticed, Tala ap Griffin, that I came with soldiers enough to see that joint edict of King Guthrum and King Alfred fulfilled within the month granted us to accomplish it. My general, Rig, has already accepted the teachings of the Christ and proudly wears the cross King Guthrum has given him.''

Tala looked from the soldiers to the dangerous man seated beside her. Edon of Warwick continued speaking horrifying words.

"Once the conversions are done, I am to staunch the wounds that cut so bitterly between neighbors on the same land. As palatine of this shire, I will hold a monthly eyre to judge and settle grievances. The morning after the new moon rises, you may bring to me your petitions, which have harried two kings. I shall deal with each charge as it is proved."

"What?" Tala gasped. "You could not possibly sit in fair judgment over my people. You jest, Viking!"

"Nay, I do not," Edon growled, not liking her reaction one bit. She glared at him as though he was something vile and unspeakable, not a polished, educated man of the world. "Make use of your days of grace as you will, Princess. Once you find yourself charged with treason before this Viking, there will be no more skulking in trees, spying upon the unwary and conducting mischief with the waters that fuel this land."

"What now?" Tala demanded scornfully. "Do you accuse me of witholding the rain and drying up the rivers?"

"Not I, Princess." Edon held back a laugh at her preposterous words. Her humor was not the issue. "It is time you learned you are not the only person capable of delivering ultimatums to kings. As you have harried Alfred, Guthrum's niece has pleaded with him for redress."

"So?" Tala replied hotly.

Edon smiled wickedly, taking a small taste of satisfaction in her discomfort over that news. She was truly naive, a mere innocent in the ways of wielding power. He leaned deliberately closer to her, inhaling her sweet fragrance as he allowed his fingertips to stroke soothingly across the satiny skin of her bare arm.

"Nor did you deny being a witch when the question was put to you at the beginning of this meal," he said huskily. "So tell me, Tala ap Griffin. How does that slipper fit now?"

Chapter Four

Tala's answer came as a resounding slap on the jarl's face. Refusing to stay and be insulted further, she bolted from his table.

Halfway to the bottom of the steps, Edon caught up with her, jerked her off her feet and flung her over his shoulder.

"You bastard, put me down! How dare you touch me! Selwyn! Stafford! I need you!" Tala screamed. She pounded her fists into the jarl's massive back, aiming for the soft flesh at his kidneys.

"Bar the gates!" Edon commanded the astonished soldiers standing in the keep's lower chamber. "Arrest any man who draws a weapon in her defense. Detain him for questioning."

Without further words, Edon spun around and marched back up the stairs and through the hall, bearing the screaming, struggling woman on his shoulder. She was not easy to contain, fighting him with all her might. What she lacked in muscle and weight she made up for in sheer determination.

The moment Edon entered his chamber and dropped her on his box bed, he caught hold of her hands and flattened her to the feather mattress. In spite of the great difference between their weights, she continued to whip about, as slippery as eels in a bowl of oil, twisting and bucking beneath him, screaming her throat raw, piercing his eardrums with her shrieks.

Her terror increased tenfold as her struggles caused her simple gown to tear from the brooches at her shoulders.

Still angered by her effrontery, by the insult she'd delivered him in slapping him publicly, Edon let her wear herself out. His grip upon her hands remained firm, keeping her spread beneath him.

Sarina bounded into the chamber and jumped on the bed. The wolfhound stuck her wet nose in the howling princess's face, whining and wiggling, distressed by the woman's ear-piercing shrieks.

"You are only making it worse for yourself," Edon said at last. He felt no sympathy whatsoever for the headstrong woman. Did she think he had no pride? Had she not given a single thought to the fact that he, too, was an atheling, the son of a king? Striking him in the face was an unforgivable insult. "Get down, Sarina!"

The wolfhound whined and nuzzled his cheek. Then, concluding that Edon would not play, she bounded off the bed and sat, thumping her tail on the floor.

Tala commanded, "Release me at once, Viking!"

"Lady," Edon warned her, his patience dwindling fast, "speak to me again in that tone of voice and I will have no choice but to teach you to respect the man you see before you."

"Strike me and I will kill you with my bare hands, Viking!" Tala gulped, struggling for her breath.

"And how will you do that, hmm?" Edon taunted. "With what weapon will you slay me, woman? Your viper's tongue? These hands that you cannot remove from my grip?"

Edon nodded to her bared breasts, exposed in the beam of moonlight that spilled into the chamber from the open window. "The only success you have had thus far is in baring your bosom. Continue the show. I shall enjoy seeing what other charms your struggles reveal."

"Barbarian!" Tala screamed. "You tricked me. I will not be mocked."

"You do not dictate terms to me, woman," he responded with terrifying severity.

"Selwyn!" Tala gave her all to one last scream, knowing full well it did her no good. In her arrogance, she had come alone. There was no valiant warrior lurking in the shadows to take down this Viking. Alone, she would defeat him or surrender to him.

She bucked in a futile attempt to unman him, thinking she would leap out the window if she got the chance. Raising her right knee only increased the intimacy of their position, centering his hips more firmly on hers.

"You are crushing me, Viking. I will be bruised from head to foot."

"The damage is of your own doing. Cease your struggling and it will go better for you."

"I would rather die now and be done with you, cur."

Edon shifted her wrists, forcing her hands into the bedding beside her head. "I think you will not die tonight, Tala ap Griffin. That would add injury to insult. I have a much different plan for you. You are to be used to heal the breach between Wessex and the Danelaw."

She clawed at his forearms, scratching at the golden bands he wore for protection. "You will not use me!" she declared vehemently, revealing the pride inherent in her soul. She needed to be taught a lesson, that much Edon saw quite clearly.

He wanted to kiss her fury from her mouth, taste her lips and slip his tongue inside. Astutely, he knew conquering her by force would not satisfy him. There was no pleasure in having his tongue or his lips bitten. So he tipped his head to the vulnerable column of her throat and tasted her heated flesh. His teeth nipped at her ear. The

sharp sound of her breath whistling against her dry lips
pleased him.

"Please get off me." Tala swallowed enough of her
pride to make a request out of necessity. He had her pinned
to the edge of his crude bed. "The wood of your bed is
cutting me in two. I do not lie."

"Open your legs and the pain will cease," Edon
drawled, preoccupied with the soft exposed flesh of her
pebbled breasts. A shiver skittered down her spine as he
deliberately stroked his chin across her nipple. Then his
hot, wet mouth closed upon her breast.

"No!" Tala jerked her head back violently. She tried to
twist out from between the wood and his hips.

The intimacy of the cradle she made for him was not
lost upon her. Nor did her altered position give her anywhere near enough relief. It made matters worse.

"Viking, you come dangerously close to violating me,"
Tala hissed, her words strained. "All of Mercia will rise
in revolt to avenge the dishonor you do me."

Edon took his own time answering. He enjoyed toying
with her breast, which was as responsive and sweet as any
he'd ever fondled. He left it a wet and quivering pebbled
peak when he raised his head at last and gazed into her
narrowed, angry eyes.

"All of what *once was Mercia* has sued for peace, Tala
ap Griffin. You are the talisman King Alfred offers to pacify the Danes. There will be no man standing forward,
challenging my rights over you. The pacts have been
sealed and accepted by two kings. You will surrender to
their will...and to mine."

"I will kill you with my bare hands if need be, Viking,"
she promised.

Edon dropped his head to her breast again. She was
powerless, but her pride was such that she would not admit
it. As he nibbled a sensitive trail across her chest and began to lave and kiss her other breast, she called down a

rain of insults upon his head, imploring her gods to avenge her and strike him dead. But no thunderbolt fell. No keening spirit took shape and form and stirred the wind.

In due time his ministrations began to have their effect. She squirmed deliciously against him, moaning involuntarily against the pleasure of his intimate touch. Through the thin linen of his tunic, Edon felt her belly tighten exquisitely and her loins begin to dampen, readying itself for the conquest that was still to come.

That she could not control her desire satisfied Edon for the moment. It was important to him to know that the woman he must marry was not immune to him physically. She would be the mother of his heirs...the sons who would inherit Warwick in the years to come. He could not bed her without pleasure there for the both of them.

"Tell me when you exhaust your font of threats."

His caustic words made Tala look sharply at his face, seeking his eyes in the shadows. Moonlight allowed her to see his tempting mouth and straight nose and the wickedly superior arch of his black eyebrows. He took liberties no man had ever dared to from her and preened like a peacock because of it.

Her heart pounded inside her chest like a drum. She could barely moisten her mouth enough to speak above her fear. "You are not going to ravish me?"

"Is that what you want? Proof that I am a barbarian?" Edon asked plainly.

"You take pleasure in mocking me."

"As I am taking my pleasure in ravishing you this very moment. What next, Princess? Shall I carry you to the cliff and chain you to the rocks above my quarry? Sue your king for a ransom? Await the brave knights of Wessex, come to slay the dragons in the caves and free you?"

"This is preposterous. We have nothing to discuss. Let me go, I implore you."

"Not until you give me assurances that you will behave

as a lady, contain yourself and sit at peace within my manse."

"I will mouth no empty promises to a Viking." She spat out the words with a full measure of scorn.

Edon straightened his arms and raised his shoulders. His movement increased the pressure of his hands upon her wrists. "Rig!"

In an instant his man appeared in the gap of the open door. "Lord, how may I serve you?"

"Bring me two strips of braided leather and a cloth suitable for gagging this woman. I tire of her vapid conversation."

"You oaf! We are not conversing." Tala jerked her right hand off the bedding, trying to slap him again.

"Your powers of deduction astonish me," Edon growled, and he slammed her arm back onto the feather bed. He gave her wrist a punishing twist to teach her the futility of her struggles. Then he grew serious, ending the game between them. "Why did the boy not come with you?" he demanded.

"Because I sent him home," Tala snapped.

"Where is your home?"

"You built a damned fortress on top of it!"

Edon dropped his elbows onto the bed beside her. Her swollen breasts were very fetching now, displayed so prettily by her uneven breathing and the dishabille of her gaping gown. Rig returned and tossed long strips of cloth and two rawhide laces onto the bed at Edon's right hand.

Tala looked to her left as the objects landed. She quickly looked back at the Viking, too aware that her heart had begun a new cadence inside her chest. His mood had changed. A moment ago his threat had contained a playful edge to it. Now the air between them throbbed with true danger.

"You wouldn't dare tie me up."

"Lady, I dare anything."

"Release me and we will begin anew."

"Nay." His eyes fixed firmly upon hers, granting no quarter. She had foolishly walked into his trap.

"You can't be allowed to wander in and out at will. My niece wants to cut you into seven pieces and store your soul in a jar. My king wants you baptized and made into a Christian. Your king wants you married with unseemly haste. And I, lady, wish to relieve my bladder. This position is becoming more untenable by the moment."

"By Anu's shrouds, you are an ass. Go and piss into the wind and leave me be, Viking."

"Shortly." Edon released her hands all at once and took up the bindings.

Tala didn't bother to resist being gagged and bound. The Viking had already won the struggle. Her hands were too numb to do any harm to him. He stuffed the cloth in her mouth and bound the gag around her face, flipped her onto her belly and tied her hands securely at the small of her back.

Smugly satisfied with his work, he slapped her bottom soundly as he removed his weight. Edon of Warwick gave the wolf a command to guard her, and departed. Tala choked on her own fury.

As uncomfortable and miserable as she was, Tala still dozed as the night lengthened. Where the Viking had taken himself to, she couldn't guess. The manse quieted quickly. Voices in the hall became muffled, their owners respecting the mewling cries of the newborn infant. The wolf fretted between spells of whining and turning round and round in a circle, her claws clicking on the floor.

Tala felt just as anxious as the beast. She had to get home. Venn would be worried sick. Stafford would be ready to call out the guard and storm the hill if Venn dared to admit where Tala had gone.

An eon later, Edon of Warwick returned. He unfastened

his breeks, stripped them from his lean hips and dropped onto the bed beside her. Tala flipped her head to the other side, glaring at him in mute entreaty.

He slid his hands behind his head and stared at the ceiling, pretending he couldn't hear her muffled groveling.

"Lady, 'tis late. Do not start your bellyaching. I do not intend to listen."

To prove that he closed his eyes and ignored her for a good long while. Tala lay absolutely still, impotently raging against the urge to kick him into the otherworld. After a long, long while he opened one eye, peeking at her. She blinked. She heard larks singing and was certain the sun would rise any moment.

The mattress shifted as he turned to his side, facing her. He lifted her diadem from the back of her head. With surprisingly gentle hands, he removed the sheer net that had held back her hair.

Edon let his fingers spread through the tangle of fiery curls gathered at the back of her head. He marveled at the soft texture of the strands and the vibrant color that moonlight could not diminish. The knot of the gag tangled in the curls.

He dismissed the churlish feeling that hounded him for having left her bound so long. Gruffly, he said, "Are you going to cooperate with me now, woman?"

Tala nodded mute agreement. Her downcast eyes did not impress him. Rebellion clearly simmered under the surface of her submission.

Edon grasped her shoulders and sat her up. Her gown fell to her waist. His breath caught in his throat at her shocking beauty and he made a vain effort to hide the effect the sight had upon him. The gods had not known what they were doing when they made women so beautiful that strong men fell weak in the knee before them. Steeling his resolve to ignore her abundantly pleasing attributes,

Edon took his knife from the table next to the bed and unsheathed the blade.

"Do not move!" he commanded in a surly voice. He cut the bonds from her wrists, then slid the blade inside the knot at the back of her head. The binding fell apart. He tossed the blade onto the bedding beside his right knee and pulled her back against his naked chest. He removed the wad of cloth from between her teeth, tossing it to the floor.

She wagged her jaw back and forth and swallowed hard several times. Edon grasped her hands, holding them before her. They were cold and stiff, her fingers swollen. Her head fell back against his shoulder as he rubbed her fingers and palms, massaging firmly.

"The pain will end shortly," he said.

Her response was a curt nod. He renewed his efforts at restoring the blood to her numb extremities. Her naked breasts brushed his hands and forearms. The soft, tempting cones stood out against the pale cloth of her gown pooled low over her hips.

Edon deliberately laid her useless hand on her thighs, knowing she would not move them voluntarily—not before the painful tingling of waking flesh abated. He stroked his hands up her bare arms and caressed her shoulders, gently massaging her neck and throat.

"You are very beautiful, Tala ap Griffin. No, do not try to speak. I will tell you what I think, and you will listen to my words because I am going to be your husband very soon. There is only one logical solution for the question of who is entitled to rule Warwick. That is to unify our separate claims by marriage. I am glad your breasts appeal to me. I want to put my hands on them and rub them like I am rubbing your hands, but you are angry and I won't. Later you will be very happy to let me touch your breasts and see you naked. You won't want to clobber me, because you will be grateful for all the pleasure I give you."

Tala swallowed. She'd been choking with that gag in her mouth. Now she couldn't muster a drop of saliva to spit in his eye. The monster deserved to have his throat slit with his own knife. She would do it, just as soon as the stinging pains in her arms abated.

Edon placed a chaste kiss upon her temple. He did not dare kiss her quivering mouth. It would be over if he did, for he could not control his desire for her much longer. He got up, reaching for his breeks and drew them on, minding the discomfort of his arousal.

King Alfred insisted she was a virgin, revered by her people and untouched even at the advanced age of twenty. She had the freedom to roam the forest of Arden—nay, all of ancient Mercia—protected by the golden torque encircling her throat. None who saw her dared molest her, for a princess of Leam was as sacred to the Celts as their Lady of the Lake herself.

Whether she was virgin or not, Edon didn't care to strain his control further by lighting a lamp and seeing her naked before him when he was fully aroused. He'd had enough sweet temptation to last him a good long while. When next he toyed with her, he would take her.

But that delight was for another day. Fastening his belt at his hips, he reached for flint and iron. He coaxed a flame onto the wick of the tin lantern, then hung the oil lamp on the hook beside his bed.

The princess of Leam's slanted amber eyes gazed at him. He stared at her breasts and the faint cinnamon freckles that glazed their plump curves and her shoulders. Cinnamon freckles were very nice.

He reached for her, saying, "Come. Stand before me and I will do what I can to fix your gown. You look a fright. My people will think I have already bedded you."

"Ass," Tala croaked as he brought her to her feet.

"Ah, ah, ah!" Edon wagged a finger under her nose. "Provoke me and I will push you onto your back and have my way with you now. I am a man. I am as weak as any other man. Your king wants this nonsense in Warwick ended, and I know exactly the way to end the squabbling between two women. I do what kings command. You have no say in the matter whatsoever, so we will not argue about such silly things again.''

Edon turned her slightly, to grasp the top of her gown and bring the halves together at her left shoulder. He unpinned the brooch and folded the cloth securing the pin. He frowned, judging his work satisfactory, then turned to her other side, repeating the process.

"There. That will work. You are much more desirable with your clothes gathered at your hips. I will not mind having a Brit with such beautiful breasts for a wife, so long as you can keep your tongue behind your teeth.''

Tala tilted her head as she glared at him. The Viking sod hadn't the good sense the gods granted the sparrows. How dare he so abuse her—a princess of Leam. She would kill him before she consented to marry him! She turned aside and reached toward the bed, grasping his knife. But when she straightened to stick it in his throat, the handle slipped out of her numb, tingling hand. The blade fell and thrummed as its point stuck in the wooden floor.

Startled by her quick move to the offense, Edon bent and retrieved his weapon. Resolving not to be so careless in the future, he put it back in its sheath, secure on the belt at his waist.

Ignoring him and angry at her own ineptness, Tala stalked out into the darkened hall. The trestle had been taken down, but a sideboard held a pitcher and cups and a wooden bowl of fruit. She filled a cup and drank it dry. By then Edon of Warwick had donned his leggings and shoes and covered his wide chest with a tunic.

"Come, you may show me the way to your home now, Tala ap Griffin. Your servants will be worried sick.''

"I'm never speaking to you again," Tala croaked in the best voice she could muster.

The Wolf of Warwick cocked his head to the side, staring at her quizzically. "Frankly, lady, I count that a relief. Women have a great tendency to chatter overly much, so I shall appreciate having one in my household who is silent. Come, my men have the horses ready. I have a great deal of work to do on the morrow."

Ignoring him completely, Tala headed down the stairs. She prayed for him to trip and fall and break his neck. When he reached the bottom floor in one piece, she realized prayers weren't the answer. She should have cast a spell.

Wise enough to outsmart most Vikings in the Danelaw, Tala gave Jarl Edon instructions to the village of Wootton instead of to the forest. Mother Wren was beside herself, pacing the parched, brown grass outside her cottage, fearing the fate that had befallen her charge in Warwick. She gave a shout of joy when she spied Tala on the jarl's mount as he rode into her yard.

Then, because the crone was matriarch to all and sundry that remained of the dwindling folk of Leam, she lit into the Viking.

"You had no right keeping my lady out to the wee hours of the morn!" the old harridan complained. She gathered the princess against her bosom, cooing over Tala as if she were Wren's very own chick.

Edon gave the cottage a good look, fixing it in his mind. He intended to return very soon and visit his bride-to-be. The more time he spent with her, the less she would resist their approaching nuptials.

"Where are the princess's guards, Selwyn and Stafford, and her brother, Venn?" he asked the old woman.

"Out!" Mother Wren snapped testily. "Searching the fens for her. Where else would they be, lord? In the loft asleep like lazy, uncaring curs? Not our brave Selwyn and Stafford. As for Venn, he may be a boy but he knows his duty to his sister."

Edon grumbled under his breath. He wanted the boy in his custody, now more than ever. If he took Venn ap Griffin back to Warwick, there'd be no argument whatsoever from Tala when the king's confessor recited the vows. "When the atheling returns, tell him I will send my man Rig to fetch him midafternoon. He may accompany me hawking."

"Oh! Venn will like that, he will." Mother Wren cackled, pretending to agree, when she knew better. Venn would spit in the Viking's eye. "Now be off with you. My lady's near to fainting as she stands."

Wren hurried Tala inside the cottage, slamming shut the half door. They both hugged each other for support, lest they collapse as they listened for the Vikings to ride away.

"My lady—" old Wren exhaled deeply, her hand pressing hard upon her heart "—this night my hair went from gray to white in the span of a moonrise. Do this to me again and I'll be laid out from stone to stone."

"Wren, you are a more splendid mummer than the stagmen of Arden Wood." Tala hugged the old woman tightly and kissed her wrinkled cheek in deepest gratitude. "Thank you, thank you. I feared you would give the game away when he demanded to know Venn's whereabouts."

Wren cackled and patted her arm. "It takes little guile to fool a Dane, child."

It wasn't long before Tala paced the cottage in high dudgeon, raising small clouds of dust on the hard-packed earth floor with her feet. She'd exchanged her royal mantle and sadly mangled gown for her hunting dress and had put her gold armbands and diadem in the casket where they remained safe between uses.

"Have you heard a single word I've said, Mother Wren?"

"Yes, yes, I heard every word." the old woman sat on her stool, yanking at her distaff. She jabbed a favorite bone on the bottom and gave it a twirl, making the stick spin. Bent fingers fed the spinning wood a hank of wool, and a thread formed in the blink of Tala's eye. "All of Leam is to become Christians and you're to marry a Viking. I heard you say it all only moments ago. What of it? Being a Christian isn't so bad."

"What of it?" Tala's hands tightened to fists. "These Vikings murdered my parents!"

"Nay, Tala. That isn't true. Jarl Edon and *his* Vikings had nothing to do with your parents' death and you know that. Just as you know you must yield to the kings' will. Tegwin has no power. Half the old stories are jumbled in his head. Why can you not listen to those who are wiser than you? We all see the end of it."

"Wren, not you, too?" Tala said sorrowfully. "Venn is trying to hold on to his birthright. He has the right to believe in the old gods of Leam, gods that made our land what it was. It isn't just a tradition to him to make gold offerings to the Lady of the Lake, it's a ritual. He believes the gods will speak to him. That their spirits show themselves in his vision dreams."

"Venn is a boy. He knows what he is taught. Send him to an abbey and he will learn of the Christ. Foster him out as your father would have done. Let Venn learn the new ways. He will adapt. You know, Saint Ninian converted all of Wessex. Why does Leam resist? The days of the druids are over."

"You don't understand, Wren. Venn refuses to abandon the last living druid. I have tried to convince him to return to Chester or go study in any abbey. He will not. Not unless I allow Tegwin to go with him."

"Then you must do something drastic."

"Such as?"

"Marry the Viking," Wren cackled. "Had I a man such

as that plowing my belly, I'd have never gone to the convent at Lyotcoyt. I saw him ride into Warwick on that black horse of his. Ooch, I'd nay let a man such as that get away…a black Dane. His mother was Irish. He'll give you sons aplenty."

Tala rolled her eyes and asked the gods for patience. Wren was so old she was addled. "You are not helping. I'd kill the Viking's sons to repay them for killing my father."

"You speak where you know not. King Alfred gave you leave to take your sisters to summer in Chester and you come to Warwick to stir up trouble in the grove. Take the Viking. It will go better for you."

"And then what? Do I turn my back on my brother? You know what will happen if I do. If I leave Venn here alone this summer, Tegwin will convince him to be the sacrifice on the night of Lughnasa."

The distaff wobbled to a stop in Mother Wren's gnarled hands. She stared balefully at the small peat fire in her hearth, which gave so little light to her rude cottage. "Truly, Tala ap Griffin, I am no help to you. Venn is of royal blood, chosen for his fate by that blood. We cannot change it. Not you or I. He will be happy in the Other World."

Tala dropped to her knees before the old woman and gripped her gnarled fingers between her hands. "Mother Wren, I love my brother. I have cared for him since he was a very little boy. I cannot let him go to the otherworld, not even if by doing that his sacrifice will save this world of mine. My life will be empty without him…as it would be without Lacey and Audrey and Gwynnth. They are all the blood I have left. They are my life, my heart, my soul."

"There, there," Mother Wren said, pulling her hands free so she could console her. "Marrying the Viking need

not end your world. The Dane is strong hearted. 'Haps he
can protect what you cannot.''

"Don't tell me to do foolish things, like accepting a
black Viking for a husband. Help me find a way to stem
the flow of change. If the Vikings could be turned back to
the Avon, then Venn could take his rightful place in this
domain. Venn is Leam's last true son. Think you of what
it would mean if he lived a full measure of years and had
sons of his own.''

"Aye.'' Old Mother Wren nodded. "He is the last of
our kings. No more and no less deserving of a long full
life than the first king to pick up a club and make all obey
him. I do not know what to tell you, child. You must seek
your answers from souls wiser than I.''

"Aye," Tala said. *But who?* she asked herself on the
long walk home through the forest in the dark of night.

The old gods did not appear to Tala. Years had passed
since the old temple in the clearing had appeared to her as
the legendary Citadel of Glass. She saw it now as only a
vitrified stone hall, emptied of its former greatness and
mysticism by the changing times.

It was not yet dawn when Tala reached the lake. She
walked far out onto the stone causeway until she stood
with water completely surrounding her. The sky was clear,
full of its fading stars. A blue, waxing moon hung low in
the western sky, its pale orb reflected a thousand times in
the tiny waves on the still, dark lake.

The water moved as it always did, with strange currents
skating from bank to bank. Swells rose midlake and ran
off to flood the fens. Whirlpools churned, then abruptly
ceased, and the black water went as flat as a griddle. There
were none alive who could divine the portends of the lake.
In ages past, the princesses of Leam could interpret each
omen they witnessed. But Tala couldn't.

The only power that had come down to her generation

was the ability to find water in dry earth. The chain of knowledge had been broken with the coming of the monks.

But it was an unheard-of catastrophe for no rain to fall between Beltane and Lughnasa. The three most fertile months of the growing season had so far passed without a drop of rain to replenish the rivers and streams.

And that tragedy had opened the ancestral mind of the people of Leam. They remembered the old rituals and sacrifices that had saved their land long years ago.

Like Tala, Venn and Mother Wren, every remaining soul born of Leam knew that if no rain fell between today and August 1, the only thing that would save them was the blood sacrifice of the atheling of Leam. The feast of the first fruits—Lughnasa—was Leam's last chance to redeem the gods' favor.

If they ignored the dire predictions of the past, in less than a generation they would all be dead.

In the fat years recently past, the ritual had dwindled to sacrificing the first grains and fruits gleaned from the fields, as a symbolic offering to guarantee the harvest. In years of dire tribulation such as this, only the sacrifice of the first blood—the son of the king or the king himself—could appease the angry gods.

Venn was the atheling of Leam. Only he could end the drought. Only his blood and body offered in sacrifice could guarantee Leam's survival past this year. That fact may as well be written in stone. Everyone knew it as truth. Venn's only salvation was rain. Plentiful rain falling in the days left in July was the only means to avert Venn's early and untimely death.

Tala had no more faith in the old ways than she had trust in the new. She didn't believe her only brother's death would bring on the rain. She didn't believe the old druid Tegwin had the power to work such magic. In her heart she believed that Venn's sacrifice would change nothing.

He would give his life and the drought would continue, unabated by divine intervention.

Tala knew even less about the new god, this Christ that her guardian, King Alfred, revered. But she knew he must be powerful if King Guthrum was willing to put his people to death if they did not accept the talisman of the cross.

If only there was someone wise and knowing she could talk to who could explain all of this to her. But she had no one. She had only this ancient lake of her ancestors, the silent spirits hidden in its depths and the confusion of her thoughts.

She prayed hard, pouring out her troubles to the Lady of the Lake. Tala sought insight and clarity, hope and solace. To make certain her desperate petition was heard, she removed her gold torque from her throat. Prayers without a sacrificial offering were an abomination to the gods.

"Lady, I beseech you. Give me a sign. Show me what I must do to save my brother's life. He is just a boy, a puny man-child of no value to you. Venn cannot bring the rain, make the seeds sprout in your earth or hold the mighty Vikings behind your river Avon. His thin body will not feed your fish for more than a day. So why must he be taken from me? I need him. I love him. Take this torque and forget my little brother. You'll be much happier with the gold."

Tala extended her torque over the water. She held her breath, waiting for the Lady of the Lake to rise up from the water and accept her offering.

The dark water at her feet moved, then churned as if gathering power. A shadowy form broke the surface at Tala's feet, throwing silvery drops onto her bare legs and breaking up the reflection of her golden torque. Her eyes followed the dark wake that bisected the still waters and her heart hammered in her throat. This was what she sought—a sign.

The fluid tension of the surface erupted in a blinding,

foamy arc of silvery water beads. Tala threw her golden torque at the breaking wave. The ring of gold spun far, far out over the black water.

A pale limb shot up from a bank of waterweeds. It snatched the gold torque in midair and splashed below the surface.

Ripples washed quickly back to the pier where Tala stood. The lake undulated softly, then stilled once more. And Tala ap Griffin burst into tears.

The precious golden torque that had declared her a princess to all of her people—that she was willing to sacrifice for the life of her brother—had been snapped out of the air not by the Lady of the Lake, but by a fish.

Chapter Five

The granary was first on Edon's scheduled tour with Embla Silver Throat the next morning. He found the dusty building well stocked and dry. All provisions stored in barrels and well-constructed crates were in good shape. Ample seed was put aside for next year's planting. Edon was a stickler for such details and always insisted upon holding back more than necessary.

Best of all, the granary was clean and rat free. Varmints were kept at bay by having numerous good mousers where they were most needed.

The deep well sunk in the center of the stockade and the one inside the keep were rank and fetid. Water for all purposes had to be carried from the Avon River, outside the gates of the fortress. The river itself had dropped five feet below the lip of the gate built to flood the moat surrounding the fortress on the deliberately raised motte of Warwick.

The absence of water in the deep moat to put out an assaulting enemy's fire made Embla Silver Throat's wooden stockade even more ridiculous, especially with so much ready stone about. Edon couldn't see how she could be so dense. And in her greed to acquire more and more land, she allowed her freemen to continue to slash and burn the woods, when the land was dry tinder!

His second order of business that morning was to stop the felling of the woods. Edon had already outlawed all fires save the cooking fires in the fortress kitchen, the hearth fires in each Viking's longhouse and the forge in the ironmaster's shed.

The stillroom wasn't as cool as it should be. Cool meant icy to a Viking, and Edon was typical in that regard. The room was located at the bottom of a declivity cut into the hill. The spring beneath had also run dry because of the drought.

The groove cut in the stone floor of the stillroom, where normally chilly water from the spring should flow freely, was covered with a layer of moss. Edon used his knife to dislodge it. His reward for that effort was a few beads of water.

He squinted in the dim light of the underground stillroom. Was it smaller than he remembered? Ten years was a long time to recall details.

"This is unusual. Springs of this sort rarely dry up," he remarked casually.

"Aye," Embla agreed testily. "Warwick's wells churn out nothing but poison or dust, thanks to the witch."

Here we go again, Edon thought. He remained on one knee, studying the chamber carved into the bedrock. The stillroom retained some but not much dampness, a quality necessary for the preservation of meats and vegetables. The trench in the floor had no pools in it, though it should. "Did you enlarge this chamber, niece?"

Embla started, surprised by his question. "No, it is as it was. I saw no need to improve it," she said gruffly.

"Thank you," Edon said.

He'd built the stillroom himself ten years ago, when he'd chosen Warwick as his home. It was curious. Rivers might alter their course, but in his experience, waters in the bedrock rarely did.

He rose to his feet, brushing off his hands. "I'd like to see the quarry next."

On their way to the granite quarry, they encountered Embla's soldiers riding out for their daily patrol. Edon spoke to the captain of his nephew Harald's disappearance. When Asgart replied, he talked of Harald in the past tense. Edon noted that.

Of course, Guthrum had told him what he believed had happened to their nephew. Edon did not want to accuse Lady Embla of murdering her husband without proof. That proof might only show up in the form of his nephew's body. Edon intended to investigate the matter thoroughly.

The truth would out eventually.

He spent the morning at the quarry, making careful notations on the drawings Maynard the Black prepared for him. Embla disdained to discuss anything with Maynard, even though he was obviously trusted by the jarl. She thought all Mercians fit only to be thralls and therefore unworthy of conversing with her. Edon was glad when the woman walked off to another part of the quarry.

"Do you see any indication of the work here at the quarry having any effect on the springs under the cliffs?"

"None, my lord," Maynard said somberly. He was always somber. Maynard dwelt in concrete reality and predictable certainties.

"And what do you make of three wells and two springs on Warwick Hill gone dry as yesterday's cake?"

Maynard shook his head. "It defies explanation, but proof of the drought is abundant. There has been no rain since the first of May, I am told. Each of the rivers we crossed in coming from Anglia were low. Low, but not empty, lord."

"And what do you make of the Leam?" Edon leaned on a rock and gazed over the forest. In the distant wood, the sun glistened and sparkled on the canopy of trees, lighting them with silver. The riverbed that meandered east toward Willoughby could be traced by the march of brown, dying trees lining its dry bank.

"Were I a gambling man," Maynard said cautiously, "I would wager someone has damned the Leam or diverted it. A river that size does not dry up in a year of no rain. Perhaps when the rains come, the springs will flow."

"You believe there must be rain above the earth for water to flow over it? How do you account for the vast quantity of water in the seas? Rock and soil are porous. Wouldn't you assume the sea presses against its shores and seeps underneath? It does not rain in Syria, yet we have both drunk from springs as sweet and as pure as fresh rain. Remember how good the water in Petra tasted to us?"

"I remember." Maynard nodded. His prominent forehead furrowed in deep ridges. "What we need is a water diviner. There were many such among the druids in years past."

"A good idea. I shall make inquiries of the Mercians. Now, let us walk to the top of the cliff and have a good look over the valley. Perhaps we can trace the watercourses from the highest mount."

"An eagle would be the best mount," Maynard suggested dryly. It was the closest he'd ever come to making a joke.

When they finished viewing Warwick valley from the highest pinnacle, Edon left Maynard to his work of plotting and mapping. The jarl strolled down into the quarry and stood beside Embla, watching her laborers toil in the pit.

Huge slabs of granite were cleanly split from the rim of the crater using the time-honored tools of fire and water. The slabs were then chiseled into quarter-ton blocks, suitable for the walls of Edon's fortress and keep.

"I don't believe I saw buildings enough at your compound to house this many stonecutters." Edon made a casual observation. It seemed ludicrous to him to consider the woman his niece when she was at least five years older than he. "Are there barracks nearby?"

"Stonecutters?" Embla countered, looking surprised by the question. "These are not the skilled masons you hired, sire. They are thralls, slaves taken in conquest of the land."

"Then let me put my question another way. Where do yonder thralls sleep?"

"There." Embla pointed to a cave in the pit.

A yawning chasm gouged out of the earth provided little shelter from the elements for the men forced to work in the quarry. They were a sorry lot, to Edon's eye.

As a commodity, slaves were as important to a large holding as its cattle, and should be as well fed and well cared for. Clearly, Embla was not of the same opinion as he about many things. Her slaves labored endlessly to the crack and rhythm of a whip. Judging from the look of their thin bodies, their food was at subsistence level.

"I see," Edon said. "Then you have more slaves tending the fields, do you?"

"Nay, the freemen have that right. Surely, Lord Edon, you have not been so long in the east that you forgot the ways of your own world?"

"No, I'm just curious about the changes here. I recall no slaves on Harald Jorgensson's last accounting, and I am new to this wergild that Guthrum has imposed."

Embla ignored the scold inherent in Edon's words. She had her scribe making the accounts ready for his immediate inspection. She would prove him in error about her there, too. She could account for every gold mark put into and taken out of the jarl's holding much better than stupid Harald ever could have. He would have given one-tenth of everything away as a tithe!

By her reckoning, the long-absent owner, Jarl Edon Halfdansson, had always made a handsome profit off her farmstead and his shire. A profit that by rights she should have kept, for it was her labor at overseeing all the work that accomplished any gain.

"The kings' wergild takes some getting used to," Embla granted. "The truth is it has little effect in a frontier where Watling Street peters out in yon miserable haunted wood. King Guthrum thinks his road an open avenue from London to Chester, but north of Warwick it comes to naught. As for the Mercians, they stay out of my way or else pay dearly for entering Warwick."

"These men—" Edon pointed to the pit "—are Mercians paying your dear price?"

"Aye. A pity they are so weak they die quickly. But there is a goodly supply, for they breed endlessly and are stupid as horses. My patrols easily replenish their numbers."

"Pray tell me what you do with women so foolish as to walk on Watling Street?"

Embla answered his appalled question without batting an eye. "There is work in the kitchens and at the looms or at whatever task they are assigned. I have found it expedient to give my thanes free use of captured Mercian women. It keeps them better controlled, and I have heard no complaints from my soldiers regarding that."

"No, I imagine you haven't," Edon murmured. "I can't help but remark upon the fact that I saw no Mercian farmsteads as I crossed the shire. There were as many Mercians as Saxons here when last I visited. Danes were the oddity. I had to pay a very high price to acquire the rights to Warwick Hill."

"Only Danes may be tenants in the Danelaw, my lord. That is Guthrum's law."

Edon thought it pointless to discuss Guthrum's law with this wife of his nephew. Her interpretation and his would never match. "I suggest we table a discussion of politics

until evening. Nothing is to be changed until I have toured
the tin and silver mines. We will do that tomorrow.''

Edon met Rig on his way down from the quarry. His
general's face was twisted with anger, his large jaw thrust
forward. Edon could tell he was grinding his teeth to keep
from cursing a blue streak. Edon dismounted and handed
Titan's reins to a stable boy. ''What has happened? Don't
spare me the news.''

''The village of Wootton is on fire.'' Rig answered in a
clipped voice. A fire of a different sort burned in his cool
blue eyes.

''How so?'' Edon asked, tamping down the alarm that
started in his chest. Tala was at Wootton...in Mother
Wren's cottage.

''I went to fetch the atheling as you commanded, lord.''
Rig spun on one heel and pointed to a group of four Vikings leaning on their axes in the shade of the ironmon-
ger's shed. Their faces were contorted with anger, matching Rig's. ''They went to Wootton to cut wood, against
your command of this morn.''

''What of Mother Wren?'' Edon asked, feeling a chill
squeeze his heart. Tala would have been sleeping in
Wren's cottage.

''Asgart claims the villagers fled into the forest. They
captured none of them, not even the old woman.''

That bit of good news relieved Edon's worries somewhat. Then Rig squared his shoulders and gave him the
rest of his news. ''The cottage where you left the princess
of Leam in the care of the old woman was empty when I
got to Wootton to inspect the fire's damage. There was no
proof that anyone was living in that abode.''

''What?'' Edon said, confused.

''I found a chest containing the lady's clothing, and her
jewels among the smoking ashes, lord. I have put it in your
keep. But that was all I found worth retrieving. There were

no furnishings or cooking pots or beds of any kind. I fear you have been tricked, lord. The princess of Leam does not live in the village of Wootton.''

''Humph!'' Edon grunted as he crossed the ward to the ironmaster's shed. So much for his plan of visiting his bride in the evening ahead. The little minx had done him in. He turned his thoughts to the problem of the burned village and the Vikings who'd disobeyed his orders. Tala would have to wait.

The Vikings were newcomers to Warwick. They were refugees from Lombardy, Danes that had been trapped in the terrible famine that had racked province after province on the Continent. Edon looked from one wary face to the other and elected the eldest of the four as their leader. ''Did you not hear my orders this morn, Viking?''

''Aye, lord, we heard you.'' The man stood his ground on crooked legs, bowed from starvation. ''I am known here as Archam the Bent. I am responsible for the fire, not my sons.''

''Why did you disobey my order?''

The four men exchanged glances. ''Our holding begins at Wootton Wood,'' the youngest answered. ''Father, tell the jarl the truth, else he will have all of our heads up on stakes.''

''Be quiet, Ranulf,'' said a brother.

''Are these your sons, Viking?'' Edon directed his words to the elder. His grizzled head rocked up and down in affirmation. Edon could not place his age; his face and throat were too wrinkled and worn by the sun and wind and the loss of a great deal of weight.

''They are each my son. Once I had ten sons all as straight and tall as you. These three are all I have left.''

''Then why would you endanger them by going against my orders?'' Edon demanded. When no answer came, he turned to Rig and commanded, ''Take the eldest beyond the palisade and cut off his head.''

All four Vikings started as Rig and his soldiers stepped forward instantly to carry out Edon's command.

"My lord!" the youngest protested, struggling to protect his brother. "We had no choice in burning the village. Asgart told us to clear the village land and plant it today. It was the only hide he would spare us."

"Aye." The father broke his proud silence, speaking from desperation. "We must plant our field now, else there will be no grain in our larder this winter. Midsummer is past."

"When did you arrive in Warwick?"

"Last full moon, Jarl Edon," said the youngest son. "We were just given our land assignment this rising."

And from the look of them, a month ago they could not have swung an axe, any one of them. "How many are you? Wives, children and thralls?" Edon asked.

"We four survived the journey overland and the voyage, lord," said the father.

"Who showed you where your holding was and gave you leave to burn your fields today?"

"Asgart of Wolverton rode out to the woodland with us and said we could plow from the top of the hill to the first stream behind the village. It was all the land there was to spare. He said to burn the cottages in our way, for the people inside were only squatters."

"We didn't want to burn them out, Lord Edon." The eldest son finally spoke in his own defense. "Lord Asgart told my father to burn the huts or else to move north to York and ask for a hide of land from someone else."

Edon was not surprised by that answer. He turned to Rig and said, "Send Thorulf to fetch Asgart. I will deal with him."

These men were being used, victimized, as were the Mercian thralls in the quarry. Edon's quarrel was not with them. Still, they had started a fire that cost a village, and someone must pay. Edon glared at all four of them and came to a summary judgment on the spot. "My man Maynard has surveyed the shire and parceled it as to my orders. There is good land, cleared and ready for planting, east of the quarry. Three of you may farm there beginning on the morrow. You, Ranulf, will pay for the damage done the village of Wootton by two months service to my general, Rig. Give your axe to your father. You will have no need of a weapon until you are released to your father's house at the end of your duty."

Edon turned to the father, asking, "Have you a longhouse, Archam the Bent?"

"Nay, we sleep under the stars. We will build a longhouse when we have land."

"Rig, take the father to Maynard. You will go to my man, Maynard the Black. He will show you the fields you may work and issue you seed to plant in your field. Do not fell any trees that you cannot use for your longhouse. I will tolerate no more fires in this shire, is that clear?"

Gratitude was not a common virtue displayed among Vikings, but these men were clearly grateful for Edon's leniency. Archam and his sons were not the type of Vikings that had gone out seeking fortunes and land forty years ago with Edon's grandfather, Ragnar Lodbok. These Vikings had been farmers all their lives. If it came to battling with axe and sword they would be hard-pressed to defend their own, much less be of good service to Edon in a war.

That was the reason he took the healthiest son into his household to be trained in weapons and fighting by Rig. Instinctively, Edon knew where the real challenge to his authority came from: Asgart, Embla's man.

It was time for the jarl of Warwick to assert his authority. Sighing, Edon dismissed the offenders. He went up to his keep and visited with his ladies and conferred with Theo, allowing him to use his mazer bowl on this occasion.

"I wish to know when it will rain and where I may find

the princess of Leam, Theo. Do not distract me with unnecessary communications from your playful spirit guides.''

Theo's fingers ran lightly around the rim of the gold cup, which hummed in a pure, sweet tone. Theo's strange, colorless eyes gazed, as they always did, off into the distance. All at once his fingers ceased circling and he dipped the tips of two into the quavering wine, silencing the melodious sound.

''Your princesses of Leam are in King Offa's hunting lodge on the bank of their lake. There are four of them. The eldest is your lady, Tala. I see her quite clearly. She is pacing back and forth and contemplates a journey. I cannot see where. She has sacrificed her torque, and her sisters are greatly distressed by that. Ah, I have it. Tala ap Griffin goes to the abbess at Loytcoyt.''

''And the atheling?'' Edon probed.

Theo shook his head. ''I cannot see the atheling. Nor do I see any rain. Not for a long time to come.''

Edon kept his fingers from drumming a staccato on the trestle top. So Tala went to the abbess at Loytcoyt, did she? Did she intend to throw herself upon the mercy of Alfred's church and beg sanctuary of the nuns? What good would that do her? Edon had no qualms about removing her from a Christian church any more than he had qualms about taking a pagan princess of Leam to wife.

''Are you certain she goes to the abbey?''

''Aye.'' Theo nodded, then frowned. ''But....''

''Well...out with it, man!''

''King Alfred comes to see her wed.''

''So now the king of Wessex comes to Warwick? Why not Guthrum as well?'' Edon scoffed.

''They both will attend the vows, Lord Edon.'' Theo picked up the goblet and consumed every drop of the white wine in its bowl, ending his reading.

Lady Eloya had remained quiet and still for the reading.

Now she rose to her feet from the bench at the end of the trestle and moved behind Edon's chair, placing her hands upon his shoulders. "Lord Edon, if you could see your face, you would be terrified by your own expression. I pity the princess when you find her."

As Eloya's hands soothed the taut muscles in Edon's neck he made a concerted effort to staunch the flow of bile churning in his stomach. He knew of the abbey at Loytcoyt. It had been built upon the bloodiest battleground he had ever seen with his own two eyes. The bodies of hundreds of Celts had formed the rubble for the abbey's foundation. The bones belonged to pagans who had refused to convert to the new religion. Heathens like Edon himself had been up till now.

Periodically this new church that preached a gospel of peace and love stirred its believers into a furor and led them in a holy war to slay all nonbelievers. Edon had escaped from Loytcoyt with his life, but not so many unbaptized Mercians of Arden Forest.

On his foreign travels, amid people like Eli and Theo and Rashid, Edon had found his own philosophy, reinforcing his core belief that life continued in spirit after death. Unlike his brother Guthrum, Edon was not quite ready to replace his host of childhood gods—Odin, Freya, Thor and Loki—for the Christian's Christ. But his travels had brought him to the point where he recognized his capricious Viking gods were not the Supreme Being. And he was pragmatic enough to keep an open mind, particularly when it was politically expedient to do so.

He reached up and patted Eloya's hand. "Thank you, love, for soothing me. I have duties to attend. Rashid, we will need your services in the ward shortly."

"Edon?" Eloya kept her hands on his shoulders. "Do not set out tracking the lady like she is a doe to be brought to ground. Give Tala time to accept her fate. She will come to love you as we all have, each in our own way."

"Eloya," Edon said impatiently, "I know what I am about. Do not tutor me as though I were still a boy in your father's court, lacking all manners or intelligence."

He stood and gathered his weapons from the sideboard, where they lay gleaming from the polish Eli had applied to them. "I will take Sarina with me," he said to his servant.

"Do you think that truly wise?" Eloya gently insisted.

"Eloya!" Edon said sharply. She gave him a chiding look, then turned to her husband, impatience with Edon radiating from her slanted sloe eyes. "Rashid, it is past time that you do something about your interfering wife," Edon continued.

Rashid paused over the medicines and unguents in his physician's casket. He, too, cast a disapproving glance at his wife of twenty years.

Eloya shrugged a pretty shoulder, undaunted by either man's scolding. "The princess will not thank you for hunting her like prey in the woods. You will want her to love Sarina in the future, not hate her.

Moving on to a more feminine task, that of sewing a smock for the new baby, Eloya settled in a chaise beside Rebecca. She ignored the men up to the point when they were armed and prepared to exit the hall.

"We will have dinner at the usual time, my lords. See that you are not late."

Chapter Six

Edon did not go out tracking Tala ap Griffin. There were too many other things that had to be done to get his holding started on the road to prosperity and civility.

Edon reestablished the guard, replacing all of Embla's captains with men of his own. The first Viking who resisted—Asgart—paid for that foolhardy transgression against Edon's authority with his life.

Edon had other reasons to slay Asgart besides his stupidity in challenging him before the assembled Vikings inside the walls of Warwick. There was the village of Wootton that had been torched—deliberately. Asgart admitted he'd ordered the burning as a sly means of flushing the princess of Leam out of hiding.

After besting Asgart in a bloody contest of swords, Edon pressed his blade to his throat and gave the man one last chance to redeem himself. "Where is the body of my nephew, Harald Jorgensson? Tell me where his bones are buried and I will spare your life."

"He is not dead yet, Jarl, but you are!" Asgart lunged sideways and plunged his sword at Edon's heart. Deflecting the blow with a powerful swing, Edon sliced the thane's head off his shoulders and sent it rolling in the dust of the ward.

Asgart's thanes looked at Edon with new respect when he calmly handed Rig his sword and walked off the field of contest to the bathhouse. The thanes gathered quickly after the fight ended, talking among themselves, deciding what they should do.

As Edon came out of the bathhouse they confronted him in the stronghold's ward.

"Jarl Edon." Their spokesman stepped forward, dropped his knee to the ground and extended the hilt of his long sword. "I am Carl Redbeard of York. Jarl Harald came to York before Lammas past and promised my men and I land and fair treatment for all Danes willing to risk the frontier.

"Your nephew, Jarl Harald Jorgensson, was a good man. He was not here when we arrived with our wives and children at Samhain. We are loyal men of Guthrum of the Danelaw. None of us know what became of the jarl. We are strong warriors as well, but we will not fight without just cause."

Edon studied the man before him, then put his hand on the hilt of the Viking's sword. "Do you swear never to raise your arm against me or mine, Carl of York?"

"Aye, Wolf of Warwick. On the blood of my three sons, I am yours to command," the soldier swore.

"Then rise, Carl of York, and go about your business. Report to my captain, Thorulf, in the morning for any change in your duties. The same applies to the rest of your men. We are at peace in Warwick and shall remain so unless King Guthrum declares otherwise. Good night."

Edon retired to his keep to take his supper.

Embla rode into the ward from the far fields at sunset and found a new order established within Warwick. New guards manned the gates of the palisade. A new captain saluted her, and the thrall who took her horse and stabled it she had never laid eyes upon before. Asgart's body lay upon a bier on the muddy bank of the Avon. Her captain's head rested on his shield.

Shaken, she charged into Edon's hall breathing fire. She found the lazy wretch at his damned board, devouring a chicken at his leisure.

"How dare you!" she shouted. "By what right do you come here, changing my guard at the gates in the middle of the day, ordering my men about, killing my soldiers? How dare you!"

She got as far as drawing her blade from her sheath before Rig jumped from his seat at Edon's table and knocked the sword cleanly from her hand with one sweep of his mighty fist. "Lady, you will curb your tongue before the jarl of Warwick," he commanded in a low, feral voice, "else get you to your hut and your loom."

Embla's breath hissed between her teeth. "You will pay for that, Rig of Sunderland." But her venom was saved for Edon. "Come, you mincing coward, I will fight you for this land Guthrum has promised me. I will show you who is the better between us."

Edon casually dropped a bone onto a porcelain platter and drew in a weary breath. "Let her go, Rig. She's just making empty threats. She has come to her senses, haven't you, niece of Guthrum of the Danelaw?"

"I'm not afraid of you," Embla shouted. "You have no real power in this shire. Listen, all of you. I have been wronged. My captain, Asgart, was a good man, loyal and true, worth the value of ten soldiers. You killed him, Edon of Warwick, and for that you must pay me a wergild."

"Ah, so such things mean something to you, do they, Embla of the Silver Throat?" Edon wiped his fingertips with a fine linen cloth, dampened with scented water. Then he rose to his feet and waited as his body servant, Eli, handed him his shield and his sword to put in his scabbard. He tested the weight in his bare hand, then looked coldly at his niece by marriage. "What value do you place on a Mercian thrall?"

"Mercian thralls have no value. They are dust beneath our feet. We are Vikings—Danes! Only freemen deserve wergild in the Danelaw."

"Very well then. Give me your value for a freeman in the Danelaw," Edon demanded as he slotted the sword in its sheath with a snap.

Embla's lip curled in disgust at Edon's Viking trappings—sword and shield, crossgartered boots and breeks sheathing his hips and thighs like a second skin. His bare chest glistened with power. His fierce face and dark coloring spoke of foreign savagery unseen in the Danelaw, but inside he was a coward, a peacemaker, a man of words, not action. Did he think her stupid? She would play his game and best him.

"A freeman is valued at five marks if he holds a tenancy, ten if he is a skilled craftman, iron worker or smith. Fifteen if he serves as a warrior to a thane, twenty if he is a Viking and mans his own oar."

"So..." Edon sighed ever so casually. He looked at his fingertips, as if thinking they needed cleaning. Embla's sneer became a growl.

"I have a claim laid before me for twenty such freemen," he said, looking up at her. "Lo and behold, I found every man at the quarry. Men who until this very evening were chained thralls in *my* quarry. I have also freed their wives and children. In fact, there are no longer any slaves in Warwick. None."

"You can't do that!" Embla shouted.

"It is already done," Edon countered without raising his voice. "The wives are gathering in my lower hall as we speak, reunited with their husbands. Do you care to go below with me, Embla Silver Throat, and listen to these men give testimony to my scribes? They are freely accounting for their crimes. Crimes that caused the forfeiture of their livelihoods and the loss of their homes, the enslavement of their wives and the murder of their children.''

"There are only outlaws from Mercia in my quarry," Embla cried in fury.

Edon's jaw set as he glared at the woman. She didn't get it. Perhaps she never would.

"You are a fool," he declared tersely. "*We are in Mercia,* damn you! Watling Street is five leagues east of Warwick! You are the one who has broken the law, angered the kings, and *I* am the one who must pay the blood price for your stupidity. Get out of my sight, before I change my mind and slit your throat!''

Embla's mouth tightened. She breathed harshly, returning the angry jarl's glare. "Who would you pay a wergild to, Lord Edon? There are no thanes of Leam remaining to lay claim to the fee. They are all dead.''

With lethal sarcasm, Edon told her, "Correct. You have wisely slain all of your enemies save one, the atheling of Leam, Prince Venn ap Griffin, ward of Alfred of Wessex.''

"No!" Embla shook her head vehemently. "The boy is dead. He was sacrificed by the druid, Tegwin. On the first of May, when the fires were lit on the hilltops, the druids slew him, as a gift to their gods to bring the spring rains to the land.''

"Has it rained since?" Edon asked bluntly.

"Nay, it has not rained in nearly a full year," Embla argued desperately. She had paid the druid good coin to slay the boy. Now this jarl intimated that the job had not been done. Had she walked into a pit of snakes? The jarl was a Viking who would not act like a Viking. What did he care for thralls or athelings, dead or alive?

"Then it is obvious, is it not?" Edon thundered, staggering Embla with the power he unleashed in his voice. "That prince was not sacrificed. Odin help me, but you are a stupid cow if you can't have reasoned that much out. The wergild will be paid, but take care, niece, I am yet of a mind to take the cost of it out of your hide. Good day, Embla. Do as Rig commands—confine yourself to the looms in your longhouse—and *do not meddle in my affairs again.*"

From the cliff overlooking the quarry, Edon could see the hidden lake in the forest only at precisely high noon. The glint of water in the distance was the closest he got to Tala ap Griffin. He had no way to relieve himself with the certain knowledge that she was indeed all right after the fire at Wootton except to go to the lake itself.

The body of water cast a sparkling reflection up into the oaks that surrounded the lake. That made them shimmer and a curious golden glow radiate from the dark, distant woods.

Even with that proof before them, not one thrall—or more specifically, not one of Embla's thralls—would admit to there being any significance to the lake. To a one they pleaded ignorance of any holy well or sacred pool in the vicinity.

Edon knew that for a lie. Ten years ago he had wandered these woods and found the lake and its myriad of spring-fed pools. He remembered a hunting lodge on the lake's bank and a mysterious, fairylike temple of stunning beauty.

All he'd cared for at the time was that the fishing had been good and the water cool and refreshing for bathing and swimming. Back then, when he was a young man of ten and nine, he would have given a year of his life to have had a desirable woman with him at that lake. He would have spent the whole day lolling in the water and making love.

Edon also remembered Arden Wood as being splendidly managed. Its undergrowth had been well trimmed, the trees coped, and the trails and pathways were clear of brush. But when he came down from the heights of Warwick Hill and began trekking through the enormous wood, searching for the lake, he spent most of a beastly hot afternoon wandering in hopeless circles.

Arden Forest was no longer a hunter's delight. It was an eerie, vast, overgrown and untended copse. Omens abounded and swung from its canopy—skulls and crossbones and evil eyes that warned away intruders. Traps and snares were set to capture the unwary. Whole sections had become impenetrable because of the density of briars and thorn bushes. The purpose of such devices was obvious: intruders were not welcome.

Inside the forest depths, Edon found it impossible to pick a direction, to locate a path, to march straight in or out or to find the lake at the center. That was a humbling, frustrating and baffling experience for him. Edon of Warwick had sailed all the known seas and navigated his way through relentless storms. He'd stood on the paved streets of Athens and walked in the shadow of the great pyramids of Cleopatra's ancestors. But he could not find the lake in the center of his own home wood.

Not even Sarina with her sensitive nose could track the princess's trail beyond the first beck crossing Fosse Way outside the stockade at Warwick. Edon needed a piece of the lady's clothing to fix the woman's scent in Sarina's capable brain. Foiled and frustrated, he returned to Warwick at sundown in a foul mood.

Rashid and Eli greeted him in the lower hall, which had become a gathering point for Edon's soldiers and captains.

"Any luck, my lord Wolf?" Eli asked, offering Edon a towel to wipe the sweat from his face and throat and a goblet of fruited wine to quench his thirst.

"None," Edon admitted, wearily handing Sarina's lead to Rashid. The wolfhound was tame and loyal, but she made the children of Warwick anxious, so Edon leashed her at the gates.

He drank the cool drink, finishing it at once, and then wiped his face and neck with the towel. "It is miserable

in the forest," he said to his men. "The gallflies swarm
and bite most viciously. A host of stinging ants inhabit the
grasses. Every fifth step there is a rotting limb hidden under the blanket of ferns, lying in wait to break a leg. That
forest has changed greatly since I last walked it ten years
ago. And I believe the changes have been deliberately
made."

"I thought as much." Rashid stood fast against Sarina's
front paws pressing on his shoulders, ruffling her ears and
scratching the thick mat of gray fur at her throat. On her
hindquarters, the wolfhound stood as tall as the man loving
her, her busy tail whacking the flagstones in pleasure.
"Down, Sarina. You have cockleburs and stickers in your
fur. I shall have to bathe and brush you, eh?"

Edon stooped to pick a handful of burrs from between
the lacing of his crossgarters. "What of the bathhouse?
Have we one adequate for our use yet?"

"Nay, lord," Eli replied. "Maynard is working on the
aqueduct with all due haste. But the river is so low it will
be another day before the water can be diverted from it. I
have drawn fresh water, heated and toted it upstairs, and
the wooden tub is full and awaits your leisure."

Edon shed his sweat-soaked tunic and used the towel to
wipe his chest and back. "I fear I smell as foul as a lath-
ered warhorse. Words cannot describe how beastly the heat
is in those woods. The steamy air presses down on you
leaching all the salts in your body. To whit, I got lost.
North was south, east became west. I couldn't see even a
scrap of the sky."

"So you didn't find the lake." Rashid walked Sarina to
the steps and released her with a command to go upstairs.

"I never came close enough to smell mud," Edon admitted.

"Perhaps you started from the wrong point," Rashid
mused.

"What point do you suggest I try? For I have limited

days to bring a princess to heel before King Alfred arrives to witness the ceremony. He will be here Saturday.'' Edon sat and began unlacing his leggings.

"At the wadi," Rashid replied. "It is dry, yes, but it once ran full of water. It seems logical that the dry river should lead you to the lake."

"Assuming that the lake is the source of the river, yes. Suppose it isn't?" Edon reasoned. "What then? Cut a straight line through the forest, chop my way to the heart of it by slashing down the trees? How long will that take? More days than I have, I'm certain."

Eli cleared his throat. Rashid lifted his shoulders in a shrug. Who could answer the Wolf of Warwick's questions? Neither of them.

Edon nodded, also stumped by the conundrum. "If all else fails, I'll still have that bath, Eli."

"As you wish, lord." Eli grinned, pleased to hear a request that he could accomplish with alacrity.

"Tala, Tala! Look what we have found!" Lacey and Audrey ran up the grassy path to Tala's pool, their voices high with the excitement of a new discovery. They burst into the clearing where Tala had gone to bathe in private, each carrying a bundle in their arms.

"What is it?" Tala quickly got to her feet, dressed in a sparkling clean gown, her wet hair hanging down her back, alarmed at what news the twins were bringing. "Is there something wrong? Are you hurt, my darlings?"

"Oh, no, Tala. Look what Lacey and I found in the woods this morning. Aren't they the most beautiful animals you've ever seen in your life?"

Each golden-haired twin opened a soft flannel in her arms and revealed a small, white-furred animal shaking against the wadded cloth pressed to her unformed chest.

Tala frowned as she sank to one knee between the twins. "What kind of an animal is it?"

"I don't know," Lacey said solemnly. "Audrey doesn't, either. We've never seen such a beast. But Tala, they're so sweet and soft. Touch this one."

"You can hold mine." Audrey lifted her animal up by its very long ears and put it in Tala's hands.

Tala inhaled, surprised by the tiny creature's lack of weight and its incredible softness. It was no bigger than a kitten. "Why, it's a tiny ball of fur. Where did it come from?"

"I don't know that, either," Audrey declared. Lacey nodded in agreement. "But they are ever so dear, and twins, too, just like me and Lacey. We can't tell them apart."

"It isn't a kitten or a puppy, but it is a baby. Oh, see how it wiggles its nose." Tala rubbed the white animal against her cheek and crooned, "Oh, it's sweet. Do you know what direction it came from? Tachbrook or Warwick?"

"No," the twins said in unison. "They move funny." Then the girls giggled and shouted together. "They hop. Hop, hop, hop!"

"Tegwin said we had to sacrifice them to Lugh at the feast of the first fruits," Audrey said matter-of-factly. "He says that is why they were found at the lake. We don't have to sacrifice them, do we, Tala? I've never seen a creature like this and neither has old Anna or Venn or Selwyn. I want to keep them."

"Yes, please, can we keep them?" Lacey pleaded.

"Wait just a moment." Tala held up both hands, begging for peace. "I don't even know what kind of animal this is. Why, it could grow to be ferocious and huge."

"Nothing this tiny could grow up to be ferocious. We will train them," Audrey argued. "Isn't that right, Lacey?"

"We'll feed them and take them for walks in the forest and clean up any mess they make. We promise, Tala.

Please! Don't let Tegwin take them to the altar over the fens. The Lady of the Lake has your torque now. She doesn't need these little animals. Tegwin's just mean.''

"Hush now. You're not drawing me into that argument before I've had a chance to even think, my ladies. First we must learn more about this animal, what it is, what it eats and how big it gets when it is fully grown. I will not make any decision before I know the facts.''

"Oh, thank you!'' Lacey threw one arm around Tala's shoulders, hugging her. Then she thrust her furry creature in her sister's face. "Give Tala a kiss, Honey.''

"You can't name yours Honey. That's what I'm going to name mine!'' Audrey howled.

"Yes, she can.'' Tala cut off that argument before they could even start. "Come, both of you, be quiet! You've disturbed the god of the pool quite enough for one afternoon. Let's go back to the temple and see if we can find someone who knows what sort of animal these are.''

There were nearly a dozen people living at the lake, but none of them—not one single person—had ever seen such odd creatures with such long and strange ears before.

They weren't shrews or muskrats or hedgehogs or cats or dogs or any kin of the foxes so numerous in the woods. They were pure white, like winter animals, made to blend into the snow.

Where they had come from when no such animal had ever existed in Arden before, Tala wanted to know. Of course, there was one person she knew of who had brought a whole collection of strange animals to Warwick. Could these living fur balls belong to Lord Edon? If so, were they valuable and rare? Should she return them as soon as possible? Audrey and Lacey would be heartbroken if asked to part with the loving little creatures.

When Venn came back from hunting, he had another look at the tiny animals and a good laugh while watching them scamper about the lodge. They could jump quite far.

He told the twins they would be good sport for hunting
and suggested they just turn them loose again, but the
twins howled and would have nothing to do with that.

Just then Mother Wren came rushing into the glen, out
of breath because she had hurried so fast. She had good
news and bad news to impart. The good news was that the
men of Wootton had come home, alive and well, freed of
the yoke of Danish slavery.

"Well, most of them returned, I tell you." Wren
wagged her apron at her reddened cheeks. She gulped
down the cup of water young Gwynnth handed her to
quench her thirst. "Ah, it's too hot for an old woman like
me to be rushing about these woods, I tell you."

"What is all this?" Tegwin demanded fiercely, scowling at Mother Wren as he came out of the vitrified temple
and crossed the scythed grass to the hunting lodge. Wren's
wild tales always upset the sanctuary's refugees or stirred
up the old warriors to go out and make battle with the
Vikings. "I've told you not to come here, old woman. One
of these days a Dane will follow you, and then where will
we be?" the druid complained.

"I didn't come to speak to you, old man." Mother Wren
gave Tegwin equal measure. She turned and addressed her
words to Tala, the rightful leader of the people of the
grove. "The new jarl, Edon, went down to the quarry in
a fury yester morn. Did you know, Tala, that his name,
Edon, means wolf cub in the Viking tongue? Why, he
spoke to every thrall, asking their names and making a list
of their crimes, demanding to know all sorts of things.
Where they were from and who their liege was."

The woman paused to take a deep breath and again flap
her apron at her ruddy face. Then she reached out and
pinched Venn's cheek, laughing gleefully. "Can ye guess
what they told him? Nay, you cannot! To a man they told
Lord Wolf their liege was the atheling of Leam, they did,

my boy! When he heard that, the Wolf of Warwick had
all their chains cut off and set them free.''

"He did not,'' Tegwin thundered, beside himself. The
interfering old biddy couldn't have told the Vikings the
atheling lived! Not when Tegwin had informed Embla Silver Throat otherwise.

"Aye, he did!'' Wren chortled. "And he promised each
one their cottage and their land back, too!''

"You are lying,'' Tegwin declared, stamping his blackthorn staff on the stones at his feet. "The woman's addled.
The sun has gone to her head. No Viking would free a
thrall.''

"By Anu's wrath, I am not addled!'' Mother Wren declared. "I heard it true from Alwin, who witnessed every
word. He told it to me and Alice of the Yellow Glen. The
new lord is a force to be reckoned with, he is, this Wolf
of Warwick.''

That brought a racket of questions and declarations from
all the people of Arden Wood. Many had strange obser-
vations of their own to add to the mystery of the new jarl
at Warwick. Some claimed to have seen a dragon slithering
across the floor of a byre, longer than the tallest Viking in
Warwick, Carl of York.

Two children had been freed that very morning and had
come running to the grove, seeking their parents. They
held everyone's attention, recounting the death of Asgart
the Horrible. The smallest even claimed to have heard Jarl
Edon order Lady Embla to tend her looms. The very idea
of Embla Silver Throat working a loom made every soul
in Arden Wood laugh uproariously. Embla Silver Throat
wouldn't know a warp from a woof or needle from thread.

Mother Wren was distracted from the gossip by the
twins and their new pets. "Upon my word, Princesses,
where'd you get those animals? There be two tasty mor-
sels, I vow.''

"We found them.'' Audrey did not offer Mother Wren

her animal; neither did Lacey. Anything that could be
skinned and boiled usually wound up in Mother Wren's
pots, they well knew.

"I imagine Embla Silver Throat had something to say
about the jarl's largess," Tala ventured, bringing the topic
back on course.

"Now there's a question," Mother Wren cackled. "I
haven't heard a peep from Warwick all day, but you can
lay odds that Embla is stewing for revenge. May she end
up like Asgart the Horrible. He stuck his big nose in where
it weren't wanted and *wheest!* Off went his head! He'd
make good boiling in my black pot, he would!"

The twins screamed when the crone slashed a quick
hand on their direction. They jumped back to the safety of
Tala's skirts.

"*Wheest,* you old fool!" Tegwin snarled, shaking so
hard that his long white beard wagged back and forth
across his belly. "Dare you come here scaring the princesses, stirring up troubles with your tales and stories? Get
you back to Wootton! Come here again and I will curse
your garden with a rain of frogs."

"Curse me with a rain of frogs, Druid, and I will set an
army of black ants to plague you!" Wren made a hex sign.

"Tegwin! Wren!" Tala commanded sharply. "That's
enough, both of you! 'Tis good news Mother Wren has
brought, if it is true. Come, Mother Wren, I'll fix you a
chamomile tea to soothe your tempers. The day is hot and
you've had a long walk."

"'Tis true. Every word, I vow," Wren declared. She
got her feet moving, accompanying Tala inside the lodge.
She had saved her bad news for Tala's ears alone. Better
that the people of Leam rejoice over the good than mourn
the bad. "You'll have to come and see the men for yourself, I imagine, my lady."

"Aye, I expect I will," Tala said plainly, not caring if
Tegwin liked that idea or not. He was the keeper of the

temple, not her keeper. And he had no right to call Mother Wren a liar; for all they knew every word she had said could be true.

"Tala, where is Gwynnth?" Venn asked before his elder sister went inside the hunting lodge with the old crone.

Tala stopped on the steps, letting Mother Wren grip her arm for support. She looked at her people, returning to their chores. "Gwynnth was here a moment ago."

"Aye, she was. She gave me a cup of cool water for my throat." Mother Wren nodded her white head vigorously.

Tala looked in the open doors of the hall, then back at the grove and the lake. Then she pointed to the causeway. "There she is, Venn. She's probably going to bathe and wash her hair at my pool. Lacey, Audrey, put those animals in a cage! I don't want them running loose, under everyone's feet."

Venn gazed at the small figure on the causeway. Something wasn't right. Tala might go off alone to her pool, but that was because she was a woman grown and required her privacy. The younger princesses were always accompanied by someone—nurses or warriors who could protect them. And why would Gwynnth go the long way to Tala's pool?

Venn decided this was good opportunity for him to exert his own independence and authority. Tala was clearly more concerned with wresting information about the jarl from Mother Wren. Gwynnth was still a child. The woods could be dangerous for a girl wandering alone.

"My lord Venn," Tegwin called to him, wagging his blackthorn staff, beckoning Venn inside the temple. Venn knew what that meant—more lessons. More hours spent reciting the same old tales over and over again. It was too hot to be trapped indoors. The sun was too bright, the day too perfect.

He shook his head and waved the old druid off. "Lessons can wait. I will return anon, Tegwin."

Venn didn't wait for a reply. He ran to the stable and let Taliesin out of his stall. Leaping onto the white stallion's back, Venn galloped off, following his little sister into the fens.

Chapter Seven

A private audience with Mother Wren convinced Tala that she must see for herself the damage done to the village of Wootton. Nor would it hurt to discover the truth behind Wren's claim that Leamurian thanes had been freed.

This time Tala wisely chose not to travel alone. She dressed with care to her station, donning her finest kirtle and a colorful, woven tunic that fell to her knees. With leggings and boots for comfortably riding astride, she took with her a guard of loyal warriors.

At Wootton, she found that seven of twenty freemen and one ealdorman had survived their arduous slavery in Embla's quarry. They milled about, looking at the smoking ruins, quite disoriented for the moment.

They had lost wives and children and homes, but they stood before the princess of Leam as free men. Each longed to pick up his life and continue, as the stoic men of Leam had done for centuries. Grateful to be free of the bonds of slavery, they tempered their words to Princess Tala with hope.

The jarl of Warwick had spoken of a lasting peace and had promised them restitution for enforced service. Four had even agreed to continue to work at Edon's quarry. Cutting the blocks of granite for his castle walls was to their liking, as was the carving and sculpting of decorations upon cornerstones and fine lintels.

The jarl's ambitious plans for his fortress intrigued Tala, as did his unexpected leniency to her people. Against the advice of her guard, she rode with them from Wootton to Warwick to seek out the jarl personally and speak to him. There was still the matter of the unsettled danegeld, as well as that of so many Danes taking up residence on land that belonged to Venn.

"Lady, you must not ride into Warwick alone. I cannot protect you if you do something so foolhardy," Selwyn insisted, riding up beside her.

As the high walls of the wooden stockade at Warwick came into view, Tala had second thoughts. Three nights before, she had been very lucky...and very foolish to go alone to meet the Viking overlord. She drew up her palfrey and nodded at Selwyn, acknowledging his sound advice.

"'Haps you are right, Selwyn. Go to the gate and give word to the jarl of Warwick that I would parley with him at King Offa's oak, one hour before sunset. Say that he must come alone, else I will not appear."

Selwyn considered her request before agreeing to it. Offa's oak was within easy range of the forest. He could protect the princess there and successfully ambush any Danes. He rode quickly up to the gates of Warwick and delivered the princess's message.

Rig was near the gates when the Leamurian warrior delivered his terse message. "Hold, sir. My lord would speak with you personally and hear the princess's words. Wait and I will fetch him."

Selwyn's eyes narrowed suspiciously, but he held his restive horse still. Glaring fiercely at the young Viking, he decided that he could take the man and six more like him should they attempt to trick him. Selwyn drew his sword and gripped it easily in his hand. "I will wait a moment, no more. Run, Viking. Fetch your jarl to me."

Rig did not waste time sparring. He ran to the keep, shouting for Edon, whom he knew was at his leisure within.

"What is it?" Edon was just coming downstairs from bathing and changing his clothes.

"There is a painted warrior at the gate. A Celt, lord, with a message from the princess. I detained him with a promise to speak directly to you. Will you come?"

"Aye." Edon grinned, putting his hand out to Eli for his sword and his shield. As he descended the steps to the yard before the keep, Edon belted his scabbard at his hips. "What sort of paint does this warrior wear?"

"Wondrous paint." Rig's blue eyes snapped. "A falcon soars on his left shoulder and a snake twists down his sword arm."

Edon's step quickened as he rounded a byre and strode to the gate. "I am Edon, Jarl of Warwick," he said the moment he spied the painted warrior seated on his horse.

"I am Selwyn of Leam."

Edon planted his feet firmly on the dirt of Fosse Way, outside his secure gate. "You serve Tala ap Griffin?"

"I do." Selwyn proudly allowed his horse to prance before the Viking, stirring the dust between them. The Viking was a giant among giants. Rumor was right. His hair was as black as Selwyn's once had been, though the Viking wore it in a womanish way, unbound and free to tangle about his shoulders. Selwyn's own great braid ran the length of his tattooed spine, a mark of his honor and courage.

"Well?" Edon put his fists to his hips, glaring at the mounted man. "What does her highness want?"

"To meet at the hour before sunset...at King Offa's oak. Come alone, Viking, or she will not appear." Selwyn delivered his terms and spurred his horse. The beast reared and pawed the air ferociously, then galloped off down the road. Selwyn's scarlet cloak billowed behind him.

"It's a trap," Rig concluded, giving voice to alarms brewing inside him.

"Find someone who knows the location of King Offa's oak," Edon replied, his mind already made up. Trap or not, he would ride out to meet the princess. Theo's predictions hung in his thoughts, warning him that the young woman was about to take flight. Going to parley with her might be his only chance to convince her to come willingly to Warwick. "You will follow me, of course, with Maynard and Thorulf, and Sarina must accompany me, but you will keep your distance, so that the princess doesn't feel threatened."

"In that case..." Rig flexed his shoulders and let his words trail off. No more needed to be said. Edon could handle a dozen men the age of the Celt. Sarina could handle their entire tribe.

They made haste to ride out, for sunset wasn't that far off. Offa's oak turned out to be the great tree they had paused at on the last leg of the journey to Warwick. Edon rode alone from the charred village of Wootton, with Sarina loping at Titan's side.

With one glance back toward her soldiers hidden in the beech wood, Tala let her horse step onto Fosse Way. Her men would not be able to hear what she and the Dane talked about, but they were there if she needed them.

Smoking Wootton was upwind and uphill. The road descended steeply, so she had a clear view of the Viking jarl the moment he passed the smoldering cottages. The yapping of the village dogs alerted her that the wolf accompanied him.

She tightened her grip upon Ariel's reins as they approached Offa's oak. Ariel caught scent of the wolf and sidestepped, tossing her head anxiously. Tala caught a clear glimpse of the black scowl on the Viking's face and knew a moment of fear. She gripped the reins tighter and gritted her teeth, telling herself she wasn't a coward.

"That's far enough, Viking!" she called out. "Come no closer, lest your wolf makes my horse bolt."

"Is it the wolf that frightens you, Princess of Leam, or the wolf's master?" Edon drew Titan to a halt and snapped his fingers at Sarina. The wolfhound sat, casting an adoring look at Edon.

Thirty feet separated them, and Tala let out a sigh of relief. She ran her hand down Ariel's withers, soothing her.

"Both," she admitted, remembering his lips burning upon her body. The memory of how easily he'd overpowered her and used her struggles to his own advantage made a blush sweep up her cheeks. She would keep to the business between them this night—her land, her people and the wergild due her.

Edon scanned the tree and its vast canopy. Sarina's alert pose and eyes directed toward the copse along the dried-up riverbed proved the princess's guard hid there, a hundred yards away.

"You have nothing to fear. Meet me halfway so that we may speak to one another without shouting," Edon commanded. "Sarina, stay."

The wolfhound dropped her front paws to the earth and thumped her tail in the dirt. Edon rode forward slowly, his eyes never moving from Tala's face.

Again her hair was neatly netted, and the lowering sun turned it to a crown of fire. Today a hammered gold band held the net in place, serving as a badge of rank. Her torque was gone from her throat, replaced by a pale ring of untanned skin.

"Good even, my lady." Edon bowed graciously as their horses met nose-to-nose on the ancient road.

"Good even, Lord Edon." Tala responded in kind, with courtesy learned at the kings' courts. "You are very prompt."

"What man would delay a moment longer than necessary for an assignation with you?"

"Only those with nothing to gain."

"Or those whose blood no longer thickens at the sight of a beautiful woman. To what do I owe the pleasure of a private meeting?"

"I wanted to thank you for releasing my thanes. You move swiftly when the cause suits your purpose."

"And what purpose is that, Lady? I gave you the terms of the kings' will. The border is to be secured between the kingdoms, the sooner the better."

"The border would be best secured by your withdrawal from Leam."

"Is it penetration that is the issue between us?" Edon asked smoothly.

"I do not believe we shall ever come to terms upon that." Tala's chin lifted and she gazed steadily into his eyes. His innuendo came close to making her blush again, but she steeled herself to give away nothing. It came as a shock to realize again that those eyes of his were not brown but blue—so dark a blue they appeared almost black in the shade of the great oak tree. "Title to Warwick Hill is yours. I will no longer dispute that. But Leam is mine, the forest is mine. Wootton is in ashes. You gave me your word that the burning would stop."

"So I did, Princess. I regret the loss of your village and am relieved to see that you were not injured in the fire," Edon said sincerely. "It gave me great alarm when I was informed of the blaze. You led me to believe you were in the care of Wren of Wootton."

Tala would leave him to believe she was in the care of every Leamurian alive before she admitted the truth—that she and her sisters and her brother no longer had any one place that they could truly call their home. What good did it do to cling to fortresses like her castle in Chester when there were not Leamurians enough to defend or protect it?

"Come with me to Warwick, Tala. We will sit down

and discuss my plans for Warwick and Leam. I will show you how our people can live together in peace."

"Plans that include a marriage?" Tala said baldly. "I think not, Viking."

The sharpness of her words struck a blow to Edon's hard-won authority. Should he remind her that only he held the power of pit and gallows in Warwickshire? His next words were testy. "Are you not a ward of King Alfred of Wessex?"

"Alfred is guardian of Leam," Tala answered calmly, making an effort not to react to the surliness inherent to his demand. "I owe the king little beyond the respect of his years. Only my father could order me to marry. Alfred cannot."

How truly naive she was, Edon thought. "Why then have you asked for this meeting? What purpose is served?"

Tala lifted her chin, meeting his frank appraisal. "I wish to know when you will pay the wergild due me."

She needed gold more than ever now. Gold to appease the Lady of the Lake and all the gods Tala offended each day with her doubts and indecision. Enough gold to appease each spirit of the earth, winds and waters. Enough to turn their greedy thoughts away from the sacrifice of a twelve-year-old boy-king. Atonement could begin with the bands at the jarl's wrists and upper arms and the twisted strands of the wolf-head torque encircling his neck. Even the angriest god would be delighted by such a priceless offering.

Edon sighed inwardly. Was gold the only thing that mattered to the little fool? "Tala, I fear you know very little of the ways of kings."

"What makes you say that?" she asked warily.

"Because it is the truth, lady." This time Edon sighed aloud. "The wergild will not give you the ease you think it will. Even did I find Embla at fault for killing all of your

thanes, their freemen and thralls, the judgment will go to
the injured king. Guthrum or Alfred will receive the wergild.''

She stared at him as if he had suddenly turned into some
sort of dragon, breathing fire at her. Horror widened her
eyes and parted her lips in dismay. "No. That cannot be.
You are wrong. That is not the way of it. I have read the
treaty.''

Edon nodded. "So have I. In fact, Tala, I have written
many such treaties for my brother Guthrum. I have spent
twenty years of my life acting as the Danelaw's good-faith
hostage, in courts and lands far, far away. The gold itself
means nothing. It is blood money, the pledge for peace,
but gold is always backed by blood. Come with me to
Warwick. There I have documents and witnesses to back
up my words with proof. I can educate you in the ways of
kings, Tala.''

She swiveled in her saddle and pointed at the smoldering cottages of Wootton. "Are you telling me that you
may burn my villages and I can receive nothing under your
kings' laws to restore the village the way it was?''

"I assured your freemen the cottages will be repaired.
Beams and thatch are easily replaced. What other services
do your peasants require? Rare and precious Welsh gold?
Silver bars from the mines in Wroxeter?''

"Welsh gold will suffice,'' Tala replied, glancing at the
handsome bands on his wrists. Surely the Lady of the Lake
would admire the fine work that went into making them.
"The kings' law is specific.''

Edon's eyes never wavered from hers. "Exactly—the
kings' law is specific. Let me clarify what the law means.''

"By all means, do,'' Tala commanded regally.

"A Dane and a Saxon meet here at this tree on their
way to a battle between the Danelaw and Wessex on the
common at Wootton. The soldiers do not like the look on
the other's face and exchange words. Words lead to blows

and they draw their swords. The Saxon slays the Viking in full view of King Alfred and King Guthrum. For the loss of one Viking warrior, Alfred of Wessex must pay Guthrum eight gold half marks. Had the Dane slain the Saxon, Guthrum would pay Alfred eight gold half marks. It is a tax, Tala.''

"What are you saying? What good is a tax?"

"The beauty of the tax is that Guthrum can turn to the soldier's commander and say, 'Why can't you control those soldiers under your command? Did you have discipline in your ranks, your men would not be killing themselves off the battlefield. They would fight only when they are told to fight against another kingdom.' It is a very simple law, lady, because of whom it holds accountable.''

Horrifically simple, Tala realized. She felt her heart sink like stone in water. What a fool she was. He must think her stupid beyond measure, demanding gold from him at every turn.

"The law holds jarls accountable, Tala. Here at Warwick I have five hundred Vikings under my command. Were Guthrum to go to war, I must provide him five hundred soldiers for war. For every man I do not provide, I owe my brother the king a wergild. That, my lady, is the king's decree."

"That changes everything," Tala said, shaken.

"Not if what you are seeking is peace. Come the new moon I will convene an eyre. You may accuse my agent, Embla Silver Throat, and she may have the right to answer all charges brought against her. Bring your witnesses and any you care to have speak on behalf of the people of Leam. The kings' treaty will be followed to the letter of the law."

"What is an eyre?" Tala asked suspiciously.

"A court of judgment authorized by the kings."

"And who is the judge of this court?"

"I am, and my decision is final."

Tala didn't like the sound of that.

"Know you this," Edon added in voice that grew harder than it had been only moments before. "Embla Silver Throat has charges of her own to lay against you. She claims the Treaty of Wedmore was broken first by Leamurian attacks upon the settlement of Warwick. She also accuses your druid, Tegwin, of murdering my nephew, Harald Jorgensson. Should you hold Harald Jorgensson captive at your temple in Arden Wood, it will not go easy on you. I will hold you accountable as a priestess of that temple."

He'd touched her vanity. Tala reacted by lifting her chin and glaring at him. "We keep no captives in our holy groves. There is no honor in that, Viking. A Celt does not shy from death by the sword any more than a Viking does. We are warriors all."

Edon regarded her proud stance in silence. She was braver and more honest than most of her people. They had common ground there, for to die a warrior's death in battle brought much honor. He nodded gravely.

"Aye, in that we are alike. But you, Tala ap Griffin, cannot draw swords against me. We are not, nor ever will be, equals on the field of battle."

"I know that, Viking," she answered without hesitating.

"Then know you this. Do you want a place in this world for your atheling, you will come with me to Warwick and make terms with me. I have told you once that your days of skulking in the forest playing fast and loose with the waters of this shire are at an end. I mean what I say."

"Are you threatening me?"

"Nay, I make no threats. I do not have to threaten to enforce my will. You have much to account for to two kings and me, beginning with the water that does not flow in that river yon."

Tala arrogantly turned in her saddle and gazed upon the dusty Leam. She looked up at the cloudless sky, then laughed at the jarl of Warwick. "You think a mere woman can control the clouds in the sky, Viking? Where is the rain that fills the rivers?"

Edon eased Titan to Tala's side and reached forward to take a firm hold upon her mount's bridle. "There is ample sun remaining for us to explore yon dry river to its source, Princess. Ride with me awhile."

Tala yanked on Ariel's bridle, but didn't dislodge Edon's grip on it. "Haven't you a rune master warning you not to tamper with the gods' will?"

"Nay, lady. I have an oracle whose predictions are ruled by the movement of wine in a gold mazer. He makes as much sense as any rune master. What have you? A druid water witch?"

"You have it wrong, Viking. I am the one empowered to witch water. That is the sacred duty of a princess of Leam, our singular duty—bringing water forth from the dry earth."

Edon noted the zeal burning in her amber eyes. She was not frightened of him, even as he aggressively took control of her mare. He laughed darkly, telling her, "I don't believe in water witches, Tala. Any man or woman with good common sense can find water under the ground. One doesn't need to be born a princess of Leam to master that skill."

"I do not mock the gods." Tala grimaced as he spurred his horse, forcing Ariel to trot at his side down the steep embankment.

"Do you pray to trees and lakes then?" Edon asked. His curiosity about her beliefs increased threefold. Did she truly believe she had the power to find water? Could she find a new source of pure water under Warwick? Or show him where to dig new wells that would flow clean and sweet? Was Embla right in accusing Tala of fouling the springs deliberately?

"Who doesn't pray to their gods?"

Edon considered her question as he ducked under the tangle of fallen beech trees that spanned the banks of the dry river. Surprisingly, she was not fighting his control of her horse, which told him much. First, that her men were nearby. Second, that the riverbed would not lead him to the lake.

When they'd cleared the brambles, he released the mare's bridle. The princess pressed her heels into her animal's sides and rode beside him.

"Well?" she demanded. "Do you pray to Odin all powerful? Have you made sacrifices to Freya and Thor?"

"Aye," Edon admitted candidly. "So I have done. But I have also traveled the world far and wide and learned that the gods are not invested in trees and streams."

"You mock me, Viking. I am not ignorant or unlettered. Nor do I live only in the forest. I have a great castle in Chester and a temple here that makes your Viking home look like a hovel. There is nothing that isn't beautiful and perfect within Arden's temple walls. We Celts have lived here in peace and prosperity for centuries. We outlasted the Romans and we will outlast you Danes, too."

Edon cast a pitying look at her determined face. She truly believed that the world would not change, when all history proved that it did. More the fool she. But he kept all hint of condescension out of his voice.

"You must make friends at Warwick with Eli, Rashid and Rebecca. Rebecca is the woman whose babe was born the day of our arrival. She grew up in a village on a desolate mountainside in a faraway land called Syria." She prays to a god she calls Yahweh. Her people were the first to believe in one god and claim to be the chosen ones."

"One god?" Tala looked at him askance, as if he had lost his wits. "Impossible. Not even the Christians profess to believe that. King Alfred always speaks of a Trinity of Gods."

Edon chuckled and nodded his head. "Then there are

Eloya and Rashid. They come from a land even wilder and more hostile to man than Rebecca does. In Persia great seas of sand sweep on as far as the eye can see. When the winds blow, it covers the earth in a choking dry fog. Eloya and Rashid are descendents of Alexander the Great. He conquered the world years before the Romans conquered Britain. Their God is named Allah, but it is the same God as Yahweh, all powerful and one.''

''This is very strange. Why do you keep such people around you?'' Tala searched Edon's face for a clue to his motives. All she could find in the handsome cast of his features was honesty and intelligence. That was most threatening of all.

''Why? So that no night in my hall will pass without learned discussions, exploring the limits of our minds and our worlds of experience. You will enjoy the variety of company we keep within my house when you are my wife.''

''I will never be your wife, Viking.'' Tala firmly shook her head. ''No princess of Leam has ever married.''

Undaunted, Edon smiled. ''Taboos are easy to break once one has taken the first step, Tala ap Griffin. What have you done with your torque?''

His perceptiveness caused Tala's eyes to narrow. Did he know what it meant for that talisman to be missing from her throat? He could not, for he was not of Leam. ''I made a gift of it to my guardian spirit, the Lady of the Lake.''

Edon's handsome face grew grave. ''Show me your lake, Tala ap Griffin.''

He would never know how tempted she was to do just that. Anxiously, Tala cast a glance back to the stand of beech trees edging the riverbed. Save Selwyn, her men were on foot. She gazed at Edon again her expression as solemn as his. His wolf ran close to them, flushing grouse from the bushes.

"I will show you my lake if you will show me each of your animals."

Edon drew his stallion up short, turning in his saddle to face her. "Which animals of mine do you wish to examine?"

"All of them, large and small." Tala's amber eyes grew dark with keen interest.

"Then I will show you all of my menagerie—my lion and apes and crocodile, rabbits and parrots. And I will tell you how each came to be part of my household and how the camels saved all of our lives in the deserts of the Holy Land. Rashid has many drawings of other creatures more curious than my camels, but you will not believe he drew them from living animals. The Mercian sisters who served in my hall thought Rashid's drawings were of bogans."

Tala swallowed. Bogans were malevolent spirits that dwelled in the fens. They emerged at night, taking hideous animal-like forms to do evil and spread death and sickness about the land. Venn's sacrificial death would put the bogan in Arden's fen to rest for a millennium. Then the rains would come and cleanse the earth, renew all life, and Leam would flourish as it always had. So claimed Tegwin.

"How do you know of bogans?" Tala asked with trepidation.

"I know of many, many things, Tala ap Griffin. Come, ride with me to Warwick. I have so much to show you."

Did she dare risk returning to Warwick with him? The hair at the back of her neck lifted and a shiver ran through her. She put aside her curiosity about other animals for the present, looking only at the wolf as it ran forward into the wood, barking joyously at a partridge it chased into flight. "How is it that a wolf has befriended you?"

The first true smile of the evening graced the Viking's handsome face, making his eyes sparkle with amusement. "Suppose I tell you that Sarina is not a wolf. She is a hound, not so different from the slick-haired mastiffs you hunt with on this isle. The sun fades, Tala. Make your decision.

"And the lake, my lord?" Tala turned the tables with ease, taunting him, "...and your test of my powers to find water?"

Edon quickly turned her challenge aside with his widening smile, "I'm a patient man in some matters...the water can wait till tomorrow. The question between us, Princess, is do you dare ride to Warwick with me?"

Chapter Eight

She dared. Casting better judgment to the wind, Tala left her guard behind in Arden wood and galloped across the sun-scorched fields alone with Jarl Edon to Warwick. Dusk settled softly on the land as they passed through the fortress's open gates. With a feeling of growing excitement, Tala dismounted outside the byre of Edon's menagerie.

Her nostrils flared at the strange scents that greeted her immediately in the dark and shadowy stable. The chaff of hay, straw and fodder tickled her nose and danced in the remaining twilight. Her ears caught the rumble of a large beast purring and the restless shuffle of others scuffling back and forth across the dry, straw-covered earth.

She and Edon came to stand before a huge tawny cat inside a cage made of stout iron bars. The beast within was hundreds of times bigger than the mild-tempered mousers of Tala's acquaintance, but it was certainly recognizable as a feline.

"Oh," she whispered reverently, face-to-face with a great cat that lazily blinked its golden eyes at her. "That is a lion."

"Aye." Edon nodded proudly.

"Why, he's huge," she said, her voice no louder than the rustle of a bird's wing.

"Rex is a lion. I do not know his age. Rashid reckons he is well past his prime, perhaps a dozen years older than I. A pasha in Alexandria had taken him captive many years ago. The light is poor this evening, but if it were earlier in the day, you would see the scars on Rex's trunk and notice that many of his great teeth are missing."

Rex ambled forward on padded feet, moving purposely toward Edon, then shook his head and roared. Tala jumped back. Oblivious to any danger whatsoever, Edon dropped to his knee and thrust his hands through the cage to grasp the beast's head and ruffle his shaggy mane. He spoke to the lion in a foreign tongue, but it was clear from the animal's response the two of them were not enemies.

Fascinated, Tala knelt beside Edon, watching his hands disappear under the tangles of the lion's mane. "You treat this beast as if it is a pet. Isn't it wild and dangerous?"

"Oh, yes, very wild and very dangerous. But to me, Rex is not so much a pet as a friend." Edon laughed. "We understand each other. The truth is, Tala ap Griffin, I could not bear to see this animal tormented night after night in the pasha's arena. The Alexandrians thought it great sport to put Rex and a bear in the same ring and let them fight to the death. So I liberated him."

"Liberated?" Tala did not know what that meant.

"I set him free." Edon got up and motioned to Tala to come with him. "But Rex has been too long in captivity or else he's grown too old to hunt for himself. In his world the lioness hunts, and he could have twenty such females in his pride. A strong lion grows fat on the kills his mates provide him. Rex is old and has lost many teeth, as I said. Some of his claws are missing. He could not win a pride of lionesses if he were returned to the wild. So we brought him with us to Britain and we feed him goats and sheep. He hasn't many years left.

"This strange beast is a camel..." And so it went as Edon took her through the byre, proudly showing her the

animals in the cages and pens. Every beast in its own
unique way had claimed some measure of the jarl's heart.

Most fascinating to Tala were his birds in wire cages—
golden finches and warblers that sang sweetly, and green
parrots that could imitate the speech of a man. Last they
came to a cage of wire and wicker that contained a great
number of the same fluffy animals Tala's little sisters had
found.

"Rabbits," Edon said with a laugh, naming the animal
for her. He opened the cage, withdrew a good-sized creature and put it in Tala's hands. "Their fur is prized in
Denmark for its softness and warmth. They make good
eating, too. Are they not common here?"

Tala smoothed her hands over the rabbit's thick pelt.
"No, they are as strange to me as your camel and crocodile."

"Ah." Edon lifted his brows in amusement at her fascination with the gentle creature. Where the fierce beasts
held his interest, hers was taken by the softest, meekest
animal. Her mothering instincts were strong and dominant.
Edon took that as a good sign.

"Then Sarina will have little luck hunting in Arden
Wood. Rabbits are her favorite food. These are what is left
of the breeding stock we brought from Byzantium. Rabbits
were rare there, too. You might see them in the woods,
since one of the cages broke on our way to Warwick. Two
or three dozen animals escaped. They are very efficient
breeders. We could well be overrun by rabbits before
long."

"Rabbits," Tala said, committing the name to memory
to tell her sisters. She handed the creature back to Edon
to return to the cage. "What do they eat?"

"Anything that grows. They can be a nuisance if they
get loose in one's newly planted fields." Edon put the
creature in the cage and secured the door. He gestured for
Tala to precede him out of the byre.

Full dark had descended, blanketing the land in a sheen of starlight. No moon had risen yet. Inside the high walls of the compound torches had been lit, some near the closed gates and some outside of the keep's great doors. The windows of the second floor glowed with soft, inviting light.

"Have you eaten, my lady?" Edon took her hand, guiding her along a darkened path toward his keep.

Tala shook her head in silent answer, searching the dark compound for their horses. They had been led away, and she hadn't given a second thought to Ariel since she'd dismounted. "It grows late. I should be on my way."

"Nay," Edon said silkily, and his hands moved to her shoulders, guiding her. "Come, my hall is well lit. There is ample food for another at my board. When the moon rises, it will be time enough for you to depart."

Tala shivered at the sensation of his rough palms clasping her shoulders. From the second floor came the music of a flute and soft laughter. She didn't want to admit that his entourage fascinated her as much as his exotic animals. Jarl Edon wasn't demanding any admissions from her. That made it easier to give in to his suggestions. The truth was, she wanted to stay with him. Somehow, she felt more alive in his company...more vital and alert.

This time they entered his hall together in friendship, Tala's hand resting firmly on his arm. The company greeted them affably, with smiles of welcome. Room was cleared at his table for Tala to sit in a place of honor beside Edon.

This time she was very much aware of the feast that had been prepared for him. Tala tried everything—the leek soup, the eels swimming in a thick, minted raisin sauce, the steamed pheasant and peppered fish, and the crusty haunch of smoked venison that was so succulent it melted on her tongue. There were olives stuffed with crab, and soft wheat bread, as well as a dark rye she enjoyed so much she ate half a loaf slathered with melted butter.

Too full to indulge further, she passed on the next course, while Edon ate heartily of rich pastries stuffed with currants and jelly, meat pies and bread puddings.

Throughout the meal his ladies talked and his men chatted. Each recounted amusing details of the day in Warwick. It was a much more jovial company this night than it had been the first time Tala had sat at the jarl's table.

"Princess." Rebecca of Hebron had noted Tala's obvious interest in her infant son. "Would you like to hold young Thomas for a while?"

Tala had thought her curiosity about the newborn would have gone without notice at the jarl's crowded table, but the proud new mother obviously knew admiration when she saw it. "He is a handsome babe. I did not mean to stare."

Rebecca smiled and gently shifted the sleeping baby into Tala's arms. The princess of Leam was a natural, knowing exactly how to handle a newborn.

"Oh, he hardly weighs anything." Tala smiled, dividing her attention between the baby and his young mother. "How thick and fine his curls are. You must be very proud."

"Thank you." Rebecca beamed at the compliment. "With such loving arms as you have, it will not be long before you have handsome sons of your own, my lady. Jarl Edon wants many sons."

"Does he?" Tala murmured, stroking the infant's soft cheek. The image Rebecca's words caused to form in her mind was not unpleasant. Tala liked children.

"Aye," Rebecca responded candidly. "I am glad the kings have ordered him to marry. Else he might never have settled in one place and taken root with only one woman."

Tala smoothed the cap of silky curls with the pads of her fingertips. This tiny human baby was so fragile and beautiful. "There is nothing I would like better than to have babes of my own, but it is not to be."

Edon shifted slightly, to lean close to her as he said, "You are wrong to doubt me, Tala. I am every bit as fecund as the Greek."

"Your fertility was never in doubt, sir." Tala lifted her gaze from the baby to Edon. "My ability to accede to your demands is. I have a duty to my people."

"Which will be well served by becoming my wife," he added quickly. "Times change, Tala. Virgin princesses no longer benefit the house of Leam. In truth, Leam is no more than a title you cling to. It does not exist as a kingdom anymore. Better that you align yourself to the house of Warwick, for I will protect what is mine."

"Better for whom, lord?" Tala asked him pointedly.

"For all of our people, yours as well as mine, Tala. There is only one solution. Through marriage we can blend what we are into a new, stronger people. Our children will inherit the lands you and I now dispute."

"What you say has some wisdom, lord, but I must remain committed to the traditions of my people. If I do any less, I forsake them."

"What traditions be those?" asked Nels of Athelney. Tala turned to the priest. Again she noticed that he wore a sword strapped to his side even at the peaceful supper table of the lord he now served.

"For one, it is my duty to offer the first grains harvested at Lughnasa, so that our harvests in the autumn will be as plentiful as the first bounty of summer."

"Making such an offering in no way interferes with your Christian duty to marry and bear children," the young bishop said firmly.

"I also value giving thanks for a productive harvest," Edon added. "I have many times witnessed Christian ceremonies blessing the beasts and the crops of the land."

"We must always thank the Good Lord for bringing us prosperity," Nels replied. "That is one way in which what was pagan is made acceptable to the church."

"It is most confusing to my mind," Tala said to Edon, "that what we have believed since the dawn of time is pagan and abhorrent to your priest's Christian beliefs, when we, in fact, celebrate the same thing."

"Paganism is rooted in polytheism," Nels of Athelney replied. "There is only one God, lord of us all."

Tala frowned and shook her head. "My cousin, King Alfred, has priests who speak of a Trinity. Now you say there is only one God."

"And his name is Allah," Rashid injected solemnly. "These infidels would mislead you, Lady Tala. Should you give me the time, I would correct the errors of your upbringing in your learned cousin's court."

"And by doing so he would guarantee you a spot in the devil incarnate's hell," replied Nels of Athelney. "My lord Edon, I must protest. We are to Christianize the district, not confuse it further."

Edon laughed and waved a magnanimous hand at the bishop. "Here we respect each other's beliefs, Nels. Tolerance is the watchword of my household. Though I understand from the lady's cousin that she practiced Alfred's faith when in residence at Winchester. Is that not so, Tala?"

The baby in Tala's arms had awoken and begun to root about. She was forced to put off answering that question directly by the necessity of returning the child to his mother. But it was amazing what she felt inside as the infant nuzzled against her breast. Little Thomas made her yearn for a child of her own.

"Well?" Edon prodded, putting Tala on the spot once the infant was moved. "Did you accommodate King Alfred's wishes when you were in his wardship, Princess?"

"Truthfully, lord?" Tala asked. How well did he actually know King Alfred?

"Aye, the truth and nothing less," Edon replied.

Tala's glance encompassed the table and that curious

collection of peoples from a startling variety of cultures and tribes. *This is the real menagerie,* she thought, *the strange peoples Edon brought together under his roof.* "I have appeased the king of Wessex's wishes, aye."

"Out of fear of reprisal?" Edon pressed deeper, seeking more truth from her than she was willing to divulge.

"No, I do not fear my kinsman's wrath. I suppose I do not wish to offend him. He is an unusual man, very wise and tolerant," Tala answered earnestly.

"Expedience is acceptable?" Edon lifted a brow. Was he mocking her gently? Tala couldn't tell.

"What are you asking?"

"Suppose a knife was at your throat and you were given a choice, be baptized or die. Which would you choose?"

"Baptism, of course. Do you call that expedience?"

"I would not call it a victory of faith," Bishop Nels answered loudly. "But I would count it a minor victory, because the seed would be planted. From a single kernel faith can grow. Give me time, Princess, and I am certain that I can show you the way to salvation."

Tala shook her head, rebuking his offer. "I have no need for this salvation you speak of because my spirit will return again in the next life. Meanwhile I tend the pool of Leam, whose waters heal. My duty is to protect and preserve, and that I shall do all the days of my life."

"Who is it that you protect, Princess?" asked the priest. "A tree-worshiping druid?"

Tala shook her head. "No."

"She protects a boy of ten and two," Edon said smoothly. "The atheling of Leam."

Tala gave a sharp glance at the man seated at her side. He was too perceptive by far. Again she wondered how well he was acquainted with her kinsman, the king of Wessex.

"Ah ha!" said the bishop, subsiding into deep thought. Edon nodded to the assembled company as he rose to his feet. "Come, my lady, the moon has risen. I will escort you safely back to your guard."

Tala had not noticed the swift passage of time, but the jarl was correct. A huge moon hovered on the brink of the starry sky, amber in color, like a polished gem. She made her farewells and accompanied Edon down the stairs to the lower floor of his keep.

A young man took up a torch, lighting their way as they moved out of doors. Edon sent the youth to fetch their horses while he and Tala waited near the compound's well.

Tala felt a moment's curiosity for the well. It was covered with wood and iron bars. There were no buckets or troughs nearby and the dirt all around it was dry.

She divined the reason it was sealed from its sulfuric scent. The water had gone bad. This year many wells had become tainted. But she sensed that less than twenty feet away, under the caprock, there was plentiful water, as sweet and pure as the water in her very own pool.

The jarl walked farther, stopping at a pleasant rise in the enclosure. There they caught a breeze and had a clear view of the pastoral valley beyond the palisade.

The air was comfortable, cooler than it had been during the long, hot summer day. No mist formed, not even above the steady flow of the river Avon. It had been a long, long time since Tala had last seen her land shrouded with fog or nourished by a mist. She missed the element and knew it was as necessary to the well-being of Leam as the water in her healing spring.

She and Edon stood awhile in companionable silence, each studying the strangely colored moon. "It's an odd moon for a peaceful summer night," Tala observed.

"*Certes.*" Edon nodded. "My oracle would call that a portend of war on my doorstep if he had eyes to see it."

"Which of the men at your board is your oracle?"

"Theo, the curly haired rascal that fathered the baby you adored."

Tala started. She turned and shot a penetrating look at the jarl. She had assumed he'd fathered the infant and that the women at his board were his concubines. Such were the practices of the Vikings. They were like the stags in the woods, fighting each other until only the strongest male stood as stud for an entire herd of does.

Reading her look exactly for what it was, Edon sobered. "No, young Thomas is not my son." He decided this was the moment to correct any further misunderstandings she harbored. "Nor are any of the women of my household my chattel or concubines. I chose not to complicate things here in Warwick."

"I see." Tala understood that men often had concubines. It was an accepted way of life in both Leam and the Danelaw, and the Celtic custom most highly frowned upon by the bishops of King Alfred's court.

"Do you?" Edon regarded her smooth face for a long moment. With a woman of such beauty as a wife, he would be hard-pressed to ever desire another woman. That was a very dangerous thought. It made him wonder if the princess of Leam knew how appealing she was.

Without thinking, he raised his hand and caught her chin with his fingers, lifting her brow to the shimmering light of the moon. "I want to kiss you, Tala ap Griffin."

He was much more honest in stating his desires than Tala. The truth was, she very much liked being in his company, being able to look at him anytime she liked, being close enough to feel that surge of blood when his arm brushed against hers or his heated gaze impacted with her sly inspections. Had she prolonged her stay as his guest, hoping for a kiss? The truthful answer was yes, she had. But she knew better than to admit to the obvious, so she made a conscious decision to be willful.

"Why?"

Edon almost laughed at her perverse question. Did she realize how quiet the compound had become? It was as though every living, breathing creature within the palisade waited to find out if the jarl of Warwick could woo the aloof and untouchable princess of Leam.

Her royal birth did not affect the beating of her heart, the scent of her skin and how both appealed to him. She was a unique woman, beautiful and desirable. Edon was surprised to discover how much that mattered. He'd been prepared to marry her and astonished to find he liked her.

His fingers spread along the line of her jaw as he slid his other arm around her back, drawing her body flush against his. Edon bent his head and captured her lips, tasting her mouth for the first time.

She yielded almost at once. Her body curved into his as perfectly as if she had been made for him. Soft breasts and warm hips cradled and welcomed him. Her sweet mouth became a flower opening. His ardent tongue made a diligent quest to ignite her fire. She had no clear idea how to kiss him to stir his passion. The art had to be taught to her. It gave Edon great pleasure to begin the first lesson.

Tala shuddered as he deepened the kiss. His arms enveloped her, making her feel small and weak against the power of his embrace and the hardness of his body pressed against hers. She did not know where to put her hands, but the urge to touch him overwhelmed her. She clasped his waist, finding the cloth of his fine tunic under her fingers. Beneath that was a netting of smooth and rippling muscle that tightened just as surely as her own belly did in response to his touch. Most delicious was the warm heat of his skin itself, resilient, smooth and soft against the pads of her fingertips.

His lips became hard, then softened wildly, and she could feel the exquisite sharpness of his closely shaved beard on her face and her lips. It was the most agonizing torment, tickling and teasing at the same time that it demanded even further surrender from her. She opened her mouth and accepted the profound intrusion of his tongue.

Far from being shocked or repelled, she found his taste as heady as his scent. Edon of Warwick was all-man, powerful and strong, stirring inside her the wants and desires of a woman in need.

One such kiss was not enough for him. He took ten kisses and gave ten more in as many hammering heartbeats. Her blood coursed in her veins, quickening.

"Come inside and bide awhile. 'Tis early yet. I'll return you to Mother Wren before the cock crows," Edon promised huskily. They were well suited as man and wife.

A shiver whipped so strongly through Tala's belly that she almost gave in. She was a virgin, five years past the age of marriage. The secrets his caresses conveyed to her body spoke of pleasures unknown yet so desired.

Then a scream broke the silence and promise of the night to come. Tala jumped away, released in the same instant the Viking jarl drew his sword.

A second scream, higher pitched and more desperate than the first, spun her around, to track the shrill plea for help to its source.

Edon located the origin before Tala did. "Stay here!" he commanded, rushing off into the darkness toward the byre that held his menagerie. Then all hell broke loose.

"Here they are," Gwynnth whispered excitedly.

"*Wheest,* Gwynnth!" Venn cast a frantic look into the dark ward of Warwick fortress. Night had come. Four fierce Vikings stood watch, two at the closed gates, two at the entrance to the keep. The evening meal was being served on the upper floor of the keep and in the longhouses inside the palisade.

"Please, Venn. I want one. Get it for me."

"Be quiet, I said. Do you want us to get caught?"

Gwynnth never gave such a silly idea a thought. No one would dare harm or touch her. She examined the cage containing the small, fluffy, long-eared animals. They had a name for the creatures now: the Danes called them rabbits. They hopped about, silent, restless, chewing on greens thrown onto the bottom of their cage. Their bright, round eyes never blinked as she poked her fingers between the iron slats of the curiously made cages.

"They come in all sorts of colors, Venn. There is a black one. That's the one I want," Gwynnth declared imperiously. "Come, take it from the cage for me."

Venn turned away from his noisy sister to look at the pens and cages in the byre. The rumbling growl of wild animals and the restless stamping of only Lugh knew what made the short hair at the back of his neck stand on end.

Something clattered and Gwynnth cried out, "Ow! It bit me!"

"Will you be quiet?" Impatient and angry, Venn started, ready to clobber the stupid girl.

Gwynnth sucked her fingers. Rabbits were jumping everywhere, bounding out the open door of the cage, hopping, scampering in all directions.

"Gwynnth, look what you've done! Quick! Help! They're getting out of the cage!"

Venn tried to scoop up several of the beasts, but before he could shove them inside, four more jumped at him, struck his chest and fell to the floor. He slammed the gate shut and stuffed the peg across its hasp.

"What goes here!" growled a Viking as he stepped into the byre and held a torch aloft. "Hey, you, boy! What do you do to the rabbits? Get out of here!"

Rabbits ran everywhere, scampering in and out of the light. Gwynnth bolted out the door opposite the shouting Viking. Cursing his own curiosity, Venn darted around a haystack.

Outside of the byre it was dark. There were buildings and structures aplenty to use as places to hide. Venn dove behind a pile of quarry stones—the huge monoliths the Vikings used to make a new wall of stone outside the wooden palisade. It was through a narrow breach in their defense that Venn and Gwynnth had entered the compound.

"Venn, I'm scared," Gwynnth wailed.

"Be quiet!" he commanded for the last time, out of patience completely. Lugh help them, if she hadn't been so greedy they wouldn't be here, risking their very lives just to get her a rabbit.

Catching hold of his sister's hand, he shoved Gwynnth over the biggest stones. "Run to Taliesin and get out of here."

Gwynnth dropped ten feet to the ground, but didn't cry out. She picked herself up and looked up at him, waiting.

"I said run!" Venn commanded. His buckskin vest snagged on a pointed stake. The sharp wood poked into his ribs. Venn winced. He tried to squeeze out the gap that Gwynnth had passed though so easily. He was too big.

"Run, Gwynnth!" he yelled at her.

Gwynnth ran. Quick as a vixen, she ducked under the brushwood stacked like cordwood along the bone-dry moat that circled the palisade.

Venn tore his jerkin free. He leaped clear of the stakes. But something went wrong. His weight shifted as he fell and he crashed onto the brush. The bones in his ankle twisted and his leg gave out. When he struggled back to his feet, he couldn't do more than hop like the rabbits in the jarl's menagerie. And halfway down the inky trail to the river bottom, Venn blundered into the cruelest Viking he'd ever in his twelve years of life known.

Unmoved by the unexpected impact, Embla Silver Throat snared a prize she'd never thought to capture—the atheling of Leam. And she knew instantly how to turn a blunder into a boon. But first she made certain the gamely limping atheling of Leam was her captive forever—by finishing a task that he'd only started. She saw to it that he broke his neck.

Chapter Nine

Edon ran to the break in the palisade where the wood wall butted against newly laid, impermeable stone. He climbed the cyclopean masonry, driven by sounds of strife over the wall. From the slick gray stone, he caught hold of the sharp, pointed stakes and pulled himself to the top.

Balancing precariously, Edon found the source of that pain-filled, bloodcurdling scream.

At the edge of the motte, Embla Silver Throat battled ferociously to subdue a captive. She yanked her opponent's head up by a hank of long hair and raised her double-edged sword high above her head.

"Stop!" Edon roared. He jumped off the twelve-foot wall, drawing his own blade in midair. "Hold your arm!" He landed on the balls of his feet, his sword ready to strike. "I said *drop your weapon!* What goes here? What are you doing outside the gates, Embla?"

"Wolf!" Embla Silver Throat spun around, clearly startled by his unexpected appearance on the scene. "What do you here?"

The boy fell to the dirt, instinctively, covering his head with his arms to protect his life.

"I asked what this is about," Edon demanded in answer. Thinking fast, Embla pointed to a leather satchel lying on the battered grass where she and the boy had been fighting. She panted, struggling to get her wind.

"I saw this ruffian at the well!" Her chest heaved, emphasizing her distress. "I watched him...try to dump...that sack in the well." She lowered her sword, breathing hard. "The wood slats...prevented him...from finishing his task."

Edon bent and secured the satchel. It weighed next to nothing. He opened it and saw its contents were naught but roots and twigs, dirty grasses.

"He saw me and ran," Embla continued.

Venn took the Vikings' discussion as his chance to crawl away. The minute he moved, Embla kicked him solidly in the ribs.

Edon heard the boy's grunt of pain and the sharp expulsion of all wind from his chest. He moved to protect the lad from the woman's vicious temper.

"That's no reason to try to kill him," Edon argued. His eyes narrowed in suspicion. "What are you doing outside the gate?" he repeated.

Embla ran her forearm across her sweaty brow. "There has been no order to remain within the gates," she countered quickly. "Forgive me for not sounding an alarm. I saw no reason to call someone to assist me. I thought it best to catch him before he got away. I believe he is in league with the witch who poisoned our well."

Edon lifted the satchel and sniffed its contents. It didn't take magical spells to poison a well. Poisonous herbs and roots would do the trick. The substances inside the sack emitted a stingingly pungent odor.

"Is it poisons, lord?" Embla asked fearfully.

"It is something potent." Edon closed the satchel. Poisons remained to be detected in better light. He sheathed his sword and took hold of the youth's jerkin, hauling him to his feet.

"Odin save us! Look, he has tattoos!" Embla exclaimed. Edon's twisting grip on the boy's leather jerkin revealed an intricately painted shoulder. "He's a murdering Celt!"

Rig came running at the forefront of a bevy of armed warriors, some carrying blazing torches above their heads. That gave Edon an immediate advantage—light so the boy could be identified. His face was common, but the dragon in flight tattooed on his shoulder was unforgettable.

Edon handed Rig the satchel of herbs. The boy clutched his ribs, seeking his second wind. Edon tightened his grip on the boy's jerkin, to get a good look at his face.

"Hold still, lad," he said warningly. "You're not going anywhere."

"Let me go," Venn demanded. "I didn't do anything! That's not my pack."

"I saw him throw it down from the palisade just before he jumped," Embla accused.

"That's a lie!" Venn gasped. His hatred for Embla Silver Throat got in the way of reason. Panic and residual pain choked him. The bitch had tried to kill him!

The Viking who'd been given the satchel examined a fistful of roots.

"Bloodroot and nightshade, Lord." Rig named the roots with mounting alarm. "There is enough poison in this satchel to kill every man, woman and child in the shire."

"It's not mine!" Venn clawed at his jerkin, ripping at the rawhide ties. The Viking jarl held the garment so tight he couldn't breathe. He had to escape somehow. Venn twisted, shifting his weight onto his left leg. Whispering an incantation to Lugh for strength, he drove his fist into the jarl's belly and broke free.

Edon was caught off guard by the punch, not that it hurt him. It didn't. The boy's garment was old. It split apart and the youth burst free of Edon's grip, leaving him holding a torn, ragged jerkin.

Furious, her rage far from spent, Embla saw her chance.

She lunged after the boy, shouting, "Stand aside, Wolf! I'll save you the trouble of dirtying your blade with the blood of a Mercian."

She swung her sword in a high arch, gathering the strength and power to decapitate the fleeing boy in one mighty stroke.

Venn's right leg buckled under him. He tumbled to the ground, magically escaping the sweep of Embla's blade as its point thudded into the earth.

"Damn you!" Edon shouted, leaping to stop a tragedy before it could happen. He grabbed Embla and shoved her aside, halting another death strike. "No! That's enough, I said!"

He straddled the boy, shielding him from further assault. "No matter his crime, no boy of Warwick will be dispatched in blind rage so long as I am jarl here!"

Venn rolled into a ball, covering his head with his arms, certain death was upon him. His heart hammered in his ears so ferociously he couldn't make sense of the Viking shouts around him.

The fierce giant who'd sniffed Embla's satchel of herbs wrenched the woman's sword from her double-fisted grip. She shrieked and cursed him.

"Rig, come to me," Edon shouted above the tumult.

"I am here, lord." Rig pushed his way through the circle of growling, angry Vikings.

Edon grasped the boy by his painted shoulder, hauling him back to his feet, then swiftly assessed him from head to toe. He was young, very young. A knot stood out on his forehead. A dark smear of blood marred his swollen mouth.

Embla had clearly delivered a harsh beating before Edon arrived. That she wasn't already sporting the boy's severed head as a trophy was a miracle.

"Take charge of this prisoner and secure him. We will investigate this alleged crime of his at first light."

"Why waste time bringing a witch to justice?" Embla stepped in front of Edon, challenging him. Every Viking drew back to listen to her shouts. "I caught him red-handed at the well. By Odin's law it is my right to take his life. I say, give him to me. Let me finish what I've begun!"

Edon scanned the crowd. Numerous warriors agreed with Embla. They condemned the boy to death without knowing if there was a scrap of evidence against him. None of them had heard the boy deny that the satchel was his. Edon had been near the well and in the ward with Tala for a good while before his scream had broken the peace. Embla's charge of tampering with the well didn't jibe with Edon's own movements. He knew something wasn't right.

"Perhaps you men came late and did not hear me," Edon raised his voice so that all present could hear him. "I said no boy or man of Warwick will be summarily killed without proof of evidence of any crime laid against him."

Rig took the boy in hand, standing fast at Edon's side against a Viking who shouted back, "What proof do you need?"

"Embla Silver Throat has told you what she saw," another stated.

"That is good enough for me," said the first.

"It is not good enough for me," Edon said forcefully. "And I am jarl here, not you or Embla Silver Throat."

Edon planted his feet wide and stuck his fists on his hips, glaring at the unruly two backing his nephew's wife. They were hotheads, longing for the days of pillage and rape, men whose blood rose easily to a fight. To them, Embla was likely a goddess, a Valkyrie who brought them valor and glory in their petty daily battles subduing the Mercians.

Scattered among the rest of the curious were Edon's well-trained soldiers, armed and dangerous and loyal to the bone. Maynard nodded as he took a stance directly beside Embla Silver Throat. One flick of Edon's head in his direction and the king's niece would be cut in two.

Embla sneered at Edon, then spat at Maynard's feet, as if saying aloud that Edon didn't dare command her death. She lifted her haughty chin and tossed her golden braids behind her shoulders.

"Well, Viking?" she demanded. "What say you? I claim that boy as my captive—my slave as forfeit for his losing our battle this night. Give him to me as any jarl would surrender a thrall taken in battle. Order me to not kill him if you will—that suits me. I'll make him wish he was dead."

The boy reacted to her words by lunging against Rig's grip, muttering something. Sarina howled deep in the trees. Edon's lion roared from within the palisade walls. Every dog and beast within hearing range set to barking and howling. The wind rose from the river and rattled the limbs of the nearby trees.

All of this happened in the span of two heartbeats. Embla took a step back. So did her brave defenders. They looked anxiously around them, as if ghosts or spirits were making all that noise. This was most curiously strange, Edon thought. This boy and Embla were not strangers to one another, but known enemies.

Edon took the ground she yielded, taking two steps forward in front of the Mercian boy.

"Come and take him, niece." Edon invited her to try, his voice carrying throughout the crowd without effort. "Come. Tell me what battle I sent you into this night? My last command to you was heard by all of my thanes and most of yours. You were ordered to tend your loom. Where is the weaving I commanded you to complete?"

Embla spat on the dirt. "I do no womanish work, Wolf of Warwick. I am Guthrum's own Valkyrie, so named

when he put this necklace round my throat. I am a warrior-
woman and can best any man among you.''

Edon laughed outright at that boast. ''By Odin's truth?
Not me, woman,'' he said, goading her deliberately.

Many that she had bested in the past now looked at her
differently. Edon counted few that did not openly admire
her gall, for she was clearly brave enough to challenge
him. Relaxing his shoulders somewhat, he took another
step forward and lifted his right hand, motioning for her
to come to him.

''I am the jarl of Warwick, Embla Silver Throat. I have
what you will never have—balls inside my breeks. Come,
test me if you dare. I'll turn you across my knee, bare your
arse before every man in Warwick and put the flat of my
sword where it will do the most good. You have walked
too far trying to wear a man's shoes. This man will put
you in your proper place, make no mistake.''

That brought laughter to the ranks, exactly as Edon intended the insult to do. Embla Silver Throat deserved humiliation to put her in her place. Not that that would bring
Harald Jorgensson back to life, Edon thought grimly.

''Go on, Silver Throat,'' called out a strapping Viking
at Maynard's side. ''Test the jarl's mettle!''

''Nay, lady, don't cross the jarl.''

''Do it. What's a blistered backside? You're tougher
than a boar's hide!'' called another, laughing rudely.

''Aye, do it,'' said another, with contempt flavoring his
voice. ''Which of us would mind seeing you beaten? It's
long past the time you got what you deserve, woman.''

''Aye,'' said another bitterly, proving there was grave
dissension in the ranks, both for and against Embla. ''How
many of us have wondered in the past just what she carries
under her skirts?''

There was moonlight enough to see raging anger burn
dark and livid on Embla's face. Edon said nothing, neither
joining the derisive laughter nor encouraging it. He wanted

the woman to back down. He saw clearly that it was not possible to pull her into his camp, cajole or win her over with time. Any hope of peace between them was gone. Edon's insult, delivered before the men she had commanded in his absence, cut too deep.

Tomorrow he would send her to Guthrum. Better that the king decide Embla's fate. If she stayed in Warwick much longer, Edon would surely have to kill her. He didn't want the blood of a woman on his hands.

Edon told Rig to take the boy away. Venn didn't want to leave this scene now and miss the final confrontation. No one had ever spoken to Embla Silver Throat the way the black-haired Viking did. Her hatred and anger could be tasted on the restless wind. Too soon, the huge blond Viking called Rig clamped his massive hands on Venn's upper arms and hauled him through the crowd.

Once the captive was removed, Edon squarely faced the remaining Vikings. He drew his sword from its sheath. With a deliberate show of power, he flexed his chest and shoulders, then rammed the point of his long sword into the earth at his feet. That gained him everyone's attention.

"Let there be no mistake!" His voice rang out loud and clear. "There is room for only one jarl at Warwick! Only one man can be invested with the power of pit and gallows. I stand before you that man. Here is my sword. Any who dare to challenge me, come, take it! Wrest the sword of power from the Wolf of Warwick."

Just yesterday every Viking in Warwick had witnessed Edon's fierce skill with the sword when Asgart's head had rolled off his unlucky shoulders. Surely, there were some who thought they could fight as well as he. Some whose arms contained the same power in the stroke of the long sword. Tension ran high through the crowd, but no man came forward to try to take Edon's weapon.

Embla stood rigid as a stone carving, battling her inner fury, knowing she could not take the jarl in a fair fight.

She vowed to Freya that the time had come for him to die.
He would beg for her mercy as did his cowardly nephew,
Harald. She would give none. No, she would torture him,
draw out his death into weeks and months of agony. The
tables would turn soon, and she would hold all the reins
of power then.

The confrontation ended. Warriors shook their heads,
scoffed or laughed and walked away. All realized there
was no need for a whole army to be gathered outside the
walls of Warwick.

The Vikings turned away. They went back to their leisure, to their suppers, to their games of chance and skill
that whiled away the evening.

In a few moments, two hundred men melted down to a
handful. The majority of those were Edon's thanes. Embla
remained rigidly where she had started her challenge. Her
breath came sharp and fast. Her eyes filled, yet she fought
bitterly against allowing the sheen of those angry tears to
show beneath her pale lashes.

That touched Edon in a way he hadn't anticipated. For
it was one thing to witness Embla's petty pride drive her
to challenge him. It was another when that same pride
shattered her shell and left her hopeless and empty. He
could not imagine what had destroyed her soul, crushed
her femininity and obliterated all traces of womanliness
from her being.

In Embla's shoes, Tala would be weeping. In Embla's
shoes, Tala would never have issued such a challenge in
the first place. What woman with any grain of love in her
heart would risk all for a scrap of earth?

Silence settled over the hill, broken by the calls of night
birds and predators prowling the nearby woods. Edon softened his stance somewhat more, but he couldn't bridge the
gap between him and his nephew's wife. The barriers
she'd throw up prevented any softening of his office. He

was the atheling. The blood royal flowed in his veins, not hers.

Still, he gave her more time to back down gracefully, to pull back behind the line she'd crossed, to apologize or beg his pardon. She let the opportunity go to waste.

He lifted his chin—a signal that he was going to speak. His words were well modulated, neither loud nor soft.

"Now is the time for you to explain what really happened between Harald Jorgensson and you, Embla. I would listen fairly to your side of the tale, withholding judgment...'haps even to letting bygones be bygones.

"My point to you is that I am not a man without mercy. If I forgive a boy for allegedly poisoning a well, I could be induced to forgive almost anything."

That momentary glaze that had softened the hardness of Embla's eyes faded as her lids brushed down and lifted. The steel inside her had been tempered in the hot furnace of her anger. Now it cooled too quickly and became brittle.

"Nearly a year ago Jarl Harald disappeared. He was lured into Ardon Wood by your whore, Tala ap Griffin."

Edon stiffened, hating the insults Embla delivered as easily as she breathed. But he made no move to stop her speech, determined to let her say her fill. He was more positive than ever that the truth of his nephew's disappearance was near at hand, only waiting to be revealed by her next words or actions.

"I can tell you exactly how he died, for I have lived here with your beloved Celts for ten years. I know my enemies far better than you, Edon Halfdansson."

Edon nodded, urging, "Go on."

"The witches ap Griffin cast powerful spells, luring men to their grove. On the night of Lughnasa, a special cake was baked of the last corn of the land. One piece was marked deliberately with a burning brand. It was offered to the male guests at their great feast of the first fruits.

Harald Jorgensson selected that piece when the food was passed.

"Because of that marked bread, my warrior was stripped naked after the meal. His head was light from the drugged mead in his cup. Then the ritual death began, but it seemed only a mummers' play at first, not real.

"The witches and the druids give all the celebrants a full share of potent mead, until their cauldron was empty. Then Harald was paraded before them, strong and virile, a man who could pleasure every witch in their forest. A man envied by the druids for his prowess and skill in battle, his strength and his bravery.

"They led him onto the causeway crossing Black Lake, to their bloody altar where the fens turn into mire. A strand of catgut was looped around his neck and knotted three times. A warrior struck him from behind, delivering a stunning blow to his temple, dazing Harald.

"The druid twisted the garrote at his throat. The veins in his neck bulged with his blood. His throat was crushed and he could no longer breathe, but he saw the bone blade they put to his gullet. He felt it sink into his swelling flesh and knew the moment his blood spurted out in a hot, thick stream.

"His heart beat strong and fierce, in a cadence matched by the drums of the mummers. Your witch held the empty caldron to catch every drop of his blood, until his very heart, that strong heart that I loved so well, emptied his veins of all the life within him.

"His feet slipped from beneath him, sinking into the black water little by little. But they held him from his boggy grave until the last drop of blood clotted. Then they let his body sink of its own accord into the mire. A triple death—stunned, garroted and drained, Lord Edon.

"A warning to you, would you but heed it. Lughnasa comes anon. Beware. The witch of Black Lake has cast her spell on you."

Finished, Embla sheathed her sword. Then she spat on the ground at Jarl Edon's feet. "Keep your pretty painted Mercian boy, Wolf of Warwick. May the both of you rot for eternity in ten Christian hells, tormented by every evil known to mankind."

Her chilling curse delivered, she swung around and walked, proud and tall, through the fortress gates, and never looked back.

Maynard gazed grimly at Edon, gauging his reaction to the woman's mad words. None who remained outside the walls of Warwick laughed, for a curse was no laughing matter to any of them.

"How do you suppose she knows that ritual?" Maynard asked in a voice pitched softly, for Edon's ears alone.

"That, my friend, is a very good question. If you find out an answer to it, tell me immediately," Edon replied. "Take charge of that satchel and gather up any roots that may have spilled from it. Nels, I will need your help, if you please."

"I am at your service, Lord Wolf." The young bishop bowed, discreetly in awe of Edon's ability to take command of a dangerous situation without faltering. "There are many devils at work this night."

"Aye, there are." Edon nodded. He quickly told the priest what he wanted him to do. Nels listened to the jarl's instructions gravely, promising that he would see to it all at the rising of the sun.

This night had proved why two kings put so much faith in the Wolf of Warwick. If he comes willingly to be baptized, Nels suspected, all of Warwick would come willingly, too. Such charismatic leaders were rare and precious, but their every action inspired their people to follow them to the very ends of the earth.

Tala's heart hammered long after the doors of the keep had slammed in her face. Edon had just sprinted off to find the reason behind that horrible scream when she was caught up by one of his soldiers and summarily returned to the keep.

The heavy oak doors were barred from without and secured within by loyal soldiers of Edon's guard permanently assigned to protect the women.

"Praise God you are safe, Princess." Lady Eloya embraced Tala in relief. Arm in arm they retreated up the steps to the security of the jarl's hall.

All the torches had been doused. Amber moonlight drenched the wide aperture of the unglazed window. Surefooted and familiar with the hall's furnishings and dimensions, Lady Eloya crossed to the clutch of frightened women gathered at the window.

Tala followed, straining her ears to make sense of the howls and shouts in the ward. All she really heard was the panic of frightened womenfolk who assumed Warwick was being attacked.

"Theo, tell us, what do you see?" Lady Eloya asked.

"No army is beating down the gate, ladies," the blind oracle said with conviction. "Hush and listen with your inner ears. You hear not the clash of iron nor can you smell bloodletting. There is no need to panic."

Tala bit hard on a knuckle of her left hand. The Vikings' women were not nearly as frightened as she was, although she, too, knew no battle was being pitched beyond the palisade. The commotion was much less intense. She moved between some servants to get a better view out the window, certain that at any moment she would see old Selwyn being dragged into the ward by his great braid of hair.

Tala wrung her hands in despair, fearing for the old warrior's life, railing at herself for her foolish impulses. When was she going to start acting the cool princess again? Why was it every time she got near the Viking jarl, all her wealth of good common sense flew right out the window?

"Look," Lady Eloya cried. "The men return!"

Tala braced her hands on the stone ledge. Lady Eloya was right. The Vikings returned. Many had doused their torches, but enough remained to light Embla Silver Throat's arrogant swagger across the breadth of the ward.

There was a prisoner.

Tala's breath was arrested. Rig of Sunderland looped an iron collar around Venn ap Griffin's throat, chaining him to the whipping post in the middle of the ward. Tala's knees weakened. If she hadn't been gripping the window ledge, she would have fallen in a heap.

What was Venn doing here? What could he possibly have done to cause Edon's best man to chain him like a wild dog? Horrified, Tala watched the Viking fasten secure irons to Venn's wrists and feet.

A small, jeering crowd had collected, of men returning from outside the fortress walls. Embla stopped at the fringes of that crowd, like a vulture waiting for the carrion to drop. No sooner did Rig turn away from completing the task of locking up the prisoner than Embla picked up a stick and began tormenting the defenseless boy, taunting Venn to fight back if he could.

Tala almost leaped out the window. Her brother nearly broke his neck, lunging the full length of the chain to get back at Embla. Tala caught herself and whirled around, shoving servants and women out of her way. The darkness in the keep swallowed her as she stumbled back toward the steps.

"Princess!" Lady Eloya cried out, alarmed. "Wait! Someone, quick, light a lamp. Princess Tala, come back."

Tala couldn't wait for a lamp to be lit. She groped for the bannister and found it, falling down the dark steps. In the cavernous lower hall, a lone lamp still burned near the door, where Eli stood guard. Tala flew at him, commanding, "Open the door! Open it, I say. Do it now or die."

She'd withdrawn her dagger from the sheath hidden under her tunic and leggings. Eli regarded her puny blade as insignificant. When she lunged at him, he caught her wrist and easily turned the point of the blade aside. "Eli, open the door!" Tala screamed at him. "The trouble is over. I must go out."

Just then the guards outside hammered on the barred doors, commanding they be opened at once.

"See?" Tala said, justified.

Unimpressed, Eli said, "You will stand back, out of the way, lady."

Summoning every ounce of patience left within her body, Tala obeyed. Her heart couldn't have beat any harder as she waited for the door to swing wide. Its iron hinges squealed in protest from the heavy oak panels' great weight. Finally, a gap appeared and Tala ran past Eli.

She came to a dead halt at an impenetrable wall just beyond the threshold, a wall made by Edon of Warwick and his henchmen, Rig, Thorulf, Rashid, Maynard the Black and Bishop Nels of Athelney. Edon put out his hands and stopped her, irately demanding, "Lady, where do you go?"

"Sweet Anu," Tala railed at the Viking jarl, "why have you put my brother in chains?"

Chapter Ten

That was the last straw. The lady was lucky the anger that flared in Edon's eyes didn't smote her dead. As it was her words left all six men standing outside Edon's keep reeling.

"Are you telling me—" growling ferociously, Edon swung his arm in an arch and pointed at the boy chained to the whipping post "—that that boy is the atheling of Leam?"

Tears stung Tala's eyes.

"Yes," she whispered desperately, falling to her knees before the Wolf of Warwick. She grasped Edon's hands, entreating him with tears. "Please, my lord, release him, and I will do anything you ask of me. I beg you, do not punish him for anything he's done. I will take his place at the whipping post, suffer willingly any punishment he has earned. You must not harm him. He is the chosen of all the gods. Should you harm one hair upon his head, Lir will release his red javelin and yellow shaft upon this land. Everything will be destroyed—every animal and bird will die a terrible death, as will all the people of Leam, Viking and Mercians alike. Please, my lord. Release him."

Edon stepped back. She was talking witchcraft again and he had little patience for that foolishness. He thrust his hands through his hair, making the long black locks stand on end. "So you want to bargain with me, do you, Tala ap Griffin?"

"My lord," she whispered, stricken by his sudden coldness. "Please, you do not know the vengeance of the gods as I do."

"Jarl Edon, I must protest," Nels interfered. "These pagan gods have no power on this Earth. Think what your brother will say if you entertain the lady's whims in this regard."

"If you please," Edon said firmly, glaring at the priest, who interfered where he shouldn't. "Let me resolve one thing at a time. The question at hand is the identity of the boy at the whipping post."

"What harm could a mere boy have done you?" Tala demanded.

"Much harm, Princess." Edon motioned to Thorulf to display the evidence in the satchel of herbs. "It was his intention to put those bitter roots in our water supply. Is that how your gods strike down their enemies, Tala ap Griffin? By sending boys to poison wells and murder innocent women and children?"

Tala started. She looked at the satchel, recognizing the roots that Thorulf displayed. She had never seen the leather pack in her life. It was not Venn's.

"No, Edon of Warwick, that is not my gods' way. They do not send boys to act on their behalf. They strike of their own accord. If my brother collected those roots, they were not for the purpose of poisoning your wells."

"How do you know that?" Edon demanded angrily.

"Because we use all roots for harmless purposes such as charms to heel illness or potions for love and prosperity. Bloodroot is a potent aphrodisiac, and it will protect any who carries it."

"It did not protect your brother this night, Tala," Edon

said ominously, lifting a skeptical eyebrow at her glib explanation.

"My point exactly, lord," she responded, undaunted.

"Then do tell me, what does a boy his age need with so many twigs of nightshade in his knapsack?" It had only one use. Let her explain that.

Tala swallowed, moistened her lips and answered, "Branwyn, the Lady of the Lake, took nightshade from her brother, Lir. He thought it only good for inspiring men to make war, but Branwyn found other uses for it, better uses. It can be used by a shape shifter or to travel into the otherworld, scan the past or see far into the future. Please, if you believe Venn brought those here to harm you, I swear I will take his punishment. Let him go, Edon. I will do anything you ask in exchange for my brother's freedom."

Tala gulped, swallowing her fear. Could she yield completely to this man? Submit her will to his for eternity?

She made her decision. "Yes, I will submit to your will in anything and everything. If you release the atheling, I am your servant all the rest of my days," Tala promised earnestly.

Edon saw then that he had won the battle between them. There would be no more talk of resisting the marriage ordered by the kings. Their marriage would join the Danes of Warwick and the Leamurians. Tala was the titular head, the sovereign of her land. It would work.

It was what Edon wanted—a marriage accomplished as ordered by the kings—but it was not what he wanted. Tala ap Griffin should be surrendering to him for love, not for fear of her brother's life. How much sweeter his reward would be then. It shouldn't have mattered how he accomplished his goal...but it did.

The woman he desired was sacrificing herself. She'd made herself an offering no different than the animals her druids slaughtered on their bloody altars. Again he took a leveling breath before he proceeded. There was no going back; time worked against him. Tomorrow Alfred could arrive at Warwick. Edon turned to the men surrounding them.

"Nels of Athelney, have you heard the princess of Leam's words to me this night? Her vow to surrender to me in all things?"

"Aye, Lord Wolf, every word," the bishop answered, perplexed by this odd turn of events.

"And you, Rig?"

"Yes, lord. I heard the princess swear to yield to your will in all things in exchange for her brother's life."

"Rashid? Maynard? Thorulf?" Edon gravely surveyed the other witnesses to Tala's urgent petition. All of them testified that they had heard her oath.

Edon nodded, satisfied. His grave expression did alter when he addressed Tala. "Then it is understood from this moment on, even when King Alfred comes, that there will be no argument over princesses of Leam being exempt from marriage. Correct?"

Edon saw her shoulders sink in defeat, but her proud chin never wavered when she reluctantly said, "Yes, my lord."

He could just as easily have taken her response as a whispered endearment. Edon couldn't believe his good fortune. A kingdom had surrendered at no more cost than a satchel of twigs.

"Very well, Tala ap Griffin, your vow to exchange your life for the atheling of Leam is so granted. Rig, go and release the boy. Nels of Athelney, I command you to take the prince with you on your journey to Evesham. You will keep the prince in your custody until he can be remanded to the care of his true guardian, Alfred of Wessex. Rise, Tala. You will come with me."

Tala pressed her hands to her tearstained face, shuddering with relief. Edon reached down and lifted her to her feet. He knew she would want to rush across the ward and smother the boy in her arms, but he decided not to allow that.

For the time being it might better serve his purpose to keep brother and sister separated. There was a great mystery afoot here. Edon intended to probe to the bottom of it.

The princess was terrified. Edon could see that clearly as he came into his hall much later in the evening. Tala sat on a cushioned chaise, staring at her hands knotted in her lap. She contributed nothing to the lively discussion that erupted upon Edon's entrance. His ladies buzzed with questions, wanting to know all the details—who the captive was, what his crime had been and what had come of Edon's summary disposal of the problem.

Edon knew what troubled his princess the most. Tala ap Griffin was consumed by the repercussions of her rash promise. She was probably wondering right now why she hadn't immediately exchanged places at the whipping post with the atheling.

The evening had cooled quite rapidly considering how very hot the day had been. Eloya sent for shawls and insisted on providing one of her best for Tala. Edon fixed a goblet of spiced mead for the princess and took it to her, joining her at the foot of the couch on which she rested.

"Drink this, Tala," he said, putting the goblet in her still hands. "It will do you good."

"What have you done with my brother?" she asked, lifting her face and casting woeful eyes up at Edon.

Edon stroked her soft cheek with the knuckles of his sword hand, touched by the wealth of sorrow and regret he saw reflected in her beautiful amber eyes. "I questioned the atheling at length regarding his activities this evening and the possessions he carried in and out of Warwick."

"The satchel that your man showed me was not Venn's," Tala told him insistently.

"It was a common sack, unremarkable in any way," Edon replied. The prince had made the same claim, so he was hearing nothing new. There was no proof that it belonged to anyone.

"Venn has many satchels, as I am sure you do also," Tala said quickly. "But he is an atheling and every possession of his is finely made by our most devoted craftsmen. Were it Venn's, it would have his crest upon it, tooled into the leather and embossing on the straps. Look…" Tala paused in her explanation to bend down and lift the hem of her tunic, exposing the leather shoes hugging her feet. "This is what I mean, lord. See the designs worked onto my boots?"

Edon looked at the trim, booted ankle she turned toward him. Her shoes were finely crafted of supple leather that folded across her ankle and laced at the calf. The tops of the boots were tooled, incised with an interlocking border of bold lines surrounding a minute dragon.

"The ap Griffin symbol is the winged dragon. It is on every one of Venn's possessions in one way or another, painted, drawn, sewn, cut or burned. If that sack were truly his, there would be a dragon on it somewhere."

Amused by her simplistic explanation of Venn's innocence, Edon smiled. He lifted his hand to her throat, touching the soft linen of her kirtle. "Are you telling me that every possession of yours is also marked, lady? Where are the winged dragons of your symbol on this kirtle?"

Tala frowned at him, her lips compressing. She set aside the goblet and lifted her fingers to the lacing at her throat, unfastening it to spread the neckline and expose the inner lining of the cloth. Turning the cloth down toward her breasts, she invited Edon to look at the carefully stitched banding that kept the linen from unraveling.

Edon would rather have looked inside and gotten a

glimpse of her breasts, but he contained himself to study the band on the garment. He saw a fine row of those curiously entwined bold lines with a tiny griffin in the heart of the vine.

Tala reached to her girdle and removed a small cloth purse from her belt, tugging on the drawstrings to open it. "Hold out your hand, please," she requested.

Accommodating her, Edon held his palm open as she emptied the contents of the silk purse. Two stones and a packet of herbs dropped into his hand. Edon touched the herbs, seeing they were knotted at the stems with thread.

"What is this?" he asked, not identifying the dried flowers or leaves in the tiny bundle.

"My flower, bluebells, lord," Tala said solemnly. "Anyone who carries bluebell is compelled to tell the truth."

"Ah ha." Edon nodded. "This is your point, then—that this herb commits you to the truth, always."

"Yes and no," Tala said somberly. "Testifying to the truth is also one of my most sacred duties as a princess of Leam. I must hold bluebells in my right hand when I sit in judgment over the disputes of my people, but as a rule the herb does compel truthfulness."

Edon nudged the two stones with his forefinger. "And what purpose does this piece of lodestone serve you, my lady?"

Tala touched the stone in turn. "That has drawing power. It will bring the thing I most want to me."

"And the pink agate?" He gently touched the small bright stone in the well of his palm.

"That contains the power to heal. It came from the bottom of my spring, the Leam, to which my powers have always been was dedicated. But truly, I do not think anything I ever did healed anyone. Leam's waters have the power, not I."

Edon took the small white purse from her hand and

returned her charms to it, noting that it also bore the crest
of the house of ap Griffin embroidered on it.

Very well, he would believe, that the satchel itself did
not belong to her brother. The boy could have gotten it
from anywhere…even Embla Silver Throat.

"Edon, I must speak with Venn." Tala laid her fingers
gently on his forearm, as if to stir him from the depth of
his thoughts. "He cannot go to Evesham just like that, on
your command. He must have his better clothes and his
horse, and Stafford must go with him."

"And who is Stafford?" Edon inquired as he lifted his
other hand to smooth a tangled red curl behind her ear.
Her white ears were so tempting, he couldn't resist following where his fingers strayed, to touch her with his lips.

"Venn's henchman." She bent her head as though she
were a reed and he the wind blowing upon her. "The same
as Rig is to you."

Distracted as he was by the shiver that raced across her
skin under his lips, it was a moment before Edon could
make a sensible reply. "You taste like honey. May I assume that Stafford is as wise as Rig? That he will know
where Prince Venn ap Griffin is when he does not come
home this night?"

Tala sighed. She didn't understand why she wasn't in
Venn's place, chained to the whipping post. Edon had
given her no explanation for their not exchanging places.

"Yes, Stafford will know where to begin his search, but
it would trouble him greatly to arrive here in the morning
and discover the atheling has been taken far from his jurisdiction. He will believe Venn has come to harm when
he does not see him outright. That could cause trouble."

"Evesham is within my jurisdiction," Edon said, very
distracted by the open collar of her kirtle and the sleek,
pliable skin of her throat. He slowly worked his way upward to her mouth, intending to kiss her very, very soon.

Tala choose her words carefully. "The people of Arden

Wood are unaware of the boundaries of your jurisdiction, lord. Most will believe our prince has disappeared into Embla's oubliette.''

"What do you mean by 'Embla's oubliette'?" Edon asked, coming instantly alert.

"Just that." Tala met the intensity of his sharp gaze without reacting to his tone. "It's a place where people are deliberately forgotten. Speak to any thrall who had the misfortune of serving her. They whisper of such a place. I've always taken the phrase to mean where the unlucky die.''

"Do you know of such a place here in Warwick?"

Tala shook her head. "You know Warwick much better than I. I have always done my best to keep my distance. It proved far healthier to stay away.''

She lapsed into silence again, deep in her own thoughts. Edon finished his drink and took the empty goblet from Tala's lax fingers and set both on a sideboard. He caught her hand in his, saying, "Come, the hour grows late. It is time we were to bed.''

Tala looked quickly up at him. She would die before admitting that the bottom had just fallen out of her stomach. Edon stood, gently tugging on her hand, insisting she get to her feet. Had she thought to gain more time to know him better before she had to sleep with him? Did her wishes matter now that she had as good as committed herself to accepting the kings' order to marry him?

Only the fact that she had given her solemn word kept Tala from jerking her hand out of his. Edon bid good-night to his company and led her to his chamber in the corner of the keep.

A servant followed with a bowl and a pitcher of water and linens for the princess to use when she washed. Edon directed the servant in placing the bowl and pitcher on a stand at the side of his bed. Then Edon opened a chest at the foot of his box bed and offered Tala the use of any of its contents. "This contains your clothing and jewelry that were salvaged from the fire at Wootton. Use whatever you need."

Tala thanked him, then shyly looked up at him. "Lord, I must send word to Mother Wren of my whereabouts. My servants—"

"Will worry, will they not?" Edon finished her thought for her. "Where should such message be sent?"

"To the priory in Loytcoyt. Wren has gone there. Just give her word that I am well. She will see to the rest."

Edon withdrew, allowing her privacy to prepare for bed.

Rig saw Edon coming down the stairs and joined him at the door of the keep for a walk under the stars. Edon liked to patrol the perimeter of the fortress each night before he retired. Rig liked to walk the length and breadth of the holding with him. Sometimes they talked the whole time. Sometimes they had little to say that hadn't already been said at some point in the day.

Under the old Viking ways it was none of Rig's business who Edon took to his bed on any given night. But since Rig's baptism, that particular foible of his unchristian overlord had become problematic. Tonight it was doubly so. Rig knew that Edon intended to keep the princess of Leam from leaving Warwick at all.

They strolled to the gate in silence, neither speaking. The guards were alert and the gates secured for the night. A rabbit hopped out from behind a stash of barrels and scampered across the ward. Edon frowned. "Someone has left a cage open, I vow."

"Aye." Rig nodded, having more important things on his mind than open rabbit cages.

"Who is in charge of the rabbits?" Edon asked, ever the stickler for details that had been delegated to others. He held everyone accountable for doing their jobs well and woe unto him who turned out to be a slacker.

"The son of the Lombard Dane—Ranulf, I think is his

name. You gave them a hide of land east of the quarry. Yesterday they put up the rails of their longhouse, but I believe Ranulf sleeps in the loft.''

"We shall see if he sleeps," Edon remarked. He turned his attention to the wall.

"While we're on the subject of sleep—" Rig found the opening he needed to speak his mind "—you may have my hammock, lord. I'll sleep quite well under the stars.''

"I have no intention of sleeping in a hammock, Rig, not when I have a perfectly good bed upstairs.''

"But the princess is in it," Rig responded flatly.

"Yes," Edon said with satisfaction. "And it took me quite long enough to get her there. Rig, you need to start making inquiries of the Mercians about Embla's oubliette. I've heard the expression bandied about. I am concerned about the last words Asgart spoke to me before he died.''

"What were they, lord?" Rig asked, frowning over Edon's response to mention of the princess. They were not man and wife in the eyes of God. With Edon's baptism coming on Saturday, when the bishop returned from Evesham, Rig had a right to be concerned about sin.

"I had my blade at his throat and his life in my hands. I offered to spare him if he would tell me where Harald Jorgensson's bones were buried.''

"Jarl Harald was a Viking. They would have burned his remains, lord, as is our old custom," Rig stated logically.

"Not if Harald had been murdered. A funeral pyre honoring him would have caused notice. No, Rig, if you do away with your enemy, you do not celebrate his passage to the otherworld with a grand conflagration...or even with a small one. You bury him quietly with few men knowing the whereabouts of the grave.''

"Ah," Rig said, nodding. "That makes sense. Yet we have investigated all fires of any note already. None looked suspicious, as I recall.''

Edon gazed at two longhouses dominating the northeast

quadrant of the compound. Embla Silver Throat's was as
quiet as a Christian abbey after vespers. The other, a barracks housing unmarried warriors, blazed with light. Vikings liked to drink and play games of chance late into the
night.

Standing in the beam of light spilling out that longhouse's door, Edon could see to the trestle beside the
hearth. The atheling of Leam and Nels of Athelney sat on
a bench, the bishop deep in passionate speech with the
silent, sullen-faced boy.

"What do you make of our prince?" Edon asked.

"I see the paint on his skin did not wash off."

"No, Thorulf told me it is permanent. It is very odd for
such work to have been done on a boy. It would signify."

"What?" Rig had come of age in the far northlands of
Caledonia, fighting the Picts. They, too, were a strange
people—going to war naked, like the Celts, and painted
with woad from head to toe.

"It signifies that young Venn is special...especially to
his clan." Edon finished the thought. "Each of his tattoos
symbolically imbue him with the powers of the dragon's
spirits. Look at him and you can almost believe that mad
tale Embla told tonight is possible."

"Mad is right. I have asked around. No one who is privy
to the rites of the druid sacrifices will say a word about
what transpires in the ceremonies. Mark my words, Edon.
That woman is unstable."

"I know. I think it best that I send her to Guthrum. It
concerns me that she spoke of the prince as though he was
a complete stranger to her. I believe she knew his identity
all along. I also believe she intended to kill him. She was
doing her best to behead him when I jumped into the fray.

"And it is possible," Edon added in afterthought, "that
the satchel in question is not the prince's contraband, but
Embla's. She gave no explanation for being outside the
gates this night. They were not open. Thorulf closed them

behind me when I rode in with the princess. I had to climb
the palisade and jump.''

Rig silently considered Edon's words. He did not trust
Embla at all.

Edon began walking again, setting the pace. They came
to the stone wall edging the motte. So far all was well.
Crickets chirped. A nightingale warbled off in the distance.
The horses hobbled in the holding pen snored as they slept
standing next to each other.

"What makes you believe she knew the prince's identity?" Rig asked.

"From the things the boy said under his breath. He was
afraid of her, but his hatred was too great to be contained.
Also Tala insisted that the leather satchel isn't his.''

"The princess will obviously do everything she can to
protect the boy. Even lie if it will aid him.''

"Yes, Rig, but that's what I find the most puzzling.
Were the boy attending the king's school, his security
would be greatly enhanced." Edon gave his opinion
bluntly. "Why risk the dangers of living in the forest, in
hostile land where an obvious enemy such as Embla could
have at any time captured the atheling?''

"I can't answer that." Rig scowled. "There must be
something here that requires his presence. Could it be as
simple as the land itself? That the prince retains ownership
by possession?''

"Could be. In fact, that makes more sense than anything
else where the boy is concerned." Edon held up his hand
abruptly, gesturing for silence. To his left he heard a scuttling noise behind a haystack. Suddenly, a youth lunged
out of the stack and pounced on a rabbit he'd flushed out
of hiding.

"Got you!" the lad declared. He scrambled to his feet,
grinning, holding the struggling rabbit by its ears. When
he saw Edon and Rig watching him, the youth changed
his hold upon the animal, supporting its wild, thumping

hindlegs with his other hand. He ducked his head in apology, saying, "Sorry to startle you, lord."

Both Edon and Rig recognized the young Viking. It was Ranulf, the youngest son of the Lombard who had set fire to Wootton. "Why are rabbits scattered about the ward, Ranulf? Were you careless in locking the cage after they were fed?"

"Oh, no, Lord Wolf." Ranulf grimaced. "Two children got into the byre and opened the cage. I chased them out, but ever since, I've had to chase down the rabbits they let loose. I think this was the last one."

"Whose children?" Edon expected parents to control their children and teach them to respect the property of others.

"They were none that I know and oddly dressed, not Viking children, Lord Wolf. It was a boy and a small girl. She had a valuable gold torque at her throat. I heard her say she wanted a black rabbit of her own. I believe they were going to steal one. But they ran off when I shouted at them. I have not seen them again, lord."

Edon accepted Ranulf's testimony as the truth and dismissed him with the admonition that there was a black-and-white rabbit still loose near the barrels stacked at the gates. He continued on his circuit of the grounds with Rig. "A boy with a girl wearing a valuable torque, eh?"

"And strangers." Rig considered that of greater importance.

"The princess told me there are no rabbits in this shire, though I know that there are hares in Britain. The native animals are not as meaty nor do they have the variety of fur of our animals," Edon murmured. "Do you suppose the prince was that boy?"

"There is one way to find out," Rig stopped and took his leave of Edon. "I'll take Ranulf to have a look at the atheling and see if he can identify the culprit."

Edon approved of that idea. Ranulf's testimony would

put a different light on the atheling's purpose for sneaking in and out of Warwick.

Edon proceeded to the bathhouse to think things over while he sat in a hot tub and washed away the day's accumulation of dirt and grime from his body. Inadequate as it was, it was still the only bathhouse within the fortress.

The new one was not even half built. Hopefully, Maynard would solve the problem of getting fresh water flowing shortly. Edon scrubbed diligently, then changed into the robe Eli had laid out for him. With nothing left to delay him from retiring and spending the balance of the night having his way with the alluringly beautiful princess of Leam, Edon returned to the keep.

Chapter Eleven

Tala prowled Edon's chamber, as restless as any of his wild animals in their cages. A window, partially glazed with diamonds of colored glass set in lead, fractured the moonlight spilling across his bed.

As interior chambers went, it was spacious, giving her plenty of room to pace and fret. She thought she could get used to looking out this window and being able to see so much of her valley at one time.

She did think about leaving, about tearing the linens on the bed into strips and making a rope to escape out the wide-open, unglazed portion of the window. Only she was too honorable to do that.

Or, she admitted, she was too curious about the night to come to risk going back on her word. She had never been with a man. The thought of staying the whole night with Edon had her stomach fluttering.

As it was, she willed him to return because the agony of waiting was too much to bear. Tala sat on the window ledge, looking at the sky. The stars hung like bright jewels in the darkness. Nothing moved. No wind sent clouds racing across the pale moon. All was still, quiet, utterly at peace.

Tala worried about her sisters, but by this time, with the

moon rising in the sky, they would be asleep in their beds, as would the servants.

No, she and Venn wouldn't be missed until morning. Then Tegwin, Selwyn and Stafford would raise a terrible alarm. Tala sighed, and could only hope that Edon fulfilled his promise to send word to Mother Wren of her whereabouts.

"What makes you sigh so deeply?" Edon asked as he quietly closed the door. Startled, Tala whirled around and bumped her head on the window frame.

"Oh! You're here!" She jumped to her feet, took one step to meet him and tripped, treading on the hem of her gown.

"So I am," Edon caught her before her ungainly pivot dumped her on the floor at his feet. It was quite nice the way she almost landed flush against his chest. "Steady there."

Self-consciously, Tala picked one foot, then the other off the folds of her gown. It was voluminous, diaphanous. It should have made her look like the most beautiful woman in the world. What it had really done was make her look like a goose. She blushed to the roots of her hair and said, "Oh."

Edon chuckled, picking her up and settling her back on the broad expanse of stone at the window. "What were you looking at, my lady?"

She dropped her hands in her lap and demurely looked at them. Edon settled onto the window ledge beside her, gazing out at the sky, giving her the chance to recover her composure. "Oh, the moon and the silver ribbon of the river. Leam valley is very beautiful from this vantage point of yours."

Edon lifted her chin with one finger, tilting her face to his. Her hair was undone, brushed and hanging down her back. It formed a scarlet river of soft, sweet waves that fell to her ankles. "I chose the view from this window, planned it from the first."

"How so?" Tala asked. "You only just arrived a few days ago. They have been building this keep for years." She shook her head, unable to believe so little time had passed. It seemed she had known him forever. Or else had been waiting for him forever.

"Oh, I was here years ago, ten in fact. At about the time the abbey at Loytcoyt was built. That was when I bought Warwick Hill."

Tala lifted her chin from his fingers. "Bought?"

"Aye." Edon nodded. "I paid a dear price for it, too. Daffyd ap Griffin haggled more gold out of me than any man I've ever bargained with. But I wanted this view of the valley. It is perfect."

"He took advantage of you," Tala said simply. "Uncle Daffyd didn't own this hill anymore than he owned the wind. Nor do you own the hill of Warwick, Edon Half-dansson. You never will."

Edon's hand dropped to his waist and rested there, his elbow thrusting out into the darkened chamber. "What are you saying, Tala ap Griffin? Do you cast your bold promise in my face now that I have let your brother go unpunished?"

"I do nothing of the sort," Tala responded, shaking her head, meeting his gaze without shying from the intensity she saw there. "I am telling you that my uncle, Daffyd ap Griffin, owned nothing, therefore he sold you nothing. The hill of Warwick never belonged to him. Nor does it belong to you, even though you build a fine stone fortress upon it."

"It is my house and I will defend it with my last breath," Edon assured her forcefully.

"I expect you will, but that does not make the land yours. The land belongs to the past, the present and the future. It is Leam in perpetuity, and it will endure beyond our lifetimes, as it endured before."

"During this lifetime, Warwick Hill shall be mine," he said resolutely. "That is the way it is to be, Tala. You may dither upon the issue all you like, but Warwick is mine, and I keep what is mine, just as I shall keep you all the rest of our days."

"I don't see why you should want that," Tala said.

"You don't?" Edon looked at her face in the moonlight. "You know you are very beautiful, don't you?"

"No more so than others." The denial was spontaneous, for she saw herself as unattainable no matter how desirable or beautiful she might be. She could not seem to look anywhere except at his mouth or the small hollow in the base of his throat, where a drop of water from his wet hair had gathered and glistened so invitingly.

Tentatively, Tala laid her fingertips on his breastbone. He wore a robe similar to hers, though the material of his was a heavier, more durable weave than this silky gown she had chosen from his trunk. Unable to resist, she touched that glistening sparkle of water and smoothed it away with the pad of her index finger.

"You have come from the river," she guessed.

"Nay, the bathhouse," Edon replied huskily, shivering at her boldly evocative, exceedingly sensuous touch.

"Ah, yes, you Vikings put much store in your bath-houses, do you not?"

"Aye, it's an exquisite pleasure, my lady."

He shook his damp hair away from his shoulders, embracing her with both hands, drawing her body against his. Her heat nourished the spark of desire flowing through him. Edon gently touched her mouth with his, kissing her with the greatest of care. She was so like a wild creature, shy and skittish, needing to be tamed to his touch before he dared allow the full intensity of his desire for her to show.

Tala shivered as his lips slowly coaxed hers to soften. Then that shiver became a shudder Edon relished, as he licked her lower lip with his tongue. He loosened the sash at her waist and slid the gown off her arms. The rustle of cloth falling to her feet whispered a counterpoint to the delicate intake of breath in her throat. He folded strong arms around her, pressing their bodies close before the open window.

The night air touched Tala's skin in a cool bath, as the heat of his hands stroked over her breasts, her belly, gripped her bottom and lifted her against the hard heat of his arousal.

"I have wanted you from the first moment I saw you, Tala ap Griffin," Edon said as he lowered his head to kiss her fully. The honesty of that admission compelled him to seek more from her. Wanting her wasn't enough. He wanted to love her, consume her, die in her arms. "Open your mouth, Tala. Yield to me."

That was the greatest taboo of her life, yet she could no more refuse to yield to Edon of Warwick than she could will herself to stop breathing. Tala closed her eyes and told herself she made this sacrifice so that Venn might live.

Her conscience demanded more honesty than that. She wanted the Wolf of Warwick the way any woman wants a man. Surrendering to his command was the most necessary pleasure she had ever experienced in her life.

His tongue thrust hot and deep inside her mouth, signaling that the duel between them had begun in earnest. She wrapped her arms around him, drawing him deeper, closer, shuddering as he shed his own robe and his naked body pressed flush against hers from thigh to breast. Hot, hard and hair-roughened skin rubbed against the soft, sleek curves of her own flesh, exciting and thrilling her.

Everywhere that her hands touched or roamed on his neck and shoulders they met solid flesh and muscle. His body fascinated and intrigued her.

His arm tightened around her hips, lifting her to carry her to his bed. There he laid her down on her back, parted her legs and settled himself in the cradle of her hips. His arousal felt hard and thick where it nestled against her womanly curls and caused a fiery burn as his weight pressed against her.

She knew there was more to this act than the mere touch of bodies pressing hotly together. She had felt pleasure before, when he'd kissed and fondled her breasts, and had not forgotten the excruciating heat it had caused in her loins. That prior experience had not taught her of the magnitude of desire his bold touch could arouse when his hand slipped freely between their bodies and daringly parted her soft nether folds.

Utterly without volition, she arched toward that delectable pleasure, blinded by the power of his hand as he coaxed a flood of desire to surge in her veins. She had not known her body could ache so, want so. Yet what exactly it was she suddenly yearned for, she did not know.

Edon sighed as her hands slipped down his chest. "Do not distract me," he whispered, then caught her breast in his mouth, kissing it, suckling with fervor. He slid his finger deep inside her, encountering the barrier that he hadn't really believed would be there.

But Tala ap Griffin's maidenhead was intact. So Edon moved slowly, bringing her to pleasure with great care. He wanted her ready for his intrusion, so that there would be little pain in their joining.

Tala gasped, then screamed, and died a little when it became so intense her whole body throbbed and tightened in shuddering completion.

"No more," she begged, pushing his hand away.

"Ah, my lady, there is much more," Edon warned her, shifting so his shaft was poised at her sweet, moist portal. He kissed her deeply, dueling with her tongue, sucking gently upon her lower lip, teaching her all that he wanted her to know about kissing. She was a willing pupil, adept and quick. Every touch he taught her she added to her growing repertoire of responses in kind.

As ripe as she was, she was unprepared for the intrusion of his shaft. He came in slowly at first, and her eyes opened and widened in shock. She gripped his upper arms tightly and cried out, "Stop!"

"Lady, I cannot." Edon caught her shoulders firmly and thrust into her, nearly seated to the hilt. She struggled to escape, but that only completed his downward drive. He trembled deliciously, forcing himself to become perfectly still, to accommodate her. "It is done, Tala."

She panted rapidly, trying to catch her breath. The sense of fullness was intense. She wanted to cry out, but withheld the shout. Bravely, she ignored the tears in her eyes. Abruptly she looked up at him and said magnanimously, "You may continue. Finish it!"

"I would be a coward did I not, lady." Edon kissed her mouth, then licked the salty tears from her eyelashes. The sheer outrageousness of her courage compelled him to cosset her tenderly. "A breaching is always difficult at first. But you will come to accommodate me with practice. We will practice this often, my darling."

Tala did not feel like his darling. The pleasure of moments ago had faded completely. She felt stabbed and deflated. This breaching hurt.

Edon caught her fingers as they flew to her mouth to press back a cry. He sought to bring her back to the pleasure at hand with deep, sensuous kisses that blinded her to the discomfort. Somehow, he controlled his lust in spite of the great pressure her tight sheath placed upon his shaft. He bent his head, kissing her pliant mouth, sucking upon her soft, giving breasts. But he could control his own overwhelming sense of urgency only so long. Thankfully, she made a few tentative thrusts forward with her own hips and widened her legs, adjusting to his intrusion.

That was the signal his body needed. He gripped her shoulders, bracing as he withdrew. Her breath caught in her throat as he plunged downward in the joy of a masculine conquest. She was so tight and firm, her muscles clenching him with every stroke. No grip was sweeter. He came with a bone-shaking, elemental force, his seed spewing inside her, filling her completely. Then he collapsed helpless as a newborn babe, spent and shuddering upon her.

Tala gasped for air, shaken by the force of their mating. Edon's weight covering her seemed the most fitting end to their joining. She reveled in his exhaustion, seeing that as the supreme triumph of her femininity. This freed her at last. She no longer need pose as the virgin princess of Leam for her people. She could pass the torch to Gwynnth.

How easy breaking a lifetime taboo really was.

In deepest gratitude, she kissed Edon's damp cheek and thanked him.

"Why do you thank me, Tala? I have hurt you abominably with my lust. I could not hold back and make this first joining easier upon you. I've been too long without a woman."

"You jest with me, surely," Tala replied. "How can you claim to be without women when you have brought so many with you to Warwick?"

Offended, Edon tweaked her nose. "I have brought many men to Warwick as well, my lady. I do not make love to their wives or their maidservants. I am a Viking, yes, but not a barbarian."

"You are a strange Viking, then. Few others I have met have any scruples whatsoever."

Edon gave her observation some thought. It was true he was not like other men, or other Vikings. He had never before felt any need to explain himself to a woman in his bed. But Tala wasn't just any woman, she was his life mate. The woman who would share his bed for the rest of

their days together. He felt a need to strengthen the bonds
between them.

He caught her hand in his, lacing their fingers together,
and looked deeply into the soft amber eyes that returned
his gaze without wavering.

"Perhaps when one starts out life as a hostage and remains so indefinitely through the years, one learns to walk
carefully wherever one goes," Edon replied, simplifying
his history for her.

"You have been a hostage?" Tala asked, taken aback
by that admission.

"Aye, before my milk teeth were all gone, I began to
serve my father, Halfdan, and then my brother Guthrum
as their emissary of good faith to the emperor of the East."
Edon shifted his weight off of her, settling her comfortably
in the crook of his arm.

"How old were you? Nine winters?"

"Nine when the ship sailed to Constantinople."

"Were you frightened?"

"I don't think I had sense enough to be frightened. I
did miss my mother terribly at first, but it became a great
adventure. It was a wonder that I wasn't washed into the
sea on my first voyage. The truth was I was well cosseted
by all the old warriors my father sent to train me in Viking
ways. I remember that when we first arrived in Constantinople, after months at sea, the emperor refused to accept
me as Halfdan's son because I look like my Irish mother."

"What changed the emperor's mind?"

"Ah, well." Edon ducked his head and smiled. "My
audacity. I think I threatened to skewer his balls with my
eating dagger for daring to name me a bastard before his
court. A Viking son can be a real terror when he wants to
prove his manhood."

"At age ten?" Tala laughed.

"Nine," Edon corrected, tweaking her nose lightly.

"You'll learn what I mean in time, when you give me sons, my lady."

Tala settled comfortably in the bend of his arm, her fingers resting against the warmth of his naked chest. "I should like to have many sons, and I do know of what you speak...regarding the pride of a son. Raising Venn has not been all that easy of a task. He..." She grew quiet, holding back her thoughts.

"He needs a man's guidance." Edon stepped in, speaking where she didn't want to reveal her private thoughts. "It can't have been easy for you, trying to raise an atheling under these circumstances, Tala. Be truthful with me. There is no reason for you to hold back from me—you will be my wife in a few days. Your brother would not have found himself in danger tonight had you brought him to my hall when first we met. Embla has true animosity toward him."

Tala considered his words. "I am aware of that. It gives all the more reason to keep Venn away from Warwick."

"He will remain at Warwick now, just as you will," Edon said without preamble. "You need not worry for his safety or your own. I have men assigned to protecting both of you."

"That is kind of you," Tala replied with downcast eyes. It *was* kind, but he did not take into consideration that their safety was something she and her own loyal vassals had always seen to in the past. "We do not wish to become a burden."

"Burden?" Edon scoffed. A frown creased his brow. He felt the urge to shake her gently, just as he'd felt the urge to throttle her when she'd thrown herself on her knees before him in supplication for her brother's life. Her reserve frustrated him, but he could see that her trust wasn't something he could gain with a kiss or a word of reassurance. He sighed over her resistance to further intimacy.

"You are no burden to me, Tala ap Griffin." Having

gotten his wind back, Edon rose from the bed and got a
wet cloth from the basin. "Here, let me tend the injury of
our mating. I fear I have hurt you."

Tala drew a sheet over her body as she tried to sit up.
"It was not unnecessary, lord."

"Be quiet." Edon pressed her onto her back and drew
away the sheet purposefully. "You will allow me to tend
you, else I cannot know when you will be healed enough
for us to enjoy another bedding."

Tala shivered as he put the wet cloth against her sore
flesh. It felt comforting, but she didn't need it and would
have preferred not to dilute the physical feelings at all.

Curious how she had always kept her physical hungers
separate from her spiritual needs. Edon confused the barriers. His hand and her heat warmed the cloth between her
legs.

"You have some blood, he remarked dispassionately
as he folded the cloth and laid a clean side against her.
Again he held it in place with the palm of his hand.

Tala rose up on her elbows, watching him. "Does that
signify?"

"Aye, it does. I shall have to go gently on you, love.
Much as I may want to make love to you again this very
moment, I will not."

He was a man whose will ruled his life. Tala did not
need more evidence of that truth. "Then how do we spend
the rest of this night together, Edon?"

He gathered up the thin sheet, which was more than
enough covering for this unusually hot summer, and settled
beside her, drawing her against his body once more. He
smoothed her long hair out of the way and kissed the sweet
white flesh beneath her ear.

"We sleep, my lady." he assured her. "But be warned,
I will make no attempt to control myself as I am doing
now when the cock crows. Close your eyes and rest."

Tala yawned and stretched. So much had happened this

day. She was tired, but thrilled by these changes in her life. She settled, cradled by his warm body so close to hers. She slept deep and long, waking to the sound of the lark singing on the windowsill.

Edon awoke to the same song. He lifted his head, blinked and said with a chuckle, "Now that, my little Mercian witch, is an omen I can live with."

Tala snuggled her cheek against Edon's chest as the little bird sang so sweetly at their window. She opened her eyes in time to see the lark take flight.

But as it flew off into the red glow of an angry, dust-choked sunrise, a hawk swept across the strange, glowing sky and struck the little bird a deadly blow. A more ominous portent of evil to come Tala had never witnessed in her life.

Embla stalked the wet stones of the dungeon, barely containing her fury.

"This is all your fault," she screamed at the badly battered man chained to the rock wall. "I was going to poison them all, but there's no chance of doing that now."

In his delirium, Harald Jorgensson could barely raise his head to acknowledge his wife's shrill charge. She marched before him, shaking her sword in her fist, ranting in a paroxysm of temper.

"You could have killed the son of a bitch ten years ago. You had your chance, but no! You were a coward then, just as you are now!"

She sheathed her sword, made her hand into a fist and struck Harald in his blackened face.

"Like everything else, I'll just have to see to it myself, won't I?" she sneered at the man's dangling head.

In truth, there was little pleasure to be had from abusing him anymore, since he no longer had the wits to fight back. Disgusted by the twisted body that hung limply from the chains attached to the wet stone wall, Embla turned away.

She kicked the bucket of stale food Eric the Tongueless periodically brought down to the dungeon.

Enough slop spilled out of it to satisfy her ire for the moment. Then she stalked out, determined to do away with Edon Halfdansson once and for all.

Gwynnth ap Griffin finally cried herself to sleep in old Anna's arms. Not that the servant could do anything to console the princess this night.

Tegwin paced back and forth between the ramp leading to the temple and the yard of King Offa's hunting lodge, stamping his blackthorn staff repeatedly in the dust. "I shall summon a plague of locusts to drive off the Vikings on Lughnasa," he vowed.

"Ha!" cackled Mother Wren. "You, Tegwin, couldn't cast a spell potent enough to raise mayflies off the reeds in the fens. Stop talking nonsense. Our princess needs us!"

"Aye," Selwyn agreed. His thick braid bobbed against his naked, tattooed back. Even the bald spot at the top of his head was tattooed, bearing a triumphant hawk in full flight onto his forehead. "It is time for a show of force and unity. That is the only thing Danes understand."

Tegwin sputtered, hating the way old Mother Wren always argued with him in front of the other elders of their clan. She was as stupid as Embla Silver Throat, always challenging his authority and refusing to recognize his importance. He held the atheling in the palm of his hand. Therein every woman in the shire made their mistake where Tegwin was concerned. This was a man's world. "I do so know how to summon the locusts. I'll show you."

"Oh, be quiet, you old fool." Mother Wren shushed him again. "You trained as a bard, not a druid, and I'm old enough to remember the difference. But I'm not so old that I have forgotten how to cast a spell that will turn you into a bullfrog if you will not mind your tongue in front of these children!"

"Now listen here, you old witch." Tegwin rattled the gold-tipped bones and shells draped around his neck. "I've been the only druid this clan has had for sixty years, I have."

Angered, Wren raised her hand, making the most powerful hex of all—the sign of the cross. Tegwin hastened behind Selwyn in case the old woman did try to turn him into a frog. All the people of the forest knew there was no witch more powerful than one who had converted to the Christ.

"What we need is a plan." Ignoring the squabbling between the two old combatants, Stafford shook his full white head, speaking gravely. "There must be order to our actions."

"'Tis market day," Anna said plainly. "I say we gather our baskets and go up the hill. Together we can distract the Vikings and free the atheling. Wren, you must leave go of your new principles and cast a counterspell to free our prince from the chains of the whipping post."

"Best we rely upon iron to cut iron, not spells." Selwyn stroked the handle of his axe fondly. A decade had passed since he'd used it for anything but cutting wood. "Our prince will not remain captive long."

"Ah!" Wren said, warming to Anna's idea. "That's it! "We will go together, all of us. Anna, wake the princesses. We must get them ready. First we will find our Tala. She will know exactly what we should do."

The abbot of Evesham Abbey, Father Bedwin, had learned the hard way to keep a vigilant lookout posted on Fosse Way. Three times Vikings from Warwick had overrun Evesham. The last attack had emptied the abbey cellars of all of their surplus wine.

For a whole year, Bedwin had been forced to celebrate the mass with a very unpalatable brew made from water and raisins as a substitute for the traditional wine.

The gentle monks had no other choice. There was no wine to be bartered or traded from any abbey or priory in the land. Because of the drought, wine, grain—all commodities—were in short supply, both in Britain and on the Continent.

Evesham, luckily, had grapevines of its own, well-established vines over a century old. Cistercian monks had tended those vines as lovingly as they tended each season's crops. Though decades had passed without a single grape ever ripening, this year's harvest would be substantial.

The unending heat and relentless sun that scorched barley and oats made grapes flourish as they had never done in Mercia before. Britain had not the clime for good wine. This was one of those years that would fill the cellars at Evesham Abbey to capacity and then some.

Father Bedwin capped his daily prayers with a plea for the Almighty to allow the hot weather to continue until the last grape was harvested at Lammas. Midsummer was well behind them.

Today the abbot walked the vineyard, humbly displaying the huge, hanging clusters of nearly purple fruit to King Alfred.

"I am surprised to see such a bounty of grapes," said the king as he mopped his brow with a linen handkerchief. "Little else flourishes in this heat."

Abbot Bedwin gravely agreed with the king. Here at the abbey the monks managed by periodically flooding their fields with water diverted from the Avon.

"And how goes your efforts to teach the farmers how to build terraces and aqueducts?" asked the king.

Alfred's curiosity was boundless. He was an exceptional ruler, concerned with promoting all the arts that made a kingdom thrive, be that animal husbandry, management of the forests or the study of Latin and Greek. His library at Winchester rivaled the Pope's. Alfred knew every book on his shelves by memory. He had another army—that of scribes, who scurried about all the land, writing down local tales and history known only by the bards of the old oral tradition. Abbot Bedwin had great respect for the king.

"We have had much success teaching our methods to the farmers south and west of the Avon, Your Majesty," Father Bedwin answered humbly. "My brothers have traveled all through the Midlands, showing the people how to build aqueducts and slope their fields so that the crops can be irrigated. I have inspected many of the farms hereabouts. We will bring in our crops, for the most part. The rivers have not dropped below ten feet anywhere in the shire."

"Devon and Dorset are in good shape, for it has rained there twice in the past month," Alfred reported. "But I fear for Kent and Sussex. The east is tinder dry, the fields barren. They will yield nothing, not even winter grass for the cattle to graze upon unless August comes in a deluge."

"We are in trying times, my king. All we can do is pray and hope the peace with the Danelaw continues. I heard there was rain north of Watling Street, near Lincoln."

"Aye, I heard the same rumor, but have had no confirmation of that from my friend King Guthrum. I am anxious to parley with him at Warwick. We have much to discuss and compare."

At the mention of Warwick, Abbot Bedwin sputtered. "You would not risk personally visiting Warwick, would you, Your Majesty?"

"Yes, I do risk it. We have agreed, Guthrum and I, to meet there on Lammas Day. We have a wedding to oversee, and I fear it will take the power of both of us to effect it. There has not been more trouble from that direction of late, has there?"

Father Bedwin displayed the palms of his callused hands, then tucked both serenely back inside the deep folds of his brown habit. "I am not one to complain about my neighbors. You know of the pagans of Arden Wood and the Vikings that raid from Warwick Hill. We do what we can in the shadow of such danger to Christianity, but I sincerely regret the last raid. We had ample warning of the barbarian attack, so we lost none of our brethren, only the wine in our cellars.''

"Embla Silver Throat." King Alfred put a name to the berserker that continued to terrorize all the abbeys in Warwickshire.

"A most bitter cross to bear is that warrior woman." Father Bedwin made a sign of the cross, in an effort to forgive the woman's cruelties, which were legion.

"She will be one of the topics of discussion between King Guthrum and me at our conference. Do you know what became of her husband, Harald Jorgensson, Abbot Bedwin? Please do not mince words or spare me any of the unpleasant details you may know.''

"No, Your Majesty, I have nothing to add about the jarl's unfortunate disappearance. It boded ill for all of Warwick, for Jarl Harald was a fair man for a Viking. I cannot say the same for his harridan wife.''

"So it is true what I hear then?" the king concluded. "That she blames all of Warwick for murdering the jarl?''

"Aye, lord, she does, and her wrath has been a hard cross to bear," the abbot admitted.

The king plucked a purple grape from a vine and tasted it, thoughtfully considering the tart flavor. Then he cleared his throat and said, "Guthrum and I meet to discuss the appropriate wergild due for the life of a king's nephew, among other things. He has written to me that some of her attacks upon the peasantry have been justified.

"We agreed upon an emissary to take control of the shire and begin holding monthly eyres. It is his youngest brother by Halfdan's last wife, the Christian princess, Mellisande of Ireland. Edon is his name. Have you met the jarl?''

"No, lord, I cannot say that I have. I have heard rumors

that the jarl arrived in Warwick a sennight ago. He brought with him a most curious retinue whose fame has spread across the shire in a matter of days.''

The king turned at the sound of running feet stamping down the path between the vines. A tonsured brother huffed onto the terrace, his brown robes hiked above his bare ankles, and his round face flushed with the heat.

''My lord king, brother abbot!'' The monk fell to his knees before them. ''Riders approach from Fosse Way out of the north. Shall I ring the alarm?''

''How many riders?'' asked the king bluntly. ''Is it a battle party?''

''Ten, sire, each on a separate mount. Warriors armed with swords and shields and battle-axes.''

The king motioned to his guard for scouts to be sent out to meet the war party before the walls. Alfred's visit to the abbey had been accomplished incognito. Only twenty loyal men had accompanied him, but he was well prepared for trouble, should it come.

''Sound your usual alarm, Abbot, and bring your brethren in from the far fields,'' he instructed the priest.

It was nearing midday, a time when the monks were scattered far out along the demesne, tending the dikes that allowed water from the Avon to flood the furrows in their ripening fields of grain. The animals were let out to graze for the day.

King Alfred continued his perusal of the vineyard, not concerned by the possibility of attack from the north. He had fought the Vikings many times with far less propitious odds.

The war party was halted outside the abbey walls. The king's scout brought only two intruders inside with him. The king immediately recognized the warrior striding toward him with a young squire dogging his heels.

Bishop Nels of Athelney, one of Alfred's oldest and dearest friends, maiched across the vineyard like a champion. They embraced heartily, clapping each other soundly on the back.

"What brings you to Evesham, Nels?" Alfred demanded of his old friend. Nels had stood by him in the dark days of his rule, when the only land Alfred could call his kingdom was the surrounded-by-a-flood, thirty-acre hill of Athelney.

The king and the bishop were as different as night and day. The handsome Saxon king towered above the bulldog-faced Celt. Yet both could fight brutally at the drop of an iron-studded gauntlet, and both had learned to cherish peace more than anything in this vexatious, temporal world.

"Trouble, what else?" Nels laughed deeply, the sound rumbling from the pit of his deep chest. He quickly grabbed hold of the squire lingering behind him. "I come from Warwick, where this quarrelsome boy's life hangs by a thread. He needs a sound beating to straighten out his thinking, but I feared I had not the right to deliver it. So I have brought him to the abbot for sanctuary."

Alfred gazed down at the young lad in the bishop's beefy grip. He looked to be a disreputable peasant by his rough clothes, and no challenge to the bishop's authority. The king's sharp eyes caught a glimpse of a woad tattoo under the boy's shirt. Nels also had tattoos under his fine linen cassock. Most Celts did.

"Sanctuary?" Alfred scoffed. "What's your name, boy?"

Venn cast a belligerent look at the Saxon and kept his jaw clamped shut. He knew better than to admit who he was to anyone. Tala would kill him if he did.

"You'll speak now, boy." Nels gave the lad a sound shake. "This is King Alfred standing before you. You'll show him the respect he deserves, else I'll take you back to Warwick and let the Danes do what they will with you."

Venn's chin jerked up, total surprise registering on his

face. The Saxon was dressed in hunting clothes not much different from the ones Venn wore every day. His golden hair was clubbed at the back of his head with a piece of leather chord and he wore neither torque nor crown as a king should wear. But the man's regal bearing gave eloquent testimony to his identity and sublime proof that the bishop spoke the truth.

"Your Majesty." Venn dropped to his knee before King Alfred. This man was his true guardian and the liege to whom Venn owed his life and his fealty. "I am Venn ap Griffin, the atheling of Leam. Your arm and your sword is sorely needed at Warwick. Vikings hold my sister imprisoned in their fortress. I fear Princess Tala has been violated, forced into an unholy alliance even as we speak. This priest will not take arms with me to slay them, though he had the men and the wherewithal to come to our aid last eve."

That was quite a mouthful for a sullen boy who hadn't spoken five civil words to Nels of Athelney in the past twelve hours.

Alfred looked to the bishop for explanation. His comrade-in-arms shook his head in wonder. "Perhaps we'd best retire to a shady spot, Alfred. This is going to take some lengthy explaining. Atheling or not, the boy stands accused of attempting to poison all of Warwick. Jarl Edon remanded him to my custody to bring to you. The young heathen and his sister are witches."

Two words in the bishop's speech told the king where things stood in Warwick. Tala was up to her old tricks, trying to scare the superstitious Vikings off her land by preying on their deep-seated pagan beliefs. He turned to the abbot, drawing the learned priest into the fold. "My good abbot, this youngster looks half-starved to my eyes. Would you be so kind as to take him to your refectory and feed him?"

"My liege, I want to fight, not eat," Venn declared

hotly. "There isn't time. We must ride with all haste back to Warwick."

Alfred fixed Venn ap Griffin with his most intense glare. He could be imperious when the need arose. "Do you dare to command your king?"

"Nay, sire, I implore you. My sister is in danger. The Wolf of Warwick will devour her."

"The Wolf of Warwick will not harm one hair on your sister's head. Tala ap Griffin is to wed Edon of Warwick by my command. You, Venn of Leam, will attend the wedding, provided I get to the bottom of this business of poisoning Warwickshire. Now, you will go with the abbot and sit and eat your fill. I will speak with you after I have sorted with the bishop what's really the trouble. Good day, boy."

Venn's eyes widened in shock. He wanted to argue that that couldn't be so. Tala married! No princess of Leam had ever married. The king turned away and walked off with the bishop. Venn's jaw sagged.

The abbot caught hold of his arm, tugging him back to his feet. Venn accompanied him to the abbey's vast kitchen. There, every kind of food a growing boy dreamed of was readily at hand. As starved as Venn was, he thought he'd died and gone to a Christian's heaven.

Chapter Twelve

It was market day at Warwick. Though she had awoken rested, the afterglow of Edon's thorough lovemaking made Tala feel lazy. She lay abed, listening to the community beyond the open window come to life.

The gates of the fortress were flung wide, allowing cart after cart to lumber across the creaking wooden bridge. Animals were driven out of their pens to the fields for the day. Oxen lowed and snorted, pulling their loads. Farmers and craftsman called out cheerful greetings to one and all, announcing their wares in bellowing voices.

Underlying the commotion of commerce was the noise of stonecutters and masons setting about their heavy, racket-producing work. The blacksmith's anvil rang. His bellows hissed as the banked embers at his forge were coaxed to life. Carpenters slammed wood ladders against the stone walls of the keep outside Edon's high window.

There was no hope for a longer, lingering sleep. Tala had to get up. She quickly washed and was in her kirtle when Lady Eloya knocked on the door, bringing her a fresh gown to wear. Eloya insisted upon doing Tala's hair and put a cushion on a stool before Tala could refuse.

This morning Tala needed the cosseting. Her body ached in the most tender places. Servants came in and stripped the jarl's bed of its linens and put fresh sheets in their place. Not a word was whispered about the blood-stained linens they took away to wash. Eloya put her hands on Tala's shoulders and gave her a comforting squeeze that as much as said welcome to womanhood.

They broke their fast to the clamoring of a righteous racket made by hammers, saws, chisels. Satisfied from the bread and cheese on the morning table, Tala went out to have a look around the ward. The fortress gates were open to one and all. She took that to mean that she could leave at will. She certainly should go to Black Lake and check on her sisters and the old ones.

Only leaving Warwick was the last thing she wanted to do, and she mentally justified her decision by imagining dire repercussions if she did leave. What would happen to Venn if she left Warwick without Edon's permission? Would Edon allow her to go if she explained about her three sisters remaining in Arden Wood?

More importantly, where was Venn? Then she remembered that Edon had told the bishop to take Venn to Evesham this morning. Assuming that that's where her brother was, Tala contented herself with wandering among the gaily decorated stalls of the merchants.

She went first to the stall of the Leam goldsmiths, for she spotted their bright awning right away. They were surprised to see her inside Warwick. All her people knew Warwick was not a safe place for a princess of Leam to be. Rather than answer questions, Tala inspected their many new items—rings and armlets, buttons and bracelets that showed their great skill.

Jacob, the diamond cutter who rented a square in the goldsmiths' stall, said to her, "My lady, King Alfred bought six stones for his lady wife and daughters yesterday in Worcester."

"He did?" Tala said, surprised to hear that her kinsman was so near to Warwick.

"Aye." Jacob nodded, proud to have news of the king's whereabouts. "He had been hunting in Malverne. You must take one of these baubles before they are all gone. It is all we have of this design, Princess."

Tala removed the jeweled pin from a brooch. "It is very beautiful, Jacob. Perhaps I can interest the jarl's ladies in your work. They linger in the keep, fussing over the baby's clothing."

"Is it true that there is a Jewess among the ladies?" Jacob asked. He was also a matchmaker among his tribe.

"Aye, Rebecca of Hebron is her name, but she is already married."

"And you, Princess? Are the rumors true that you will soon wed?"

"When did you hear that?" Tala was startled by the question.

"Days ago, in Loytcoyt. May I offer my felicitations." Jacob bowed obsequiously, the tight curls of his forelocks bobbing before his prominent ears. "You must accept the matched brooches as a wedding present from my house to yours."

"I couldn't possibly accept so grand a gift, Jacob, and you know that." Tala put the brooch back in the jewel merchant's hand. He was not her subject and owed her no tithe. The goldsmiths, on the other hand, did. They hovered nearby, staring at her so intently they were almost rude, and listening openly to her words with Jacob.

"Is it true, my lady? the elder of the two brothers asked. "Do you break custom and take a husband? Where is your torque that we made for your coming of age?"

Edon overheard the goldsmiths ask their questions and saw how Tala self-consciously touched her neck when reminded of her missing badge of rank. She did not have to explain to them what she had done with her torque. He came to her side and put a proprietary hand on her shoulder.

"The princess's torque had a flaw in it that scratched her delicate skin," he told the smiths. "Show me what you have that is better made."

Both smiths took exception to the jarl's words, for there were no finer torques in the world than those they created for the princesses of Leam. They exchanged a look between them, then the younger brother brought forth a heavy rosewood casket from beneath his stall. He set it on the trestle, produced an iron key and unlocked the hasp.

Inside the casket were four torques on a velvet tray. Only one was crafted of the three-wire, nine-strand gold necessary for a royal Leamurian ornament. The smiths folded their arms across their chests and allowed Edon to choose what he liked, smug in their certainty that he would not know the difference.

The gold of each torque glistened in the morning sun. Edon unerringly took the finest one from the cloth-lined tray. It was heavy and pure, the twisted strands malleable in his hands.

Tala held her breath as he handled the sacred neck ornament. Yesterday she would have considered it a fitting gift for Branwyn, the Lady of the Lake. Yesterday Tala had been a virgin and fit to act as a go-between for her people to the goddess. Today she was not. The weight of that sin colored her throat and face. She could not look at Edon or either of the goldsmiths to save her soul.

"This is of excellent work," Edon said after a moment's close inspection. "But I do not like the fobs at the ends. Have you any wolf heads?"

"Ah," said the smiths in unison, having come prepared for just such a request from the new jarl, "yes, lord, we do."

"Show them to me," Edon commanded.

One lifted the upper tray, which was cleverly inserted in the casket that contained the torques. Under it was a whole collection of cast heads—fierce wolves, snarling wolves, thoughtful wolves, sleeping wolves and young wolves. Each was a perfect pair to cap the ends of any torque in the tray above.

Edon considered the heads and the weight of the nine-stranded torque in his hand. It was too heavy an ornament for Tala's slender neck, and a wolf head simply did not suit her. But then her torque must have been of a similar weight and it had been capped with winged dragons.

He chose the young wolves and ordered the goldsmiths to change the heads on the torque in his hand. Then he took another one, of three strands of gold beautifully chased, and put that around Tala's neck.

"Oh, no, Edon, you mustn't." She began to remove the torque the instant he fitted the ornament around her throat, but he caught her hands, stilling them.

"Be quiet, Tala," he said sternly. Then he lifted her chin and considered the fit and the style. "This will do for my lady. I also need rings for her hand and mine as well, a matched set. I like that design with the interlocking bars."

He selected a Celtic wedding-band set. They were a tradition among her people, for couples who married for love.

"As you wish, lord." The smiths bowed, asking to size their fingers before Edon and Tala left to visit another stall. He allowed the fitting, then tucked Tala's hand firmly on his arm and walked with her down the row of stalls.

"I wondered where you had gotten yourself off to, my lady," he said by way of directing the topic of discussion. Theo had divined what she'd done with her torque, but it remained to be explained *why* she had done such a drastic thing. That was what Edon wanted most to know.

He put the question to her. "You never did tell me why you sacrificed your torque. This one is not so fine, but I see your people expect to see you properly adorned. I have never seen so many men give a single woman such out-

rageous looks all at one time. What is the symbolism I am
missing?''

Tala touched the lightweight necklace at her throat.
"Thank you for the gift, lord. I will see that you are re-
imbursed the cost."

Why she had cast her sacred badge of rank into the lake
was a matter between herself and the goddess. At the time
she had not realized what it would mean to her people.
She saw now that they thought the Viking lord had
stripped her of her honor. That he had in effect raped her
as his warriors raped their land.

Tala could do nothing about setting the gossip straight
until after Lughnasa. Likewise, Edon's answers had to wait
until then as well. If she admitted the truth to him, she
knew Edon would interfere with Venn's destiny.

This marriage talk covered her people's sense of shame.
Princesses of Leam did not marry. Those who broke taboo
eventually were ostracized, shunned and went to live in
the glens alone. Some had become powerful witches,
feared and revered. Morgan le Fey was one.

"You will not repay me for any gift I present you,"
Edon said severely, refusing her offer. "Let us go and look
among the cloth merchants. You have need of clothing
suitable for Warwick. I will set Eloya and Rebecca to work
making you new garments as soon as we have chosen good
cloth."

"Are you plying me with the gifts of a leman, lord?
Paying me for the service I rendered to you last night?"

Edon stopped dead in his tracks, his hand tightening on
Tala's arm. He whirled her around before him, determined
to make her answer him. "What did you say?"

What she had said did not bear repeating. Certainly not
in a louder voice to make her meaning and intent any more
clear than it had been the first time. Edon's faculties were
sharp and intact. He knew exactly what she meant, and it
made him livid that she would think of herself in that way.

Didn't she understand she would be his wife? A husband *had* the right to buy gifts for his wife.

Tala twisted her arm, fighting the tight grasp of his fingers. She would not stoop to arguing with him in public. Shamefaced, she gathered Eloya's gown in her fists and ran from Edon before either of them could publicly embarrass themselves further.

As she dodged among the crowds, Vikings and Mercians alike, she heard Edon shout her name and knew that he would follow her. The issue between them was honor.

But in the clear light of day there was none to be had. She had betrayed her people so that she could enjoy the pleasures of the flesh in the Wolf of Warwick's bed.

Now she saw what she had done for what it was.

Desperate for a place of sanctuary, Tala stood on the apex of Warwick Hill, needing the one thing she could never find within these walls: the solace of her glen, her spring and the healing waters of Leam—balm for her troubled soul.

No wonder the Lady of the Lake refused to answer her urgent prayers. She must have known the wickedness Tala harbored in her heart and the lust she bore a Viking jarl.

The troop of mummers arrived well before midday. All work in the shire seemed to have stopped completely with their arrival. Inside the palisade walls the ranks swelled to an immense crowd. Rig had no idea where all these people had come from. Nor had he realized that market day in the shire would cause him so much grief.

Lord Edon was in a rare mood, as wildly angry as his namesake the wolf, and the people of Warwick sensed this. He prowled the crowd like the dangerous predator, hunting the missing princess.

Tala had vanished into thin air. Rig had with his own eyes seen the princess of Leam disappear. One minute she had been standing at the top of the hill, the next she had bent down and grasped a handful of dust and blown it to the four winds.

Rig was not the only Viking who had witnessed her skillful spell casting. Thorulf and Maynard had also harkened to Edon's shout to stop the woman and had given chase with him through the crowd.

They had closed in upon her when she stopped running—on the peak of the raised motte. There she had blown dust into their eyes and blinded all of them, conjuring up a great whirlwind. Perhaps she *was* a witch, Rig thought. Grains of sand still stung his eyes, and he had not caught so much as a glimpse of her skirts since.

Edon strode across the ward to where Rig stood, rubbing his irritated eyes in dismay. He did not believe in spells, Tala must be hiding somewhere!

"No one has seen her go out the gates," Edon snarled. He trusted Maynard's guards on duty there. They were good men, reliable and true, not given to drink. If they said the princess of Leam had not walked out the gates of Warwick then she hadn't. "Have the grounds been thoroughly searched?"

"Aye," Rig answered. It had been done.

"Keep searching. Don't stop until she's found."

What he would do with her when he found her was the question. Edon stalked into the keep, prowling up the steps to the second floor with a heavy, telling tread. Eloya and Rebecca looked up at him when he came into the upper hall. Both gathered their sewing and fled out of sight to Eloya's chamber.

Distraught, Edon poured himself a goblet of wine and stood consuming it, quenching his raging thirst. "Well?" he demanded when he had slammed the silver cup back onto the board and turned to find Blind Theo before him.

"She does not wish to be found, Wolf," Theo said bluntly.

"Why?" Edon scowled. It was a wasted expression, for

Theo could not see the anger suffusing Edon's hurt face. Where had Tala gone? Why did she hide from him? When would she come back, and what would he do if she did not?

"You must consider this a time for licking one's wounds," Theo advised. "Someone offended the princess. I sense it was a look she was given, though I cannot be certain. Her status is at issue and she is troubled. She will surface before nightfall."

Edon groaned. He wanted her in his arms now!

He vowed to get roaring drunk in the meantime and woe unto her when she came to ground. Edon grasped the Persian brass pitcher and filled his goblet to the rim.

"There are visitors at the gate asking for you." Theo abruptly turned, his sightless eyes fixed on the unseen.

"I don't give a damn for visitors at the gate. The ward is overrun with a multitude of visitors I didn't invite." Edon grabbed the cup and hoisted it to his mouth, watching Theo twist his head quizzically, the way Sarina did when she listened to sounds Edon could not hear.

"Shall I go to greet them in your stead?" Theo asked.

"Do that." Edon dropped onto a chaise, snatching the pitcher of wine in hand and draining the cup in his other hand in one gulp.

Theo carefully took up his long white staff of supple aspen. He began to shuffle and tap his way toward the stairs, nimble and certain of his path. They were settled in for good if Theo knew his way about Warwick without a servant cleaving to his side.

It wasn't Theo's maneuvering that troubled Edon. It was Tala's. Why had she likened his gift of gold to the coins paid a prostitute?

Tala didn't need an oracle to tell her when Edon came inside the keep. She heard every word he spoke to Theo and each of Theo's replies. Nor did the Greek need his second sight to delve into her whereabouts. The ladies and Theo all knew she was in Edon's chamber, trying to control her sobbing.

These tears humiliated her more than she could publicly bear. She was not a woman easily given to shedding tears. When Edon came into the hall, Tala quickly wiped her face and blew her nose as softly as she could to clear her head. That was it. She resolved to cry no more for her lost virtue.

It was time she faced the truth squarely. She was no longer an exalted princess of Leam, the repository of her people's dreams and prayers. She was an ordinary woman now, free to accept the man she had chosen. She need not hang her head in shame or allow other people to give her looks that lessened her self-worth.

She pressed her hands onto the bedding and stood up, squaring her shoulders and straightening the folds of her gown. It was a beautiful gown, with a soft green sheath that hung gracefully from the two brooches fastening the shoulders. The neckline of Tala's kirtle was square. She lifted her chin and touched the gold torque at her throat, tucked the handkerchief inside her sleeve and went into the hall to speak to Edon.

He had a goblet tilted to his mouth. A moment passed before he lowered it enough to see her standing just beyond the sprawl of his long legs on the chaise.

The cup did a funny thing—it dropped once, then dropped again, though no wine splashed out onto Edon's sleeveless tunic. Then he slammed the cup onto the table at his side, and he did spill the wine in the brass pitcher when he dropped that beside the goblet.

His eyes glowed like a wolf's in the forest as he lunged to his feet in front of her. "By Odin's breath, you are a witch!"

Tala took a step back as he came at her. His hard hands clenched her waist, yanking her to him in a crushing grip.

His mouth slashed across hers in a kiss that spoke of need and want so overwhelming that it shook her to her toes.

Deliberately, Tala spread her fingers into the soft waves of black hair that graced his temples. She opened her mouth, accepting the intrusion of his tongue, matching his fervor and heat.

He kissed her hard, desperately, conveying more than need—a loss, perhaps, the abandonment that he'd felt when she'd vanished from his sight. It could be so easy to blind an enraged man, to cast a spell that confused him and left him turning about, lost and incoherent. Tala held back from taking such advantage against him. If either of them was spellbound, it was she. Her heart was melting under his fierce, possessive gaze. No shield or armor, spell or potion could be called upon to protect her from falling deeply in love with him.

Edon thrust his fingers into the braids coiled at the back of her neck and pulled her head back. He stared into her bewitching amber eyes and growled, "Don't you practice your witchery on me, lady!"

Tala didn't shy from his terrifying power. She caught his ears and brought his mouth down to hers, kissing him with the same need and abandon he had wielded. Caution was thrown to the wind.

Edon's arm tightened across her hips. He straightened abruptly, tossing her over his shoulder. He stalked into his chamber, slammed the door shut at his back. The oak popped loudly in its frame. Tala shivered as she slid down his chest, her skirts hiking up from the pressure of his arm against her flesh.

Edon pushed her backward onto his bed, splitting her milk white thighs as he covered her. He caught the top of her gown and ripped it open. He exposed her breasts with no more force than she used in her frantic efforts to unfasten his breeks.

He sprang free in her unskilled hands, consumed with

the desire to get inside her and stay there for the rest of eternity.

He tasted of wine and temper. That was more than good enough for Tala. She wanted to be conquered, wanted the ghosts and demons haunting her to be exorcised completely. Edon was real. Edon was life. Edon was her passion's wolf, stalking her to his lair, curling up inside her and devouring her heart.

He was a man who could throw back his head and laugh at the gods, mock them all and make their petty vanities insignificant fears to be chased away like bad dreams plaguing a silly child. She clung to him, clung to his strength and let him wreak his havoc upon her. But it wasn't havoc...it was loving—sweet and fierce, filled with the essence of life.

In that swirling, heady maelstrom of surrender, Tala realized the truth—she loved the Wolf of Warwick.

She loved Edon Halfdansson. She would sacrifice everything to remain with him, surrender her life to protect him. Her soul, her heart and her mind opened to shower him in that love without reservation. With the deliberate and conscious release of the tightly cocooned emotions locked inside her came undescribable joy and a feeling of pure happiness that she'd never in her life experienced.

"Edon!" Tala said over and over again, showering his face with kisses, touching him, curling into him. She was happy, complete and at one with him, sated on every level possible. He was her perfect mate, made for her.

Neither noticed the fierce heat inside the closed chamber until they were both spent and exhausted, lying tangled together in a sweat-soaked heap.

Edon lifted the damp braids from the back of her neck and kissed her shoulder. She drew her nails down his chest, leaving little marks that would fade when their skin cooled—if it ever did.

Their clothes lay in rags on the bed and the floor, destroyed in their fit of passion. Ruefully, Tala eyed Lady Eloya's green gown and knew she would have to replace the cloth. She told herself she would see to that some other market day.

Leaving Edon's lair held no appeal whatsoever.

Edon caught hold of her hip and rolled her over on his chest, propping her chin above his with his thumb. "What are you thinking, woman?"

Tala straddled his hips, pressed her hands into the bedding and straightened up as far as his arm at her back would allow. "That I shall stay in my wolf's lair for the rest of eternity."

"Best you think again if you seek to hide your beauty from the world, kitten." He grinned cheekily. Oh, but the pointed way her breasts hung above his head inviting his mouth to savor them again. Tempted too much, he lifted his head to catch the nearest with his mouth and pulled her down so that he could suckle at his leisure.

Her moist belly arched against him, and his shaft sprang back to life, renewed with a vigor that made his blood pound in his ears. He had heard her say his name a hundred times. That delighted him more than anything in the world.

Laughing, Edon rolled her onto her back, trying to regain control of his raging desire for her. She was too newly his, too new to such wild lovemaking. To take her again would be callous beyond belief. He laid his hand on her belly and lifted his mouth from her breast.

"Be still," he said sternly.

Tala's hands dropped from his chest and arm. "I have displeased you," she said, stricken.

"No, you have pleased me beyond my wildest dreams," Edon said very firmly.

He was in control now. The red haze of lust was abating enough that he could think what he was doing. Not one coherent thought to her own pleasure had entered his brain until now and she wasn't going to drive that thought blindly out of his mind again.

"I want to kiss you." Tala slipped her hand behind his head to pull his mouth back to hers. "I like kissing very much."

"It has its place." Edon shook her hand away as easily as he shook the heavy hair at his nape behind his shoulders. He straightened above her, picking her up under her arms, lifting her higher onto the bed. Then he put both of his knees between her lovely white legs and separated them while he sat back on his heels.

Beautiful hot sunlight revealed all of her luscious body to his gaze. The damp curls at the apex of her thighs were as red as the tangled and frayed braids spilling across the sheets under her head. Her breasts were swollen and full from his lovemaking, her nipples hardened wet nubs in their rosy areolas. He laid his hand on her belly and circled her navel, gently kneading the soft swell between her hipbones.

"What are you doing?" Tala asked, feeling uncertain. His gaze no longer lingered on her face or even her breasts. He was looking at her most intently…there, at that… She hadn't a word for what exactly he looked at, but she could feel the heat of his gaze burning on her flesh. And the way his hand slowly circled her belly was like a monstrous tease. He came closer and closer to her curls, grazing them with his knuckles, tormentingly close, but not close enough. "Edon, I asked what you're doing?"

"Be quiet, Tala. I am going to teach you a woman's pleasure and I don't want to be distracted. You haven't screamed for me, and I want to hear you shout that you love me at the top of your voice. I want every man in Warwickshire to envy me when I enter you again. I want them all to know that the Wolf of Warwick has his mate at his mercy. I want you to shudder and shake, and need me as much as I need you. That is what making love is all about. So just be quiet and I will do all the work. There will be no spells involved and no witchcraft. I don't need any herbs or potions or magic words.''

She shivered as his nails raked through the curls, fluffing them, tangling in them. She sank her teeth into her lower lip as his left hand came into play, stroking slowly up the inside of her right thigh.

"Edon, this is very embarrassing. It's broad daylight. It's wrong. You shouldn't be looking at me like that.''

"Looking like what? Like I am a starving man and this is the first meal I've been offered in a month?'' His hands came together at her nether lips, one hand parted the petals and the other slipped inside her, probing as he'd done last night in the dark.

Tala tensed and sat up, grasping his wrists. "Don't,'' she whispered desperately. Dear Branwyn help her, she could see the tops of people's heads out the window.

She'd distracted him enough that Edon looked where she had looked. Way off in the distance beyond the palisade there were men in the distant fields. He grinned as he looked back at the panic in her liquid eyes. "Lie down, Tala, and no one will see you. They cannot see what I see.'' He found the spot he was looking for and caught it firmly between his powerful fingers, tugging it tautly, settling his thumb over the tiny button.

The sinewy chord in it fattened as his thumb circled round and round. Tala grabbed the sheet and threw it over her head. Edon chuckled and pulled the sheet away from her face, then he set to work stoking her fire. He wanted her to burn for him as badly as he burned for her.

She shot upright again when he put his mouth to her and kissed her. He put his arm across her belly and held her down, without explaining why he needed to exercise such restraint. She was as wet and sweet as honey, thick with her own cream, bucking under the pleasure of his tongue bringing her to the pinnacle of desire. Her hips

arched against him, her buttocks lifting with those sharp
undulating jerks that told of her coming explosion.

He opened his eyes to watch her belly spasm and her
head twist frantically back and forth on the bed. Sweat
glistened from her every pore, wetting her thighs where
they squeezed and relaxed upon his head. Still his tongue
kept laving her. He slid two fingers inside her tight sheath,
giving her the slow, steady thrusts that touched her womb,
suckling her nubbin the way he had attended her breasts
in each love duel prior to this.

What he wanted now with single-minded purpose was
her complete submission to his tuition. He played her body
like a well-strung harp, making her every muscle sing with
pleasure. Her breath came in sharp, quick gasps, hampered
by the fist she had crammed in her mouth to keep her
moans to herself.

He knew exactly the moment the explosion inside her
came. The walls of her womb tightened ferociously on his
fingers the way he'd felt her body clench on his shaft and
drive him to exploding inside her. Instantly afterward
every muscle in her lower body began to shake and tremble. Edon withdrew his fingers and walked up her body on
his hands and knees. He paused a moment above her,
watching her taut expression dissolve as she opened her
eyes, panting.

"You still haven't screamed." He took her hand from
her mouth and laid her limp arm beside her head, gripping
her wrist lightly. "Bring your knees to my waist, Tala, and
lock your ankles behind my back."

The inside of her thighs quivered as they clasped him.
She was compliant, obedient. Edon braced himself with
his right hand, reached down and settled his aching shaft
at her portal. One downward stroke sank him to the hilt.
The scream he'd wanted to hear erupted from her lips.

Edon smoothed her hair away from her face with the
palm of his hand and caught her chin in his fingers, tilting

her face up to meet his. A tender smile creased the corners of his eyes. His voice was soft and comforting as he said, "Now, my love, is time for kissing."

His mouth played over hers, applying soft kisses, gently nipping at her lips, their tongues mating, dueling, dancing together. He let her rest beneath him, his weight contained on the fulcrum of her hips, the penetration deep and quiet, the beast in him dormant for the moment. It was a tender quiet, a quiet to be savored, waiting to build to an enormous, satisfying release for each of them.

Again Edon smoothed back the damp tangles of silky hair that clung to her brow and cheek. "Do you still want me, Tala?" he asked almost hesitantly.

She lifted her hand and rubbed the backs of her fingers across his cheek. "Aye, I do. More with each moment that passes between us."

Reveling in the sweetness of her, Edon dipped his head to her shoulder, allowing both of her hands complete freedom to stroll across his back and sides, caressing him the way he'd worshiped her. He slid his hands under her back, grasping her shoulders, and began to undulate his hips with a slow, steady rhythm—deep even strokes that gave him more pleasure than he'd ever known.

Her body was simply perfect for him, built to respond to his, to cushion and resist him. She matched the tempo of his rhythm each time it changed. Her breath caught in her throat in a little gasp. Edon lifted his head and kissed her neck, planted his elbows and tightened his hands on her shoulders, to pull her downward with each stroke, to increase the power of their mating.

Instinctively her knees tightened at his hips. Her hands flattened on his back and caught hold of the flexing muscles in his shoulders. Her belly slapped against his, then became concave and rounded again with each upward thrust.

"That's it." Edon encouraged her to work as hard as

he did. "Bear down on me, Tala. Inside, make your womb grab hold and squeeze now." His head dropped with the exquisite pleasure of her motion.

He held back, certain that it would be well worth the agony now to wait for her. Her breath had become completely erratic, catching inside her, expelling in frantic moans.

"Edon, please!" she cried.

"Not yet." He shook his hair out of his eyes, lifted his shoulders completely from her and dug his hands into the wood frame of the box bed for support.

Her eyes opened, desperation in them. "Edon!"

"No," he commanded, locking his jaw against release. The pace doubled. The whole frame of the bed danced on its stout legs, knocking like four devils on the wood floor.

"Edon!" Tala screamed.

"Not yet!" He shut his eyes fiercely, refusing to be tempted by her delirious beauty. Just when he thought he could push his control to a new height, her womb wrested the last of his will from him. It clamped upon him, gripping him in midstroke, and that unbelievable, inexpressible contraction began that spent him completely and milked him of every ounce of seed inside his body.

"My Lord!" Tala yelled.

"Yes!" Edon's shout was the last gasp of a dying man's exploding heart. "Odin, save me!"

He collapsed in a blaze of pleasured pain from which there surely would never be any reprieve.

Edon was so still and motionless after he collapsed that Tala thought he was dead. The room was like the iron-master's furnace, blazing with heat and sun pouring directly onto them from the west.

Tala couldn't move. Morbid cramps seized hold of her thighs as she lay pinned beneath Edon. Her breath came in scary little pants that didn't begin to satisfy her need for more air.

But inside her, where all of her feelings had centered completely, there was this wonderful throbbing that went on and on.

She closed her eyes and reveled in it. When she did that, the sun and the heat felt so, so good. Edon's weight felt like the most soothing coverlet she'd ever snuggled under in her life.

"Tala, be still. I have nothing left. Nothing, you greedy witch." His lips moved against her neck. He was alive. His chest inflated just a little, pressing down on hers. He groaned like a man mortally wounded.

"Don't move," she whispered, content as they were.

"As if I could."

Edon took a deep breath, gathering what little strength he had. He opened his eyes mere slits to find this wicked redhead in his bed, wearing nothing but a sated, cat-ate-the-cream smile. Odin help him!

He brought his hand to his face, rubbing it, and moistened his lips. Still, he hadn't the strength to move.

"Edon..." Tala swallowed. "I don't think I will ever be able to leave this room. You have taught me what you meant about hearing me scream. I am probably going to have to think long and hard about how to manage this. Surely there must be a law written about just how smug and arrogant a man is allowed to be."

Edon chuckled. He couldn't laugh. Not yet. He managed to tug gently on her hair. "I will find a very large sack to put over your head so that you do not have to look people in the eye when they congratulate me for having made you scream out my name.

Tala curled up her fingers and hit him. He caught her hand and brought it to his mouth, kissing the poor little weak fist that couldn't wound a gnat at this moment.

His rakish smile melted Tala's heart. What was she going to do? It was too late to turn back. She'd already fallen in love with him. "Don't let your prowess go to your head," she warned him, coming to her senses at last. She found enough strength left inside her to tighten her fist when Edon turned her hand over to kiss the palm.

"Thank you, Tala. That was a splendid tryst." Edon laid her hand on her chest between her breasts.

"A tryst?" she echoed, chilled by that word.

He looked out the window to judge the time. The sun could now be seen in the shaped glass at the top of the window frame. Colored light danced on the stone wall and the floor at the far corner of the chamber. It was nearing the third hour after noon.

"I'm thirsty, Tala. Get up and fetch me a cup of water."

"You jest, Viking," she mumbled. She was still reeling from their lovemaking being called a tryst…as if what had happened in his bed was of no import whatsoever.

Edon tilted his head on his folded hands, looking at her. How like a cat she was, sprawled in the sun, soaking in the rays. Would her white belly freckle if she lay here long enough, absolutely naked? Her legs were brown from the sun and freckled, too. All her freckles were very nice, but her white, white belly was the nicest of all.

She hadn't moved a muscle since he'd placed her hand between her breasts.

"Are you going to fetch my water, woman?" Edon asked.

Tala opened her eyes and looked at him. His smugness needed lessoning. "Do I have to? When I can get up from this bed, it will be to go and see my brother…or else to go to the privy…"

"Ah, ha." Edon sat up and swung his legs off the bed. He stood abruptly in one smooth motion, rising to his full, impressive height without any seeming effort at all. "So now you want to go to the privy and take off for Evesham to see your brother, do you? He is just a boy whom you have spoiled abominably and who hasn't been away from your skirts for one full day. What happened to that declaration of yours that you could never leave this chamber or look any of my men in the eye?''

"I never said that," Tala countered, sitting up as he poured a cup of water from the pitcher. She held out her hand, expecting to be served.

Edon frowned. "That is what you meant. That is why I said I would provide you with a big sack to wear over your head. All my men have heard you scream for me to satisfy you, Tala ap Griffin. You may not have noticed how quiet it became outdoors when you were screaming, but I heard the silence. The bed jumped three feet across the floor with the racket you caused. See, look behind you and you will see it is a full arm's length farther from the wall. You are naught but a little woman with puny strength, but you can yell louder than an Irish banshee when you take your pleasure.''

Her face flooded with color, but best to Edon's eye was that the blush began at her breasts and spread upward into her throat. Some of it even ran down onto her midriff, making her white, white belly attract his eye again. The little wretch noticed the direction his hungry eyes moved and she snatched up the sheet and drew it across her.

Edon drained the cup of water and set it down. Restored, he reached across her foot and caught the sheet, yanking it off her.

"Give that back, you cur." Tala caught hold of a corner of the sheet. "I won't sit here naked for you to drool at like some rheumy-eyed old man!''

"You won't?" Edon snapped the cloth out of her hands, rolled the sheet into a ball and threw it out the window.

Tala gasped, shocked that he would do such a thing. She dragged her hand through her hair, looking about her for her clothes. Edon saw the direction of her gaze and beat her to her kirtle. In one step he had the garment in hand, rolling it into a tighter ball than he had the sheet.

"You wouldn't dare," Tala exclaimed as she got off the bed. He wouldn't, would he?

Edon packed the wadded cloth tighter, his eyebrow lifted in a dark arch. "What good are clothes to a princess who never expects to leave this room?" he demanded. "Who expects to be served hand and foot by those who come inside these walls? I asked for a drink of water from you and you refused, but you held out your hand, demanding the cup of water I poured for myself. If you want this kirtle, you had better come and get it before I throw it to the rabble beneath this window. There are many out there that would save it as a reminder of the screams they heard coming out this window today."

Tala's lower lip started to tremble. She looked to the window, but didn't dare come away from the protection of the solid stone wall. For the love of Branwyn, she was naked. "Why are you being so cruel to me?"

Edon hardened his heart against her impending storm of tears. "Why are you so thoughtless?"

That stopped the tears before they spilled. "I'm not," she said insistently.

"You are," he retorted.

"Then go ahead. Throw my kirtle out the window. Maybe some poor wretch who hasn't got anything but a scratchy wool rag to wear will catch it. What do I care? I have plenty of kirtles. What makes you think I need to wear anything at all, Viking? I can cast a spell and walk out of here just as I am and no one will know the difference except you."

Tala ran her hand through her hair one more time, then spun around on her bare foot and marched to the door. She caught the iron handle in her fist and yanked.

Edon tossed the kirtle over his shoulder, not caring if it went out the window or not. "If you open that door and walk out of this room naked, spell or no spell, you will be one very sorry princess."

Shaking her hair so that more of it would fall and give her some covering, Tala said over her shoulder, ''Viking, what makes you so certain that I am not already one very sorry princess?''

The line drawn in the quicksand between them, she yanked open the oak door and walked out.

Chapter Thirteen

An instant later Tala slammed the door shut at her back. Nearly blind with anger, she took two steps into Edon's hall and froze.

The hall was not empty!

It should have been. It was the middle of the afternoon. Over a thousand people attended the market. Every one of Edon's entourage should have been outdoors, haggling with the merchants and farmers. Tala should have had the time to gather her wits, or at least cast a spell of invisibility about her once she had slammed Jarl Edon's bedchamber door.

Pride should have girded her with a cloak of protection before she even thought to cast a spell. There was not a heartbeat of time to accomplish anything. Before her was a hall filled to standing room only. The slamming door caused every head in the hall to swing her direction. Tala's nakedness kept those heads turned while eyes widened, focused and outright stared.

"Oh, dear," Lady Eloya murmured, as King Alfred rose from Edon's high-backed chair. Rashid touched Eloya's arm and silence fell as the king put out his hand and stopped the withdrawal of a deadly blade from the scabbard at Venn ap Griffin's waist.

"Let me go, sire," the young prince yelled. "I told you we'd come too late. I'll kill the bastard!"

"You will do nothing of the kind," the king commanded.

Tala gulped. She had two choices in that instant. She could continue forward, throw herself at her cousin's feet and beg his protection, or she could turn around, swallow the pride she had left and retreat to the Viking, thereby allowing Edon to gloat over her stupidity all the rest of her miserable days.

Knowing full well that it was going to cost her a much deserved beating no matter which route she chose, she opted for the king. He had shown mercy in the past.

Time seemed to have come to a complete standstill. No one moved as Tala strode across the hall and came to a stop within striking distance of King Alfred's long arm. She dropped to her knee before the king, bowing her head deeply. Some of her tangled, sleep-mussed hair fell across her shoulders and covered her nakedness.

She brought both her hands together, her bent arms covering her breasts, saying urgently, "Your Majesty, forgive me. I throw myself upon your mercy."

By Anu's shroud, she wanted to die. She wanted Lugh to split the floor of the keep and open a hole in the earth to swallow her up in the otherworld. The ripe scent of her own body rose up to torment her more. Tala kept her downcast eyes on the planks of unvarnished wood before the king. She didn't dare look above the scuffling feet of her brother, struggling to free himself from the king's soldier who forcibly contained him.

"For the love of God, someone give me my cloak," Alfred said in a choked voice. Immediately, the king's steward produced Alfred's ermine-lined cloak and dropped the heavy cloth across Tala's shoulders. She clutched it around her, mortified, beginning to shake at her own tenacity. Oh, what she would give to roll back time one-

quarter of an hour, to be back in that bed when Edon had
asked her for a drink of water!

"Marshal, clear this hall!" Alfred's shout broke the
spell-shocked inertia. Instantly, people jumped into pur-
poseful motion. Venn lunged free of the soldier restraining
him, whipped his dagger out of its sheath and ran at the
closed door of Edon's bedchamber.

"Nels!" Alfred commanded, "Take that boy out! Tie
him back to the whipping post if he gives you one bit of
trouble. Tala ap Griffin, get on your feet. You had the
audacity to march into this room as naked as the day you
were born. Rise up now and stand before me and account
for what you think you're doing in this shire! I gave you
leave to go to Chester, did I not?"

"Your Majesty?" Tala looked up, terrified.

Venn gave a fierce shout as he was captured and his
weapon wrenched out of his hand. Bishop Nels himself
wrapped him in an armlock and wrestled him to the stairs.
Venn roared a protest that would have credited the lion in
Edon's menagerie.

The king's guards and Edon's hustled the curious down
the narrow steps to the lower floor after the bishop. They
could not get people moving anywhere near fast enough
to suit Tala or King Alfred.

"I said stand up!" Alfred roared.

Tala jerked upright, unaided, trembling from head to
foot. Never in her life had her knees rattled so hard. She
made herself look at her cousin. Alfred was twelve years
the older, but he had spent half of his life commanding an
army. She had never feared his wrath before. She did now.
Her eyes darted to the only escape from this keep, the
stairwell. Her jaw moved up and down but no words could
come out of her throat. She wet her lips as the last head
slipped out of sight down the stairs.

"My lord cousin, forgive me, please." Tala choked, rattled by the fierce expression on Alfred's face. She saw that

she had embarrassed him as much as she had embarrassed herself. "This is not what it seems."

His intelligent brow lowered ominously. "Then you'd best tell me quick just what you did hope to accomplish by this little drama...so obviously staged for my benefit?"

"I have not staged anything," Tala answered quickly. "On my word, Alfred, I did not know you were here. I thought the whole keep empty."

"With the noise of forty people in the very next chamber?" Alfred countered, pointing to an empty hourglass standing on Edon's laden trestle. "I turned that over myself when the wait for your dalliance to end became tedious."

Flaming color shot into Tala's cheeks. "You've been here nearly an hour, sire?"

Alfred almost raised his arm to strike her for her interminable gall. Did she think him a fool? He clenched his teeth and growled, "I arrived at midday and was met by a blind man who invited me into this hall. He informed me that you and the jarl were otherwise occupied."

Abashed, Tala said earnestly, "On my soul, Cousin, I did not know that. I heard nothing beyond the walls of that room."

The door at Tala's back opened. Alfred's piercing blue eyes shifted to take a summary of Edon. He came into the king's presence clothed, wearing breeks and boots and crossgartered leggings. Tala slid a sideways look at him and saw that he'd even honored the king by putting on a proper tunic, with sleeves and a standing collar at his throat. Her fingers tightened on Alfred's robe, pulling it closer about her chest.

Edon went straight to the king and put his knee to the floor. He made a humble obeisance, solicitously taking the king's hand and kissing his ring. "Your Majesty, forgive me for not being present at your arrival. You were not expected before the morrow."

"How can that be credited when you knew my ward would come to me breathing tales of his sister's dishonoring? Don't give me any of your smooth palavering, Wolf. Stand up and face me man-to-man. I commanded you to marry the princess of Leam, not seduce her."

"You hadn't the right to order him to marry me?" Tala started.

"I have every right!" Alfred shouted.

Edon glared at Tala and issued a warning as an aside as he got to his feet. "I told you not to open that door, Princess!"

"No, you told me that I would be sorry if I walked out of the room, and I told you I was already sorry. Alfred, how could you command this Viking to marry me when you know full well the traditions of my people? Why would you do that?"

"You are my ward, Tala ap Griffin, and it is my right to command that you accept such husband as I see fit. I also commanded you to take lessons with the abbess at Loytcoyt to see that your sisters were baptized and to attend Mass daily. I made it clear that I would not tolerate any more nonsense in the groves. I also commanded you not to teach those girls to become witches, healers or seers."

"What girls are we talking about?" Edon interrupted.

"The three sisters to the atheling and your bride, Warwick. Where are they? My best guess tells me they aren't at Loytcoyt Abbey where they should be, are they, Tala?"

"No, sire," She shook her head.

"Just as I thought." Alfred's displeasure was evident by the dark scowl marring his handsome face. "Then I have not arrived here any too soon. The wedding takes place day after tomorrow, Tala ap Griffin, and you have no say whatsoever in refusing it. Test my will on that accord if you dare.

"It is not too late to order you taken to the whipping

post and flogged for your audacity. I will leave punishing your brazenness to the jarl's discretion. It is clear to me that your boldness results from a power play between the two of you. And I will tell Jarl Edon very frankly my opinion of this matter.''

The king paused. His eyes condemned her for whatever willfulness he perceived in this odd, unaccountable situation.

''Return to your boudoir and repair your appearance. Do not venture out again in my presence without attending to your station as the bearer of the title to the land of Leam requires. Such exalted status deserves more than you have given it.''

The will to fight deserted Tala. Her heart was crushed, trampled under kingly edicts and Edon's callous seduction. She would have given up all of Leam for love, provided the Viking would have left her self-respect intact. Tala realized that Edon had been ordered to get control of her land. Wasn't bedding the eldest daughter of the last king of Leam the surest way to do that?

Edon of Warwick would never love her. He was marrying her only because of a whim of state. Nothing in the real world was what Tala thought it was. The simple denial of a cup of water, in his eyes, had made her seem thoughtless and unworthy of the Wolf of Warwick's esteem. What man of any standing would want her now that she'd debased herself completely before the king and his court?

It saddened her. There would be no redress for Leam. They were all to be sacrificed so that Alfred could have a lasting peace with the Danelaw. The gods would not rally to Leam's aid. The gods were dead. The final truth was that Tala had known it in her heart for a long, long time.

Not long after the king dismissed her, Lady Eloya and her maids were sent to the bathhouse to attend Tala. Tala

wasn't fooled by the womens' solicitous manner; she was
under close watch.

Tala wanted to tell Alfred and Edon it wasn't necessary.
If left to her own devices, she wasn't going to open a vein.
The time-honored route out of deep disgrace practiced by
the Romans had no appeal to her, even now. But being
watched so carefully wasn't making this interminable day
any shorter.

The water was too hot and the sauna beastly. Tala was
given some sort of penitent's robe to wear after her bath.
She concluded from that that it was only a matter of time
before she was to be publicly flogged and cast out of the
community.

Lost in her own dreary thoughts, she couldn't pay any
attention to the fact that Warwick kept getting more and
more crowded during the rest of the sweltering afternoon.
All the remaining folk of Leam came to the fortress. They
openly mixed with newly freed Mercian thralls, Vikings
and the king's retinue of soldiers and monks from
Evesham Abbey.

Too late Tala learned that Mother Wren, Anna and Tegwin had come with the little princesses for market day.
Selwyn and Stafford wisely declined to come within the
walls of Warwick, where their tattoos and uncut braids
would draw immediate attention to the party.

But Tala's sisters' gold torques made them stand out in
the crowd as well. Before too long, King Alfred himself
learned of their presence in the crowded palisade. His
guards swooped down upon them. Alfred didn't mince his
words. Tala had failed to serve him properly in the capacity of a good Christian guardian.

Her sisters had their torques removed. They were
handed up to Alfred's horse guard and taken immediately
from Warwick to a convent of the king's choosing. Edon
tried to dissuade Alfred from taking the girls away by offering to stand in Tala's stead as a proper guardian for

them. King Alfred flatly refused to consider his offer. Edon was as much a pagan as Tala.

After the girls' abrupt departure, the king told Venn and Tala that their sisters would dedicate the rest of their growing years to his Christ. When they came of age, Alfred alone would decide who their husbands would be.

In one tumultuous decision, the king abolished the house of Leam.

With her sisters' golden torques in his fist, Alfred scanned the crowd gathered on the hill of Warwick. He read their mood and sensed a moral victory at hand. He seized the moment. Using the torques as a lure, Alfred of Wessex led all of Warwick down to the banks of the river Avon. All save a handful of Vikings who remained loyal to Embla Silver Throat. She and her guard escaped into the woodlands below Warwick and were not seen again that day in the fortress.

The long day's sun sank steadily in the west. The citizenry of Leam were ripe for a conversion. Even Edon's Vikings, mostly refugees from disease and famine rampant on the Continent, were of a mood to accept a change.

Resolutely, King Alfred marched to the river and stood before it, speaking to the gathered people. He knew that most had followed him just to see what he would do with the torques. He knew many of them believed that Branwyn's silken arm would rise from the water to catch the golden necklaces when he threw them in the water. And he knew they would sink like stones. Nothing more would happen—save that their hopes would be lost. It was up to Alfred to give these people something symbolic to replace their loss.

Alfred spoke eloquently of the old myths, resigning those tales to the realm of fantasy alongside legends of Arthur and Merlin. At exactly the right moment in his impassioned speech, he negligently tossed the three gold torques into the middle of the river Avon.

No miracle occurred. The gold sank in the water and disappeared forever.

Alfred used that demonstration to offer the people of Leam and the pagan Vikings a new beginning—baptism, life everlasting and eternal salvation by the grace of God Almighty. Then he turned to Bishop Nels of Athelney.

The bishop spoke to the struggles the Celts of Britain had suffered through the years. Even as distraught as she was, Tala noticed that Venn was completely spellbound by his words.

Nels of Athelney knew how to speak to all—the sad, hopeless Celts like Tala, the humbled-by-adversity Vikings and the downtrodden Mercians, who weren't Angles or Saxons or Celts but some bastardized mixture of them all. In his moving speech, Nels transformed the old gods into saints of Christianity.

Tala was old enough to have heard many of his most persuasive points argued before. She wasn't enthralled by hearing her legendary Lady of the Lake transmigrate from Branwyn to blessed Saint Brigid. Nonetheless, she knew that the bishop played to the desires of the people, granting them a boon. The cult of the virgins would continue, reborn under the auspices of a saint, blessed by association with the Holy Mother of God.

These Christians assimilated everything. All pagan celebrations were now sacred days drawn into the church rituals. To become a Christian all one had to do was say aye to the Lord and be baptized.

With the crowd whipped to a fervor, Bishop Nels called upon the priests and monks of Evesham Abbey to assist him in conducting baptisms in the river Avon.

For Tala, the immersion in the tepid Avon seemed anticlimatic. She couldn't shake off the feeling that she was trapped in a bad dream from which there was no waking.

King Alfred stood waist deep in the water, acting as godfather to Edon, Venn and Tala.

Edon was dunked first and came out renamed John.
Venn came up sputtering and choking on a mouthful of
water, reborn as Samuel. Tala would just as soon have
stayed under and floated away to her lady's bower in the
waterweeds. She was lifted from the watery grave not even
fighting the sting of fluid saturating her airways. King Alfred pounded her on her back and named her Mary, then
presented them each with a golden crucifix.

Alfred turned to welcome the next convert as Tala
dashed river water out of her eyes. The current tugged on
her knees. A shiver crossed her shoulders. She looked at
the horizon and gave thanks that sundown had come. Finally, this awful, interminable day was nearly over.

Edon caught hold of her wrist and without a word began
pulling her toward the Avon's muddy bank. His grip allowed her only one hand to press back the weight of her
wet hair from her face. She plucked at her penitent's robe,
trying to lift it off her breasts as Edon hauled her to the
shore.

The sun dipping to the horizon turned into another ominous, heat-scorched sunset—bloodred and angry. When
Tala looked down to pull on the wet cloth, she could see
her nipples and the curls between her thighs. She shivered,
cold in spite of the blistering heat.

Edon yanked harder on her arm, then looked over his
shoulder to see what was holding her back. He growled
out a thoroughly unchristian curse, pulling her out of the
water completely.

The wet shroud was plastered to her legs and clung to
her hips and belly. A vein throbbed maddeningly in his
forehead. Edon thought she may as well have come down
to the river to be baptized as she'd walked into his hall,
flaunting her body before the king and his court—naked.

He'd had enough. Edon stopped in the mud beside the
river and jerked his tunic off. Growling, he dragged the

garment roughly over Tala's head, stuffing her arms inside
the sleeves. Last, he gave the hem of his garment a violent
tug, pulling it down to cover the tops of her thighs. Satisfied, he grabbed her wrist and marched resolutely up the
hill to Warwick.

The keep was ominously quiet. Eloya and Rebecca
looked up from their sewing, dismayed as Edon and Tala
entered the hall drenched to the skin. Rashid, Theo and Eli
stood at the window, dispassionate observers of the spectacle of conversion. They had chosen to remain outcasts,
committed to their individual beliefs.

Driven to execute some act of vengeance to reclaim authority within his own domain, Edon pulled on Tala across
the hall behind him. He shoved open the door to his chamber, dragged her inside and shut it behind them.

Time had come for a reckoning.

The chamber was nearly dark, for the red sunset was
fading fast. No lamps or candles burned. Tala saw in a
glance that Eloya's efficient army of servants had swept
through the chamber. The bed was sheeted, returned to its
normal place against the stone wall, and the smell of sex
and lust was gone.

Tala began carefully peeling off Edon's tunic. She laid
the soaked garment on the window ledge, spreading it out
to dry.

Then she stepped away from the window and caught up
a handful of her wet, shapeless penitent's robe.

"Don't go any further," Edon warned.

He let the lid to his sea chest fall open with a bang.
Tala's fingers unintentionally tightened on the cotton in
her hands. Edon looked down at her bare ankles. Then he
slapped the scabbard he held in his right hand against his
leg. "I said stop right there!"

Tala let go of the cloth. It fell into place again, covering
her feet. She didn't know what to do with her hands so

she just let them hang at her sides. She didn't say a word. Neither did he.

He watched her breasts rise and fall, lifting the gossamer cloth away from her ribs and stomach. He looked long and intently at the wet fabric that stuck to her thighs and outlined the cleft between them. She watched his shoulders flex as he folded the tongue of the belt up to the buckle, doubling the strap. He stretched the belt between his hands, mentally measuring its length, then gripped the buckle firmly.

Then, satisfied with his preparations, he looked at her. "What was the last thing I told you before you went out the door, Princess?"

Tala thrust out her chin. "You said if I opened the door and walked out naked, spell or no spell, that I would be one very sorry princess."

"Are you?"

"Yes."

"Good. That's a start. Come here and kneel down beside the bed. You don't need to lift your skirt. You're as good as naked with that wet cloth clinging to you."

"What happens if I say no?"

"Say no and find out," he urged in a dire tone.

"Edon, I didn't know the king was out there."

"It makes no difference to me what you knew. This is not between your king and you. It is between us. I will be obeyed and respected in my house."

Tala nodded her head slightly. That was the first commandment of life. She had punished her brother and her sisters for defying her, used a strap—not unlike the one Edon held—on both Venn and Gwynnth. For the most part, they were obedient and loving, curious children. When they were willful or deliberately careless she carried out her parental duty. A necessary whipping hadn't harmed them. But these thoughts were only making her remember the terrible pain of losing them.

Alfred had taken the girls from her without compassion? She hadn't had time to explain to them what brought about the king's decision. He hadn't even allowed Tala to embrace or tell the girls how much she loved them, that she would always love them. But kings and distance and time couldn't stop love or end it.

Edon ground his teeth at the silent tears that ran down her cheeks and dripped onto the sackcloth. She brought her left hand to her face and wiped away a stream, sniffed deeply and nodded again.

"Very well," she said, and lifted her proud chin once more as she moved forward. She would not beg or grovel before him. She did intend to have her say, even if he beat her more for it. "I did not strut into a crowded hall, showing myself to every man and woman present, to shame you or embarrass you."

"So what was your intention, lady? Your actions as much as said that you would never be ruled by me, but only by your pride and vanity. That is the real issue between us. The reason why you have left me no recourse except to beat you."

He'd hit the mark with those words. It had been her pride and injured vanity that had driven her out that door, more the fool she.

"I am accustomed to being the final authority in Leam, my lord." She looked down at his feet. "I find it difficult to defer to the will of another."

It was a wonder that Edon didn't strangle her right then. He shouted at her, "And look what that has cost you! Had you worked with your king, done the things he asked you to do, would your sisters have been summarily taken from you today?"

Tala gulped as she shook her head. "I don't know."

"Yes, you do know, Tala." Edon let his temper have full reign. It was time the angry words were said. Time she came to grips with true authority. "Don't play games with words. I won't stand for that! Who rules this land?"

"The king." She granted that admission and immediately couched it with a justification. "But it was his duty to protect me and my sisters so that our way of life could continue. Instead, he offered my people's land to a Viking overlord on the promise of marriage in Alfred's church. Your motives are as base and secretive as Alfred's."

"My motives have always been stated and open, Tala. I wanted Leam from the first moment I spied it."

"That is your way...the Viking way. You take—with no thought given to whom what you covet truly belongs. It is not the Christian motto Do Unto Others that Viking sons are taught in infancy, it is Take From Others Before They Take From You! You could have let me be, with my family and my people, in our forest and at peace."

Affronted, Edon countered, "Lady, it was you who came out of the forest spying. You who came to my hall delivering ultimatums. You who made yourself a nuisance with your petitions of redress to two kings, focusing all attention upon what was happening in the peaceful shire of Warwick. A good man was sent here to rule, Harald Jorgensson. I have proof from your people and mine that he was a fair and compassionate overlord, allowing Mercians and Danes to coexist equitably. You stirred up the waters of rebellion and distrust by slaughtering my sister's son, the nephew of my king at your blood sacrifice on Lughnasa."

"That's a lie!" Tala shouted back.

"It is not!" Edon forced her to yield precious ground as he backed her into the chamber's stone corner with his flaring temper. "Why else would two kings from different realms have taken such interest in the doings of a small sect of Celtic pagans?"

"Because they covet this land."

"No! Edon shouted at the top of his voice. "Because

one king, the new convert, was convinced that the beliefs he now holds dear were being insulted deep in the woodlands of his frontier. Guthrum believes your rituals are devil worship. Blood sacrifice of another human being is the worst evil in a world that holds each human life as sacred as God himself.''

''We had nothing to do with Jarl Harald Jorgensson's death!'' Tala insisted furiously. ''Who accuses us of such a thing?''

''That is irrelevant, Tala. The point is the kings believe your ancient rituals prevail, and I know that you continue to make sacrifices at the lake in Arden Wood.''

''You know nothing of the kind,'' she argued heatedly.

''Then tell me where your golden torque is this very moment.''

Edon let his words hang in the throbbing air between them, knowing full well she would not answer with anything that came near the truth. Then he told her exactly where the golden torque was.

''It is at the bottom of Black Lake, because you made an offering of the most sacred and valuable possession you had to the Lady of the Lake. Isn't it?''

Shaken by his acumen, Tala gasped, ''How do you know that?''

Her words and expression confirmed Edon's suspicion. Heaven help her if Embla Silver Throat proved right in her accusation of how Harald had died. For Edon would hold all of the druids and their priestesses responsible for his nephew's life. The mystery was slowly beginning to unravel, though the finger of guilt pointed not in the direction he had thought it would.

''How I know things isn't the issue, lady. Your cupidity is.''

''Cupidity! The only lust between us is yours, Wolf of Warwick! Make no mistake, that bond is severed. Now that I see you for what you are, all affairs between us are over. I will have nothing further to do with you."

"I'm talking bloodlust, lady. Harald Jorgensson was my kinsman, and if you had anything to do with his disappearance or the taking of his life, I will hold you accountable."

"You fool." Tala shook her head and said the last civil words she ever intended to speak to the Wolf of Warwick for the rest of her life. "If you would but search your own holding, you would know what became of Harald Jorgensson. My people and I are innocent of his blood."

"Best you hope the balance of my investigation proves that true, Tala ap Griffin. Your pretty denial changes nothing. As to affairs between you and me, we are to be married on Lammas, two days hence. All lands and properties that you claim in your brother's name will, at the moment of our marriage, become mine to hold and dispose of as I see fit."

"You will have to drag me screaming and kicking to the altar, Viking," Tala promised.

"I don't think that will be as difficult to accomplish as you predict." Edon cracked the leather belt against his leg. "One way or another you will learn to submit to a higher authority. If force is the only language you can understand, then I will use force ruthlessly against you."

"If you touch me now, I will never forgive you, Viking."

"Princess, if I didn't use force now, I would never forgive myself. Your willful and deliberate manipulations have pushed both of us to that impasse. Believe me, you will think long and hard about the consequences of your thoughtlessness in the future."

Tala put her shoulder blades to the cold wall at her back, staring at him in the twilight, her head moving ever so slightly in a negating motion. Her racing heart told her to say *Edon, don't,* but her uncompromising pride wouldn't allow the petition out of her locked throat. She was a princess of Leam, *a violated virgin priestess of the Lady of the Lake.*

She knew what dangers he deliberately courted by tempting the gods in raising his hand against her. All reason commanded that she warn him of the danger. Yet the Ceremony of Baptism they had just been through had mockingly proclaimed that her gods were dead. Christ was now almighty. Why should she waste her breath warning him of pagan dangers he wouldn't believe?

"Then do it, Viking. Take your vengeance for my thoughtless insult against you. The sooner you have done with it, the sooner I may be quit of you forever."

"Therein lies the gravest error in your thinking, Princess. You will not be quit of me until the vows of marriage spoken between us have been fulfilled." With those words, Edon tremulously raised the strap in his hand, not knowing what to do next. She had left him no other alternative with her stubborn refusal to yield to his authority.

Chapter Fourteen

The lightning struck without warning. In one heartbeat, the brilliant bolt of light zigzagged across the stones at the top of the window, jumped to the belt buckle in Edon's hand and shot across the room, exploding into the iron bolts affixed to the hinges on the oak door.

The seasoned oak burst into flame. Edon flew across the room, thrown against the stone wall, and sank in a heap. His scabbard belt ignited midair and fell to the floor. Tala slammed into the corner as the deafening clap of thunder shook the roof, walls and floor of the keep.

An irreverent thought flashed in her mind: *If this is a sign from the gods, it is too little and too late. The damage has been done hours ago...by the king of Wessex...not the Wolf of Warwick!*

Across the room, Edon's black hair spiked around his head like the ruff of an indignant cock. Tala blinked again and again to clear her blurred sight, and nothing changed. Edon didn't move. The acrid smell of burning hair and flesh didn't stop stinging Tala's nose.

The door burst open. Eli rushed in, yelling, "Lord Edon!" He saw Edon crumpled before the open window, Tala in the corner and the flaming belt on the floor in between.

The servant grabbed the pitcher of water from the sideboard and threw its contents on the fire. That was when
he saw the flames near the iron studs on the oak door. He
yelled, "Fire, fire, fire!"

Tala shielded her eyes with her hand. Rashid ran into
the room, saw Edon and dropped to his side. Eli grabbed
the pitcher of water and dashed its contents at the burning
door. Rig brought his axe and hacked at the smoldering
wood. Eli threw a bowl of water at Edon's face, and
Rashid slapped his cheeks. His red skin turned white where
the blows struck.

Somehow Tala got her arms and legs to work. She
crawled to where Rashid had stretched out Edon's long
body. His lids were half-open but his blue eyes had rolled
up into his head. Rashid pressed his ear to Edon's naked
chest. He sat back abruptly, made a hard fist and slammed
it with all his might into Edon's breastbone. Then he bent
and listened for a heartbeat.

"Edon!" Tala gulped. An irrational fear took hold of
her, telling her Edon was dead. The gods had proved once
more why it was taboo to touch a sacred princess of Leam.
Rashid drove his fist into Edon's chest again, a violent
blow that made the jarl's flaccid arms bounce off the floor.

"Edon!" Tala grasped his ears and shook his head.
"Edon!"

She looked at Rashid. The Persian met her eyes resign-
edly. "I can do nothing, Princess. He is gone."

"No!" Tala shouted, shoving the Persian away. "Don't
you dare hit him again. You're killing him! Edon, Edon!"
She threw herself over Edon to protect him, to love him,
to shake him back to life. "Edon!"

"Princess," Rashid said softly, grasping her shoulders,
trying to pull her back.

"No!" Tala gathered Edon to her, lifting his head and
shoulders from the floor. She wrapped her arms around
him as tightly as she could. She rocked him back and forth,

crooning in his ear, kissing his face, crying, frantic to keep him with her. She kissed his soft lips and tried to breathe her life into his, blowing her breath into his lungs. "Edon, please. You can't leave me. I have nothing left but you! I love you. Edon, please."

His warm body remained slack in her arms. His head rolled back, his jaw lax, his blue tongue lifeless and inert inside the mouth that she loved so much to kiss. By all the gods of the earth, she loved him. She could not lose him!

Rashid cast a concerned look at Rig and Eli, and the three of them, loyal men who themselves loved Edon as much as life, stood back, allowing the princess of Leam privacy to grieve.

Lady Eloya pushed her way through the gathering crowd and bent to wrap a warm shawl around the princess's pale shoulders. She hugged her and kissed the top of the Tala's head, then turned and, with tears filling her eyes, went to break the sad news to Theo and Rebecca.

Tala heard the winds howl and scream as they raged through the keep. She lifted her cheek from Edon's brow, turning to her inner sight for answers. Thunder rocked the heavens from Warwick to the Citadel of Glass at Black Lake.

In a vision swimming before her eyes, Tala saw Tegwin standing at the high altar, his blackthorn staff raised to the heavens. He summoned all the demons from the other-world with the chant of an ancient and powerful curse, bidding them come forth in wind and thunder and wreak their vengeance upon Leam's enemies.

"Tegwin, no!" Tala screamed. "No! I forbid it! Branwyn, I command you, stop Tegwin! Give Edon back to me! This man is mine. I have chosen him. I love him! Give him back. You cannot take him from me!"

She threw out her hand, envisioning it knocking the druid's blackthorn staff out of his grasp. The howling wind assaulting Warwick abated.

Edon took a breath.

Tala wrapped him tightly in her arms, rocking him gently back and forth, crooning a soft song of love in his ear, whispering her litany of thanksgiving. He was alive. The Wolf of Warwick lived.

Rashid and Rig were the first to realize the change. Knowing a miracle had ruptured the cosmos, Rig fell to his knees and fervently prayed. Rashid called to Eli to help him move Edon. They took him from Tala's arms and laid him on the bed, covering him quickly with a warm blanket.

Oblivious to her wet clothes, Tala crawled onto the bed to be with Edon, to touch him and silently celebrate his return to life. There she stayed until King Alfred and his priests arrived.

"You must come with me, Princess," Lady Eloya insisted then. She tightened the shawl around Tala's shoulders and drew her off the bed. "The danger is past. Edon will be all right now. Rashid will protect him. I will protect you. You are safe now. Come along, my child."

Somehow Eloya managed to keep the princess from making eye contact with the king. The fury in the princess's eyes was a sight to behold—terrifying really. Only the powers in the heavens knew what sort of wrath the princess of Leam was capable of at that moment. Eloya guided her through the crowded hall and into her own chamber. She told Olga to fetch her towels and lotions. Anastacia was sent to bring clean clothes and shoes. Eloya took up a brush and began to smooth the tangles out of the princess's hair.

Confused, Rebecca paced the floor before the wide, north-facing window in Eloya's room, racking her baby to quiet it after the fierce and sudden storm. "There are clouds high to the north. For all the wind and thunder, there has not been a drop of rain. Perhaps it will come."

"No." Tala shook her head. "The storm is over. There will be no rain in Warwick." Not before her brother gave his blood to the land to renew it. The die was cast. She had been a fool to doubt the power of the gods. And ten times more a fool to question their existence.

"How do you know?" Rebecca asked, stopping to pat Thomas's back and look at the princess.

"I just know," she answered.

"Let us talk about something else," Eloya said, giving Rebecca a telling look.

The woman nodded and came to Tala, stretching out her arms. "Would you like to hold Thomas, Tala? He's quiet now. I think he might even go to sleep."

"Oh, yes." Tala exhaled in relief.

She carefully gathered the baby up and rocked him much the same way she had comforted and reassured Edon, letting him know that she forgave him. She was going to miss her family, but now she knew she would someday have them back. Just as she had Edon back. Alfred would come to his senses.

When the princess's hair was neatly restored to order and the baby put to bed, Lady Eloya sent the others out of the room. "See to supper, Rebecca. It has been a very long and trying day. The men need to eat. Do what you can."

After the door closed, Eloya took up a fine kirtle, saying, "Now, let's get you dressed in something that suits your station. You are the Jarl of Warwick's woman."

"I can do it, Eloya," Tala said, her confidence returning with each moment that passed. "I'm not helpless. I've been fending for myself since I was a child."

"Do you want me to leave you, Princess?"

"No, of course not. I just don't want you to think you have to serve me. I can do very well for myself." Tala took the kirtle in hand and examined it. "This is new?"

"Yes, Rebecca and I just made it for you. We were hoping to have it finished before your wedding."

"Oh," Tala said, touched by the women's generosity. "Thank you. I could save it until then. This robe is dry now. Perhaps I could just put a surcoat over it. That would work, wouldn't it?"

"I want to throw that rag away," Eloya said plainly. "It is only fit for rags."

"It is rather crude, isn't it?" Tala tugged at the shapeless sack. Then she took it off, handed it to Eloya and drew the soft linen kirtle onto her arms. The sleeves were closely fitted. A soft ribbon closed the kirtle above her breasts. The long skirt flowed wide at her ankles. "Oh, this is much better. I will tell Rebecca how much I appreciate it."

Eloya folded the damp, muddy baptismal robe and handed Tala an outer gown of russet-colored samite. The rich cloth suited the princess, bringing color to her cheeks. Her soft boots had been cleaned and were perfect with the gown. Eloya was satisfied. She took the torque off Tala's neck, made an adjustment to it, then put it back.

"We shall play this game the king of Wessex's way, shall we, Princess Tala? You will wear the torque like this, hmm? The cross looks very pretty at your throat. Alfred does have exceptional taste in jewelry."

"Despite what he has put me through this day, he is a good king," Tala said as Eloya passed her a polished silver hand mirror to look at herself.

"Yes, I dare say his motives are better than most. He is human and there lies any man's frailties. He ordered Edon to beat you, Princess."

Tala paused to consider Eloya's words. After a moment, she gave back the mirror as she shook her head very firmly. "No, Eloya, I know my cousin. As a king, Alfred is most often too humane. Maybe that is why I have gone to the lengths that I have to hold Leam for Venn. Alfred would levy a fine. The beating must have been Edon's idea, to bring me back to my senses. I had given up. Edon was right.''

Eloya looked into Tala's brown eyes and saw that tenderness tempered the anger simmering inside her. She could have been a queen in her own right, but that was not to be. Eloya was not fooled; she thought Tala didn't want the power she did have. Alfred was a lucky man, for Tala could have commanded her gods to strike him dead.

Tala looked up suddenly at Eloya, a small frown puckering her brow. ''No,'' she said very firmly. ''I can't do that, Eloya. The only thing I have ever been able to do is intercede. Sometimes they listen to me. Shall we go now and join the men?''

''If you are ready.'' Eloya deferred to her.

''I want to see Edon.''

He was seated at the end of the table in a low-backed chair drawn up beside the high one, which had been given to Alfred. Edon was still pale and shaken. Two spots of color appeared on his cheeks when Tala came into the room. Rig immediately got up from the seat at Edon's left side, surrendering the wolf-head chair to Tala.

''Fetch a cushion,'' Edon told him. Before Tala reached his side, the cushion was in place on the wooden seat.

''So you will still cosset her?'' King Alfred asked as he rose to his feet with the rest of the men as the ladies took their places at the table.

''Of course.'' Edon bowed his head slightly to the king, then turned to take Tala's hand and guide her to her seat. ''She is to be my wife. I will cherish her all my days.''

High color stained Tala's cheeks, and her eyes were downcast as Edon gripped her fingers and bent close to whisper in her ear. ''I thought you were never coming out.''

Tala's lips flexed at the corners, then she briefly looked

up at his eyes, saying, "But I had to come out and hear your men praise you for making me scream, lord."

"Humph!" Edon coughed. He cast a quick look at Tala's eyes and caught the loving twinkle just before it faded. "So much for seeking your forgiveness, eh?"

"You may seek it later," Tala told him primly.

Edon delayed taking his seat until the king did. Then Alfred turned to Lady Eloya and engaged her in conversation. "What did you think of the strange lightning this eve, my lady? Have you seen such displays in your country?"

"A desert storm is liable to conjure anything, your majesty," Eloya answered wisely. "Though I would rank this night's display as unusual. That lightning went from one end of this hall to the other. It quite frightened the life out of me. Were you told we thought Lord Edon dead?"

"He looks quite hale to me." Alfred studied Edon, then turned his scrutiny upon his kinswoman. He had an approving nod for her jewelry, worn as he specified, though he wasn't fooled that she would ever be anything but a pagan in her heart. The old ways were too ingrained in her.

She was making a great effort to appear subdued, her wild hair coiled at her nape, her gown modest and comely. If the Viking jarl remained firm, Alfred thought Tala's wildness could be tamed. "Did you think you were dead, Lord John?"

"No, of course not." Edon scoffed at such an idea. "Although my chest hurts...here." He put his left hand over his heart. His right hand, Tala saw, was bandaged. "I was stunned by the concussion. My ears have only just quit ringing."

"And you, Mary?" Alfred turned to Tala, addressing her by her baptismal name, "Were you also affected by the bolt of lightning that broke the stone above the window?"

"It broke a stone?" Tala said, turning to Edon.

"That's not exactly true," the jarl interjected. "The stone had a flaw in it that I noticed when I inspected the keep the first time. I had the masons fit an iron bar across the top of the lintel before the carpenters hung the window frame. Lightning tends to gravitate toward iron."

"Like a lodestone has drawing power?" Tala sought clarification. She searched his face for confirmation that he was truly recovered.

"Exactly," Edon answered. "It's the same principle."

"I'm certain living on the highest hill in the shire must have something to do with it as well." Alfred offered his own wry observation. "Had I been the one struck by lightning, I'd give consideration to building my home elsewhere and keep Warwick for defense."

"That is one way to look at my castle's position." Edon removed his palm from the sore spot on his chest. "One I shall certainly keep in mind as the work continues."

"Beware the next storm," Venn ap Griffin muttered from across the table.

Tala started. Edon was very aware of her sharp intake of breath as he turned to the atheling. "What did you say?"

"He meant prepare for the next storm," Tala interjected deliberately.

The interference kept the jarl from making immediate eye contact with her brother. Edon frowned as he shifted his gaze across the table.

The atheling bent over the food in front of him, revealing no sign of the malice Edon had heard in his voice. Nels of Athelney leaned toward the boy's ear, giving him private counsel. Edon felt that tingling of flesh behind his ears that had preceded the lightning strike. He had ignored it then, but he did not ignore it now.

"If a boy is old enough to sit at the table with men, he

is old enough to speak for himself, Tala,'' Edon responded testily.

"His command of Danish is limited.'' Tala offered a lame excuse. Her teeth caught the corner of her lip and her eyes were full of concern as they met Edon's again. "Sometimes Venn mistakes common words.''

"He spoke in English.'' Edon frowned, unable to take his gaze from Tala's compelling amber eyes. He couldn't think what she wanted of him, but knew her brother had been out of line. Again his ears pricked. Tiny spots of light danced before his eyes and the small hairs at the nape of his neck began to rise. If he were in a battle, he would know he was about to be attacked from behind. He spun around, looking for Embla Silver Throat, anticipating her behind him with a knife in her hand.

This was preposterous, he thought. He reached for the goblet of wine before him and drained it.

They were witches, both the atheling and the princess. Surely they could not control the elements or his thoughts...and she made excuses for the boy, protected him. There was something else troubling Edon, but he couldn't put his finger on it. Something Tala had said to him a long time ago...something about their gods protecting the atheling—or her. If he could only remember...

To ease his mind, Edon motioned to Rig, calling him to his side. "Where is Embla?" he whispered.

"Getting drunk in her longhouse,'' Rig answered.

"You are keeping her under close watch while the king is here?'' Edon said.

"Aye, Lord, she does not move from her house without a tail following her every move,'' Rig assured him.

"Good,'' Edon said. "Keep it that way.'' He turned back to Tala.

Edon clenched his right hand, crushing the bandage, feeling the stabbing pull of the buckle-shaped burn embedded in his palm. Had Tala used witchcraft to stop him?

This whole day had been remarkable. How much of it was caused by her spell casting, her witchery?

Tala raised her hand and rubbed her brow. She shook her head once, then looked him straight in the eye and whispered so only Edon could hear her speak at the noisy table, "I didn't bring the lightning. I couldn't hurt you."

Knowing, certain she had read his thoughts, Edon said, "Then who did? What did?"

She dropped her hand to her lap and shrugged. "I don't know. I'm tired and confused. Maybe tomorrow I can provide you the answers you seek."

"How?" By casting more spells? *How can I control a woman who can prevent my arm from being raised against her?* That question had troubled Edon since he'd returned to consciousness. How could any man hold his own against a woman protected by the gods? It left him reeling in confusion, angry and hurt.

Tala self-consciously touched the heavy cross at her throat, cast a surreptitious look at the king, making certain Alfred was deep in conversation with others at the table. Edon repeated his demand. "How will you find this answer to my questions?"

"Come with me to Black Lake. I will show you all of my powers."

"Very well," Edon snapped, feeling vulnerable and testy. Heretofore, he hadn't believed in dark powers, evil or witchcraft, and he wouldn't start now. He refused to fear her. Fearing her endangered the love he felt for her. "We will go to the lake on the morrow. Now let me eat in peace."

Her eyes held his as she solemnly suggested, "Mayhaps my ancestors knew what they were doing when they made it a taboo for a princess of Leam to mate."

Edon had no patience for that line of ignorant reasoning. He refused to credit taboos and omens and silly superstitions. He picked up a rib from his platter and bit into it.

Midway through chewing the morsel he said, "Logic and reason can explain every event."

Tala watched him swallow and take a second bite, a bigger one that he would have to chew longer. Watching the way he hunched his shoulders over his food made her remember the way his shoulders curved as he bent to take her breast in his mouth, so greedy and hungry.

She loved him, but it was all wrong. It was totally irrational, defying all explanation. The Wolf was going to marry her in King Alfred's church. If her pagan gods had a fit over a baptism and a justified near beating, what would they do over a marriage?

It was all Tala could do not to dissolve into a fit of hysterical laughter. She was going to marry him. She would dare her gods to stop her. Remembering how he had looked with his spirit leaving his body brought the terror of losing him back to her. No, she would give Leam away to stay with Edon of Warwick. That was a certainty.

Edon tore off the last bit of meat with his teeth, then cast the bone to the platter. He grabbed a damp linen napkin and wiped his fingers and mouth, then leaned back against his chair, cocked his left arm on the rest and stared at her. His bandaged right hand rested on the trestle. The exposed fingertips tapped impatiently on the wood.

"My household is run by rules and order. Everyone has a purpose, and work to do. Your purpose is to see to my comfort and to provide me sons."

Tala smiled, envisioning a black-haired, blue-eyed daughter the very image of him. They would have two daughters before she would produce that coveted son. "And daughters?"

"Aye, several of those. But I will raise them not to be little witches who manipulate grown men into becoming mush-brained imbeciles, as you do. Lord, I'm already talking like an idiot. Go to bed, Tala. I want to sit and talk of war and law with my men and the king. You interfere."

"By your command, my lord." Tala lowered her eyes in a parody of submission. "I shall leave you to your talk."

Edon caught her arm as she started to rise and said in her white ear, "Do not bait me, woman."

"Beast." Tala replied without heat, and tugged her sleeve from his fingers, then stood. She took her leave of the king and Edon. Lady Eloya and Rebecca withdrew with her.

Venn ap Griffin excused himself to go out to the privy. It was the only way he could think of to escape the hall and try to reach Tala alone. He felt like a dog on a leash, chained to the priest's side. When the women left the hall, the talk turned to topics that held the men's interest. Venn finally managed to slip away.

The Vikings' other women stayed too close to his sister. Venn ran across the ward and hid in the shadow of a long-house. He felt certain Tala would come to him, that she would recognize his signal, the song of a lark.

The women walked to the privy together, then stopped to talk near the sealed well. Rebecca wanted to sit awhile. Eloya joined her. Tala cocked her ear to the sound of a bird call, a lark warbling. She searched for its source. It came again when she faced Embla Silver Throat's long-house.

"Was it me or did either of you sense something amiss at the table?" Rebecca asked.

"No, it wasn't just you," Eloya told her. "No one told the king what really happened to Edon. He thought him only stunned."

"Then it was a miracle, wasn't it?" Rebecca concluded.

"The king would say so, if he knew the truth of the affair." Tala bent to look close at the boards covering the well. "Why do we not use this well?"

"The water went bad the day we arrived," Rebecca told

her. "It was most inconvenient. Eloya and I were in the bathhouse and the sluices were running quite well. Then it just stopped. Out here the water dropped and then rose again, but it was full of mud and silt. Edon deemed it unfit to drink. Our servants have carted water from the river ever since, but Maynard is working on a new aqueduct."

"I see," Tala said. "You have to dig another well."

"Where?" Eloya asked simply.

Tala looked over the motte. The question was elementary; she walked ten paces and stopped. She heard the whistle again, closer to her, and realized it had to be Venn. She couldn't see him, but he knew how to use the shadows to remain invisible. So did she.

"Here," she said to Eloya.

"Stay right there," Eloya commanded, and hopped to her feet, gathering a handful of small stones. She hurried to Tala and then set the stones in a circle around where she stood. "How deep do you think the water is?"

"Oh, not far. Ten feet, more or less, just under the caprock."

"You are brilliant." Eloya hugged her and then reached over and tapped a stone wall that was under construction. "This is the first wall of our bathhouse—our ladies-only bathhouse. I will tell Maynard to reverse the walls, to enclose this spot. That way we will have water first. He is never going to get an aqueduct to bring water to the top of this hill. Men think they know everything, but they don't." Eloya tapped her forehead knowingly and grinned.

Embla Silver Throat stepped out her door in time to see the three women stroll back to the jarl's palace. She crossed her arms, considering the usefulness of the two foreign women. Both were adept with the needle, but made womanly clothes that had no practical use for a warrior. Embla's one vanity was clothes that flattered her own strong body. All the Vikings of Warwick had lusted after

her until those women came. Now they looked at the foreign women and talked about bedding them.

Embla turned to Eric the Tongueless and said, "Which
of the foreign women do you want to bed? The little one
or the new mother?"

Eric grinned gruesomely, making a motion of rocking a
baby. Embla smiled, wicked with hate. "She has big
breasts and so much milk her babe grows fat. Come to me
at sunrise and I will let you tote my water to the bathhouse.
I will make certain you see her breasts and her brown
belly."

Eric nodded his head energetically as he kicked aside a
dog and reached for the pail of table scraps it had been
eating. He grunted noisily, smacking his lip in anticipation
of what Embla promised him. He followed Embla around
the side of the longhouse.

There was a root cellar under her byre. Inside the byre
she lit a torch and threw back a tarp, which covered a
heavy plank door fitted over the cellar. The crude stairs it
hid were wet and slick. Embla went down them surefoot-
edly, unerringly knowing her way into the cave.

Venn held himself perfectly still until the glimmer of
Embla's torch quit bouncing on the cavern's wet walls.
His heart had begun to hammer in his throat as she'd uncovered the hidden door in her cellar. Instinctively, he
knew what he was seeing...the entrance to her oubliette.
All the thralls knew about it, but no one knew where it
was. They said her husband, Harald Jorgensson, was imprisoned there.

Venn saw his chance to gain a major victory. King Alfred would reward him handsomely if he found proof of
what had happened to Jarl Harald. If he found the jarl's
bones inside Warwick, Venn could prove once and for all
that no one born of Leam had had anything to do with
Harald's death. That way Tala could collect the wergild

due her. Maybe she wouldn't even have to marry the Viking.

He was momentarily torn between meeting Tala and following Embla. He made up his mind to act now. Tala would wait. He eased down the twisting stairs, one careful step at a time.

At the steps of the keep Tala stopped. Where was Venn hiding? Why didn't he signal her again? Worried, she cast a concerned glance at Eloya and Rebecca, then caught her hand to her throat, saying, "My necklace! I've lost it."

"No, you haven't," Rebecca said.

"No, the cross. It fell off. I have to find it. I must wear it in front of the king. It must have fallen."

"We'll come help you look." Eloya turned from the door.

"No, no, you needn't do that. I'll find it right away. I thought I felt something fall when I waited for you at the privy. I won't be but a moment. Go in. I'll be right behind you."

The fortress gates were closed. Twice as many guards stood duty, because a king was in residence. Eloya knew nothing untoward could happen. "Go on then. If anyone asks, I'll just say you were delayed."

"I won't be but a moment," Tala promised again.

She hurried across the ward, expecting Venn to come out of the shadows immediately, now that she was alone. The guards at the gate saw her. Tala stopped at the well, pretending to look for something lost. She softly whistled the lark's song. There was no answer. She moved away from the well, into the northern quadrant. Venn did not step out from any building.

She walked closer to the longhouse, whispering, "Venn? Where are you?"

All her senses told her not to go closer to that dwelling.

Evil emanated from it the way spores burst from poisonous mushrooms.

Two of the Vikings at the gate began walking toward her. Tala looked at them to make certain they were men she recognized. One was Edon's captain, Maynard the Black. He said quite sternly, "What do you out here alone, Princess?"

"I lost the cross my kinsman gave me," Tala said. Where was Venn? "There were lights in Embla's house when the ladies and I were walking."

"You did not walk to this quarter," Maynard said, proving that he'd kept a careful eye on Tala's movements. "I will light a torch and help you look."

Tala tightened her fingers on the cross in her palm. "It must be there by the well." She retreated. Maynard paced every step with her. His soldier ran to fetch a torch and bring light to aid the search. While Maynard circled opposite her, Tala bent down, running her fingers through the grass that grew thick in the damp earth beside the stones. "Here it is! I have found it!"

She straightened, holding the crucifix in her palm.

"You have good eyes, lady. Come." Maynard offered her his arm. "I will return you to the keep."

Tala slipped her fingers under his strong arm, grateful for it. She did not look back toward that dark house. She did not want to look into the evil it contained. If Venn had half the sense she thought he did, he would not linger there, either.

Chapter Fifteen

The king joined the hunting party that went out at first light to bring in game for the feast of Lammas. There was much to be done in preparation for the celebration of the first fruits of harvest, a day set apart since time immemorial.

Inside and outside Warwick work began early. Vikings, Mercians and Leamurians went to the fields and meadows to cull the first harvest. Tala and the jarl of Warwick lay abed behind their closed door. Venn ap Griffin ate his fill of the lean pickings at the jarl's morning table.

The Christians fasted on this day in preparation for the morrow's holy day.

Venn did not understand this required fast any more than he understood the symbolism behind the rituals. Blood was the most sacred sacrifice a people could offer the gods. The Christians substituted wine for blood and called that sacrifice.

The atheling of Leam made do with the mead in kegs kept for the guards. The honeyed beer tasted better with each tankard Venn pulled. It made him swagger, pleased with all he'd accomplished in the night.

Unlike the rest of the baptized populace, Venn's newly gained state of grace did not make him revel in joy. He sank deeper and deeper into righteous anger. King Alfred had gone too far. Edon of Warwick had also gone too far. The compounded insults against his elder sister had been tripled by the king's autocratic abduction of Venn's three little sisters.

He was only a boy in size and strength, but Venn ap Griffin had long begun to think the thoughts of a man. He knew only one way to address the harm done his family. That was to strike back at the injustice swiftly and exact his own retribution.

He held no fear of consequence, certain that King Alfred's laws could not affect him. Venn's fate was sealed. Tomorrow night, when the shadow of the earth obliterated the full moon of Lughnasa, his spirit would soar into the otherworld, free to come again in whatever form pleased him.

He had made up his mind he would come back as a roe deer. As a stag bearing twelve points on his antlers, he would rule the forests completely.

Unlike his sister, Venn enjoyed his freedom within and without the walls of Warwick. No guards were set to keep watch upon him, to follow his movements or keep track of what he did. He had to account for his whereabouts only to the bishop.

He went downhill to the beech wood, where he knew Selwyn and Stafford kept watch a safe distance away. Their cloaks made the two warriors invisible in the early shadows, but Venn had no trouble locating them.

"What is it you wish us to do, lord?" Selwyn asked after they exchanged greetings.

"Take Embla Silver Throat captive. Hold her in the dungeon at the lake until King Guthrum arrives. He will be here by noon on the morrow, Lughnasa. That is when Tala will wed the Viking...after the celebration of the High Mass.

"I will parley with this Guthrum of the Danelaw and

offer to exchange my prisoner, Embla Silver Throat, provided Guthrum can convince King Alfred to return my
sisters immediately to Leam. Believe me, the Vikings'
king will want Embla back. What she has done to Harald
Jorgensson is grounds for revenge."

"You have been to the oubliette?" Selwyn gasped,
astounded.

"Aye," Venn said. "After the kings agree to my terms,
I will show Lord Edon where his nephew has been imprisoned lo these many months."

"You will be showing him Harald's bones." Selwyn
did not warm to any plan that put the atheling at risk. "The
jarl will not thank you for that."

"Nay, he is not dead yet. Only nearly so."

"Then why do we not rescue him and take *him* captive?" Stafford, the cautious warrior, asked. "Harald Jorgensson would bring a better ransom than Embla Silver
Throat."

Venn frowned at the man. The questions did not challenge him, only troubled him. "He is in a cave directly
under Silver Throat's longhouse. It would take more than
the three of us to bring him into the light alive. He is far
gone, delirious."

"All the more reason to give such dreadful news to the
jarl himself. His gratitude will know no bounds."

"I don't want the Viking's thanks," Venn said resolutely. "I want his pain. He has dishonored Tala. For that,
Wessex and Warwick must pay. They force her to wed
against our customs."

At that news, Selwyn and Stafford burst forth with angry
words. Venn shrugged his shoulders, accepting what he
could not change. "Tala has no choice except to stay with
the jarl now that she is no longer a virgin. Else when I am
gone, she would become a witch of the wood. The Wolf
will protect her with his life and no harm will come to her.
One of the little ones can take Tala's place. Gwynnth is

of age and knows most of Tala's duties. Alfred will return my sisters, as that will become a condition for his peace to continue. He has based all of his aspirations on maintaining this uneasy peace of his. I am certain of that.''

"I saw you and the princess go willingly into the river,'' Stafford said solemnly.

"It meant nothing.''

"Then why do it?''

"They took my sword and my knife.'' Venn raised his hands from his sides, displaying the fact that he was weaponless. "What choice did any of us have when the king and his bishop came to the river wearing their weapons? The jarl's guards made it clear we would be baptized or die. I was not born to die at the end of a Viking sword.''

"Nay, you are the last son of Leam and you will be remembered through the years.'' Stafford nodded his white head gravely. "These Saxons will pass from the Earth, washed away by the coming flood.''

Venn vigorously agreed. "Their God cannot bring the rain or fill their wells. Only Lugh and I can do that. Little did Alfred know that he appeased our gods with the sacrificed torques of my sisters that preceded his Christians rite. As for Tala and I, we merely had an extra bath. The Mercians had much need of it.''

The old soldiers laughed at the rude joke. Then Venn continued outlining his plan. He was just a boy but he knew how to be crafty.

Edon slept late. He awoke flat on his back and brought his hand to his eyes to rub them, wincing when he curled his fingers. Yawning, he opened his eyes and looked at his palm. A dark, painful blister formed an imprint of his scabbard buckle. The wound reminded him of all that had happened the day before.

He jerked to the side, fearing his bed empty, certain that

the princess of Leam had somehow fled during the night while he slept.

Tala ap Griffin lay beside him, sound asleep. That both reassured and disturbed him. No sheet covered either of them, for the night had been muggy throughout. Tala was unclothed, but Edon felt no urge to pull her to him, to taste the pleasures of the flesh with her.

Too many barriers impeded intimacy between them. When he'd come to bed last night, he'd lain beside her silently, not touching her in any way. He could no longer deny the obvious. Her gods could still protect her. The pleasure she stirred in him could destroy him.

Edon got up to relieve himself, then took the lid off a jar of salve and applied it to his wounded palm. He was winding a bandage around his hand when Tala awoke. She groaned as she sat up, sleepily staring out the window at the day.

"Oh my, 'tis late," she said. She turned her head to Edon and looked at him as he clumsily tucked the end of the long bandage into a fold at his wrist. "Do you need help?"

"Nay, I've managed." Edon dismissed her brusquely. He caught up his breeks, stepping into them. As he fastened the ties at his waist, he said over his shoulder, "Get up, lazy bones, it's a long walk to the lake."

Tala yawned and stretched before she rose to her feet. "'Tis not that far, and we can ride."

Edon watched her pour water from the pitcher.

"We walk," he said, ending that discussion. Best she learn he meant what he said. He rubbed the bruises in the center of his chest as he selected a jerkin from his trunk. Then he sat on the edge of the bed to lace his crossquarters and fasten them. He was much slower than usual, hampered by his hand. Hampered by a strange lethargy that affected all his movements.

One image remained very strong in his mind—that of

leaving his body and looking down at the floor of his chamber, the way a bird might look down on the people inside when it flew in through a window. It spooked Edon to have seen himself lying there lifeless, as Tala bent over his body, rocking him back and forth. He'd watched her kiss him and plead with him, and had heard her vow over and over that she loved him.

She'd been hysterical, distraught, he told himself, and distressed women were liable to say anything. In the trying moments that followed the lightning strike, she hadn't been herself.

In his trunk, Tala found her own leggings and garters and those well-fitted breeks she favored for riding. Over that she donned a sleeveless tunic that she belted at her narrow waist with a colorful sash. Her small white purse with the two stones and twist of bluebells hung from the red sash. Last she took his wooden comb and wet it, then pulled it through the fall of hair topping her braids, smoothing the fraying that had come about while she slept.

She came to Edon as he stood, putting on the jerkin. "I'll do that." She took the laces from his hand and threaded them through embroidered grommets in the soft leather, drawing the vest closed across his chest.

Edon studied the top of her bent head while she finished the task. Then he caught her chin with his bandaged hand and lifted her face. Her cheeks were pale and there were smudges under her eyes. Neither spoke; they simply stood close, looking into the other's face.

"What do you?" Tala asked hesitantly.

"I am looking for your measure," Edon replied gravely.

"And what is that?" she said in a voice that was not as self-assured as the first question had been.

"Your measure. I would know if you will push me to the limits of my control again, lady. Are we done with the tests of whose will is the stronger between us?"

Tala tried to duck her head and remove her chin from

his grasp. Edon detained her, making her keep eye contact
with him. "Warwick is yours," she said at last. "I will
defer to you in the future."

Edon wasn't convinced. "You as much as granted that
when you bargained for your brother's life. I learned to
my cost what a grievous mistake it was not to place you
in his chains at the whipping post."

"I mean it this time," Tala said.

"So your tears were false then? You were playing on
my emotions."

"I was afraid for Venn."

"Answer the question I asked, Tala. Were your tears
false?"

"No."

"Then your promise was."

"No." Her chin wagged back and forth against the restraint of his thumb and curled forefinger. He could see
the anguish in her soulful amber eyes. She compressed her
lips. "You were right. I gave my promise without thinking
how I would react when Venn was no longer in danger. I
have been his only protector too long, my lord."

"And what way is it that you go now, lady?"

She lowered her amber gaze to look at his mouth and
his chin. Her tongue appeared in a quick motion, damp-
ening her lips. It was a very sensual movement, but Edon
hardened his heart against temptation. "I would like to try
it your way, Edon."

"My way is Christian now, Tala. I am committed, because I gave my solemn word to this Almighty God of
King Alfred's. I don't pledge myself lightly. Tomorrow
when I take the vows that bind me to you as a husband,
those will be as solemnly given as any oath I have sworn
in my life. I have much to learn about these new ways and
I don't know that I will be a good Christian. God will
judge me someday. One thing I know for certain is that
he will not find me a man who fell back on his word."

Tala's eyebrows drew together in puzzlement. Her teeth caught a corner of her lip and worried it. The gesture was a habit that Edon found endearing. He wanted to kiss that ragged corner, but it was better that he did not.

"I have heard Christians pledge to take no other mate for life," she said. "What of your concubines? What will you do with them if I am to be the only woman in your bed?"

"What concubines? Do you think I sleep with the wives of my soldiers and advisors? I have told you before that Rebecca is wife to Theo the Greek. Lady Eloya, who serves as my housekeeper and chatelaine, is most definitely married to Rashid, and theirs is a commitment until death do them part. The other women are her servants. You are the only woman I have bedded in Warwick. When you become my wedded wife, you will be the only woman I bed until the day I die. What more can you ask of me?"

"I don't know," Tala said. She could ask for love, but she didn't dare. "It is not the way of my people. Marriage contracts are made and often dissolved freely. We Celts can be shallow and self-serving, but we are not hypocrites like the Christians, who swear falsely when they pledge to be faithful all the days of their lives. Were I to make a pledge of fidelity, I would hold to it."

"And so will I," Edon said solemnly.

He dropped his head and briefly touched her lips with his. It was a chaste kiss, passionless but tender. Then he let go of her chin and stepped back from her, motioning to the door. "Shall we go out now?"

Tala deferred to him. "As you command, lord."

As they ate a small morning repast, Edon filled a knapsack with provisions to be eaten when they reached the lake. His recent experience in Arden Wood told him they would not come to water until well after midday. The arduous hike would not bring them back to Warwick until evening.

Food was a requirement. He had no measure for Tala's stamina. Nor did he want to be saddled with a weak or fainting woman on a lengthy, hot march. They set out immediately, walking at a brisk pace. A good hour passed before they left the fields behind, where laborers paced the furrows, selectively searching out ripened heads of grain.

Moments after crossing the dusty Leam riverbed, Tala and he were in deep woods. The canopy became a high, thick roof blocking out the intense sunlight. The floor of the forest was thick with ferns and small flowering plants that thrived in dense shade.

For all the shadows, the forest was miserably hot. Ferns crackled under Edon's feet, almost as dry as the grasses that grew in the open meadows under the broiling sun. The drought made a difference in the woods, too.

Edon saw no clear pathways. Tala's quick and sure step convinced him she was familiar with the way she traveled. They quickly came to a peculiar break in the land—a rocky escarpment thrusting straight up from the forest floor, like a sheared-off mountain cleaved by a giant's axe. The top boasted a stand of rowan trees and seven upright standing stones. At the base of the cliff grew limes.

Tala led Edon to one side, where the cliff fell back to the earth. There a thicket of briars nourished by a sluggish beck made any forward progress impossible. Edon put his knee to the earth and cupped his hands in the water, assuaging his thirst and splashing more of the cool liquid on his face and throat to wash away his sweat.

"Are you lost, Tala?" Edon asked finally.

Tala watched a few drops of water fall off his chin and dot the soft suede of his jerkin. She smiled, and shook her head, then stepped onto a stone that poked out of the leafy debris. A narrow passage appeared through the briars.

Edon gazed at passage and rock, knowing there was a lever and fulcrum hidden under the stone.

"It's not very wide, but Mother Wren passes without getting scratched. Can you squeeze through?"

"Aye," Edon said doubtfully. "Were I an armless dwarf." He turned sideways and crouched, having concluded he had to go first while she stood on the fulcrum. Midway in, he called back, "How do you get in?"

"Oh, there's a trick to it. Keep going."

She kept a careful eye on his progress, watching the thorns catch at his vest. He'd forgotten he carried the knapsack and had to wrench the cloth free. The moment he stepped into a clearing before an oak grove, Tala released the fulcrum. The gap closed behind him with the cracking and shivering of branches. Spiny leaves again formed an impenetrable wall.

"Tala!" Edon shouted. "Where's the other end of the mechanism?"

"There isn't one. Wait right there!" Tala called from beyond the hedgerow. "I'll join you before you see the sun above the top of the oak trees."

Her laugh told him two things: she didn't want him to know the quickest way into her grove, and she was delighted that she'd played him for a fool. Edon looked at the oaks and the sky above them. The sun was still low enough to be hidden by the trees. The hedgerow fanned out as far as he could see in both directions.

He sat down and waited, taking the knapsack from his back. Clumps of yellow goatsbeard grew abundantly in the rock-strewn clearing. The grass was short, heavily grazed. Numerous droppings told him this was stabling ground for horses. It looked more like the woodland he remembered.

The wait had become tedious by the time Tala emerged from under the great oaks. She'd changed her clothes and freed her hair from its braids. Her slender body, gowned in a scanty dress, was bare armed and bare legged. A coronet of blue violets and rosy mallows encircled her head.

"My apologies, Lord Edon," she said uncertainly. "I wanted to welcome you to Arden Wood properly, my lord."

He started to tell her that he hadn't come here for a romp with a woodland nymph. He rose to his feet and the sun burst over the top of the oaks and blinded him. When he put up his hand to shade his eyes, she chortled in delight.

"Ah, I'm not late. I came exactly when I promised." She caught hold of his hand. That felt strange; he wasn't used to anyone holding it. Instead of leading, she walked beside him. "I have displeased you."

It was a flat statement, not a question. He gazed at her upturned face. "No, you do not displease me. You puzzle me. We did not come here to play. I agreed to do this because you implied I would find answers to the questions I asked you yesterday."

"Yes." Tala nodded.

"Are you a witch, Tala ap Griffin?"

"Some people say so. I don't see my powers as witchcraft. Come, it is easier to show you what I mean than to explain it. Do you know of the legends of King Arthur and his magician, Merlin?"

"I have heard a hundred tales, each more fantastic than the last. Which part of the epic do you wish to discuss?"

"None of it—all of it." Tala shrugged. "Some say Merlin was born being able to see into men's hearts and foretell the future. All other things he learned by shape shifting, by becoming the owl, the deer, the salmon in the stream."

Edon stopped walking. The oaks had thinned and the lake shimmered before him. Its placid surface lay as motionless as a platter of polished silver. The sight took him back ten years, seeing the lake exactly as he'd seen it as a youth. The bank was much wider, the level of the water lowered by the long drought.

On the distant shore, swans paddled in and out of a stand of reeds, dipping into the still water to eat the rich vegetation.

"It is nearly as I remember," Edon said at last, "save for one thing. Ten years ago there was a spire marking where a temple once stood. It was in ruins when I saw it, but I could tell it had been a very beautiful shrine. The shape of it was a horseshoe, the two sides folding around the upright spire. I expect water affected the building. Wood and wattle and daub disintegrates. That's a pity."

"The ruin you describe is known as the Citadel of Glass by my people. You don't see it now?"

"No. Isn't the Citadel of Glass the castle of the Lady of the Lake, according to legend?"

"So it is," Tala agreed. "It is said that only the pure of heart can see the citadel. You are very fortunate to have seen it. King Alfred has also seen it."

"Has he?"

"Yes. The year he turned ten and seven. He came here to be healed of an infirmity that troubles his belly."

"You know this for a fact?" Edon said.

"Yes, I was there. I witnessed all of it. I was just a small girl, not as old as my youngest sisters, Lacey and Audrey, but I already knew that Alfred would be a great and magnificent king. If you ask him of this, he will confirm that every word I say is true."

"Ahh." Edon sighed. She told an intriguing story, but that's all it was. "You said he came here to be cured of the ague that affects his bowels. But he was not cured. He is troubled by that affliction to this day."

"That was Alfred's choice. He refused the cure. He was very young and steeped in the myths of his beloved church. His brother was king and Alfred was his general, the commander of all the king's troops. It was too great a responsibility to put on the shoulders of so young a man. That was what made him sick."

"Why did he refuse the cure?"

"I believe he had a vision of the troubles of the king of Britain—maybe all of the kings, past, present and future. He stood close to the throne and knew that it cost a man his life to be king. Alfred wanted to live. So he went away from Leam and would not take the waters. To this day he will drink none of the healing water of Leam."

Tala's head tilted more in that quizzical manner as she continued to stare intently at Edon's face, watching his eyes and every facet of his expression. He laughed bluntly and tapped her nose. "What are you looking for? Have I grown a huge wart on the end of my nose?"

"No, you haven't. You really don't see it, do you?"

Edon's momentary playfulness faded. He looked at the sparkling lake and then back at her lovely face. "See what, Tala? I see much. A lake that is more beautiful than any ford in Denmark. A hut and a clearing where too many animals have eaten the grass to the roots. The sun and a cloudless sky."

He laughed again, that short, clipped laugh that was more a bark or a scoff than true laughter. "Am I supposed to see a great glass spire and pinnacle with a golden altar floating above the middle of the lake?"

"It is there," Tala assured him. "Not in the middle, no, but to the left of King Offa's hunting lodge."

"There is nothing there," Edon replied firmly. "Your imagination intrigues me. Now why bring King Offa into the tale?"

"He explains how Alfred and I are related. Offa's mother was from the clan of the white dragons, and his daughter married into the golden dragons, Alfred's clan."

Again Edon touched her nose. "Are there no bears up your family tree?"

"There could be. There is now to be a wolf."

"Ah, so there is." Edon's gaze returned to the lake. He swung the pack off his shoulder, tossing it to the grassy knoll beside an oak. Then he settled on the grass, saying "I would be content to spend out my days here. It is a spellbinding sight. The water is low. Is the fishing still good?"

Tala opened the knapsack and took out a tin cup. "Aye, the fish bite when they may. We never go hungry. I'll get you a drink of water."

Edon expected her to go to the lake, but she went instead to one of the nearby streams. She came back with the cup brimming and knelt beside him. Edon propped his good hand on the ground, taking the cup from her in his bandaged right hand. Tala sat on her heels, waiting.

The cup was so full, water soaked the bandage as he quenched his thirst. It was cold and pure, deliciously fresh from an underground spring.

"Do you want some?" Edon offered.

"No, drink your fill. There is plenty more."

"Ah, so this water you will fetch and carry for me, will you?" Edon drained the cup and handed it back to her. "Don't get up. I'm quite satisfied for now."

"The bandage is wet. Let me unwind it and hang it to dry."

"Now I'm getting suspicious, little witch. What game do you play?" Edon extended his hand, intently watching her unwind the wet bandage.

"I am not playing a game. I am trying to answer your questions," Tala explained as she unrolled the cloth. She flipped it out in a long arc, then took it to the nearest oak and hung it over a low limb.

Edon flexed his fingers and looked into the palm of his hand. He grew very still and silent, until Tala sat down beside him. "Damn you, you've done it again," he exclaimed.

"What have I done?" Tala said calmly.

"Look at my hand," Edon commanded.

Tala did not need to look. "I gave you a cup of water from the Leam. The burn on your hand has healed."

Edon exposed his hand again. It was damp. There was a healed pink scar where that morning there had been angry, painful blisters.

"The bruises on your chest are also gone, because the waters of the Leam heal, Edon. They always have and always will. It is not my power. Not my spell casting. I'm only the water bearer, naught else," Tala said solemnly. "What are you doing?" she added, when, without a word, he got to his feet and reached down for her arm, pulling her up.

"Be quiet," Edon growled. When she resisted his tight hold on her upper arm, he picked her up and tossed her across his shoulder. The excesses of yesterday had left a score of passion marks on her body. Her short dress put a bruise on her thigh at his eye level. Edon strode to the stream he'd watched her get the water from and followed it up a small rise to a barrier of rocks, where a stream collected into the pool where she had gotten the water.

"What is it you intend to do, Edon?" Tala demanded.

"Conduct a test of my own device, lady." Without giving her a chance to say another word he tossed her into the pool.

Tala sank like a stone, then came up sputtering, her hair and her crown of flowers streaming in her eyes. "You miserable Viking!" She smote the water in front of her, splashing a silvery arc onto his chest, soaking his jerkin. "I ought to turn you into a frog!"

"Do it." Edon laughed as he tugged the wet garment over his head. "Do it quick, before I take off my boots."

"Don't you dare climb in here! This is my pool and I don't share it with any man!" Tala turned away, paddling to the wall opposite him. No mortar held the stones together. Moss grew thick in and around the cracks. "And you will not desecrate my pool doing what you're thinking of doing, Edon Warwick!''

It took too much time to unwind crossgarters and remove boots. Edon was only reaching for the ties of his breeks when she climbed out of the water on the other side of the pool. Her short gown clung to her body. Her skin was as smooth and unblemished as it had been the first time he'd seen her naked. She stood on the flat rocks shaking an angry fist.

''Oh! You make me so mad I could spit!'' Then she did just that and then ran away.

Edon froze and waited for the hammer to fall. He was absolutely certain he was going to turn into a huge, fat bullfrog. A frog that would be swamped by the crumpled collapse of his breeks around his ears as he shrank to a frog's size and had to hop away.

When nothing of that sort happened, Edon blushed over his giving in to such superstitious thoughts. Then he threw back his head and laughed at his own gullibility.

Chapter Sixteen

King Alfred climbed onto the horse a foot soldier held for him, very pleased at the outcome of the hunt. He had personally taken place in a footrace to bring a wild boar to ground. The pursuit had exhilarated him, and as he looked back at the many bearers shouldering the spoils of the hunt, he was satisfied.

There would be a great feast on Lammas at Warwick. That the whole shire, Vikings and pagans alike, had converted was certainly an event well worth celebrating.

The jarl's best man, Rig of Sunderland, spurred his mount to come to Alfred's side. "Are you ready to ride back to the fortress, Lord King?" Rig asked.

"Aye." Alfred grinned, looking younger than his thirty-two hard-lived years. "We've done well, Rig. Lord Edon will be surprised by the bounty on his board on the morrow."

"There are plentiful beasts in Arden Wood," Rig commented. "I just wish it would rain. The horses will grow lean without oats."

Suddenly Alfred raised his hand in a signal for silence. Rig cocked his head and listened. They were not far from Fosse Way. Sometimes outlaws that lived in the woods attacked unwary travelers. Both he and the king spurred their horses and galloped toward the road. The king's guard followed at their heels.

They burst out of the forest at the clearing where King Offa's oak sheltered a goodly portion of Fosse Way. A dazed Viking stood under the oak, howling like a madman.

"What is the trouble here, man?" King Alfred shouted. The bawling man held two horses by their reins and rubbed his big head with the palm of his left hand.

"Oh, that is Eric the Tongueless, Your Majesty," Rig said as he drew up beside the king and dismounted. "He cannot talk and his wits are addled. An ax cleaved his head years ago. Be calm, Eric."

Eric started when he saw the mighty Rig standing before him. He put up his hand in a gesture of submission, then bawled like an overgrown baby.

"Eric!" Rig grasped his shoulder and shook it. "Be a man! Why do you weep? What happened?"

Eric made frantic gestures with his hands, pointing to Embla's fine horse and empty saddle, then he made violent motions of fighting and pointed to the woods.

"What do you make of it, Rig?" the king asked, concerned for the witless man.

"It would appear that he and his mistress, Embla Silver Throat, were attacked. Is that right, Eric?"

Eric nodded emphatically and ran his fingers over his shoulders and arms, then pointed to a Celtic symbol scratched into the trunk of the old tree.

Rig patiently watched the mute man's hand motions. Some of it made sense, but most didn't. "Were you attacked by painted warriors?"

At that Eric ran to the tree and slapped his hand on the hex sign.

"Ah, Celts." Rig completed the word picture that Eric's frantic gestures seemed to indicate. "I think I know what he's going on about. There are some old Celt warriors. I've seen one or two. They never cut their hair, but wear it in great long plaits hanging down their back, hence Eric's pointing to his back. They are also painted, Lord King—tattooed from head to toe. with the animals that Eric's gestures are trying to explain. The gist of his story is that they have taken Embla Silver Throat.''

Alfred wanted to say "good riddance" but that was not a Christian thing to do so he said nothing. Rig urged Eric the Tongueless onto a mount and they brought the man back to Warwick with them. Eric immediately went to Embla's longhouse, drew his sword and sat before her door, wailing and moaning, apparently grief stricken by his loss.

"What should we do about this, Rig?" King Alfred asked.

"I can send men to search the woods, but you know as well as I that we will find very little. It is too easy to get lost in Arden Wood. I'd best talk to Edon. Embla is his niece by marriage.''

"I think we should send for my ward, Venn ap Griffin. He was to spend the day with Nels, studying catechism. If he has painted warriors on the loose in the forest, I want to know about them," said the king resolutely.

Rig sent for the bishop and the atheling. The boy, the bishop assured them, had spent the whole day indoors with him, diligently applying himself to the study of the Bible.

Venn insisted he knew nothing about any outlaws.

Further interrogation was forestalled by the arrival of King Guthrum, a day sooner than anticipated. Venn was glad to see the Viking king arrive. Lessons in catechism ended for him when Bishop Nels went straight out to greet to the king of the Danelaw, welcoming him with open arms.

All Venn had to do now was wait for Edon. The boy kept a close watch, waiting for the right moment to make his move and parley with a king.

Tala and Edon had no sooner returned to the fortress at sundown than they were told Embla Silver Throat was missing and King Guthrum was not a happy visitor. Tala found that last an understatement. The king was livid. He lashed out at Edon the moment they stepped into Edon's hall.

"Do you know what this whelp has done?" Guthrum shouted at the top of his voice. "Oh, to think that such a viper lives under my own protection. Explain yourself, Edon, lest I have your head torn off your shoulders and posted on a stake outside the walls of this cursed keep."

"What on earth are you shouting about, brother? And yes, I am just as happy to see you!" Edon dropped his hand from Tala's waist and strode across the hall to confront his older brother. In a rage, Guthrum was terrifying and hard to placate.

Guthrum had the atheling by the cloth at his neck and shook him viciously. "This miscreant—who took the vows of Christianity only yesterday at my sponsor's behest—has just whispered in my ear that he wants to make a devil's pact with me!"

Edon gave a quick look at Venn ap Griffin's ruddy face. Guthrum was nigh onto choking the twelve-year-old to death. "And what sort of bargain has the boy offered you?"

"Harald Jorgensson in exchange for this atheling's three virgin sisters!" Guthrum thundered.

"What?" King Alfred jumped to his feet, incensed. He hadn't known what the boy had whispered to the other king just as Edon entered the hall.

"Harald Jorgensson!" Edon stiffened. He glared at Venn and cut a sharp look back at Tala, silently advising her to stay quiet. "What do you know about our nephew, boy?"

Venn grasped at his throat, where the Viking king's fierce grip clamped the cloth of his jerkin like a vise.

"For heaven's sake, Athelstan, let him go so he may

speak,'' King Alfred demanded, calling Guthrum by his
baptismal name.

Guthrum did not want to let the boy go. He wanted to
choke the life out of him. He shook him harder to make
his point clear, then released his hold. Venn nearly collapsed on the trestle table, coughing and choking. He
rubbed his hand across his windpipe.

"Speak up!" thundered both kings.

"Nay," Venn croaked. "Not before you both give your
word that you will return my sisters."

"And why should I do that?" Alfred yelled furiously.
Now he was as angry as Guthrum, and rightly so. No boy
was going to coerce him into doing what was irresponsible.

"Because if you do not...I will not show King Guthrum
where his nephew has been kept low these many months."
Venn played his trump smugly, certain both kings would
have to yield in order to gain the knowledge Venn had so
carefully collected. They both wanted the missing Viking
jarl, and only Venn ap Griffin knew where the man was.

"Boy, do you threaten me?" Guthrum cuffed Venn so
hard he knocked the prince off his feet.

"Hold! My lords! Killing the boy does not get information from him." Edon stepped into the fray, to intervene
as best he could. He put himself between Guthrum and the
belligerent youth.

"I'll do more than box his ears, by God," Guthrum
insisted, drawing back his meaty fist again.

"Brother, please!" Edon held up a calming hand, begging for peace. "Let me reason with him. The two of you
roaring like bears only makes him more unwilling to cooperate. Please, go down to the lower hall and compose
yourselves. I'll get to the bottom of this."

Both kings were so angry that they stalked downstairs,
vowing not to be swayed no matter what Edon wormed
out of the degenerate boy.

"You ask him what he's done with Embla Silver

Throat!'' King Alfred called out as he urged King Guthrum down the steps. "He put his warriors on her trail this afternoon and kidnapped her. I'll stake my crown on that, I will.''

Edon pulled up a stool and set Venn on it. He waited until the hall cleared before he sat down beside the atheling, poured a goblet of mead and handed the drink to Venn to soothe his abused throat. The boy looked scared, as well he should. But like his sister, he had a backbone made of tempered steel.

Ap Griffins, Edon was coming to realize, had never learned the fine art of compromise or retreat. That might explain why they were a family of royal orphans.

The boy thirstily drank all of the mead, so Edon poured him a second cup. While Venn drank that, Edon folded his arms across his chest and waited. Venn set the drained goblet on the trestle. His fingers trembled. Wary eyes darted up to Edon's.

"Now, suppose you tell me just what's going on, Venn ap Griffin," Edon suggested in a calm, rational voice.

Venn flashed a look at his sister, who hovered nearby, then turned to Edon. "I found the jarl last night."

"Where is he?"

"Where everyone knows he would be. In Embla Silver Throat's oubliette."

Edon took a deep breath. "There is no such place."

"Oh, aye, there is, and I know the way to it." Venn stiffened, recovering his purpose. "He is not dead, Edon Halfdansson, not yet."

"Then I suggest that you show me where this oubliette is, for I take it from your tone that it is only a matter of time before Jarl Harald *will* be dead. I would not speak on your behalf if my nephew dies."

There was steel in the jarl's voice. Venn blinked impassively at him, undaunted. "There are my sisters..." he said, proving that age was not a factor in having a single-minded sense of purpose.

"What is it you want for your sisters?"

"I want them returned to Leam," Venn said resolutely. "Or to Warwick, as you would call it. That will suit me. If they are to be converted as I have been, then command your kings to send tutors here. I want them with Tala."

Edon cast a glance at Tala and saw that she listened attentively to her brother's efforts at striking a bargain. But she was clearly very puzzled by his words and did not know what had prompted the boy's actions this day. "Very well," Edon said summarily. "I will put your petition to the kings. More than that I cannot do. Lead me to this oubliette?"

"Not yet." Venn shook his head. "You must promise me that you will see my sisters grown, and that if and when they are married to men of their station, that they are not abused or mistreated. Promise me that."

"Why should I promise that when they have a brother who will see to such needs more carefully than I?"

"Because I may not be here to see to it," Venn said simply. He lifted his shoulders, adding, "Who knows what the morrow brings? I will be content if you give me your word to do what I ask."

There was something very disturbing about the boy's fatalism, but that wasn't the issue Edon needed to address at this moment.

"Very well, you have my word, Venn ap Griffin." Edon gave the assurance Venn wanted. "I will do everything in my power to see to it that your sisters are well taken care of, all of their days, in so far as I may be alive to do so. As you say, who knows what the morrow may bring."

Tala watched the two of them shake hands, sealing the bond between them. She knew better than to interfere. Venn was on his own in this regard, and she knew why. His time was limited. If the eclipse of the moon happened on Lughnasa, as Tegwin predicted, Venn would consent to becoming the final sacrifice. She realized that he was determined to settle his affairs, to be prepared.

Saddened by what she could not stop, Tala retreated to the company of the women and waited. They were all subdued, quiet. Rebecca remained seated nearest the window, where she could see out into the ward and give back reports.

Time seemed to have come to a standstill. Outside, the full moon appeared in the night sky. It lay on the horizon, a heavy orb the color of blood, orange and red.

"What do you suppose it means?" Rebecca asked of her husband, the blind oracle.

"I think we worry overmuch on the colors of the moon." Theo touched his son's cradle, setting it gently back into motion to keep the sleeping infant at peace. If prescience gave him any inkling of the events to unfold, he kept his thoughts to himself.

Distracted by what she saw outside, Rebecca called over her shoulder, "They are coming out of Embla Silver Throat's byre. Edon and Rig carry a litter between them. Rashid, I think you will be needed very soon."

The badly battered and abused jarl was taken first to the bathhouse, where he was washed and covered with clean linens, before he was brought upstairs into the keep. King Guthrum wept over him, clearly moved by the emaciated and starved body of his nephew and the unnecessary suffering he had gone through.

Rashid attended the jarl, doing what he could for the festering sores that scored the Viking's body, applying liniments and poultices where they would do the most good. Lady Eloya prepared him a nourishing soup and sat beside the withered man, carefully tipping a small cup of the strengthening broth to his lips, aiding him in drinking it.

Harald was so weakened and frail that it was feared, as Venn had implied, that he would not live through the night.

King Guthrum summoned Bishop Nels to him, commanding that his sister's only son be shriven, forgiven of his sins, so that he could obtain a just reward in heaven.

Edon and King Alfred had remained downstairs, deep in a private discussion. Venn joined his sister near the window of the hall and the two of them sat watching the moon rise high into the sky. Venn took hold of Tala's hand.

"I must go, Tala," he said quietly, calm and convinced of his purpose. "Lughnasa's full moon is upon us."

Tala did not look at her brother immediately. Instead she held his warm, young hand very tightly, feeling his pulse beating under her fingertips. "Stay," she whispered. "Let this moon pass and remain with me."

"I cannot." Venn shook his head resolutely. "It is my duty. Tegwin told me the land has shriveled as much as it can. Did you see the baskets of grain and corn the gleaners brought to the keep as offerings for the morrow's first fruits? Leam will starve if I do not summon the rain."

"Nay, we will not," Tala responded. "The monks at Evesham have found ways to use the water from the rivers."

"Nay, Tala. The rivers are dying, too. Don't tell me what isn't so. Leam will cease to exist if I do not go. All of you will begin to die this winter, as so many people have done in the land of the Franks and the Lombards. No, I must do my part."

"But what if this Christian God, the Almighty Father, is stronger than our old gods?" Tala argued earnestly.

For a moment Venn considered her words, then his doubts returned and he shook his head. "It is the only thing I can do, and it is the best thing I can do. I am the chosen one."

He removed his hand from her tight grip and stood up, looking to the right and left to see who remained in the hall. The moment was right. Not even a servant lingered in Edon's hall as Venn bounded onto the window ledge.

"Look for me in Arden Wood, sister. If I see you, I will give you a sign. You'll know it is I, come again, when you next meet a grown stag bearing twelve points on its rack, honoring each of my twelve years in this cycle of life. Farewell."

The atheling sprang out the window. He landed in the dusty ward at the base of the keep. Tala bent out across the windowsill, watching his last salute. He sprinted to the open gates of the fortress, then was gone, lost in the strange, unaccountable moonlight.

Tala forced herself to sit back down on her stool. She clamped her hands tightly in her lap, willing herself not to cry. She should be happy, rejoicing in the things that had come true. Everything was as the old druid, Tegwin, had predicted. Venn ap Griffin, the last boy-king, had gone willingly to his sacrifice. No greater love could any king show, than to die for his people.

An hour passed before Edon came quietly to Tala, taking the vacant seat at her side. He gripped the fingers that had last held her brother's hand. "Tala, answer me this. Can the water of your spring be transported? I fear Harald will not live through this night."

Tala took a deep breath. It was one thing to heal a small wound such as a burn or a bruise at the spring itself. She wasn't sure even Branwyn could cure the ills that had befallen the nephew of Guthrum, king of the Danelaw. His blood might be too thin, his time on earth already sealed on the wheel of life.

"What is it you want, Edon? To bring water from the Leam here to Warwick?"

"Aye, for I know Harald would not survive a journey to the well. Will it work, Tala? Can we fetch water here, enough to see Harald regain his strength?"

"We can try." She nodded.

"Then let's do it," Edon said resolutely. He called to
Rig and ordered their horses saddled and brought to the
keep.

The earth's shadow was just beginning to fall across the
moon as they rode out of Warwick. Tala led the Vikings
to her woodland, passing King Offa's Oak, then leaving
the road as they galloped into the forest.

Edon looked only once at the sky, noting that an eclipse
of the moon was taking place. Rig made the sign of the
cross over his chest before he followed on Edon's heels,
galloping into the dark and haunted wood behind the Celtic
princess.

Tala wasted no time taking them on a roundabout trail;
she headed straight up the dried riverbed. Even in the di-
minishing light of an eclipse, Edon saw how many trees
were dying for lack of water. It wasn't very long after that
they reached the lake.

They trotted up to the same pool that Edon had dumped
Tala in so unceremoniously that very morning. He and Rig
dismounted and began filling goatskin vessels with water
from the healing stream. Tala sat on Ariel, her gaze fixed
elsewhere, looking over the lake.

Then a scream pierced the air.

Edon dropped his goatskin and reached for his sword as
he rushed to the edge of the lake. The water, blacker than
soot staining an ironmaster's forge, lay still and ominous
like a huge black granite gravestone. Yet Edon could see
nothing to fight or defend.

He went back to Tala's pool and filled the goatskin.
Edon looked up as he put the stopper in the bag. Ominous
clouds rolled rapidly above the oaks. The wind gathered
force, tossing the uppermost branches back and forth angrily.

Again that inhuman scream pierced the air. Edon identified it as a woman's scream—and one full of terror. This

time, Edon listened for the direction of the scream. It came from across the lake, near King Offa's hunting lodge. Bounding onto Titan's back, Edon called to Rig, "Attend me!"

"No, wait!" Tala came to life, fearing that Edon would interfere in the gods' will. She galloped after him, hot on his heels, to the hunting lodge on the opposite bank.

If it was an illusion of the intense darkness, unhampered by any natural light from the moon, Edon didn't ask, but he saw the temple very clearly. He dismounted outside it, at a long ramp that cut a straight path into the heart of the vast structure beside the lake.

He could not fathom how he'd been tricked in the daylight into believing that the temple no longer existed. For it was there, solid and very much real, very much a ruin in the coal black night.

Its vitrified spire rose twenty feet above the lake between two sheltering oaks. Rounded sides formed a great semicircular amphitheater.

In the center stood an altar constructed of gleaming obsidian, the color of the shadows. The altar held only one object, a black iron cauldron.

Again that scary scream split the air and made the hackles rise on Edon's neck. He spun around, searching for something or someone to fight with his drawn sword. There was no one, no warriors come to bar his path and keep him from entering the temple or walking cautiously up the ramp. Rig followed, staying within the reach of Edon's arm, guarding his back.

They came to the end of the ramp, where it fell sharply away from the raised altar. Before them was a horrendous pit, glistening in the terrifying darkness. Its entire surface was slick and smooth, deliberately glazed by the heat of tremendous fire.

The steep walls were solidly vitrified. Had there been light, Edon knew he would see reflected back at him his

own image. Some ancient inferno had turned all the walls
and structures of this place into a slick, mirrorlike glass.
No wonder he'd only seen the trees!

And then he saw her. At the bottom of the pit, Embla
Silver Throat hacked at walls too steep, too solid and too
slippery to climb. An iron grate sealed the mouth of the
pit.

"Help me!" she screamed. "Odin, All Father, help me!
Ayeeiiiaa! Freya, Loki, come aid me!"

She had no weapons to use against the terrors that she
faced in the bottom of the deep pit. She chopped at her
own shadowy image with her fists and feet.

There were neither druid priests, nor others to witness
her suffering. She foolishly fought against her own night
terrors, wearing herself out by fighting whatever invisible
demons tormented her in the pit's awesome darkness.

"Tegwin, I know you're up there, you bastard. Come
help me! Damn your eyes, I've paid you good coin to kill
that boy! Where are you? Tegwin! Tegwin! I'll kill you
for this!"

Rig dropped his hand on Edon's shoulder as the two of
them put away their swords. The last sliver of the moon
slipped into shadow and the eclipse became total.

"She is mad," Rig said uneasily.

They could hear the woman throw her whole body
against the wall. Her hands pounded at unseen sights, and
she cursed violently, calling upon Harald Jorgensson to
take up arms against her. She vowed to kill him anew,
slowly and surely.

Edon cast a glance up at the threatening sky, where the
eclipsed moon glowed a deep, dark red. The wind tore at
the treetops, scattered leaves and dirt across the ground.

"She will keep well enough inside there until the morrow," Edon said dispassionately. "Let us attend our purpose. Harald may yet live to dispense his own justice. I
would not cheat him of that pleasure. We will come back

with ropes and get her out once we've taken this water to Harald.''

Edon turned, looking for Tala. "Get our horses and the water," he called to Rig as he ran down the long ramp. He saw Tala far out on the lake, walking across the water.

"Tala!" Edon shouted.

With the rising of the violent wind, the water in Black Lake changed temperament. It churned in turbulent upheaval. Waves swelled and crashed against its raw, drought-exposed banks. They lashed at Edon as though to drive him back up the shore.

Far, far away from him, on the water's roiling surface, Tala seemed to float above the tempest. He could see her feet move across the tops of spumy whitecaps. It was as though she stepped on the crests themselves and was held up above the thickening maelstrom by some miracle.

Fear set a huge hammer banging in Edon's heart. Logic told him nothing was as it appeared at Black Lake. He cupped his hands to his mouth, yelling, "Tala!"

Surely his eyes deceived him! She could not be walking on the water, for that would be a miracle! But when she did not turn and come back to him, Edon rushed forward, headless of the danger to himself. Sink or swim, he was going after her. "Tala!"

He splashed straight after her, his feet sinking into the choppy waves only to stay right on top of the water...like Tala did! It wasn't sand or dirt under his feet in the water, but stone. Flat rocks supported his full weight—carefully laid stone over which the glistening, turbulent waves swirled and eddied—but the depth of the water above the stones rose no higher than his knees.

Then he made the connection, saw what he hadn't been able to see before. The stone ramp to the temple crossed the lake and the fens! It was a causeway. Feeling ten times a fool, Edon ran after her, his footing sure as he closed the gap between them.

He caught up with her on the far edge of the lake, where
the fen was thick and deep, the raw peat exposed and rank
from the drought. Edon grabbed hold of her arms, encasing
her in his sure grip. "Where do you go?"

"There!" Tala pointed woodenly ahead, to a clearing
encircled by oaks. Torchlight cast an eerie glow under the
wind-tossed oaks. Edon saw a dozen giant stags, walking
upright on two legs. He saw they were men in costumes—
mummers, naught else.

In the center of their circle stood an old man in the
vestments of a druid. A beard white with age touched his
belly. To each side of the druid stood two old Celtic warriors. Edon recognized the one, Selwyn, whose painted
torso he'd admired at the gates of Warwick.

"What goes here?" Edon asked quietly, holding fast to
Tala. He felt the hair on the back of his neck crawl. He
looked for Rig and saw him coming round the lake, leading their horses. "Tell me, Tala, what are they doing?"

She took a shuddering breath, mesmerized by the rite
exposed before them. Her young brother mounted a stone
platform above the fen, wearing only a breechclout. The
tattoo on his shoulder stood out starkly against the white
flesh of his thin, naked chest.

At the boy's throat was the most magnificent torque
Edon had ever seen in his life—made of a gold so pure it
seemed like a wreath of fire encircling Venn's slender
neck.

The druid raised his hands high in prayer and solemnly
removed the gold torque from the atheling's body. In its
place he wrapped a slender knotted cord, a garrote under
which he slipped a shaved piece of wood.

Embla Silver Throat's description of the Lughnasa sacrifice came back to Edon with haunting clarity. He lurched,
certain that he knew exactly what he was seeing. His fingers dug into Tala's shoulders.

"What in the name of God are they doing?"

"They sacrifice Venn's royal blood to the power and mercy of the gods. He will bring the rain," Tala whispered. Then her hands flew to her mouth and she broke down, weeping, crying silently in heartbreaking sorrow.

"That's idiocy!" Edon countered. "Any fool can see its going to rain torrents at any moment. This is obscene, an abomination against the baptism we received yesterday."

Tala pressed her hands against Edon's mouth, vainly trying to still him. "No, let it be, Edon. Do not interfere. You will provoke the gods. They will not spare your life a second time."

"The hell you say!" Edon swore as he pushed her hands away. "I'm stopping this."

He ran into the clearing as Venn raised a basket of grain to the sky. Lightning swept beneath the scudding clouds. The air crackled. The scent of rain invaded the fen. The oaks tossed violently as Venn held his gift of the first fruits aloft. Thunder rumbled from the thickening clouds, drowning out the boy's offertory prayers.

The stag men began to chant and sway. The druid raised his staff aloft as Venn poured the grain and corn onto the dried, crackling peat. The black pools were long gone, caked with the black mud that coated the dried-up bog. The soft, unstable earth cracked under Edon's feet as he strode to the center of the grove and drew his sword.

"Stop this nonsense! Venn ap Griffin, get down from that altar this moment!"

"Lord Edon!" Venn practically choked on the words. The spell cast by Tegwin and the chanting mummers was momentarily broken.

"How dare you, Viking!" Tegwin shouted. "Seize him and throw him in the pit!

"No!" Venn commanded. "You will leave this Viking be!"

"I'm glad you said that, boy." Edon reached up and

grabbed hold of Venn's skinny arm, yanking him to the queasy ground at his side. "Otherwise, it would go very bad for you when we return to Warwick."

"Seize him, I say!" Tegwin commanded. Stafford and Selwyn hesitated, not knowing who to obey, their atheling or the druid.

"No!" Venn put his thin body in front of Edon, shielding him. "I said you will not harm this Viking, Tegwin. Stafford, Selwyn, hear me! Lord Edon is to look after my sisters."

"Don't be a fool, boy!" Tegwin snarled. "That Viking can do nothing in this life or in the one that comes after. Kill him, I said!" He pushed Stafford and Selwyn forward, gesturing furiously at the stone clubs they had in their hands. "Do it, I say! Crush his head! Time is of the essence! We must finish the sacrifice."

Stafford's white brow lowered in concern. This ritual wasn't going the way it should. The whole sequence was out of order. Stafford had learned it as a boy not much older than Venn. There was no oak cake and no mistletoe. Tegwin hadn't recited a single prayer correctly in its entirety. Stafford was old, older than any man in the glen, but his memory was clear and sharp.

"Kill the Viking!" Tegwin screamed. He jerked Venn's gold torque out of a pocket of his robe, holding it aloft. "This gold torque to the man who kills the Viking!"

"I'd like to see one of you old men try." Edon cut his sword through the air, making it whistle and the stag men fall back. He jerked Venn behind him and made a threatening motion at Tegwin with his sword.

"I know you, you old faker," Edon continued. "You're no more a real druid than I am. You've been in league with Embla Silver Throat right from the start. She paid you to kill this boy. And you come to this grove tonight performing this blasphemy!"

"Kill him!" Tegwin screeched. "Damn him to the other world! Don't listen to him! He lies!"

When none of the old soldiers moved to take on Edon, desperation drove Tegwin to seek divine aid. "O Esus! Shake the earth where this unbeliever stands. Smote him, oh great and mighty Taranis, god of thunder and light! I call on you, Teutates, return to your people. Give us back our lands this Viking invader has stolen! Restore the waters to Leam!"

"What jibberish!" Edon snarled in disgust. He caught hold of Venn's arm and shook him. "Can't you see that he's naught but a mad old man? Has he offered your torque to the god of the water? No, he hid it inside his cloak so he could sell it tomorrow! Then he offers it to these old men so they'd get up the nerve to take me on. The damned old fool was down at the river yesterday, being baptized like everyone else. He doesn't believe any of it, Venn. He's just hedging his bets and working one side against the other. Don't be a fool twice, boy."

"My lord." Venn's eyes were not on Tegwin or Edon. They were on the terrible sky that was becoming more violent and frightening by the moment.

Edon shook him again. "Listen to me, boy—this old fool is trying to kill you. For what? So that ten old men can dance around all night in deer heads, wagging their antlers and getting drunk?"

Edon reached over and grabbed the nearest stag man, jerking his costume off his head. Under the brown robes was a bald, fat man. "Who is this? Lucius the baker? What power does he have?"

Edon gave the old man a boot in the seat of his breeks, sending him tumbling to the ground.

"My lord," Venn cried out, pointing at the sky behind Tegwin.

The old druid had climbed onto the sacrifice stone and stood like Moses on Mount Sinai with his arms upraised,

his garments blowing in the wind that whipped viciously
through the trees.

"Come, Taranis, show your wrath! Kill the Viking!"
Tegwin shook his staff at the tumultuous, lowering storm.
A huge black cloud melded the storm to the lake—forging
both into one great elemental force, like the gruesome bogan of their collective nightmares. "I command you—"

Lightning struck the staff in Tegwin's upraised hand.
The old man flew out of his sandals, suspended for an
electrifying moment. Then he crashed to the ground, his
clothing and hair on fire. His death scream rent the air.

The stag men tumbled backward, knocked off their feet
by the concussion of the lightning. Their fiery brands fell
to the earth, landing on the dry layers of exposed peat,
bursting into flames. In a heartbeat each mummer was
screaming and rolling as their robes and crackling stag
heads caught flame.

The wild wind spread the fire like quicksilver across the
parched bracken. Every dry, brittle oak circling the grove
burst into flame.

The grisly, gruesome nightmare grew more macabre as
flames spread outward, leaping from tree to tree. The burning stag men panicked and ran, howling, trying to shed
deer-head masks and long robes.

Dragging Venn toward his sister, Edon shouted, "The
Almighty God has spoken, boy. He's saying get out of
here, now!"

Chapter Seventeen

If it hadn't been for the fire erupting all around them, Edon would most definitely have taken the time at Black Lake to bang Tala's and her little brother's heads together. Maybe that would have put some sense into each of them.

As it was, Rig, Tala, Venn and Edon had all they could handle to escape the rising wall of flames the wind drove at them. The fire swept across the fields of exposed peat, cutting off all retreat back to the causeway. Their only escape was west through the woods. Even so, the raging forest fire jumped ahead of their retreat more than once.

In desperation, they fled to the shallow river Avon, dismounting and leading their horses into the center of current, taking its winding course to Warwick.

By the time they reached the fortress, the total eclipse of the moon had passed. The fire in Arden Wood cast an eerie glow over the whole valley as they climbed the high hill at Warwick. The storm clouds thickened. Ash, cinders and acrid smoke filled the air. A dozen great fires burned in the forest.

Thunder rolled and lightning smote the valley. Terrible clouds filled the entire sky, yet the rain held back. What signal nature waited for, Edon didn't know. He was just thankful they made it back to the fortress.

It took six stout Vikings on each of the heavy gates to close them against the driving wind. Dirt from the arid fields swept up in the wind, stinging eyes and searing skin.

As he dismounted and surrendered his horse to a stable boy, Edon cast a worried look toward his menagerie's byre. The nearest fire was leagues to the west. The wind howled. God alone knew what damage was coming.

Edon told the men on guard to keep a sharp watch and to let him know if the wind changed direction. Rig caught the skins of healing water from their saddles and slung them over his shoulders, following Edon, Tala and Venn.

Venn didn't waste his energy trying to speak against the raging wind as Edon manhandled him into the keep. Inside it was another matter. There the howling wind was stopped by the thick stone walls.

The atheling yanked his arm free of Edon's fierce grip and snarled, "Now we're doomed, Viking."

"Are we?" Edon snapped. "And how is that?" He relaxed now that the keep's doors behind them were shut and barred. "And how is that?"

"It will never rain," the boy said purposefully.

"Never?" Edon cocked a skeptical brow at that dire prediction. Apparently the boy was stupid as well as stubborn.

"*Never!*" Venn said in disgust. "Tala, you explain it to him!"

Edon relieved Rig of the water-filled goatskins. "Explanations can wait. Rig, put two of my best guards on this boy with the orders not to allow him out of their sight for any reason. Let's get this water upstairs."

The two kings and the bishop knelt beside the bed where Jarl Harald lay. The Viking's once-handsome face was at peace, no longer twisted in agony or pain. The kings were united in prayer for his soul. A dozen candles flickered in the chamber, filling it with the scent of beeswax, sweet and potent and sacred.

Another deafening clap of thunder rumbled over the top of the fortress, and the most splendid thing happened. The rains let loose. Huge drops struck the slate tiles on the roof, wet the keep's outer walls and splashed on the windowsill. The next gust of wind brought the scent of a blessing— dry earth turning wet.

Certain that he'd come too late, Edon slipped across the room and took hold of the shutters to close them as quietly as he could. He paused to look out the window at the parched valley. Off in the distance the fire raged in the heart of Arden Wood, a great conflagration. The onslaught of rain did nothing to stop it.

"Uncle...Edon?" A voice spoke from behind his back. "Don't close the shutters. I have been too long in the land of the dead. Let me see the sky."

Edon spun around, shocked to hear Harald speak in so strong and clear a voice. "Harald! Was that you?"

The sick man lifted his pale hand from the blankets at his side. "Aye, it is I. Come, let me touch you and see you in the candles. Guthrum tells me you have come to the Lord."

Edon dropped to one knee beside the bed and took Harald's pale hand in his own. His best and dearest friend from childhood was no more than skin and bones. But the eyes inside Harald's shrunken sockets were intelligent and bright. His spirit shone out from inside him.

"Where is Embla?"

"She is trapped in Arden Wood. There is a fire there. I could do nothing to save her." Edon shook his head, not willing to tell Harald more than that.

Harald sighed and closed his eyes. He lifted his fingers toward Guthrum, motioning to him. "Tell him, please."

Guthrum cleared his throat, his face grave and concerned. "Harald accompanied me to Wedmore as my heir. It was there, under the tutelage of Bishop Nels, that we both came to acknowledge our faith and were baptized.

Embla was against it. Harald thought in time she would give up her pagan ways.'' Guthrum held open his hands. "I suspected her from the first…but without proof I could not act.''

"You must forgive her,'' Harald said firmly. "She thought me weak for my faith, for forgiving her every injury she did against me. She tried to raise demons in me, but she failed. I am alive because I never lost my faith that God would save me.''

Edon looked at Rig and motioned to Tala to come forward. He put a goatskin of healing water in her hands. Tala held it a moment, hesitating, unsure of what she should do. Then she turned to Bishop Nels and gave him the skin, asking him to bless the water.

She wanted to kiss Edon, cover him with kisses of thanks. He'd saved her brother. It didn't bother her if Venn sulked about being cheated of his fate. He was so young and had so much to learn. So did she. Now, thanks to a Viking, she had the chance to start anew, to bring her family together again. To heal her land and her people.

All three sacks of water were blessed and then Harald's bandages were removed so that the sores from his chains could be washed and cleansed in the water of the Leam. He asked for cup after cup of the sweet, pure water to drink. Tala and Edon watched as Rashid tended the jarl's wounds.

"You will be up and on your feet in no time," Rashid assured Harald. "Once we've put some meat back on your bones.''

"I will hold you to that, for I expect Brother Bedwin at Evesham will have much work for me to do. I'm going back there, Guthrum. It is the only place on this Earth that I have ever felt completely at peace. Now that Edon is home, you must make him see that Warwick prospers. I am going to devote the rest of my life to God.''

"Evesham Abbey has prospered quite well," King Alfred interjected. "Did you know, Guthrum, that they will bring in a mighty crop of grapes this year on account of the unseasonably hot weather? Just listen to that rain, my friends, and give thanks!"

Later, after the occupants of the crowded keep quieted for the night, Tala stood at Edon's windows watching rain pour from the sky. Deep glistening puddles made little lakes in the fenced ward. At the base of Warwick Hill the river rose in its banks, filling as each beck and stream that fed into it gushed with life again.

"I want to go play in the rain like a child." Tala leaned out the window to touch the rainwater that cascaded off the roof. "I never thought to see anything so wonderful again in my lifetime."

Edon frowned as he wrapped his arms around her waist and pulled her back. "You're a foolish woman, lady, to even suggest going out and playing in this torrent. Once struck by lightning, I won't risk it twice."

Tala wrapped her wet hands over his dry ones and squeezed. "You risked it all this night, Wolf of Warwick, defying the old gods."

"I won't make light of your beliefs, Tala. I am just thankful that I was there and could stop a travesty from happening. Your brother was duped. Tegwin had other reasons to kill him. Embla bribed him. She knew of Venn's rightful claim to Leam and wanted him out of the way, just as she wanted Harald out of her way. Thorulf searched her byre and longhouse. She was stealing from the shire, hoarding gold and silver."

"I don't understand why she turned against her own husband. Jarl Harald was a handsome, virile man."

"Yes." Edon nodded. "But when he began to pay a regular tithe to the church, Embla saw that as taking money from her coffers. As my managers of Warwick they were

entitled to one-twentieth of the profits of this shire. She
wanted it all."

"It was greed that made her do the horrible things she
did?" Tala asked.

"Aye." Edon rubbed his chin over the top of her head.
She felt so right in his arms. So perfect. "In truth, I believe
she intended to kill me as well. Thorulf's search of her
longhouse found a second satchel of nightshade and bloodroot—an identical pack to the one she accused Venn of
bringing into Warwick."

"Lord, she could have poisoned us all!" Tala whispered.

"Had your brother not accidentally bumped into her
when she was trying to sneak back into the fortress unnoticed from collecting the roots, she might well have done
just that. But once the roots were discovered there were
too many witnesses for her to risk trying to poison our
food or drink. We were very lucky that night."

"Some would say you have been blessed with much
good fortune," Tala said. She looked up at his solemn
face. "It is only a miracle you and Venn were not killed
by lightning in the grove this night. You were not all that
far from the spot where Tegwin stood."

"Ah, but that's where I know better, love. I made doubly certain that I did not raise my hand or my sword to
attract the lightning, as he did. I learned my lesson the first
time. I dare say your druid has gotten his just reward. Tala,
he was going to murder your brother. Don't you feel angry
about that?"

Tala sighed deeply. "Aye, I have always been against
such dreadful sacrifice from the first I heard of it. But when
the old legends are recited and a young boy is convinced
that such a sacrifice is his heroic destiny...well, my
thoughts on the matter don't carry much weight. Venn
knew he could never become a king like our ancestors
were, but as a sacrificial victim, he would be revered for-

ever as a great and noble boy-king. I did everything I could to sway him from believing Tegwin. Only each day that the drought continued, Venn began to think that to bring the rain was a wonderful thing.''

"Tegwin played on Venn's fears." Edon sighed. "I don't relish returning to the lake on the morrow to collect Embla's body. But she must have a proper burial. As caught up as he is in forgiving all harm done him, Harald will likely have it no other way.''

"You don't have to go yourself, do you?'' Tala asked him, concerned.

"We'll see. Perhaps Rig can manage it.''

Edon turned her around in his arms and kissed her mouth. She was willing and pliable. Though he wanted to press her into yielding to him, Edon settled for placing a soft and tender kiss on each of her temples and letting her retire to bed. He had much to get ready for the morrow, and it was important that they keep a good watch on the rising river and the fire in the forest.

Walking the perimeter of the fortress wouldn't satisfy Edon that all was well in Warwick this wild night. He and Rig road out again, traveling up Fosse Way as far as Watling Street and returning via the trail beside the river.

It rained the whole time they were out, hard and steady rain. The Avon was rising, but not dangerously so. From his final survey of the valley from the top of his hill, he saw that the fire in the forest was finally out.

First thing in the morning, Rig promised to take a patrol into the woods and search the temple for Embla Silver Throat. Both Edon and Rig privately hoped that the patrol would return bringing the bitter woman's remains for burial. But they both were guarded in their thoughts, wanting to see her body before they accepted her death as a fact. In that pit, she could have survived the fire.

It was very late when Edon crawled into bed beside Tala and gathered her close in his arms. It was still raining, a steady, nourishing rain that quenched the earth's deep thirst.

Edon closed his eyes and listened to the rain. In just a few days, his Warwick would be green again, the way it should be. He went to sleep contented, certain that all things were as they should be in the heavens and on earth.

He woke to empty arms and an empty bed.

Instantly, Edon remembered two things that he'd tried to remember before and couldn't. The first was Tala's prediction of what would happen to Leam if any man should lay hands on the atheling of Leam—that the land would be smote from end to end, laid desolate and ruined by the wrath of Leam's ancient gods. The second was Theo's prediction that the princess of Leam had made plans to flee to the abbess at Loytcoyt.

Groaning with regret, Edon jumped out of bed and threw open the shutters to look over Warwick. One glance at the world outside his windows told him both predictions had come true. The proof was as evident as the collapse of Embla's flimsy palisade wall.

The stockade had fallen victim to the winds and drenching rain. The forest fire had been extinguished by the rain, but not before the flames had consumed nearly all of Arden Wood. The forest Edon saw from his window was a charred ruin.

The peaceful river that meandered through the valley had become a flood by daylight. Cursing his foul luck, Edon shouted for Eli as he snatched up his breeks and began to dress.

Eli, who slept on the sill of the jarl's door every night, opened the door, ready to be of service to Edon. "Lord?"

"Fetch Maynard to me at once!" Edon growled. The servant whipped about, scuttling out as Edon sat and began lacing the garters on his boots. With the deluge of rain still falling from the heavily laden skies, Edon knew to dress for the elements. His feet wouldn't be dry again until he collapsed in bed that night. He had every intention of entering that bed a newly wedded husband, exercising his marital rights.

Maynard arrived as Edon stood fastening his belt and scabbard at his hips. He wasn't encumbering himself with his long sword today. If it came to fighting, it would have to be done at close range.

"You sent for me, Lord Edon?" Maynard presented a rigid salute, prepared for any order to come his way.

"I did," Edon replied in clipped tones. "Where is the atheling?"

"On his knees in the chapel between King Guthrum and King Alfred, lord."

"Are you absolutely certain of that?" Edon asked harshly.

"I saw all three enter the north barracks myself before I answered your summons. The bishop has turned that building into his residence and chapel since his arrival, Lord Edon."

Slightly flustered by Maynard's confident answers, Edon brought other urgent events forward, checking to see if his captain remained on his toes. "And what is being done about the collapsed gates and palisade? Who has taken a count of how many animals escaped their pens or were stolen from the stables?"

"Thorulf is out checking the pens and I have personally been to the menagerie and seen that the beasts are fed and contented in their cages. The wooden wall may be down, but the fortress is secure. No one lays abed, lord. We have been hard at work since the wall fell a good two hours ago."

Edon simmered, wondering if his captain was chiding him for having slept through disaster. "Well, Maynard, my good man, since you know everyone's business and appear to have everything within this keep well in hand, where is my bride this bright and cheerful morning?''

Maynard the Black's dimple almost flashed in his cheek, but he managed to keep his smile to himself. The jarl was in a testy mood. He withheld the urge to comment on the upcoming nuptials. That would only antagonize Edon more. Instead, Maynard answered simply, ''Eli brought heated water upstairs for the princess's bath. She and Lady Eloya are currently bemoaning some flaw in your bride's complexion. They have also sent an urgent request to the priests and the kings to command the sun to shine and the mud to dry before noon. Hence the gentlemen in question have repaired to the chapel to pray for a small and very temporary break in the deluge, lord.''

''Humph!'' Edon grunted darkly. He jerked his chin up, his blue eyes flashing at the soldier. ''Are you telling me that the princess of Leam is in this building?''

''Yes, lord,'' Maynard said with certainty. ''Where else should she be on her wedding day? And may I be the first to offer you my most sincere congratulations, my lord Wolf? The princess of Leam will be an exquisite bride.''

Edon whipped a tunic over his head. He flashed a dismissive nod at Maynard and advanced from the bedchamber into the hall.

The morning trestle was set against the long east wall. Rain splattered in the huge west window, where a pair of carpenters were applying finishing touches to the frame that would hold the stained-glass window Edon had brought all the way from Constantinople to grace his hall. The jarl snatched a pear from a bowl as he passed the table, striding in a deliberate course to Lady Eloya's chamber.

A whole gaggle of servants crowded that room. Every trunk and chest that held even so much as a scrap of cloth stood open around the airy chamber. A painted screen in the far corner prevented Edon from seeing who was actually in the bathing tub. The rose scent of oil of attar conflicted with the tang of lemons in dominating the air of Eloya's chamber. Edon's ears were assaulted by oohs and aahs and giggles, the prattle of too many women.

Oblivious to the tittering servants, Edon strode to the painted screen and pulled it aside. Both Tala and Eloya started—Tala looking up at him from a steaming tub of foaming bubbles in which she was delightfully naked, Eloya stiffening as she coated the princess's shoulders with a thick white cream.

"What the devil are you women doing?"

"My lord!" Eloya said, affronted by his intrusion. She straightened and reached for a length of toweling to cover Tala's nudity. Edon lifted a peremptory hand, dismissing her.

Tala was much more blasé about his unannounced arrival. In a glance she saw that Edon only had eyes for her, and those eyes were riveted to the wet curves of her breasts, which were just hidden from his sight by the press of her soap-covered arm in the deep bath water.

"We are bleaching away my freckles, my lord," she told him plainly, motioning to the cream Eloya had applied to her shoulders, arms and throat.

"Freckles?" Edon felt as if he was staggering. A rush of feminine scents assaulted his nose—of perfumes and oils, and all those hidden, secret unguents women used to make themselves alluring. God help him, he couldn't stand it!

"I forbid it!" he barked, bristling just like his animals did when they were threatened. "Do not remove one single freckle from my lady's skin, Eloya!"

"But—"

"Not one!" Edon commanded.

His face flushed a dark red, giving testimony to how flustered he was. He had truly woken up believing Tala had run away from him.

Tala was here, in his keep, making herself beautiful just

for him. He wanted to reach down and grab her, take her out of that tub and cart her wet, beautiful body back to his bed on the other side of the keep. But...he couldn't.

She hadn't run away to Loytcoyt Abbey.

Theo's prediction was false. Tala smiled at him and Edon almost shamed himself with the intensity of his desire for her. Mastering control of himself, he bowed to her and her silly tub and preparations. He would wait until she was his wife under Alfred and Guthrum's law. And he vowed privately that if he ever caught her in such admirable dishabille again, he would dismiss all servants and retainers from the room and have his way with her on the spot.

"Am I to take that to mean that you like freckles, Edon?" Tala asked quietly, thrilled by the admiration she saw in the Viking's eyes.

"Of course, I like freckles—your freckles. On you, my lady, they are the most splendid ornament of all."

Tala smiled at him, and the gloomy, dismal day suddenly seemed bright and more beautiful than any day of his life. Nodding curtly, his orders delivered, Edon turned about and marched back into the hall.

If Theo's sightless eyes could twinkle, they did so as Edon sat down beside him at the trestle. The jarl was clearly famished, starved as a newly risen wintering bear this morning.

"I sense in you a rare mood, my lord," Theo said good naturedly.

"Don't start with me, you miserable soothsayer," Edon said purposefully, reaching for a loaf of crusty bread and breaking it in half. "Horrible dreams jolted me out of a most pleasant sleep this morning...all because of your misguided attempts at prophecy with a mazer cup."

"My misguided attempts at prophecy!" Theo flattened his broad hand on his chest. "An oracle can only tell what he sees. It's not my fault that you insist on altering events to suit yourself. I've always said that prophecy is an opportunity to effect a change. Perhaps you'd care for a reading this morning.''

Edon stopped him from reaching for the golden cup that always hung from a chain at his belt. "No," Edon said firmly. "I've got a wall to see repaired and a flooding river to monitor. That's enough for one day.''

"Oh, I do not think you need trouble yourself with the river today,'' Theo assured him. "I saw to it that everyone was well prepared for a possible flood on Lammas. Today we need only worry about getting you married.''

It did Edon no good to wish that were so. He had plenty more things to worry about, namely Embla Silver Throat. He needed to find Rig and see if the Viking woman's body had been found.

Edon sighed, then cast a quick look at the closed door across the hall. It was going to be the longest day of his life. Of that fact he was absolutely certain.

Chapter Eighteen

Theo proved correct in his assessment at the breakfast table: the shire was prepared for a flood. As Edon and Rig rode about the countryside through the continuing rain, it soon became evident that the farmers had moved their stock away from the pastures nearest the river. Fortunately, lowlands that were underwater were not the most productive and fertile of fields. The bulk of Warwick's harvest was safe from the Avon's rising water.

Water flowed in the Leam again. That torrent ran too fast for them to take the shortcut into Arden Wood to assess the damage to the forest. However, the fire damage certainly made it easier to pass through the woods. The hedgerow was gone, as were most of the great trees.

The old temple ruin was not invisible this morning. A heavy layer of black ash coated the spire and the ramp. King Offa's hunting lodge was gutted by the fire. Several feet of water had collected in the bottom of the pit where Edon had last seen Embla Silver Throat fighting her invisible enemies.

There was no body to be recovered from the pit.

"I don't like this," Rig said as they turned their horses toward the grove. "That woman could be anywhere if she's alive."

"That's a big if," Edon countered. "Assume she found some way to get out of the pit, the odds are she perished in the fire when it swept through the forest."

Edon's conclusion was logical. The destruction went on for leagues in all directions. "Thank God for the rain. Otherwise this whole valley would still be burning."

They continued their search, although the rain hampered their inspection. They could not go into the fens. The bog was underwater and the ground unstable. "Tomorrow is soon enough to send a detail here to bury the dead at the grove."

"Aye." Edon nodded, turning his horse and whistling to Sarina to heel. "Let's return to Warwick. I'll want to wash the stench of this fire away before I am wed."

The biggest surprise of the morning came when Edon returned to Warwick. A patrol of King Alfred's guard had returned, bringing the three little princesses of Leam to attend their sister's wedding. The girls were solemnly chaperoned by an old nun, Mother Wren. Edon was very surprised to learn that the Leamurian woman was actually the abbess of Loytcoyt Abbey.

As the morning progressed the rain began to let up and people set out from their cottages and longhouses for Warwick. No one wanted to miss attending Lammas Day's High Mass with two kings. Vikings and Mercians alike brought the best of their young animals and the first fruits of their summer labors to be blessed by the bishop.

Bishop Nels prepared to celebrate the Mass outdoors. Just before noon, the rain let up to a light, misty drizzle.

Edon took his place in the assembly before the altar. Rig and Maynard stood at his sides. Flanking them were Rashid, Eli and Thorulf, all looking extremely handsome in their very best native garments. Sensing something important was happening, Sarina trotted out and began to nose around, sniffing inquiringly at everyone. She also was at her best, newly bathed and brushed till her thick coat shone. She finally came to stand at Edon's side and thump her tail approvingly against his legs as the wedding procession emerged from the keep.

Venn ap Griffin had been chosen to lead the procession, bearing the bishop's tallest crucifix. Behind him walked his little sisters. Each carried a small basket filled with wildflowers that they cast about for their sister to walk upon as she came solemnly to Edon's side.

The smell of wet earth mingled with the fragrant, mystical scent of burning frankincense as the bishop circled the altar, blessing all the people gathered around it. But to Edon, nothing could diminish the alluring perfumes of the beautiful woman at his side.

Eloya's skills were evident in Tala's breathtaking appearance. Her red-gold hair shone in a crown of natural braids carefully wound around her head. A gown of royal blue silk clung to her curves so lovingly that the sight of her had taken Edon's breath away.

The animals and the fruits of Warwick were blessed before the Mass. Afterward Bishop Nels urged Edon and Tala forward, and the words of the ceremony of marriage were spoken over them. Edon vowed to love, honor and cherish Tala all the days of his life, then he slipped a ring of Welsh gold onto her finger, saying, "With this ring, I thee wed."

Tala hesitated a moment when it was her turn to repeat her vows in the Christian ceremony. In the old ways her and Edon's hands would have been scored with a knife so that their blood would flow and then they would have been securely bound together. As their blood mingled, it would have made them one. She shook her head, clearing away all thought of the old traditions. For in the old days, she would never have married. She would have spent her life serving the people by making their offerings of gold trinkets to the Lady of the Lake.

She turned and took the ring Eloya held out to her and

repeated after the priest, "I, Tala ap Griffin, take you, Edon, son of Halfdan, as my lawfully wedded husband, from this day forward, until death do us part." Then she slipped the gold ring on his finger, looked up into the brilliant shine of his beautiful blue eyes and said, "With this ring, I thee wed."

"I pronounce you man and wife. What God has brought together, let no man put asunder." Bishop Nels raised his hands in a blessing. "You may kiss the bride," he said to Edon.

Edon took Tala in his arms and kissed her soundly. Neither one of them paid much attention to the shouts and cheers of celebration that surrounded them. All that mattered was this kiss and their union.

Afterward the festivities began in earnest, undaunted by the damp day. It rained hard all afternoon and evening. The bonfire wouldn't stay lit, but no one seemed to notice the loss of that old custom. It certainly didn't hamper the dancing or the drinking, especially not by the hearty Viking revelers.

The Danes weren't the only ones consuming Edon's sweet wines. Ruddy-faced from the vintage he'd consumed, Venn ap Griffin stumbled up on the raised dais. He paused under the bright awning where Tala and Edon sat high and dry as they presided over the feast. Venn swept a jaunty feathered cap off his brow and bowed low to the newly wedded couple. Then he struck a pose that was anything but gracious, folding his arms across his chest and thrusting out his jaw.

"I've come to a decision, sister!" Venn announced. His voice was too loud, his tone belligerent. The gleam in his eyes bespoke a challenge.

"And what decision is that, brother?" Tala asked gently.

Edon, who held the Greek motto Moderation In All Things as his own personal philosophy, set aside the double-handled cup of wine he shared with Tala. Her fingers came over his arm in a gesture of restraint.

Venn drew himself up to his full height and puffed out his skinny chest. "I won't take no for an answer, either!"

"And what is it that I won't be saying no to little brother?" Tala inquired softly, so as not to draw any more attention than necessary to Venn's peculiar behavior. Not many of the revelers were paying him any mind, thank heaven.

"You just won't," he declared imperiously, his voice rising in a squeak.

Edon's growl startled Venn. The boy wobbled crookedly for a moment before making a serious and very inebriated effort at straightening his shoulders. Then he cast a hasty frown at Edon's fierce face and focused one eye back on Tala. "Saints preserve you, sister, I don't know how you will live with that man all the rest of your days. He scares the piss out of me! But listen, sister, I've made up my mind and I'm going to do it, even if you forbid it. King Alfred says I may, so that's that. I'm going."

That said, Venn tried to spin about and march off. Only he stumbled on the dais, and if it hadn't been for Rig catching him, Venn would have fallen face first in the dirt.

"Hold on there, boy." Rig held Venn up and turned him around to face the pair seated at the high board.

"Thank you, Rig." Tala nodded regally, dismissing the attendant. "Venn, where is it you think you are going?"

"I told you!" he almost shouted. Except Edon had started to stand up, and that made Venn lurch to the side and clap his mouth shut. Then he scrambled back up onto the dais and he bent over Tala's arm, whispering in her ear, "I'm going to Rome with Bishop Nels."

"What!" Tala exclaimed.

This time it was Edon's hand that touched her arm, in a gesture that said eloquently *be still.* "What is it that

Bishop Nels will do with a bothersome little pagan like you at his side in Rome, young man?''

Affronted by Edon's question, Venn looked right at him and said, ''Why, he's going to introduce me to the pope and the curia, and let me read all the testaments of the saints. Alfred says I may go, so please say yes, Tala. I do so want to go. Bishop Nels knows more than any man alive. I'll come back, but when I do, maybe I'll be a priest like him. Say yes, will you?''

Tala, who had spent so much of her life worrying about this brother of hers, didn't know what to answer. Again she felt that overwhelming need to hold the boy tightly in her arms, to protect him from each and every danger. But she kept her arms at her sides as she watched her anxious brother wobble ever so slightly because he'd had a glass too much of the supper wine. She turned to Edon and looked at him for direction.

Edon's face was solemn, and his eyes met hers levelly. He gave an almost imperceptible nod of his head.

Tala resumed her inspection of her brother. She saw that he was serious—perhaps more serious than he'd ever been in his short life. ''Rome is a very long way from Warwick, isn't it, Venn?''

''Aye, but that's good. There's so much to learn and see, Tala. I want to see it all...as your Viking has done. More than that, I want to learn it all. Read every book and study with every teacher. Rome's the center of the whole world, Tala. I humbly implore you, do say yes.''

''Yes,'' she answered.

That stunned the boy. He fell back, shock causing him to blink repeatedly. ''Yes? Do you mean it? You'll let me go? You've not let me leave Arden since Papa died.''

Tala suddenly saw where she had made her gravest mistake. By trying so hard to retain possession of Leam against the invaders, she had almost lost sight of what was most important to her—the person her brother was to become. "Yes, you may go to Rome with Bishop Nels."

Venn dropped to his knees before her, wobbling a little as he took both her hands in his and kissed them. "Thank you, sister. I'm glad we didn't have to fight about it. Take care of her, Viking."

The boy lurched onto his feet, then ran into the dancing crowd of merrymakers.

Tala smiled a little worriedly at her brother's abrupt departure. "I think he's consumed too much of your wine, Edon."

"I don't think, I know he has." Edon laughed. "What say you we let these revels continue without us?" The time had come that they could slip away and not be missed. Edon took her hand in his, pulling her onto her feet. "What do you say, wife of the Wolf of Warwick?"

"I thought you'd never ask." Tala leaned into his side and kissed him hungrily.

Edon took her hand and laid it on his arm, proudly walking with her through the wet and very merry crowd toward the keep. Soon they reached the dry and crowded interior of the lower hall. Both kings held reign there, sharing anecdotes of the trials and tribulations of their courts with most of Edon's close entourage.

A few ribald comments and totally unnecessary pieces of advice were tossed toward the bride and groom as they made sure and steady progress upstairs to the sanctuary of their private room.

The second floor was completely deserted. Not even a servant lingered in the unlit shadows of the upper hall. Everyone was outside or downstairs enjoying the feast and celebration. That was exactly the way Edon had ordered it. He wanted some time alone with Tala, and the only way it seemed he could accomplish that was to ban his entire household from the second floor of the keep. He was very pleased to see his orders fulfilled, right down to his request for a private meal to be set out on the trestle for the two of them.

Six precious tallow candles in a Roman candelabra graced the end of the linen-covered table. Two chairs were set at the very end. Edon graciously settled Tala in the wolf's-head seat and took his place beside her.

"What is this?" she asked shyly.

"A private supper," Edon replied. He lifted a cover from a silver dish, revealing an array of finger foods that they both would enjoy. There were plump purple grapes, a gift from the abbot of Evesham. Delicious slivers of smoked ham were rolled around olives with red pimentos. Crusty rolls had been stuffed with wedges of the most delicious cheeses to be had in the entire isle.

Neither one of them was very hungry for food, but the small meal provided an interlude between the commotion of the crowd and the intimacy of being alone.

Tala peeled a grape, neatly removing the seeds before she popped the plump fruit into Edon's mouth.

"Are you content, my lady?" he asked.

"Aye, I am content. I am nearly bursting, I've eaten and drunk so much."

"I do not want you to complain later that I have not satisfied your every need." He placed a small kiss at the corner of her eye and let the heady scent of her perfume tease his nose.

Tala's fingers drifted to his chest, gently plying the soft embroidered chambray against his skin. Neither of the kings had worn a garment so finely made, nor looked so handsome to her eyes.

Edon let his lips trail across her cheek and softly kiss her pliant mouth. It opened willingly, but he kept his desire under firm control, determined to take his time wooing her. The thrill she stirred within him was nearly magical in the way it made his blood hum in his veins.

But beside the consummation of their marriage there

was one thing more that he needed from her—one thing she withheld that he wanted more than anything he'd ever wanted in his life. How or when her love had become so important to him, he couldn't say. He just knew that without it, their union in the marriage bed would be a hollow victory.

"There is one thing that bothers me, my lady."

"And what is that?" Tala asked frankly.

"You have neatly avoided any mention of wanting or expecting love from this marriage of ours." Edon held her hand against his chest, cradling her warm fingers in his callused one. "I do recall hearing you say clearly that you would honor and obey me all of your days, but I did not hear you say that you would love me."

Tala looked stricken by his words. "But I did," she insisted, too quickly to suit Edon.

"Nay, you merely mouthed the word, skipping over it as swiftly as you could." Edon turned her hand over, exposing her palm. "I spoke at length of my feelings about this marriage of ours before. In my land there are time-honored customs that unite a husband and wife, as there are customs your people hold dear. Without them—that is, without holding to the traditions that we are accustomed to—there is not the feeling of solidity to the marriage ceremony. The vows ring hollow."

Tala's expression was as grave and serious as Edon's. "Go on."

Edon's eyes were bright as a boy's when they came back to Tala's. "The thing is, I want very much for you to be my wife in all ways. I want no reservations between us, nothing to hold us back from becoming the partners and lovers that we have the potential to be."

Again he paused, as though finding the right words were difficult for him. In the moment of silence Tala spoke. "There are some customs in this new service that were what I expected."

"And what was that?" Edon asked.

Tala touched the ring he'd placed on her finger. "The symbol of eternity, a ring of gold that has no beginning and no end."

"Ah, yes, that," Edon acknowledged, touching his own ring.

Tala leaned a little closer to him and placed her fingers on his lips. "And the kiss sealing the union between us. That was very nice and certainly all that I expected."

Edon smiled as her fingers slowly moved down his jaw to touch the cleft in his chin. "I, too, expected such a kiss to seal our bargain, making the union perfect."

He kissed her again, more deeply and intently. He pulled back some moments later and summoned the courage to say, "There is no reason for me not to believe that someday you will come to love me, is there?"

How could she possibly not love him? Tala thought. She'd given over to her feelings the night he'd been struck by lightning. The thought of losing him to death had devastated her. She frowned as she studied his face in the soft glow of the precious candles gracing the trestle. Her dimples flashed briefly. "No, no reason at all."

Edon let out a deep breath. "There was one custom that was missing for me. I fear I am too newly baptized not to need something more than mystical smoke and Latin blessings. I am a Viking, a man of the sword, a conqueror." He removed his dagger from his waist. "There is one Viking custom lacking, and without it no life pledge between us is valid."

Edon took her hand in his and lightly scored the plump mound of Venus beneath her thumb. Tala's hiss made him bend his head and kiss the small wound, but he did not release her fingers as he cut his own palm. Then he clasped her hand in his, so that their blood flowed together.

"By the blood that beats in my heart I will protect you. By the mingling of our blood, our spirits are one from this day forward, our bodies united in this world forever, my woman, my wife, my love.'' Then he leaned against her and kissed her once more, his need and desire becoming heady and strong.

''Oh, Edon,'' Tala whispered, pulling him as close to her as he could be.

''I love you, Tala ap Griffin, wife of Edon Halfdansson. No, hush, be quiet. You don't need to tell me you love me.'' Edon gathered her into his arms as he stood up. Her own arms tightened around his shoulders and she kissed him hard, enticing him to near madness. He laughed, saying, ''I heard your frantic cries the night I was struck by lightning. 'Haps the need to scream your love for me will come over you very soon, hmm? And this time nothing will stop me from gloating when my men congratulate me for making you yell how much you love me at the top of your voice.''

''How touching, Jarl Edon.'' Embla Silver Throat sneered as she came forward out of the dark shadows of the hall. ''As Odin is my judge, I can stand no more of this loathsome pulchritude. Set the witch on her feet and raise your hands over your heads. Both of you! The game is ended. I'm taking over and the two of you are as good as dead.''

Chapter Nineteen

Edon very carefully set Tala on her feet. The woman in the shadows had come armed. She had a Welsh longbow in hand, a barbed arrow cocked and aimed with deadly precision at Tala's breast. Edon had no reason to doubt Embla's accuracy with the weapon, especially not at such close range.

"That's good," Embla said smoothly, advancing carefully out of the midnight shadows. "Put the knife down on the table, Edon—slowly. No fast moves or I might be tempted to pierce the witch's arm with this arrow. It's poisoned, you know, but you might have guessed that... seeing as how you ransacked my possessions. And though I can promise you that a nick on the arm isn't fatal, I can also assure you that her death will be agonizingly long and lingering."

"What is it you want?" Edon carefully shifted away from the trestle, to gain the space to maneuver clear of the chairs and stools scattered about the hall. "How is it you escaped your pit?"

"So that was you I saw on the rim tormenting me, was it?" She tossed her head back, casting a wealth of tangled blond hair out of her eyes. Even in the half shadows of romantic candlelight, it was clear she had been through hell and back. Her hair and clothes were scorched by fire and mud clung to her legs. "Had you come to gloat? Too soon, you fool. You led my devoted Eric straight to me."

Embla tensed as Edon caught Tala's arm. Embla let her arrow fly, and it sped across the room, landing in the back of Edon's chair with a chilling thud. Tala yelped as Edon jerked her clear of the arrow's path, pushing her behind him.

Eric the Tongueless lunged from the darkness and grabbed Tala, whipping her away from Edon's protection. The giant slapped his hand across Tala's mouth, silencing her piercing scream of alarm.

"Good boy, Eric!" Embla laughed gloatingly, at Edon. She notched another arrow in the bow as she commanded, "Stand where you are, Wolf of Warwick! Don't be such a coward! It isn't the woman I'm going to kill first. It's you!"

"Why, Embla? What makes you think this will accomplish anything?" Edon straightened, not bothering to glance back at Tala. He'd heard the scrape of a steel blade leaving its sheath and knew without having to look behind him that the silent giant held a knife at her throat. "What is it you want, niece? The kings will never let you live to claim Warwick now."

"Oh, aye, that's a fearsome truth, isn't it?" Embla growled throatily, her voice clearly abused by smoke and fire. "Here you are, come to reap the fruits of my labor, the wealth of this shire, its mines and bounty. You ruined everything. You even managed to kill the damn druid who served me even better than that braggart Asgart. Do you have any idea of the amount of gold that lies in the mud of the river Leam?"

Edon laughed bluntly. "I don't see you wearing any of it."

"Wear it? What kind of fool do you think I am? I've had every pound melted into ingots. Once the river Leam was drained, it yielded tons of gold coins and jewelry, the torques of every king and princess of Leam since the bloody-minded Celts began their sacrifices a thousand years ago. I'd only just begun dredging it when that witch showed up at Offa's lodge at Beltane and began stirring up her people."

Edon glared at the woman. "So what has stopped you from taking your gold and leaving Warwick? Why have you come back? You'll never depart alive now."

"On the contrary, you are going to make certain that I leave Warwick very much alive. All of my ingots are carefully concealed inside the walls of this monstrosity of yours. Eric, quit fondling that woman's breasts and tie her up. Do the work you need to do!" Embla ordered. "Then tie the jarl's hands very tightly behind his back and see that a garrote is knotted at his throat."

Tala's heart hammered in her chest. She feared for Edon's life. Embla would not let him live, she knew that. The lumbering Viking sheathed his knife, then jerked Tala around. She saw Harald Jorgensson staggering to his feet in the doorway of his sickroom. At the same time Sarina bounded up the open stairs, a dark and fearsome growl coming from her throat.

Eric grunted in alarm. Tala grabbed his hand as he raised it and sank her teeth deep into his filthy palm. She freed one arm and dug her fingers into his eyes. Howling, the giant struck out at her with his other fist.

Edon heard the scuffle break out behind him. His weapons hung on the wall at Embla's back—his shield and swords, pikes and battle axes.

Embla saw his glance go to the wall behind her. She stepped to the side, her back to the open door where Harald Jorgensson stood on his feet—a pale apparition, apprising the scene before him.

"Do it, Harald!" Edon shouted. "Now, Sarina!"

Embla spun around. "Nay!" she screamed when she saw her husband standing in the doorway. "You're dead!"

"Nay, Embla, lay down your bow!" Harald rasped. "Your reign of terror is at an end."

Sarina sprang at the Viking woman, her growl deadly and terrifying. Embla's bow swiveled from Harald to the dog. Harald, too, lunged at her, his weak fist grazing the hand that held the bow steady. Embla's poisoned arrow thudded into the wooden door at her husband's back. She screamed as the hound sank her teeth into her arm.

Then all hell erupted. Edon caught his sword in hand, spun around and, yelling like a wild berserker, went after the man that tormented his wife. Rig, Maynard and Thorulf burst into the hall, hot on the wolfhound's tail. Edon's sword cracked down on Eric the Tongueless's shoulder as he drew back his arm to strike Tala again.

Eric's arm dropped. His howl matched Embla Silver Throat's shrieks as the dog tore her necklace from her throat and ripped into flesh and blood.

Turning on Edon, Eric flashed his dagger in his left hand, lunging forward.

"No!" Tala screamed. "No!" She leaped onto the mute's back, dragging him back. Edon's sword thrust upward, puncturing the villain's belly. He let go of his sword, jumped back and swept Tala away.

Eric fell forward onto the hilt of the sword. Ten inches of bloody steel poked out of his back, where Tala had been clinging to him mere seconds ago.

Edon lifted Tala higher in the air, roaring at the top of his voice, "Don't you ever do that again!" He shook her fiercely, then crushed her in his arms, overcome by the terror of what could have happened to her as his moving blade impaled Eric. "You little fool!"

"Hold, Sarina, stop!" Jarl Harald fell to the floor, grasping the wolfhound's neck, trying to pull her off the woman struggling underneath the dog.

Tala threw her arms around Edon's head and neck. "Oh, my love, I nearly lost you for good."

Edon allowed her to rain a hundred desperate kisses on his face, his brow, his cheeks and his mouth. It made no difference in the rage frozen on his features. He could have killed her. Didn't she realize that?

"Edon!" Harald shouted in desperation. "Call off your dog!"

Rashid and Thorulf both issued commands to the enraged wolfhound. Their combined strength hauling on Sarina's collar wasn't enough to pull her off. Edon patted Tala's cheeks, examined her belly and her arms, making certain she was all in one piece and all right before he looked to the struggle between his men and the hound. He needed the time to compose himself.

"*À moi*, Sarina, heel!" Edon softly issued the only command the wolfhound would obey. Sarina barked wildly a moment more, then turned and padded on clicking paws to Edon's side. She sniffed his hands, whining, thumping her tail on a piece of furniture, awaiting his approval.

"Good dog, Sarina!" Edon had to let go of Tala to calm his pet and praise her. The wolfhound woofed and jumped up, putting her paws on his shoulders, licking his face. "Now sit."

Edon then guided Tala to his chair and set her down, kissing her trembling mouth. Raising one finger in a command to stay, he turned to assess the damage to his house.

"That was a surprise I could have done without."

The jarl's dry understatement brought the attention of each of his captains to him. Rig, Maynard and Thorulf cast uneasy, sheepish looks between them.

Harald collapsed at the side of the woman he had married. Rashid bent over Embla, pressing a thick, folded cloth to the woman's bleeding throat. Embla stared at the blood on her chest with horrified eyes.

"Damn you, Embla," Harald cursed her. "You just don't know when to give up, do you? Send for a priest!"

A strangulated sound gurgled from her mouth.

Tala turned away, sickened by the sight of so much blood and horror, and saw Venn and Bishop Nels burst into the upper hall at the same time.

"What's happened?" Venn came to Tala, asking questions, confused by what he saw and agitated because he had missed all of the action. The warriors had formed a solid flank between Jarl Harald and his wife and Edon. King Guthrum moved to Edon's side, putting his hand on his shoulder.

"Clear this hall," the king commanded. "Edon, take your bride from the sight of this. I'll handle it from here."

Edon nodded, accepting his brother's command. He turned to Tala and assisted her to her feet. Rig and Eli rushed ahead of him, bringing lanterns, checking that the chamber was empty of all threat and danger.

"I need water to wash," Edon said as he guided Tala inside the bedchamber. She was shaking badly as he set her down on the edge of the bed. He gripped her hands in his as he knelt before her. "Are you all right, my love?"

"No," Tala said as she burst into tears. She threw her arms around his shoulders, clasping him to her. "That bitch was going to kill you!"

Edon slipped his arm around Tala's waist, holding her as tightly as she held him. "Don't be foolish, love, I'm not so easy to harm. It was a mad thing for her to try to do—to kill me in my own house. There, there now, be quiet. Stop this crying."

"But Edon..." Tala shook her head and kissed both of his cheeks. "I hadn't told you that I love you. Don't do that to me again! I could have died from fear of losing you."

"Ah, that bad, was it, love?" Edon chuckled, delighted by the hard-won although frantic declaration of her love. "If that is what it takes to get you to admit what you feel for me, then I shall have some villain tucked behind every door in Warwick, just so you will scream you love me when I have defeated the lout.''

Tala dashed her hand across her eyes, sniffed and leaned back, looking at his undamaged face. "You will do no such thing!" she commanded. She touched his brow, smoothing his black hair away from his eyes. "Why do you call me 'love'?"

"What else am I to call the only woman who means everything to me? Do you realize that you attacked a man four times your size with nothing more than your teeth and your fingers?" Edon caught her hands and kissed the backs of her knuckles. "You, a puny little princess, trying to kill a Viking with your bare hands."

"He was going to hurt you." she replied, justifying her actions.

Edon lifted his hand to touch the swelling bump on her cheek, where Eric had struck her very hard. The rage inside him bubbled to the surface. He took hold of Tala's hands and held them still between them. His face was dark and very serious. "You will never do that again, understand? Say that you do, Tala, because I don't think my heart could take another near miss like that."

Tala wasn't certain she knew just what he was talking about. She swallowed and nodded her head. She thought the best thing to do was just agree with him. "Yes, Edon," she said. "I understand."

He could tell by the fear and confusion in her eyes that she really didn't comprehend. Maybe she thought bodies were made of solid bone and that tempered steel didn't go through human flesh the way a table knife slipped through butter. He took a deep breath, feeling calmer. Perhaps a little more explanation and she would understand his point. Sometimes there was no help except to fight things out and settle them once and for all. Though he wanted to live in peace with everyone, he couldn't guarantee that everyone in this world would live in peace with him.

"The point is, love, I had everything under control. That

scream of yours alerted everyone downstairs that there was trouble. Harald was resting in his room and I knew Sarina would come to my aid shortly. You didn't need to jump on Eric's back to protect me from his puny knife. I can fight very well. But I prefer to fight on my own terms and at my own pace. Is that clear?''

"Yes, Edon," Tala said.

She still didn't get it. Edon shook his head. "In the future, should you ever find yourself in the same shire as I am when a fight erupts, you will keep perfectly still. You will not stick your fingers in someone's eyes, pull his ears or bite his fingers and hands."

Tala's fingers wiggled inside the tight restraint of his grip. Edon tugged on them, holding her still.

"Yes, Edon," she said, as if right on a cue. His scowl deepened.

"More important, lady, you will never, ever jump on the back of any man I am fighting. This is the only time you will ever hear me issue such an order. I am perfectly capable of settling my disputes without your assistance. Understood?''

Tala tilted her chin a little, staring at his eyes, then she nodded. Since he wouldn't let go of her hands, she leaned forward and kissed his mouth again. This time she lingered over his hard mouth, which didn't soften, not one little bit. She lifted her head and said, "You are so supremely arrogant, Viking!''

Tala kissed him again, and this time his strong arms encased her so completely she thought the life was going to be squeezed out of her.

"And you are a wild woman, perfectly suited to an arrogant Viking." Edon lifted her in his arms as he rose to his feet. She clung to him, refusing to release his mouth, deepening the kiss between them.

A moment or two later, Edon heard the door shut at his back. He lifted his head and looked as his wife's face. "Come, love, Eli has left enough water to wash the scent of battle from both our hands. The night is now ours to enjoy. Nothing will intrude again, I promise you.''

"Nothing?" Tala asked as she began to pull the laces out of his tunic.

"Nothing," Edon said with grave assurance. To make doubly certain that fact was truth, he put the bar on the door, guaranteeing their absolute privacy. Tala suppressed a small chuckle, preferring to remain as grave and serious as he was.

"Can you command the sun not to rise in the morning so that this night of ours might never end?" she challenged.

"I can command people, not Apollo. It's Lughnasa Night. We must make haste if we are to enjoy each other's finest fruits. Shall I turn my hourglass and make you a wager that you'll be howling out my name before the last sands have run out?"

Tala lifted her chin and gave him a sultry smile.

"You may issue any challenge you feel up to declaring. I shall do my part to see that the sands run very, very slowly."

"Ah!" Edon tapped her nose gently. "So I am to be utterly at the mercy of my Mercian witch for all eternity, am I? You will cast spells on hourglasses to slow the sands, will you? Take unfair advantage of me and my prowess in bed?"

"You spoke the words of your own spell, binding our spirits from this day forward until death do us part. I am yours through eternity." Tala wound her arms around his neck. "You may have all the love I have in my heart. I wouldn't have you any other way, my love and my Viking."

"So be it." Edon smiled as he sealed their bargain with a kiss. Then he turned over the hourglass and set out on the first of a lifetime of delights to come, one sweet, loving hour at a time.

* * * * *

Author note

This whole book evolved out of one snippit in the Anglo-Saxon Chronicles, wherein King Ella of Deria (York) slew Halfdan by throwing him in a pit full of snakes. In retaliation, Halfdan's sons carved a blood eagle on Ella's back. They cut his ribs free from his spine and spread his lungs on his back and watched the man die. This is, of course, too brutal for our day and age, but in my original notes Tala and Venn were King Ella's children. That plot twist didn't work.

Romancing history is what writing historical novelists do. I personally like the gory details. It's safe so long as I'm in my twentieth-century bungalow, far removed from the reality of those times. I hope you enjoyed my take on existing legends. If you'd like information on upcoming books or what's been published in the past, check out my home page. You can read reviews and send me e-mail at: http//www.NAinc.com/mayne

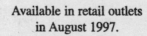

HARLEQUIN WOMEN KNOW ROMANCE WHEN THEY SEE IT.

And they'll see it on **ROMANCE CLASSICS**, the new 24-hour TV channel devoted to romantic movies and original programs like the special **Romantically Speaking—Harlequin™ Goes Prime Time.**

Romantically Speaking—Harlequin™ Goes Prime Time introduces you to many of your favorite romance authors in a program developed exclusively for Harlequin® readers.

Watch for **Romantically Speaking—Harlequin™ Goes Prime Time** beginning in the summer of 1997.

If you're not receiving ROMANCE CLASSICS, call your local cable operator or satellite provider and ask for it today!

ROMANCE CLASSICS

Escape to the network of your dreams.

See Ingrid Bergman and Gregory Peck in *Spellbound* on Romance Classics.

Free Gift Offer

With a Free Gift proof-of-purchase from any Harlequin® book, you can receive a beautiful cubic zirconia pendant.

This stunning marquise-shaped stone is a genuine cubic zirconia—accented by an 18" gold tone necklace.
(Approximate retail value $19.95)

Send for yours today...
compliments of ◆HARLEQUIN®

To receive your free gift, a cubic zirconia pendant, send us one original proof-of-purchase, photocopies not accepted, from the back of any Harlequin Romance®, Harlequin Presents®, Harlequin Temptation®, Harlequin Superromance®, Harlequin Intrigue®, Harlequin American Romance®, or Harlequin Historicals® title available at your favorite retail outlet, together with the Free Gift Certificate, plus a check or money order for $1.65 U.S./$2.15 CAN. (do not send cash) to cover postage and handling, payable to Harlequin Free Gift Offer. We will send you the specified gift. Allow 6 to 8 weeks for delivery. Offer good until December 31, 1997, or while quantities last. Offer valid in the U.S. and Canada only.

Free Gift Certificate

Name: _____

Address: _____

City: _____ State/Province: _____ Zip/Postal Code: _____

Mail this certificate, one proof-of-purchase and a check or money order for postage and handling to: HARLEQUIN FREE GIFT OFFER 1997. In the U.S.: 3010 Walden Avenue, P.O. Box 9071, Buffalo NY 14269-9057. In Canada: P.O. Box 604, Fort Erie, Ontario L2Z 5X3.

084-KEZR